East of Eden

John Steinbeck was born in Salinas, California, in 1902.
After studying science at Stanford University he worked
successively as labourer, druggist, caretaker, fruit-picker and
surveyor. His first novel, *Cup of Gold* (1929), was about
Morgan the pirate. *The Grapes of Wrath* (1939), his most
popular book, tells of a migratory family seeking work in
California; it was awarded the Pulitzer Prize, and has been
compared in its influence to *Uncle Tom's Cabin*. His other
novels include *East of Eden*, *Of Mice and Men*, *The Pearl*,
Sweet Thursday and *Cannery Row*, all published in Pan Books.
Also available in Pan are several collections of his short stories,
and *Journal of a Novel*, *The East of Eden Letters*. In 1962
Steinbeck was awarded the Nobel Prize for Literature.
He died in 1968.

Also by
John Steinbeck in Pan Books

The Grapes of Wrath
Of Mice and Men
Cannery Row
Sweet Thursday
The Moon Is Down
The Pearl
Burning Bright
The Log from the Sea of Cortez
The Winter of Our Discontent
The Short Reign of Pippin IV
To a God Unknown
The Long Valley
Tortilla Flat
Once There Was a War

Journal of a Novel
Travels with Charley

John Steinbeck

East of Eden

Pan Books in association with
William Heinemann

First British edition published 1952 by William Heinemann Ltd
This edition published 1963 by Pan Books Ltd,
Cavaye Place, London SW10 9PG, in association with
William Heinemann Ltd
12th printing 1978
All rights reserved
ISBN 0 330 30001 6
Printed in Great Britain by
Richard Clay (The Chaucer Press) Ltd, Bungay, Suffolk

PASCAL COVICI

Dear Pat,

You came upon me carving some kind of little figure out of wood and you said, 'Why don't you make something for me?'

I asked you what you wanted, and you said, 'A box.'

'What for?'

'To put things in.'

'What things?'

'Whatever you have,' you said.

Well, here's your box. Nearly everything I have is in it, and it is not full. Pain and excitement are in it, and feeling good or bad and evil thoughts and good thoughts – the pleasure of design and some despair and the indescribable joy of creation.

And on top of these are all the gratitude and love I have for you.

And still the box is not full.

JOHN

CONTENTS

East of Eden

Part One

CHAPTER 1

I

THE SALINAS Valley is in Northern California. It is a long narrow swale between two ranges of mountains, and the Salinas River winds and twists up the centre until it falls at last into Monterey Bay.

I remember my childhood names for grasses and secret flowers. I remember where a toad may live and what time the birds awaken in the summer – and what trees and seasons smelled like – how people looked and walked and smelled even. The memory of odours is very rich.

I remember that the Gabilan Mountains to the east of the valley were light gay mountains full of sun and loveliness and a kind of invitation, so that you wanted to climb into their warm foothills almost as you want to climb into the lap of a beloved mother. They were beckoning mountains with a brown grass love. The Santa Lucias stood up against the sky to the west and kept the valley from the open sea, and they were dark and brooding – unfriendly and dangerous. I always found in myself a dread of west and a love of east. Where I ever got such an idea I cannot say, unless it could be that the morning came over the peaks of the Gabilans and the night drifted back from the ridges of the Santa Lucias. It may be that the birth and death of the day had some part in my feeling about the two ranges of mountains.

From both sides of the valley little streams slipped out of the hill canyons and fell into the bed of the Salinas River. In the winter of wet years the streams ran full-freshet, and they swelled the river until sometimes it raged and boiled, bank-full, and then it was a destroyer. The river tore the edges of the farm lands and washed whole acres down; it toppled barns and houses into itself, to go floating and bobbing away. It trapped cows and pigs and sheep and drowned them in its muddy brown water and carried them to the sea. Then when the late spring came, the river drew in from its edges and the sandbanks appeared. And in the summer the river didn't run at all above ground. Some pools would be left in the deep swirl places under a high bank. The tules and grasses grew back, and willows straightened up with the flood débris in their upper branches. The Salinas was only a part-time river. The summer sun drove it underground. It was not a fine river at all, but it was the only one we had, and so we boasted about it – how dangerous it was in a wet winter and how dry it was in a dry summer. You can boast about anything if it's all you have. Maybe the less you have, the more you are required to boast.

The floor of the Salinas Valley, between the ranges and below the foothills, is level because this valley used to be the bottom of a hundred-mile inlet from the sea. The river mouth at Moss Landing was centuries ago the entrance to this long inland water. Once, fifty miles down the valley, my father bored a well. The drill came up first with topsoil and then with gravel and then with white sea sand full of shells and even pieces of whalebone. There were twenty feet of sand and then black earth again, and even a piece of redwood, that imperishable wood that does not rot. Before the inland sea the valley must have been a forest. And those things had happened right under our feet. And it seemed to me sometimes at night that I could feel both the sea and the redwood forest before it.

On the wide level acres of the valley the topsoil lay deep and fertile. It required only a rich winter of rain to make it break forth in grass and flowers. The spring flowers in a wet year were unbelievable. The whole valley floor, and the foothills too, would be carpeted with lupins and poppies. Once a woman told me that coloured flowers would seem more bright if you added a few white flowers to give the colours definition. Every petal of blue lupin is edged with white, so that a field of lupins is more blue than you can imagine. And mixed with these were splashes of California poppies. These too are of a burning colour – not orange, not gold, but if pure gold were liquid and could raise a cream, that golden cream might be like the colour of the poppies. When their season was over the yellow mustard came up and grew to a great height. When my grandfather came into the valley the mustard was so tall that a man on horseback showed only his head above the yellow flowers. On the uplands the grass would be strewn with buttercups, with hen-and-chickens, with black-centred yellow violets. And a little later in the season there would be red and yellow stands of Indian paintbrush. These were the flowers of the open spaces exposed to the sun.

Under the live oaks, shaded and dusky, the maidenhair flourished and gave a good smell, and under the mossy banks of the watercourses whole clumps of five-fingered ferns and goldybacks hung down. Then there were harebells, tiny lanterns, cream white and almost sinful-looking, and these were so rare and magical that a child, finding one, felt singled out and special all day long.

When June came the grasses headed out and turned brown, and the hills turned a brown which was not brown but a gold and saffron and red – an indescribable colour. And from then on until the next rains the earth dried and the streams stopped. Cracks appeared on the level ground. The Salinas River sank under its sand. The wind blew down the valley, picking up dust and straws, and grew stronger and harsher as it went south. It stopped in the evening. It was a rasping nervous wind, and the dust particles cut into a man's skin and burned his eyes. Men working in the fields wore goggles and tied handkerchiefs around their noses to keep the dirt out.

The valley land was deep and rich, but the foothills wore only a skin of topsoil no deeper than the grass roots; and the farther up the hills you went, the thinner grew the soil, with flints sticking through, until at the brush line it was a kind of dry flinty gravel that reflected the hot sun blindingly.

I have spoken of the rich years when the rainfall was plentiful. But there were dry years too, and they put a terror on the valley. The water came in a thirty-year cycle. There would be five or six wet and wonderful years when there might be nineteen to twenty-five inches of rain, and the land would shout with grass. Then would come six or seven pretty good years of twelve to sixteen inches of rain. And then the dry years would come, and sometimes there would be only seven or eight inches of rain. The land dried up and the grasses headed out miserably a few inches high and great bare scabby places appeared in the valley. The live oaks got a crusty look and the sagebrush was grey. The land cracked and the springs dried up and the cattle listlessly nibbled dry twigs. Then the farmers and the ranchers would be filled with disgust for the Salinas Valley. The cows would grow thin and sometimes starve to death. People would have to haul water in barrels to their farms just for drinking. Some families would sell out for nearly nothing and move away. And it never failed that during the dry years the people forgot about the rich years, and during the wet years they lost all memory of the dry years. It was always that way.

9

And that was the long Salinas Valley. Its history was like that of the rest of the state. First there were Indians, an inferior breed without energy, inventiveness, or culture, a people that lived on grubs and grasshoppers and shellfish, too lazy to hunt or fish. They ate what they could pick up and planted nothing. They pounded bitter acorns for flour. Even their warfare was a weary pantomime.

Then the hard, dry Spaniards came exploring through, greedy and realistic, and their greed was for gold or God. They collected souls as they collected jewels. They gathered mountains and valleys, rivers and whole horizons, the way a man might now gain title to building lots. These tough, dried-up men moved restlessly up the coast and down. Some of them stayed on grants as large as principalities, given to them by Spanish kings who had not the faintest idea of the gift. These first owners lived in poor feudal settlements, and their cattle ranged freely and multiplied. Periodically the owners killed the cattle for their hides and tallow and left the meat to the vultures and coyotes.

When the Spaniards came they had to give everything they saw a name. This is the first duty of any explorer – a duty and a privilege. You must name a thing before you can note it on your hand-drawn map. Of course they were religious people, and the men who could read and write, who kept the records and drew the maps, were the tough untiring priests who travelled with the soldiers. Thus the first names of places were saints' names or religious holidays celebrated at stopping places. There are many saints, but they are not inexhaustible, so that we find repetitions in the first namings. We have San Miguel, St Michael, San Ardo, San Bernardo, San Benito, San Lorenzo, San Carlos, San Francisquito. And then the holidays – Natividad, the Nativity; Nacimiente, the Birth; Soledad, the Solitude. But places were also named from the way the expedition felt at the time: Buena Esperanza, good hope; Buena Vista because the view was beautiful; and Chualar because it was pretty. The descriptive names followed: Paso de los Robles because of the oak trees; Los Laureles for the laurels; Tularcitos because of the reeds in the swamp; and Salinas for the alkali which was white as salt.

Then places were named after animals and birds seen – Gabilanes for the hawks which flew in those mountains; Topo for the mole; Los Gatos for the wild cats. The suggestions sometimes came from the nature of the place itself : Tassajara, a cup and saucer; Laguna Seca, a dry lake; Corral de Tierra for a fence of earth; Paraiso because it was like Heaven.

Then the Americans came – more greedy because there were more of them. They took the lands, remade the laws to make their titles good. And farmholds spread over the land, first in the valleys and then up the foothill slopes, small wooden houses roofed with redwood shakes, corrals of split poles. Wherever a trickle of water came out of the ground a house sprang up and a family began to grow and multiply. Cuttings of red geraniums and rose bushes were planted in the door-yards. Wheel tracks of buckboards replaced the trails, and fields of corn and barley and wheat squared out of the yellow mustard. Every ten miles along the travelled routes a general store and blacksmith shop happened, and these became the nuclei of little towns, Bradley, King City, Greenfield.

The Americans had a greater tendency to name places after people than had the Spaniards. After the valleys were settled the names of places refer more to things which happened there, and these to me are the most fascinating of all names because each name suggests a story that has been forgotten. I think of Bolsa Neuva, a new purse; Morocojo, a lame Moor (who was he and how did he get there?); Wild Horse Canyon and Mustang Grade and Shirt Tail Canyon. The names of places carry a charge of the people who named them, reverent or irreverent, descriptive, either poetic or disparaging. You can name anything San Lorenzo, but Shirt Tail Canyon or the Lame Moor is something quite different.

The wind whistled over the settlements in the afternoon, and the farmers began to set out mile-long wind-breaks of eucalyptus to keep the ploughed topsoil from blowing away. And this is about the way the Salinas Valley was when my grandfather brought his wife and settled in the foothills to the east of King City.

CHAPTER 2

I

I M U S T depend on hearsay, on old photographs, on stories told, and on memories which are hazy and mixed with fable in trying to tell you about the Hamiltons. They were not eminent people, and there are few records concerning them except for the usual papers on birth, marriage, land ownership, and death.

Young Samuel Hamilton came from the north of Ireland and so did his wife. He was the son of small farmers, neither rich nor poor, who had lived on one landhold and in one stone house for many hundreds of years. The Hamiltons managed to be remarkably well educated and well read; and, as is so often true in that green country, they were connected and related to very great people and very small people, so that one cousin might be a baronet and another cousin a beggar. And of course they were descended from the ancient kings of Ireland, as every Irishman is.

Why Samuel left the stone house and the green acres of his ancestors I do not know. He was never a political man, so it is not likely a charge of rebellion drove him out, and he was scrupulously honest, which eliminates the police as prime movers. There was a whisper – not even a rumour but rather an unsaid feeling – in my family that it was love drove him out, and not love of the wife he married. But whether it was too successful love or whether he left in pique at unsuccessful love, I do not know. We always preferred to think it was the former. Samuel had good looks and charm and gaiety. It is hard to imagine that any country Irish girl refused him.

He came to the Salinas Valley full-blown and hearty, full of inventions and energy. His eyes were very blue, and when he was tired one of them wandered outwards a little. He was a big man but delicate in a way. In the dusty business of ranching he seemed always immaculate. His hands were clever. He was a good blacksmith and carpenter and woodcarver, and he could improvise anything with bits of wood and metal. He was for ever inventing a new way of doing an old thing and doing it better and quicker, but he never in his whole life had any talent for making money. Other men who had the talent took Samuel's tricks and sold them and grew rich, but Samuel barely made wages all his life.

I don't know what directed his steps towards the Salinas Valley. It was an unlikely place for a man from a green country to come to, but he came about thirty years before the turn of the century and he brought with him his tiny Irish wife, a tight hard little woman humourless as a chicken. She had a dour Presbyterian mind and a code of morals that pinned down and beat the brains out of nearly everything that was pleasant to do.

I do not know where Samuel met her, how he wooed her, married. I think there must have been some other girl printed somewhere in his heart, for he was a man of love and his wife was not a woman to show her feelings. And in spite of this, in all the years from his youth to his death in the Salinas Valley, there was no hint that Samuel ever went to any other woman.

When Samuel and Liza came to the Salinas Valley all the level land was taken, the rich bottoms, the little fertile creases in the hills, the forests, but there was still marginal land to be homesteaded, and in the barren hills, to the east of what is now King City, Samuel Hamilton homesteaded.

He followed the usual practice. He took a quarter-section for himself and a quarter-section for his wife, and since she was pregnant he took a quarter-section for the child. Over the years nine children were born, four boys and five girls, and with each birth another quarter-section was added to the ranch, and that makes eleven quarter-sections, or seventeen hundred and sixty acres.

If the land had been any good the Hamiltons would have been rich people. But the acres were harsh and dry. There were no springs, and the crust of topsoil was so thin that the flinty bones stuck through. Even the sagebrush struggled to exist, and the oaks were dwarfed from lack of moisture. Even in reasonably good years there was so little feed that the cattle kept thin running about looking for enough to eat. From their barren hills the Hamiltons could look down to the west and see the richness of the bottom land and the greenness around the Salinas River.

Samuel built his house with his own hands, and he built a barn and a blacksmith shop. He found quite soon that even if he had ten thousand acres of hill country he could not make a living on the bony soil without water. His clever hands built a well-boring rig, and he bored wells on the lands of luckier men. He invented and built a threshing machine and moved through the bottom farms in harvest time, threshing the grain his own farm would not raise. And in his shop he sharpened ploughs and mended harrows and welded broken axles and shod horses. Men from all over the district brought him tools to mend and

13

to improve. Besides, they loved to hear Samuel talk of the world and its thinking, of the poetry and philosophy that were going on outside the Salinas Valley. He had a rich deep voice, good both in song and in speech, and while he had no brogue there was a rise and a lilt and a cadence to his talk that made it sound sweet in the ears of the taciturn farmers from the valley bottom. They brought whisky too, and out of sight of the kitchen window and the disapproving eye of Mrs Hamilton they took hot nips from the bottle and nibbled cuds of green wild anise to cover the whisky breath. It was a bad day when three or four men were not standing around the forge, listening to Samuel's hammer and his talk. They called him a comical genius and carried his stories carefully home, and they wondered at how the stories spilled out on the way, for they never sounded the same repeated in their own kitchens.

Samuel should have been rich from his well rig and his threshing machine and his shop, but he had no gift for business. His customers, always pressed for money, promised payment after harvest, and then after Christmas, and then after – until at last they forgot it. Samuel had no gift for reminding them. And so the Hamiltons stayed poor.

The children came along as regularly as the years. The few overworked doctors of the county did not often get to the ranches for a birth unless the joy turned nightmare and went on for several days. Samuel Hamilton delivered all his own children and tied the cords neatly, spanked the bottoms and cleaned up the mess. When his youngest was born with some small obstruction and began to turn black, Samuel put his mouth against the baby's mouth and blew air in and sucked it out until the baby could take over for himself. Samuel's hands were so good and gentle that neighbours from twenty miles away would call on him to help with a birth. And he was equally good with mare, cow, or woman.

Samuel had a great black book on an available shelf and it had gold letters on the cover – *Dr Gunn's Family Medicine*. Some pages were bent and beat up from use, and others were never opened to the light. To look through *Dr Gunn* is to know the Hamiltons' medical history. These are the used sections – broken bones, cuts, bruises, mumps, measles, back-ache, scarlet fever, diphtheria, rheumatism, female complaints, hernia, and of course everything to do with pregnancy and the birth of children. The Hamiltons must have been either lucky or moral, for the sections on gonorrhea and syphilis were never opened.

14

Samuel had no equal for soothing hysteria and bringing quiet to a frightened child. It was the sweetness of his tongue and the tenderness of his soul. And just as there was a cleanness about his body, so there was a cleanness in his thinking. Men coming to his blacksmith shop to talk and listen dropped their cursing for a while, not from any kind of restraint but automatically, as though this were not the place for it.

Samuel kept always a foreignness. Perhaps it was in the cadence of his speech, and this had the effect of making men, and women too, tell him things they would not tell to relatives or close friends. His slight strangeness set him apart and made him safe as a repository.

Liza Hamilton was a very different kettle of fish. Her head was small and round and it held small round convictions. She had a button nose and a hard little set-back chin, a gripping jaw set on its course even though the angels of God argued against it.

Liza was a good plain cook, and her house – it was always her house – was brushed and pummelled and washed. Bearing her children did not hold her back very much – two weeks at the most she had to be careful. She must have had a pelvic arch of whalebone, for she had big children one after the other.

Liza had a finely developed sense of sin. Idleness was a sin, and card playing, which was a kind of idleness to her. She was suspicious of fun, whether it involved dancing or singing or even laughter. She felt that people having a good time were wide open to the devil. And this was a shame, for Samuel was a laughing man, but I guess Samuel was wide open to the devil. His wife protected him whenever she could.

She wore her hair always pulled tight back and bunned behind in a hard knot. And since I can't remember how she dressed, it must have been that she wore clothes that matched herself exactly. She had no spark of humour and only occasionally a blade of cutting wit. She frightened her grandchildren because she had no weakness. She suffered bravely and uncomplainingly through life, convinced that that was the way her God wanted everyone to live. She felt that rewards came later.

II

When people first came to the West, particularly from the owned and fought-over farmlets of Europe, and saw so much land to be had for the signing of a paper and the building of a foundation, an itching land-greed seemed to come over them. They

15

wanted more and more land – good land if possible, but land anyway. Perhaps they had filaments of memory of feudal Europe where great families became and remained great because they owned things. The early settlers took up land they didn't need and couldn't use; they took up worthless land just to own it. And all proportions changed. A man who might have been well-to-do on ten acres in Europe was rat-poor on two thousand in California.

It wasn't very long until all the land in the barren hills near King City and San Ardo was taken up, and ragged families were scattered through the hills, trying their best to scratch a living from the thin flinty soil. They and the coyotes lived clever, despairing, sub-marginal lives. They landed with no money, no equipment, no tools, no credit, and particularly with no knowledge of the new country and no technique for using it. I don't know whether it was a divine stupidity or a great faith that let them do it. Surely such venture is nearly gone from the world. And the families did survive and grow. They had a tool or a weapon that is also nearly gone, or perhaps it is only dormant for a while. It is argued that because they believed thoroughly in a just, moral God they could put their faith there and let the smaller securities take care of themselves. But I think that because they trusted themselves and respected themselves as individuals, because they knew beyond doubt that they were valuable and potentially moral units – because of this they could give God their own courage and dignity and then receive it back. Such things have disappeared perhaps because men do not trust themselves any more, and when that happens there is nothing left except perhaps to find some strong sure man, even though he may be wrong, and to dangle from his coat-tails.

While many people came to the Salinas Valley penniless, there were others who, having sold out somewhere else, arrived with money to start a new life. These usually bought land, but good land, and built their houses of planed lumber, and had carpets and coloured-glass diamond panes in their windows. There were numbers of these families and they got the good land of the valley and cleared the yellow mustard away and planted wheat.

Such a man was Adam Trask.

CHAPTER 3

I

ADAM TRASK was born on a farm on the outskirts of a little town which was not far from a big town in Connecticut. He was an only son, and he was born six months after his father was mustered into a Connecticut regiment in 1862. Adam's mother ran the farm, bore Adam, and still had time to embrace a primitive theosophy. She felt that her husband would surely be killed by the wild and barbarous rebels, and she prepared herself to get in touch with him in what she called the beyond. He came home six weeks after Adam was born. His right leg was off at the knee. He stumped in on a crude wooden leg he himself had carved out of beechwood. And already it was splitting. He had in his pocket and placed on the parlour table the lead bullet they had given him to bite while they cut off his frayed leg.

Adam's father Cyrus was something of a devil – had always been wild – drove a two-wheeled cart too fast, and managed to make his wooden leg seem jaunty and desirable. He had enjoyed his military career, what there was of it. Being wild by nature, he had liked his brief period of training and the drinking and gambling and whoring that went with it. Then he marched south with a group of replacements, and he enjoyed that too – seeing the country and stealing chickens and chasing rebel girls up into the haystacks. The grey, despairing weariness of protracted manoeuvres and combat did not touch him. The first time he saw the enemy was at eight o'clock one spring morning, and at eight-thirty he was hit in the right leg by a heavy slug that mashed and splintered the bones beyond repair. Even then he was lucky, for the rebels retreated and the field surgeons moved up immediately. Cyrus Trask did have his five minutes of horror while they cut the shreds away and sawed the bone off square and burned the open flesh. The tooth-marks in the bullet proved that. And there was considerable pain while the wound healed under the unusually septic conditions in the hospitals of that day. But Cyrus had vitality and swagger. While he was carving his beechwood leg and hobbling about on a crutch, he contracted a particularly virulent dose of the clap from a negro girl who whistled at him from under a pile of lumber and charged him ten cents. When he had his new leg, and painfully knew his condition, he hobbled about for days, looking for the

17

girl. He told his bunk-mates what he was going to do when he found her. He planned to cut off her ears and her nose with his pocket-knife and get his money back. Carving on his wooden leg he showed his friends how he would cut her. 'When I finish her she'll be a funny-looking bitch,' he said. 'I'll make her so a drunk Indian won't take out after her.' His light-of-love must have sensed his intentions, for he never found her. By the time Cyrus was released from the hospital and the army, his gonorrhea was dried up. When he got home to Connecticut there remained only enough of it for his wife.

Mrs Trask was a pale, inside-herself woman. No heat of sun ever reddened her cheeks, and no open laughter raised the corners of her mouth. She used religion as a therapy for the ills of the world and of herself, and she changed the religion to fit the ill. When she found that the theosophy she had developed for communication with a dead husband was not necessary, she cast about for some new unhappiness. Her search was quickly rewarded by the infection Cyrus brought home from the war. And as soon as she was aware that a condition existed, she devised a new theology. Her god of communication became a god of vengeance – to her the most satisfactory deity she had devised so far – and, as it turned out, the last. It was quite easy for her to attribute her condition to certain dreams she had experienced while her husband was away. But the disease was not punishment enough for her nocturnal philandering. Her new god was an expert in punishment. He demanded of her a sacrifice. She searched her mind for some proper egotistical humility and almost happily arrived at the sacrifice – herself. It took her two weeks to write her last letters with revisions and corrected spelling. In it she confessed to crimes she could not possibly have committed and admitted faults far beyond her capacity. And then, dressed in a secretly made shroud, she went out on a moonlight night and drowned herself in a pond so shallow that she had to get down on her knees in the mud and hold her head under water. This required great will-power. As the warm unconsciousness finally crept over her, she was thinking with some irritation of how her white lawn shroud would have mud down the front when they pulled her out in the morning. And it did.

Cyrus Trask mourned for his wife with a keg of whisky and three old army friends who had dropped in on their way home to Maine. Baby Adam cried a good deal at the beginning of the wake, for the mourners, not knowing about babies, had neglected to feed him. Cyrus soon solved the problem. He dipped a rag in

18

whisky and gave it to the baby to suck, and after three or four dippings young Adam went to sleep. Several times during the mourning period he awakened and complained and got the dipped rag again and went to sleep. The baby was drunk for two days and a half. Whatever may have happened in his developing brain, it proved beneficial to his metabolism: from that two and a half days he gained an iron health. And when at the end of three days his father finally went out and bought a goat, Adam drank the milk greedily, vomited, drank more, and was on his way. His father did not find the reaction alarming, since he was doing the same thing.

Within a month Cyrus Trask's choice fell on the seventeen-year-old daughter of a neighbouring farmer. The courtship was quick and realistic. There was no doubt in anybody's mind about his intentions. They were honourable and reasonable. Her father abetted the courtship. He had two younger daughters, and Alice, the eldest, was seventeen. This was her first proposal.

Cyrus wanted a woman to take care of Adam. He needed someone to keep house and cook, and a servant cost money. He was a vigorous man and needed the body of a woman, and that too cost money – unless you were married to it. Within two weeks Cyrus had wooed, wedded, bedded, and impregnated her. His neighbours did not find his action hasty. It was quite normal in that day for a man to use up three or four wives in a normal lifetime.

Alice Trask had a number of admirable qualities. She was a deep scrubber and a corner-cleaner in the house. She was not very pretty, so there was no need to watch her. Her eyes were pale, her complexion sallow, and her teeth crooked, but she was extremely healthy and never complained during her pregnancy. Whether she liked children or not no one ever knew. She was not asked, and she never said anything unless she was asked. From Cyrus's point of view this was possibly the greatest of virtues. She never offered any opinion or statement, and when a man was talking she gave a vague impression of listening while she went about doing the housework.

The youth, inexperience, and taciturnity of Alice Trask all turned out to be assets for Cyrus. While he continued to operate his farm as such farms were operated in the neighbourhood, he entered on a new career – that of the old soldier. And that energy which had made him wild now made him thoughtful. No one now outside the War Department knew the quality and duration of his service. His wooden leg was at once a certificate of proof of his soldiering and a guarantee that he wouldn't ever have to do it again. Timidly he began to tell Alice about his campaigns, but as his technique grew so did his battles. At the very first he knew he was lying, but it was not long before he was equally sure that every one of his stories was true. Before he had entered the service he had not been much interested in warfare; now he bought every book about war, read every report, subscribed to the New York papers, studied maps. His knowledge of geography had been shaky and his information about the fighting non-existent; now he became an authority. He knew not only the battles, movements, campaigns, but also the units involved, down to the regiments, their colonels, and where they originated. And from telling he became convinced that he had been there.

All of this was a gradual development, and it took place while Adam was growing to boyhood and his young half-brother behind him. Adam and little Charles would sit silent and respectful while their father explained how every general thought and planned and where they had made their mistakes and what they should have done. And then – he had known it at the time – he had told Grant and McClellan where they were wrong and had begged them to take his analysis of the situation. Invariably they refused his advice and only afterwards was he proved right.

There was one thing Cyrus did not do, and perhaps it was clever of him. He never once promoted himself to non-commissioned rank. Private Trask he began, and Private Trask he remained. In the total telling, it made him at once the most mobile and ubiquitous private in the history of warfare. It made it necessary for him to be in as many as four places at once. But perhaps instinctively he did not tell those stories close to each other. Alice and the boys had a complete picture of him: a private soldier, and proud of it, who not only happened to be where every spectacular and important action was taking place but who wandered freely into staff meetings and joined or dissented in the decisions of general officers.

The death of Lincoln caught Cyrus in the pit of the stomach. Always he remembered how he felt when he first heard the news. And he could never mention it or hear of it without quick tears in his eyes. And while he never actually said it, you got the indestructible impression that Private Cyrus Trask was one of Lincoln's closest, warmest, and most trusted friends. When Mr Lincoln wanted to know about the army, the real army, not those prancing dummies in gold braid, he turned to Private Trask.

How Cyrus managed to make this understood without saying it was a triumph of insinuation. No one would call him a liar. And this was mainly because the lie was in his head, and any truth coming from his mouth carried the colour of the lie.

Quite early he began to write letters and then articles about the conduct of the war, and his conclusions were intelligent and convincing. Indeed, Cyrus developed an excellent military mind. His criticisms both of the war as it had been conducted and of the army organization as it persisted were irresistibly penetrating. His articles in various magazines attracted attention. His letters to the War Department, printed simultaneously in the newspapers, began to have a sharp effect in decisions on the army. Perhaps if the Grand Army of the Republic had not assumed political force and direction his voice might not have been heard so clearly in Washington, but the spokesman for a block of nearly a million men was not to be ignored. And such a voice in military matters Cyrus Trask became. It came about that he was consulted in matters of army organization, in officer relationships, in personnel and equipment. His expertness was apparent to everyone who heard him. He had a genius for the military. More than that, he was one of those responsible for the organization of the GAR as a cohesive and potent force in the national life. After several unpaid offices in that organization, he took a paid secretaryship which he kept for the rest of his life. He travelled from one end of the country to the other, attending conventions, meetings, and encampments. So much for his public life.

His private life was also laced through with his new profession. He was a man devoted. His house and farm he organized on a military basis. He demanded and got reports on the conduct of his private economy. It is probable that Alice preferred it this way. She was not a talker. A terse report was easiest for her. She was busy with the growing boys and with keeping the house clean and the clothes washed. Also, she had to conserve her energy, though she did not mention this in any of her reports. Without warning her energy would leave her, and she would have to sit down and wait until it came back. In the night she would be drenched with perspiration. She knew perfectly well that she had what was called consumption, would have known even if she was not reminded by a hard, exhausting cough. And she did not know how long she would live. Some people wasted on for quite a few years. There wasn't any rule about it. Perhaps she didn't dare to mention it to her husband. He had

21

devised a method of dealing with sickness which resembled punishment. A stomach-ache was treated with a purge so violent that it was a wonder anyone survived it. If she had mentioned her condition, Cyrus might have started a treatment which would have killed her off before her consumption could have done it. Besides, as Cyrus became more military, his wife learned the only technique through which a soldier can survive. She never made herself noticeable, never spoke unless spoken to, performed what was expected and no more, and tried for no promotions. She became a rear rank private. It was much easier that way. Alice retired to the background until she was barely visible at all.

It was the little boys who really caught it. Cyrus had decided that even though the army was not perfect, it was still the only honourable profession for a man. He mourned the fact that he could not be a permanent soldier because of his wooden leg, but he could not imagine any career for his sons except the army. He felt a man should learn soldiering from the ranks, as he had. Then he would know what it was about from experience, not from charts and textbooks. He taught them the manual of arms when they could barely walk. By the time they were in grade school, close-order drill was as natural as breathing and as hateful as hell. He kept them hard with exercises, beating out the rhythm with a stick on his wooden leg. He made them walk for miles, carrying knapsacks loaded with stones to make their shoulders strong. He worked constantly on their marksmanship in the wood-lot behind the house.

11

When a child first catches adults out – when it first walks into his grave little head that adults do not have divine intelligence, that their judgements are not always wise, their thinking true, their sentences just – his world falls into panic desolation. The gods are fallen and all safety gone. And there is one sure thing about the fall of gods: they do not fall a little; they crash and shatter or sink deeply into green muck. It is a tedious job to build them up again; they never quite shine. And the child's world is never quite whole again. It is an aching kind of growing.

Adam found his father out. It wasn't that his father changed, but that some new quality came to Adam. He had always hated the discipline, as every normal animal does, but it was just and true and inevitable as measles, not to be denied or cursed, only

22

to be hated. And then – it was very fast, almost a click in the brain – Adam knew that, for him at least, his father's methods had no reference to anything in the world but his father. The techniques and training were not designed for the boys at all but only to make Cyrus a great man. And the same click in the brain told Adam that his father was not a great man, that he was, indeed, a very strong-willed and concentrated little man wearing a huge busby. Who knows what causes this – a look in the eye, a lie found out, a moment of hesitation? – then god comes crashing down in a child's brain.

Young Adam was always an obedient child. Something in him shrank from violence, from contention, from the silent shrieking tensions that can rip at a house. He contributed to the quiet he wished for by offering no violence, no contention and to do this he had to retire into secretness, since there is some violence in everyone. He covered his life with a veil of vagueness, while behind his quiet eyes a rich full life went on. This did not protect him from assault but it allowed him an immunity.

His half-brother, Charles, only a little over a year younger, grew up with his father's assertiveness. Charles was a natural athlete, with instinctive timing and co-ordination and the competitor's will to win over others, which makes for success in the world.

Young Charles won all contests with Adam whether they involved skill, or strength, or quick intelligence, and won them so easily that quite early he lost interest and had to find his competition among other children. Thus it came about that a kind of affection grew between the two boys, but it was more like an association between brother and sister than between brothers. Charles fought any boy who challenged or slurred Adam and usually won. He protected Adam from his father's harshness with lies and even with blame-taking. Charles felt for his brother the affection one has for helpless things, for blind puppies and new babies.

Adam looked out of his covered brain – out of the long tunnels of his eyes – at the people of his world. His father, a one-legged natural force at first, installed justly to make little boys feel littler and stupid boys aware of their stupidity; and then – after god had crashed – he saw his father as the policeman laid on by birth, the officer who might be circumvented, or fooled, but never challenged. And out of the long tunnels of his eyes Adam say his half-brother Charles as a bright being of another species, gifted with muscle and bone, speed and alertness, quite on a different plane, to be admired as one admires the sleek lazy danger of a black leopard, not by any chance to be compared with oneself. And it would no more have occurred to Adam to confide in his brother – to tell him the hunger, the grey dreams, the plans and silent pleasures that lay at the back of the tunnelled eyes – than to share his thoughts with a lovely tree or a pheasant in flight. Adam was glad of Charles the way a woman is glad of a fat diamond, and he depended on his brother in the way that same woman depends on the diamond's glitter and the self-security tied up in its worth; but love, affection, empathy, were beyond conception.

Towards Alice Trask, Adam concealed a feeling that was akin to a warm shame. She was not his mother – that he knew because he had been told many times. Not from things said but from the tone in which other things were said, he knew that he had once had a mother and that she had done some shameful thing, such as forgetting the chickens or missing the target on the range in the wood-lot. And as a result of her fault she was not here. Adam thought sometimes that if he could only find out what sin it was she had committed, why, he would sin it too – and not be here.

Alice treated the boys equally, washed them and fed them, and left everything else to their father, who had let it be known clearly and with finality that training the boys physically and mentally was his exclusive province. Even praise and reprimand he would not delegate. Alice never complained, quarrelled, laughed, or cried. Her mouth was trained to a line that concealed nothing and offered nothing too. But once when Adam was quite small he wandered silently into the kitchen. Alice did not see him. She was darning socks and she was smiling. Adam retired secretly and walked out of the house and into the wood-lot to a sheltered place behind a stump that he knew well. He settled deep between the protecting roots. Adam was as shocked as though he had come upon her naked. He breathed excitedly, high against his throat. For Alice had been naked – she had been smiling. He wondered how she had dared such wantonness. And he ached towards her with a longing that was passionate and hot. He did not know what it was about, but all the long lack of holding, of rocking, of caressing, the hunger for breast and nipple, and the softness of a lap, and the voice-tone of love and compassion, and the sweet feeling of anxiety – all these were in his passion, and he did not know it because he did not know that such things existed, so how could he miss them.

Of course it occurred to him that he might be wrong, that some misbegotten shadow had fallen across his face and warped his seeing. And so he cast back to the sharp picture in his head and knew that the eyes were smiling too. Twisted light could do one or the other but not both.

He stalked her then, game-wise, as he had the woodchucks on the knoll when day after day he had lain lifeless as a young stone and watched the old wary chucks bring their children out to sun. He spied on Alice, hidden, and from unsuspected eye-corner, and it was true. Sometimes when she was alone, and knew she was alone, she permitted her mind to play in a garden, and she smiled. And it was wonderful to see how quickly she could drive the smile to earth the way the woodchucks holed their children.

Adam concealed his treasure deep in his tunnels, but he was inclined to pay for his pleasure with something. Alice began to find gifts – in her sewing basket, in her worn-out purse, under her pillow – two cinnamon pinks, a bluebird's tail-feather, half a stick of green sealing wax, a stolen handkerchief. At first Alice was startled, but then that passed, and when she found some unsuspected present the garden smile flashed and disappeared the way a trout crosses a knife of sunshine in a pool. She asked no questions and made no comment.

Her coughing was very bad at night, so loud and disturbing that Cyrus had at last to put her in another room or he would have got no sleep. But he did visit her very often – hopping on his one bare foot, steadying himself with hand on wall. The boys could hear and feel the jar of his body through the house as he hopped to and from Alice's bed.

As Adam grew he feared one thing more than any other. He feared the day he would be taken and enlisted in the army. His father never let him forget that such a time would come. He spoke of it often. It was Adam who needed the army to make a man of him. Charles was pretty near a man already. And Charles was a man, and a dangerous man, even at fifteen, and when Adam was sixteen.

III

The affection between the two boys had grown with the years. It maybe that part of Charles's feeling was contempt, but it was a protective contempt. It happened that one evening the boys were playing peewee, a new game to them, in the door-yard. A small

25

pointed stick was laid on the ground, then struck near one end with a bat. The small stick flew into the air and then was batted as far as possible.

Adam was not good at games. But by some accident of eye and timing he beat his brother at peewee. Four times he drove the peewee farther than Charles did. It was a new experience to him, and a wild flush came over him, so that he did not watch and feel out his brother's mood as he usually did. The fifth time he drove the peewee it flew humming like a bee far out in the field. He turned happily to face Charles and suddenly he froze deep in his chest. The hatred in Charles's face frightened him. 'I guess it was just an accident,' he said lamely. 'I bet I couldn't do it again.'

Charles set his peewee, struck it, and, as it rose into the air, struck at it and missed. Charles moved slowly towards Adam, his eyes cold and non-committal. Adam edged away in terror. He did not dare to turn and run, for his brother could outrun him. He backed slowly away, his eyes frightened and his throat dry. Charles moved close and struck him in the face with his bat. Adam covered his bleeding nose with his hands, and Charles swung his bat and hit him in the ribs, knocked the wind out of him, swung at his head and knocked him out. And as Adam lay unconscious on the ground Charles kicked him heavily in the stomach and walked away.

After a while Adam became conscious. He breathed shallowly because his chest hurt. He tried to sit up and fell back at the wrench of the torn muscles over his stomach. He saw Alice looking out, and there was something in her face that he had never seen before. He did not know what it was, but it was not soft or weak, and it might be hatred. She saw that he was looking at her, dropped the curtains into place, and disappeared. When Adam finally got up from the ground and moved, bent over, into the kitchen, he found a basin of hot water standing ready for him and a clean towel beside it. He could hear his step-mother coughing in her room.

Charles had one great quality. He was never sorry – ever. He never mentioned the beating, apparently never thought of it again. But Adam made very sure that he didn't win again – at anything. He had always felt the danger in his brother, but now he understood that he must never win unless he was prepared to kill Charles. Charles was not sorry. He had very simply fulfilled himself.

Charles did not tell his father about the beating, and Adam

did not, and surely Alice did not, and yet he seemed to know. In the months that followed he turned a gentleness on Adam. His speech became softer towards him. He did not punish him any more. Almost nightly he lectured him, but not violently. And Adam was more afraid of the gentleness than he had been at the violence, for it seemed to him that he was being trained as a sacrifice, almost as though he was being subjected to kindness before death, the way victims intended for the gods were cuddled and flattered so that they might go happily to the stone and not outrage the gods with unhappiness.

Cyrus explained softly to Adam the nature of a soldier. And though his knowledge came from research rather than experience, he knew and he was accurate. He told his son of the sad dignity that can belong to a soldier, how he is necessary in the light of all the failures of man – the penalty of our frailties. Perhaps Cyrus discovered these things in himself as he told them. It was very different from the flag-waving, shouting bellicosity of his younger days. The humilities are piled on a soldier, so Cyrus said, in order that he may, when the time comes, be not too resentful of the final humility – a meaningless and dirty death. And Cyrus talked to Adam alone and did not permit Charles to listen.

Cyrus took Adam to walk with him one late afternoon, and the black conclusions of all of his study and his thinking came out and flowed with a kind of thick terror over his son. He said, 'I'll have you know that a soldier is the most holy of all humans because he is the most tested – most tested of all. I'll try to tell you. Look now – in all of history men have been taught that killing of men is an evil thing not to be countenanced. Any man who kills must be destroyed because this is a great sin, maybe the worst sin we know. And then we take a soldier and put murder in his hands and we say to him, "Use it well, use it wisely." We put no checks on him. Go out and kill as many of a certain kind or classification of your brothers as you can. And we will reward you for it because it is a violation of your early training.'

Adam wet his dry lips and tried to ask and failed and tried again. 'Why do they have to do it?' he said. 'Why is it?'

Cyrus was deeply moved and he spoke as he had never spoken before. 'I don't know,' he said. 'I've studied and maybe learned how things are, but I'm not even close to why they are. And you must not expect to find that people understand what they do. So many things are done instinctively, the way a bee makes

27

honey or a fox dips his paws in a stream to fool dogs. A fox can't say why he does it, and what bee remembers winter or expects it to come again? When I knew you had to go I thought to leave the future open so you could dig out your own findings, and then it seemed better if I could protect you with the little I know. You'll go in soon now – you've come to the age.'

"I don't want to,' said Adam quickly.

'You'll go in soon,' his father went on, not hearing. 'And I want to tell you so you won't be surprised. They'll first strip off your clothes, but they'll go deeper than that. They'll shuck off any little dignity you have – you'll lose what you think of as your decent right to live and to be let alone to live. They'll make you live and eat and sleep and shit close to other men. And when they dress you up again you'll not be able to tell yourself from the others. You can't even wear a scrap or pin a note on your breast to say, "This is me – separate from the rest." '

'I don't want to do it,' said Adam.

'After a while,' said Cyrus, 'you'll think no thought the others do not think. You'll know no word the others can't say. And you'll do things because the others do them. You'll feel the danger in any difference whatever – a danger to the whole crowd of like-thinking, like-acting men.'

'What if I don't?' Adam demanded.

'Yes,' said Cyrus, 'sometimes that happens. Once in a while there is a man who won't do what is demanded of him, and do you know what happens? The whole machine devotes itself coldly to the destruction of his difference. They'll beat your spirit and your nerves, your body and your mind, with iron rods until the dangerous difference goes out of you. And if you can't finally give in, they'll vomit you up and leave you stinking outside – neither part of themselves nor yet free. It's better to fall in with them. They only do it to protect themselves. A thing so triumphantly illogical, so beautifully senseless as an army can't allow a question to weaken it. Within itself, if you do not hold it up to other things for comparison and derision, you'll find slowly, surely, a reason and a logic and a kind of dreadful beauty. A man who can accept it is not a worse man always, and sometimes is a much better man. Pay good heed to me, for I have thought long about it. Some men there are who go down the dismal wrack of soldiering, surrender themselves and become faceless. But these had not much face to start with. And maybe you're like that. But there are others who go down, submerge in the common slough, and then rise more themselves than they

28

were, because – because they have lost a littleness of vanity and have gained all the gold of the company and the regiment. If you can go down so low, you will be able to rise higher than you can conceive, and you will know a holy joy, a companionship almost like that of a heavenly company of angels. Then you will know the quality of men even if they are inarticulate. But until you have gone way down you can never know this.'

As they walked back towards the house Cyrus turned left and entered the wood-lot among the trees, and it was dusk. Suddenly Adam said, 'You see that stump there, sir? I used to hide between the roots on the far side. After you punished me I used to hide there, and sometimes I went there just because I felt bad.'

'Let's go and see the place,' his father said. Adam led him to it, and Cyrus looked down at the nest-like hole between the roots. 'I knew about it long ago,' he said. 'Once when you were gone a long time I thought you must have such a place, and I found it because I felt the kind of a place you would need. See how the earth is tamped and the little grass is torn? And while you sat in there you stripped little pieces of bark to shreds. I knew it was the place when I came upon it.'

Adam was staring at his father in wonder. 'You never came here looking for me,' he said.

'No,' Cyrus replied. 'I wouldn't do that. You can drive a human too far. I wouldn't do that. Always you must leave a man one escape before death. Remember that! I knew, I guess, how hard I was pressing you. I didn't want to push you over the edge.'

They moved restlessly off through the trees. Cyrus said, 'So many things I want to tell you. I'll forget most of them. I want to tell you that a soldier gives up so much to get something back. From the day of a child's birth he is taught by every circumstance, by every law and rule and right, to protect his own life. He starts with that great instinct, and everything confirms it. And then he is a soldier and he must learn to violate all of this – he must learn coldly to put himself in the way of losing his own life without going mad. And if you can do that – and, mind you, some can't – then you will have the greatest gift of all. Look, son,' Cyrus said earnestly, 'nearly all men are afraid, and they don't even know what causes their fear – shadows, perplexities, dangers without names or numbers, fear of a faceless death. But if you can bring yourself to face not shadows but real death, described and recognizable, by bullet or sabre, arrow or lance, then you need never be afraid again, at least not in the same way you were before. Then you will be a man set apart from other men, safe where other men may cry in terror. This is the great reward. Maybe this is the only reward. Maybe this is the final purity all ringed with filth. It's nearly dark. I'll want to talk to you again tomorrow night when both of us have thought about what I've told you.'

But Adam said, 'Why don't you talk to my brother? Charles will be going. He'll be good at it, much better than I am.'

'Charles won't be going,' Cyrus said. 'There'd be no point in it.'

'But he would be a better soldier.'

'Only outside on his skin,' said Cyrus. 'Not inside. Charles is not afraid, so he could never learn anything about courage. He does not know anything outside himself, so he could never gain the things I've tried to explain to you. To put him in an army would be to let loose things which in Charles must be chained down, not let loose. I would not dare to let him go.'

Adam complained, 'You never punished him, you let him live his own life, you praised him, you did not haze him, and now you let him stay out of the army.' He stopped, frightened at what he had said, afraid of the rage or the contempt or the violence his words might let loose.

His father did not reply. He walked on out of the wood-lot, and his head hung down so that his chin rested on his chest, and the rise and fall of his hip when his wooden leg struck the ground was monotonous. The wood leg made a side-semicircle to get ahead when its turn came.

It was completely dark by now, and the golden light of the lamps shone out from the open kitchen window. Alice came to the doorway and peered out, looking for them, and then she heard the uneven footsteps approaching and went back to the kitchen.

Cyrus walked to the kitchen stoop before he stopped and raised his head. 'Where are you?' he asked.

'Here – right behind you – right here.'

'You asked a question. I guess I'll have to answer. Maybe it's good and maybe it's bad to answer. You're not clever. You don't know what you want. You have no proper fierceness. You let other people walk over you. Sometimes I think you're a weakling who will never amount to a dog turd. Does that answer your question? I love you better. I always have. This may be a bad thing to tell you, but it's true. I love you better. Else why would I have given myself the trouble of hurting you? Now shut your mouth and go to your supper. I'll talk to you tomorrow night. My leg aches.'

There was no talk at supper. The quiet was disturbed only by the slup of soup and gnash of chewing, and his father waved his hand to try to drive the moths away from the chimney of the kerosene lamp. Adam thought his brother watched him secretly. And he caught an eye-flash from Alice when he looked up suddenly. After he had finished eating, Adam pushed back his chair. 'I think I'll go for a walk,' he said.

Charles stood up. 'I'll go with you.'

Alice and Cyrus watched them go out of the door, and then she asked one of her rare questions. She asked nervously, 'What did you do?'

'Nothing,' he said.

'Will you make him go?'

'Yes.'

'Does he know?'

Cyrus stared bleakly out of the open door into the darkness. 'Yes, he knows.'

'He won't like it. It's not right for him.'

'It doesn't matter,' Cyrus said, and he repeated loudly, 'It doesn't matter,' and his tone said, 'Shut your mouth. This is not your affair.' They were silent a moment, and then he said almost in a tone of apology, 'It isn't as though he were your child.'

Alice did not reply.

The boys walked down the dark rutty road. Ahead they could see a few pinched lights where the village was.

'Want to go in and see if anything's stirring at the inn?' Charles asked.

'I hadn't thought of it,' said Adam.

'Then what the hell are you walking out at night for?'

'You didn't have to come,' said Adam.

Charles moved close to him. 'What did he say to you this afternoon? I saw you walking together. What did he say?'

'He just talked about the army – like always.'

'Didn't look like that to me,' Charles said suspiciously. 'I saw him leaning close, talking the way he talks to men – not telling, talking.'

'He was telling,' Adam said patiently, and he had to control his breath, for a little fear had begun to press up against his stomach. He took as deep a gulp of air as he could and held it to push back at the fear.

'What did he tell you?' Charles demanded again.

'About the army and how it is to be a soldier.'

'I don't believe you,' said Charles. 'I think you're a goddam mealy-mouthed liar. What're you trying to get away with?'

'Nothing,' said Adam.

Charles said harshly, 'Your crazy mother drowned herself. Maybe she took a look at you. That'd do it.'

Adam let out his breath gently, pressing down the dismal fear. He was silent.

Charles cried, 'You're trying to take him away! I don't know how you're going about it. What do you think you're doing?'

'Nothing,' said Adam.

Charles jumped in front of him so that Adam had to stop, his chest almost against his brother's chest. Adam backed away, but carefully, as one backs away from a snake.

'Look at his birthday!' Charles shouted. 'I took six bits and I bought him a knife made in Germany – three blades and a corkscrew, pearl-handled. Where's that knife? Do you ever see him use it? Did he give it to you? I never even saw him hone it. Have you got that knife in your pocket? What did he do with it? "Thanks," he said, like that. And that's the last I heard of a pearl-handled German knife that cost six bits.'

Rage was in his voice and Adam felt the creeping fear; but he knew also that he had a moment left. Too many times he had seen the destructive machine that chopped down anything standing in its way. Rage came first and then a coldness, a possession; non-committal eyes and a pleased smile and no voice at all, only a whisper. When that happened murder was on the way, but cool, deft murder, and hands that worked precisely, delicately. Adam swallowed saliva to dampen his dry throat. He could think of nothing to say that would be heard, for once in rage his brother would not listen, would not even hear. He bulked darkly in front of Adam, shorter, wider, thicker, but still not crouched. In the starlight his lips shone with wetness, but there was no smile yet and his voice still raged.

'What did you do on his birthday? You think I didn't see? Did you spend six bits or even four bits. You brought him a mongrel pup you had picked up in the wood-lot. You laughed like a fool and said it would make a good bird dog. That dog sleeps in his room. He plays with it while he's reading. He's got it all trained. And where's the knife? "Thanks," he said, just

"Thanks".' Charles spoke in a whisper and his shoulders dropped.

Adam made one desperate jump backwards and raised his hands to guard his face. His brother moved precisely, each foot planted firmly. One fist lanced delicately to get the range, and then the bitter-frozen work – a hard blow in the stomach, and Adam's hands dropped; then four punches to the head. Adam felt the bone and gristle of his nose crunch. He raised his hands again and Charles drove at his heart. And all this time Adam looked at his brother as the condemned look hopelessly and puzzled at the executioner.

Suddenly, to his own surprise, Adam launched a wild, over-hand, harmless swing which had neither force nor direction. Charles ducked in and under it and the helpless arm went around his neck. Adam wrapped his arms around his brother and hung close to him, sobbing. He felt the square fists whipping nausea into his stomach and still he held on. Time was slowed to him. With his body he felt his brother move sideways to force his legs apart. And he felt the knee come up, past his knees, scraping his thighs, until it crashed against his testicles and flashing white pain ripped and echoed through his body. His arms let go. He bent over and vomited, while the cold killing went on.

Adam felt the punches on temples, cheeks, eyes. He felt his lip split and tatter over his teeth, but his skin seemed thickened and dull, as though he were encased in heavy rubber. Dully he wondered why his legs did not buckle, why he did not fall, why un-consciousness did not come to him. The punching continued eternally. He could hear his brother panting with the quick ex-plosive breath of a sledge-hammer man, and in the sick starlit dark he could see his brother through the tear-watered blood that flowed from his eyes. He saw the innocent, non-committal eyes, the small smile on wet lips. And as he saw these things – a flash of light and darkness.

Charles stood over him, gulping air like a run-out dog. And then he turned and walked quickly back, towards the house, kneading his bruised knuckles as he went.

Consciousness came back quick and frightening to Adam. His mind rolled in a painful mist. His body was heavy and thick with hurt. But almost instantly he forgot his hurts. He heard quick footsteps on the road. The instinctive fear and fierceness of a rat came over him. He pushed himself up on his knees and dragged himself off the road to the ditch that kept it drained. There was a foot of water in the ditch, and the tall

33

grass grew up from its sides. Adam crawled quietly into the water, being very careful to make no splash.

The footsteps came close, slowed, moved on a little, came back. From his hiding-place Adam could see only a darkness in the dark. And then a sulphur match was struck and burned a tiny blue until the wood caught, lighting his brother's face grotesquely from below. Charles raised the match and peered around, and Adam could see the hatchet in his right hand.

When the match went out the night was blacker than before. Charles moved slowly on and struck another match, and on and struck another. He searched the road for signs. At last he gave it up. His right hand rose and he threw the hatchet far off into the field. He walked rapidly away towards the pinched lights of the village.

For a long time Adam lay in the cool water. He wondered how his brother felt, wondered whether now that his passion was chilling he would feel panic or sorrow or sick conscience or nothing. These things Adam felt for him. His conscience bridged him to his brother and did his pain for him the way at other times he had done his homework.

Adam crept out of the water and stood up. His hurts were stiffening and the blood was dried in a crust on his face. He thought he would stay outside in the darkness until his father and Alice went to bed. He felt that he could not answer any questions, because he did not know any answers, and trying to find one was harsh to his battered mind. Dizziness edged with blue lights came fringing his forehead, and he knew that he would be fainting soon.

He shuffled slowly up the road with wide-spread legs. At the stoop he paused, looked in. The lamp hanging by its chain from the ceiling cast a yellow circle and lighted Alice and her mending-basket on the table in front of her. On the other side his father chewed a wooden pen and dipped it in an open ink bottle and made entries in his black record book.

Alice, glancing up, saw Adam's bloody face. Her hand rose to her mouth and her fingers hooked over her lower teeth.

Adam drag-footed up one step and then the other and supported himself in the doorway.

Then Cyrus raised his head. He looked with a distant curiosity. The identity of the distortion came to him slowly. He stood up, puzzled and wondering. He stuck the wooden pen in the ink bottle and wiped his fingers on his trousers. 'Why did he do it?' Cyrus asked softly.

34

Adam tried to answer, but his mouth was caked and dry. He licked his lips and started them bleeding again. 'I don't know,' he said.

Cyrus stumped over to him and grasped him by the arm so fiercely that he winced and tried to pull away. 'Don't lie to me! Why did he do it? Did you have an argument?'

'No.'

Cyrus wrenched at him. 'Tell me! I want to know. Tell me! You'll have to tell me. I'll make you tell me! Goddam it, you're always protecting him! Don't you think I know that? Did you think you were fooling me? Now tell me, or by God I'll keep you standing there all night!'

Adam cast about for an answer. 'He doesn't think you love him.'

Cyrus released the arm and hobbled back to his chair and sat down. He rattled the pen in the ink bottle and looked blindly at his record book. 'Alice,' he said, 'help Adam to bed. You'll have to cut his shirt off, I guess. Give him a hand.' He got up again, went to the corner of the room where the coats hung on nails and, reaching behind the garments, brought out his shotgun, broke it to verify its load, and clumped out of the door.

Alice raised her hand as though she would hold him back with a rope of air. And her rope broke and her face hid her thoughts. 'Go in your room,' she said. 'I'll bring some water in a basin.'

Adam lay on the bed, a sheet pulled up to his waist, and Alice patted the cuts with a linen handkerchief dipped in warm water. She was silent for a long time and then she continued Adam's sentence as though there had never been an interval, 'He doesn't think his father loves him. But you love him – you always have.'

Adam did not answer her.

She went on quietly, 'He's a strange boy. You have to know him – all rough shell, all anger until you know.' She paused to cough, leaned down and coughed, and when the spell was over her cheeks were flushed and she was exhausted. 'You have to know him,' she repeated. 'For a long time he has given me little presents, pretty things you wouldn't think he'd even notice. But he doesn't give them right out. He hides them where he knows I'll find them. And you can look at him for hours and he won't ever give the slightest sign he did it. You have to know him.'

She smiled at Adam and he closed his eyes.

CHAPTER 4

I

CHARLES STOOD at the bar in the village inn and Charles was laughing delightedly at the funny stories the night-stranded drummers were telling. He got out his tobacco sack with its meagre jingle of silver and bought the men a drink to keep them talking. He stood and grinned and rubbed his split knuckles. And when the drummers, accepting his drink, raised their glasses and said, 'Here's to you,' Charles was delighted. He ordered another drink for his new friends, and then he joined them for some kind of deviltry in another place.

When Cyrus stumped out into the night he was filled with a kind of despairing anger at Charles. He looked on the road for his son, and he went to the inn to look for him, but Charles was gone. It is probable that if he had found him that night he would have killed him, or tried to. The direction of a big act will warp history, but probably all acts do the same in their degree, down to a stone stepped over in the path or a breath caught at sight of a pretty girl or a finger-nail nicked in the garden soil.

Naturally it was not long before Charles was told that his father was looking for him with a shotgun. He hid out for two weeks, and when he finally did return, murder had sunk back to simple anger and he paid his penalty in overwork and a false, theatrical humility.

Adam lay four days in bed, so stiff and aching that he could not move without a groan. On the third day his father gave evidence of his power with the military. He did it as a poultice to his own pride and also as a kind of prize for Adam. Into the house, into Adam's bedroom, came a captain of cavalry and two sergeants in dress uniform of blue. In the door-yard their horses were held by two privates. Lying in his bed, Adam was enlisted in the army as a private in the cavalry. He signed the Articles of war and took the oath while his father and Alice looked on. And his father's eyes glistened with tears.

After the soldiers had gone his father sat with him a long time. 'I've put you in the cavalry for a reason,' he said. 'Barrack life is not a good life for long. But the cavalry has work to do. I made sure of that. You'll like going for the Indian country.

There's action coming. I can't tell you how I know. There's fighting on the way.'

'Yes, sir,' Adam said.

11

It has always seemed strange to me that it is usually men like Adam who have to do the soldiering. He did not like fighting to start with, and far from learning to love it, as some men do, he felt an increasing revulsion for violence. Several times his officers looked closely at him for malingering, but no charge was brought. During these five years of soldiering Adam did more detail work than any man in the squadron, but if he killed an enemy it was an accident of ricochet. Being a marksman and sharpshooter, he was peculiarly fitted to miss. By this time the Indian fighting had become like dangerous cattle-drives – the tribes were forced into revolt, driven and decimated, and the sad, sullen remnants settled on starvation lands. It was not nice work, but, given the pattern of the country's development, it had to be done.

To Adam, who was an instrument, who saw not the future farms but only the torn bellies of fine humans, it was revolting and useless. When he fired his carbine to miss he was committing treason against his unit, and he didn't care. The emotion of non-violence was building in him until it became a prejudice like any other thought-stultifying prejudice. To inflict any hurt on anything for any purpose became inimical to him. He became obsessed with this emotion, for such it surely was, until it blotted out any possible thinking in its area. Indeed he was commended three times and then decorated for bravery.

As he revolted more and more from violence, his impulse took the opposite direction. He ventured his life a number of times to bring in wounded men. He volunteered for work in field hospitals even when he was exhausted from his regular duties. He was regarded by his comrades with contemptuous affection and the unspoken fear men have of impulses they do not understand.

Charles wrote to his brother regularly – of the farm and the village, of sick cows and a foaling mare, of the added pasture and the lightning-struck barn, of Alice's choking death from her consumption and his father's move to a permanent paid position in the GAR in Washington. As with many people, Charles, who could not talk, wrote with fullness. He set down his loneliness

37

and his perplexities, and he put on paper many things he did not know about himself.

During the time Adam was away he knew his brother better than ever before or afterwards. In the exchange of letters there grew a closeness neither of them could have imagined.

Adam kept one letter from his brother, not because he understood it completely but because it seemed to have a covered meaning he could not get at. 'Dear Brother Adam,' the letter said, 'I take my pen in hand to hope you are in good health' – he always started this way to ease himself gently into the task of writing. 'I have not had your answer to my last letter, but I presume you have other things to do – ha! ha! The rain came wrong and damned the apple blossoms. There won't be many to eat next winter but I will save what I can. Tonight I cleaned the house and it is wet and soapy and maybe not any cleaner. How do you suppose Mother kept it the way she did? It does not look the same. Something settles down on it. I don't know what, but it will not scrub off. But I have spread the dirt around more evenly anyways. Ha! ha!

'Did Father write you anything about his trip? He's gone clean out to San Francisco in California for an encampment of the Grand Army. The Secty. of War is going to be there, and Father is to introduce him. But this is not any great shucks to Father. He has met the President, three, four times and even been to supper to the White House. I would like to see the White House. Maybe you and me can go together when you come home. Father could put us up for a few days and he would be wanting to see you anyways.

'I think I better look around for a wife. This is a good farm, and even if I'm no bargain there's girls could do worse than this farm. What do you think? You did not say if you are going to come live home when you get out of the army. I hope so. I miss you.'

The writing stopped there. There was a scratch on the page and a splash of ink and then it went on in pencil, but the writing was different.

In pencil it said, 'Later. Well, right there the pen give out. One of the points broke off. I'll have to buy another pen-point in the village – rusted right through.'

The words began to flow more smoothly. 'I guess I should wait for a new pen-point and not write with a pencil. Only I was sitting here in the kitchen with the lamp on and I guess I got to thinking and it come on late – after twelve, I guess, but I never looked. Old Black Joe started crowing out in the hen-house. Then Mother's rocking-chair cricked for all the world like she was sitting in it. You know I don't take truck with that, but it set me minding backwards, you know how you do some-times. I guess I'll tear this letter up maybe, because what's the good of writing stuff like this.'

The words began to race now as though they couldn't get out fast enough. 'If I'm to throw it away I'd just as well set it down,' the letter said. 'It's like the whole house was alive and had eyes everywhere, and like there was people behind the door just ready to come in if you looked away. It kind of makes my skin crawl. I want to say – I want to say – I mean, I never understood – well why our father did it. I mean, why didn't he like that knife I bought for him on his birthday. Why didn't he? It was a good knife and he needed a good knife. If he had used it or even honed it, or took it out of his pocket and looked at it – that's all he had to do. If he'd liked it I wouldn't have took out after you. I had to take out after you. Seems like to me my mother's chair is rocking a little. It's just the light. I don't take any truck with that. Seems like to me there's something not finished. Seems like when you half finished a job and can't think what it was. Some-thing didn't get done. I shouldn't be here. I ought to be wan-dering around the world instead of sitting here on a good farm looking for a wife. There is something wrong, like it didn't get finished, like it happened too soon and left something out. It's me should be where you are and you here. I never thought like this before. Maybe because it's late – it's later than that. I just looked out and it's first dawn. I don't think I fell off to sleep. How could the night go so fast? I can't go to bed now. I couldn't sleep anyways.'

The letter was not signed. Maybe Charles forgot he had in-tended to destroy it and sent it along. But Adam saved it for a time, and whenever he read it again it gave him a chill and he didn't know why.

CHAPTER 5

O N T H E ranch the little Hamiltons began to grow up, and every year there was a new one. George was a tall handsome boy, gentle and sweet, who had from the first a kind of courtliness. Even as a little boy he was polite and what they used to call 'no trouble'. From his father he inherited the neatness of clothing and body and hair, and he never seemed ill-dressed even when he was. George was a sinless boy and grew to be a sinless man. No crime of commission was ever attributed to him, and his crimes of omission were only misdemeanours. In his middle life, at about the time such things were known about, it was discovered that he had pernicious anaemia. It is possible that his virtue lived on a lack of energy.

Behind George, Will grew along, dumpy and stolid. Will had little imagination but he had great energy. From childhood on he was a hard worker, if anyone would tell him what to work at, and once told he was indefatigable. He was a conservative, not only in politics but in everything. Ideas he found revolutionary, and he avoided them with suspicion and distaste. Will lived to live so that no one could find fault with him, and to do that he had to live as nearly like other people as possible.

Maybe his father had something to do with Will's distaste for either change or variation. When Will was a growing boy, his father had not been long enough in the Salinas Valley to be thought of as an 'old-timer'. He was in fact a foreigner and an Irishman. At that time the Irish were much disliked in America. They were looked upon with contempt, particularly on the East Coast, but a little of it must have seeped out to the West. And Samuel had not only variability but was a man of ideas and innovations. In small cut-off communities such a man is always regarded with suspicion until he has proved he is no danger to the others. A shining man like Samuel could, and can, cause a lot of trouble. He might, for example, prove too attractive to the wives of men who knew they were dull. Then there were his education and his reading, the books he bought and borrowed, his knowledge of things that could not be eaten or worn or co-habited with, his interest in poetry and his respect for good writing. If Samuel had been a rich man like the Thornes or the Delmars, with their big houses and wide flat lands, he would have had a great library.

40

The Delmars had a library – nothing but books in it and panelled in oak. Samuel, by borrowing, had read many more of the Delmars' books than the Delmars had. In that day an educated rich man was acceptable. He might send his sons to college without comment, might wear a vest and white shirt and tie in the day-time of a week-day, might wear gloves and keep his nails clean. And since the lives and practices of rich men were mysterious, who knows what they could use or not use? But a poor man – what need had he for poetry or for painting or for music not fit for singing or dancing? Such things did not help him bring in a crop or keep a scrap of cloth on his children's backs. And if in spite of this he persisted, maybe he had reasons which would not stand the light of scrutiny.

Take Samuel, for instance. He made drawings of work he intended to do with iron or wood. That was good and understandable, even enviable. But on the edges of the plans he made other drawings, sometimes trees, sometimes faces or animals or bugs, sometimes just figures that you couldn't make out at all. And these caused men to laugh with embarrassed uneasiness. Then, too, you never knew in advance what Samuel would think or say or do – it might be anything.

The first few years after Samuel came to Salinas Valley there was a vague distrust of him. And perhaps Will as a little boy heard talk in the San Lucas store. Little boys don't want their fathers to be different from other men. Will might have picked up his conservatism right then. Later, as the other children came along and grew, Samuel belonged to the valley, and it was proud of him in the way a man who owns a peacock is proud. They weren't afraid of him any more, for he did not seduce their wives or lure them out of sweet mediocrity. The Salinas Valley grew fond of Samuel, but by that time Will was formed.

Certain individuals, not by any means always deserving, are truly beloved of the gods. Things come to them without their effort or planning. Will Hamilton was one of these. And the gifts he received were the ones he could appreciate. As a growing boy Will was lucky. Just as his father could not make money, Will could not help making it. When Will Hamilton raised chickens and his hens began to lay, the price of eggs went up. As a young man, when two of his friends who ran a little store came to the point of despondent bankruptcy, Will was asked to lend them a little money to tide them over the quarter's bills, and they gave him a one-third interest for a pittance. He was not niggardly. He gave them what they asked for. The store was on its feet within one year, expanding in two, opening branches in three, and its descendants, a great mercantile system, now dominate a large part of the area.

Will also took over a bicycle-and-tool shop for a bad debt. Then a few rich people of the valley bought automobiles, and his mechanic worked on them. Pressure was put on him by a determined poet whose dreams were brass, cast iron, and rubber. This man's name was Henry Ford, and his plans were ridiculous if not illegal. Will grumblingly accepted the southern half of the valley as his exclusive area, and within fifteen years the valley was two-deep in Fords and Will was a rich man driving a Marmon.

Tom, the third son, was most like his father. He was born in fury and he lived in lightning. Tom came headlong into life. He was a giant in joy and enthusiasms. He didn't discover the world and its people, he created them. When he read his father's books, he was the first. He lived in a world shining and fresh and as uninspected as Eden on the sixth day. His mind plunged like a colt in a happy pasture, and when later the world put up fences he plunged against the wire, and when the final stockade surrounded him, he plunged right through it and out. And as he was capable of giant joy, so did he harbour huge sorrow, so that when his dog died, the world ended.

Tom was as inventive as his father but he was bolder. He would try things his father would not dare. Also, he had a large concupiscence to put the spurs in his flanks, and this Samuel did not have. Perhaps it was his driving sexual need that made him remain a bachelor. It was a very moral family he was born into. It might be that his dreams and his longing, and his outlets, for that matter, made him feel unworthy, drove him sometimes whining into the hills. Tom was a nice mixture of savagery and gentleness. He worked inhumanly, only to lose in effort his crushing impulses.

The Irish do have a despairing quality of gaiety, but they have also a dour and brooding ghost that rides on their shoulders and peers in on their thoughts. Let them laugh too loudly, it sticks a long finger down their throats. They condemn themselves before they are charged, and this makes them defensive always.

When Tom was nine years old he worried because his pretty little sister Mollie had an impediment in her speech. He asked her to open her mouth wide and he saw that a membrane under her tongue caused the trouble. 'I can fix that,' he said. He led her to a secret place far from the house, whetted his pocket-knife on a stone, and cut the offending halter of speech. And then he ran away and was sick.

The Hamilton house grew as the family grew. It was designed to be unfinished, so that lean-tos could jut out as they were needed. The original room and kitchen soon disappeared in a welter of these lean-tos.

Meanwhile Samuel got no richer. He developed a very bad patent habit, a disease many men suffer from. He invented a part of a threshing machine, better, cheaper, and more efficient than any in existence. The patent attorney ate up his little profit for the year. Samuel sent his models to a manufacturer, who promptly rejected the plans and used the method. The next few years were kept lean by the suing, and the drain stopped only when he lost the suit. It was his first sharp experience with the rule that without money you cannot fight money. But he had caught the patent fever, and year after year the money made by threshing and by smithing was drained off in patents. The Hamilton children went barefoot, and their overalls were patched and food was sometimes scarce, to pay for the crisp blue-prints with cogs and planes and elevations.

Some men think big and some think little. Samuel and his sons Tom and Joe thought big and George and Will thought little. Joseph was the fourth son – a kind of mooning boy, greatly beloved and protected by the whole family. He early discovered that a smiling helplessness was his best protection from work. His brothers were tough hard workers, all of them. It was easier to do Joe's work than to make him do it. His mother and father thought him a poet because he wasn't any good at anything else. And they so impressed him with this that he wrote glib verses to prove it. Joe was physically lazy, and probably mentally lazy too. He day-dreamed out his life, and his mother loved him more than the others because she thought he was helpless. Actually he was the least helpless, because he got exactly what he wanted with a minimum of effort. Joe was the darling of the family.

In feudal times an ineptness with sword and spear headed a young man for the Church: in the Hamilton family Joe's inability properly to function at farm and forge headed him for a higher education. He was not sickly or weak but he did not lift very well; he rode horses badly and detested them. The whole family laughed with affection when they thought of Joe trying to learn to plough; his tortuous first furrow wound about like a flatland stream, and his second furrow touched his first only once and then to cross it and wander off.

Gradually he eliminated himself from every farm duty. His mother explained that his mind was in the clouds, as though this were some singular virtue.

When Joe had failed at every job, his father in despair put him to herding sixty sheep. This was the least difficult job of all and the one classically requiring no skill. All he had to do was to stay with the sheep. And Joe lost them – lost sixty sheep and couldn't find them where they were huddled in the shade of a dry gulch. According to the family story, Samuel called the family together, girls and boys, and made them promise to take care of Joe after he was gone, for if they did not Joe would surely starve.

Interspersed with the Hamilton boys were five girls: Una the oldest, a thoughtful studious, dark girl; Lizzie – I guess Lizzie must have been the oldest since she was named after her mother – I don't know much about Lizzie. She early seemed to find a shame for her family. She married young and went away and thereafter was seen only at funerals. Lizzie had a capacity for hatred and bitterness unique among the Hamiltons. She had a son, and when he grew up and married a girl Lizzie didn't like she did not speak to him for many years.

Then there was Dessie, whose laughter was so constant that everyone near her was glad to be there because it was more fun to be with Dessie than with anyone else.

The next sister was Olive, my mother. And last was Mollie, who was a little beauty with lovely blonde hair and violet eyes.

These were the Hamiltons, and it was almost a miracle how Liza, skinny little biddy that she was, produced them year after year and fed them, baked bread, made their clothes, and clothed them with good manners and iron morals too.

It is amazing how Liza stamped her children. She was completely without experience in the world, she was unread and, except for the one long trip from Ireland, untravelled. She had no experience with men save only her husband, and that she looked upon as a tiresome and sometimes painful duty. A good part of her life was taken up with bearing and raising. Her total intellectual association was the Bible, except the talk of Samuel and her children, and to them she did not listen. In that one book she had her history and her poetry, her knowledge of people and things, her ethics, her morals, and her salvation. She never studied the Bible or inspected it; she just read it. The many

44

places where it seems to refute itself did not confuse her in the least. And finally she came to a point where she knew it so well that she went right on reading it without listening.

Liza enjoyed universal respect because she was a good woman and raised good children. She could hold up her head anywhere. Her husband and her children and her grandchildren respected her. There was a nail-hard strength in her, a lack of any compromise, a rightness in the face of all opposing wrongness, which made you hold her in a kind of awe but not in warmth.

Liza hated alcoholic liquors with an iron zeal. Drinking alcohol in any form she regarded as a crime against a properly outraged deity. Not only would she not touch it herself, but she resisted its enjoyment by anyone else. The result naturally was that her husband Samuel and all her children had a good lusty love for a drink.

Once when he was very ill Samuel asked, 'Liza, couldn't I have a glass of whisky to ease me?'

She set her little hard chin. 'Would you go to the throne of God with liquor on your breath? You would not!' she said.

Samuel rolled over on his side and went about his illness without ease.

When Liza was about seventy her elimination slowed up and her doctor told her to take a tablespoon of port wine for medicine. She forced down the first spoonful, making a crooked face, but it was not so bad. And from that moment she never drew a completely sober breath. She always took the wine in a tablespoon, it was always medicine, but after a time she was doing over a quart a day and she was a much more relaxed and happy woman.

Samuel and Liza Hamilton got all of their children raised and well towards adulthood before the turn of the century. It was a whole clot of Hamiltons growing up on the ranch to the east of King City. And they were American children and young men and women. Samuel never went back to Ireland and gradually he forgot it entirely. He was a busy man. He had no time for nostalgia. The Salinas Valley was the world. A trip to Salinas sixty miles to the north at the head of the valley was event enough for a year, and the incessant work on the ranch, the care and feeding and clothing of his bountiful family, took most of his time – but not all. His energy was large.

His daughter Una had become a brooding student, tense and dark. He was proud of her wild, exploring mind. Olive was preparing to take county examinations after a stretch in the secondary school in Salinas. Olive was going to be a teacher, an honour like having a priest in the family in Ireland. Joe was to be sent to college because he was no damn good at anything else. Will was well along the way to accidental fortune. Tom bruised himself on the world and licked his cuts. Dessie was studying dressmaking, and Mollie, pretty Mollie, would obviously marry some well-to-do man.

There was no question of inheritance. Although the hill ranch was large it was abysmally poor. Samuel sunk well after well and could not find water on his own land. That would have made the difference. Water would have made them comparatively rich. The one poor pipe of water pumped up from deep near the house was the only source; sometimes it got dangerously low, and twice it ran dry. The cattle had to come from the far fringe of the ranch to drink and then go out again to feed.

All in all it was a good firm-grounded family, permanent, and successfully planted in the Salinas Valley, not poorer than many and not richer than many either. It was a well-balanced family with its conservatives and its radicals, its dreamers and its realists. Samuel was well pleased with the fruit of his loins.

CHAPTER 6

I

AFTER ADAM joined the army and Cyrus moved to Washington, Charles lived alone on the farm. He boasted about getting himself a wife, but he did not go about doing it by the usual process of meeting girls, taking them to dances, testing their virtues or otherwise, and finally slipping feebly into marriage. The truth of it was that Charles was abysmally timid of girls. And, like most shy men, he satisfied his normal needs in the anonymity of the prostitute. There is great safety for a shy man with a whore. Having been paid for, and in advance, she has become a commodity, and a shy man can be gay with her and even brutal to her. Also, there is none of the horror of the possible turn-down which shrivels the guts of timid men.

The arrangement was simple and reasonably secret. The owner of the inn kept three rooms on his top floor for transients, which he rented to girls for two-week periods. At the end of two weeks a new set of girls took their place. Mr Hallam, the innkeeper, had no part in the arrangement. He could almost say with truth that he didn't know anything about it. He simply collected five times the normal rent for his three rooms. The girls were assigned, procured, moved, disciplined, and robbed by a whoremaster named Edwards, who lived in Boston. His girls moved in a slow circuit among the small towns, never staying anywhere more than two weeks. It was an extremely workable system. A girl was not in town long enough to cause remark either by citizen or town marshal. They stayed pretty much in the rooms and avoided public places. They were forbidden on pain of beating to drink or make noise or to fall in love with anyone. Meals were served in their rooms, and the clients were carefully screened. No drunken man was permitted to go up to them. Every six months each girl was given one month of vacation to get drunk and raise hell. On the job, let a girl be disobedient to the rules, and Mr Edwards personally stripped her, gagged her, and horsewhipped her within an inch of her life. If she did it again she found herself in jail, charged with vagrancy and public prostitution.

The two-week stands had another advantage. Many of the girls were diseased, and a girl had nearly always gone away by the time her gift had incubated in a client. There was no one for a man to get mad at. Mr Hallam knew nothing about it, and Mr Edwards never appeared publicly in his business capacity. He had a very good thing in his circuit.

The girls were all pretty much alike – big, healthy, lazy, and dull. A man could hardly tell there had been a change. Charles Trask made it a habit to go to the inn at least once every two weeks, to creep up to the top floor, do his quick business, and return to the bar to get mildly drunk.

The Trask house had never been gay, but lived in only by Charles it took on a gloomy, rustling decay. The lace curtains were grey, the floors, although swept, grew sticky and dank. The kitchen was lacquered – walls, windows, and ceiling – with grease from the frying-pans.

The constant scrubbing by the wives who had lived there and the bi-annual deep-seated scouring had kept the dirt down. Charles rarely did more than sweep. He gave up sheets on his bed and slept between blankets. What good to clean the house when there was no one to see it? Only on the nights he went to the inn did he wash himself and put on clean clothes.

Charles developed a restlessness that got him out at dawn. He worked the farm mightily because he was lonely. Coming in from his work, he gorged himself on fried food and went to bed and to sleep in the resulting torpor.

His dark face took on the serious expressionlessness of a man who is nearly always alone. He missed his brother more than he missed his mother and father. He remembered quite inaccurately the time before Adam went away as the happy time, and he wanted it to come again.

During the years he was never sick, except of course for the chronic indigestion which was universal, and still is, with men who live alone, cook for themselves, and eat in solitude. For this he took a powerful purge called Father George's Elixir of Life.

One accident he did have in the third year of his aloneness. He was digging out rocks and sledding them to the stone wall. One large boulder was difficult to move. Charles prised it with a long iron bar, and the rock bucked and rolled back again and again. Suddenly he lost his temper. The little smile came on his face, and he fought the stone as though it were a man, in silent fury. He drove his bar deep behind it and threw his whole weight back. The bar slipped and its upper end crashed against his forehead. For a few moments he lay unconscious in the field and then he rolled over and staggered, half-blinded, to the house. There was a long torn welt on his forehead from hairline to a point between his eyebrows. For a few weeks his head was bandaged over a draining infection, but that did not worry him. In that day pus was thought to be benign, a proof that a wound was healing properly. When the wound did heal, it left a long and crinkled scar, and while most scar tissue is lighter than the surrounding skin, Charles's scar turned dark brown. Perhaps the bar had forced iron rust under the skin and made a kind of tattoo.

The wound had not worried Charles, but the scar did. It looked like a long fingermark laid on his forehead. He inspected it often in the little mirror by the stove. He combed his hair down over his forehead to conceal as much of it as he could. He conceived a shame for his scar; he hated his scar. He became restless when anyone looked at it, and fury rose in him if any question was asked about it. In a letter to his brother he put down his feeling about it.

'It looks,' he wrote, 'like somebody marked me like a cow. The damn thing gets darker. By the time you get home it will maybe be black. All I need is one going the other way and I would look like a Papist on Ash Wednesday. I don't know why it bothers me. I got plenty other scars. It just seems like I was marked. And when I go into town, like to the inn, why, people are always looking at it. I can hear them talking about it when they don't know I can hear. I don't know why they're so damn curious about it. It gets so I don't feel like going in town at all.'

11

Adam was discharged in 1885 and started to beat his way home. In appearance he had changed little. There was no military carriage about him. The cavalry didn't act that way. Indeed some units took pride in sloppy posture.

Adam felt that he was sleep-walking. It is a hard thing to leave any deeply routined life, even if you hate it. In the morning he awakened on a split second and lay awaiting reveille. His calves missed the hub of leggings and his throat felt naked without its tight collar. He arrived in Chicago, and there, for no reason, rented a furnished room for a week, stayed in it for two days, went to Buffalo, changed his mind, and moved to Niagara Falls. He didn't want to go home and he put it off as long as possible. Home was not a pleasant place in his mind. The kind of feelings he had had there were dead in him, and he had a reluctance to bring them to life. He watched the falls by the hour. Their roar stupefied and hypnotized him.

One evening he felt a crippling loneliness for the close men in barracks and tent. His impulse was to rush into a crowd for warmth, any crowd. The first crowded public place he could find was a little bar, thronged and smoky. He sighed with pleasure, almost nestled in the human clot the way a cat nestles into a woodpile. He ordered whisky and drank it and felt warm and good. He did not see or hear. He simply absorbed the contact.

As it grew late and the men began to drift away, he became fearful of the time when he would have to go home. Soon he was alone with the bar-tender, who was rubbing and rubbing the mahogany of the bar and trying with his eyes and his manner to get Adam to go.

'I'll have one more,' Adam said.

The bar-tender set the bottle out. Adam noticed him for the first time. He had a strawberry mark on his forehead.

'I'm a stranger in these parts,' said Adam.

'That's what we mostly get at the falls,' the bar-tender said.

'I've been in the army. Cavalry.'

'Yeah!' the bar-tender said.

49

Adam felt suddenly that he had to impress the man, had to get under his skin some way. 'Fighting Indians,' he said. 'Had some great times.'

The man did not answer him.

'My brother has a mark on his head.'

The bar-tender touched the strawberry mark with his fingers. 'Birthmark,' he said. 'Gets bigger every year. Your brother got one?'

'His came from a cut. He wrote me about it.'

'You notice this one of mine looks like a cat?'

'Sure it does.'

'That's my nickname, Cat. Had it all my life. They say my old lady must of been scared by a cat when she was having me.'

'I'm on my way home. Been away a long time. Won't you have a drink?'

'Thanks. Where you staying?'

'Mrs May's boarding-house.'

'I know her. What they tell is she fills you up with soup so you can't eat much meat.'

'I guess there are tricks to every trade,' said Adam.

'I guess that's right. There's sure plenty in mine.'

'I bet that's true,' said Adam.

'But the one trick I need I haven't got. I wisht I knew that one.'

'What is it?'

'How the hell to get you to go home and let me close up.'

Adam stared at him, stared at him and did not speak.

'It's a joke,' the bar-tender said uneasily.

'I guess I'll go home in the morning,' said Adam. 'I mean my real home.'

'Good luck,' the bar-tender said.

Adam walked through the dark town, increasing his speed as though loneliness sniffed along behind him. The sagging front steps of his boarding-house creaked a warning as he climbed them. The hall was gloomed with the dot of yellow light from an oil-lamp turned down so low that it jerked expiringly.

The landlady stood in her open doorway and her nose made a shadow to the bottom of her chin. Her cold eyes followed Adam as do the eyes of a front-painted portrait, and she listened with her nose for the whisky that was in him.

'Good night,' said Adam.

She did not answer him.

At the top of the first flight he looked back. Her head was raised, and now her chin made a shadow on her throat and her eyes had no pupils.

His room smelled of dust dampened and dried many times. He picked a match from his block and scratched it on the side of the block. He lighted the shank of candle in the japanned candlestick and regarded the bed – as spineless as a hammock and covered with a dirty patchwork quilt, the cotton batting spilling from the edges.

The porch steps complained again, and Adam knew the woman would be standing in her doorway ready to spray in-hospitality on the new arrival.

Adam sat down in a straight chair and put his elbows on his knees and supported his chin in his hands. A lodger down the hall began a patient, continuing cough against the quiet night.

And Adam knew he could not go home. He had heard old soldiers tell of doing what he was going to do.

'I just couldn't stand it. Didn't have no place to go. Didn't know nobody. Wandered around and pretty soon I got in a panic like a kid, and first thing I knowed I'm begging the ser-geant to let me back in – like he was doing me a favour.'

Back in Chicago, Adam re-enlisted and asked to be assigned to his old regiment. On the train going west the men of his squadron seemed very dear and desirable.

While he waited to change trains in Kansas City, he heard his name called and a message was shoved into his hand – orders to report to Washington to the office of the Secretary of War. Adam in his five years had absorbed rather than learned never to wonder about an order. To an enlisted man the high far gods in Washington were crazy, and if a soldier wanted to keep his sanity he thought about generals as little as possible.

In due course Adam gave his name to a clerk and went to sit in an ante-room. His father found him there. It took Adam a moment to recognize Cyrus, and much longer to get used to him. Cyrus had become a great man. He dressed like a great man – black broadcloth coat and trousers, wide black hat, over-coat with a velvet collar, ebony cane which he made to seem a sword. And Cyrus conducted himself like a great man. His speech was slow and mellow, measured and unexcited, his ges-tures were wide, and new teeth gave him a vulpine smile out of all proportion to his emotion.

After Adam had realized that this was his father he was still puzzled. Suddenly he looked down – no wooden leg. The leg was straight, bent at the knee, and the foot was clad in a polished kid congress gaiter. When he moved there was a limp, but not a clumping wooden-legged limp.

Cyrus saw the look. 'Mechanical,' he said. 'Works on a hinge. Got a spring. Don't even limp when I set my mind to it. I'll show it to you when I take it off. Come along with me.'

Adam said, 'I'm under orders, sir. I'm to report to Colonel Wells.'

'I know you are. I told Wells to issue the orders. Come along.'

Adam said uneasily, 'If you don't mind, sir, I think I'd better report to Colonel Wells.'

His father reversed himself. 'I was testing you,' he said grandly. 'I wanted to see whether the army has any discipline these days. Good boy. I knew it would be good for you. You're a man and a soldier, my boy.'

'I'm under orders, sir,' said Adam. This man was a stranger to him. A faint distaste arose in Adam. Something was not true. And the speed with which doors opened straight to the Colonel, the obsequious respect of that officer, the words, 'The Secretary will see you now, sir,' did not remove Adam's feeling.

'This is my son, a private soldier, Mr Secretary – just as I was – a private soldier in the United States Army.'

'I was discharged a corporal, sir,' said Adam. He hardly heard the exchange of compliments. He was thinking, 'This is the Secretary of War. Can't he see that this isn't the way my father is? He's play-acting. What's happened to him? It's funny the Secretary can't see it.'

They walked to the small hotel where Cyrus lived, and on the way Cyrus pointed out the sights, the buildings, the spots of history, with the expansiveness of a lecturer. 'I live in a hotel,' he said. 'I've thought of getting a house, but I'm on the move so much it wouldn't hardly pay. I'm all over the country most of the time.'

The hotel clerk couldn't see either. He bowed to Cyrus, called him 'Senator', and indicated that he would give Adam a room if he had to throw someone out.

'Send a bottle of whisky to my room, please.'

'I can send some chipped ice if you like.'

'Ice!' said Cyrus. 'My son is a soldier.' He rapped his leg with his stick and it gave forth a hollow sound. 'I have been a soldier – a private soldier. What do we want ice for?'

Adam was amazed at Cyrus's accommodation. He had not

only a bedroom but a sitting-room beside it, and the toilet was in a closet right in the bedroom.

Cyrus sat down in a deep chair and sighed. He pulled up his trouser leg and Adam saw the contraption of iron and leather and hardwood. Cyrus unlaced the leather sheath that held it on his stump and stood the travesty-on-flesh beside his chair. 'It gets to pinching pretty bad,' he said.

With the leg off, his father became himself again, the self Adam remembered. He had experienced the beginning of contempt, but now the childhood fear and respect and animosity came back to him, so that he seemed a little boy testing his father's immediate mood to escape trouble.

Cyrus made his preparations, drank his whisky, and loosened his collar. He faced Adam. 'Well?'

'Sir?'

'Why did you re-enlist?'

'I – I don't know, sir. I just wanted to.'

'You don't like the army, Adam.'

'No, sir.'

'Why did you go back?'

'I didn't want to go home.'

Cyrus sighed and rubbed the tips of his fingers on the arms of his chair. 'Are you going to stay in the army?' he asked.

'I don't know, sir.'

'I can get you into West Point. I have influence. I can get you discharged so you can enter West Point.'

'I don't want to go there.'

'Are you defying me?' Cyrus asked quietly.

Adam took a long time to answer, and his mind sought escape before he said, 'Yes, sir.'

Cyrus said, 'Pour me some whisky, son,' and when he had it he continued, 'I wonder if you know how much influence I really have. I can throw the Grand Army at any candidate like a sock. Even the President likes to know what I think about public matters. I can get senators defeated and I can pick appointments like apples. I can make men and I can destroy men. Do you know that?'

Adam knew more than that. He knew that Cyrus was defending himself with threats. 'Yes, sir. I've heard.'

'I could get you assigned to Washington – assigned to me even – teach you your way about.'

'I'd rather go back to my regiment, sir.' He saw the shadow of loss darken his father's face.

'Maybe I made a mistake. You've learned the dumb resistance of a soldier.' He sighed. 'I'll get you ordered to your regiment. You'll rot in barracks.'

'Thank you, sir.' After a pause Adam asked, 'Why didn't you bring Charles here?'

'Because I — No, Charles is better where he is – better where he is.'

Adam remembered his father's tone and how he looked. And he had plenty of time to remember, because he did rot in barracks. He remembered that Cyrus was lonely and alone – and knew it.

III

Charles had looked forward to Adam's return after five years. He had painted the house and the barn, and as the time approached he had a woman in to clean the house, to clean it to the bone.

She was a clean, mean old woman. She looked at the dust-grey rotting curtains, threw them out, and made new ones. She dug grease out of the stove that had been there since Charles's mother died. And she leached the walls of a brown shiny nastiness deposited by cooking-fat and kerosene lamps. She pickled the floors with lye, soaked the blankets in sal soda, complaining the whole time to herself, 'Men – dirty animals. Pigs is clean compared. Rot in their own juice. Don't see how no woman ever marries them. Stink like measles. Look at oven – pie juice from Methusaleh.'

Charles had moved into a shed where his nostrils would not be assailed by the immaculate but painful smells of lye and soda and ammonia and yellow soap. He did, however, get the impression that she didn't approve of his housekeeping. When finally she grumbled away from the shining house Charles remained in the shed. He wanted to keep the house clean for Adam. In the shed where he slept were the tools of the farm and the tools for their repair and maintenance. Charles found that he could cook his fried and boiled meals more quickly and efficiently on the forge than he could on the kitchen stove. The bellows forced quick flaring heat from the coke. A man didn't have to wait for a stove to heat up. He wondered why he had never thought of it before.

Charles waited for Adam, and Adam did not come. Perhaps Adam was ashamed to write. It was Cyrus who told Charles in an angry letter about Adam's re-enlistment against his wishes. And Cyrus indicated that, in some future, Charles could visit him in Washington, but he never asked him again.

Charles moved back to the house and lived in a kind of savage filth, taking a satisfaction in overcoming the work of the grumbling woman.

It was a year before Adam wrote to Charles – a letter of embarrassed newsiness building his courage to say, 'I don't know why I signed again. It was like somebody else doing it. Write soon and tell me how you are.'

Charles did not reply until he had received four anxious letters, and then he replied coolly, 'I didn't hardly expect you anyway,' and he went on with a detailed account of farm and animals.

Time had got in its work. After that Charles wrote right after New Year's Day and received a letter from Adam written right after New Year's Day. They had grown so apart that there was little mutual reference and no questions.

Charles began to keep one slovenly woman after another. When they got on his nerves he threw them out the way he would sell a pig. He didn't like them and had no interest in whether or not they liked him. He grew away from the village. His contacts were only with the inn and the postmaster. The village people might denounce his manner of life, but one thing he had which balanced his ugly life even in their eyes. The farm had never been so well run. Charles cleared land, built up his walls, improved his drainage, and added a hundred acres to the farm. More than that, he was planting tobacco, and a long new tobacco barn stood impressively behind the house. For these things he kept the respect of his neighbours. A farmer cannot think too much evil of a good farmer. Charles was spending most of his money and all of his energy on the farm.

CHAPTER 7

I

ADAM SPENT his next five years doing the things an army uses to keep its men from going insane – endless polishing of metal and leather, parade and drill and escort, ceremony of bugle and flag, a ballet of business for men who aren't doing anything. In 1886 the big packing-house strike broke out in Chicago and Adam's regiment entrained, but the strike was settled before they were needed. In 1888 the Seminoles, who had never signed a peace treaty, stirred restlessly, and the cavalry entrained again; but the Seminoles retired into their swamps and were quiet, and the dream-like routine settled on the troops again.

Time interval is a strange and contradictory matter in the mind. It would be reasonable to suppose that a routine time or an eventless time would seem interminable. It should be so, but it is not. It is the dull eventless times that have no duration whatever. A time splashed with interest, wounded with tragedy, crevassed with joy – that's the time that seems long in the memory. And this is right when you think about it. Eventlessness has no posts to drape duration on. From nothing to nothing is no time at all.

Adam's second five years were up before he knew it. It was late in 1890, and he was discharged with sergeant's stripes in the Presidio in San Francisco. Letters between Charles and Adam had become great rarities, but Adam wrote his brother just before his discharge, 'This time I'm coming home,' and that was the last Charles heard of him for over three years.

Adam waited out the winter, wandering up the river to Sacramento, ranging in the valley of the San Joaquin, and when the spring came Adam had no money. He rolled a blanket and started slowly eastward, sometimes walking and sometimes with groups of men on the rods under slow-moving freight-cars. At night he jungled up with wandering men in the camping places on the fringes of towns. He learned to beg, not for money but for food. And before he knew it he was a bindlestiff himself.

Such men are rare now, but in the nineties there were many of them, wandering men, lonely men, who wanted it that way. Some of them ran from responsibilities and some felt driven out of society by injustice. They worked a little, but not for long. They stole a little, but only food and occasionally needed garments from a wash-line. They were all kinds of men – literate men and ignorant men, clean men and dirty men – but all of them had restlessness in common. They followed warmth and avoided great heat and great cold. As the spring advanced they tracked it eastward, and the first frost drove them west and south. They were brothers to the coyote which, being wild, lives close to man and his chicken-yards: they were near towns but not in them. Associations with other men were for a week or for a day and then they drifted apart.

Around the little fires where communal stew bubbled there was all manner of talk and only the personal was unmentionable. Adam heard of the development of the IWW with its angry angels. He listened to philosophic discussions, to metaphysics, to aesthetics, to impersonal experience. His companions for the night might be a murderer, an unfrocked priest or one who had unfrocked himself, a professor forced from his warm berth by a dull faculty, a lone driven man running from memory, a fallen archangel and a devil in training, and each contributed bits of thought to the fire as each contributed carrots and potatoes and onions and meat to the stew. He learned the technique of shaving with broken glass, of judging a house before knocking to ask for a hand-out. He learned to avoid or get along with hostile police and to evaluate a woman for her warmth of heart.

Adam took pleasure in the new life. When autumn touched the trees he had got as far as Omaha, and without question or reason or thought he hurried west and south, fled through the mountains and arrived with relief in Southern California. He wandered by the sea from the border north as far as San Luis Obispo, and he learned to pilfer the tide pools for abalones and eels and mussels and perch, to dig the sandbars for clams, and to trap a rabbit in the dunes with a noose of fish-line. And he lay in the sun-warmed sand, counting the waves.

Spring urged him east again, but more slowly than before. Summer was cool in the mountains, and the mountain people were kind as lonesome people are kind. Adam took a job on a widow's outfit near Denver and shared her table and her bed humbly until the frost drove him south again. He followed the Rio Grande past Albuquerque and El Paso through the Big Bend, through Laredo to Brownsville. He learned Spanish words for food and pleasure, and he learned that when people are very poor they still have something to give and the impulse to give it. He developed a love for poor people he could not have conceived if he had not been poor himself. And by now he was an expert tramp, using humility as a working principle. He was lean and sun-darkened, and he could withdraw his own personality until he made no stir of anger or jealousy. His voice had grown soft, and he had merged many accents and dialects into his own speech, so that his speech did not seem foreign anywhere. This was the great safety of the tramp, a protective veil. He rode the trains very infrequently, for there was a growing anger against tramps, based on the angry violence of the IWW and aggravated by the fierce reprisals against them. Adam was picked up for vagrancy. The quick brutality of police and prisoners frightened him and drove him away from the gatherings of tramps. He travelled alone after that and made sure that he was shaven and clean.

When spring came again he started north. He felt that his time of rest and peace was over. He aimed north towards Charles and the weakening memories of his childhood.

Adam moved rapidly across interminable East Texas, through Louisiana and the butt ends of Mississippi and Alabama, and into the flank of Florida. He felt that he had to move quickly. The negroes were poor enough to be kind, but they could not trust any white man no matter how poor, and the poor white men had a fear of strangers.

Near Tallahassee he was picked up by sheriff's men, judged vagrant, and put on a road gang. That's how the roads were built. His sentence was six months. He was released and instantly picked up again for a second six months. And now he learned how men can consider other men as beasts and that the easiest way to get along with such men was to be a beast. A clean face, an open face, an eye raised to meet an eye – these drew attention and attention drawn brought punishment. Adam thought how a man doing an ugly or a brutal thing has hurt himself and must punish someone for the hurt. To be guarded at work by men with shotguns, to be shackled by the ankle at night to a chain, were simple matters of precaution, but the savage whippings for the least stir of will, for the smallest shred of dignity or resistance, these seemed to indicate that guards were afraid of prisoners, and Adam knew from his years in the army that a man afraid is a dangerous animal. And Adam, like anyone in the world, feared what whipping would do to his body and his spirit. He drew a curtain around himself. He removed expression from his face, light from his eyes, and silenced his speech. Later he was not so much astonished that it had happened to him but that he had been able to take it and with a minimum of pain. It was much more horrible afterwards than when it was happening. It is a triumph of self-control to see a man whipped until the muscles of his back show white and glistening through the cuts and to give no sign of pity or anger or interest. And Adam learned this.

People are felt rather than seen after the first few moments. During his second sentence on the roads of Florida, Adam reduced his personality to a minus. He caused no stir, put out no vibration, became as nearly invisible as it is possible to be. And when the guards could not feel him, they were not afraid of him. They gave him the jobs of cleaning the camps, of handing out the slops to the prisoners, of filling the water buckets.

Adam waited until three days before his second release. Right after noon that day he filled the water buckets and went back to the little river for more. He filled his buckets with stones and sank them, and then he eased himself into the water and swam a long way down-stream, rested and swam farther down. He kept moving in the water until at dusk he found a place under a bank with bushes for cover. He did not get out of the water.

Late in the night he heard the hounds go by, covering both sides of the river. He had rubbed his hair hard with green leaves to cover human odour. He sat in the water with his nose and eyes clear. In the morning the hounds came back, disinterested, and the men were too tired to beat the banks properly. When they were gone, Adam dug a piece of water-logged fried saw-belly out of his pocket and ate it.

He had schooled himself against hurry. Most men were caught bolting. It took Adam five days to cross the short distance into Georgia. He took no chances, held back his impatience with an iron control. He was astonished at his ability.

On the edge of Valdosta, Georgia, he lay hidden until long after midnight, and he entered the town like a shadow, crept to the rear of a cheap store, forced a window slowly so that the screws of the lock were pulled from the sun-rotted wood. Then he replaced the lock but left the window open. He had to work by moonlight drifting through dirty windows. He stole a pair of cheap trousers, a white shirt, black shoes, black hat, and an oil-skin raincoat, and he tried on each article for fit. He forced himself to make sure nothing looked disturbed before he climbed out of the window. He had taken nothing which was not heavily stocked. He had not even looked for the cash drawer. He lowered the window carefully and slipped from shadow to shadow in the moonlight.

He lay hidden during the day and went in search of food at night – turnips, a few ears of corn from a crib, a few windfall apples – nothing that would be missed. He broke the newness of the shoes with rubbed sand and kneaded the raincoat to destroy its newness. It was three days before he got the rain he needed, or in his extreme caution felt he needed.

The rain started late in the afternoon. Adam huddled under his oilskin, waiting for the dark to come, and when it did he walked through the dripping night into the town of Valdosta. His black hat was pulled down over his eyes and his yellow oilskin was strapped tight against his throat. He made his way to the station and peered through a rain-blurred window. The station agent, in green eyeshade and black alpaca work-sleeves, leaned through the ticket window, talking to a friend. It was twenty minutes before the friend went away. Adam watched him off the platform. He took a deep breath to calm himself and went inside.

11

Charles received very few letters. Sometimes he did not inquire at the post office for weeks. In February of 1894 when a thick letter came from a firm of attorneys in Washington the postmaster thought it might be important. He walked out to the Trask farm, found Charles cutting wood, and gave him the letter. And since he had taken so much trouble, he waited around to hear what the letter said.

Charles let him wait. Very slowly he read all five pages, went back and read them again, moving his lips over the words. Then he folded it up and turned towards the house.

The postmaster called after him, 'Anything wrong, Mr Trask?'

'My father is dead,' Charles said, and he walked into the house and closed the door.

'Took it hard,' the postmaster reported in town. 'Took it real hard. Quiet man. Don't talk much.'

In the house Charles lighted the lamp, although it was not dark yet. He laid the letter on the table, and he washed his hands before he sat down to read it again.

There hadn't been anyone to send him a telegram. The attorneys had found his address among his father's papers. They were sorry – offered their condolences. And they were pretty excited too. When they had made Trask's will they thought he might

60

have a few hundred dollars to leave his sons. That is what he looked to be worth. When they inspected his bank-books they found that he had over ninety-three thousand dollars in the bank and ten thousand dollars in good securities. They felt very different about Mr Trask then. People with that much money were rich. They would never have to worry. It was enough to start a dynasty. The lawyers congratulated Charles and his brother Adam. Under the will, they said, it was to be shared equally. After the money they listed the personal effects left by the deceased: five ceremonial swords presented to Cyrus at various GAR conventions, an olivewood gavel with a gold plate on it, a Masonic watch charm with a diamond set in the dividers, the gold caps from the teeth he had out when he got his plates, watch (silver), gold-headed stick, and so forth.

Charles read the letter twice more and cupped his forehead in his hands. He wondered about Adam. He wanted Adam home.

Charles felt puzzled and dull. He built up the fire and put the frying-pan to heat and sliced thick slices of salt pork into it. Then he went back to stare at the letter. Suddenly he picked it up and put it in the drawer of the kitchen table. He decided not to think of the matter at all for a while.

Of course he thought of little else, but it was a dull circular thinking that came back to the starting point again and again: Where had he got it?

When two events have something in common, in their natures or in time or place, we leap happily to the conclusion that they are similar, and from this tendency we create magics and store them for re-telling. Charles had never before had a letter delivered at the farm in his life. Some weeks later a boy ran out to the farm with a telegram. Charles always connected the letter and the telegram the way we group two deaths and anticipate a third. He hurried to the village railroad station, carrying the telegram in his hand.

'Listen to this,' he said to the operator.

'I already read it.'

'You did?'

'It comes over the wire,' said the operator. 'I wrote it down.'

'Oh! Yes, sure. "Urgent need you telegraph me one hundred dollars. Coming home. Adam."'

'Came collect,' the operator said. 'You owe me sixty cents.'

'Valdosta, Georgia – I never heard of it.'

'Neither'd I, but it's there.'

'Say, Carlton, how do you go about telegraphing money?'

'Well, you bring me a hundred and two dollars and sixty cents and I send a wire telling the Valdosta operator to pay Adam one hundred dollars. You owe me sixty cents too.'

'I'll pay – say, how do I know it's Adam? What's to stop anybody from collecting it?'

The operator permitted himself a smile of worldliness. 'Way we go about it, you give me a question couldn't nobody else know the answer. So I send both the question and the answer. Operator asks this fella that question, and if he can't answer he don't get his money.'

'Say, that's pretty cute. I better think up a good one.'

'You better get the hundred dollars while Old Breen still got the window open.'

Charles was delighted with the game. He came back with the money in his hand. 'I got the question,' he said.

'I hope it ain't your mother's middle name. Lot of people don't remember.'

'No, nothing like that. It's this. "What did you give father on his birthday just before you went in the army?"'

'It's a good question, but it's long as hell. Can't you cut it down to ten words?'

'Who's paying for it? Answer is, "A pup."'

'Wouldn't nobody guess that,' said Carlton. 'Well, it's you paying, not me.'

'Be funny if he forgot,' said Charles. 'He wouldn't ever get home.'

III

Adam came walking out from the village. His shirt was dirty and the stolen clothes were wrinkled and soiled from having been slept in for a week. Between the house and the barn he stopped and listened for his brother, and in a moment he heard him hammering at something in the big new tobacco barn. 'Oh, Charles!' Adam called.

The hammering stopped, and there was silence. Adam felt as though his brother were inspecting him through the cracks in the barn. Then Charles came out quickly and hurried to Adam and shook hands.

'How are you?'

'Fine,' said Adam.

'Good God, you're thin!'

'I guess I am. And I'm years older too.'

Charles inspected him from head to foot. 'You don't look prosperous.'

'I'm not.'

'Where's your valise?'

'I haven't got one.'

'Jesus Christ! Where've you been?'

'Mostly wandering about all over.'

'Like a hobo?'

'Like a hobo.'

After all the years and the life that had made creased leather out of Charles's skin and redness in his dark eyes, Adam knew from remembering that Charles was thinking of two things – the questions and something else.

'Why didn't you come home?'

'I just got to wandering. Couldn't stop. It gets into you. That's a real bad scar you've got there.'

'That's the one I wrote you about. Gets worse all the time. Why didn't you write? Are you hungry?' Charles's hands itched into his pockets and out and touched his chin and scratched his head.

'It may go away. I saw a man once – bar-tender – he had one that looked like a cat. It was a birthmark. His nickname was Cat.'

'Are you hungry?'

'Sure. I guess I am.'

'Plan to stay home now?'

'I – I guess so. Do you want to get to it now?'

'I – I guess so,' Charles echoed him. 'Our father is dead.'

'I know.'

'How the hell do *you* know?'

'Station agent told me. How long ago did he die?'

' 'Bout a month.'

'What of?'

'Pneumonia.'

'Buried here?'

'No. In Washington. I got a letter and newspapers. Carried him on a caisson with a flag over it. The Vice-President was there and the President sent a wreath. All in the papers. Pictures too – I'll show you. I've got it all.'

Adam studied his brother's face until Charles looked away. 'Are you mad at something?' Adam asked.

'What should I be mad at?'

'It just sounded —'

63

'I've got nothing to be mad at. Come on, I'll get you something to eat.'

'All right. Did he linger long?'

'No. It was galloping pneumonia. Went right out.'

Charles was covering up something. He wanted to tell it, but he didn't know how to go about it. He kept hiding in words. Adam fell silent. It might be a good thing to be quiet and let Charles sniff and circle until he came out with it.

'I don't take much stock in messages from the beyond,' said Charles. 'Still, how can you know? Some people claim they've had messages – old Sarah Whitburn. She swore. You just don't know what to think. You didn't get a message, did you? Say, what the hell's bit off your tongue?'

Adam said, 'Just thinking.' And he was thinking with amazement; 'Why, I'm not afraid of my brother! I used to be scared to death of him, and I'm not any more. Wonder why not. Could it be the army? Or the chain gang? Could it be Father's death? Maybe – but I don't understand it.' With the lack of fear, he knew he could say anything he wanted to, whereas before he had picked over his words to avoid trouble. It was a good feeling he had, almost as though he himself had been dead and resurrected.

They walked into the kitchen he remembered and didn't remember. It seemed smaller and dingier. Adam said almost gaily, 'Charles, I been listening. You want to tell me something and you're walking around it like a terrier around a bush. You better tell before it bites you.'

Charles's eyes sparked with anger. He raised his head. His force was gone. He thought with desolation, 'I can't lick him any more. I can't.'

Adam chuckled. 'Maybe it's wrong to feel good when our father's just died, but, you know, Charles, I never felt better in my whole life. I never felt so good. Spill it, Charles. Don't let it chew on you.'

Charles asked, 'Did you love our father?'

'I won't answer you until I know what you're getting at.'

'Did you or didn't you?'

'What's that got to do with you?'

'Tell me.'

The creative free boldness was all through Adam's bones and brain. 'All right, I'll tell you. No. I didn't. Sometimes he scared me. Sometimes – yes, sometimes I admired him, but most of the time I hated him. Now tell me why you want to know.'

Charles was looking down at his hands. 'I don't understand,'

64

he said. 'I just can't get it through my head. He loved you more than anything in the world.'

'I don't believe that.'

'You don't have to. He liked everything you brought him. He didn't like me. He didn't like anything I gave him. Remember the present I gave him, the pocket-knife? I cut and sold a load of wood to get that knife. Well, he didn't even take it to Washington with him. It's right in his bureau right now. And you gave him that pup. It didn't cost you a thing. Well, I'll show you a picture of that pup. It was at his funeral. A colonel was holding it – it was blind, couldn't walk. They shot it after the funeral.'

Adam was puzzled by the fierceness of his brother's tone. 'I don't see,' he said. 'I don't see what you're getting at.'

'I loved him,' said Charles. And, for the first time that Adam could remember, Charles began to cry. He put his head down in his arms and cried.

Adam was about to go to him when a little of the old fear came back. No, he thought, if I touched him he would try to kill me. He went to the open doorway and stood looking out, and he could hear his brother's sniffling behind him.

It was not a pretty farm near the house – never had been. There was litter about it, an unkemptness, a run-downness, a lack of plan; no flowers, and bits of paper and scraps of wood scattered about on the ground. The house was not pretty either. It was a well-built shanty for shelter and cooking. It was a grim farm and a grim house, unloved and unloving. It was no home, no place to long for or to come back to. Suddenly Adam thought of his step-mother – as unloved as the farm, inadequate, clean in her way, but no more wife than the farm was a home.

His brother's sobbing had stopped. Adam turned. Charles was looking blankly straight ahead. Adam said, 'Tell me about Mother.'

'She died. I wrote you.'

'Tell me about her.'

'I told you. She died. It's so long ago. She wasn't your Mother.'

The smile Adam had once caught on her face flashed up in his mind. Her face was projected in front of him.

Charles's voice came through the image and exploded it. 'Will you tell me one thing – not quick – think before you tell me, and maybe don't answer unless it's true, your answer.' Charles moved his lips to form the question in advance. 'Do you think it would be possible for our father to be – dishonest?'

'What do you mean?'

'Isn't that plain enough? I said it plain. There's only one meaning to dishonest.'

'I don't know,' said Adam. 'I don't know. No one ever said it. Look what he got to be. Stayed overnight in the White House. The Vice-President came to his funeral. Does that sound like a dishonest man? Come on, Charles,' he begged, 'tell me what you've been wanting to tell me from the minute I got here.'

Charles wet his lips. The blood seemed to have gone out of him, and with it energy and all ferocity. His voice became a monotone. 'Father made a will. Left everything equal to me and you.'

Adam laughed. 'Well, we can always live on the farm. I guess we won't starve.'

'It's over a hundred thousand dollars,' the dull voice went on.

'You're crazy. More like a hundred dollars. Where would he get it?'

'It's no mistake. His salary with the GAR was a hundred and thirty-five dollars a month. He paid his own room and board. He got five cents a mile and hotel expenses when he travelled.'

'Maybe he had it all the time and we never knew.'

'No, he didn't have it all the time.'

'Well, why don't you write to the GAR and ask? Someone there might know.'

'I wouldn't dare,' said Charles.

'Now look! Don't go off half-cocked. There's such a thing as speculation. Lots of men struck it rich. He knew big men. Maybe he got in on a good thing. Think of the men who went to the gold rush in California and came back rich.'

Charles's face was desolate. His voice dropped so that Adam had to lean close to hear. It was as toneless as a report. 'Our father went into the Union Army in June, 1862. He had three months' training here in this state. That makes it September. He marched south. October twelfth he was hit in the leg and sent to the hospital. He came home in January.'

'I don't see what you're getting at.'

Charles's words were thin and sallow. 'He was not at Chancellorsville. He was not at Gettysburg or the Wilderness or Richmond or Appomattox.'

'How do you know?'

'His discharge. It came down with his other papers.'

Adam sighed deeply. In his chest, like beating fists, was a surge of joy. He shook his head almost in disbelief.

Charles said, 'How did he get away with it? How in hell did he get away with it? Nobody ever questioned it. Did you? Did I? Did my mother? Nobody did. Not even in Washington.'

Adam stood up. 'What's in the house to eat? I'm going to warm up something.'

'I killed a chicken last night. I'll fry it if you can wait.'

'Anything quick?'

'Some salt pork and plenty of eggs.'

'I'll have that,' said Adam.

They left the question lying there, walked mentally around it, stepped over it. Their words ignored it, but their minds never left it. They wanted to talk about it and could not. Charles fried salt pork, warmed up a skillet of beans, fried eggs.

'I ploughed the pasture,' he said. 'Put in rye.'

'How did it do?'

'Just fine, once I got the rocks out.' He touched his forehead. 'I got this damn thing trying to pry out a stone.'

'You wrote about that,' Adam said. 'Don't know whether I told you your letters meant a lot to me.'

'You never wrote much what you were doing,' said Charles.

'I guess I didn't want to think about it. It was pretty bad, most of it.'

'I read about the campaigns in the papers. Did you go on those?'

'Yes. I didn't want to think about them. Still don't.'

'Did you kill Injuns?'

'Yes, we killed Injuns.'

'I guess they're real ornery.'

'I guess so.'

'You don't have to talk about it if you don't want to.'

'I don't want to.'

They ate their dinner under the paraffin lamp. 'We'd get more light if I would only get around to washing that lampshade.'

'I'll do it,' said Adam. 'It's hard to think of everything.'

'It's going to be fine having you back. How would you like to go to the inn after supper?'

'Well, we'll see. Maybe I'd like just to sit awhile.'

'I didn't write about it in a letter, but they've got girls at the inn. I didn't know but you'd like to go in with me. They change every two weeks. I didn't know but you'd like to look them over.'

'Girls?'

'Yes, they're upstairs. Makes it pretty handy. And I thought you just coming home —'

'Not tonight. Maybe later. How much do they charge?'

'A dollar. Pretty nice girls mostly.'

'Maybe later,' said Adam. 'I'm surprised they let them come in.'

'I was too at first. But they worked out a system.'

'You go often?'

'Every two or three weeks. It's pretty lonesome here, a man living alone.'

'You wrote once you were thinking of getting married.'

'Well, I was. Guess I didn't find the right girl.'

All around the main subject the brothers beat. Now and then they would almost step into it, and quickly pull away, back into crops and local gossip and politics and health. They knew they would come back to it sooner or later. Charles was more anxious to strike in deep that Adam was, but then Charles had had the time to think of it, and to Adam it was a new field of thinking and feeling. He would have preferred to put it over until another day, and at the same time he knew his brother would not permit him to.

Once he said openly, 'Let's sleep on that other thing.'

'Sure, if you want to,' said Charles.

Gradually they ran out of escape talk. Every acquaintance was covered and every local event. The talk lagged and the time went on.

'Feel like turning in?' Adam asked.

'In a little while.'

They were silent, and the night moved restlessly about the house, nudging them and urging them.

'I sure would like to've seen that funeral,' said Charles.

'Must have been pretty fancy.'

'Would you care to see the clippings from the papers? I've got them all in my room.'

'No. Not tonight.'

Charles squared his chair round and put his elbows on the table. 'We'll have to figure it out,' he said nervously. 'We can put it off all we want, but we goddam well got to figure what we're going to do.'

'I know that,' said Adam. 'I guess I just wanted some time to think about it.'

'Would that do any good? I've had time, lots of time, and I just went in circles. I tried not to think about it, and I still went in circles. You think time is going to help?'

'I guess not. I guess not. What do you want to talk about

first? I guess we might as well get into it. We're not thinking about anything else.'

'There's the money,' said Charles. 'Over a hundred thousand dollars – a fortune.'

'What about the money?'

'Well, where did it come from?'

'How do I know? I told you he might have speculated. Somebody might have put him on to a good thing there in Washington.'

'Do you believe that?'

'I don't believe anything,' Adam said. 'I don't know, so what can I believe?'

'It's a lot of money,' said Charles. 'It's a fortune left to us. We can live the rest of our lives on it, or we can buy a hell of a lot of land and make it pay. Maybe you didn't think about it, but we're rich. We're richer than anybody hereabouts.'

Adam laughed. 'You say it like it was a jail sentence.'

'Where did it come from?'

'What do you care?' Adam asked. 'Maybe we should just settle back and enjoy it.'

'He wasn't at Gettysburg. He wasn't at any goddam battle in the whole war. He was hit in a skirmish. Everything he told was lies.'

'What are you getting at?' said Adam.

'I think he stole the money,' Charles said miserably. 'You asked me and that's what I think.'

'Do you know where he stole it?'

'No.'

'Then why do you think he stole it?'

'He told lies about the war.'

'What?'

'I mean, if he lied about the war – why, he could steal.'

'How?'

'He held jobs in the GAR – big jobs. He maybe could have got into the treasury, rigged the books.'

Adam sighed. 'Well, if that's what you think, why don't you write to them and tell them? Have them go over the books. If it's true we could give back the money.'

Charles's face was twisted and the scar on his forehead showed dark. 'The Vice-President came to his funeral. The President sent a wreath. There was a line of carriages half a mile long and hundreds of people on foot. And do you know who the pallbearers were?'

'What are you digging at?'

'S'pose we found out he's a thief. Then it would come out how he never was at Gettysburg or anyplace else. Then everybody would know he was a liar too, and his whole life was a goddam lie. Then even if sometimes he did tell the truth, nobody would believe it was the truth.'

Adam sat very still. His eyes were untroubled, but he was watchful. 'I thought you loved him,' he said calmly. He felt released and free.

'I did. I do. That's why I hate this – his whole life gone – all gone. And his grave – they might even dig it up and throw him out.' His words were ragged with emotion. 'Didn't you love him at all?' he cried.

'I wasn't sure until now,' said Adam. 'I was all mixed up with how I was supposed to feel. No. I did not love him.'

'Then you don't care if his life is spoiled and his poor body rooted up and – oh, my God almighty!'

Adam's brain raced, trying to find words for his feeling. 'I don't have to care.'

'No, you don't,' Charles said bitterly. 'Not if you didn't love him, you don't. You can help kick him in the face.'

Adam knew that his brother was no longer dangerous. There was no jealousy to drive him. The whole weight of his father was on him, but it was his father and no one could take his father away from him.

'How will you feel, walking in town, after everyone knows?' Charles demanded. 'How will you face anybody?'

'I told you I don't care. I don't have to care because I don't believe it.'

'You don't believe what?'

'I don't believe he stole any money. I believe in the war he did just what he said he did and was just where he said he was.'

'But the proof – how about the discharge?'

'You haven't any proof that he stole. You just made that up because you don't know where the money came from.'

'His army papers —'

'They could be wrong,' Adam said. 'I believe they are wrong. I believe in my father.'

'I don't see how you can.'

Adam said, 'Let me tell you. The proofs that God does not exist are very strong, but in lots of people they are not as strong as the feeling that He does.'

70

'But you said you did not love our father. How can you have faith in him if you didn't love him?'

'Maybe that's the reason,' Adam said slowly, feeling his way. 'Maybe if I had loved him I would have been jealous of him. You were. Maybe – maybe love makes you suspicious and doubting. Is it true that when you love a woman you are never sure – never sure of her because you aren't sure of yourself? I can see it pretty clearly. I can see how you loved him and what it did to you. I did not love him. Maybe he loved me. He tested me and hurt me and punished me and finally he sent me out like a sacrifice, maybe to make up for something. But he did not love you, and so he had faith in you. Maybe – why, maybe it's a kind of reverse.'

Charles stared at him. 'I don't understand,' he said.

'I'm trying to,' said Adam. 'It's a new thought to me. I feel good. I feel better maybe than I have ever felt in my whole life. I've got rid of something. Maybe sometimes I'll get what you have, but I haven't got it now.'

'I don't understand,' Charles said again.

'Can you see that I don't think our father was a thief? I don't believe he was a liar.'

'But the papers —'

'I won't look at the papers. Papers are no match at all for my faith in my father.'

Charles was breathing heavily. 'Then you would take the money?'

'Of course.'

'Even if he stole it?'

'He did not steal it. He couldn't have stolen it.'

'I don't understand,' said Charles.

'You don't? Well, it does seem that maybe this might be the secret of the whole thing. Look, I've never mentioned this – do you remember when you beat me up just before I went away?'

'Yes.'

'Do you remember later? You came back with a hatchet to kill me.'

'I don't remember very well. I must have been crazy.'

'I didn't know then, but I know now – you were fighting for your love.'

'Love?'

'Yes,' said Adam. 'We'll use the money well. Maybe we'll stay here. Maybe we'll go away – maybe to California. We'll have to see what we'll do. And of course we must set up a monument to our father – a big one.'

'I couldn't ever go away from here,' said Charles.

'Well, let's see how it goes. There's no hurry. We'll feel it out.'

CHAPTER 8

I

I BELIEVE there are monsters born in the world to human parents. Some you can see, misshapen and horrible, with huge heads or tiny bodies; some are born with no arms, no legs, some with three arms, some with tails or mouths in odd places. They are accidents and no one's fault, as used to be thought. Once they were considered the visible punishment for concealed sins.

And just as there are physical monsters, can there not be mental or psychic monsters born? The face and body may be perfect, but if a twisted gene or malformed egg can produce physical monsters, may not the same process produce a malformed soul?

Monsters are variations from the accepted normal to a greater or a less degree. As a child may be born without an arm, so one may be born without kindness or the potential of conscience. A man who loses his arms in an accident has a great struggle to adjust himself to the lack, but one born without arms suffers only from people who find him strange. Having never had arms, he cannot miss them. Sometimes when we are little we imagine how it would be to have wings, but there is no reason to suppose it is the same feeling birds have. No, to a monster the norm must seem monstrous, since everyone is normal to himself. To the inner monster it must be even more obscure, since he has no visible thing to compare with others. To a man born without conscience, a soul-stricken man must seem ridiculous. To a criminal, honesty is foolish. You must not forget that a monster is only a variation, and that to a monster the norm is monstrous.

It is my belief that Cathy Ames was born with the tendencies, or lack of them, which drove and forced her all of her life. Some balance wheel was misweighted, some gear out of ratio. She was not like other people, never was from birth. And just as a cripple may learn to utilize his lack so that he becomes more effective in a limited field than the uncrippled, so did Cathy, using her difference, make a painful and bewildering stir in her world.

There was a time when a girl like Cathy would have been called possessed by the devil. She would have been exorcised to cast out the evil spirit, and if after many trials that did not work, she would have been burned as a witch for the good of the community. The one thing that may not be forgiven a witch is her ability to distress people, to make them restless and uneasy and even envious.

As though nature concealed a trap, Cathy had from the first a face of innocence. Her hair was gold and lovely; wide-set hazel eyes with upper lids that drooped made her look mysteriously sleepy. Her nose was delicate and thin, and her cheekbones high and wide, sweeping down to a small chin so that her face was heart-shaped. Her mouth was well shaped and well lipped but abnormally small – what used to be called a rosebud. Her ears were very little, without lobes, and they pressed so close to her head that even with her hair combed up they made no silhouette. They were thin flaps sealed against her head.

Cathy always had a child's figure even after she was grown, slender, delicate arms and hands – tiny hands. Her breasts never developed very much. Before her puberty the nipples turned inward. Her mother had to manipulate them out when they became painful in Cathy's tenth year. Her body was a boy's body, narrow-hipped, straight-legged, but her ankles were thin and straight without being slender. Her feet were small and round and stubby, with fat insteps almost like little hoofs. She was a pretty child and she became a pretty woman. Her voice was huskily soft, and it could be so sweet as to be irresistible. But there must have been some steel cord in her throat, for Cathy's voice could cut like a file when she wished.

Even as a child she had some quality that made people look at her, then look away, then look back at her, troubled at something foreign. Something looked out of her eyes, and was never there when one looked again. She moved quietly and talked little, but she could enter no room without causing everyone to turn towards her.

She made people uneasy but not so that they wanted to go away from her. Men and women wanted to inspect her, to be close to her, to try to find what caused the disturbance she distributed so subtly. And since this had always been so, Cathy did not find it strange.

Cathy was different from other children in many ways, but

one thing in particular set her apart. Most children abhor difference. They want to look, talk, dress, and act exactly like all of the others. If the style of dress is an absurdity, it is pain and sorrow to a child not to wear that absurdity. If necklaces of pork chops were accepted, it would be a sad child who could not wear pork chops. And this slavishness to the group normally extends into every game, every practice, social or otherwise. It is a protective coloration children utilize for their safety.

Cathy had none of this. She never conformed in dress or conduct. She wore whatever she wanted to. The result was that quite often other children imitated her.

As she grew older the group, the herd, which is any collection of children, began to sense what adults felt, that there was something foreign about Cathy. After a while only one person at a time associated with her. Groups of boys and girls avoided her as though she carried a nameless danger.

Cathy was a liar, but she did not lie the way most children do. Hers was no day-dream lying, when the thing imagined is told and, to make it seem more real, told as real. That is just ordinary deviation from external reality. I think the difference between a lie and a story is that a story utilizes the trappings and appearance of truth for the interest of the listener as well as of the teller. A story has in it neither gain nor loss. But a lie is a device for profit or escape. I suppose if that definition is strictly held to, then a writer of stories is a liar – if he is financially fortunate.

Cathy's lies were never innocent. Their purpose was to escape punishment, or work, or responsibility, and they were used for profit. Most liars are tripped up either because they forget what they have told or because the lie is suddenly faced with an incontrovertible truth. But Cathy did not forget her lies, and she developed the most effective method of lying. She stayed close enough to the truth so that one could never be sure. She knew two other methods also – either to interlard her lies with truth or to tell a truth as though it were a lie. If one is accused of a lie and it turns out to be the truth, there is a backlog that will last a long time and protect a number of untruths.

Since Cathy was an only child her mother had no close contrast in the family. She thought all children were like her own. And since all parents are worriers she was convinced that all her friends had the same problems.

Cathy's father was not so sure. He operated a small tannery in a town in Massachusetts, which made a comfortable, careful living if he worked very hard. Mr Ames came in contact with other children away from his home and he felt that Cathy was not like other children. It was a matter more felt than known. He was uneasy about his daughter but he could not have said why.

Nearly everyone in the world has appetites and impulses, trigger emotions, islands of selfishness, lusts just beneath the surface. And most people either hold such things in check or indulge them secretly. Cathy knew not only these impulses in others but how to use them for her own gain. It is quite possible that she did not believe in any other tendencies in humans, for while she was preternaturally alert in some directions she was completely blind in others.

Cathy learned when she was very young that sexuality with all its attendant yearnings and pains, jealousies and taboos, is the most disturbing impulse humans have. And in that day it was even more disturbing than it is now, because the subject was unmentionable and unmentioned. Everyone concealed that little hell in himself, while publicly pretending it did not exist – and when he was caught up in it he was completely helpless. Cathy learned that by the manipulation and use of this one part of people she could gain and keep power over nearly anyone. It was at once a weapon and a threat. It was irresistible. And since the blind helplessness seems never to have fallen on Cathy, it is probable that she had very little of the impulse herself and indeed felt a contempt for those who did. And when you think of it in one way, she was right.

What freedom men and women could have, were they not constantly tricked and trapped and enslaved and tortured by their sexuality! The only drawback in that freedom is that without it one would not be a human. One would be a monster.

At ten Cathy knew something of the power of the sex impulse and began coldly to experiment with it. She planned everything coldly, foreseeing difficulties and preparing for them.

The sex play of children has always gone on. Everyone, I guess, who is not abnormal has foregathered with little girls in some dim leafy place, in the bottom of a manger, under a willow, in a culvert under a road – or at least has dreamed of doing so. Nearly all parents are faced with the problem sooner or later, and then the child is lucky if the parent remembers his own childhood. In the time of Cathy's childhood, however, it was harder. The parents, denying it in themselves, were horrified to find it in their children.

On a spring morning when with late-surviving dew the young grass bristled under the sun, when the warmth crept into the ground and pushed the yellow dandelions up, Cathy's mother finished hanging the washed clothes on the line. The Ameses lived on the edge of town, and behind their house were barn and carriage house, vegetable garden, and fenced paddock for two horses.

Mrs Ames remembered having seen Cathy stroll away towards the barn. She called for her, and when there was no answer she thought she might have been mistaken. She was about to go into the house when she heard a giggle from the carriage house. 'Cathy!' she called. There was no answer. An uneasiness came over her. She reached back in her mind for the sound of the giggle. It had not been Cathy's voice. Cathy was not a giggler.

There is no knowing how or why dread comes on a parent. Of course many times apprehension arises when there is no reason for it at all. And it comes most often to the parents of only children, parents who have indulged in black dreams of loss.

Mrs Ames stood still, listening. She heard soft secret voices and moved quietly towards the carriage house. The double doors were closed. The murmur of voices came from inside, but she could not make out Cathy's voice. She made a quick stride and pulled the doors open and the bright sun crashed inside. She froze, mouth open, at what she saw. Cathy lay on the floor, her skirts pulled up. She was naked to the waist, and beside her two boys about fourteen were kneeling. The shock of the sudden light froze them too. Cathy's eyes were blank with terror. Mrs Ames knew the boys, knew their parents.

Suddenly one of the boys leaped up, darted past Mrs Ames, and ran around the corner of the house. The other boy helplessly edged away from the woman and with a cry rushed through the doorway. Mrs Ames clutched at him, but her fingers slipped from his jacket and he was gone. She could hear his running footsteps outside.

Mrs Ames tried to speak and her voice was a croaking whisper. 'Get up!'

Cathy stared blankly up at her and made no move. Mrs Ames saw that Cathy's wrists were tied with a heavy rope. She screamed and flung herself down and fumbled at the knots. She carried Cathy into the house and put her to bed.

The family doctor, after he had examined Cathy, could find no evidence that she had been mistreated. 'You can just thank God you got there in time,' he said over and over to Mrs Ames.

Cathy did not speak for a long time. Shock, the doctor called it. And when she did come out of the shock Cathy refused to talk. When she was questioned her eyes widened until the whites showed all around the pupils and her breathing stopped and her body grew rigid and her cheeks reddened from holding her breath.

The conference with the parents of the boys was attended by Dr Williams. Mr Ames was silent most of the time. He carried the rope which had been around Cathy's wrists. His eyes were puzzled. There were things he did not understand, but he did not bring them up.

Mrs Ames settled down to a steady hysteria. She had been there. She had seen. She was the final authority. And out of her hysteria a sadistic devil peered. She wanted blood. There was a kind of pleasure in her demands for punishment. The town, the country, must be protected. She put it on that basis. She had arrived in time, thank God. But maybe the next time she would not; and how would other mothers feel? And Cathy was only ten years old.

Punishments were more savage then than they are now. A man truly believed that the whip was an instrument of virtue. First singly and then together the boys were whipped, whipped to raw cuts.

Their crime was bad enough, but the lies proved an evil that not even the whip could remove. And their defence was from the beginning ridiculous. Cathy, they said, had started the whole thing, and they had each given her five cents. They had not tied her hands. They said they remembered that she was playing with a rope.

Mrs Ames said it first and the whole town echoed it. 'Do they mean to say she tied her own hands? A ten-year-old child?'

If the boys had owned up to the crime they might have escaped some of the punishment. Their refusal brought a torturing rage not only to their fathers, who did the whipping, but to the whole community. Both boys were sent to a house of correction with the approval of their parents.

'She's haunted by it,' Mrs Ames told the neighbours. 'If she could only talk about it, maybe she would get better. But when I ask her about it – it's like it came right back to her and she goes into shock again.'

The Ameses never spoke of it to her again. The subject was closed. Mr Ames very soon forgot his haunting reservations. He would have felt bad if two boys were in the house of correction for something they did not do.

After Cathy had fully recovered from her shock, boys and girls watched her from a distance and then moved closer, fascinated by her. She had no girl crushes, as is usual at twelve and thirteen. Boys did not want to take the chance of being ragged by their friends for walking home from school with her. But she exercised a powerful effect on both boys and girls. And if any boy could come on her alone, he found himself drawn to her by a force he could neither understand nor overcome.

She was dainty and very sweet and her voice was low. She went for long walks by herself, and it was a rare walk when some boy did not blunder out of a wood-lot and come on her by accident. And while whispers went scurrying about, there is no knowing what Cathy did. If anything happened, only vague whispers followed, and this in itself was unusual at an age when there are many secrets and none of them kept long enough to raise a cream.

Cathy developed a little smile, just a hint of a smile. She had a way of looking sideways and down that hinted to a lone boy of secrets he could share.

In her father's mind another question stirred, and he shoved it down deep and felt dishonest for thinking about it at all. Cathy had remarkable luck in finding things – a gold charm, money, a little silken purse, a silver cross with red stones said to be rubies. She found many things, and when her father advertised in the weekly *Courier* about the cross no one ever claimed it.

Mr William Ames, Cathy's father, was a covert man. He rarely told the thoughts in his mind. He wouldn't have dared so far to expose himself to the gaze of his neighbours. He kept the little flame of suspicion to himself. It was better if he didn't know anything, safer, wiser, and much more comfortable. As for Cathy's mother, she was so bound and twisted in a cocoon of gauzy half-lies, warped truth, suggestions, all planted by Cathy, that she would not have known a true thing if it had come to her.

III

Cathy grew more lovely all the time. The delicate blooming skin, the golden hair, the wide-set, modest, and yet promising eyes, the little mouth full of sweetness, caught attention and held it. She finished the eight grades of grammar school with such a good record that her parents entered her in the small high school, although in that time it was not usual for a girl to go on with her studies. But Cathy said she wanted to be a teacher, which delighted her mother and father, for this was the one profession of dignity open to a girl of a good but not well-to-do family. Parents took honour from a daughter who was a teacher.

Cathy was fourteen when she entered high school. She had always been precious to her parents, but with her entrance into the rarities of algebra and Latin she climbed into clouds where her parents could not follow. They had lost her. They felt that she was transported to a higher order.

The teacher of Latin was a pale intense young man who had failed in divinity school and yet had enough education to teach the inevitable grammar, Caesar, Cicero. He was a quiet young man who warmed his sense of failure to his bosom. Deep in himself he felt that he had been rejected by God, and for cause.

For a time it was noticed that a flame leaped in James Grew and some force glowed in his eyes. He was never seen with Cathy and no relationship was even suspected.

James Grew became a man. He walked on his toes and sang to himself. He wrote letters so persuasive that the directors of his divinity school looked favourably on re-admitting him.

And then the flame went out. His shoulders, held so high and square, folded dejectedly. His eyes grew feverish and his hands twitched. He was seen in church at night, on his knees, moving his lips over prayers. He missed school and sent word that he was ill when it was known that he was walking all alone in the hills beyond the town.

One night, late, he tapped on the door of the Ames house. Mr Ames complained his way out of bed, lighted a candle, flung an overcoat over his night-gown, and went to the door. It was a wild and crazy-looking James Grew who stood before him, his eyes shining and his body one big shudder.

'I've got to see you,' he said hoarsely to Mr Ames.

'It's after midnight,' Mr Ames said sternly.

'I've got to see you alone. Put on some clothes and come outside. I've got to talk to you.'

'Young man, I think you're drunk or sick. Go home and get some sleep. It's after midnight.'

'I can't wait. I've got to talk to you.'

'Come down to the tannery in the morning,' said Mr Ames,

79

and he closed the door firmly on the reeling caller and stood inside, listening. He heard the wailing voice, 'I can't wait. I can't wait,' and then the feet dragged slowly down the steps.

Mr Ames shielded the candlelight away from his eyes with his cupped hand and went back to bed. He thought he saw Cathy's door close very silently, but perhaps the leaping candlelight had fooled his eyes, for a portière seemed to move too.

'What in the world?' his wife demanded when he came back to the bedside.

Mr Ames didn't know why he answered as he did – perhaps to save discussion. 'A drunken man,' he said. 'Got the wrong house.'

'I don't know what the world is coming to,' said Mrs Ames.

As he lay in the darkness after the light was out he saw the green circle left in his eyes by the candle flame, and in its whirling, pulsing flame he saw the frantic, beseeching eyes of James Grew. He didn't go back to sleep for a long time.

In the morning a rumour ran through the town, distorted here and there, added to, but by afternoon the story clarified. The sexton had found James Grew stretched on the floor in front of the altar. The whole top of his head blown off. Beside him lay a shotgun, and beside it the piece of stick with which he had pushed the trigger. Near him on the floor was a candlestick from the altar. One of the three candles was still burning. The other two had not been lighted. And on the floor were two books, the hymnal and the Book of Common Prayer, one on top of the other. The way the sexton figured it, James Grew had propped the gun-barrel on the books to bring it in line with his temple. The recoil of the discharge had thrown the shotgun off the books.

A number of people remembered having heard an explosion early in the morning, before daylight. James Grew left no letter. No one could figure why he had done it.

Mr Ames's first impulse was to go to the coroner with his story of the midnight call. Then he thought, 'What good would it do? If I knew anything it would be different. But I don't know a single thing.' He had a sick feeling in his stomach. He told himself over and over that it was not his fault. 'How could I have helped it? I don't even know what he wanted.' He felt guilty and miserable.

At dinner his wife talked about the suicide and he couldn't eat. Cathy sat silent, but no more silent than usual. She ate with little dainty nips and wiped her mouth often on her napkin.

Mrs Ames went over the matter of the body and the gun in detail. 'There's one thing I meant to speak of,' she said. 'That drunken man who came to the door last night – could that have been young Grew?'

'No,' he said quickly.

'Are you sure? Could you see him in the dark?'

'I had a candle,' he said sharply. 'Didn't look anything like, had a big beard.'

'No need to snap at me,' she said. 'I just wondered.'

Cathy wiped her mouth, and when she laid her napkin on her lap she was smiling.

Mrs Ames turned to her daughter. 'You saw him every day in school, Cathy. Has he seemed sad lately? Did you notice anything that might mean —'

Cathy looked down at her plate and then up. 'I thought he was sick,' she said. 'Yes, he has looked bad. Everybody was talking in school today. And somebody – I don't remember who – said that Mr Grew was in some kind of trouble in Boston. I didn't hear what kind of trouble. We all liked Mr Grew.' She wiped her lips delicately.

That was Cathy's method. Before the next day was out everybody in town knew that James Grew had been in trouble in Boston, and no one could possibly imagine that Cathy had planted the story. Even Mrs Ames had forgotten where she heard it.

IV

Soon after her sixteenth birthday a change came over Cathy. One morning she did not get up for school. Her mother went into her room and found her in bed, staring at the ceiling. 'Hurry, you'll be late. It's nearly nine.'

'I'm not going.' There was no emphasis in her voice.

'Are you sick?'

'No.'

'Then hurry, get up.'

'I'm not going.'

'You must be sick. You've never missed a day.'

'I'm not going to school,' Cathy said calmly. 'I'm never going to school again.'

Her mother's mouth fell open. 'What do you mean?'

'Not ever,' said Cathy and continued to stare at the ceiling.

'Well, we'll just see what your father has to say about that!'

With all our work and expense, and two years before you get your certificate!' Then she came close and said softly, 'You aren't thinking of getting married?'

'No.'

'What's that book you're hiding?'

'Here! I'm not hiding it.'

'Oh! *Alice in Wonderland*. You're too big for that.'

Cathy said, 'I can get to be *so* little you can't even see me.'

'What in the world are you talking about?'

'Nobody can find me.'

Her mother said angrily, 'Stop making jokes. I don't know what you're thinking of. What does Miss Fancy think she is going to do?'

'I don't know yet,' said Cathy. 'I think I'll go away.'

'Well, you just lie there, Miss Fancy, and when your father comes home he'll have a thing or two to say to you.'

Cathy turned her head very slowly and looked at her mother. Her eyes were expressionless and cold. And suddenly Mrs Ames was afraid of her daughter. She went out quietly and closed the door. In her kitchen she sat down and cupped her hands in her lap and stared out of the window at the weathering carriage house.

Her daughter had become a stranger to her. She felt, as most parents do at one time or another, that she was losing control, that the bridle put in her hands for the governing of Cathy was slipping through her fingers. She did not know that she had never had any power over Cathy. She had been used for Cathy's purposes always. After a while Mrs Ames put on a bonnet and went to the tannery. She wanted to talk to her husband away from the house.

In the afternoon Cathy rose listlessly from her bed and spent a long time in front of the mirror.

That evening Mr Ames, hating what he had to do, delivered a lecture to his daughter. He spoke of her duty, her obligation, her natural love for her parents. Towards the end of his speech he was aware that she was not listening to him. This made him angry and he fell into threats. He spoke of the authority God had given him over his child and of how this natural authority had been armed by the state. He had her attention now. She looked him right in the eyes. Her mouth smiled a little, and her eyes did not seem to blink. Finally he had to look away, and this enraged him further. He ordered her to stop her nonsense.

Vaguely he threatened her with whipping if she did not obey him.

He ended on a note of weakness. 'I want you to promise me that you will go to school in the morning and stop your foolishness.'

Her face was expressionless. The little mouth was straight. 'All right,' she said.

Later that night Mr Ames said to his wife with an assurance he did not feel, 'You see, it just needs a little authority. Maybe we've been too lax. But she has been a good child. I guess she forgot who's boss. A little sternness never hurt anybody.' He wished he were as confident as his words.

In the morning she was gone. Her straw travelling basket was gone and the best of her clothing. Her bed was neatly made. The room was impersonal – nothing to indicate that a girl had grown up in it. There were no pictures, no mementos, none of the normal clutter of growing. Cathy had never played with dolls. The room had no Cathy imprint.

In his way Mr Ames was an intelligent man. He clapped on his derby hat and walked quickly to the railroad station. The station agent was certain. Cathy had taken the early morning train. She had bought a ticket for Boston. He helped Mr Ames write a telegram to the Boston police. Mr Ames bought a round-trip ticket and caught the nine-fifty to Boston. He was a very good man in a crisis.

That night Mrs Ames sat in the kitchen with the door closed. She was white and she gripped the table with her hands to control her shaking. The sound, first of the blows and then of the screaming, came clearly to her through the closed doors.

Mr Ames was not good at whipping because he had never done it. He lashed at Cathy's legs with the buggy whip, and when she stood quietly staring at him with calm cold eyes he lost his temper. The first blows were tentative and timid, but when she did not cry he slashed at her sides and shoulders. The whip licked and cut. In his rage he missed her several times or got too close so that the whip wrapped around her body.

Cathy learned quickly. She found him out and knew him, and once she had learned she screamed, she writhed, she cried, she begged, and she had the satisfaction of feeling the blows instantly become lighter.

Mr Ames was frightened at the noise and hurt he was creating. He stopped. Cathy dropped back on the bed, sobbing. And if he had looked, her father would have seen that there were no tears in her eyes, but rather the muscles of her neck were tight and there were lumps just under her temples where the jaw muscles knotted.

He said, 'Now will you ever do that again?'

'No, oh, no! Forgive me,' Cathy said. She turned over on the bed so that her father could not see the coldness in her face.

'See you remember who you are. And don't forget what I am.'

Cathy's voice caught. She produced a dry sob. 'I won't forget,' she said.

In the kitchen Mrs Ames wrestled her hands. Her husband put his fingers on her shoulder.

'I hated to do it,' he said. 'I had to. And I think it did her good. She seems like a changed girl to me. Maybe we haven't bent the twig enough. We've spared the rod. Maybe we were wrong.' And he knew that although his wife had insisted on the whipping, although she had forced him to whip Cathy, she hated him for doing it. Despair settled over him.

v

There seemed no doubt that it was what Cathy needed. As Mr Ames said, 'It kind of opened her up.' She had always been tractable but now she became thoughtful too. In the weeks that followed she helped her mother in the kitchen and offered to help more than was needed. She started to knit an afghan for her mother, a large project that would take months. Mrs Ames told the neighbours about it. 'She has such a fine colour sense – rust and yellow. She's finished three squares already.'

For her father Cathy kept a ready smile. She hung up his hat when he came in and turned his chair properly under the light to make it easy for him to read.

Even in school she was changed. Always she had been a good student, but now she began to make plans for the future. She talked to the principal about examinations for her teaching certificate, perhaps a year early. And the principal looked over her record and thought she might well try it with hope of success. He called on Mr Ames at the tannery to discuss it.

'She didn't tell us any of this,' Mr Ames said proudly.

'Well, maybe I shouldn't have told you. I hope I haven't ruined a surprise.'

Mr and Mrs Ames felt that they had blundered on some magic which solved all of their problems. They put it down to an unconscious wisdom which comes only to parents. 'I never saw such a change in a person in my life,' Mr Ames said.

'But she was always a good child,' said his wife. 'And have you noticed how pretty she's getting? Why, she's almost beautiful. Her cheeks have so much colour.'

'I don't think she'll be teaching school long, with her looks,' said Mr Ames.

It was true that Cathy glowed. The childlike smile was constantly on her lips while she went about her preparations. She had all the time in the world. She cleaned the cellar and stuffed papers all around the edges of the foundation to block the draught. When the kitchen door squeaked she oiled the hinges and then the lock that turned too hard, and while she had the oil-can out she oiled the front-door hinges too. She made it her duty to keep the lamps filled and their chimneys clean. She invented a way of dipping the chimneys in a big can of kerosene she had in the basement.

'You'd have to see it to believe it,' her father said.

And it wasn't only at home either. She braved the smell of the tannery to visit her father. She was just past sixteen and of course he thought of her as a baby. He was amazed at her questions about business.

'She's smarter than some men I could name,' he told his foreman. 'She might be running the business some day.'

She was interested not only in the tanning processes but in the business end too. Her father explained the loans, the payments, the billing, and the pay-roll. He showed her how to open the safe and was pleased that after the first try she remembered the combination.

'The way I look at it is this,' he told his wife. 'We've all of us got a little of the Old Nick in us. I wouldn't want a child that didn't have some gumption. The way I see it, that's just a kind of energy. If you just check it and keep it in control, why, it will go in the right direction.'

Cathy mended all of her clothes and put her things in order.

One day in May she came home from school and went directly to her knitting needles. Her mother was dressed to go out. 'I have to go to the Altar Guild,' she said. 'It's about the cake sale next week. I'm chairman. Your father wondered if you would go by the bank and pick up the money for the pay-roll and take it to the tannery. I told him about the cake sale so I can't do it.'

'I'd like to,' said Cathy.

'They'll have the money ready for you in a bag,' said Mrs Ames, and she hurried out.

Cathy worked quickly but without hurry. She put on an old apron to cover her clothes. In the basement she found a jelly jar with a top and carried it out to the carriage house, where the tools were kept. In the chicken-yard she caught a little pullet, took it to the block and chopped its head off, and held the writhing neck over the jelly jar until it was half full of blood. Then she carried the quivering pullet to the manure pile and buried it deep. Back in the kitchen she took off the apron and put it in the stove and poked the coals until a flame sprang up on the cloth. She washed her hands and inspected her shoes and stockings and wiped a dark spot from the toe of her right shoe. She looked at her face in the mirror. Her cheeks were bright with colour and her eyes shone and her mouth turned up in its small childlike smile. On her way out she hid the jelly jar under the lowest part of the kitchen steps. Her mother had not been gone even ten minutes.

Cathy walked lightly, almost dancing, round the house and into the street. The trees were breaking into leaf and a few early dandelions were in yellow flower on the lawns. Cathy walked gaily towards the centre of the town, where the bank was. And she was so fresh and pretty that people walking turned and looked after her when she had passed.

VI

The fire broke out at about three o'clock in the morning. It rose, flared, roared, crashed, and crumbled in on itself almost before anyone noticed it. When the volunteers ran up, pulling their hose-cart, there was nothing for them to do but wet down the roofs of the neighbouring houses to keep them from catching fire.

The Ames house had gone up like a rocket. The volunteers and the ordinary audience fires attract looked around at the lighted faces, trying to see Mr and Mrs Ames and their daughter. It came to everyone at once that they were not there. People gazed at the broad ember-bed and saw themselves and their children in there, and hearts rose up and pumped against throats. The volunteers began to dump water on the fire almost as though they might even so late save some corporeal part of the family. The frightened talk ran through the town that the whole Ames family had burned.

By sunrise everyone in town was tight-packed about the smoking black pile. Those in front had to shield their faces against the heat. The volunteers continued to pump water to cool off the charred mess. By noon the coroner was able to throw wet planks down and probe with a crowbar among the sodden heaps of charcoal. Enough remained of Mr and Mrs Ames to make sure there were two bodies. Near neighbours pointed out the approximate place where Cathy's room had been, but although the coroner and any number of helpers worked over the débris with a garden rake they could find no tooth or bone.

The chief of the volunteers meanwhile had found the door-knobs and lock of the kitchen door. He looked at the blackened metal, puzzled, but not quite knowing what puzzled him. He borrowed the coroner's rake and worked furiously. He went to the place where the front door had been and raked until he found that lock, crooked and half melted. By now he had his own small crowd, who demanded, 'What are you looking for, George?' and 'What did you find, George?'

Finally the coroner came over to him. 'What's on your mind, George?'

'No keys in the locks,' the chief said uneasily.

'Maybe they fell out.'

'How?'

'Maybe they melted.'

'The locks didn't melt.'

'Maybe Bill Ames took them out.'

'On the inside?' He held up his trophies. Both bolts stuck out.

Since the owner's house was burned and the owner ostensibly burned with it, the employees of the tannery, out of respect, did not go to work. They hung around the burned house, offering to help in any way they could, feeling official and generally getting in the way.

It wasn't until afternoon that Joel Robinson, the foreman, went down to the tannery. He found the safe open and papers scattered all over the floor. A broken window showed how the thief had entered.

Now the whole complexion changed. So, it was not an accident. Fear took the place of excitement and sorrow, and anger, brother of fear, crept in. The crowd began to spread.

They had not far to go. In the carriage house there was what is called 'signs of a struggle' – in this case a broken box, a shattered carriage lamp, scraped marks in the dust, and straw on the floor. The onlookers might not have known these as signs of a struggle had there not been a quantity of blood on the floor.

The constable took control. This was his province. He pushed and herded everyone out of the carriage house. 'Want to gum up all these clues?' he shouted at them. 'Now you all stay clear outside the door.'

He searched the room, picked up something, and in a corner found something else. He came to the door, holding his discoveries in his hands—a blood-spattered blue hair-ribbon and a cross with red stones. 'Anybody recognize these here?' he demanded.

In a small town where everyone knows everyone it is almost impossible to believe that one of your acquaintances could murder anyone. For that reason, if the signs are not pretty strong in a particular direction, it must be some dark stranger, some wanderer from the outside world where such things happen. Then the hobo camps are raided and vagrants brought in and hotel registers scrutinized. Every man who is not known is automatically suspected. It was May, remember, and the wandering men had only recently taken to the roads, now that the warming months let them spread their blankets by any watercourse. And the gypsies were out too—a whole caravan less than five miles away. And what a turning out those poor gypsies got!

The ground for miles around was searched for new-turned earth, and likely pools were dragged for Cathy's body. 'She was so pretty,' everyone said, and they meant that in themselves they could see a reason for carrying Cathy off. At length a bumbling hairy half-wit was brought in for questioning. He was a fine candidate for hanging because not only did he have no alibis, he could not remember what he had done at any time in his life. His feeble mind sensed that these questioners wanted something of him and, being a friendly creature, he tried to give it to them. When a baited and set question was offered to him, he walked happily into the trap and was glad when the constable looked happy. He tried manfully to please these superior beings. There was something very nice about him. The only trouble with his confession was that he confessed too much in too many directions. Also, he had constantly to be reminded of what he was supposed to have done. He was really pleased when he was indicted by a stern and frightened jury. He felt that at last he amounted to something.

There were, and are, some men who become judges whose love for the law and for its intention of promoting justice has the quality of love for a woman. Such a man presided at the examination before plea – a man so pure and good that he cancelled out a lot of wickedness with his life. Without the prompting the culprit was used to, his confession was nonsense. The judge questioned him and found out that although the suspect was trying to follow instructions he simply could not remember what he did, whom he killed, how or why. The judge sighed wearily and motioned him out of the courtroom and crooked his fingers at the constable.

'Now look here, Mike,' he said, 'you shouldn't do a thing like that. If that poor fellow had been just a little smarter you might have got him hanged.'

'He said he did it.' The constable's feelings were hurt, because he was a conscientious man.

'He would have admitted climbing the golden stairs and cutting St Peter's throat with a bowling ball,' the judge said. 'Be more careful, Mike. The law was designed to save, not to destroy.'

In all such local tragedies time works like a damp brush on water-colour. The sharp edges blur, the ache goes out of it, the colours melt together, and from the many separated lines a solid grey emerges. Within a month it was not so necessary to hang someone, and within two months nearly everybody discovered that there wasn't any real evidence against anyone. If it had not been for Cathy's murder, fire and robbery might have been a coincidence. Then it occurred to people that without Cathy's body you couldn't prove anything even though you thought she was dead.

Cathy left a scent of sweetness behind her.

CHAPTER 9

I

MR EDWARDS carried on his business of whoremaster in an orderly and unemotional way. He maintained his wife and his two well-mannered children in a good house in a good neighbourhood in Boston. The children, two boys, were entered on the books at Groton when they were infants.

Mrs Edwards kept a dustless house and controlled her servants. There were of course many times when Mr Edwards had to be away from home on business, but he managed to live an amazingly domestic life and to spend more evenings at home than you could imagine. He ran his business with a public accountant's neatness and accuracy. He was a large and powerful man, running a little to fat in his late forties, and yet in surprisingly good condition for a time when a man wanted to be fat if only to prove he was a success.

He had invented his business – the circuit route through the small towns, the short stay of each girl, the discipline, the percentages. He felt his way along and made few mistakes. He never sent his girls into the cities. He could handle the hungry constables of the villages, but he had respect for the experienced and voracious big-city police. His ideal stand was a small town with a mortgaged hotel and no amusements, one where his only competition came from wives and an occasional wayward girl. At this time he had ten units. Before he died at sixty-seven of strangulation on a chicken bone, he had groups of four girls in each of thirty-three small towns in New England. He was better than well fixed – he was rich; and the manner of his death was in itself symbolic of success and well-being.

At the present time the institution of the whorehouse seems to a certain extent to be dying out. Scholars have various reasons to give. Some say that the decay of morality among girls has dealt the whorehouse its death-blow. Others, perhaps more idealistic, maintain that police supervision on an increased scale is driving the houses out of existence. In the late days of the last century and the early part of this one, the whorehouse was an accepted if not openly discussed institution. It was said that its existence protected decent women. An unmarried man could go to one of these houses and evacuate the sexual energy which was making him uneasy and at the same time maintain the popular attitudes about the purity and loveliness of women. It was a mystery, but then there are many mysterious things in our social thinking.

These houses ranged from palaces filled with gold and velvet to the crummiest cribs where the stench would drive a pig away. Every once in a while a story would start about how young girls were stolen and enslaved by the controllers of the industry, and perhaps many of the stories were true. But the great majority of whores drifted into their profession through laziness and stupidity. In the houses they had no responsibility. They were fed and clothed and taken care of until they were too old, and then they were kicked out. This ending was no deterrent. No one who is young is ever going to be old.

Now and then a smart girl came into the profession, but she usually moved up to better things. She got a house of her own or worked successfully at blackmail or married a rich man. There was even a special name for the smart ones. They were grandly called courtesans.

Mr Edwards had no trouble either in recruiting or in controlling his girls. If a girl was not properly stupid, he threw her out. He did not want very pretty girls either. Some local young man might fall in love with a pretty whore and there would be hell to pay. When any of his girls became pregnant they had the choice of leaving or of being aborted so brutally that a fair proportion died. In spite of this the girls usually chose abortion.

It was not always smooth sailing for Mr Edwards. He did have his problems. At the time of which I am telling you he had been subjected to a series of misfortunes. A train wreck had killed off two units of four girls each. Another of his units he lost to conversion when a small-town preacher suddenly caught fire and began igniting the townsfolk with his sermons. The swelling congregation had to move out of the church and into the fields. Then, as happens so often, the preacher turned over his hole-card, the sure-fire card. He predicted the date of the end of the world, and the whole county moved bleating in on him. Mr Edwards went to the town, took the heavy quirt from his suitcase, and whipped the girls unmercifully; instead of seeing things his way, the girls begged for more whipping to wipe out their fancied sins. He gave up in disgust, took their clothes, and went back to Boston. The girls achieved a certain prominence when they went naked to the camp meeting to confess and testify. That is how Mr Edwards happened to be interviewing and recruiting numbers of girls instead of picking one up here and there. He had three units to rebuild from the ground.

I don't know how Cathy Ames heard about Mr Edwards. Perhaps a hack driver told her. The word got around when a girl really wanted to know. Mr Edwards had not had a good morning when she came into his office. The pain in his stomach he ascribed to a halibut chowder his wife had given him for supper the night before. He had been up all night. The chowder had blown both ways and he still felt weak and crampy.

For this reason he did not take in all at once the girl who called herself Catherine Amesbury. She was far too pretty for his business. Her voice was low and throaty, she was slight, almost delicate, and her skin was lovely. In a word she was not Mr

Edwards's kind of girl at all. If he had not been weak he would have rejected her instantly. But while he did not look at her very closely during the routine questioning, mostly about relatives who might cause trouble, something in Mr Edwards's body began to feel her. Mr Edwards was not a concupiscent man, and besides he never mixed his professional life with his private pleasures. His reaction startled him. He looked up, puzzled, at the girl, and her eyelids dipped sweetly and mysteriously, and there was just a suggestion of a sway on her lightly padded hips. Her little mouth wore a cat smile. Mr Edwards leaned forward at his desk, breathing heavily. He realized that he wanted this one for his own.

'I can't understand why a girl like you —' he began, and fell right into the oldest conviction in the world – that the girl you are in love with can't possibly be anything but true and honest.

'My father is dead,' Catherine said modestly. 'Before he died he had let things go to pieces. We didn't know he had borrowed money on the farm. And I can't let the bank take it away from my mother. The shock would kill her.' Catherine's eyes dimmed with tears. 'I thought maybe I could make enough to keep up the interest.'

If ever Mr Edwards had a chance it was now. And indeed a little warning buzz did sound in his brain, but it was not loud enough. About eighty per cent of the girls who came to him needed money to pay off a mortgage. And Mr Edwards made it an unvarying rule not to believe anything his girls said at any time, beyond what they had for breakfast, and they sometimes lied about that. And here he was, a big, fat, grown-up whore-master, leaning his stomach against his desk while his cheeks darkened with blood and excited chills ran up his legs and thighs.

Mr Edwards heard himself saying, 'Well now, my dear, let's talk this over. Maybe we can figure some way for you to get the interest money.' And this to a girl who had simply asked for a job as a whore – or had she?

11

Mrs Edwards was persistently if not profoundly religious. She spent a great part of her time with the mechanics of her church, which did not leave her time for either its background or its effects. To her, Mr Edwards was in the importing business, and even if she had known – which she probably did – what business he was really in, she would not have believed it. And this is another mystery. Her husband had always been to her a coldly thoughtful man who made few and dutiful physical demands on her. If he had never been warm, he had never been cruel either. Her dramas and her emotions had to do with the boys, with the vestry, and with food. She was content with her life and thankful. When her husband's disposition began to disintegrate, causing him to be restless and snappish, to sit staring and then to rush out of the house in a nervous rage, she ascribed it first to his stomach and then to business reverses. When by accident she came upon him in the bathroom, sitting on the toilet and crying softly to himself, she knew he was a sick man. He tried quickly to cover his red brimming eyes from her scrutiny. When neither herb teas nor physics cured him she was helpless.

If in all the years Mr Edwards had heard about anyone like himself he would have laughed. For Mr Edwards, as cold-blooded a whoremaster as ever lived, had fallen hopelessly, miserably in love with Catherine Amesbury. He rented a sweet little brick house for her, and then gave it to her. He bought her every imaginable luxury, over-decorated the house, kept it over-warm. The carpeting was too deep and the walls were crowded with heavy-framed pictures.

Mr Edwards had never experienced such misery. As a matter of business he had learned so much about women that he did not trust one for a second. And since he deeply loved Catherine and love requires trust, he was torn to quivering fragments by his emotion. He had to trust her and at the same time he did not trust her. He tried to buy her loyalty with presents and with money. When he was away from her, he tortured himself with the thought of other men slipping into her house. He hated to leave Boston to check up on his units because this would leave Catherine alone. To a certain extent he began to neglect his business. It was his first experience with this kind of love and it nearly killed him.

One thing Mr Edwards did not know, and could not know because Catherine would not permit it, was that she was faithful to him in the sense that she did not receive or visit other men. To Catherine, Mr Edwards was as cold a business proposition as his units were to him. And as he had his techniques, so had she hers. Once she had him, which was very soon, she managed always to seem lightly dissatisfied. She gave him an impression of restlessness, as though she might take flight at any moment. When she knew he was going to visit her, she made it a point to be out and to come in glowing as from some incredible experience. She complained a good deal about the difficulties of avoiding the lecherous looks and touches of men in the street who could not keep away from her. Several times she ran frightened into the house, having barely escaped a man who had followed her. When she would return in the late afternoon and find him waiting for her she would explain, 'Why, I was shopping. I have to go shopping, you know.' And she made it sound like a lie.

In their sexual relations she convinced him that the result was not quite satisfactory to her, that if he were a better man he could release a flood of unbelievable reaction in her. Her method was to keep him continually off balance. She saw with satisfaction his nerves begin to go, his hands take to quivering, his loss of weight, and the wild glazed look in his eyes. And when she delicately sensed the near approach of insane, punishing rage, she sat in his lap and soothed him and made him believe for a moment in her innocence. She could convince him.

Catherine wanted money, and she set about getting it as quickly and as easily as she could. When she had successfully reduced him to a pulp, and Catherine knew exactly when the time had come, she began to steal from him. She went through his pockets and took any large notes she found. He didn't dare accuse her for fear she would go away. The presents of jewellery he gave her disappeared, and although she said she had lost them, he knew they had been sold. She padded the grocery bills, added to the prices of clothes. He could not bring himself to stop it. She did not sell the house, but she mortgaged it for every penny she could get.

One evening his key did not fit in the lock of the front door. She answered his pounding after a long time. Yes, she had changed the locks because she had lost her key. She was afraid, living alone. Anyone could get in. She would get him another key – but she never did. He always had to ring the bell after that, and sometimes it took a long time for her to answer, and at other times his ring was not answered at all. There was no way for him to know whether she was at home or not. Mr Edwards had her followed – and she did not know how often.

Mr Edwards was essentially a simple man, but even a simple man has complexities which are dark and twisted. Catherine was clever, but even a clever woman misses some of the strange corridors in a man.

She made only one bad slip, and she had tried to avoid that

one. As was proper, Mr Edwards had stocked the pretty little nest with champagne. Catherine had from the first refused to touch it.

'It makes me sick,' she explained. 'I've tried it and I can't drink it.'

'Nonsense,' he said. 'Just have one glass. It can't hurt you.'

'No, thank you. No, I can't drink it.'

Mr Edwards thought of her reluctance as a delicate, a ladylike quality. He had never insisted until one evening when it occurred to him that he knew nothing about her. Wine might loosen her tongue. The more he thought of it, the better the idea seemed to him.

'It's not friendly of you not to have a glass with me.'

'I tell you, it doesn't agree with me.'

'Nonsense.'

'I tell you I don't want it.'

'This is silly,' he said. 'Do you want me to be angry with you?'

'No.'

'Then drink a glass.'

'I don't want it.'

'Drink it.' He held a glass for her, and she retreated from it.

'You don't know. It's not good for me.'

'Drink it.'

She took the glass and poured it down and stood still, quivering, seeming to listen. The blood flowed to her cheeks. She poured another glass for herself and another. Her eyes became set and cold. Mr Edwards felt a fear of her. Something was happening to her which neither she nor he could control.

'I didn't want to do it. Remember that,' she said calmly.

'Maybe you'd better not have any more.'

She laughed and poured herself another glass. 'It doesn't matter now,' she said. 'More won't make much difference.'

'It's nice to have a glass or so,' he said uneasily.

She spoke to him softly. 'You fat slug,' she said. 'What do you know about me? Do you think I can't read every rotten thought you ever had? Want me to tell you? You wonder where a nice girl like me learned tricks. I'll tell you. I learned them in cribs – you hear? – cribs. I've worked in places you never even heard of – four years. Sailors brought me little tricks from Port Said. I know every nerve in your lousy body and I can use them.'

'Catherine,' he protested, 'you don't know what you're saying.'

'I could see it. You thought I would talk. Well, I'm talking.'

She advanced slowly towards him, and Mr Edwards overcame his impulse to edge away. He was afraid of her, but he sat still. Directly in front of him she drank the last champagne in her glass, delicately struck the rim on the table, and jammed the ragged edge against his cheek.

And then he did run from the house, and he could hear her laughing as he went.

III

Love to a man like Mr Edwards is a crippling emotion. It ruined his judgement, cancelled his knowledge, weakened him. He told himself she was hysterical and tried to believe it, and it was made easier for him by Catherine. Her outbreak had terrified her, and for a time she made every effort to restore his sweet picture of her.

A man so painfully in love is capable of self-torture beyond belief. Mr Edwards wanted with all his heart to believe in her goodness, but he was forced not to, as much by his own particular devil as by her outbreak. Almost instinctively he went about learning the truth and at the same time disbelieved it. He knew, for instance, that she would not put her money in a bank. One of his employees, using a complicated set of mirrors, found out the place in the cellar of the little brick house where she did keep it.

One day a clipping came from the agency he employed. It was an old newspaper account of a fire from a small-town weekly. Mr Edwards studied it. His chest and stomach turned to molten metal and a redness glowed in his head behind his eyes. There was real fear mixed up in his love, and the precipitate from the mixing of these two is cruelty. He staggered dizzily to his office couch and lay face down, his forehead against the cool black leather. For a time he hung suspended, hardly breathing. Gradually his brain cleared. His mouth tasted salty, and there was a great ache of anger in his shoulders. But he was calm and his mind cut its intention through time like a sharp beam of a searchlight through a dark room. He moved slowly, checking his suitcase just as he always did when he started out to inspect his units – clean shirts and underwear, a night-gown and slippers, and the heavy quirt with the lash curving around the end of the suitcase.

He moved heavily up the little garden in front of the brick house and rang the bell.

Catherine answered it immediately. She had on her coat and hat.

'Oh!' she said. 'What a shame! I must go out for a while.'

Mr Edwards put down his suitcase. 'No,' he said.

She studied him. Something was changed. He lumbered past her and went down into the cellar.

'Where are you going?' Her voice was shrill.

He did not reply. In a moment he came up again, carrying a small oak box. He opened his suitcase and put the box inside.

'That's mine,' she said softly.

'I know.'

'What are you up to?'

'I thought we'd go for a little trip.'

'Where? I can't go.'

'Little town in Connecticut. I have some business there. You told me once you wanted to work. You're going to work.'

'I don't want to now. You can't make me. Why, I'll call the police!'

He smiled so horribly that she stepped back from him. His temples were thudding with blood. 'Maybe you'd rather go to your home town,' he said. 'They had a big fire there several years ago. Do you remember that fire?'

Her eyes probed and searched him, seeking a soft place, but his eyes were flat and hard. 'What do you want me to do?' she asked quietly.

'Just come for a little trip with me. You said you wanted to work.'

She could think of only one plan. She must go along with him and wait for a chance. A man couldn't always watch. It would be dangerous to thwart him now – best go along with it and wait. That always worked. It always had. But his words had given Catherine real fear.

In the small town they got off the train at dusk, walked down its one dark street and on out into the country. Catherine was wary and watchful. She had no access to his plan. In her purse she had a thin-bladed knife.

Mr Edward thought he knew what he intended to do. He meant to whip her and put her in one of the rooms at the inn, whip her and move her to another town, and so on until she was of no use any more. Then he would throw her out. The local constable would see to it that she did not run away. The knife did not bother him. He knew about that.

The first thing he did when they stopped in a private place

between a stone wall and a fringe of cedars was to jerk the purse from her hand and throw it over the wall. That took care of the knife. But he didn't know about himself, because in all his life he had never been in love with a woman. He thought he only meant to punish her. After two slashes the quirt was not enough. He dropped it on the ground and used his fists. His breathing came out in squealing whines.

Catherine did her best not to fall into panic. She tried to duck his threshing fists or at least to make them ineffective, but at last fear overcame her and she tried to run. He leaped at her and brought her down, and by then his fists were not enough. His frantic hand found a stone on the ground and his cold control was burst through with a red roaring wave.

Later he looked down on her beaten face. He listened for her heart-beat and could hear nothing over the thumping of his own. Two complete and separate thoughts ran in his mind. One said, 'Have to bury her, have to dig a hole and put her in it.' And the other cried like a child, 'I can't stand it. I couldn't bear to touch her.' Then the sickness that follows rage overwhelmed him. He ran from the place, leaving his suitcase, leaving the quirt, leaving the oak box of money. He blundered away in the dusk, wondering only where he could hide his sickness for a while.

No question was ever asked of him. After a time of sickness to which his wife ministered tenderly, he went back to his business and never again let the insanity of love come near him. A man who can't learn from experience is a fool, he said. Always afterwards he had a kind of fearful respect for himself. He had never known that the impulse to kill was in him.

That he had not killed Catherine was an accident. Every blow had been intended to crush her. She was a long time unconscious and a long time half-conscious. She realized her arm was broken and she must find help if she wanted to live. Wanting to live forced her to drag herself along the dark road, looking for help. She turned in at a gate and almost made the steps of the house before she fainted. The roosters were crowing in the chicken-house and a grey rim of dawn lay on the east.

CHAPTER 10

I

WHEN TWO men live together they usually maintain a kind of shabby neatness out of incipient rage at each other. Two men alone are constantly on the verge of fighting, and they know it. Adam Trask had not been home long before the tensions began to build up. The brothers saw too much of each other and not enough of anyone else.

For a few months they were busy getting Cyrus's money in order and out at interest. They travelled together to Washington to look at the grave, good stone and on top an iron star with seal and a hole on the top in which to insert the stick for a little flag on Decoration Day. The brothers stood by the grave a long time, then they went away and they didn't mention Cyrus.

If Cyrus had been dishonest he had done it well. No one asked questions about the money. But the subject was on Charles's mind.

Back on the farm Adam asked him, 'Why don't you buy some new clothes? You're a rich man. You act like you're afraid to spend a penny.'

'I am,' said Charles.

'Why?'

'I might have to give it back.'

'Still harping on that? If there was anything wrong, don't you think we'd have heard about it by now?'

'I don't know,' said Charles. 'I'd rather not talk about it.'

But that night he brought up the subject again. 'There's one thing bothers me,' he began.

'About the money?'

'Yes, about the money. If you make that much money there's bound to be a mess.'

'How do you mean?'

'Well, papers and account books and bills of sale, notes, figuring – well, we went through Father's things and there wasn't none of that.'

'Maybe he burned it up.'

'Maybe he did,' said Charles.

The brothers lived by a routine established by Charles, and he never varied it. Charles awakened on the stroke of four-thirty as surely as though the brass pendulum of the clock had nudged

99

him. He was awake, in fact, a split second before four-thirty. His eyes were open and had blinked once before the high gong struck. For a moment he lay still, looking up into the darkness and scratching his stomach. Then he reached to the table beside his bed and his hand fell exactly on the block of sulphur matches lying there. His fingers pulled a match free and struck it on the side of the block. The sulphur burned its little blue bead before the wood caught. Charles lighted the candle beside his bed. He threw back his blanket and got up. He wore long grey underwear that bagged over his knees and hung loose around his ankles. Yawning, he went to the door, opened it, and called, 'Half past four, Adam. Time to get up. Wake up.'

Adam's voice was muffled. 'Don't you ever forget?'

'It's time to get up.' Charles slipped his legs into his trousers and hunched them up over his hips. 'You don't have to get up,' he said. 'You're a rich man. You can lay in bed all day.'

'So are you. But we still get up before daylight.'

'You don't have to get up,' Charles repeated. 'But if you're going to farm, you'd better farm.'

Adam said ruefully, 'So we're going to buy more land so we can do more work.'

'Come off it,' said Charles. 'Go back to bed if you want to.'

Adam said, 'I bet you couldn't sleep if you stayed in bed. You know what I bet? I bet you get up because you want to, and then you take credit for it – like taking credit for six fingers.'

Charles went into the kitchen and lighted the lamp. 'You can't lay in bed and run a farm,' he said, and he knocked the ashes through the grate of the stove and tore some paper over the exposed coals and blew until the flame started.

Adam was watching him through the door. 'You wouldn't use a match,' he said.

Charles turned angrily. 'You mind your own goddam business. Stop picking at me.'

'All right,' said Adam. 'I will. And maybe my business isn't here.'

'That's up to you. Any time you want to get out, you go right ahead.'

The quarrel was silly but Adam couldn't stop it. His voice went on without his willing it, making angry and irritating words. 'You're damn right I'll go when I want,' he said. 'This is my place as much as yours.'

'Then why don't you do some work on it?'

'Oh, Lord!' Adam said. 'What are we fussing about? Let's not fuss.'

'I don't want trouble,' said Charles. He scooped lukewarm mush into two bowls and spun them on the table.

The brothers sat down. Charles buttered a slice of bread, gouged out a knifeful of jam and spread it over the butter. He dug butter for his second slice and left a slop of jam on the butter roll.

'Goddam it, can't you wipe your knife? Look at that butter!'

Charles laid his knife and the bread on the table and placed his hands palm down on either side. 'You better get off the place,' he said.

Adam got up. 'I'd rather live in a pigsty,' he said, and he walked out of the house.

11

It was eight months before Charles saw him again. Charles came in from work and found Adam sloshing water on his hair and face from the kitchen bucket.

'Hello,' said Charles. 'How are you?'

'Fine,' said Adam.

'Where'd you go?'

'Boston.'

'No place else?'

'No. Just looked at the city.'

The brothers settled back to their old life, but each took precautions against anger. In a way each protected the other and so saved himself. Charles, always the early riser, got breakfast ready before he awakened Adam. And Adam kept the house clean and started a set of books on the farm. In this guarded way they lived for two years before their irritation grew beyond control again.

On a winter evening Adam looked up from his account book. 'It's nice in California,' he said. 'It's nice in the winter. And you can raise anything there.'

'Sure you can raise it. But when you got it, what are you going to do with it?'

'How about wheat? They raise a lot of wheat in California.'

'The rust will get to it,' said Charles.

'What makes you so sure? Look, Charles, things grow so fast in California they say you have to plant and step back quick or you'll get knocked down.'

Charles said, 'Why the hell don't you go there? I'll buy you out any time you say.'

Adam was quiet then, but in the morning while he combed his hair and peered in the small mirror he began it again.

'They don't have any winter in California,' he said. 'It's just like spring all the time.'

'I like the winter,' said Charles.

Adam came towards the stove. 'Don't be cross,' he said.

'Well, stop picking at me. How many eggs?'

'Four,' said Adam.

Charles placed seven eggs on top of the warming oven and built his fire carefully of small pieces of kindling until it burned fiercely. He put the skillet down next to the flame. His sullenness left him as he fried the bacon.

'Adam,' he said, 'I don't know whether you notice it, but it seems like every other word you say is California. Do you really want to go?'

Adam chuckled. 'That's what I'm trying to figure out,' he said. 'I don't know. It's like getting up in the morning. I don't want to get up, but I don't want to stay in bed either.'

'You sure make a fuss about it,' said Charles.

Adam went on, 'Every morning in the army that damned bugle would sound. And I swore to God if I ever got out I would sleep till noon every day. And here I get up a half-hour before reveille. Will you tell me, Charles, what in hell we're working for?'

'You can't lay in bed and run a farm,' said Charles. He stirred the hissing bacon around with a fork.

'Take a look at it,' Adam said earnestly. 'Neither one of us has got a chick or a child, let alone a wife. And the way we're going it don't look like we ever will. We don't have time to look around for a wife. And here we're figuring to add the Clark place to ours if the price is right. What for?'

'It's a damn fine piece,' said Charles. 'The two of them together would make one of the best farms in this section. Say! You thinking of getting married?'

'No. And that's what I'm talking about. Come a few years and we'll have the finest farm in this section. Two lonely old farts working our tails off. Then one of us will die off and the fine farm will belong to one lonely old fart, and then he'll die off —'

'What the hell are you talking about?' Charles demanded. 'Fellow can't get comfortable. You make me itch. Get it out — what's on your mind?'

'I'm not having any fun,' said Adam. 'Or anyway I'm not having enough. I'm working too hard for what I'm getting, and I don't have to work at all.'

'Well, why don't you quit?' Charles shouted at him. 'Why don't you get the hell out? I don't see any guards holding you. Go down to the South Seas and lay in a hammock if that's what you want.'

'Don't be cross,' said Adam quietly. 'It's like getting up. I don't want to get up and I don't want to stay down. I don't want to stay here and I don't want to go away.'

'You make me itch,' said Charles.

'Think about it, Charles. You like it here?'

'Yes.'

'And you want to live here all your life?'

'Yes.'

'Jesus, I wish I had it that easy. What do you suppose is the matter with me?'

'I think you've got knocker fever. Come in to the inn tonight and get it cured up.'

'Maybe that's it,' said Adam. 'But I never took much satisfaction in a whore.'

'It's all the same,' Charles said. 'You shut your eyes and you can't tell the difference.'

'Some of the boys in the regiment used to keep a squaw around. I had one for a while.'

Charles turned to him with interest. 'Father would turn in his grave if he knew you was squawing around. How was it?'

'Pretty nice. She'd wash my clothes and mend and do a little cooking.'

'I mean the other – how was that?'

'Good. Yes, good. And kind of sweet – kind of soft and sweet. Kind of gentle and soft.'

'You're lucky she didn't put a knife in you while you were asleep.'

'She wouldn't. She was sweet.'

'You've got a funny look in your eye. I guess you were kind of gone on that squaw.'

'I guess I was,' said Adam.

'What happened to her?'

'Smallpox.'

'You didn't get another one?'

Adam's eyes were pained. 'We piled them up like they were

103

logs, over two hundred, arms and legs sticking out. And we piled brush on top and poured coal oil on.'

'I've heard they can't stand smallpox.'

'It kills them,' said Adam. 'You're burning the bacon.'

Charles turned quickly back to the stove. 'It'll just be crisp,' he said, 'I like it crisp.' He shovelled the bacon out on a plate and broke the eggs in the hot grease and they jumped and fluttered their edges to brown lace and made clucking sounds.

'There was a school-teacher,' Charles said. 'Prettiest thing you ever saw. Had little tiny feet. Bought all her clothes in New York. Yellow hair, and you never saw such little feet. Sang too, in the choir. Everybody took to going to church. Damn near stampeded getting into church. That was quite a while ago.'

' 'Bout the time you wrote about thinking of getting married?'

Charles grinned. 'I guess so. I guess there wasn't a young buck in the county didn't get the marrying fever.'

'What happened to her?'

'Well, you know how it is. The women got kind of restless with her here. They got together. First thing you knew they had her out. I heard she wore silk underwear. Too hoity-toity. School board had her out half way through the term. Feet no longer than that. Showed her ankles too, like it was an accident. Always showing her ankles.'

'Did you get to know her?'

'No. I only went to church. Couldn't hardly get in. Girl that pretty's no right in a little town. Just makes people uneasy. Causes trouble.'

Adam said, 'Remember that Samuels girl? She was real pretty. What happened to her?'

'Same thing. Just caused trouble. She went away. I heard she's living in Philadelphia. Does dressmaking. I heard she gets ten dollars just for making one dress.'

'Maybe we ought to get away from here,' Adam said.

Charles said, 'Still thinking of California?'

'I guess so.'

Charles's temper tore in two. 'I want you out of here!' he shouted. 'I want you to get off the place. I'll buy you or sell you or anything. Get out, you son-of-a-bitch —' He stopped. 'I guess I don't mean that last. But goddam it, you make me nervous.'

'I'll go,' said Adam.

In three months Charles got a coloured picture-postcard of the bay at Rio, and Adam had written on the back with a splottery pen, 'It's summer here when it's winter there. Why don't you come down?'

Six months later there was another card, from Buenos Aires. 'Dear Charles – my God this is a big city. They speak French and Spanish both. I'm sending you a book.'

But no book came. Charles looked for it all the following winter and well into the spring. And instead of the book Adam arrived. He was brown and his clothes had a foreign look.

'How are you?' Charles asked.

'Fine. Did you get the book?'

'No.'

'I wonder what happened to it? It had pictures.'

'Going to stay?'

'I guess so. I'll tell you about that country.'

'I don't want to hear about it,' said Charles.

'Christ, you're mean,' said Adam.

'I can just see it all over again. You'll stay around a year or so and then you'll get restless and you'll make me restless. We'll get mad at each other and then we'll get polite to each other – and that's worse. Then we'll blow up and you'll go away again, and then you'll come back and we'll do it all over again.'

Adam asked, 'Don't you want me to stay?'

'Hell, yes,' said Charles. 'I miss you when you're not here. But I can see how it's going to be just the same.'

And it was just that way. For a while they reviewed old times, for a while they recounted the times when they were apart, and finally they lapsed into the long ugly silences, the hours of speechless work, the guarded courtesy, the flashes of anger. There were no boundaries to time, so that it seemed endless passing.

On an evening Adam said, 'You know, I'm going to be thirty-seven. That's half a life.'

'Here it comes,' said Charles. 'Wasting your life. Look, Adam, could we not have a fight this time?'

'How do you mean?'

'Well, if we run true to form we'll fight for three or four weeks, getting you ready to go away. If you're getting restless, couldn't you just go away and save all the trouble?'

Adam laughed and the tension went out of the room. 'I've got a pretty smart brother,' he said. 'Sure, when I get the itch bad enough I'll go without fighting. Yes, I like that. You're getting rich, aren't you, Charles?'

'I'm doing all right. I wouldn't say rich.'

'You wouldn't say you bought four buildings and the inn in the village?'

'No, I wouldn't say it.'

'But you did. Charles, you've made this about the prettiest farm anywhere about. Why don't we build a new house – bath-tub and running water and a water-closet? We're not poor people any more. Why, they say you're nearly the richest man in this section.'

'We don't need a new house,' Charles said gruffly. 'You take your fancy ideas away.'

'It would be nice to go to the toilet without going outside.'

'You take your fancy ideas away.'

Adam was amused. 'Maybe I'll build a pretty little house right over by the wood-lot Say, how would that be? Then we wouldn't get on each other's nerves.'

'I don't want it on the place.'

'The place is half mine.'

'I'll buy you out.'

'But I don't have to sell.'

Charles's eyes blazed. 'I'll burn your goddam house down.'

'I believe you would,' Adam said, suddenly sobered. 'I believe you really would. What are you looking like that for?'

Charles said slowly, 'I've thought about it a lot. And I've wanted for you to bring it up. I guess you aren't ever going to.'

'What do you mean?'

'You remember when you sent me a telegram for a hundred dollars?'

'You bet I do. Saved my life, I guess. Why?'

'You never paid it back.'

'I must have.'

'You didn't.'

Adam looked down at the old table where Cyrus had sat, knocking on his wooden leg with a stick. And the old oil-lamp was hanging over the centre of the table, shedding its unstable yellow light from the round Rochester wick.

Adam said slowly, 'I'll pay you in the morning.'

'I gave you plenty of time to offer.'

'Sure you did, Charles. I should have remembered.' He

paused, considering, and at last he said, 'You don't know why I needed the money.'

'I never asked.'

'And I never told. Maybe I was ashamed. I was a prisoner, Charles. I broke jail – I escaped.'

Charles's mouth was open. 'What are you talking about?'

'I'm going to tell you. I was a tramp and I got taken up for vagrancy and put on a road gang – leg-irons at night. Got out in six months and picked right up again. That's how they get their roads built. I served three days less than the second six months and then I escaped – got over the Georgia line, robbed a store for clothes, and sent you the telegram.'

'I don't believe you,' Charles said. 'Yes, I do. You don't tell lies. Of course I believe you. Why didn't you tell me?'

'Maybe I was ashamed. But I'm more ashamed that I didn't pay you.'

'Oh, forget it,' said Charles. 'I don't know why I mentioned it.'

'Good God, no. I'll pay you in the morning.'

'I'll be damned,' said Charles. 'My brother a jail-bird!'

'You don't have to look so happy.'

'I don't know why,' said Charles, 'but it makes me kind of proud. My brother a jail-bird! Tell me this, Adam – why did you wait till just three days before they let you go to make your break?'

Adam smiled. 'Two or three reasons,' he said. 'I was afraid if I served out my time, why, they'd pick me up again. And I figured if I waited till the end they wouldn't expect me to run away.'

'That makes sense,' said Charles. 'But you said there was one more reason.'

'I guess the other was the most important,' Adam said, 'and it's the hardest to explain. I figured I owed the state six months. That was the sentence. I didn't feel right about cheating. I only cheated three days.'

Charles exploded with laughter. 'You're a crazy son-of-a-bitch,' he said with affection. 'But you say you robbed a store.'

'I sent the money back with ten per cent interest,' Adam said.

Charles leaned forward. 'Tell me about the road gang, Adam.'

'Sure I will, Charles. Sure I will.'

CHAPTER 11

I

CHARLES HAD more respect for Adam after he knew about the prison. He felt the warmth for his brother you can feel only for one who is not perfect and therefore no target for your hatred. Adam took some advantage of it too. He tempted Charles.

'Did you ever think, Charles, that we've got enough money to do anything we want to do?'

'All right, what do we want?'

'We could go to Europe, we could walk around Paris.'

'What's that?'

'What's what?'

'I thought I heard someone on the stoop.'

'Probably a cat.'

'I guess so. Have to kill off some of them pretty soon.'

'Charles, we could go to Egypt and walk around the Sphinx.'

'We could stay right here and make some good use of our money. And we could get to hell out to work and make some use of the day. Those goddam cats!' Charles jumped to the door and yanked it open and said, 'Get!' Then he was silent, and Adam saw him staring at the steps. He moved beside him.

A dirty bundle of rags and mud was trying to worm its way up the steps. One skinny hand clawed slowly at the stairs. The other dragged helplessly. There was a caked face with cracked lips and eyes peering out of swollen, blackened lids. The forehead was laid open, oozing blood back into the matted hair.

Adam went down the stairs and kneeled beside the figure. 'Give me a hand,' he said. 'Come on, let's get her in. Here – look out for that arm. It looks broken.'

She fainted when they carried her in.

'Put her in my bed,' Adam said. 'Now I think you better go for the doctor.'

'Don't you think we better hitch up and take her in?'

'Move her? No. Are you crazy?'

'Maybe not as crazy as you. Think about it a minute.'

'For God's sake, think about what?'

'Two men living alone and they've got this in their house.'

Adam was shocked. 'You don't mean it.'

'I mean it all right. I think we better take her in. It'll be all over the county in two hours. How do you know what she is?

108

How'd she get here? What happened to her? Adam, you're taking an awful chance.'

Adam said coldly, 'If you don't go now, I'll go and leave you here.'

'I think you're making a mistake. I'll go, but I tell you we'll suffer for it.'

'I'll do the suffering,' said Adam. 'You go.'

After Charles left, Adam went to the kitchen and poured hot water from the tea-kettle into a basin. In his bedroom he dampened a handkerchief in the water and loosened the caked blood and dirt on the girl's face. She reeled up to consciousness and her blue eyes glinted at him. His mind went back – it was this room, this bed. His step-mother was standing over him with a damp cloth in her hand, and he could feel the little running pains as the water cut through. And she had said something over and over. He heard it, but he could not remember what it was.

'You'll be all right,' he said to the girl. 'We're getting a doctor. He'll be here right off.'

Her lips moved a little.

'Don't try to talk,' he said. 'Don't try to say anything.' As he worked gently with his cloth a huge warmth crept over him. 'You can stay here,' he said. 'You can stay here as long as you want. I'll take care of you.' He squeezed out the cloth and sponged her matted hair and lifted it out of the gashes in her scalp.

He could hear himself talking as he worked, almost as though he were a stranger listening. 'There, does that hurt? The poor eyes – I'll put some brown paper over your eyes. You'll be all right. That's a bad one on your forehead. I'm afraid you'll have a scar there. Could you tell me your name? No, don't try. There's lots of time. There's lots of time. Do you hear that? That's the doctor's rig. Wasn't that quick?' He moved to the kitchen door. 'In here, Doc. She's in here,' he called.

11

She was very badly hurt. If there had been X-rays in that time the doctor might have found more injuries than he did. As it was he found enough. Her left arm and three ribs were broken and her jaw was cracked. Her skull was cracked too, and the teeth on the left side were missing. Her scalp was ripped and torn and her forehead laid open to the skull. So much the doctor could see and identify. He set her arm, taped her ribs, and sewed up her scalp. With a pipette and an alcohol flame he bent a glass tube to go through the aperture where a tooth was missing so that she could drink and take liquid food without moving her cracked jaw. He gave her a large shot of morphine, left a bottle of opium pills, washed his hands, and put on his coat. His patient was asleep before he left the room.

In the kitchen he sat down at the table and drank the hot coffee Charles put in front of him.

'All right, what happened to her?' he asked.

'How do we know?' Charles said truculently. 'We found her on our porch. If you want to see, go look at the marks on the road where she dragged herself.'

'Know who she is?'

'God, no.'

'You go upstairs at the inn – is she anybody from there?'

'I haven't been there lately. I couldn't recognize her in that condition, anyway.'

The doctor turned his head towards Adam. 'You ever see her before?'

Adam shook his head slowly.

Charles said harshly, 'Say, what you mousing around at?'

'I'll tell you, since you're interested. That girl didn't fall under a harrow even if she looks that way. Somebody did that to her, somebody who didn't like her at all. If you want the truth, somebody tried to kill her.'

'Why don't you ask her?' Charles said.

'She won't be talking for quite a while. Besides, her skull is cracked, and God knows what that will do to her. What I'm getting at is, should I bring the sheriff into it?'

'No!' Adam spoke so explosively that the two looked at him. 'Let her alone. Let her rest.'

'Who's going to take care of her?'

'I am,' said Adam.

'Now, you look here —' Charles began.

'Keep out of it!'

'It's my place as much as yours.'

'Do you want me to go?'

'I didn't mean that.'

'Well, I'll go if she has to go.'

The doctor said, 'Steady down. What makes you so interested?'

'I wouldn't put a hurt dog out.'

'You wouldn't get mad about it either. Are you holding something back? Did you go out last night? Did you do it?'

'He was here all night,' said Charles. 'He snores like a goddam train.'

Adam said, 'Why can't you let her be? Let her get well.'

The doctor stood up and dusted his hands. 'Adam,' he said, 'your father was one of my oldest friends. I know you and your family. You aren't stupid. I don't know why you don't recognize ordinary facts, but you don't seem to. Have to talk to you like a baby. That girl was assaulted. I believe whoever did it tried to kill her. If I don't tell the sheriff about it, I'm breaking the law. I admit I break a few, but not that one.'

'Well, tell him. But don't let him bother her until she's better.'

'It's not my habit to let my patients be bothered,' the doctor said. 'You still want to keep her here?'

'Yes.'

'Your funeral. I'll look in tomorrow. She'll sleep. Give her water and warm soup through the tube if she wants it.' He stalked out.

Charles turned on his brother. 'Adam, for God's sake, what is this?'

'Let me alone.

'What's got into you?'

'Let me alone – you hear? Just let me alone.'

'Christ!' said Charles, and spat on the floor and went restlessly and uneasily to work.

Adam was glad he was gone. He moved about the kitchen, washed the breakfast dishes, and swept the floor. When he had put the kitchen to rights he went in and drew a chair up to the bed. The girl snored thickly through the morphine. The swelling was going down on her face, but the eyes were blackened and swollen. Adam sat very still, looking at her. Her set and splinted arm lay on her stomach, but her right arm lay on top of the coverlet, the fingers curled like a nest. It was a child's hand, almost a baby's hand. Adam touched her wrist with his finger, and her fingers moved a little in reflex. Her wrist was warm. Secretly then, as though he were afraid he might be caught, he straightened her hand and touched the little cushion pads on the fingertips. Her fingers were pink and soft, but the skin on the back of her hand seemed to have an underbloom like a pearl. Adam chuckled with delight. Her breathing stopped and he became electrically alert – then her throat clicked and the rhythmed snoring continued. Gently he worked her hand and arm under the cover before he tiptoed out of the room.

For several days Cathy lay in a cave of shock and opium. Her skin felt like lead, and she moved very little because of the pain. She was aware of movement around her. Gradually her head and her eyes cleared. Two young men were with her, one occasionally and the other a great deal. She knew that another man who came in was the doctor, and there was also a tall lean man, who interested her more than any of the others, and the interest grew out of fear. Perhaps in her drugged sleep she had picked something up and stored it.

Very slowly her mind assembled the last days and rearranged them. She saw the face of Mr Edwards, saw it lose its placid self-sufficiency and dissolve into murder. She had never been so afraid before in her life, but she had learned fear now. And her mind sniffed about like a rat looking for an escape. Mr Edwards knew about the fire. Did anyone else? And how did he know? A blind nauseating terror rose in her when she thought of that.

From things she heard she learned that the tall man was the sheriff and wanted to question her, and that the young man named Adam was protecting her from the questioning. Maybe the sheriff knew about the fire.

Raised voices gave her the cue to her method. The sheriff said, 'She must have a name. Somebody must know her.'

'How could she answer? Her jaw is broken.' Adam's voice.

'If she's right-handed she could spell out the answers. Look here, Adam, if somebody tried to kill her I'd better catch him while I can. Just give me a pencil and let me talk to her.'

Adam said, 'You heard the doctor say her skull was cracked. How do you know she can remember?'

'Well, you give me a paper and pencil and we'll see.'

'I don't want you to bother her.'

'Adam, goddam it, it doesn't matter what you want. I'm telling you I want a paper and pencil.'

Then the other young man's voice. 'What's the matter with you? You make it sound like it was you who did it. Give him a pencil.'

She had her eyes closed when the three men came quietly into her room.

'She's asleep,' Adam whispered.

She opened her eyes and looked at them.

The tall man came to the side of the bed. 'I don't want to

bother you, Miss. I'm the sheriff. I know you can't talk, but will you just write some things on this?'

She tried to nod and winced with pain. She blinked her eyes rapidly to indicate assent.

'That's the girl,' said the sheriff. 'You see? She wants to.' He put the tablet on the bed beside her and moulded her fingers around the pencil. 'There we are. Now. What is your name?'

The three men watched her face. Her mouth grew thin and her eyes squinted. She closed her eyes and the pencil began to move. 'I don't know,' it scrawled in huge letters.

'Here, now there's a fresh sheet. What do you remember?'

'All black. Can't think,' the pencil wrote before it went over the edge of the tablet.

'Don't you remember who you are, where you came from? Think!'

She seemed to go through a great struggle and then her face gave up and became tragic. 'No. Mixed up. Help me.'

'Poor child,' the sheriff said. 'I thank you for trying, anyway. When you get better we'll try again. No, you don't have to write any more.'

The pencil wrote, 'Thank you,' and fell from her fingers.

She had won the sheriff. He ranged himself with Adam. Only Charles was against her. When the brothers were in her room, and it took two of them to help her on the bed-pan without hurting her, she studied Charles's dark sullenness. He had something in his face that she recognized, that made her uneasy. She saw that he touched the scar on his forehead very often, rubbed it, and drew its outline with his fingers. Once he caught her watching. He looked guiltily at his fingers. Charles said brutally, 'Don't you worry. You're going to have one like it, maybe even a better one.'

She smiled at him, and he looked away. When Adam came in with her warm soup Charles said, 'I'm going in town and drink some beer.'

III

Adam couldn't remember ever having been so happy. It didn't bother him that he did not know her name. She had said to call her Cathy, and that was enough for him. He cooked for Cathy, going through recipes used by his mother and his step-mother.

Cathy's vitality was great. She began to recover very quickly. The swelling went out of her cheeks and the prettiness of

113

convalescence came to her face. In a short time she could be helped to a sitting position. She opened and closed her mouth very carefully, and she began to eat soft foods that required little chewing. The bandage was still on her forehead, but the rest of her face was little marked except for the hollow cheek on the side where the teeth were missing.

Cathy was in trouble and her mind ranged for a way out of it. She spoke little, even when it was not so difficult.

One afternoon she heard someone moving around in the kitchen. She called, 'Adam, is it you?'

Charles's voice answered, 'No, it's me.'

'Would you come in here just for a minute, please?'

He stood in the doorway. His eyes were sullen.

'You don't come in much,' she said.

'That's right.'

'You don't like me.'

'I guess that's right too.'

'Will you tell me why?'

He struggled to find an answer. 'I don't trust you.'

'Why not?'

'I don't know. And I don't believe you lost your memory.'

'But why should I lie?'

'I don't know. That's why I don't trust you. There's something – I almost recognize.'

'You never saw me in your life.'

'Maybe not. But there's something that bothers me – that I ought to know. And how do you know I never saw you?'

She was silent, and he moved to leave. 'Don't go,' she said. 'What do you intend to do?'

'About what?'

'About me.'

He regarded her with a new interest. 'You want the truth?'

'Why else should I ask?'

'I don't know, but I'll tell you. I'm going to get you out of here just as soon as I can. My brother's turned fool, but I'll bring him round if I have to lick him.'

'Could you do that? He's a big man.'

'I could do it.'

She regarded him levelly. 'Where is Adam?'

'Gone in town to get some more of your goddam medicine.'

'You're a mean man.'

'You know what I think? I don't think I'm half as mean as you are under that nice skin. I think you're a devil.'

She laughed softly. 'That makes two of us,' she said. 'Charles, how long do I have?'

'For what?'

'How long before you put me out? Tell me truly.'

'All right, I will. About a week or ten days. Soon as you can get around.'

'Suppose I don't go.'

He regarded her craftily, almost with pleasure at the thought of combat. 'All right, I'll tell you. When you had all that dope you talked a lot, like in your sleep.'

'I don't believe that.'

He laughed, for he had seen the quick tightening of her mouth. 'All right, don't. And if you just go about your business as soon as you can, I won't tell. But if you don't, you'll know all right, and so will the sheriff.'

'I don't believe I said anything bad. What could I say?'

'I won't argue with you. And I've got work to do. You asked me and I told you.'

He went outside. Back of the hen-house he leaned over and laughed and slapped his leg. 'I thought she was smarter,' he said to himself. And he felt more easy than he had for days.

IV

Charles had frightened her badly. And if he had recognized her, so had she recognized him. He was the only person she had ever met who played it her way. Cathy followed his thinking, and it did not reassure her. She knew that her tricks would not work with him, and she needed protection and rest. Her money was gone. She had to be sheltered, and would have to be, for a long time. She was tired and sick, but her mind went skipping among possibilities.

Adam came back from town with a bottle of Pain Killer. He poured a tablespoonful. 'This will taste horrible,' he said. 'It's good stuff though.'

She took it without protest, did not even make much of a face about it. 'You're good to me,' she said. 'I wonder why. I've brought you trouble.'

'You have not. You've brightened up the whole house. Never complain or anything, hurt as bad as you are.'

'You're so good, so kind.'

'I want to be.'

'Do you have to go out? Couldn't you stay and talk to me?'

115

'Sure I could. There's nothing so important to do.'

'Draw up a chair, Adam, and sit down.'

When he was seated she stretched her right hand towards him, and he took it in both of his. 'So good and kind,' she repeated. 'Adam, you keep promises, don't you?'

'I try to. What are you thinking about?'

'I'm alone and I'm afraid,' she cried. 'I'm afraid.'

'Can't I help you?'

'I don't think anyone can help me.'

'Tell me and let me try.'

'That's the worst part. I can't even tell you.'

'Why not? If it's a secret I won't tell it.'

'It's not my secret, don't you see?'

'No, I don't.'

Her fingers gripped his hand tightly. 'Adam, I didn't ever lose my memory.'

'Then why did you say —'

'That's what I'm trying to tell you. Did you love your father, Adam?'

'I guess I revered him more than loved him.'

'Well, if someone you revered were in trouble, wouldn't you do anything to save him from destruction?'

'Well, sure. I guess I would.'

'Well, that's how it is with me.'

'But how did you get hurt?'

'That's part of it. That's why I can't tell.'

'Was it your father?'

'Oh, no. But it's all tied up together.'

'You mean, if you tell me who hurt you, then your father will be in trouble?'

She sighed. He would make up the story himself. 'Adam, will you trust me?'

'Of course.'

'It's an awful thing to ask.'

'No, it isn't, not if you're protecting your father.'

'You understand, it's not my secret. If it were I'd tell you in a minute.'

'Of course I understand. I'd do the same thing myself.'

'Oh, you understand so much.' Tears welled up in her eyes. He leaned down towards her, and she kissed him on the cheek.

'Don't you worry,' he said, 'I'll take care of you.'

She lay back against the pillow. 'I don't think you can.'

'What do you mean?'

'Well, your brother doesn't like me. He wants me to get out of here.'

'Did he tell you that?'

'Oh, no. I can just feel it. He hasn't your understanding.'

'He has a good heart.'

'I know that, but he doesn't have your kindness. And when I have to go – the sheriff is going to begin asking questions and I'll be all alone.'

He stared into space. 'My brother can't make you go. I own half of this farm. I have my own money.'

'If he wanted me to go I would have to. I can't spoil your life.'

Adam stood up and strode out of the room. He went to the back door and looked out on the afternoon. Far off in the field his brother was lifting stones from a sled and piling them on the stone wall. Adam looked up at the sky. A blanket of herring clouds was rolling in from the east. He sighed deeply and his breath made a tickling, exciting feeling in his chest. His ears seemed suddenly clear, so that he heard the chickens cackling and the east wind blowing over the ground. He heard horses' hoofs plodding on the road and far-off pounding on wood where a neighbour was shingling a barn. And all these sounds related into a kind of music. His eyes were clear too. Fences and walls and sheds stood staunchly out in the yellow afternoon, and they were related too. There was change in everything. A flight of sparrows dropped into the dust and scrabbled for bits of food and then flew off like a grey scarf twisting in the light. Adam looked back at his brother. He had lost track of time and he did not know how long he had been standing in the doorway.

No time had passed. Charles was still struggling with the same large stone. And Adam had not released the full, held breath he had taken when time stopped.

Suddenly he knew joy and sorrow felted into one fabric. Courage and fear were one thing too. He found that he had started to hum a droning little tune. He turned, walked through the kitchen, and stood in the doorway, looking at Cathy. She smiled weakly at him, and he thought, What a child! What a helpless child! and a surge of love filled him.

'Will you marry me?' he asked.

Her face tightened and her hand closed convulsively.

'You don't have to tell me now,' he said. 'I want you to think about it. But if you would marry me I could protect you. No one could hurt you again.'

Cathy recovered an instant. 'Come here, Adam. There, sit down. Here, give me your hand. That's good, that's right.' She raised his hand and put the back of it against her cheek. 'My dear,' she said brokenly. 'Oh, my dear. Look, Adam, you have trusted me. Now will you promise me something? Will you promise not to tell your brother you have asked me?'

'Ask you to marry me? Why shouldn't I?'

'It's not that. I want this night to think. I'll want maybe more than this night. Could you let me do that?' She raised her hand to her head. 'You know, I'm not sure I can think straight. And I want to.'

'Do you think you might marry me?'

'Please, Adam. Let me alone to think. Please, my dear.'

He smiled and said nervously, 'Don't make it long. I'm kind of like a cat up a tree so far he can't come down.'

'Just let me think. And, Adam – you're a kind man.'

He went outside and walked towards where his brother was loading stones.

When he was gone Cathy got up from her bed and moved unsteadily to the bureau. She leaned forward and looked at her face. The bandage was still on her forehead. She raised the edge of it enough to see the angry red underneath. She had not only made up her mind to marry Adam but she had so decided before he had asked her. She was afraid. She needed protection and money. Adam could give her both. And she could control him – she knew that. She did not want to be married, but for the time being it was a refuge. Only one thing bothered her. Adam had a warmth towards her which she did not understand since she had none towards him, nor had ever experienced it towards anyone. And Mr Edwards had really frightened her. That had been the only time in her life she had lost control of a situation. She determined never to let it happen again. She smiled to herself when she thought what Charles would say. She felt a kinship to Charles. She didn't mind his suspicion of her.

v

Charles straightened up when Adam approached. He put his palms against the small of his back and massaged the tired muscles. 'My God, there's lots of rocks,' he said.

'Fellow in the army told me there's valleys in California – miles and miles – and you can't find a stone, not even a little one.'

'There'll be something else,' said Charles. 'I don't think there's any farm without something wrong with it. Out in the Middle West it's locusts, someplace else it's tornadoes. What's a few stones?'

'I guess you're right. I thought I would give you a hand.'

'That's nice of you. I thought you'd spend the rest of your life holding hands with that in there. How long is she going to stay?'

Adam was on the point of telling him of his proposal, but the tone of Charles's voice made him change his mind.

'Say,' Charles said, 'Alex Platt came by a little while ago. You'd never think what happened to him. He's found a fortune.'

'How do you mean?'

'Well, you know the place on his property where that clump of cedars sticks out – you know, right on the county road?'

'I know. What about it?'

'Alex went in between those trees and his stone wall. He was hunting rabbits. He found a suitcase and a man's clothes all packed nice. Soaked up with rain, though. Looked like it had been there some time. And there was a wooden box with a lock, and when he broke it open there was near four thousand dollars in it. And he found a purse too. There wasn't anything in it.'

'No name or anything?'

'That's the strange part – no name; no name on the clothes, no labels on the suits. It's just like the fellow didn't want to be traced.'

'Is Alex going to keep it?'

'He took it in to the sheriff, and the sheriff is going to advertise it, and if nobody answers, Alex can keep it.'

'Somebody's sure to claim it.'

'I guess so. I didn't tell Alex that. He's feeling so good about it. That's funny about no labels – not cut out, just didn't have any.'

'That's a lot of money,' Adam said. 'Somebody's bound to claim it.'

'Alex hung around for a while. You know, his wife goes around a lot.' Charles was silent. 'Adam,' he said finally, 'we got to have a talk. The whole county's doing plenty of talking.'

'What about? What do you mean?'

'Goddam it, about that – that girl. Two men can't have a girl living with them. Alex says the women are pretty riled up about it. Adam, we can't have it. We live here. We've got a good name.'

'You want me to throw her out before she's well?'

'I want you to get rid of her – get her out. I don't like her.'

'You never have.'

'I know it. I don't trust her. There's something – something – I don't know what it is, but I don't like it. When you going to get her out?'

'Tell you what,' Adam said slowly. 'Give her one more week and then I'll do something about her.'

'You promise?'

'Sure I promise.'

'Well, that's something. I'll get the word to Alex's wife. From there on she'll handle the news. Good Lord, I'll be glad to have the house to ourselves again. I don't suppose her memory's come back?'

'No,' said Adam.

VI

Five days later, when Charles had gone to buy some calf feed, Adam drove the buggy to the kitchen steps. He helped Cathy in, tucked the blanket around her knees, and put another around her shoulders. He drove to the county seat and was married to her by a justice of the peace.

Charles was home when they returned. He looked sourly at them when they came into the kitchen. 'I thought you'd took her in to put her on the train.'

'We got married,' Adam said simply.

Cathy smiled at Charles.

'Why? Why did you do it?'

'Why not? Can't a man get married?'

Cathy went quickly into the bedroom and closed the door.

Charles began to rave. 'She's no damned good, I tell you. She's a whore.'

'Charles!'

'I tell you, she's just a two-bit whore. I wouldn't trust her with a bit piece – why, that bitch, that slut!'

'Charles, stop it! Stop it, I tell you! Keep your filthy mouth shut about my wife!'

'She's no more a wife than an alley cat.'

Adam said slowly, 'I think you're jealous, Charles. I think you wanted to marry her.'

'Why, you goddam fool! Me jealous? I won't live in the same house with her!'

Adam said evenly, 'You won't have to. I'm going away. You can buy me out if you want. You can have the farm. You always wanted it. You can stay here and rot.'

Charles's voice lowered. 'Won't you get rid of her? Please, Adam. Throw her out. She'll tear you to pieces. She'll destroy you, Adam, she'll destroy you!'

'How do you know so much about her?'

Charles's eyes were bleak. 'I don't,' he said, and his mouth snapped shut.

Adam did not even ask Cathy whether she wanted to come out for dinner. He carried two plates into the bedroom and sat beside her.

'We're going to go away,' he said.

'Let me go away. Please, let me. I don't want to make you hate your brother. I wonder why he hates me!'

'I think he's jealous.'

Her eyes narrowed. 'Jealous?'

'That's what it looks like to me. You don't have to worry. We're getting out. We're going to California.'

She said quietly, 'I don't want to go to California.'

'Nonsense. Why, it's nice there, sun all the time and beautiful.'

'I don't want to go to California.'

'You are my wife,' he said softly. 'I want you to go with me.'

She was silent and did not speak of it again.

They heard Charles slam out the door, and Adam said, 'That will be good for him. He'll get a little drunk and he'll feel better.'

Cathy modestly looked at her fingers. 'Adam, I can't be a wife to you until I'm well.'

'I know,' he said. 'I understand. I'll wait.'

'But I want you to stay with me. I'm afraid of Charles. He hates me so.'

'I'll bring my cot in here. Then you can call me if you're frightened. You can reach out and touch me.'

'You're so good,' she said. 'Could we have some tea?'

'Why, sure, I'd like some myself.' He brought the steaming cups and went back for the sugar bowl. He settled himself in a chair near her bed. 'It's pretty strong. Is it too strong for you?'

'I like it strong.'

He finished his cup. 'Does it taste strange to you? It's got a funny taste.'

Her hand flew to her mouth. 'Oh, let me taste it.' She sipped the dregs. 'Adam,' she cried, 'you got the wrong cup – that was mine. It had my medicine in it.'

He licked his lips. 'I guess it can't hurt me.'

'No, it can't.' She laughed softly. 'I hope I don't need to call you in the night.'

'What do you mean?'

'Well, you drank my sleeping medicine. Maybe you wouldn't wake up easily.'

Adam went down into a heavy opium sleep, though he fought to stay awake. 'Did the doctor tell you to take this much?' he asked thickly.

'You're just not used to it,' she said.

Charles came back at eleven o'clock. Cathy heard his tipsy footsteps. He went into his room, flung off his clothes, and got into bed. He grunted and turned, trying to get comfortable, and then he opened his eyes. Cathy was standing by his bed. 'What do you want?'

'What do you think? Move over a little.'

'Where's Adam?'

'He drank my sleeping medicine by mistake. Move over a little.'

He breathed harshly. 'I already been with a whore.'

'You're a pretty strong boy. Move over a little.'

'How about your broken arm?'

'I'll take care of that. It's not your worry.'

Suddenly Charles laughed. 'The poor bastard,' he said, and he threw back the blanket to receive her.

Part Two

CHAPTER 12

YOU CAN see how this book has reached a great boundary that was called 1900. Another hundred years were ground up and churned, and what had happened was all muddied by the way folks wanted it to be – more rich and meaningful the farther back it was. In the books of some memories it was the best time that ever sloshed over the world – the old time, the gay time, sweet and simple, as though time were young and fearless. Old men who didn't know whether they were going to stagger over the boundary of the century looked forward to it with distaste. For the world was changing, and sweetness was gone, and virtue too. Worry had crept on a corroding world, and what was lost – good manners, ease, and beauty? Ladies were not ladies any more, and you couldn't trust a gentleman's word.

There was a time when people kept their fly-buttons fastened. And man's freedom was boiling off. And even childhood was not good any more – not the way it was. No worry then but how to find a good stone, not round exactly but flattened and water-shaped, to use in a sling pouch cut from a discarded shoe. Where did all the good stones go, and all simplicity?

A man's mind vagued up a little, for how can you remember the feeling of pleasure or pain or choking emotion? You can remember only that you had them. An elder man might truly recall through water the delicate doctor-testing of little girls, but such a man forgets, and wants to, the acid emotion eating at the spleen so that a boy had to put his face flat down in the young wild oats and drum his fists against the ground and sob 'Christ! Christ!' Such a man might say, and did, 'What's that damned kid lying out there in the grass for? He'll catch a cold.'

Oh, strawberries don't taste as they used to and the thighs of women have lost their clutch!

And some men eased themselves like setting hens into the nest of death.

History was secreted in the glands of a million historians. We must get out of this banged-up century, some said, out of this cheating, murderous century of riot and secret death, of scrabbling for public lands and damn well getting them by any means at all.

Think back, recall our little nation fringing the oceans, torn with complexities, too big for its britches. Just got going when the British took us on again. We beat them, but it didn't do us much good. What we had was a burned White House and ten thousand widows on the public pension list.

Then the soldiers went to Mexico and it was a kind of painful picnic. Nobody knows why you go to a picnic to be uncomfortable when it is so easy and pleasant to eat at home. The Mexican War did two good things though. We got a lot of western land, damn near doubled our size, and besides that it was a training ground for generals, so that when the sad self-murder settled on us the leaders knew the techniques for making it properly horrible.

And then the arguments:

Can you keep a slave?

Well, if you bought him in good faith, why not?

Next they'll be saying a man can't have a horse. Who is it wants to take my property?

And there we were, like a man scratching at his own face and bleeding into his own beard.

Well, that was over and we got slowly up off the bloody ground and started westward.

There came boom and bust, bankruptcy, depression.

Great public thieves came along and picked the pockets of everyone who had a pocket.

To hell with that rotten century!

Let's get it over and the door closed shut on it! Let's close it like a book and go on reading! New chapter, new life. A man will have clean hands once we get the lid slammed shut on that stinking century. It's a fair thing ahead. There's no rot on this clean new hundred years. It's not stacked, and any bastard who deals seconds from this new deck of years – why, we'll crucify him head-down over a privy.

Oh, but strawberries will never taste so good again and the thighs of women have lost their clutch!

CHAPTER 13

I

SOMETIMES A kind of glory lights up the mind of a man. It happens to nearly everyone. You can feel it growing or preparing like a fuse burning towards dynamite. It is a feeling in the stomach, a delight of the nerves, of the forearms. The skin tastes the air, and every deep-drawn breath is sweet. Its beginning has the pleasure of a great stretching yawn; it flashes in the brain and the whole world glows outside your eyes. A man may have lived all of his life in the grey, and the land and trees of him dark and sombre. The events, even the important ones, may have trooped by, faceless and pale. And then – the glory – so that a cricket song sweetens his ears, the smell of the earth rises chanting to his nose, and dappling light under a tree blesses his eyes. Then a man pours outward, a torrent of him, and yet he is not diminished. And I guess a man's importance in the world can be measured by the quality and number of his glories. It is a lonely thing, but it relates us to the world. It is the mother of all creativeness, and it sets each man separate from all other men.

I don't know how it will be in the years to come. There are monstrous changes taking place in the world, forces shaping a future whose face we do not know. Some of these forces seem evil to us, perhaps not in themselves but because their tendency is to eliminate other things we hold good. It is true that two men can lift a bigger stone than one man. A group can build automobiles quicker and better than one man, and bread from a huge factory is cheaper and more uniform. When our food and clothing and housing are all born in the complication of mass production, mass method is bound to get into our thinking and to eliminate all other thinking. In our time mass or collective production has entered our economics, our politics, and even our religion, so that some nations have substituted the idea collective for the idea God. This in my time is the danger. There is great tension in the world, tension towards a breaking point, and men are unhappy and confused.

At such a time it seems natural and good to me to ask myself these questions. What do I believe in? What must I fight for and what must I fight against?

Our species is the only creative species, and it has only one creative instrument, the individual mind and spirit of a man. Nothing was ever created by two men. There are no good collaborations, whether in music, in art, in poetry, in mathematics, in philosophy. Once the miracle of creation has taken place, the group can build and extend it, but the group never invents anything. The preciousness lies in the lonely mind of a man.

And now the forces marshalled around the concept of the group have declared a war of extermination on that preciousness, the mind of man. By disparagement, by starvation, by repressions, forced direction, and the stunning hammer-blows of conditioning, the free, roving mind is being pursued, roped, blunted, drugged. It is a sad suicidal course our species seems to have taken.

And this I believe: that the free, exploring mind of the individual human is the most valuable thing in the world. And this I would fight for: the freedom of the mind to take any direction it wishes, undirected. And this I must fight against: any idea, religion, or government which limits or destroys the individual. This is what I am and what I am about. I can understand why a system built on a pattern must try to destroy the free mind, for that is one thing which can by inspection destroy such a system. Surely I can understand this, and I hate it and I will fight against it to preserve the one thing that separates us from the uncreative beasts. If the glory can be killed, we are lost.

II

Adam Trask grew up in greyness, and the curtains of his life were like dusty cobwebs, and his days a slow file of half-sorrows and sick dissatisfactions, and then, through Cathy, the glory came to him.

It doesn't matter that Cathy was what I have called a monster. Perhaps we can't understand Cathy, but on the other hand we are capable of many things in all directions, of great virtues and great sins. And who in his mind has not probed the black water?

Maybe we all have in us a secret pond where evil and ugly things germinate and grow strong. But this culture is fenced, and the swimming brood climbs up only to fall back. Might it not be that in the dark pools of some men the evil grows strong enough to wriggle over the fence and swim free? Would not such a man be our monster, and are we not related to him in our hidden water? It would be absurd if we did not understand both angels and devils, since we invented them.

Whatever Cathy may have been, she set off the glory in Adam. His spirit rose flying and released him from fear and bitterness and rancid memories. The glory lights up the world and changes it the way a star-shell changes a battleground. Perhaps Adam did not see Cathy at all, so lighted was she by his eyes. Burned in his mind was an image of beauty and tenderness, a sweet and holy girl, precious beyond thinking, clean and loving, and that image was Cathy to her husband, and nothing Cathy did or said could warp Adam's Cathy.

She said she did not want to go to California and he did not listen, because *his* Cathy took his arm and started first. So bright was his glory that he did not notice the sullen pain in his brother, did not see the glinting in his brother's eyes. He sold his share of the farm to Charles, for less than it was worth, and with that and his half of his father's money he was free and rich.

The brothers were strangers now. They shook hands at the station, and Charles watched the train pull out and rubbed his scar. He went to the inn, drank four quick whiskies, and climbed the stairs to the top floor. He paid the girl and then could not perform. He cried in her arms until she put him out. He raged at his farm, forced it, added to it, drilled and trimmed, and his boundaries extended. He took no rest, no recreation, and he became rich without pleasure and respected without friends.

Adam stopped in New York long enough to buy clothes for himself and Cathy before they climbed on the train which bore them across the continent. How they happened to go to the Salinas Valley is very easy to understand.

In that day the railroads – growing, fighting among themselves, striving to increase and to dominate – used every means to increase their traffic. The companies not only advertised in the newspapers, they issued booklets and broadsides describing and picturing the beauty and richness of the West. No claim was too extravagant – wealth was unlimited. The Southern Pacific Railroad, headed by the wild energy of Leland Stanford, had begun to dominate the Pacific Coast not only in transportation but in politics. Its rails extended down the valleys. New towns sprang up, new sections were opened and populated, for the company had to create customers to get custom.

The long Salinas Valley was part of the exploitation. Adam had seen and studied a fine colour broadside which set forth the valley as that region which heaven unsuccessfully imitated. After reading the literature, anyone who did not want to settle in the Salinas Valley was crazy.

Adam did not rush at his purchase. He bought a rig and drove around, meeting the earlier comers, talking of soil and water, climate and crops, prices and facilities. It was not speculation with Adam. He was here to settle, to found a home, a family, perhaps a dynasty.

Adam drove exuberantly from farm to farm, picked up dirt and crumbled it in his fingers, talked and planned and dreamed. The people of the valley liked him and were glad he had come to live there, for they recognized a man of substance.

He had only one worry, and that was for Cathy. She was not well. She rode around the country with him, but she was listless. One morning she complained of feeling ill and stayed in her room in the King City hotel while Adam drove into the country. He returned at about five in the afternoon to find her nearly dead from loss of blood. Luckily Adam found Dr Tilson at his supper and dragged him from his roast beef. The doctor made a quick examination, inserted a packing, and turned to Adam.

'Why don't you wait downstairs?' he suggested.

'Is she all right?'

'Yes. I'll call you pretty soon.'

Adam patted Cathy's shoulder, and she smiled up at him.

Dr Tilson closed the door behind him and came back to the bed. His face was red with anger. 'Why did you do it?'

Cathy's mouth was a thin tight line.

'Does your husband know you are pregnant?'

Her head moved slowly from side to side.

'What did you do it with?'

She stared up at him.

He looked around the room. He stepped to the bureau and picked up a knitting-needle. He shook it in her face. 'The old offender – the old criminal,' he said. 'You're a fool. You've nearly killed yourself and you haven't lost your baby. I suppose you took things too, poisoned yourself, inserted camphor, kerosene, red pepper. My God! Some of the things you women do!'

Her eyes were as cold as glass.

He pulled a chair up beside her bed. 'Why don't you want to have the baby?' he asked softly. 'You've got a good husband. Don't you love him? Don't you intend to speak to me at all? Tell me, damn it! Don't turn mulish.'

Her lips did not move and her eyes did not flicker.

'My dear,' he said, 'can't you see? You must not destroy life. That's the one thing gets me crazy. God knows I lose patients

128

because I don't know enough. But I try – I always try. And then I see a deliberate killing.' He talked rapidly on. He dreaded the sick silence between his sentences. This woman puzzled him. There was something inhuman about her. 'Have you met Mrs Laurel? She's wasting and crying for a baby. Everything she has or can get she would give to have a baby, and you – you try to stab yours with a knitting-needle. All right,' he cried, 'you won't speak – you don't have to. But I'm going to tell you. The baby's safe. Your aim was bad. And I'm telling you this – you're going to have that baby. Do you know what the law in this state has to say about abortion? You don't have to answer, but you listen to me! If this happens again, if you lose this baby and I have any reason to suspect monkey business, I will charge you, I will testify against you, and I will see you punished. Now I hope you have sense enough to believe me, because I mean it.'

Cathy moistened her lips with a little pointed tongue. The cold went out of her eyes and a weak sadness took its place. 'I'm sorry,' she said. 'I'm sorry. But you don't understand.'

'Then why don't you tell me?' His anger disappeared like mist. 'Tell me, my dear.'

'It's hard to tell. Adam is so good, so strong. I am – well, I'm tainted. Epilepsy.'

'Not you!'

'No, but my grandfather and my father – and my brother.' She covered her eyes with her hands. 'I couldn't bring that to my husband.'

'Poor child,' he said. 'My poor child. You can't be certain. It's more than probable that your baby will be fine and healthy. Will you promise me not to try any more tricks?'

'Yes.'

'All right then. I won't tell your husband what you did. Now lie back and let me see if the bleeding's stopped.

In a few minutes he closed his satchel and put the knitting-needle in his pocket. 'I'll look in tomorrow morning,' he said.

Adam swarmed on him as he came down the narrow stairs into the lobby. Dr Tilson warded off a flurry of 'How is she? Is she all right? What caused it? Can I go up?'

'Whoa, hold up – hold up.' And he used his trick, his standard joke. 'Your wife is sick.'

'Doctor —'

'She has the only good sickness there is —'

'Doctor —'

129

'Your wife is going to have a baby.' He brushed past Adam and left him staring. Three men sitting round the stove grinned at him. One of them observed dryly, 'If it was me now – why, I'd invite a few, maybe three, friends to have a drink.' His hint was wasted. Adam bolted clumsily up the narrow stairs.

Adam's attention narrowed to the Bordoni ranch a few miles south of King City, almost equidistant, in fact, between San Lucas and King City.

The Bordonis had nine hundred acres left of a grant of ten thousand acres which had come to Mrs Bordoni's great-grand-father from the Spanish crown. The Bordonis were Swiss, but Mrs Bordoni was the daughter and heiress of a Spanish family that had settled in the Salinas Valley in very early times. And as happened with most of the old families, the land slipped away. Some was lost in gambling, some chipped off for taxes, and some acres torn off like coupons to buy luxuries – a horse, a diamond, or a pretty woman. The nine hundred remaining acres were the core of the original Sanchez grant, and the best of it too. They straddled the river and tucked into the foothills on both sides, for at this point the valley narrows and then opens out again. The original Sanchez house was still usable. Built of adobe, it stood in a tiny opening in the foothills, a miniature valley fed by a precious ever-running spring of sweet water. That of course was why the first Sanchez had built his seat there. Huge live oaks shaded the valley, and the earth had a richness and a greenness foreign to this part of the country. The walls of the low house were four feet thick, and the round pole rafters were tied on with rawhide ropes which had been put on wet. The hide shrank and pulled joist and rafter tight together, and the leather ropes became hard as iron and nearly imperishable. There is only one drawback to this building method. Rats will gnaw at the hide if they are let.

The old house seemed to have grown out of the earth, and it was lovely. Bordoni used it for a cow barn. He was a Swiss, an immigrant, with his national passion for cleanliness. He distrusted the thick mud walls and built a frame house some distance away, and his cows put their heads out of the deep recessed windows of the old Sanchez house.

The Bordonis were childless, and when the wife died in ripe years a lonely longing for his Alpine past fell on her husband. He wanted to sell the ranch and go home. Adam Trask refused to buy in a hurry, and Bordoni was asking a big price and using the selling method of pretending not to care whether he sold or not. Bordoni knew Adam was going to buy his land long before Adam knew it.

Where Adam settled he intended to stay and to have his unborn children stay. He was afraid he might buy one place and then see another he liked better, and all the time the Sanchez place was drawing him. With the advent of Cathy, his life extended long and pleasantly ahead of him. But he went through all the motions of carefulness. He drove and rode and walked over every foot of the land. He put a post-hole auger down through the subsoil to test and feel and smell the under earth. He inquired about the small wild plants of field and riverside and hill. In damp places he knelt down and examined the game tracks in the mud, mountain lion and deer, coyote and wild cat, skunk and racoon, weasel and rabbit, all overlaid with the pattern of quail tracks. He threaded among willows and sycamores and wild blackberry vines in the river-bed, patted the trunks of live oaks and scrub oak, madrone, laurel, toyon.

Bordoni watched him with squinting eyes and poured tumblers of red wine squeezed from the grapes of his small hillside vineyard. It was Bordoni's pleasure to get a little drunk every afternoon. And Adam, who had never tasted wine, began to like it.

Over and over he asked Cathy's opinion of the place. Did she like it? Would she be happy there? And he didn't listen to her noncommittal answers. He thought that she linked arms with his enthusiasm. In the lobby of the King City hotel he talked to the men who gathered around the stove and read the papers sent down from San Francisco.

'It's water I think about,' he said one evening. 'I wonder how deep you'd have to go to bring in a well.'

A rancher crossed his denim knees. 'You ought to go see Sam Hamilton,' he said. 'He knows more about water than anybody around here. He's a water witch and a well-digger too. He'll tell you. He's put down half the wells in this part of the valley.'

His companion chuckled. 'Sam's got a real legitimate reason to be interested in water. Hasn't got a goddam drop of it on his own place.'

'How do I find him?' Adam asked.

'I'll tell you what. I'm going to have him make some angle-irons. I'll take you with me if you want. You'll like Mr Hamilton. He's a fine man.'

'Kind of comical genius,' his companion said.

They went to the Hamilton ranch in Louis Lippo's buckboard – Louis and Adam Trask. The iron straps rattled around in the box, and a leg of venison, wrapped in wet burlap to keep it cool, jumped around on top of the iron. It was customary in that day to take some substantial lump of food as a present when you went calling on a man, for you had to stay to dinner unless you wished to insult his house. But a few guests could set back the feeding plans for the week if you did not build up what you destroyed. A quarter of pork or a rump of beef would do. Louis had cut down the venison and Adam provided a bottle of whisky.

'Now, I'll have to tell you,' Louis said. 'Mr Hamilton will like that, but Mrs Hamilton has got a skunner on it. If I was you I'd leave it under the seat, and when we drive around to the shop, why, then you can get it out. That's what we always do.'

'Doesn't she let her husband take a drink?'

'No bigger than a bird,' said Louis. 'But she's got brass-bound opinions. Just you leave the bottle under the seat.'

They left the valley road and drove into the worn and rutted hills over a set of wheel tracks gullied by the winter rains. The horses strained into their collars and the buckboard rocked and swayed. The year had not been kind to the hills, and already in June they were dry and the stones showed through the short, burned feed. The wild oats had headed out barely six inches above the ground, as though with knowledge that if they didn't make seed quickly they wouldn't get to seed at all.

'It's not likely-looking country,' Adam said.

'Likely? Why, Mr Trask, it's country that will break a man's heart and eat him up. Likely! Mr Hamilton has a sizeable piece and he'd of starved to death on it with all those children. The ranch don't feed them. He does all kinds of jobs, and his boys are starting to bring in something now. It's a fine family.'

Adam stared at a line of dark mesquite that peeked out of a draw. 'Why in the world would he settle on a place like this?'

Louis Lippo, as does every man, loved to interpret, to a stranger particularly, if no native was present to put up an argument. 'I'll tell you,' he said. 'Take me – my father was Italian. Came here after the trouble but he brought a little money. My place isn't very big but it's nice. By father bought it. He picked it out. And take you – I don't know how you're fixed and wouldn't ask, but they say you're trying to buy the old Sanchez place and

Bordoni never gave anything away. You're pretty well fixed or you wouldn't even ask about it.'

'I'm comfortably off,' said Adam modestly.

'I'm talking the long way round,' said Louis. 'When Mr and Mrs Hamilton came into the valley they didn't have a pot to piss in. They had to take what was left – government land that nobody else wanted. Twenty-five acres of it won't keep a cow alive even in good years, and they say the coyotes move away in bad years. There's people say they don't know how the Hamiltons lived. But of course Mr Hamilton went right to work – that's how they lived. Worked as a hired hand till he got his threshing machine built.'

'Must have made a go of it. I hear of him all over.'

'He made a go of it all right. Raised nine children. I'll bet he hasn't got four bits laid away. How could he?'

One side of the buckboard leaped up, rolled over a big round stone and dropped down again. The horses were dark with sweat and lathered under collar and britching.

'I'll be glad to talk to him,' said Adam.

'Well, sir, he raised one fine crop – he had good children and he raised them fine. All doing well – maybe except Joe. Joe – he's the youngest – they're talking about sending him to college, but all the rest are doing fine. Mr Hamilton can be proud. The house is just on the other side of the next rise. Don't forget and bring out that whisky – she'll freeze you to the ground.'

The dry earth was ticking under the sun and the crickets rasped. 'It's a real god-forsaken country,' said Louis.

'Makes me feel mean,' said Adam.

'How's that?'

'Well, I'm fixed so I don't have to live on a place like this.'

'Me too, and I don't feel mean. I'm just goddam glad.'

When the buckboard topped the rise Adam could look down on the little cluster of buildings which composed the Hamilton seat – a house with many lean-tos, a cow shed, a shop, and a wagon shed. It was a dry and sun-eaten sight – no big trees and a small hand-watered garden.

Louis turned to Adam, and there was just a hint of hostility in his tone. 'I want to put you straight on one or two things, Mr Trask. There's people that when they see Samuel Hamilton the first time might get the idea he's full of bull. He don't talk like other people. He's an Irishman. And he's all full of plans – a hundred plans a day. And he's all full of hope. My Christ, he'd have to be to live on this land! But you remember this – he's a fine worker, a good blacksmith, and some of his plans work out. And I've heard him talk about things that were going to happen, and they did.'

Adam was alarmed at the hint of threat. 'I'm not a man to run another man down,' he said, and he felt that suddenly Louis thought of him as a stranger and an enemy.

'I just wanted you to get it straight. There's some people come in from the East and they think if a man hasn't got a lot of money he's no good.'

'I wouldn't think of —'

'Mr Hamilton maybe hasn't got four bits put away, but he's our people and he's as good as we got. And he's raised the nicest family you're likely to see. I just want you to remember that.'

Adam was on the point of defending himself, and then he said, 'I'll remember. Thanks for telling me.'

Louis faced round front again. 'There he is – see, out by the shop? He must of heard us.'

'Has he got a beard?' Adam asked, peering.

'Yes, got a nice beard. It's turning white fast, beginning to grizzle up.'

They drove past the frame house and saw Mrs Hamilton looking out of the window at them, and they drew up in front of the shop where Samuel stood waiting for them.

Adam saw a big man, bearded like a patriarch, his greying hair stirring in the air like thistledown. His cheeks above his beard were pink where the sun had burned his Irish skin. He wore a clean blue shirt, overalls, and a leather apron. His sleeves were rolled up, and his muscular arms were clean too. Only his hands were blackened from the forge. After a quick glance Adam came back to the eyes, light blue and filled with a young delight. The wrinkles around them were drawn in radial lines inwards by laughter.

'Louis,' he said, 'I'm glad to see you. Even in the sweetness of our little heaven here, we like to see our friends.' He smiled at Adam, and Louis said, 'I brought Mr Adam Trask to see you. He's a stranger from down east, come to settle.'

'I'm glad,' said Samuel. 'We'll shake another time. I wouldn't soil your hand with these forge hooks.'

'I brought some strap iron, Mr Hamilton. Would you make some angles for me? The whole frame of my header bed is fallen to hell.'

'Sure I will, Louis. Get down, get down. We'll put the horses to the shade.'

'There's a piece of venison behind, and Mr Trask brought a little something.'

Samuel glanced towards the house. 'Maybe we'll get out the "little something" when we've got the rig behind the shed.'

Adam could hear the singing lilt of his speech and yet could detect no word pronounced in a strange manner except perhaps in sharpened *t*'s and *l*'s held high on the tongue.

'Louis, will you out-span your team? I'll take the venison in. Liza will be glad. She likes a venison stew.'

'Any of the young ones home?'

'Well, no, they aren't. George and Will came home for the week-end, and they all went last night to a dance up Wild Horse Canyon at the Peach Tree school-house. They'll come trooping back by dusk. We lack a sofa because of that. I'll tell you later – Liza will have a vengeance on them – it was Tom did it. I'll tell you later.' He laughed and started towards the house, carrying the wrapped deer's haunch. 'If you want you can bring the "little something" into the shop, so you don't let the sun glint on it.'

They heard him calling as he came near the house. 'Liza, you'll never guess. Louis Lippo has brought a piece of venison bigger than you.'

Louis drove in behind the shed, and Adam helped him take the horses out, tie up the tugs, and halter them in the shade. 'He meant that about the sun shining on the bottle,' said Louis.

'She must be a holy terror.'

'No bigger than a bird, but she's brass-bound.'

' "Out-span," ' Adam said, 'I think I've heard it said that way, or read it.'

Samuel rejoined them in the shop. 'Liza will be happy if you will stay to dinner,' he said.

'She didn't expect us,' Adam protested.

'Hush, man. She'll make some extra dumplings for the stew. It's a pleasure to have you here. Give me your straps, Louis, and let's see how you want them.'

He built a chip fire in the black square of the forge and pulled a bellows breeze on it and then fed wet coke over with his fingers until it glowed. 'Here, Louis,' he said, 'wave your wing on my fire. Slow, man, slow and even.' He laid the strips of iron on the glowing coke. 'No, sir, Mr Trask, Liza's used to cooking for nine starving children. Nothing can startle her.' He tonged the iron to more advantageous heat, and he laughed. 'I'll take that last back as a holy lie,' he said. 'My wife is rumbling like round

135

stones in the surf. And I'll caution the both of you not to mention the word "sofa". It's a word of anger and sorrow to Liza.'

'You said something about it,' Adam said.

'If you knew my boy Tom, you'd understand it better, Mr Trask. Louis knows him.'

'Sure I know him,' Louis said.

Samuel went on, 'My Tom is a hell-bent boy. Always takes more on his plate than he can eat. Always plants more than he can harvest. Pleasures too much, sorrows too much. Some people are like that. Liza thinks I'm like that. I don't know what will come of Tom. Maybe greatness, maybe the noose – well, Hamiltons have been hanged before. And I'll tell you about that some time.'

'The sofa,' Adam suggested politely.

'You're right. I do, and Liza says I do, shepherd my words like rebellious sheep. Well, came the dance at the Peach Tree school and the boys, George, Tom, Will, and Joe, all decided to go. And of course the girls were asked. George and Will and Joe, poor simple boys, each asked one lady friend, but Tom – he took too big a helping as usual. He asked two Williams sisters, Jennie and Belle. How many screw-holes do you want, Louis?'

'Five,' said Louis.

'All right. Now I must tell you, Mr Trask, that my Tom has all the egotism and self-love of a boy who thinks he's ugly. Mostly lets himself go fallow, but comes a celebration and he garlands himself like a maypole, and he glories like spring flowers. This takes him quite a piece of time. You notice the wagon house was empty? George and Will and Joe started early and not so beautiful as Tom. George took the rig, Will had the buggy, and Joe got the little two-wheeled cart.' Samuel's eyes shone with pleasure. 'Well then, Tom came out as shy and shining as a Roman emperor and the only thing left with wheels was a hay-rake, and you can't take even one Williams sister on that. For good or bad, Liza was taking her nap. Tom sat on the steps and thought it out. Then I saw him go to the shed and hitch up two horses and take the double-tree off the hay-rake. He wrestled the sofa out of the house and ran a fifth-chain under the legs – the fine goose-neck horsehair sofa that Liza loves better than anything. I gave it to her to rest on before George was born. The last I saw, Tom went dragging up the hill, reclining at his ease on the sofa to get the Williams girls. And, oh, Lord, it'll be worn thin as a wafer from scraping by the time he gets it back.' Samuel put down his tongs and placed his hands on his hips the better to laugh. 'And Liza has the smoke of brimstone coming out her nostrils. Poor Tom.'

Adam said, smiling, 'Would you like to take a little something?'

'That I would,' said Samuel. He accepted the bottle and took a quick swallow of whisky and passed it back.

'*Uisquebaugh* – it's an Irish word – whisky, water of life – and so it is.'

He took the red straps to his anvil and punched screw-holes in them and bent the angles with his hammer and the forked sparks leaped out. Then he dipped the iron hissing into his half-barrel of black water. 'There you are,' he said, and threw them on the ground.

'I thank you,' said Louis. 'How much will that be?'

'The pleasure of your company.'

'It's always like that,' Louis said helplessly.

'No, when I put your new well down you paid my price.'

'That reminds me – Mr Trask here is thinking of buying the Bordoni place – the old Sanchez grant – you remember?'

'I know it well,' said Samuel. 'It's a fine piece.'

'He was asking about water, and I told him you knew more about that than anybody around here.'

Adam passed the bottle, and Samuel took a delicate sip and wiped his mouth on his forearm above the soot.

'I haven't made up my mind,' said Adam. 'I'm just asking some questions.'

'Oh, Lord, man, now you've put your foot in it. They say it's a dangerous thing to question an Irishman because he'll tell you. I hope you know what you're doing when you issue me a licence to talk. I've heard two ways of looking at it. One says the silent man is the wise man and the other that a man without words is a man without thought. Naturally I favour the second – Liza says to a fault. What do you want to know?'

'Well, take the Bordoni place. How deep would you have to go to get water?'

'I'd have to see the spot – some places thirty feet, some places a hundred and fifty, and in some places clear to the centre of the world.'

'But you could develop water?'

'Nearly every place except my own.'

'I've heard you have a lack here.'

'Heard? Why, God in heaven must have heard! I've screamed it loud enough.'

'There's a four-hundred-acre piece beside the river. Would there be water under it?'

'I'd have to look. It seems to me it's an odd valley. If you'll hold your patience close, maybe I can tell you a little bit about it, for I've looked at it and poked my stinger down into it. A hungry man gorges with his mind – he does indeed.'

Louis Lippo said, 'Mr Trask is from New England. He plans to settle here. He's been west before, though – in the army, fighting Indians.'

'Were you now? Then it's you should talk and let me learn.'

'I don't want to talk about it.'

'Why not? God help my family and my neighbours if I had fought the Indians!'

'I didn't want to fight them, sir.' The 'sir' crept in without his knowing it.

'Yes, I can understand that. It must be a hard thing to kill a man you don't know and don't hate.'

'Maybe that makes it easier,' said Louis.

'You have a point, Louis. But some men are friends with the whole world in their hearts, and there are others that hate themselves and spread their hatred around like butter on hot bread.'

'I'd rather you told me about this land,' Adam said uneasily, for a sick picture of piled-up bodies came into his mind.

'What time is it?'

Louis stepped out and looked at the sun. 'Not past ten o'clock.'

'If I get started I have no self-control. My son Will says I talk to trees when I can't find a human vegetable.' He sighed and sat down on a nail-keg. 'I said it was a strange valley, but maybe that's because I was born in a green place. Do you find it strange, Louis?'

'No, I never been out of it.'

'I've dug in it plenty,' Samuel said. 'Something went on under it – maybe still going on. There's an ocean bed underneath, and below that another world. But that needn't bother a farming man. Now, on top is good soil, particularly on the flats. In the upper valley it is light and sandy, but mixed in with that, the top sweetness of the hills that washed down on it in the winters. As you go north the valley widens out, and the soil gets blacker and heavier and perhaps richer. It's my belief that marshes were there once, and the roots of centuries rotted into the soil and made it black and fertilized it. And when you turn it up, a little greasy clay mixes and holds it together. That's from about Gonzales north to the river mouth. Off the sides, around Salinas and Blanco and Castroville and Moss Landing, the marshes are still there. And when one day those marshes are drained off, that will be the richest of all land in this red world.'

'He always tells what it will be like some day,' Louis threw in.

'Well, a man's mind can't stay in time the way his body does.'

'If I'm going to settle here I need to know about how and what will be,' said Adam. 'My children, when I have them, will be on it.'

Samuel's eyes looked over the heads of his friends, out of the dark forge to the yellow sunlight. 'You'll have to know that under a good part of the valley, some places deep, and others pretty near the surface, there's a layer called hard-pan. It's a clay, hard-packed, and it feels greasy too. Some places it is only a foot thick, and more in others. And this hard-pan resists water. If it were not there the winter rains would go soaking down and dampen the earth, and in the summer it would rise up to the roots again. But when the earth above the hard-pan is soaked full, the rest runs fresheting off or stands rotting on top. And that's one of the main curses of our valley.'

'Well, it's a pretty good place to live in, isn't it?'

'Yes, it is, but a man can't entirely rest when he knows it could be richer. I've thought that if you could drive thousands of holes through it to let the water in, it might solve it. And then I tried something with a few sticks of dynamite. I punched a hole through the hard-pan and blasted. That broke it up and the water could get down. But, God in heaven, think of the amount of dynamite! I've read that a Swede – the same man who invented dynamite – has got a new explosive stronger and safer. Maybe that might be the answer.'

Louis said half derisively and half with admiration, 'He's always thinking about how to change things. He's never satisfied with the way they are.'

Samuel smiled at him. 'They say man lived in trees one time. Somebody had to get dissatisfied with a high climb or your feet would not be touching flat ground now.' And then he laughed again. 'I can see myself sitting on my dust heap making a world in my mind as surely as God created this one. But God saw his world. I'll never see mine except – this way. This will be a valley of great richness one day. It could feed the world, and maybe it will. And happy people will live here, thousands and thousands — ' A cloud seemed to come over his eyes and his face set in sadness and he was silent.

'You make it sound like a good place to settle,' Adam said. 'Where else could I raise my children with that coming?'

Samuel went on, 'There's a thing I don't understand. There's a blackness on this valley. I don't know what it is, but I can feel it. Sometimes on a white blinding day I can feel it cutting off the sun and squeezing the light out of it like a sponge.' His voice rose. 'There's a black violence on this valley. I don't know – I don't know. It's as though some old ghost haunted it out of the dead ocean below and troubled the air with unhappiness. It's as secret as hidden sorrow. I don't know what it is, but I see it and feel it in the people here.'

Adam shivered. 'I just remembered I promised to get back early. Cathy, my wife, is going to have a baby.'

'But Liza's getting ready.'

'She'll understand when you tell her about the baby. My wife is feeling poorly. And I thank you for telling me about the water.'

'Have I depressed you with my rambling?'

'No, not at all – not at all. It's Cathy's first baby and she's miserable.'

Adam struggled all night with his thoughts, and the next day he drove out and shook hands with Bordoni and the Sanchez place was his.

CHAPTER 14

I

THERE IS so much to tell about the Western country in that day that it is hard to know where to start. One thing sets off a hundred others. The problem is to decide which one to tell first.

You remember that Samuel Hamilton said his children had gone to a dance at the Peach Tree school. The country schools were the centres of culture then. The Protestant churches in the towns were fighting for their existence in a country where they were newcomers. The Catholic church, first on the scene and deeply dug in, sat in comfortable tradition while the missions were gradually abandoned and their roofs fell in and pigeons roosted on the stripped altars. The library (in Latin and Spanish) of the San Antonio Mission was thrown into a granary, where the rats ate off the sheepskin bindings. In the country the repository of art and science was the school, and the schoolteacher shielded and carried the torch of learning and of beauty. The school-house was the meeting place for music, for debate. The polls were set in the school-house for elections. Social life, whether it was the crowning of a May queen, the eulogy to a dead president, or an all-night dance, could be held nowhere else. And the teacher was not only an intellectual paragon and a social leader, but also the matrimonial catch of the countryside. A family could indeed walk proudly if a son married the schoolteacher. Her children were presumed to have intellectual advantages both inherited and conditioned.

The daughters of Samuel Hamilton were not destined to become work-destroyed farm wives. They were handsome girls and they carried with them the glow of their descent from the kings of Ireland. They had a pride that transcended their poverty. No one ever thought of them as deserving pity. Samuel raised a distinctly superior breed. They were better read and better bred than most of their contemporaries. To all of them Samuel communicated his love of learning, and he set them apart from the prideful ignorance of their time. Olive Hamilton became a teacher. That meant she left home at fifteen and went to live in Salinas, where she could go to secondary school. At seventeen she took county board examinations, which covered all the arts and sciences, and at eighteen she was teaching school at Peach Tree.

In her school there were pupils older and bigger than she was. It required great tact to be a school-teacher. To keep order among the big undisciplined boys without pistol and bull whip was a difficult and dangerous business. In one school in the mountains a teacher was raped by her pupils.

Olive Hamilton had not only to teach everything, but to all ages. Very few youths went past the eighth grade in those days, and what with farm duties some of them took fourteen or fifteen years to do it. Olive had also to practise a rudimentary medicine, for there were constant accidents. She sewed up knife cuts after a fight in the school-yard. When a small barefooted boy was bitten by a rattlesnake, it was her duty to suck his toe to draw the poison out.

She taught reading to the first grade and algebra to the eighth. She led the singing, acted as a critic of literature, wrote the social notes that went weekly to the *Salinas Journal*. In addition, the whole social life of the area was in her hands, not only graduation exercises, but dances, meetings, debates, chorals, Christmas and May Day festivals, patriotic exudations on Decoration Day and the Fourth of July. She was on the election board and headed and held together all charities. It was far from an easy job, and it had duties and obligations beyond belief. The teacher had no private life. She was watched jealously for any weakness of character. She could not board with one family for more than one term, for that would cause jealousy – a family gained social ascendancy by boarding the teacher. If a marriageable son belonged to the family where she boarded a proposal was automatic; if there was more than one claimant, vicious fights occurred over her hand. The Aguita boys, three of them, nearly clawed each other to death over Olive Hamilton. Teachers rarely lasted very long in the country schools. The work was so hard and the proposals so constant that they married within a very short time.

This was a course Olive Hamilton determined she would not take. She did not share the intellectual enthusiasms of her father, but the time she had spent in Salinas determined her not to be a ranch wife. She wanted to live in a town, perhaps not so big as Salinas, but at least not a cross-roads. In Salinas, Olive had experienced niceties of living, the choir and vestments, Altar Guild, and bean suppers of the Episcopal church. She had partaken of the arts – road companies of plays and even operas, with their magic and promise of an aromatic world outside. She had gone to parties, played charades, competed in poetry readings, joined a chorus and orchestra. Salinas had tempted her. There she could go to a party dressed for the party, and come home in the same dress, instead of rolling her clothes in a saddlebag and riding ten miles, then unrolling and pressing them.

Busy though she was with her teaching, Olive longed for the metropolitan life, and when the young man who had built the flour mill in King City sued properly for her hand, she accepted him subject to a long and secret engagement. The secrecy was required because if it were known there would be trouble among the young men in the neighbourhood.

Olive had not her father's brilliance, but she did have a sense of fun, together with her mother's strong and undeviating will. What light and beauty could be forced down the throats of her reluctant pupils, she forced.

There was a wall against learning. A man wanted his children to read, to figure, and that was enough. More might make them

142

dissatisfied and flighty. And there were plenty of examples to prove that learning made a boy leave the farm to live in the city – to consider himself better than his father. Enough arithmetic to measure land and lumber and to keep accounts, enough writing to order goods and write to relatives, enough reading for newspapers, almanacs and farm journals, enough music for religious and patriotic display – that was enough to help a boy and not to lead him astray. Learning was for doctors, lawyers, and teachers, a class set off and not considered related to other people. There were some sports, of course, like Samuel Hamilton, and he was tolerated and liked, but if he had not been able to dig a well, shoe a horse, or run a threshing machine, God knows what would have been thought of the family.

Olive did marry her young man and did move, first to Paso Robles, then to King City, and finally to Salinas. She was as intuitive as a cat. Her acts were based on feelings rather than thoughts. She had her mother's firm chin and button nose and her father's fine eyes. She was the most definite of any of the Hamiltons except her mother. Her theology was a curious mixture of Irish fairies and an Old Testament Jehovah whom in her later life she confused with her father. Heaven was to her a nice home ranch inhabited by her dead relatives. External realities of a frustrating nature she obliterated by refusing to believe in them, and when one resisted her disbelief she raged at it. It was told of her that she cried bitterly because she could not go to two dances on one Saturday night. One was in Greenfield and the other in San Lucas – twenty miles apart. To have gone to both and then home would have entailed a sixty-mile horseback ride. This was a fact she could not blast with her disbelief, and so she cried with vexation and went to neither dance.

As she grew older she developed a scattergun method for dealing with unpleasant facts. When I, her only son, was sixteen I contracted pleural pneumonia, in that day a killing disease. I went down and down, until the wing-tips of the angels brushed my eyes. Olive used her scattergun method of treating pleural pneumonia, and it worked. The Episcopalian minister prayed with and for me, the Mother Superior and nuns of the convent next to our house held me up to Heaven for relief twice a day, a distant relative who was a Christian Science reader held the thought for me. Every incantation, magic, and herbal formula known was brought out, and she got two good nurses and the town's best doctors. Her method was practical. I got well. She was loving and firm with her family, three girls and me, trained us to housework, dish-washing, clothes-washing, and manners. When angered she had a terrible eye which could blanch the skin off a bad child as easily as if he were a boiled almond.

When I recovered from my pneumonia it came time for me to learn to walk again. I had been nine weeks in bed, and the muscles had gone lax and the laziness of recovery had set in. When I was helped up, every nerve cried, and the wound in my side, which had been opened to drain the pus from the pleural cavity, pained horribly. I fell back in bed, crying, 'I can't do it! I can't get up!'

Olive fixed me with her terrible eye. 'Get up!' she said. 'Your father has worked all day and sat up all night. He has gone into debt for you. Now get up!'

And I got up.

Debt was an ugly word and an ugly concept to Olive. A bill unpaid past the fifteenth of the month was a debt. The word had connotations of dirt and slovenliness and dishonour. Olive, who truly believed that her family was the best in the world, quite snobbishly would not permit it to be touched by debt. She planted that terror of debt so deeply in her children that even now, in a changed economic pattern where indebtedness is a part of living, I become restless when a bill is two days overdue. Olive never accepted the instalment plan when it became popular. A thing bought by instalments was a thing you did not own and for which you were in debt. She saved for things she wanted, and this meant that the neighbours had new gadgets as much as two years before we did.

II

Olive had great courage. Perhaps it takes courage to raise children. And I must tell you what she did about the First World War. Her thinking was not international. Her first boundary was the geography of her family, second her town, Salinas, and finally there was a dotted line, not clearly defined, which was the county line. Thus she did not quite believe in the war, not even when Troop C, our militia cavalry, was called out, loaded its horses on a train, and set out for the open world.

Martin Hopps lived round the corner from us. He was wide, short, red-haired. His mouth was wide, and he had red eyes. He was almost the shyest boy in Salinas. To say good morning to him was to make him itch with self-consciousness. He belonged to Troop C because the armoury had a basket-ball court.

If the Germans had known Olive and had been sensible they would have gone out of their way not to anger her. But they didn't know or they were stupid. When they killed Martin Hopps they lost the war, because that made my mother mad and she took out after them. She had liked Martin Hopps. He had never hurt anyone. When they killed him Olive declared war on the German Empire.

She cast about for a weapon. Knitting helmets and socks was not deadly enough for her. For a time she put on a Red Cross uniform and met other ladies similarly dressed in the armoury, where bandages were rolled and reputations unrolled. This was all right, but it was not driving at the heart of the Kaiser. Olive wanted blood for the life of Martin Hopps. She found her weapon in Liberty bonds. She had never sold anything in her life beyond an occasional angel cake for the Altar Guild in the basement of the Episcopal church, but she began to sell bonds by the bale. She brought ferocity to her work. I think she made people afraid not to buy them. And when they did buy from Olive she gave them a sense of actual combat, of putting a bayonet in the stomach of Germany.

As her sales sky-rocketed and stayed up, the Treasury Department began to notice this new Amazon. First there came mimeographed letters of commendation, then real letters signed by the Secretary of the Treasury, and not with a rubber stamp either. We were proud, but not so proud as when prizes began to arrive, a German helmet (too small for any of us to wear), a bayonet, a jagged piece of shrapnel set on an ebony base. Since we were not eligible for armed conflict beyond marching with wooden guns, our mother's war seemed to justify us. And then she outdid herself, and outdid everyone in our part of the country. She quadrupled her already fabulous record and she was awarded the fairest prize of all – a ride in an army aeroplane.

Oh, we were proud kids! Even vicariously this was an eminence we could hardly stand. But my poor mother – I must tell you that there are certain things in the existence of which my mother did not believe, against any possible evidence to the contrary. One was a bad Hamilton and another was the aeroplane. The fact that she had seen them didn't make her believe in them one bit more.

In the light of what she did I have tried to imagine how she felt. Her soul must have crawled with horror, for how can you fly in something that does not exist? As a punishment the ride would have been cruel and unusual, but it was a prize, a gift, an honour, and an eminence. She must have looked into our eyes and seen the shining idolatry there and understood that she was trapped. Not to have gone would have let her family down. She was surrounded, and there was no honourable way out save death. Once she had decided to go up in the non-existent thing she seemed to have had no idea whatever that she would survive it.

Olive made her will – took lots of time with it and had it checked to be sure it was legal. Then she opened her rosewood box wherein were the letters her husband had written to her in courtship and since. We had not known he wrote poetry to her, but he had. She built a fire in the grate and burned every letter. They were hers, and she wanted no other human to see them. She bought all new underwear. She had a horror of being found dead with mended or, worse, unmended underclothes. I think perhaps she saw the wide twisted mouth and embarrassed eyes of Martin Hopps on her and felt that in some way she was re-imbursing him for his stolen life. She was very gentle with us and did not notice a badly washed dinner-plate that left a greasy stain on the dish-towel.

This glory was scheduled to take place at the Salinas Race Track and Rodeo Grounds. We were driven to the track in an army automobile, feeling more solemn and golden than at a good funeral. Our father was working at the Spreckles Sugar Factory, five miles from town, and could not get off, or perhaps didn't want to, for fear he could not stand the strain. But Olive had made arrangements, on pain of not going up, for the plane to try to fly as far as the sugar factory before it crashed.

I realize now that the several hundred people who had gathered simply came to see the aeroplane, but at that time we thought they were there to do my mother honour. Olive was not a tall woman and at that age she had begun to put on weight. We had to help her out of the car. She was probably stiff with fright, but her little chin was set.

The plane stood in the field around which the race track was laid out. It was appallingly little and flimsy – an open-cockpit biplane with wooden struts, tied with piano wire. The wings were covered with canvas. Olive was stunned. She went to the side as an ox to the knife. Over the clothes she was convinced were her burial clothes two sergeants slipped on a coat, a padded coat, and a flight coat, and she grew rounder and rounder with each layer. Then a leather helmet and goggles, and with her little button of a nose and her pink cheeks you really had something.

She looked like a goggled ball. The two sergeants hoisted her bodily into the cockpit and wedged her in. She filled the opening completely. As they strapped her in she suddenly came to life and began waving frantically for attention. One of the soldiers climbed up, listened to her, came over to my sister Mary, and led her to the side of the plane. Olive was tugging at the thick padded flight glove on her left hand. She got her hands free, took off her engagement ring with its tiny diamond, and handed it down to Mary. She set her gold wedding ring firmly, pulled the gloves back on, and faced the front. The pilot climbed into the front cockpit, and one of the sergeants threw his weight on the wooden propeller. The little ship taxied away and turned, and down the field it roared and staggered into the air, and Olive was looking straight ahead and probably her eyes were closed.

We followed it with our eyes as it swept up and away, leaving a lonesome silence behind it. The bond committee, the friends and relatives, the simple unhonoured spectators didn't think of leaving the field. The plane became a speck in the sky towards Spreckles and disappeared. It was fifteen minutes before we saw it again flying serenely and very high. Then to our horror it seemed to stagger and fall. It fell endlessly, caught itself, climbed, and made a loop. One of the sergeants laughed. For a moment the plane steadied and then it seemed to go crazy. It barrel-rolled, made Immelmann turns, inside and outside loops, and turned over and flew over the field upside down. We could see the black bullet which was our mother's helmet. One of the soldiers said quietly, 'I think he's gone nuts. She's not a young woman.'

The aeroplane landed steadily enough and ran up to the group. The motor died. The pilot climbed out, shaking his head in perplexity. 'Goddamdest woman I ever saw,' he said. He reached up and shook Olive's nerveless hand and walked hurriedly away.

It took four men and quite a long time to get Olive out of the cockpit. She was so rigid they could not bend her. We took her home and put her to bed, and she didn't get up for two days.

What had happened came out slowly. The pilot talked some and Olive talked some, and both stories had to be put together before they made sense. They had flown out and circled the Spreckles Sugar Factory as ordered – circled it three times so that our father would be sure to see, and then the pilot thought of a joke. He meant no harm. He shouted something, and his

147

face looked contorted. Olive could not hear over the noise of the engine. The pilot throttled down and shouted, 'Stunt?' It was a kind of joke. Olive saw his goggled face and the slip-stream caught his word and distorted it. What Olive heard was the word 'stuck'.

Well, she thought, here it is, just as I knew it would be. Here was her death. Her mind flashed to see if she had forgotten anything – will made, letters burned, new underwear, plenty of food in the house for dinner. She wondered whether she had turned out the light in the back room. It was all in a second. Then she thought there might be an outside chance of survival. The young soldier was obviously frightened and fear might be the worst thing that could happen to him in handling the situation. If she gave way to the panic that lay on her heart it might frighten him more. She decided to encourage him. She smiled brightly and nodded to give him courage, and then the bottom fell out of the world. When he levelled out of his loop the pilot looked back again and shouted, 'More?'

Olive was way beyond hearing anything, but her chin was set and she was determined to help the pilot so that he would not be too afraid before they hit the earth. She smiled and nodded again. At the end of each stunt he looked back, and each time she encouraged him. Afterwards he said over and over, 'She's the goddamdest woman I ever saw. I tore up the rule book and she wanted more. Good Christ, what a pilot she would have made!'

CHAPTER 15

I

ADAM SAT like a contented cat on his land. From the entrance to the little draw under a giant oak, which dipped its roots into underground water, he could look out over the acres lying away to the river and across to an alluvial flat and then up the rounded foothills on the western side. It was a fair place even in the summer when the sun laced into it. A line of river willows and sycamores banded it in the middle, and the western hills were yellow-brown with feed. For some reason the mountains to the west of the Salinas Valley have a thicker skin of earth on them than have the eastern foothills, so that the grass is richer there. Perhaps the peaks store rain and distribute it more evenly, and perhaps, being more wooded, they draw more rainfall.

Very little of the Sanchez, now Trask, place was under cultivation, but Adam in his mind could see the wheat growing tall and squares of green alfalfa near the river. Behind him he could hear the rackety hammering of the carpenters, brought all the way from Salinas to rebuild the old Sanchez house. Adam had decided to live in the old house. Here was a place in which to plant his dynasty. The manure was scraped out, the old floors torn up, neck-rubbed window casings ripped away. New sweet wood was going in, pine sharp with resin and velvety redwood and a new roof of long split shakes. The old thick walls sucked in coat after coat of whitewash made with lime in salt water, which, as it dried, seemed to have a luminosity of its own.

He planned a permanent seat. A gardener had trimmed the ancient roses, planted geraniums, laid out the vegetable flat, and brought the living spring in little channels to wander back and forth through the garden. Adam foretasted comfort for himself and his descendants. In a shed, covered with tarpaulins, lay the crated heavy furniture sent from San Francisco and carted out from King City.

He would have good living too. Lee, his pigtailed Chinese cook, had made a special trip to Pajaro to buy the pots and kettles and pans, kegs, jars, copper, and glass for his kitchen. A new pigsty was building far from the house and down-wind, with chicken and duck runs near and a kennel for the dogs to keep the coyotes away. It was no quick thing Adam contemplated, to be finished and ready in a hurry. His men worked deliberately and slowly. It was a long job. Adam wanted it well done. He inspected every wooden joint, stood off to study paint samples on a shingle. In the corner of his room catalogues piled up – catalogues for machinery, furnishings, seeds, fruit trees. He was glad now that his father had left him a rich man. In his mind a darkness was settling over his memory of Connecticut. Perhaps the hard flat light of the West was blotting out his birthplace. When he thought back to his father's house, to the farm, the town, to his brother's face, there was a blackness over all of it. And he shook off the memories.

Temporarily he had moved Cathy into the white-painted, clean spare house of Bordoni, there to await the home and the child. There was no doubt whatever that the child would be finished well before the house was ready. But Adam was un-hurried.

'I want it built strong,' he directed over and over. 'I want it to last – copper nails and hard wood – nothing to rust or rot.'

He was not alone in his preoccupation with the future. The whole valley, the whole West was that way. It was a time when the past had lost its sweetness and its sap. You'd go a good long road before you'd find a man, and he very old, who wished to bring back a golden past. Men were notched and comfortable in the present, hard and unfruitful as it was, but only as a doorstep into a fantastic future. Rarely did two men meet, or three stand in a bar, or a dozen gnaw tough venison in camp, that the valley's future, paralysing in its grandeur, did not come up, not as conjecture but as a certainty.

'It'll be – who knows? maybe in our lifetime,' they said.

And people found happiness in the future according to their present lack. Thus a man might bring his family down from a hill ranch in a drag – a big box nailed on oaken runners which pulled bumping down the broken hills. In the straw of the box his wife would brace the children against the tooth-shattering, tongue-biting crash of the runners against stone and ground. And the father would set his heels and think, 'When the roads come in – then will be the time. Why, we'll sit high and happy in a surrey and get clear into King City in three hours – and what more in the world could you want than that?'

Or let a man survey his grove of live-oak trees, hard as coal and hotter, the best firewood in the world. In his pocket might be a newspaper with a squib: 'Oak cord wood is bringing ten dollars a cord in Los Angeles.' Why, hell, when the railroad puts a branch out here, I could lay it down neat, broke up and sea-soned, right beside the track, for a dollar and a half a cord. Let's go the whole hog and say the Southern Pacific will charge three-fifty to carry it. There's still five dollars a cord, and there's three thousand cords in that little grove alone. That's fifteen thousand dollars right there.

There were others who prophesied, with rays shining on their foreheads, about the sometime ditches that would carry water all over the valley – who knows? maybe in our lifetime – or deep wells with steam engines to pump the water up out of the guts of the world. Can you imagine? Just think what this land would raise with plenty of water! Why, it will be a frigging garden!

Another man, but he was crazy, said that some day there'd be a way, maybe ice, maybe some other way, to get a peach like this here I got in my hand clear to Philadelphia.

In the towns they talked of sewers and inside toilets, and some already had them; and arc lights on the street corner – Salinas had those – and telephones. There wasn't any limit, no boundary at all, to the future. And it would be so a man wouldn't have room to store his happiness. Contentment would flood raging down the valley like the Salinas River in March of a thirty-inch year.

They looked over the flat, dry, dusty valley and the ugly mushroom towns and they saw a loveliness – who knows? maybe in our lifetime. That's one reason you couldn't laugh too much at Samuel Hamilton. He let his mind range more deliciously than any other, and it didn't sound so silly when you heard what they were doing in San Jose. Where Samuel went haywire was wondering whether people would be happy when all that came.

Happy? He's haywire now. Just let us get it, and we'll show you happiness.

And Samuel could remember hearing of a cousin of his mother's in Ireland, a knight and rich and handsome, and anyway shot himself on a silken couch, sitting beside the most beautiful woman in the world who loved him.

'There's a capacity for appetite,' Samuel said, 'that a whole heaven and earth of cake can't satisfy.'

Adam Trask nosed some of his happiness into futures, but there was present contentment in him too. He felt his heart smack up against his throat when he saw Cathy sitting in the sun, quiet, her baby growing, and a transparency to her skin that made him think of the angels on Sunday School cards. Then a breeze would move her bright hair, or she would raise her eyes, and Adam would swell out in his stomach with a pressure of ecstasy that was close kin to grief.

If Adam rested like a sleek fed cat on his land, Cathy was catlike too. She had the inhuman attribute of abandoning what she could not get and of waiting for what she could get. These two gifts gave her great advantages. Her pregnancy had been an accident. When her attempt to abort herself failed and the doctor threatened her, she gave up that method. This does not mean that she reconciled herself to pregnancy. She sat it out as she would have weathered an illness. Her marriage to Adam had been the same. She was trapped and she took the best possible way out. She had not wanted to go to California either, but other plans were denied her for the time being. As a very young child she had learned to win by using the momentum of her opponent. It was easy to guide a man's strength where it was impossible to resist him. Very few people in the world could have known that Cathy did not want to be where she was and in the condition she was. She relaxed and waited for the change she knew must come some time. Cathy had the one quality required of a great and successful criminal: she trusted no one, confided in no one. Her self was an island. It is probable that she did not even look at Adam's new land or building house, or turn his towering plans to reality in her mind, because she did not intend to live here after her sickness was over, after her trap opened. But to his questions she gave proper answers; to do otherwise would be waste motion, and dissipated energy, and foreign to a good cat.

'See, my darling, how the house lies – windows looking down the valley?'

'It's beautiful.'

'You know, it may sound foolish, but I find myself trying to think the way old Sanchez did a hundred years ago. How was the valley then? He must have planned so carefully. You know, he had pipes? He did – made out of redwood with a hole bored or burned through to carry the water from the spring. We dug up some pieces of it.'

'That's remarkable,' she said. 'He must have been clever.'

'I'd like to know more about him. From the way the house sets, the trees he left, the shape and proportion of the house, he must have been a kind of artist.'

'He was a Spaniard, wasn't he? They're artistic people, I've heard. I remember in school about a painter – no, he was a Greek.'

'I wonder where I could find out about old Sanchez.'

'Well, somebody must know.'

'All of his work and planning, and Bordoni kept cows in the house. You know what I wonder about most?'

'What, Adam?'

'I wonder if he had a Cathy and who she was.'

She smiled and looked down and away from him. 'The things you say.'

'He must have had! He must have had. I never had energy or direction or – well, even a very great desire to live before I had you.'

'Adam, you embarrass me. Adam, be careful. Don't joggle me, it hurts.'

'I'm sorry. I'm so clumsy.'

'No, you're not. You just don't think. Should I be knitting or sewing, do you suppose? I'm so comfortable just sitting.'

'We'll buy everything we need. You just sit and be comfortable. I guess in a way you're working harder than anyone here. But the pay – the pay is wonderful!'

'Adam, the scar on my forehead isn't going to go away, I'm afraid.'

'The doctor said it would fade in time.'

'Well, sometimes it seems to be getting fainter, and then it comes back. Don't you think it's darker today?'

'No, I don't.'

But it was. It looked like a huge thumb-print, even to whorls of wrinkled skin. He put his finger near, and she drew her head away.

'Don't,' she said. 'It's tender to the touch. It turns red if you touch it.'

'It will go away. Just takes a little time, that's all.'

She smiled as he turned, but when he walked away her eyes were flat and directionless. She shifted her body restlessly. The baby was kicking. She relaxed and all her muscles loosened. She waited.

Lee came near where her chair was set under the biggest oak tree. 'Missy likee tea?'

'No – yes, I would too.'

Her eyes inspected him and her inspection could not penetrate the dark brown of his eyes. He made her uneasy. Cathy had always been able to shovel into the mind of any man and dig up his impulses and his desires. But Lee's brain gave and repelled like rubber. His face was lean and pleasant, his forehead broad, firm, and sensitive, and his lips curled in a perpetual smile. His long black glossy braided queue, tied at the bottom with a narrow piece of black silk, hung over his shoulder and moved rhythmically against his chest. When he did violent work he curled his queue on top of his head. He wore narrow cotton trousers, black heel-less slippers, and a frogged Chinese smock. Whenever he could he hid his hands in his sleeves as though he were afraid for them, as most Chinese did in that day.

'I bling litta table,' he said, bowed slightly, and shuffled away.

Cathy looked after him, and her eyebrows drew down in a scowl. She was not afraid of Lee, yet she was not comfortable with him either. But he was a good and respectful servant – the best. And what harm could he do her?

The summer progressed and the Salinas River retired underground or stood in green pools under high banks. The cattle lay drowsing all day long under the willows and only moved out at night to feed. An umber tone came to the grass. And the afternoon winds blowing inevitably down the valley started a dust that was like fog and raised it into the sky almost as high as the mountain tops. The wild oat roots stood up like nigger-heads where the winds blew the earth away. Along a polished earth, pieces of straw and twigs scampered until they were stopped by some rooted thing; and little stones rolled crookedly before the wind.

It became more apparent than ever why old Sanchez had built his house in the little draw, for the wind and the dust did not penetrate, and the spring, while it diminished, still gushed a head of cold clear water. But Adam, looking out over his dry dust-obscured land, felt the panic the Eastern man always does at first in California. In a Connecticut summer two weeks without rain is a dry spell and four a drought. If the countryside is not green it is dying. But in California it does not ordinarily rain at all between the end of May and the first of November. The Eastern man, though he has been told, feels the earth is sick in the rainless months.

Adam sent Lee with a note to the Hamilton place to ask Samuel to visit him and discuss the boring of some wells on his new place.

Samuel was sitting in the shade, watching his son Tom design and build a revolutionary coon trap, when Lee drove up in the Trask cart. Lee folded his hands in his sleeves and waited. Samuel read the note. 'Tom,' he said, 'do you think you could keep the estate going while I run down and talk water with a dry man?'

'Why don't I go with you? You might need some help.'

'At talking? – that I don't. It won't come to digging for some time, if I'm any judge. With wells there's got to be a great deal of talk – five or six hundreds words for every shovel of dirt.'

'I'd like to go – it's Mr Trask, isn't it? I didn't meet him when he came here.'

'You'll do that when the digging starts. I'm older than you. I've got first claim on the talk. You know, Tom, a coon is going to reach his pretty little hand through here and let himself out. You know how clever they are.'

'See this piece here? It screws on and turns down here. You couldn't get out of that yourself.'

'I'm not so clever as a coon. I think you've worked it out, though. Tom, boy, would you saddle Doxology while I go tell your mother where I'm going?'

'I bling lig,' said Lee.

'Well, I have to come home some time.'

'I bling back.'

'Nonsense,' said Samuel. 'I'll lead my horse in and ride back.'

Samuel sat in the buggy beside Lee, and his clobber-footed saddle-horse shuffled clumsily behind.

'What's your name?' Samuel asked pleasantly.

'Lee. Got more name. Lee papa family name. Call Lee.'

'I've read quite a lot about China. You born in China?'

'No. Born here.'

Samuel was silent for quite a long time while the buggy lurched down the wheel track towards the dusty valley. 'Lee,' he said at last, 'I mean no disrespect, but I've never been able to figure why you people still talk pidgin when an illiterate baboon from the black bogs of Ireland, with a head full of Gaelic and a tongue like a potato, learns to talk a poor grade of English in ten years.'

Lee grinned. 'Me talkee Chinese talk,' he said.

'Well, I guess you have your reasons. And it's not my affair. I hope you'll forgive me if I don't believe it, Lee.'

Lee looked at him and the brown eyes under their rounded upper lids seemed to open and deepen until they weren't foreign any more, but man's eyes, warm with understanding. Lee chuckled. 'It's more than a convenience,' he said. 'It's even more than self-protection. Mostly we have to use it to be understood at all.'

Samuel showed no sign of having observed any change. 'I can understand the first two,' he said thoughtfully, 'but the third escapes me.'

Lee said, 'I know it's hard to believe, but it has happened so often to me and to my friends that we take it for granted. If I should go up to a lady or a gentleman, for instance, and speak as I am doing now, I wouldn't be understood.'

'Why not?'

'Pidgin they expect, and pidgin they'll listen to. But English from me they don't listen to, and so they don't understand it.'

'Can that be possible? How do I understand you?'

'That's why I'm talking to you. You are one of the rare people who can separate your observation from your preconception. You see what is, where most people see what they expect.'

'I hadn't thought of it. And I've not been so tested as you, but what you say has a handle of truth. You know, I'm very glad to talk to you. I've wanted to ask so many questions.'

'Happy to oblige.'

'So many questions. For instance, you wear the queue. I've read that it is a badge of slavery imposed by conquest by the Manchus on the Southern Chinese.'

'That is true.'

'Then why in the name of God do you wear it here, where the Manchus can't get at you?'

'Talkee Chinese talk. Queue Chinese fashion – you savvy?'

Samuel laughed loudly. 'That does have the green touch of convenience,' he said. 'I wish I had a hidey-hole like that.'

'I'm wondering whether I can explain,' said Lee. 'Where there is no likeness of experience it's very difficult. I understand you were not born in America.'

'No, in Ireland.'

'And in a few years you can almost disappear; while I, who was born in Grass Valley, went to school and several years to the University of California, have no chance of mixing.'

'If you cut your queue, dressed and talked like other people?'

'No. I tried it. To the so-called whites I was still a Chinese, but an untrustworthy one; and at the same time my Chinese friends steered clear of me. I had to give it up.'

Lee pulled up under a tree, got out, and unfastened the check rein. 'Time for lunch,' he said. 'I made a package. Would you like some?'

'Sure I would. Let me get down in the shade there. I forget to eat sometimes, and that's strange because I'm always hungry. I'm interested in what you say. It has a sweet sound of authority. Now it peeks into my mind that you should go back to China.'

Lee smiled satirically at him. 'In a few minutes I don't think you'll find a loose bar I've missed in a lifetime of search. I did go back to China. My father was a fairly successful man. It didn't work. They said I looked like a foreign devil; they said I spoke like a foreign devil. I made mistakes in manners, and I didn't know delicacies that had grown up since my father left. They wouldn't have me. You can believe it or not – I'm less foreign here than I was in China.'

'I'll have to believe you because it's reasonable. You've given me things to think about until at least February twenty-seventh. Do you mind my questions?'

'As a matter of fact, no. The trouble with pidgin is that you get to thinking in pidgin. I write a great deal to keep my English up. Hearing and reading aren't the same as speaking and writing.'

'Don't you ever make a mistake? I mean, break into English?'

'No, I don't. I think it's a matter of what is expected. You look at a man's eyes, you see that he expects pidgin and a shuffle, so you speak pidgin and shuffle.'

'I guess that's right,' said Samuel. 'In my own way I tell jokes because people come all the way to my place to laugh. I try to be funny for them even when the sadness is on me.'

'But the Irish are said to be a happy people, full of jokes.'

'There's your pidgin and your queue. They're not. They're a dark people with a gift for suffering way past their deserving. It's said that without whisky to soak and soften the world, they'd kill themselves. But they tell jokes because it's expected of them.'

Lee unwrapped a little bottle. 'Would you like some of this? Chinee drink ng-ka-py.'

'What is it?'

'Chinee blandy. Stlong dlink – as a matter of fact it's a brandy with a dosage of wormwood. Very powerful. It softens the world.'

Samuel sipped from the bottle. 'Tastes a little like rotten apples,' he said.

'Yes, but nice rotten apples. Taste it back along your tongue towards the roots.'

Samuel took a big swallow and tilted his head back. 'I see what you mean. That *is* good.'

'Here are some sandwiches, pickles, cheese, a can of buttermilk.'

'You do well.'

'Yes, I see to it.'

Samuel bit into a sandwich. 'I was shuffling over half a hundred questions. What you said brings the brightest one up. You don't mind?'

'Not at all. The only thing I do want to ask of you is not to talk this way when other people are listening. It would only confuse them and they wouldn't believe it anyway.'

'I'll try,' said Samuel. 'If I slip, just remember that I'm a comical genius. It's hard to split a man down the middle and always to reach for the same half.'

'I think I can guess what your next question is.'

'What?'

'Why am I content to be a servant?'

'How in the world did you know?'

'It seemed to follow.'

'Do you resent the question?'

'Not from you. There are no ugly questions except those clothed in condescension. I don't know where being a servant came into disrepute. It is the refuge of a philosopher, the food of the lazy, and, properly carried out, it is a position of power, even of love. I can't understand why more intelligent people don't take it as a career – learn to do it well and reap its benefits. A good servant has absolute security, not because of his master's kindness, but because of habit and indolence. It's a hard thing for a man to change spices or lay out his own socks. He'll keep a bad servant rather than change. But a good servant, and I am an excellent one, can completely control his master, tell him what to think, how to act, whom to marry, when to divorce, reduce him to terror as a discipline, or distribute happiness to him, and finally be mentioned in his will. If I had wished I could have robbed, stripped, and beaten anyone I've worked for and come away with thanks. Finally, in my circumstances I am unprotected. My master will defend me, protect me. You have to work and worry. I work less and worry less. And I am a good servant. A bad one does no work and does no worrying, and he still is fed, clothed, and protected. I don't know any profession where the field is so cluttered with incompetents and where excellence is so rare.'

Samuel leaned towards him, listening intently.

Lee went on, 'It's going to be a relief after that to go back to pidgin.'

'It's a very short distance to the Sanchez place. Why did we stop so near?' Samuel asked.

'Allee time talkee. Me Chinee number one boy. You leddy go now?'

'What? Oh, sure. But it must be a lonely life.'

'That's the only fault with it,' said Lee. 'I've been thinking of going to San Francisco and starting a little business.'

'Like a laundry? Or a grocery store?'

'No. Too many Chinese laundries and restaurants. I thought perhaps a bookstore. I'd like that, and the competition wouldn't be too great. I probably won't do it, though. A servant loses his initiative.'

158

In the afternoon Samuel and Adam rode over the land. The wind came up as it did every afternoon, and the yellow dust ran into the sky.

'Oh, it's a good piece,' Samuel cried. 'It's a rare piece of land.'

'Seems to me it's blowing away bit by bit,' Adam observed.

'No, it's just moving over a little. You lose some to the James ranch but you get some from the Southeys.'

'Well, I don't like the wind. Makes me nervous.'

'Nobody likes wind for very long. It makes animals nervous and restless too. I don't know whether you noticed, but a little farther up the valley they're planting windbreaks of gum trees. Eucalyptus – comes from Australia. They say the gums grow ten feet a year. Why don't you try a few rows and see what happens? In time they should back up the wind a little, and they make grand firewood.'

'Good idea,' Adam said. 'What I really want is water. This wind would pump all the water I could find. I thought if I could bring in a few wells and irrigate, the topsoil wouldn't blow away. I might try some beans.'

Samuel squinted into the wind. 'I'll try to get you water if you want,' he said. 'And I've got a little pump I made that will bring it up fast. It's my own invention. A windmill is a pretty costly thing. Maybe I could build them for you and save you some money.'

'That's good,' said Adam, 'I wouldn't mind the wind if it worked for me. And if I could get water I might plant alfalfa.'

'It's never brought much of a price.'

'I wasn't thinking of that. Few weeks ago I took a drive up around Greenfield and Gonzales. Some Swiss have moved in there. They've got nice little dairy herds and they get four crops of alfalfa a year.'

'I heard about them. They brought in Swiss cows.'

Adam's face was bright with plans. 'That's what I want to do. Sell butter and cheese and feed the milk to the pigs.'

'You're going to bring credit to the valley,' Samuel said. 'You're going to be a real joy to the future.'

'If I can get water.'

'I'll get you water if there's any to be got. I'll find it. I brought my magic wand.' He patted a forked stick tied to his saddle.

Adam pointed to the left where a wide flat place was covered with a low growth of sagebrush. 'Now then,' he said, 'thirty-six acres and almost as level as a floor. I put an auger down. Topsoil averages three and a half feet, sand on top and loam within plough reach. Think you could get water there?'

'I don't know,' Samuel said. 'I'll see.'

He dismounted, handed his reins to Adam, and untied his forked wand. He took the forks in his two hands and walked slowly, his arms out and stretched before him and the wand-tip up. His steps took a zigzag course. Once he frowned and backed up a few steps, then shook his head and went on. Adam rode slowly along behind, leading the other horse.

Adam kept his eyes on the stick. He saw it quiver and then jerk a little, as though an invisible fish were tugging at a line. Samuel's face was taut with attention. He continued on until the point of the wand seemed to be pulled strongly downward against his straining arms. He made a slow circle, broke off a piece of sagebrush, and dropped it on the ground. He moved well outside his circle, held up his stick again, and moved inward towards his marker. As he came near it, the point of the stick was drawn down again. Samuel sighed and relaxed and dropped his wand on the ground. 'I can get water here,' he said. 'And not very deep. The pull was strong, plenty of water.'

'Good,' said Adam. 'I want to show you a couple more places.'

Samuel whittled out a stout piece of sagewood and drove it into the soil. He made a split on the top and fitted a crosspiece on for a mark. Then he kicked the brittle brush down in the area so he could find his marker again.

On a second try three hundred yards away the wand seemed nearly torn downwards out of his hands. 'Now there's a whole world of water here,' he said.

The third try was not so productive. After half an hour he had only the slightest sign.

The two men rode slowly back towards the Trask house. The afternoon was golden, for the yellow dust in the sky gilded the light. As always, the wind began to drop as the day waned, but it sometimes took half the night for the dust to settle out of the air. 'I knew it was a good place,' Samuel said. 'Anyone can see that. But I didn't know it was that good. You must have a great drain under your land from the mountains. You know how to pick land, Mr Trask.'

Adam smiled. 'We had a farm in Connecticut,' he said. 'For six generations we dug stones out. One of the first things I remember is sledding stones over to the walls. I thought that was the way all farms were. It's strange to me and almost sinful here. If you wanted a stone, you'd have to go a long way for it.'

'The ways of sin are curious,' Samuel observed. 'I guess if a man had to shuck off everything he had, inside and out, he'd manage to hide a few little sins somewhere for his own discomfort. They're the last things we'll give up.'

'Maybe that's a good thing to keep us humble. The fear of God in us.'

'I guess so,' said Samuel. 'And I guess humility must be a good thing, since it's a rare man who has not a piece of it, but when you look at humbleness it's hard to see where its value rests unless you grant that it is a pleasurable pain and very precious. Suffering – I wonder has it been properly looked at.'

'Tell me about your stick,' Adam said. 'How does it work?'

Samuel stroked the fork now tied to his saddle strings. 'I don't really believe in it, save that it works.' He smiled at Adam. 'Maybe it's this way. Maybe I know where the water is, feel it in my skin. Some people have a gift in this direction or that. Suppose – well, call it humility, or a deep disbelief in myself, forced me to do a magic to bring up to the surface the thing I know anyway. Does that make any sense to you?'

'I'd have to think about it,' said Adam.

The horses picked their own way, heads hung low, reins loosened against the bits.

'Can you stay the night?' Adam asked.

'I can, but better not. I didn't tell Liza I'd be away the night. I'd not like to give her a worry.'

'But she knows where you are.'

'Sure she knows. But I'll ride home tonight. It doesn't matter the time. If you'd like to ask me to supper I'd be glad. And when do you want me to start on the wells?'

'Now – as soon as you can.'

'You know it's no cheap thing, indulging yourself with water. I'd have to charge you fifty cents or more a foot, depending on what we find down there. It can run into money.'

'I have the money. I want the wells. Look, Mr Hamilton —'

' "Samuel" would be easier.'

'Look, Samuel, I mean to make a garden of my land. Remember my name is Adam. So far I've had no Eden, let alone been driven out.'

'It's the best reason I ever heard for making a garden,' Samuel exclaimed. He chuckled. 'Where will the orchard be?'

Adam said, 'I won't plant apples. That would be looking for accidents.'

'What does Eve say to that? She has a say, you remember. And Eves delight in apples.'

'Not this one.' Adam's eyes were shining. 'You don't know this Eve. She'll celebrate my choice. I don't think anyone can know her goodness.'

'You have a rarity. Right now I can't recall any greater gift.'

They were coming near to the entrance to the little side valley in which was the Sanchez house. They could see the rounded green tops of the great live oaks.

'Gift,' Adam said softly. 'You can't know. No one can know. I had a grey life, Mr Hamilton – Samuel. Not that it was bad compared to other lives, but it was nothing. I don't know why I tell you this.'

'Maybe because I like to hear.'

'My mother – died – before my memory. My step-mother was a good woman but troubled and ill. My father was a stern, fine man – maybe a great man.'

'You couldn't love him?'

'I had the kind of feeling you have in church, and not a little fear in it.'

Samuel nodded. 'I know – and some men want that.' He smiled ruefully. 'I've always wanted the other. Liza says it's the weak thing in me.'

'My father put me in the army, in the West, against the Indians.'

'You told me. But you don't think like a military man.'

'I wasn't a good one. I seem to be telling you everything.'

'You must want to. There's always a reason.'

'A soldier must want to do the things we had to do – or at least be satisfied with them. I couldn't find good enough reasons for killing men and women, nor understand the reasons when they were explained.'

They rode on in silence for a time. Adam went on, 'I came out of the army like dragging myself muddy out of a swamp. I wandered for a long time before going home to a remembered place I did not love.'

'Your father?'

'He died, and home was a place to sit around or work around, waiting for death the way you might wait for a dreadful picnic.'

'Alone?'

'No, I have a brother.'

'Where is he – waiting for the picnic?'

'Yes – yes, that's exactly what. Then Cathy came. Maybe I will tell you some time when I can tell and you want to hear.'

'I'll want to hear,' Samuel said. 'I eat stories like grapes.'

'A kind of light spread out from her. And everything changed colour. And the world opened out. And a day was good to awaken to. And there were no limits to anything. And the people of the world were good and handsome. And I was not afraid any more.'

'I recognize it,' Samuel said. 'That's an old friend of mine. It never dies, but sometimes it moves away, or you do. Yes, that's my acquaintance – eyes, nose, mouth, and hair.'

'All this coming out of a little hurt girl.'

'And not out of you?'

'Oh, no, or it would have come before. No, Cathy brought it, and it lives around her. And now I've told you why I want the wells. I have to repay somehow for value received. I'm going to make a garden so good, so beautiful, that it will be a proper place for her to live and a fitting place for her light to shine on.'

Samuel swallowed several times, and he spoke with a dry voice out of a pinched-up throat. 'I can see my duty,' he said. 'I can see it plainly before me if I am any kind of man, any kind of friend to you.'

'What do you mean?'

Samuel said satirically, 'It's my duty to take this thing of yours and kick it in the face, then raise it up and spread slime on it thick enough to blot out its dangerous light.' His voice grew strong with vehemence. 'I should hold it up to you muck-covered and show you its dirt and danger. I should warn you to look closer until you can see how ugly it really is. I should ask you to think of inconstancy and give you examples. I should give you Othello's handkerchief. Oh, I know I should. And I should straighten out your tangled thought, show you that the impulse is grey as lead and rotten as a dead cow in wet weather. If I did my duty well, I could give you back your bad old life and feel good about it, and welcome you back to the musty membership in the lodge.'

'Are you joking? Maybe I shouldn't have told —'

'It is the duty of a friend. I had a friend who did the duty once for me. But I'm a false friend. I'll get no credit for it among my peers. It's a lovely thing, preserve it, and glory in it. And I'll dig your wells if I have to drive my rig to the black

163

centre of the earth. I'll squeeze water out like juice from an orange.'

They rode under the great oaks and towards the house. Adam said, 'There she is, sitting outside.' He shouted, 'Cathy, he says there's water – lots of it.' Aside he said excitedly, 'Did you know she's going to have a baby?'

'Even at this distance she looks beautiful,' Samuel said.

IV

Because the day had been hot, Lee set a table outside under an oak tree, and as the sun neared the western mountains he padded back and forth from the kitchen, carrying the cold meats, pickles, potato salad, coconut cake, and peach pie which were supper. In the centre of the table he placed a gigantic stoneware pitcher full of milk.

Adam and Samuel came from the wash-house, their hair and faces shining with water, and Samuel's beard was fluffy after its soaping. They stood at the trestle table and waited until Cathy came out.

She walked slowly, picking her way as though she were afraid she would fall. Her full skirt and apron concealed to a certain extent her swelling abdomen. Her face was untroubled and childlike, and she clasped her hands in front of her. She had reached the table before she looked up and glanced from Samuel to Adam.

Adam held her chair for her. 'You haven't met Mr Hamilton, dear,' he said.

She held out her hand. 'How do you do?' she said.

Samuel had been inspecting her. 'It's a beautiful place,' he said, 'I'm glad to meet you. You are well, I hope?'

'Oh, yes. Yes, I'm well.'

The men sat down. 'She makes it formal whether she wants to or not. Every meal is a kind of occasion,' Adam said.

'Don't talk like that,' she said. 'It isn't true.'

'Doesn't it feel like a party to you, Samuel?' he asked.

'It does so, and I can tell you there's never been such a candidate for a party as I am. And my children – they're worse. My boy Tom wanted to come today. He's spoiling to get off the ranch.'

Samuel suddenly realized that he was making his speech last to prevent silence from falling on the table. He paused, and the silence dropped. Cathy looked down at her plate while she ate a

164

sliver of roast lamb. She looked up as she put it between her small sharp teeth. Her wide-set eyes communicated nothing. Samuel shivered.

'It isn't cold, is it?' Adam asked.

'Cold? No. A goose walked over my grave, I guess.'

'Oh, yes. I know that feeling.'

The silence fell again. Samuel waited for some speech to start up, knowing in advance that it would not.

'Do you like our valley, Mrs Trask?'

'What? Oh, yes.'

'If it isn't impertinent to ask, when is your baby due?'

'In about six weeks,' Adam said. 'My wife is one of those paragons – a woman who does not talk very much.'

'Sometimes a silence tells the most,' said Samuel, and he saw Cathy's eyes leap up and down again, and it seemed to him that the scar on her forehead grew darker. Something had flicked her the way you'd flick a horse with the braided string popper on a buggy whip. Samuel couldn't recall what he had said that had made her give a small inward start. He felt a tenseness coming over him that was somewhat like the feeling he had just before the water wand pulled down, an awareness of something strange and strained. He glanced at Adam and saw that he was looking raptly at his wife. Whatever was strange was not strange to Adam. His face had happiness on it.

Cathy was chewing a piece of meat, chewing with her front teeth. Samuel had never seen anyone chew that way before. And when she had swallowed, her little tongue flicked round her lips. Samuel's mind repeated, 'Something – something – can't find what it is. Something wrong,' and the silence hung on the table.

There was a shuffle behind him. He turned. Lee set a teapot on the table and shuffled away.

Samuel began to talk to push the silence away. He told how he had first come to the valley fresh from Ireland, but within a few words neither Cathy nor Adam was listening to him. To prove it, he used a trick he had devised to discover whether his children were listening when they begged him to read to them and would not let him stop. He threw in two sentences of nonsense. There was no response from either Adam or Cathy. He gave up.

He bolted his supper, drank his tea scalding hot, and folded his napkin. 'Ma'am, if you'll excuse me, I'll ride off home. And I thank you for your hospitality.'

'Good night,' she said.

Adam jumped to his feet. He seemed torn out of a reverie. 'Don't go now. I hoped to persuade you to stay the night.'

'No, thank you, but that I can't. And it's not a long ride. I think – of course, I know – there'll be a moon.'

'When will you start the wells?'

'I'll have to get my rig in order, do a piece of sharpening, and put my house in order. In a few days I'll send the equipment with Tom.'

The life was flowing back into Adam. 'Make it soon,' he said. 'I want it soon. Cathy, we're going to make the most beautiful place in the world. There'll be nothing like it anywhere.'

Samuel switched his gaze to Cathy's face. It did not change. The eyes were flat and the mouth with its small up-curve at the corners was carven.

'That will be nice,' she said.

For just a moment Samuel had an impulse to do or say something to shock her out of her distance. He shivered again.

'Another goose?' Adam asked.

'Another goose.' The dusk was falling and already the tree forms were dark against the sky. 'Good night, then.'

'I'll walk down with you.'

'No, stay with your wife. You haven't finished your supper.'

'But I — '

'Sit down, man. I can find my own horse, and if I can't I'll steal one of yours.' Samuel pushed Adam gently down in his chair. 'Good night. Good night. Good night, ma'am.' He walked quickly towards the shed.

Old platter-foot Doxology was daintily nibbling hay from the manger with lips like two flounders. The halter chain clinked against the wood. Samuel lifted down his saddle from the big nail where it hung by one wooden stirrup and swung it over the broad back. He was lacing the latigo through the cinch rings when there was a small stir behind him. He turned and saw the silhouette of Lee against the last light from the open shadows.

'When you come back?' the Chinese asked softly.

'I don't know. In a few days or a week. Lee, what is it?'

'What is what?'

'By God, I got creepy! Is there something wrong here?'

'What do you mean?'

'You know damn well what I mean.'

'Chinee boy jus' workee – not hear, not talkee.'

'Yes. I guess you're right. Sure, you're right. Sorry I asked

166

you. It wasn't very good manners.' He turned back, slipped the bit in Dox's mouth, and laced the big flop-ears into the head-stall. He slipped the halter and dropped it in the manger. 'Good night, Lee,' he said.

'Mr Hamilton —'

'Yes?'

'Do you need a cook?'

'On my place I can't afford a cook.'

'I'd work cheap.'

'Liza would kill you. Why – you want to quit?'

'Just thought I'd ask,' said Lee. 'Good night.'

v

Adam and Cathy sat in the gathering dark under the tree.

'He's a good man,' Adam said. 'I like him. I wish I could persuade him to take over here and run this place – kind of superintendent.'

Cathy said, 'He's got his own place and his own family.'

'Yes, I know. And it's the poorest land you ever saw. He could make more at wages from me. I'll ask him. It does take a time to get used to a new country. It's like being born again and having to learn all over. I used to know from what quarter the rains came. It's different here. And once I knew in my skin whether wind would blow, when it would be cold. But I'll learn. It just takes a little time. Are you comfortable, Cathy?'

'Yes.'

'One day, and not too far away, you'll see the whole valley green with alfalfa – see it from the fine big windows of the finished house. I'll plant rows of gum trees, and I'm going to send away for seeds and plants – put in a kind of experimental farm. I might try lichee nuts from China. I wonder if they would grow here. Well, I can try. Maybe Lee would tell me. And once the baby's born you can ride over the whole place with me. You haven't really seen it. Did I tell you? Mr Hamilton is going to put up windmills, and we'll be able to see them turning from here.' He stretched his legs out comfortably under the table. 'Lee should bring candles,' he said. 'I wonder what's keeping him.'

Cathy spoke very quietly. 'Adam, I didn't want to come here. I am not going to stay here. As soon as I can I will go away.'

'Oh, nonsense.' He laughed. 'You're like a child away from

167

home for the first time. You'll love it once you get used to it and the baby is born. You know, when I first went away to the army I thought I was going to die of home-sickness. But I got over it. We all get over it. So don't say silly things like that.'

'It's not a silly thing.'

'Don't talk about it, dear. Everything will change after the baby is born. You'll see. You'll see.'

He capped his hands behind his head and looked up at the faint stars through the tree branches.

CHAPTER 16

I

SAMUEL HAMILTON rode back home in a night so flooded with moonlight that the hills took on the quality of the white and dusty moon. The trees and earth were moon-dry, silent and airless and dead. The shadows were black without shading and the open places white without colour. Here and there Samuel could see secret movement, for the moon-feeders were at work – the deer which browse all night when the moon is clear and sleep under thickets in the day. Rabbits and field-mice and all other small hunted creatures that feel safer in the concealing light crept and hopped and crawled and froze to resemble stones or small bushes when ear or nose suspected danger. The predators were working too – the long weasels like waves of brown light; the cobby wild cats crouching near to the ground, almost invisible except when their yellow eyes caught light and flashed for a second; the foxes sniffling with pointed up-raised noses for a warm-blooded supper; the raccoon padding near still water, talking frogs. The coyotes nuzzled along the slopes and, torn with sorrow-joy, raised their heads and shouted their feeling, half keen, half laughter, at their goddess moon. And over all the shadowy screech owls sailed, drawing a smudge of shadowy fear below them on the ground. The wind of the afternoon was gone and only a little breeze like a sigh was stirred by the restless thermals of the warm, dry hills.

Doxology's loud off-beat footsteps silenced the night people until after he had passed. Samuel's beard glinted white, and his greying hair stood up high on his head. He had hung his black hat on his saddle horn. An ache was on the top of his stomach, an apprehension that was like a sick thought. It was a *Weltsch-*

merz – which we used to call 'Welshrats' – the world sadness that rises into the soul like a gas and spreads despair so that you probe for the offending event and can find none.

Samuel went back in his mind over the fine ranch and the indications of water – no Welshrats could come out of that unless he sheltered a submerged envy. He looked in himself for envy and could find none. He went on to Adam's dream of a garden like Eden and to Adam's adoration of Cathy. Nothing there unless – unless his secret mind brooded over his own healed loss. But that was so long ago he had forgotten the pain. The memory was mellow and warm and comfortable, now that it was all over. His loins and his thighs had forgotten hunger.

As he rode through the light and dark of tree-shade and open his mind moved on. When had the Welshrats started crawling in his chest? He found it then – and it was Cathy, pretty, tiny, delicate Cathy. But what about her? She was silent, but many women were silent. What was it? Where had it come from? He remembered that he had felt an imminence akin to the one that came to him when he held the water wand. And he remembered the shivers when the goose walked over his grave. Now he had pinned it down in time and place and person. It had come at dinner and it had come from Cathy.

He built her face in front of him and studied her wide-set eyes, delicate nostrils, mouth smaller than he liked but sweet, small firm chin, and back to her eyes. Were they cold? Was it her eyes? He was circling to the point. The eyes of Cathy had no message, no communication of any kind. There was nothing recognizable behind them. They were not human eyes. They reminded him of something – what was it? – some memory, some picture. He strove to find it and then it came of itself.

It rose out of the years complete with all its colours and its cries, its crowded feelings. He saw himself, a very little boy, so small that he had to reach high for his father's hand. He felt the cobbles of Londonderry under his feet and the crush and gaiety of the one big city he had seen. A fair, it was, with puppet shows and stalls of produce and horses and sheep penned right in the street for sale or trade or auction, and other stalls of bright-coloured knick-knackery, desirable and, because his father was gay, almost possessable.

And then the people turned like a strong river, and they were carried along a narrow street as though they were chips on a flood tide, pressure at chest and back and the feet keeping up. The narrow street opened out to a square, and against the grey wall of a building there was a high structure of timbers and a noosed rope hanging down.

Samuel and his father were pushed and bunted by the water of people, pushed closer and closer. He could hear in his memory ear his father saying, 'It's no thing for a child. It's no thing for anybody, but less for a child.' His father struggled to turn, to force his way back against the flood wave of people. 'Let us out. Please let us out. I've a child here.'

The wave was faceless and it pushed without passion. Samuel raised his head to look at the structure. A group of dark-clothed, dark-hatted men had climbed up on the high platform. And in their midst was a man with golden hair, dressed in dark trousers and a light blue shirt open at the throat. Samuel and his father were so close that the boy had to raise his head high to see.

The golden man seemed to have no arms. He looked out over the crowd and then looked down, looked right at Samuel. The picture was clear, lighted and perfect. The man's eyes had no depth – they were not like other eyes, not like the eyes of a man.

Suddenly there was quick movement on the platform, and Samuel's father put both his hands on the boy's head so that his palms cupped over the ears and his fingers met behind. The hands forced Samuel's head down and forced his face tight in against his father's black best coat. Struggle as he would, he could not move his head. He could see only a band of light around the edges of his eyes and only a muffled roar of sound came to his ears through his father's hands. He heard heart-beats in his ears. Then he felt his father's hands and arms grow rigid with set muscles, and against his face he could feel his father's deep-caught breathing and then deep intake and held breath, and his father's hands, trembling.

A little more there was to it, and he dug it up and set it before his eyes in the air ahead of the horse's head – a worn and battered table at a pub, loud talk and laughter. A pewter mug was in front of his father, and a cup of hot milk, sweet and aromatic with sugar and cinnamon, before himself. His father's lips were curiously blue and there were tears in his father's eyes.

'I'd never have brought you if I'd known. It's not fit for any man to see, and sure not for a small boy.'

'I didn't see any,' Samuel piped. 'You held my head down.'

'I'm glad of that.'

'What was it?'

'I'll have to tell you. They were killing a bad man.'

'Was it the golden man?'

'Yes, it was. And you must put no sorrow on him. He had to be killed. Not once but many times he did dreadful things – things only a fiend could think of. It's not his hanging sorrows me but that they make a holiday of it that should be done secretly, in the dark.'

'I saw the golden man. He looked right down at me.'

'For that even more I thank God he's gone.'

'What did he do?'

'I'll never tell you nightmare things.'

'He had the strangest eyes, the golden man. They put me in mind of a goat's eyes.'

'Drink your sweety-milk and you shall have a stick with ribbons and a long whistle like silver.'

'And the shiny box with a picture into it?'

'That also, so you drink up your sweety-milk and beg no more.'

There it was, mined out of the dusty past.

Doxology was climbing the last rise before the hollow of the home ranch and the big feet stumbled over stones in the roadway.

It was the eyes, of course, Samuel thought. Only twice in my life have I seen eyes like that – not like human eyes. And he thought, 'It's the night and the moon. Now what connection under heaven can there be between the golden man hanged so long ago and the sweet little bearing mother? Liza's right. My imagination will get me a passport to hell one day. Let me dig this nonsense out, else I'll be searching that poor child for evil. This is how we can get trapped. Now think hard and then lose it. Some accident of eye shape and eye colour, it is. But no, that's not it. It's a look and has no reference to shape or colour. Well, why is a look evil, then? Maybe such a look may have been some time on a holy face. Now, stop this romancing and never let it trouble again – ever.' He shivered. I'll have to set up a goose fence around my grave, he thought.

And Samuel Hamilton resolved to help greatly with the Salinas Valley Eden, to make a secret guilt-payment for his ugly thoughts.

II

Liza Hamilton, her apple cheeks flaming red, moved like a caged leopard in front of the stove when Samuel came into the kitchen in the morning. The oakwood fire roared up past an open damper to heat the oven for the bread, which lay white and rising in the pans. Liza had been up before dawn. She always was. It was just as sinful to her to lie abed after light as it was to be abroad after dark. There was no possible virtue in either. Only one person in the world could with impunity and without crime lie between her crisp ironed sheets after dawn, after sun-up, even to the far reaches of mid-morning, and that was her youngest and last born, Joe.

Only Tom and Joe lived on the ranch now. And Tom, big and red, already cultivating a fine flowing moustache, sat at the kitchen table with his sleeves rolled down as he had been mannered. Liza poured thick batter from a pitcher on to a soapstone griddle. The hot cakes rose like little hassocks, and small volcanoes formed and erupted on them until they were ready to be turned. A cheerful brown, they were, with tracings of darker brown. And the kitchen was full of the good sweet smell of them.

Samuel came in from the yard where he had been washing himself. His face and beard gleamed with water, and he turned down the sleeves of his blue shirt as he entered the kitchen. Rolled-up sleeves at the table were not acceptable to Mrs Hamilton. They indicated either an ignorance or a flouting of the niceties.

'I'm late, Mother,' Samuel said.

She did not look round at him. Her spatula moved like a striking snake and the hot cakes settled their white sides hissing on the soapstone. 'What time was it you came home?' she asked.

'Oh, it was late – late. Must have been near eleven. I didn't look, fearing to waken you.'

'I did not waken,' Liza said grimly. 'And maybe you can find it healthy to rove all night, but the Lord God will do what He sees fit about that.' It was well known that Liza Hamilton and the Lord God held similar convictions on nearly every subject. She turned and reached and a plate of crisp hot cakes lay between Tom's hands. 'How does the Sanchez place look?' she asked.

Samuel went to his wife, leaned down from his height, and kissed her round red cheek. 'Good morning, Mother. Give me your blessing.'

'Bless you,' said Liza automatically.

Samuel sat down at the table and said, 'Bless you, Tom. Well, Mr Trask is making great changes. He's fitting up the old house to live in.'

Liza turned sharply from the stove. 'The one where the cows and pigs have slept the years?'

'Oh, he's ripped out the floors and window casings. All new and new painted.'

'He'll never get the smell of pigs out,' Liza said firmly. 'There's a pungency left by a pig that nothing can wash out or cover up.'

'Well, I went inside and looked around, Mother, and I could smell nothing except paint.'

'When the paint dries you'll smell pig,' she said.

'He's got a garden laid out with spring water running through it, and he's set a place apart for flowers, roses and the like, and some of the bushes are coming clear from Boston.'

'I don't see how the Lord God puts up with such waste,' she said grimly. 'Not that I don't like a rose myself.'

'He said he'd try to root some cuttings for me,' Samuel said.

Tom finished his hot cakes and stirred his coffee. 'What kind of a man is he, Father?'

'Well, I think he's a fine man – has a good tongue and a fair mind. He's given to dreaming — '

'Hear now the pot blackguarding the kettle,' Liza interrupted.

'I know, Mother, I know. But have you ever thought that my dreaming takes the place of something I haven't? Mr Trask has practical dreams and the sweet dollars to make them solid. He wants to make a garden of his land, and he will do it too.'

'What's his wife like?' Liza asked.

'Well, she's very young and very pretty. She's quiet, hardly speaks, but then she's having her first baby soon.'

'I know that,' Liza said. 'What was her name before?'

'I don't know.'

'Well, where did she come from?'

'I don't know.'

She put his plate of hot cakes in front of him and poured coffee in his cup and refilled Tom's cup. 'What did you learn, then? How does she dress?'

'Why, very nice, pretty – a blue dress and a little coat, pink but tight about the waist.'

'You've an eye for that. Would you say they were made clothes or store-bought?'

'Oh, I think store-bought.'

'You would not know,' Liza said firmly. 'You thought the travelling suit Dessie made to go to San Jose was store-bought.'

'Dessie's the clever love,' said Samuel. 'A needle sings in her hands.'

Tom said, 'Dessie's thinking of opening a dressmaking shop in Salinas.'

'She told me,' Samuel said. 'She'd make a great success of it.'

'Salinas?' Liza put her hands on her hips. 'Dessie didn't tell me.'

'I'm afraid we've done bad service to our dearie,' Samuel said. 'Here she wanted to save it for a real tin-plate surprise to her mother and we've leaked it like wheat from a mouse-hole sack.'

'She might have *told* me,' said Liza. 'I don't like surprises. Well, go on – what was she doing?'

'Who?'

'Why, Mrs Trask, of course.'

'Doing? Why, sitting, in a chair under an oak tree. Her time's not far.'

'Her hands, Samuel, her hands – what was she doing with her hands?'

Samuel searched his memory. 'Nothing, I guess. I remember – she had little hands and she held them clasped in her lap.'

Liza sniffed. 'Not sewing, not mending, not knitting?'

'No, Mother.'

'I don't know that it's a good idea for you to go over there. Riches and idleness, devil's tools, and you've not a very sturdy resistance.'

Samuel raised his head and laughed with pleasure. Sometimes his wife delighted him, but he could never tell her how. 'It's only the riches I'll be going there for, Liza. I meant to tell you after breakfast so you could sit down to hear. He wants me to bore four or five wells for him, and maybe put windmills and storage tanks.'

'Is it all talk? Is it a windmill turned by water? Will he pay you or will you come back excusing as usual. "He'll pay when his crops comes in," ' she mimicked. ' "He'll pay when his rich uncle dies." It's my experience, Samuel, and should be yours, that if they don't pay presently they never pay at all. We could buy a valley farm with your promises.'

'Adam Trask will pay,' said Samuel. 'He's well fixed. His father left him a fortune. It's a whole winter of work, Mother. We'll lay something by and we'll have a Christmas to scrape the stars. He'll pay fifty cents a foot, and the windmills, Mother. I can make everything but the casings right here. I'll need the boys to help. I want to take Tom and Joe.'

'Joe can't go,' she said. 'You know he's delicate.'

'I thought I might scrape off some of his delicacy. He can starve on delicacy.'

'Joe can't go,' she said finally. 'And who is to run the ranch while you and Tom are gone?'

'I thought I'd ask George to come back. He doesn't like a clerk's job even if it is in King City.'

'Like it he may not, but he can take a measure of discomfort for eight dollars a week.'

'Mother,' Samuel cried, 'here's our chance to scratch our name in the First National Bank! Don't throw the weight of your tongue in the path of fortune. Please, Mother!'

She grumbled to herself all morning over her work while Tom and Samuel went over the boring equipment, sharpened bits, drew sketches of windmills new in design, and measured for timbers and redwood water-tanks. In the mid-morning Joe came out to join them, and he became so fascinated that he asked Samuel to let him go.

Samuel said, 'Off-hand I'd say I'm against it, Joe. Your mother needs you here.'

'But I want to go, Father. And don't forget, next year I'll be going to college in Palo Alto. And that's going away, isn't it? Please let me go. I'll work hard.'

'I'm sure you would if you could come. But I'm against it. And when you talk to your mother about it, I'll thank you to let it slip that I'm against it. You might even throw in that I refused you.'

Joe grinned, and Tom laughed aloud.

'Will you let her persuade you?' Tom asked.

Samuel scowled at his sons. 'I'm a hard-opinioned man,' he said. 'Once I've set my mind, oxen can't stir me. I've looked at it from all angles and my word is – Joe can't go. You wouldn't want to make a liar of my word, would you?'

'I'll go and talk to her now,' said Joe.

'Now, son, take it easy,' Samuel called after him. 'Use your head. Let her do most of it. Meanwhile I'll set my stubborn up.'

Two days later the big wagon pulled away, loaded with timbers and tackle. Tom drove four horses, and beside him Samuel and Joe sat swinging their feet.

CHAPTER 17

I

WHEN I said Cathy was a monster it seemed to me that it was so. Now I have bent close with a glass over the small print of her and re-read the footnotes, and I wonder if it was true. The trouble is that since we cannot know what she wanted, we will never know whether or not she got it. If, rather than running towards something, she ran away from something, we can't know whether she escaped. Who knows but that she tried to tell someone or everyone what she was like and could not, for lack of a common language? Her life may have been her language, formal, developed, indecipherable. It is easy to say she was bad, but there is little meaning unless we know why.

I've built the image in my mind of Cathy, sitting quietly waiting for her pregnancy to be over, living on a farm she did not like, with a man she did not love.

She sat in her chair under the oak tree, her hands clasped each to each in love and shelter. She grew very big – abnormally big, even at a time when women gloried in big babies and counted extra pounds with pride. She was misshapen; her belly, tight and heavy and distended, made it impossible for her to stand without supporting herself with her hands. But the great lump was local. Shoulders, neck, arms, hands, face, were unaffected, slender and girlish. Her breasts did not grow and her nipples did not darken. There was no quickening of milk glands, no physical planning to feed the newborn. When she sat behind a table you could not see that she was pregnant at all.

In that day there was no measuring of pelvic arch, no testing of blood, no building with calcium. A woman gave a tooth for a child. It was the law. And a woman was likely to have strange tastes, some said for filth, and it was set down to the Eve nature still under sentence for original sin.

Cathy's odd appetite was simple compared to some. The carpenters, repairing the old house, complained that they could not keep the lumps of chalk with which they coated their chalk lines. Again and again the scored hunks disappeared. Cathy stole them and broke them in little pieces. She carried the chips in her apron pocket, and when no one was about she crushed the soft lime between her teeth. She spoke very little. Her eyes were

176

remote. It was as though she had gone away, leaving a breathing doll to conceal her absence.

Activity surged around her. Adam went happily about building and planning his Eden. Samuel and his boys brought in a well at forty feet and put down the new-fangled expensive metal casing, for Adam wanted the best.

The Hamiltons moved their rig and started another hole. They slept in a tent beside the work and cooked over a campfire. But there was always one or another of them riding home for a tool or with a message.

Adam fluttered like a bewildered bee confused by too many flowers. He sat by Cathy and chatted about the pieplant roots just come in. He sketched for her the new fan blade Samuel had invented for the windmill. It had a variable pitch and was an unheard-of thing. He rode out to the well rig and slowed the work with his interest. And naturally, as he discussed wells with Cathy, his talk was all of birth and child care at the well head. It was a good time for Adam, the best time. He was the king of his wide and spacious life. And summer passed into a hot and fragrant autumn.

11

The Hamiltons at the well rig had finished their lunch of Liza's bread and rat cheese and venomous coffee cooked in a can over the fire. Joe's eyes were heavy and he was considering how he could get away into the brush to sleep for a while.

Samuel knelt in the sandy soil, looking at the torn and broken edges of his bit. Just before they had stopped for lunch the drill had found something thirty feet down that had mangled the steel as though it were lead. Samuel scraped the edge of the blade with his pocket-knife and inspected the scrapings in the palm of his hand. His eyes shone with a childlike excitement. He held out his hand and poured the scrapings into Tom's hand.

'Take a look at it, son. What do you think it is?'

Joe wandered over from his place in front of the tent. Tom studied the fragments in his hand. 'Whatever it is, it's hard,' he said. 'Couldn't be a diamond that big. Looks like metal. Do you think we've bored into a buried locomotive?'

His father laughed. 'Thirty feet down,' he said admiringly.

'It looks like tool steel,' said Tom. 'We haven't got anything that can touch it.' Then he saw the far-away joyous look on his

177

father's face and a shiver of shared delight came to him. The Hamilton children loved it when their father's mind went free. Then the world was peopled with wonders.

Samuel said, 'Metal, you say. You think, steel. Tom, I'm going to make a guess and then I'm going to get an assay. Now hear my guess – and remember it. I think we'll find nickel in it, and silver maybe, and carbon and manganese. How I would like to dig it up! It's in sea sand. That's what we've been getting.'

Tom said, 'Say, what do you think it is with – nickel and silver — '

'It must have been long thousand centuries ago,' Samuel said, and his sons knew he was seeing it. 'Maybe it was all water here – an inland sea with the seabirds circling and crying. And it would have been a pretty thing if it happened at night. There would come a line of light and then a pencil of white light and then a tree of blinding light drawn in a long arc from heaven. Then there'd be a great waterspout and a big mushroom of steam. And your ears would be staggered by the sound because the roaring cry of its coming would be on you at the same time the water exploded. And then it would be black night again because of the blinding light. And gradually you'd see the killed fish coming up, showing silver in the starlight, and the crying birds would come to eat them. It's a lonely, lovely thing to think about, isn't it?'

He made them see it as he always did.

Tom said softly, 'You think it's a meteorite, don't you?'

'That I do, and we can prove it by assay.'

Joe said eagerly, 'Let's dig it up.'

'You dig it, Joe, while we bore for water.'

Tom said seriously, 'If the assay showed enough nickel and silver, wouldn't it pay to mine it?'

'You're my own son,' said Samuel. 'We don't know whether it's big as a house or little as a hat.'

'But we could probe down and see.'

'That we could if we did it secretly and hid our thinking under a pot.'

'Why, what do you mean?'

'Now, Tom, have you no kindness towards your mother? We give her enough trouble, son. She's told me plain that if I spend any more money patenting things, she'll give us trouble to remember. Have pity on her! Can't you see her shame when you ask her what we're doing? She's a truthful woman, your mother. She'd have to say, "They're at digging up a star." ' He laughed happily. 'She'd never live it down. And she'd make us smart. No pies for three months.'

Tom said, 'We can't get through it. We'll have to move to another place.'

'I'll put some blasting powder down,' said his father, 'and if that doesn't crack it aside we'll start a new hole.' He stood up. 'I'll have to go home for powder and to sharpen the drill. Why don't you boys ride along with me and we'll give Mother a surprise so that she'll cook the whole night and complain. That way she'll dissemble her pleasure.'

Joe said, 'Somebody's coming, coming fast.' And indeed they could see a horseman riding towards them at full gallop, but a curious horseman who flopped about on his mount like a tied chicken. When he came a little closer they saw that it was Lee, his elbows waving like wings, his queue lashing about like a snake. It was surprising that he stayed on at all and still drove the horse at full tilt. He pulled up, breathing heavily. 'Missy Adam say come! Miss Cathy bad – come quick, Missy yell, scream.'

Samuel said, 'Hold on, Lee. When did it start?'

'Mebbe bleakfus time.'

'All right. Calm yourself. How is Adam?'

'Missy Adam clazy. Cly – laugh —make vomit.'

'Sure,' said Samuel. 'These new fathers. I was one once. Tom, throw a saddle on for me, will you?'

Joe said, 'What is it?'

'Why, Mrs Trask is about to have her baby. I told Adam I'd stand by.'

'You?' Joe asked.

Samuel levelled his eyes on his youngest son. 'I brought both of you into the world,' he said. 'And you've given no evidence you think I did a bad service to the world. Tom, you get all the tools gathered up. And go back to the ranch and sharpen the metal. Bring back the box of powder that's on the shelf in the tool-shed, and go easy with it as you love your arms and legs. Joe, I want you to stay here and look after things.'

Joe said plaintively, 'But what will I do here alone?'

Samuel was silent for a moment. Then he said, 'Joe, do you love me?'

'Why, sure.'

'If you heard I'd committed some great crime, would you turn me over to the police?'

'What are you talking about?'

'Would you?'

'No.'

'All right, then. In my basket, under my clothes, you'll find two books – new, so be gentle with them. It's two volumes by a man the world is going to hear from. You can start reading if you want and it will raise up your lid a little. It's called *The Principles of Psychology* and it's by an Eastern man named William James. No relation to the train robber. And, Joe, if you ever let on about the books I'll run you off the ranch. If your mother ever found out I spent the money on them she'd run me off the ranch.'

Tom led a saddled horse to him. 'Can I read it next?'

'Yes,' said Samuel, and he slipped his leg lightly over the saddle. 'Come on, Lee.'

The Chinese wanted to break into a gallop, but Samuel restrained him. 'Take it easy, Lee. Birthing takes longer than you think, mostly.'

For a time they rode in silence, and then Lee said, 'I'm sorry you bought those books. I have the condensed form, in one volume, the textbook. You should have borrowed it.'

'Have you now? Do you have many books?'

'Not many here – thirty or forty. But you're welcome to any of them you haven't read.'

'Thank you, Lee. And you may be sure I'll look the first moment I can. You know, you could talk to my boys. Joe's a little flighty, but Tom's all right and it would do him good.'

'It's a hard bridge to cross, Mr Hamilton. Makes me timid to talk to a new person, but I'll try if you say so.'

They walked the horses rapidly towards the little draw of the Trask place. Samuel said, 'Tell me, how is it with the mother?'

'I'd rather you saw for yourself and thought for yourself,' Lee said. 'You know, when a man lives alone as much as I do, his mind can go off on an irrational tangent just because his social world is out of kilter.'

'Yes, I know. But I'm not lonely and I'm on a tangent too. But maybe not the same one.'

'You don't think I imagine it, then?'

'I don't know what it is, but I'll tell you for your reassurance that I've a sense of strangeness.'

'I guess that's all it is with me too,' said Lee. He smiled. 'I'll tell you how far it got with me, though. Since I've come here I find myself thinking of Chinese fairy tales my father told me. We Chinese have a well-developed demonology.'

'You think she is a demon?'

'Of course not,' said Lee. 'I hope I'm a little beyond such silliness. I don't know what it is. You know, Mr Hamilton, a servant develops an ability to taste the wind and judge the climate of the house he works in. And there's a strangeness here. Maybe that's what makes me remember my father's demons.'

'Did your father believe in them?'

'Oh, no. He thought I should know the background. You Occidentals perpetuate a good many myths too.'

Samuel said, 'Tell me what happened to set you off. This morning, I mean.'

'If you weren't coming I would try,' said Lee. 'But I would rather not. You can see for yourself. I may be crazy. Of course Mr Adam is strung so tight he may snap like a banjo string.'

'Give me a little hint. It might save time. What did she do?'

'Nothing. That's just it. Mr Hamilton, I've been at births before, a good many of them, but this is something new to me.'

'How?'

'It's – well – I'll tell you the one thing I can think of. This is much more like a bitter, deadly combat than a birth.'

As they rode into the draw and under the oak trees Samuel said, 'I hope you haven't got me in a state, Lee. It's a strange day, and I don't know why.'

'No wind,' said Lee. 'It's the first day in the month when there hasn't been wind in the afternoon.'

'That's so. You know, I've been so close to the details I've paid no attention to the clothing of the day. First we find a buried star and now we go to dig up a mint-new human.' He looked up through the oak branches at the yellow-lit hills. 'What a beautiful day to be born in!' he said. 'If signs have their fingers on a life, it's a sweet life coming. And, Lee, if Adam plays true, he'll be in the way. Stay close, will you? In case I need something. Look, the men, the carpenters, are sitting under that tree.'

'Mr Adam stopped the work. He thought the hammering might disturb his wife.'

Samuel said, 'You stay close. That sounds like Adam playing true. He doesn't know his wife probably couldn't hear God Himself beating a tattoo on the sky.'

The workmen sitting under the tree waved to him. 'How do, Mr Hamilton. How's your family?'

'Fine, fine. Say, isn't that Rabbit Holman? Where've you been, Rabbit?'

181

'Went prospecting, Mr Hamilton.'

'Find anything, Rabbit?'

'Hell, Mr Hamilton, I couldn't even find the mule I went out with.'

They rode on towards the house. Lee said quickly, 'If you ever get a minute, I'd like to show you something.'

'What is it, Lee?'

'Well, I've been trying to translate some old Chinese poetry into English. I'm not sure it can be done. Will you take a look?'

'I'd like to, Lee. Why, that would be a treat for me.'

III

Bordoni's white frame house was very quiet, almost broodingly quiet, and the blinds were pulled down. Samuel dismounted at the stoop, untied his bulging saddlebags, and gave his horse to Lee. He knocked and got no answer and went in. It was dusky in the living-room after the outside light. He looked in the kitchen, scrubbed to the wood grain by Lee. A grey stoneware pilon coffee-pot grunted on the back of the stove. Samuel tapped lightly on the bedroom door and went in.

It was almost pitch-black inside, for not only were the blinds down but blankets were tacked over the windows. Cathy was lying in the big four-poster bed, and Adam sat beside her, his face buried in the coverlet. He raised his head and looked blindly out.

Samuel said pleasantly, 'Why are you sitting in the dark?'

Adam's voice was hoarse. 'She doesn't want the light. It hurts her eyes.'

Samuel walked into the room and authority grew in him with each step. 'There will have to be light,' he said. 'She can close her eyes. I'll tie a black cloth over them if she wants.' He moved to the window and grasped the blanket to pull it down, but Adam was upon him before he could yank.

'Leave it. The light hurts her,' he said fiercely.

Samuel turned on him. 'Now, Adam, I know what you feel. I promised you I'd take care of things, and I will. I only hope one of those things isn't you.' He pulled the blanket down and rolled up the blind to let the golden afternoon light in.

Cathy made a little mewing sound from the bed, and Adam went to her. 'Close your eyes, dear. I'll put a cloth over your eyes.'

Samuel dropped his saddlebags in a chair and stood beside the bed. 'Adam,' he said firmly, 'I'm going to ask you to go out of the room and to stay out.'

'No, I can't. Why?'

'Because I don't want you in the way. It's considered a sweet practice for you to get drunk.'

'I couldn't.'

Samuel said, 'Anger's a slow thing in me and disgust is slower, but I can taste the beginnings of both of them. You'll get out of the room and give me no trouble or I'll go away and you'll have a basket of trouble.'

Adam went finally, and from the doorway Samuel called, 'And I don't want you bursting in if you hear anything. You wait for me to come out.' He closed the door, noticed there was a key in the lock, and turned it. 'He's an upset, vehement man,' he said. 'He loves you.'

He had not looked at her closely until now. And he saw true hatred in her eyes, unforgiving, murderous hatred.

'It'll be over before long, dearie. Now tell me, has the water broke?'

Her hostile eyes glared at him and her lips raised snarling from her little teeth. She did not answer him.

He stared at her. 'I did not come by choice except as a friend,' he said. 'It's not a pleasure to me, young woman. I don't know your trouble and minute by minute I don't care. Maybe I can save you some pain – who knows? I'm going to ask you one more question. If you don't answer, if you put that snarling look on me I'm going out and leave you to welter.'

The words struck into her understanding like lead shot dropped in water. She made a great effort. And it gave him a shivering to see her face change, the steel leave her eyes, the lips thicken from line to bow, and the corners turn up. He noticed a movement of her hands, the fists unclench and the fingers turn pinkly upwards. Her face became young and innocent and bravely hurt. It was like one magic-lantern slide taking the place of another.

She said softly, 'The water broke at dawn.'

'That's better. Have you had hard labour?'

'Yes.'

'How far apart?'

'I don't know.'

'Well, I've been in this room fifteen minutes.'

'I've had two little ones – no big ones since you came.'

'Fine. Now where's your linen?'

'In that hamper over there.'

'You'll be all right, dearie,' he said gently.

He opened his saddlebags and took out a thick rope covered with blue velvet and looped at either end. On the velvet hundreds of little pink flowers were embroidered. 'Liza sent you her pulling rope to use,' he said. 'She made it when our first-born was preparing. What with our children and friends', this rope has pulled a great number of people into the world.' He slipped one of the loops over each of the footposts of the bed.

Suddenly her eyes glazed and her back arched like a spring and the blood started to her cheeks. He waited for her cry or scream and looked apprehensively at the closed door. But there was no scream – only a series of grunting squeals. After a few seconds her body relaxed and the hatefulness was back in her face.

The labour struck again. 'There's a dear,' he said soothingly. 'Was it one or two? I don't know. The more you see, the more you learn no two are alike. I'd better get my hands washed.'

Her head threshed from side to side. 'Good, good, my darling,' he said. 'I think it won't be long till your baby's here.' He put his hand on her forehead where her scar showed dark and angry. 'How did you get the hurt on your head?' he asked.

Her head jerked up and her sharp teeth fastened on his hand across the back and up into the palm near the little finger. He cried out in pain and tried to pull his hands away, but her jaw was set and her head twisted and turned, mangling his hand the way a terrier worries a sack. A shrill snarling came from her set teeth. He slapped her on the cheek and it had no effect. Automatically he did what he would have done to stop a dog fight. His left hand went to her throat and he cut off her wind. She struggled and tore at his hand before her jaws unclenched and he pulled his hand free. The flesh was torn and bleeding. He stepped back from the bed and looked at the damage her teeth had done. He looked at her with fear. And when he looked, her face was calm again and young and innocent.

'I'm sorry,' she said quickly. 'Oh, I'm sorry.'

Samuel shuddered.

'It was the pain,' she said.

Samuel laughed shortly. 'I'll have to muzzle you, I guess,' he said. 'A collie bitch did the same to me once.' He saw the hatred look out of her eyes for a second and then retreat.

Samuel said, 'Have you got anything to put on it? Humans are more poisonous than snakes.'

'I don't know.'

'Well, have you got any whisky? I'll pour some whisky on it.'

'In the second drawer.'

He splashed whisky on his bleeding hand and kneaded the flesh against the alcohol sting. A strong quaking was in his stomach and a sickness rose up against his eyes. He took a swallow of whisky to steady himself. He dreaded to look back at the bed. 'My hand won't be much good for a while,' he said.

Samuel told Adam afterwards, 'She must be made of whalebone. The birth happened before I was ready. Popped like a seed. I'd not the water ready to wash him. Why, she didn't even touch the pulling rope to bear down. Pure whalebone, she is.' He tore at the door, called Lee and demanded warm water. Adam came charging into the room. 'A boy!'. Samuel cried. 'You've got a boy! Easy,' he said, for Adam had seen the mess in the bed and a green was rising in his face.

Samuel said, 'Send Lee in here. And you, Adam, if you still have the authority to tell your hands and feet what to do, get to the kitchen and make me some coffee. And see the lamps are filled and the chimneys clean.'

Adam turned like a zombie and left the room. In a moment Lee looked in. Samuel pointed to the bundle in a laundry basket. 'Sponge him off in warm water, Lee. Don't let a draught get on him. 'Lord! I wish Liza were here. I can't do everything at once.'

He turned back to the bed. 'Now, dearie, I'll get you cleaned up.'

Cathy was bowed again, snarling in her pain. 'It'll be over in a little,' he said. 'Take a little time for the residue. And you're so quick. Why, you didn't even have to pull on Liza's rope.' He saw something, stared, and went quickly to work. 'Lord God in Heaven, it's another one!'

He worked fast, and as with the first the birth was incredibly quick. And again Samuel tied the cord. Lee took the second baby, washed it, wrapped it, and put it in the basket.

Samuel cleaned the mother and shifted her gently while he changed the linen on the bed. He found in himself a reluctance to look in her face. He worked as quickly as he could, for his bitten hand was stiffening. He drew a clean white sheet up to her chin and raised her to slip a fresh pillow under her head. At last he had to look at her.

Her golden hair was wet with perspiration but her face had

185

changed. It was stony, expressionless. At her throat the pulse fluttered visibly.

'You have two sons,' Samuel said. 'Two fine sons. They aren't alike Each one born separate in his own sack.'

She inspected him coldly and without interest.

Samuel said, 'I'll show your boys to you.'

'No,' she said without emphasis.

'Now, dearie, don't you want to see your sons?'

'No. I don't want them.'

'Oh, you'll change. You're tired now, but you'll change. And I'll tell you now – this birth was quicker and easier than I've seen ever in my life.'

The eyes moved from his face. 'I don't want them. I want you to cover the windows and take the light away.'

'It's weariness. In a few days you'll feel so different you won't remember.'

'I'll remember. Go away. Take them out of the room. Send Adam in.'

Samuel was caught by her tone. There was no sickness, no weariness, no softness. His words came out without his will. 'I don't like you,' he said and wished he could gather the words back into his throat and into his mind. But his words had no effect on Cathy.

'Send Adam in.'

In the little living-room Adam looked vaguely at his sons and went quickly into the bedroom and shut the door. In a moment came the sound of tapping. Adam was nailing the blankets over the windows again.

Lee brought coffee to Samuel. 'That's a bad-looking hand you have there,' he said.

'I know. I'm afraid it's going to give me trouble.'

'Why did she do it?'

'I don't know. She's a strange thing.'

Lee said, 'Mr Hamilton, let me take care of that. You could lose an arm.'

The life went out of Samuel. 'Do what you want, Lee. A frightened sorrow has closed down over my heart. I wish I were a child so I could cry. I'm too old to be afraid like this. And I've not felt such despair since a bird died in my hand by a flowing water long ago.'

Lee left the room and shortly returned, carrying a small ebony box carved with twisting dragons. He sat by Samuel and from his box took a wedge-shaped Chinese razor. 'It will hurt,' he said softly.

186

'I'll try to bear it, Lee.'

The Chinese bit his lips, feeling the inflicted pain in himself while he cut deeply into the hand, opened the flesh around the toothmarks front and back, and trimmed the ragged flesh away until good red blood flowed from every wound. He shook a bottle of yellow emulsion labelled Hall's Cream Salve and poured it into the deep cuts. He saturated a handkerchief with the salve and wrapped the hand. Samuel winced and gripped the chair arm with his good hand.

'It's mostly carbolic acid,' Lee said. 'You can smell it.'

'Thank you, Lee. I'm being a baby to knot up like this.'

'I don't think I could have been so quiet,' said Lee. 'I'll get you another cup of coffee.'

He came back with two cups and sat down by Samuel. 'I think I'll go away,' he said. 'I never went willingly to a slaughter-house.'

Samuel stiffened. 'What do you mean?'

'I don't know. The words came out.'

Samuel shivered. 'Lee, men are fools. I guess I hadn't thought about it, but Chinese men are fools too.'

'What made you doubt it?'

'Oh, maybe because we think of strangers as stronger and better than we are.'

'What do you want to say?'

Samuel said, 'Maybe the foolishness is necessary, the dragon fighting, the boasting, the pitiful courage to be constantly knocking a chip off God's shoulder, and the childish cowardice that makes a ghost of a dead tree beside a darkening road. Maybe that's good and necessary, but—'

'What do you want to say?' Lee repeated patiently.

'I thought some wind had blown up the embers of my foolish mind,' Samuel said. 'And now I hear in your voice that you have it too. I feel wings over this house. I feel a dreadfulness coming.'

'I feel it too.'

'I know you do, and that makes me take less than my usual comfort in my foolishness. This birth was too quick, too easy – like a cat having kittens. And I fear for these kittens. I have dreadful thoughts gnawing to get into my brain.'

'What do you want to say?' Lee asked a third time.

'I want my wife,' Samuel cried. 'No dreams, no ghosts, no foolishness. I want her here. They say miners take canaries into the pits to test the air. Liza has no truck with foolishness.

187

And, Lee, if Liza sees a ghost, it's a ghost and not a fragment of a dream. If Liza feels trouble we'll bar the doors.'

Lee got up and went to the laundry basket and looked down at the babies. He had to peer close, for the light was going fast. 'They're sleeping,' he said.

'They'll be squalling soon enough. Lee, will you hitch up the rig and drive to my place for Liza? Tell her I need her here. If Tom's still there, tell him to mind the place. If not, I'll send him in the morning. And if Liza doesn't want to come, tell her we need a woman's hand here and a woman's clear eyes. She'll know what you mean.'

'I'll do it,' said Lee. 'Maybe we're scaring each other, like two children in the dark.'

'I've thought of that,' Samuel said. 'And, Lee, tell her I hurt my hand at the well head. Do not, for God's sake, tell her how it happened.'

'I'll get some lamps lit and then I'll go,' said Lee. 'It will be a great relief to have her here.'

'That it will, Lee. That it will. She'll let some light into this cellar hole.'

After Lee drove away in the dark, Samuel picked up a lamp in his left hand. He had to set it on the floor to turn the knob of the bedroom door. The room was in pitch-blackness, and the yellow lamplight streamed upward and did not light the bed.

Cathy's voice came strong and edged from the bed. 'Shut the door. I do not want the light. Adam, go out! I want to be in the dark – alone.'

Adam said hoarsely, 'I want to stay with you.'

'I do not want you.'

'I will stay.'

'Then stay. But don't talk any more. Please close the door and take the lamp away.'

Samuel went back to the living-room. He put the lamp on the table by the laundry basket and looked in on the small sleeping faces of the babies. Their eyes were pinched shut and they sniffled a little in discomfort at the light. Samuel put his forefinger down and stroked the hot foreheads. One of the twins opened his mouth and yawned prodigiously and settled back to sleep. Samuel moved the lamp and then went to the front door and opened it and stepped outside. The evening star was so bright that it seemed to flare and crumple as it sank towards the western mountains. The air was still and Samuel could smell the day-heated sage. The night was very dark. Samuel started when he heard a voice speaking out of the blackness.

'How is she?'

'Who is it?' Samuel demanded.

'It's me, Rabbit.' The man emerged and took form in the light from the doorway.

'The mother, Rabbit? Oh, she's fine.'

'Lee said twins.'

'That's right – twin sons. You couldn't want better. I guess Mr Trask will tear the river up by the roots now. He'll bring in a crop of candy canes.'

Samuel didn't know why he changed the subject. 'Rabbit, do you know what we bored into today? A meteorite.'

'What's that, Mr Hamilton?'

'A shooting star that fell a million years ago.'

'You did? Well, think of that! How did you hurt your hand?'

'I almost said on a shooting star.' Samuel laughed. 'But it wasn't that interesting. I pinched it in the tackle.'

'Bad?'

'No, not bad.'

'Two boys,' said Rabbit. 'My old lady will be jealous.'

'Will you come inside and sit, Rabbit?'

'No, no; thank you. I'll get out to sleep. Morning seems to come earlier every year I live.'

'That it does, Rabbit. Good night then.'

Liza Hamilton arrived about four in the morning. Samuel was asleep in his chair, dreaming that he had gripped a red-hot bar of iron and could not let go. Liza awakened him and looked at his hand before she even glanced at the babies. While she did well the things he had done in a lumbering, masculine way, she gave him his orders and packed him off. He was to get up this instant, saddle Doxology, and ride straight for King City. No matter what time it was, he must wake up that good-for-nothing doctor and get his hand treated. If it seemed all right he could go home and wait. And it was a criminal thing to leave your last-born, and he little more than a baby himself, sitting there by a hole in the ground with no one to care for him. It was a matter which might even engage the attention of the Lord God Himself.

If Samuel craved realism and activity, he got it. She had him off the place by dawn. His hand was bandaged by eleven and

189

he was in his own chair at his own table by five in the afternoon, sizzling with fever, and Tom was boiling a hen to make chicken soup for him.

For three days Samuel lay in bed, fighting the fever phantoms and putting names to them too, before his great strength broke down the infection and drove it caterwauling away.

Samuel looked up at Tom with clear eyes and said: 'I'll have to get up,' tried it and sat weakly back, chuckling – the sound he made when any force in the world defeated him. He had an idea that even when beaten he could steal a little victory by laughing at defeat. And Tom brought him chicken soup until he wanted to kill him. The lore has not died out of the world, and you will still find people who believe that soup will cure any hurt or illness and is no bad thing to have for the funeral either.

IV

Liza stayed away a week. She cleaned the Trask house from the top clear down into the grain of the wooden floors. She washed everything she could bend enough to get into a tub and sponged the rest. She put the babies on a working basis and noted with satisfaction that they howled most of the time and began to gain weight. Lee she used like a slave since she didn't quite believe in him. Adam she ignored since she couldn't use him for anything. She did make him wash the windows and then did it again after he had finished.

Liza sat with Cathy just enough to come to the conclusion that she was a sensible girl who didn't talk very much or try to teach her grandmother to suck eggs. She also checked her over and found that she was perfectly healthy, not injured and not sick, and that she would never nurse the twins. 'And just as well too,' she said. 'Those great lummoxes would chew a little thing like you to the bone.' She forgot that she was smaller than Cathy and had nursed every one of her own children.

On Saturday afternoon Liza checked her work, left a list of instructions as long as her arm to cover every possibility from colic to an inroad of grease ants, packed her travelling basket, and had Lee drive her home.

She found her house a stable of filth and abomination and she set to cleaning it with the violence and disgust of a Hercules at labour. Samuel asked questions of her in flight.

190

How were the babies?

They were fine, growing.

How was Adam?

Well, he moved around as if he was alive but he left no evidence. The Lord in his wisdom gave money to very curious people, perhaps because they'd starve without.

How was Mrs Trask?

Quiet, lackadaisical, like most rich Eastern women (Liza had never known a rich Eastern woman), but on the other hand docile and respectful. 'And it's a strange thing,' Liza said. 'I can find no real fault with her save perhaps a touch of laziness, and I don't like her very much. Maybe it's that scar. How did she get it?'

'I don't know,' said Samuel.

Liza levelled her forefinger like a pistol between his eyes. 'I'll tell you something. Unbeknowst to herself, she's put a spell on her husband. He moons around her like a sick duck. I don't think he's given the twins a thorough good look yet.'

Samuel waited until she went by again. He said, 'Well, if she's lazy and he's moony, who's going to take care of the sweet babies? Twin boys take a piece of looking after.'

Liza stopped in mid-swoop, drew a chair close to him, and sat resting her hands on her knees. 'Remember I've never held the truth lightly if you don't believe me,' she said.

'I don't think you could lie, dearie,' he said, and she smiled, thinking it a compliment.

'Well, what I'm to tell you might weigh a little heavy on your belief if you did not know that.'

'Tell me.'

'Samuel, you know that Chinese with his slanty eyes and his outlandish talk and that braid?'

'Lee? Sure I know him.'

'Well, wouldn't you say off-hand he was a heathen?'

'I don't know.'

'Come now, Samuel, anybody would. But he's not.' She straightened up.

'What is he?'

She tapped his arm with an iron finger. 'A Presbyterian, and well up – well up, I say, when you dig it out of that crazy talk. Now what do you think of that?'

Samuel's voice was unsteady with trying to clamp his laughter in. 'No!' he said.

'And I say yes. Well now, who do you think is looking after

the twins? I wouldn't trust a heathen from here to omega – but a Presbyterian – he learned everything I told him.'

'No wonder they're taking on weight,' said Samuel.

'It's a matter for praise and it's a matter for prayer.'

'We'll do it too,' said Samuel. 'Both.'

v

For a week Cathy rested and gathered her strength. On Saturday of the second week of October she stayed in her bedroom all morning. Adam tried the door and found it locked.

'I'm busy,' she called, and he went away.

Putting her bureau in order, he thought, for he could hear her opening drawers and closing them.

In the later afternoon Lee came to Adam where he sat on the stoop. 'Missy say I go King City buy nursery bottle,' he said uneasily.

'Well, do it then,' said Adam. 'She's your mistress.'

'Missy say not come back mebbe Monday. Take —'

Cathy spoke calmly from the doorway. 'He hasn't had a day off for a long time. A rest would do him good.'

'Of course,' said Adam. 'I just didn't think of it. Have a good time. If I need anything I'll get one of the carpenters.'

'Men go home, Sunday.'

'I'll get the Indian. Lopez will help.'

Lee felt Cathy's eyes on him. 'Lopez dlunk. Find bottle whisky.'

Adam said petulantly, 'I'm not helpless, Lee. Stop arguing.'

Lee looked at Cathy standing in the doorway. He lowered his eyelids. 'Mebbe I come back late,' he said, and he thought he saw two dark lines appear between her eyes and then disappear. He turned away. 'Goo-by,' he said.

Cathy went back to her room as the evening came down. At seven-thirty Adam knocked. 'I've got you some supper, dear. It's not much.' The door opened as though she had been standing waiting. She was dressed in her neat travelling dress, the jacket edged in black braid, black velvet lapels, and large jet buttons. On her head was a wide straw hat with a tiny crown; long jet-headed hatpins held it on. Adam's mouth dropped open.

She gave him no chance to speak. 'I'm going away now.'

'Cathy, what do you mean?'

'I told you before.'

'You didn't.'

'You didn't listen. It doesn't matter.'

'I don't believe you.'

Her voice was dead and metallic. 'I don't give a damn what you believe. I'm going.'

'The babies —'

'Throw them in one of your wells.'

He cried in panic, 'Cathy, you're sick. You can't go – not from me – not from me.'

'I can do anything to you. Any woman can do anything to you. You're a fool.'

The word got through his haze. Without warning, his hands reached for her shoulders and he thrust her backwards. As she staggered he took the key from the inside of the door, slammed the door shut, and locked it.

He stood panting, his ear close to the panel, and a hysterical sickness poisoned him. He could hear her moving quietly about. A drawer was opened, and the thought leaped in him – she's going to stay. And then there was a little click he could not place. His ear was almost touching the door.

Her voice came from so near that he jerked his head back. He heard richness in her voice. 'Dear,' she said softly, 'I didn't know you would take it so. I'm sorry, Adam.'

His breath burst hoarsely out of his throat. His hand trembled, trying to turn the key, and it fell out on the floor after he had turned it. He pushed the door open. She stood three feet away. In her right hand she held his .44 Colt, and the black hole of the barrel pointed at him. He took a step towards her, saw that the hammer was back.

She shot him. The heavy slug struck him in the shoulder and flattened and tore out a piece of his shoulder-blade. The flash and roar smothered him, and he staggered back and fell to the floor. She moved slowly towards him, cautiously, as she might towards a wounded animal. He stared up into her eyes, which inspected him impersonally. She tossed the pistol on the floor beside him and walked out of the house.

He heard her steps on the porch, on the crisp dry oak leaves on the path, and then he could hear her no more. And the monotonous sound that had been there all along was the cry of the twins, wanting their dinner. He had forgotten to feed them.

CHAPTER 18

I

HORACE QUINN was the new deputy sheriff appointed to look after things around the King City district. He complained that his new job took him away from his ranch too much. His wife complained even more, but the truth of the matter was that nothing much had happened in a criminal way since Horace had been deputy. He had seen himself making a name for himself and running for sheriff. The sheriff was an important officer. His job was less flighty than that of district attorney, almost as permanent and dignified as superior court judge. Horace didn't want to stay on the ranch all his life, and his wife had an urge to live in Salinas, where she had relatives.

When the rumours, repeated by the Indian and the carpenters, that Adam Trask had been shot reached Horace, he saddled up right away and left his wife to finish butchering the pig he had killed that morning.

Just north of the big sycamore tree where the Hester road turns off to the left, Horace met Julius Euskadi. Julius was trying to decide whether to go quail hunting or to King City and catch the train to Salinas to shake some of the dust out of his britches. The Euskadis were well-to-do, handsome people of Basque extraction.

Julius said, 'If you'd come along with me, I'd go into Salinas. They tell me that right next door to Jenny's, two door from the Long Green, there's a new place called Faye's. I heard it was pretty nice, run like San Francisco. They've got a piano player.'

Horace rested his elbow on his saddle horn and stirred a fly from his horse's shoulder with his rawhide quirt. 'Some other time,' he said. 'I've got to look into something.'

'You wouldn't be going to Trask's, would you?'

'That's right. Did you hear anything about it?'

'Not to make any sense. I heard Mr Trask shot himself in the shoulder with a forty-four and then fired everybody on the ranch. How do you go about shooting yourself in the shoulder with a forty-four, Horace?'

'I don't know. Them Easterners are pretty clever. I thought I'd go up and find out. Didn't his wife just have a baby?'

'Twins, I heard,' said Julius. 'Maybe they shot him.'

'One hold the gun and the other pull the trigger? Hear anything else?'

'All mixed up, Horace. Want some company?'

'I'm not going to deputize you, Julius. Sheriff says the supervisors are raising hell about the pay-roll. Hornby out in the Alisal deputized his great-aunt and kept her in posse three weeks just before Easter.'

'You're fooling!'

'No, I'm not. And you get no star.'

'Hell, I don't want to be a deputy. Just thought I'd ride along with you for company. I'm curious.'

'Me too. Glad to have you, Julius. I can always fling the oath around your neck if there's any trouble. What do you say the new place is called?'

'Faye's. Sacramento woman.'

'They do things pretty nice in Sacramento,' and Horace told how they did things in Sacramento as they rode along.

It was a nice day to be riding. As they turned into the Sanchez draw they were cursing the bad hunting in recent years. Three things are never any good – farming, fishing, and hunting – compared to other years, that is. Julius was saying, 'Christ, I wish they hadn't killed off all the grizzly bears. In eighteen-eighty my grandfather killed one up by Pleyto weighed eighteen hundred pounds.'

A silence came on them as they rode in under the oaks, a silence they took from the place itself. There was no sound, no movement.

'I wonder if he finished fixing up the old house,' Horace said.

'Hell no. Rabbit Holman was working on it, and he told me Trask called them all in and fired them. He told them not to come back.'

'They say Trask has got a pot of money.'

'I guess he's well fixed, all right,' said Julius. 'Sam Hamilton is sinking four wells – if he didn't get fired too.'

'How is Mr Hamilton? I ought to go up to see him.'

'He's fine. Full of hell as ever.'

'I'll have to go up and pay him a visit,' said Horace.

Lee came out on the stoop to meet them.

Horace said, 'Hello, Ching Chong. Bossy man here?'

'He sick,' Lee said.

'I'd like to see him.'

'No see. He sick.'

'That's enough of that,' said Horace. 'Tell him Deputy Sheriff Quinn wants to see him.'

Lee disappeared, and in a moment he was back. 'You come,' he said. 'I take horsy.'

Adam lay in the four-poster bed where the twins had been born. He was propped high with pillows, and a mound of home-devised bandages covered his left breast and shoulder. The room reeked of Hall's Cream Salve.

Horace said later to his wife, 'And if you ever saw death still breathing, there it was.'

Adam's cheeks hugged the bone and pulled the skin of his nose tight and skinny. His eyes seemed to bulge out of his head and to take up the whole upper part of his face, and they were shiny with sickness, tense and myopic. His bony right hand kneaded a fistful of coverlet.

Horace said, 'Howdy, Mr Trask. Heard you got hurt.' He paused, waiting for an answer. He went on, 'Just thought I'd drop around and see how you were doing. How'd it happen?'

A look of transparent eagerness came over Adam's face. He shifted slightly in the bed.

'If it hurts to talk you can whisper,' Horace added helpfully.

'Only when I breathe deep,' Adam said softly. 'I was cleaning my gun and it went off.'

Horace glanced at Julius and then back. Adam saw the look and a little colour of embarrassment rose in his cheeks.

'Happens all the time,' said Horace. 'Got the gun around?'

'I think Lee put it away.'

Horace stepped to the door. 'Hey there, Ching Chong, bring the pistol.'

In a moment Lee poked the gun butt-first through the door. Horace looked at it, swung the cylinder out, poked the cartridges out, and smelled the empty brass cylinder of the one empty shell. 'There's better shooting cleaning the damn things than pointing them. I'll have to make a report to the county, Mr Trask. I won't take up much of your time. You were cleaning the barrel, maybe with a rod, and the gun went off and hit you in the shoulder?'

'That's right, sir,' Adam said quickly.

'And, cleaning it, you hadn't swung out the cylinder?'

'That's right.'

'And you were poking the rod in and out with the barrel pointed towards you with the hammer cocked?'

Adam's breath rasped in a quick intake.

196

Horace went on, 'And it must have blowed the rod right through you and took off your left hand too.' Horace's pale sun-washed eyes never left Adam's face. He said kindly, 'What happened, Mr Trask? Tell me what happened.'

'I tell you truly it was an accident, sir.'

'Now you wouldn't have me write a report like I just said. The sheriff would think I was crazy. What happened?'

'Well, I'm not very used to guns. Maybe it wasn't just like that, but I was cleaning it and it went off.'

There was a whistle in Horace's nose. He had to breathe through his mouth to stop it. He moved slowly up from the foot of the bed, nearer to Adam's head and staring eyes. 'You came from the East not very long ago, didn't you, Mr Trask?'

'That's right. Connecticut.'

'I guess people don't use guns very much there any more.'

'Not much.'

'Little hunting?'

'Some.'

'So you'd be more used to a shotgun?'

'That's right. But I never hunted much.'

'I guess you didn't hardly use a pistol at all, so you didn't know how to handle it.'

'That's right,' Adam said eagerly. 'Hardly anybody there has a pistol.'

'So when you came here you bought that forty-four because everybody out here has a pistol and you were going to learn how to use it.'

'Well, I thought it might be a good thing to learn.'

Julius Euskadi stood tensely, his face and body receptive, listening but uncommunicative.

Horace sighed and looked away from Adam. His eyes brushed over and past Julius and came back to his hands. He laid the gun on the bureau and carefully lined the brass and lead cartridges beside it. 'You know,' he said, 'I've only been a deputy a little while. I thought I was going to have some fun with it and maybe in a few years run for sheriff. I haven't got the guts for it. It isn't any fun to me.'

Adam watched him nervously.

'I don't think anybody's ever been afraid of me before – mad at me, yes – but not afraid. It's a mean thing, makes me feel mean.'

Julius said irritably, 'Get to it. You can't resign right this minute.'

'The hell I can't – if I want to. All right! Mr Trask, you served in the United States Cavalry. The weapons of the cavalry are carbines and pistols. You —' He stopped and swallowed. 'What happened, Mr Trask?'

Adam's eyes seemed to grow larger, and they were moist and edged with red. 'It was an accident,' he whispered.

'Anybody see it? Was your wife with you when it happened?'

Adam did not reply, and Horace saw that his eyes were closed. 'Mr Trask,' he said. 'I know you're a sick man. I'm trying to make it as easy on you as I can. Why don't you rest now while I have a talk with your wife?' He waited a moment and then turned to the doorway, where Lee still stood. 'Ching Chong, tell Missy I would admire to talk to her a few minutes.'

Lee did not reply.

Adam spoke without opening his eyes. 'My wife is away on a visit.'

'She wasn't here when it happened?' Horace glanced at Julius and saw a curious expression on Julius's lips. The corners of his mouth were turned slightly up in a sardonic smile. Horace thought quicky, 'He's ahead of me. He'd make a good sheriff.' 'Say,' he said, 'that's kind of interesting. Your wife had a baby – two babies – two weeks ago, and now she's gone on a visit. Did she take the babies with her? I thought I heard them a little while ago.' Horace leaned over the bed and touched the back of Adam's clenched right hand. 'I hate this, but I can't stop now. Trask!' he said loudly, 'I want you to tell me what happened. This isn't nosiness. This is the law. Now, damn it, you open your eyes and tell me or, by Christ, I'll take you in to the sheriff even if you are hurt.'

Adam opened his eyes, and they were blank like a sleep-walker's eyes. And his voice came out without rise or fall, without emphasis, and without any emotion. It was as though he pronounced perfectly words in a language he did not understand.

'My wife went away,' he said.

'Where did she go?'

'I don't know.'

'What do you mean?'

'I don't know where she went.'

Julius broke in, speaking for the first time. 'Why did she go?'

'I don't know.'

Horace said angrily, 'You watch it, Trask. You're playing

pretty close to the edge and I don't like what I'm thinking. You must know why she went away.'

'I don't know why she went.'

'Was she sick? Did she act strange?'

'No.'

Horace turned. 'Ching Chong, do you know anything about this?'

'I go King City Satdy. Come back mebbe twelve night. Find Missy Tlask on floor.'

'So you weren't here when it happened?'

'No, ma'am.'

'All right, Trask, I'll have to get back to you. Open up that blind a little, Ching Chong, so I can see. There, that's better. Now I'm going to do it your way first until I can't any more. Your wife went away. Did she shoot you?'

'It was an accident.'

'All right, an accident, but was the gun in her hand?'

'It was an accident.'

'You don't make it very easy. But let's say she went away and we have to find her – see? – like a kid's game. You're making it that way. How long have you been married?'

'Nearly a year.'

'What was her name before you married her?'

There was a long pause, and then Adam said softly, 'I won't tell. I promised.'

'Now you watch it. Where did she come from?'

'I don't know.'

'Mr Trask, you're talking yourself right into the county jail. Let's have a description. How tall was she?'

Adam's eyes gleamed. 'Not tall – little and delicate.'

'That's just fine. What colour hair? Eyes?'

'She was beautiful.'

'Was.'

'Is.'

'Any scars?'

'Oh, God, no. Yes – a scar on her forehead.'

'You don't know her name, where she came from, where she went, and you can't describe her. And you think I'm a fool.'

Adam said, 'She had a secret. I promised I wouldn't ask her. She was afraid for someone.' And without warning Adam began to cry. His whole body shook, and his breath made little sounds. It was hopeless crying.

Horace felt misery rising in him. 'Come on in the other room,

Julius,' he said, and led the way into the living-room. 'All right, Julius, tell me what you think. Is he crazy?'

'I don't know.'

'Did he kill her?'

'That's what jumped into my mind.'

'Mine too,' said Horace. 'My God!' He hurried into the bedroom and came back with the pistol and the shells. 'I forgot them,' he apologized. 'I won't last long in this job.'

Julius asked, 'What are you going to do?'

'Well, I think it's beyond me. I told you I wouldn't put you on the pay-roll, but hold up your right hand.'

'I don't want to get sworn in, Horace. I want to go to Salinas.'

'You don't have any chance, Julius. I'll have to arrest you if you don't get your goddam hand up.'

Julius reluctantly put up his hand and disgustedly repeated the oath. 'And that's what I get for keeping you company,' he said. 'My father will skin me alive. All right, what do we do now?'

Horace said, 'I'm going to run to papa. I need the sheriff. I'd take Trask in, but I don't want to move him. You've got to stay, Julius. I'm sorry. Have you got a gun?'

'Hell, no.'

'Well, take this one, and take my star.' He unpinned it from his shirt and held it out.

'How long do you think you'll be gone?'

'Not any longer than I can help. Did you ever see Mrs Trask, Julius?'

'No, I didn't.'

'Neither did I. And I've got to tell the sheriff that Trask doesn't know her name or anything. And she's not very big and she is beautiful. That's one hell of a description! I think I'll resign before I tell the sheriff, because he's sure as hell going to fire me afterwards. Do you think he killed her?'

'How the hell do I know?'

'Don't get mad.'

Julius picked up the gun and put the cartridges back in the cylinder and balanced it in his hand. 'You want an idea, Horace?'

'Don't it look like I need one?'

'Well, Sam Hamilton knew her – he took the babies, Rabbit says. And Mrs Hamilton took care of her. Why don't you ride out there on your way and find out what she really looked like.'

'I think maybe you better keep that star,' said Horace. 'That's good. I'll get going.'

'You want me to look around?'

'I want you just to see that he doesn't get away – or hurt himself. Understand? Take care of yourself.'

11

About midnight Horace got on a freight train in King City. He sat up in the cab with the engineer, and he was in Salinas the first thing in the morning. Salinas was the county seat, and it was a fast-growing town. Its population was due to cross the two thousand mark any time. It was the biggest town between San Jose and San Luis Obispo, and everyone felt that a brilliant future was in store for it.

Horace walked up from the Southern Pacific Depot and stopped in the Chop House for breakfast. He didn't want to get the sheriff out so early and rouse ill-will when it wasn't necessary. In the Chop House he ran into young Will Hamilton, looking pretty prosperous in a salt-and-pepper business suit.

Horace sat down at the table with him. 'How are you, Will?'

'Oh, pretty good.'

'Up here on business?'

'Well, yes, I do have a little deal on.'

'You might let me in on something some time.' Horace felt strange talking like this to such a young man, but Will Hamilton had an aura of success about him. Everybody knew he was going to be a very influential man in the county. Some people exude their futures, good or bad.

'I'll do that, Horace. I thought the ranch took all your time.'

'I could be persuaded to rent it if anything turned up.'

Will leaned over the table. 'You know, Horace, our part of the county has been pretty much left out. Did you ever think of running for office?'

'What do you mean?'

'Well, you're a deputy – did you ever think of running for sheriff?'

'Why, no, I didn't.'

'Well, you think about it. Just keep it under your hat. I'll look you up in a couple of weeks and we'll talk about it. But keep it under your hat.'

'I'll certainly do that, Will. But we've got an awful good sheriff.'

'I know. That's got nothing to do with it. King City hasn't got a single county officer – you see?'

'I see. I'll think about it. Oh, by the way I stopped by and saw your father and mother yesterday.'

Will's face lighted up. 'You did? How were they?'

'Just fine. You know, your father is a real comical genius.'

Will chuckled. 'He made us laugh all the time we were growing up.'

'But he's a smart man too, Will. He showed me a new kind of windmill he's invented – goddamdest thing you ever saw.'

'Oh, Lord!' said Will, 'here come the patent attorneys again!'

'But this is good,' said Horace.

'They're all good. And the only people who make any money are the patent lawyers. Drives my mother crazy.'

'I guess you've got a point there.'

Will said, 'The only way to make any money is to sell something somebody else makes.'

'You've got a point there Will, but this is the goddamdest windmill you ever saw.'

'He took you in, did he, Horace?'

'I guess he did. But you wouldn't want him to change, would you?'

'Oh, Lord, no!' said Will. 'You think about what I said.'

'All right.'

'And keep it under your hat,' said Will.

The sheriff's job was not an easy one, and that county which, out of the grab bag of popular elections, pulled a good sheriff was lucky. It was a complicated position. The obvious duties of the sheriff – enforcing the law and keeping the peace – were far from the most important ones. It was true that the sheriff represented armed force in the county, but in a community seething with individuals a harsh or stupid sheriff did not last long. There were water rights, boundary disputes, astray arguments, domestic relations, paternity matters – all to be settled without force of arms. Only when everything else failed did a good sheriff make an arrest. The best sheriff was not the best fighter but the best diplomat. And Monterey County had a good one. He had a brilliant gift for minding his own business.

Horace went into the sheriff's office in the old county jail about ten minutes after nine. The sheriff shook hands and discussed the weather and the crops until Horace was ready to get down to business.

'Well, sir,' Horace said finally, 'I had to come up to get your advice.' And he told his story in great detail – what everybody had said and how they looked and what time it was – everything.

After a few moments the sheriff closed his eyes and laced his fingers together. He punctuated the account occasionally by opening his eyes, but he made no comment.

'Well, there I was on a limb,' Horace said. 'I couldn't find out what happened. I couldn't even find out what the woman looked like. It was Julius Euskadi got the idea I should go to see Sam Hamilton.'

The sheriff stirred, crossed his legs, and inspected the job. 'You think he killed her.'

'Well, I did. But Mr Hamilton kind of talked me out of it. He says Trask hasn't got it in him to kill anybody.'

'Everybody's got it in him,' the sheriff said. 'You just find his trigger and anybody will go off.'

'Mr Hamilton told me some funny things about her. You know, when he was taking her babies she bit him on the hand. You ought to see the hand, like a wolf got him.'

'Did Sam give you a description?'

'He did, and his wife did.' Horace took a piece of paper from his pocket and read a detailed description of Cathy. Between the two of them the Hamiltons knew pretty much everything physical there was to know about Cathy.

When Horace finished, the sheriff sighed. 'They both agreed about the scar?'

'Yes, they did. And both of them remarked about how sometimes it was darker than other times.'

The sheriff closed his eyes again and he leaned back in his chair. Suddenly he straightened up, opened a drawer of his roll-top desk, and took out a pint of whisky. 'Have a drink,' he said.

'Don't mind if I do. Here's looking at you.' Horace wiped his mouth and handed back the pint. 'Got any ideas?' he asked.

The sheriff took three big swallows of whisky, corked the pint, and put it back in the drawer before he replied. 'We've got a pretty well-run county,' he said. 'I get along with the constables, give them a hand when they need it, and they help me out when I need it. You take a town growing like Salinas, and strangers in and out all the time – could have trouble if we didn't watch it pretty close. My office gets along fine with the local people.' He looked Horace in the eye. 'Don't get restless. I'm not making a speech. I just want to tell you how it is. We don't drive people. We've got to live with them.'

'Did I do something wrong?'

'No, you didn't, Horace. You did just right. If you hadn't come to town or if you had brought Mr Trask in, we'd of been in one hell of a mess. Now hold on. I'm going to tell you —'

'I'm listening,' said Horace.

'Over across the tracks down by Chinatown there's a row of whorehouses.'

'I know that.'

'Everybody knows it. If we closed them up they'd just move. The people want those houses. We keep an eye on them so not much bad happens. And the people that run those houses keep in touch with us. I've picked up some wanted men from tips I got down there.'

Horace said, 'Julius told me —'

'Now wait a minute. Let me get all this said so we won't have to go back over it. About three months ago a fine-looking woman came in to see me. She wanted to open a house here and wanted to do it right. Came from Sacramento. Ran a place there. She had letters from some pretty important people – straight record – never had any trouble. A pretty damn good citizen.'

'Julius told me. Name of Faye.'

'That's right. Well, she opened a nice place, quiet, well run. It was about time old Jenny and the Nigger had some competition. They were mad as hell about it, but I told them just what I told you. It's about time they had some competition.'

'There's a piano player.'

'Yes, there is. Good one too – blind fella. Say, are you going to let me tell this?'

'I'm sorry,' said Horace.

'That's all right. I know I'm slow, but I'm thorough. Anyways, Faye turned out to be just what she looks like, a good solid citizen. Now there's one thing a good quiet whorehouse is more scared of than anything else. Take a flighty randy girl runs off from home and goes in a house. Her old man finds her and he begins to shovel up hell. Then the churches get into it, and the women, and pretty soon that whorehouse has got a bad name and we've got to close it up. You understand?'

'Yeah!' Horace said softly.

'Now don't get ahead of me. I hate to tell something you already thought out. Faye sent me a note Sunday night. She's got a girl and she can't make much out of her. What puzzles Faye is that this kid looks like a runaway girl except she's a goddam good whore. She knows all the answers and all the tricks. I went down and looked her over. She told me the usual bull, but I can't find a thing wrong with her. She's of age and nobody's made a complaint.' He spread his hands. 'Well, there it is. What do we do about it?'

'You're pretty sure it's Mrs Trask?'

The sheriff said, 'Wide-set eyes, yellow hair, and a scar on her forehead, and she came in Sunday afternoon.'

Adam's weeping face was in Horace's mind. 'God all mighty! Sheriff, you got to get somebody else to tell him. I'll quit before I do.'

The sheriff gazed into space. 'You say he didn't even know her name, where she came from. She really bull-shitted him, didn't she?'

'The poor bastard,' Horace said. 'The poor bastard is in love with her. No, by God, somebody else has got to tell him. I won't.'

The sheriff stood up. 'Let's go down to the Chop House and get a cup of coffee.'

They walked along the street in silence for a while. 'Horace,' the sheriff said, 'if I told some of the things I know, this whole goddam county would go up in smoke.'

'I guess that's right.'

'You said she had twins?'

'Yeah, twin boys.'

'You listen to me, Horace. There's only three people in the world that knows – her and you and me. I'm going to warn her that if she ever tells I'll brush her arse out of this county so fast it'll burn. And, Horace – if you should ever get an itchy tongue, before you tell anybody, even your wife, why, you think about those little boys finding out their mother is a whore.'

III

Adam sat in his chair under the big oak tree. His left arm was expertly bandaged against his side so that he could not move his shoulder. Lee came out carrying the laundry basket. He set it on the ground beside Adam and went back inside.

The twins were awake, and they both looked blindly and earnestly up at the wind-moved leaves of the oak tree. A dry oak leaf came whirling down and landed in the basket. Adam leaned over and picked it out.

He didn't hear Samuel's horse until it was almost upon him, but Lee had seen him coming. He brought a chair out and led Doxology away towards the shed.

Samuel sat down quietly, and he didn't trouble Adam by looking at him too much, and he didn't trouble him by not looking at him. The wind freshened in the tree-tops and a fringe of it ruffled Samuel's hair. 'I thought I'd better get back to the wells,' Samuel said softly.

Adam's voice had gone rusty from lack of use. 'No,' he said, 'I don't want any wells. I'll pay you for the work you did.'

Samuel leaned over the basket and put his finger against the small palm of one of the twins and the fingers closed and held on. 'I guess the last bad habit a man will give up is advising.'

'I don't want advice.'

'Nobody does. It's a giver's present. Go through the motions, Adam.'

'What motions?'

'Act out being alive like a play. And after a while, a long while, it will be true.'

'Why should I?' Adam asked.

Samuel was looking at the twins. 'You're going to pass something down, no matter what you do or if you do nothing. Even if you let yourself go fallow, the weeds will grow and the brambles. Something will grow.'

Adam did not answer, and Samuel stood up. 'I'll be back,' he said. 'I'll be back again and again. Go through the motions, Adam.'

In the back of the shed Lee held Doxology while Sam mounted. 'There goes your bookstore, Lee,' he said.

'Oh, well,' said the Chinese, 'maybe I didn't want it much, anyway.'

CHAPTER 19

I

A NEW country seems to follow a pattern. First come the openers, strong and brave and rather childlike. They can take care of themselves in a wilderness, but they are naïve and helpless against men, and perhaps that is why they went out in the first place. When the rough edges are worn off the new land, business men and lawyers come in to help with the development – to solve problems of ownership, usually by removing the temptations to themselves. And finally comes culture, which is entertainment, relaxation, transport out of the pain of living. And culture can be on any level, and is.

The church and the whorehouse arrived in the Far West simultaneously. And each would have been horrified to think it was a different facet of the same thing. But surely they were both intended to accomplish the same thing: the singing, the devotion, the poetry of the churches took a man out of his bleakness for a time, and so did the brothels. The sectarian Churches came in swinging, cocky and loud and confident. Ignoring the laws of debt and repayment, they built churches which couldn't be paid for in a hundred years. The sects fought evil, true enough, but they also fought each other with a fine lustiness. They fought at the turn of a doctrine. Each happily believed all the others were bound for hell in a basket. And each for all its bumptiousness brought with it the same thing: the Scripture on which our ethics, our art and poetry, and our relationships are built. It took a smart man to know where the difference lay between the sects, but anyone could see what they had in common. And they brought music – maybe not the best, but the form and sense of it. And they brought conscience, or, rather, nudged the dozing conscience. They were not pure, but they had a potential of purity, like a soiled white shirt. And any man could make something pretty fine of it within himself. True enough, the Reverend Billing, when they caught up with him, turned out to be a thief, an adulterer, a libertine, and a zoophilist, but that didn't change the fact that he had communicated some good things to a great number of receptive people. Billing went to jail, but no one ever arrested the good things he had released. And it doesn't matter much that his motive was impure. He used good material and some of it stuck. I use Billing only as an outrageous example. The honest preachers had energy and go. They fought the devil, no holds barred, boots and eye-gouging permitted. You might get the idea that they howled truth and beauty the way a seal bites out the National Anthem on a row of circus horns. But some of the truth and beauty remained, and the anthem was recognizable. The sects did more than this, though. They built the structure of social life in the Salinas Valley. The church supper is the grandfather of the country club, just as the Thursday poetry reading in the basement under the vestry sired the little theatre.

While the churches, bringing the sweet smell of piety for the soul, came in prancing and farting like brewery horses in bock-beer time, the sister evangelism, with release and joy for the body, crept in silently and greyly, with its head bowed and its face covered.

You may have seen the spangled palaces of sin and fancy dancing in the false West of the movies, and maybe some of them existed – but not in the Salinas Valley. The brothels were quiet, orderly, and circumspect. Indeed, if after hearing the ecstatic shrieks of climactic conversion against the thumping beat of the melodeon you had stood under the window of a whorehouse and listened to the low decorous voices, you would have been likely to confuse the identities of the two ministries. The brothel was accepted while it was not admitted.

I will tell you about the solemn courts of love in Salinas. They were about the same in other towns, but the Salinas Row has a pertinence to this telling.

You walked west on Main Street until it bent. That's where Castroville Street crossed Main. Castroville Street is now called Market Street. God knows why. Streets used to be named for the place they aimed at. Thus Castroville Street, if you followed it nine miles, brought you to Castroville, Alisal Street to Alisal, and so forth.

Anyway, when you came to Castroville Street you turned right. Two blocks down, the Southern Pacific tracks cut diagonally across the street on their way south, and a street crossed Castroville Street from east to west. And for the life of me I cannot remember the name of that street. If you turned left on that street and crossed the tracks you were in Chinatown. If you turned right you were on the Row.

It was a black 'dobe street, deep shining mud in winter and hard as rutted iron in summer. In the spring the tall grass grew along it sides – wild oats and mallow weeds and yellow mustard mixed in. In the early morning the sparrows shrieked over the horse manure in the street.

Do you remember hearing that, old men? And do you remember, how an easterly breeze brought odours in from Chinatown, roasting pork and punk and black tobacco and yen shi? And do you remember the deep blatting stroke of the great gong in the Joss House, and how its tone hung in the air so long?

Remember, too, the little houses, unpainted, unrepaired? They seemed very small, and they tried to efface themselves in outside neglect, and the wild overgrown front yards tried to hide them from the street. Remember how the blinds were always drawn with little lines of yellow light around their edges? You could hear only a murmur from within. Then the front door would open to admit a country boy, and you'd hear laughter and perhaps the soft sentimental tone of an open-face piano with a piece of toilet chain across the strings, and then the door would close it off again.

Then you might hear horses' hoofs on the dirt street, and Pet Bulene would drive his hack up in front, and maybe four or five portly men would get out – great men, rich or official, bankers maybe, or the court-house gang. And Pet would drive round the corner and settle down in his hack to wait for them. Big cats would ripple across the street to disappear in the tall grass.

And then – remember? – the train whistle and the boring light and a freight from King City would go stomping across Castroville Street and into Salinas and you could hear it sighing at the station. Remember?

Every town has its celebrated madams, eternal women to be sentimentalized down the years. There is something very attractive to men about a madam. She combines the brains of a business man, the toughness of a prize-fighter, the warmth of a companion, the humour of a tragedian. Myths collect round her, and, oddly enough, not voluptuous myths. The stories remembered and repeated about a madam cover every field but the bedroom. Remembering, her old customers picture her as philanthropist, medical authority, bouncer, and poetess of the bodily emotions without being involved with them.

For a number of years Salinas had sheltered two of these treasures: Jenny, sometimes called Fartin' Jenny, and the Nigger, who owned and operated the Long Green. Jenny was a good companion, a keeper of secrets, a giver of secret loans. There is a whole literature of stories about Jenny in Salinas.

The Nigger was a handsome, austere woman with snow-white hair and a dark and awful dignity. Her brown eyes, brooding deep in her skull, looked out on an ugly world with philosophic sorrow. She conducted her house like a cathedral dedicated to a sad but erect Priapus. If you wanted a good laugh and a poke in the ribs, you went to Jenny's and got your money's worth; but if the sweet world-sadness close to tears crept out of your immuttable loneliness, the Long Green was your place. When you came out of there you felt that something pretty stern and important had happened. It was no jump in the hay. The dark beautiful eyes of the Nigger stayed with you for days.

When Faye came down from Sacramento and opened her house there was a flurry of animosity from the two incumbents.

They got together to drive Faye out, but they discovered she was not in competition.

Faye was the motherly type, big-breasted, big-hipped, and warm. She was a bosom to cry on, a soother and a stroker. The iron sex of the Nigger and the tavern bacchanalianism of Jenny had their devotees, and they were not lost to Faye. Her house became the refuge of young men puling in puberty, mourning over lost virtue, and aching to lose some more. Faye was the re-assurer of misbegotten husbands. Her house took up the slack for frigid wives. It was the cinnamon-scented kitchen of one's grandmother. If any sexual thing happened to you at Faye's you felt it was an accident but forgivable. Her house led the youths of Salinas into the thorny path of sex in the pinkest, smoothest way. Faye was a nice woman, not very bright, highly moral, and easily shocked. People trusted her and she trusted everyone. No one could want to hurt Faye once he knew her. She was no competition to the others. She was a third phase.

Just as in a store or on a ranch the employees are images of the boss, so in a whorehouse the girls are very like the madam, partly because she hires that kind and partly because a good madam imprints her personality on the business. You could stay a very long time at Faye's before you would hear an ugly or sug-gestive word spoken. The wanderings to the bedrooms, the pay-ments, were so soft and casual they seemed incidental. All in all she ran a hell of a fine house, as the constable and the sheriff knew. Faye contributed heavily to every charity. Having a revul-sion against disease, she paid for regular inspection of her girls. You had less chance of contracting a difficulty at Faye's than with your Sunday School teacher. Faye soon became a solid and desirable citizen of the growing town of Salinas.

11

The girl Kate puzzled Faye – she was so young and pretty, so ladylike, so well educated. Faye took her into her own inviolate bedroom and questioned her far more than she would if Kate had been another kind of girl. There were always women knock-ing on the door of a whorehouse, and Faye recognized most of them instantly. She could tick them off – lazy, vengeful, lustful, unsatisfied, greedy, ambitious. Kate didn't fall into any of these classes.

'I hope you don't mind my asking you all these questions,' she said. 'It just seems so strange that you should come here. Why, you could get a husband and a surrey and a corner house in town with no trouble at all, no trouble at all.' And Faye rolled her wedding band round and round on her fat little finger.

Kate smiled shyly. 'It's so hard to explain. I hope you won't insist on knowing. The happiness of someone very near and dear to me is involved. Please don't ask me.'

Faye nodded solemnly. 'I've known things like that. I had one girl who was supporting her baby, and no one knew for a long, long time. That girl has a fine house and a husband in – there, I nearly told you where. I'd cut out my tongue before I'd tell. Do you have a baby, dear?'

Kate looked down to try to conceal the shine of tears in her eyes. When she could control her throat she whispered, 'I'm sorry, I can't talk about it.'

'That's all right. That's all right. You just take your time.'

Faye was not bright, but she was far from stupid. She went to the sheriff and got herself cleared. There was no sense in taking chances. She knew something was wrong about Kate, but if it didn't harm the house it really wasn't Faye's business.

Kate might have been a chiseller, but she wasn't. She went to work right away. And when customers come back again and again and ask for a girl by name, you know you've got something. A pretty face won't do that. It was quite apparent to Faye that Kate was not learning a new trade.

There are two things it is good to know about a new girl: first, will she work? and second, will she get along with the other girls? There's nothing will upset a house like an ill-tempered girl.

Faye didn't have long to wonder about the second question. Kate put herself out to be pleasant. She helped the other girls keep their rooms clean. She served them when they were sick, listened to their troubles, answered them in matters of love, and as soon as she had some, loaned them money. You couldn't want a better girl. She became best friend to everyone in the house.

There was no trouble Kate would not take, no drudgery she was afraid of, and, in addition, she brought business. She soon had her own group of regular customers. Kate was thoughtful too. She remembered birthdays and always had a present and a cake with candles. Faye realized she had a treasure.

People who don't know think it is easy to be a madam – just sit in a big chair and drink beer and take half the money the girls make, they think. But it's not like that at all. You have to feed the girls – that's groceries and a cook. Your laundry problem is quite a bit more complicated than that of a hotel. You have to keep the girls well and as happy as possible, and some of them can get pretty ornery. You have to keep suicide at an absolute minimum, and whores, particularly the ones getting along in years, are flighty with a razor; and that gets your house a bad name.

It isn't so easy, and if you have waste too you can lose money. When Kate offered to help with the marketing and planning of meals Faye was pleased, although she didn't know when the girl found time. Well, not only did the food improve, but the grocery bills came down one-third the first month Kate took over. And the laundry – Faye didn't know what Kate said to the man but that bill suddenly dropped twenty-five per cent. Faye didn't see how she ever got along without Kate.

In the late afternoon before business they sat together in Faye's room and drank tea. It was much nicer since Kate had painted the woodwork and put up lace curtains. The girls began to realize that there were two bosses, not one, and they were glad, because Kate was very easy to get along with. She made them turn more tricks but she wasn't mean about it. They'd as likely as not have a big laugh over it.

By the time a year had passed Faye and Kate were like mother and daughter. And the girls said, 'You watch – she'll own this house some day.'

Kate's own hands were always busy, mostly at drawn work on the sheerest of lawn handkerchiefs. She could make beautiful initials. Nearly all the girls carried and treasured her handkerchiefs.

Gradually a perfectly natural thing happened. Faye, the essence of motherliness, began to think of Kate as her daughter. She felt this in her breast and in her emotions, and her natural morality took hold. She did not want her daughter to be a whore. It was a perfectly reasonable sequence.

Faye thought hard how she was going to bring up the subject. It was a problem. It was Faye's nature to approach any subject sideways. She could not say, 'I want you to give up whoring.'

She said, 'If it is a secret, don't answer, but I've always meant to ask you. What did the sheriff say to you – good Lord, is it a year ago? How the time goes! Quicker as you get older, I think. He was nearly an hour with you. He didn't – but of course not. He's a family man. He goes to Jenny's. But I don't want to pry into your affairs.'

212

'There's no secret at all about that,' said Kate. 'I would have told you. He told me I should go home. He was very nice about it. When I explained that I couldn't, he was very nice and understanding.'

'Did you tell him why?' Faye asked jealously.

'Of course not. Do you think I would tell him when I won't tell you? Don't be silly, darling. You're such a funny little girl.'

Faye smiled and snuggled contentedly down in her chair.

Kate's face was in repose, but she was remembering every word of that interview. As a matter of fact she rather liked the sheriff. He was direct.

III

He had closed the door of her room, glanced round with the quick recording eye of a good policeman – no photographs, none of the personal articles which identify, nothing but clothes and shoes.

He sat down on her little cane rocking chair and his buttocks hung over on each side. His fingers got together in conference, talking to one another like ants. He spoke in an unemotional tone, almost as though he weren't much interested in what he was saying. Maybe that was what impressed her.

At first she put on her slightly stupid demure look, but after a few of his words she gave that up and bored him with her eyes, trying to read his thought. He neither looked in her eyes nor avoided them. But she was aware that he was inspecting her as she inspected him. She felt his glance go over the scar on her forehead almost as though he had touched it.

'I don't want to make a record,' he said quietly. 'I've held office a long time. About one more term will be enough. You know, young woman, if this were fifteen years back I'd do some checking, and I guess I'd find something pretty nasty.' He waited for some reaction from her but she did not protest. He nodded his head slowly. 'I don't want to know,' he said. 'I want peace in this county, and I mean all kinds of peace, and that means people getting to sleep at night. Now I haven't met your husband,' he said, and she knew he noticed the slight movement of her tightening muscles. 'I hear he's a very nice man. I hear also that he's pretty hard hit.' He looked into her eyes for a moment. 'Don't you want to know how bad you shot him?'

'Yes,' she said.

'Well, he's going to get well – smashed his shoulder, but he's going to get well. That Chink is taking pretty good care of him. Course I don't think he'll lift anything with his left arm for quite a spell. A forty-four tears hell out of a man. If the Chink hadn't come back he'd of bled to death, and you'd be staying with me in the jail.'

Kate was holding her breath, listening for any hint of what was coming and not hearing any hints.

'I'm sorry,' she said quietly.

The sheriff's eyes became alert. 'Now that's the first time you've made a mistake,' he said. 'You're not sorry. I knew somebody like you once – hung him twelve years ago in front of the county jail. We used to do that here.'

The little room with its dark mahogany bed, its marble-top washstand with bowl and pitcher and a door for the pot, its wallpaper endlessly repeating little roses – little roses – the little room was silent, the sound sucked out of it.

The sheriff was staring at a picture of three cherubim – just heads, curly-haired, limpid-eyed, with wings about the size of pigeons' wings growing out of where their necks would be. He frowned. 'That's a funny picture for a whorehouse,' he said.

'It was here,' said Kate. Apparently the preliminaries were over now.

The sheriff straightened up, undid his fingers, and held the arms of his chair. Even his buttocks pulled in a little. 'You left a couple of babies,' he said. 'Little boys. Now you calm down. I'm not going to try to get you to go back. I guess I'd do quite a bit to keep you from going back. I think I know you. I could just run you over the county line and have the next sheriff run you, and that could keep up till you landed splash in the Atlantic Ocean. But I don't want to do that. I don't care how you live as long as you don't give me any trouble. A whore is a whore.'

Kate asked evenly, 'What is it you do want?'

'That's more like it,' the sheriff said. 'Here's what I want. I notice you changed your name. I want you to keep your new name. I guess you made up someplace you came from – well, that's where you came from. And your reason – that's when you're maybe drunk – you keep your reason about two thousand miles away from King City.'

She was smiling a little, and not a forced smile. She was beginning to trust this man and to like him.

'One thing I thought of,' he said. 'Did you know many people around King City?'

214

'No.'

'I heard about the knitting-needle,' he said casually. 'Well, it could happen that somebody you knew might come in here. That your real hair colour?'

'Yes.'

'Dye it black for a while. Lots of people look like somebody else.'

'How about this?' She touched her scar with a slender finger.

'Well, that's just a – what is that word? What is that goddam word? I had it this morning.'

'Coincidence?'

'That's it – coincidence.' He seemed to be finished. He got out tobacco and papers and rolled a clumsy, lumpy cigarette. He broke out a sulphur match and struck it on the block and held it away until its acrid blue flame turned yellow. His cigarette burned crookedly up the side.

Kate said, 'Isn't there a threat? I mean, what you'll do if I —'

'No, there isn't. I guess I could think up something pretty ornery, though, if it came to that. No, I don't want you – what you are, what you do, or what you say – to hurt Mr Trask or his boys. You figure you died and now you're somebody else and we'll get along fine.'

He stood up and went to the door, then turned. 'I've got a boy – he'll be twenty this year; big nice-looking fellow with a broken nose. Everybody likes him. I don't want him in here. I'll tell Faye to. Let him go to Jenny's. If he comes in, you tell him to go to Jenny's.' He closed the door behind him.

Kate smiled down at her fingers.

IV

Faye twisted round in her chair to reach a piece of brown pan-ocha studded with walnuts. When she spoke it was around a mouth full of candy. Kate wondered uneasily whether she could read minds, for Faye said, 'I still don't like it as well. I said it then and I say it again. I liked your hair blonde better. I don't know what got into you to change it. You've got a fair complexion.'

Kate caught a single thread of hair with fingernails of thumb and forefinger and gently drew it out. She was very clever. She told the best lie of all – the truth. 'I didn't want to tell you,' she said. 'I was afraid I might be recognized and that would hurt someone.'

Faye got up out of her chair and went to Kate and kissed her. 'What a good child it is,' she said. 'What a thoughtful dear.'

Kate said, 'Let's have some tea. I'll bring it in.' She went out of the room, and in the hall on the way to the kitchen she rubbed the kiss from her cheek with her fingertips.

Back in her chair, Faye picked out a piece of panocha with a whole walnut showing through. She put it in her mouth and bit into a piece of walnut shell. The sharp, pointed fragment hit a hollow tooth and whanged into the nerve. Blue lights of pain flashed through her. Her forehead became wet. When Kate came back with teapot and cups on a tray Faye was clawing at her mouth with a crooked finger and whimpering in agony.

'What is it?' Kate cried.

'Tooth – nutshell.'

'Here, let me see. Open and point.' Kate looked into the open mouth then went to the nut bowl on the fringed table for a nut pick. In a fraction of a second she had dug out the shell and laid it in the palm of her hand. 'There it is.'

The nerve stopped shrieking and the pain dropped to an ache. 'Only that big? It felt like a house. Look, dear,' said Faye, 'open that second drawer where my medicine is. Bring the paregoric and a piece of cotton. Will you help me pack this tooth?'

Kate brought the bottle and pushed a little ball of saturated cotton into the tooth with the point of the nut pick. 'You ought to have it out.'

'I know. I will.'

'I have three teeth missing on this side.'

'Well, you'd never know it. That made me feel all shaky. Bring me the Pinkham, will you?' She poured herself a slug of the vegetable compound and sighed with relief. 'That's a wonderful medicine,' she said. 'The woman who invented it was a saint.'

CHAPTER 20

I

IT WAS a pleasant afternoon. Frémont's Peak was lighted pinkly by the setting sun, and Faye could see it from her window. From over on Castroville Street came the sweet sound of jingling horse bells from an eight-horse grain team down from the ridge. The cook was fighting pots in the kitchen. There was a rubbing sound on the wall and then a gentle tap on the door.

'Come in, Cotton Eye,' Faye called.

The door opened and the crooked little cotton-eyed piano player stood in the entrance, waiting for a sound to tell him where she was.

'What is it you want?' Faye asked.

He turned to her. 'I don't feel good, Miss Faye. I want to crawl into my bed and not do no playing tonight.'

'You were sick two nights last week, Cotton Eye. Don't you like your job?'

'I don't feel good.'

'Well, all right. But I wish you'd take better care of yourself.'

Kate said softly, 'Let the gong alone for a couple of weeks, Cotton Eye.'

'Oh, Miss Kate. I didn't know you was here. I ain't been smoking.'

'You've been smoking,' Kate said.

'Yes, Miss Kate, I will sure let it alone. I don't feel good.' He closed the door, and they could hear his hand rubbing along the wall to guide him.

Faye said, 'He told me he'd stopped.'

'He hasn't stopped.'

'The poor thing,' said Faye, 'he doesn't have much to live for.'

Kate stood in front of her. 'You're so sweet,' she said. 'You believe in everybody. Some day if you don't watch, or I don't watch for you, someone will steal the roof.'

'Who'd want to steal from me?' asked Faye.

Kate put her hand on Faye's plump shoulders. 'Not everyone is as nice as you are.'

Faye's eyes glistened with tears. She picked up a handkerchief from the chair beside her and wiped her eyes and patted delicately at her nostrils. 'You're like my own daughter, Kate,' she said.

'I'm beginning to believe I am. I never knew my mother. She died when I was small.'

Faye drew a deep breath and plunged into the subject.

'Kate, I don't like you working here.'

'Why not?'

Faye shook her head, trying to find words. 'I'm not ashamed. I run a nice house. If I didn't somebody else might run a bad house. I don't do anybody any harm. I'm not ashamed.'

'Why should you be?' asked Kate.

'But I don't like you working. I just don't like it. You're sort of my daughter. I don't like my daughter working.'

'Don't be silly, darling,' said Kate. 'I have to – here or somewhere else. I told you. I have to have the money.'

'No, you don't.'

'Of course I do. Where else could I get it?'

'You could be my daughter. You could manage the house. You could take care of things for me and not go upstairs. I'm not always well, you know.'

'I know you're well, poor darling. But I have to have money.'

'There's plenty for both of us, Kate. I could give you as much as you make and more, and you'd be worth it.'

Kate shook her head sadly. 'I do love you,' she said. 'And I wish I could do what you want. But you need your little reserve, and I – well, suppose something should happen to you? No, I must go on working. Do you know, dear, I have five regulars tonight?'

A jar of shock struck Faye. 'I don't want you to work.'

'I have to, Mother.'

The word did it. Faye burst into tears, and Kate sat on the arm of her chair and stroked her cheek and wiped her streaming eyes. The outburst sniffled to a close.

The dusk was settling deeply on the valley. Kate's face was a glow of lightness under her dark hair. 'Now you're all right. I'll go and look in on the kitchen and then dress.'

'Kate, can't you tell your regulars you're sick?'

'Of course not, Mother.'

'Kate, it's Wednesday. Probably won't be anybody in after one o'clock.'

'The Woodmen of the World are having a do.'

'Oh, yes. But on Wednesday – the Woodmen won't be here after two.'

'What are you getting at?'

'Kate, when you close, you tap on my door. I'll have a little surprise for you.'

'What kind of a surprise?'

'Oh, a secret surprise! Will you ask the cook to come in as you go by the kitchen?'

'Sounds like a cake surprise.'

'Now don't ask questions, darling. It's a surprise.'

Kate kissed her. 'What a dear you are, Mother.'

When she had closed the door behind her Kate stood for a moment in the hall. Her fingers caressed her pointed chin. Her eyes were calm. Then she stretched her arms over her head and strained her body in a luxurious yawn. She ran her hands slowly down her sides from right under her breasts to her hips. Her mouth corners turned up a little, and she moved towards the kitchen.

11

The few regulars drifted in and out and two drummers walked down the Line to look them over, but not a single Woodman of the World showed up. The girls sat yawning in the parlour until two o'clock, waiting.

What kept the Woodmen away was a sad accident. Clarence Monteith had a heart attack right in the middle of the closing ritual and before supper. They laid him out on the carpet and dampened his forehead until the doctor came. Nobody felt like sitting down to the doughnut supper. After Dr Wilde had arrived and looked Clarence over, the Woodmen made a stretcher by putting flagpoles through the sleeves of two overcoats. On the way home Clarence died, and they had to go for Dr Wilde again. And by the time they had made plans for the funeral and written the piece for the *Salinas Journal*, nobody had any heart for a whorehouse.

The next day, when they found out what had happened, the girls all remembered what Ethel had said at ten minutes to two.

'My God!' Ethel had said, 'I never heard it so quiet. No music, cat's got Kate's tongue. It's like setting up with a corpse.'

Later Ethel was impressed with having said it – almost as if she knew.

Grace had said, 'I wonder what cat's got Kate's tongue. Don't you feel good? Kate – I said, don't you feel good?'

Kate started. 'Oh! I guess I was thinking of something.'

'Well, I'm not,' said Grace. 'I'm sleepy. Why don't we close up? Let's ask Faye if we can't lock up. There won't be a Chink in tonight. I'm going to ask Faye.'

Kate's voice cut in on her. 'Let Faye alone. She's not well. We'll close up at two.'

'That clock's way wrong,' said Ethel. 'What's the matter with Faye?'

Kate said, 'Maybe that's what I was thinking about. Faye's not well. I'm worried to death about her. She won't show it if she can help it.'

'I thought she was all right,' Grace said.

219

Ethel hit the jackpot again. 'Well, she don't look good to me. She's got a kind of flush. I noticed it.'

Kate spoke very softly. 'Don't you girls ever let her know I told you. She wouldn't want you to worry. What a dear she is!'

'Best goddam house I ever hustled,' said Grace.

Alice said, 'You better not let her hear you talk words like that.'

'Balls!' said Grace. 'She knows all the words.'

'She don't like to hear them – not from us.'

Kate said patiently, 'I want to tell you what happened. I was having tea with her late this afternoon and she fainted dead away. I do wish she'd see a doctor.'

'I noticed she had a kind of bright flush,' Ethel repeated. 'That clock's way wrong but I forget which way.'

Kate said, 'You girls go to bed. I'll lock up.'

When they were gone Kate went to her room and put on her pretty new print dress that made her look like a little girl. She brushed and braided her hair and let it hang behind in one thick pigtail tied with a little white bow. She patted her cheeks with Florida water. For a moment she hesitated, and then from the top bureau drawer she took a little gold watch that hung from a fleur-de-lis pin. She wrapped it in one of her fine lawn handkerchiefs and went out of the room.

The hall was very dark, but a rim of light showed under Faye's door. Kate tapped softly.

Faye called, 'Who is it?'

'It's Kate.'

'Don't you come in yet. You wait outside. I'll tell you when.' Kate heard a rustling and a scratching in the room. Then Faye called, 'All right. Come in.'

The room was decorated. Japanese lanterns with candles in them hung on bamboo sticks at the corners, and red crêpe paper twisted in scallops from the centre to the corners to give the effect of a tent. On the table with candlesticks around it was a big white cake and a box of chocolates, and beside these a basket with a magnum of champagne peeking out of crushed ice. Faye wore her best lace dress and her eyes were shiny with emotion.

'What in the world?' Kate cried. She closed the door. 'Why, it looks like a party!'

'It is a party. It's a party for my dear daughter.'

'It's not my birthday.'

Faye said, 'In a way maybe it is.'

'I don't know what you mean. But I brought you a present.'

She laid the folded handkerchief in Faye's lap. 'Open it carefully,' she said.

Faye held the watch up. 'Oh, my dear, my dear! You crazy child! No, I can't take it.' She opened the face and then picked open the back with her fingernail. It was engraved – 'To C. with all my heart from A.'

'It was my mother's watch,' Kate said softly. 'I would like my new mother to have it.'

'My darling child! My darling child!'

'Mother would be glad.'

'But it's my party. I have a present for my dear daughter, but I'll have to do it in my own way. Now, Kate, you open the bottle of wine and pour two glasses while I cut the cake. I want it to be fancy.'

When everything was ready Faye took her seat behind the table. She raised her glass. 'To my daughter – may you have long life and happiness.' And when they had drunk Kate proposed, 'To my mother.'

Faye said, 'You'll make me cry – don't make me cry. Over on the bureau, dear. Bring the little mahogany box. There, that's the one. Now put it on the table here and open it.'

In the polished box lay a rolled white paper tied with a red ribbon. 'What in the world is it?' Kate asked.

'It's my gift to you. Open it.'

Kate very carefully untied the red ribbon and unrolled the tube. It was written elegantly with shaded letters, and it was well and carefully drawn and witnessed by the cook.

'All my worldly goods without exception to Kate Albey because I regard her as my daughter.'

It was simple, direct and legally irreproachable. Kate read it three times, looked back at the date, studied the cook's signature. Faye watched her, and her lips were parted in expectation. When Kate's lips moved, reading, Faye's lips moved.

Kate rolled the paper and tied the ribbon around it and put it in the box and closed the lid. She sat in her chair.

Faye said at last, 'Are you pleased?'

Kate's eyes seemed to peer into and beyond Faye's eyes – to penetrate the brain behind the eyes. Kate said quietly, 'I'm trying to hold on, Mother. I didn't know anyone could be so good. I'm afraid if I say anything too quickly or come too close to you, I'll break to pieces.'

It was more dramatic than Faye had anticipated, quiet and electric. Faye said, 'It's a funny present, isn't it?'

'Funny? No, it isn't funny.'

'I mean, a will is a strange present. But it means more than that. Now you are my real daughter I can tell you. I – no, *we* – have cash and securities in excess of sixty thousand dollars. In my desk are notations of accounts and safe-deposit boxes. I sold the place in Sacramento for a very good price. Why are you so silent, child? Is something bothering you?'

'A will sounds like death. That's thrown a pall.'

'But everyone should make a will.'

'I know, Mother.' Kate smiled ruefully. 'A thought crossed my mind. I thought of all your kin coming in angrily to break such a will as this. You can't do this.'

'My poor little girl, is that what's bothering you? I have no folks. As far as I know, I have no kin. And if I did have some – who would know? Do you think you are the only one with secrets? Do you think I use the name I was born with?'

Kate looked long and levelly at Faye.

'Kate,' she cried, 'Kate, it's a party. Don't be sad! Don't be frozen!'

Kate got up, gently pulled the table aside, and sat down on the floor. She put her cheek on Faye's knee. Her slender fingers traced a gold thread on the skirt through its intricate leaf pattern. And Faye stroked Kate's cheek and hair and touched her strange ears. Shyly Faye's fingers explored the borders of the scar.

'I think I've never been so happy before,' said Kate.

'My darling. You make me happy too. Happier than I have ever been. Now I don't feel alone. Now I feel safe.'

Kate picked delicately at the gold thread with her fingernails.

They sat in the warmth for a long time before Faye stirred. 'Kate,' she said, 'we're forgetting. It's a party. We've forgotten the wine. Pour it, child. We'll have a little celebration.'

Kate said uneasily, 'Do we need it, Mother?'

'It's good. Why not? I like to take on a little load. It lets the poison out. Don't you like champagne, Kate?'

'Well, I never have drunk much. It's not good for me.'

'Nonsense. Pour it, darling.'

Kate got up from the floor and filled the glasses.

Faye said, 'Now drink it down. I'm watching you. You're not going to let an old woman get silly by herself.'

'You're not an old woman, Mother.'

'Don't talk – drink it. I won't touch mine until yours is

222

empty.' She held her glass until Kate had emptied hers, then gulped it. 'Good, that's good,' she said. 'Fill them up. Now, come on, dear – down the rat-hole. After two or three the bad things go away.'

Kate's chemistry screamed against the wine. She remembered, and she was afraid.

Faye said, 'Now let me see the bottom, child – there. You see how good it is? Fill up again.'

The transition came to Kate almost immediately after the second glass. Her fear evaporated, her fear of anything disappeared. This was what she had been afraid of, and now it was too late. The wine had forced a passage through all the carefully built barriers and defences and deceptions and she didn't care. The thing she had learned to cover and control was lost. Her voice became chill and her mouth was thin. Her wide-set eyes slitted and grew watchful and sardonic.

'Now you drink – Mother – while I watch,' she said. 'There's a – dear. I'll bet you can't drink two without stopping.'

'Don't bet me, Kate. You'd lose. I can drink six without stopping.'

'Let me see you.'

'If I do, will you?'

'Of course.'

The contest started, and a puddle of wine spread out over the table-top and the wine went down in the magnum.

Faye giggled. 'When I was a girl – I could tell you stories maybe you wouldn't believe.'

Kate said, 'I could tell stories nobody would believe.'

'You? Don't be silly. You're a child.'

Kate laughed. 'You never saw such a child. This is a child – yes – a child!' She laughed with a thin penetrating shriek.

The sound got through the wine that was muffling Faye. She centred her eyes on Kate. 'You look so strange,' she said. 'I guess it's the lamplight. You look different.'

'I am different.'

'Call me "Mother", dear.'

'*Mother – dear.*'

'Kate, we're going to have such a good life.'

'You bet we are. You don't even know. You don't know.'

'I've always wanted to go to Europe. We could get on a ship and have nice clothes – dresses from Paris.'

'Maybe we'll do that – but not now.'

'Why not, Kate? I have plenty of money.'

'We'll have plenty more.'

Faye spoke pleadingly. 'Why don't we go now? We could sell the house. With the business we've got, we could get maybe ten thousand dollars for it.'

'No.'

'What do you mean, no? It's my house. I can sell it.'

'Did you forget I'm your daughter?'

'I don't like your tone, Kate. What's the matter with you? Is there any more wine?'

'Sure, there's a little. Look at it through the bottle. Here, drink it out of the bottle. That's right – Mother – spill it down your neck. Get it in under your corset, Mother, against your fat stomach.'

Faye wailed, 'Kate, don't be mean! We were feeling so nice. What do you want to go and spoil it for?'

Kate wrenched the bottle from her hand. 'Here, give me that.' She tipped it up and drained it and dropped it on the floor. Her face was sharp and her eyes glinted. The lips of her little mouth were parted to show her small sharp teeth, and the canines were longer and more pointed than the others. She laughed softly. 'Mother – dear Mother – I'm going to show you how to run a whorehouse. We'll fix the grey slugs that come in here and dump their nasty little loads – for a dollar. We'll give them pleasure, Mother dear.'

Faye said sharply, 'Kate, you're drunk. I don't know what you're talking about.'

'You don't, Mother dear? Do you want me to tell you?'

'I want you to be sweet. I want you to be like you were.'

'Well, it's too late. I didn't want to drink the wine. But you, you nasty fat worm, you made me. I'm your dear, sweet daughter – don't you remember? Well, I remember how surprised you were that I had regulars. Do you think I'll give them up? Do you think they give me a mean little dollar in quarters? No, they give me ten dollars, and the price is going up all the time. They can't go to anybody else. Nobody else is any good for them.'

Faye wept like a child. 'Kate,' she said, 'don't talk like that. You're not like that. You're not like that.'

'Dear Mother, sweet fat Mother, take down the pants of one of my regulars. Look at the heelmarks on the groin – very pretty. And the little cuts that bleed for a long time. Oh, Mother dear, I've got the sweetest set of razors all in a case – and so sharp, so sharp.'

Faye struggled to get out of her chair. Kate pushed her back.

'And do you know, Mother dear, that's the way this whole house is going to be. The price will be twenty dollars, and we'll make the bastards take a bath. We'll catch the blood on white silk handkerchiefs – Mother dear – blood from the little knotted whips.'

In her chair Faye began to scream hoarsely. Kate was on her instantly with a hard hand cupped over her mouth. 'Don't make a noise. There's a good darling. Get snot all over your daughter's hand – but no noise.' Tentatively she took her hand away and wiped it on Faye's skirt.

Faye whispered, 'I want you out of the house. I want you out. I run a good house without nastiness. I want you out.'

'I can't go, Mother. I can't leave you alone, poor dear.' Her voice chilled. 'Now I'm sick of you. Sick of you.' She took a wineglass from the table, went to the bureau, and poured paregoric until the glass was half full. 'Here, Mother, drink it. It will be good for you.'

'I don't want to.'

'There's a good dear. Drink it.' She coaxed the fluid into Faye. 'Now one more swallow – just one more.'

Faye mumbled thickly for a while and then she relaxed in her chair and slept, snoring thickly.

III

Dread began to gather in the corners of Kate's mind, and out of dread came panic. She remembered the other time and a nausea swept through her. She gripped her hands together, and the panic grew. She lighted a candle from the lamp and went unsteadily down the dark hall to the kitchen. She poured dry mustard in a glass, stirred water into it until it was partly fluid, and drank it. She held on to the edge of the sink while the paste went burning down. She retched and strained again and again. At the end of it, her heart was pounding and she was weak – but the wine was overcome and her mind was clear.

She went over the evening in her mind, moving from scene to scene like a sniffing animal. She bathed her face and washed out the sink and put the mustard back on the shelf. Then she went back to Faye's room.

The day was coming fast. Kate sat beside the bed and watched so that it stood black against the sky. Faye was still snoring in her chair. Kate watched her for a few moments and then she fixed Faye's bed. Kate dragged and strained and lifted the dead

225

weight of the sleeping woman. On the bed Kate undressed Faye and washed her face and put her clothes away.

The day was coming fast. Kate sat beside the bed and watched the relaxed face, the mouth open, lips blowing in and out.

Faye made a restless movement and her dry lips slobbered a few thick words and sighed off to a snore again.

Kate's eyes became alert. She opened the top bureau drawer and examined the bottles which constituted the medicine chest of the house – paregoric, Pain Killer, Lydia Pinkham, iron wine tonic, Hall's Cream Salve, Epsom salts, castor oil, ammonia. She carried the ammonia bottle to the bed, saturated a handkerchief, and, standing well away, held the cloth over Faye's nose and mouth.

The strangling, shocking fumes went in, and Faye came snorting and fighting out of her black web. Her eyes were wide and terrified.

Kate said, 'It's all right, Mother. It's all right. You had a nightmare. You had a bad dream.'

'Yes, a dream,' and then sleep overcame her again and she fell back and began to snore, but the shock of the ammonia had lifted her up nearer consciousness and she was more restless. Kate put the bottle back in its drawer. She straightened the table, mopped up the spilled wine, and carried the glasses to the kitchen.

The house was dusky with dawn light creeping in around the edges of the blinds. The cook stirred in his lean-to behind the kitchen, groping for his clothes and putting on his clodhopper shoes.

Kate moved quietly She drank two glasses of water and filled the glass again and carried it back to Faye's room and closed the door. She lifted Faye's right eyelid, and the eye looked rakishly up at her, but it was not rolled back in her head. Kate acted slowly and precisely. She picked up the handkerchief and smelled it. Some of the ammonia had evaporated but the smell was still sharp. She laid the cloth lightly over Faye's face, and when Faye twisted and turned and came near to waking, Kate took the handkerchief away and let Faye sink back. This she did three times. She put the handkerchief away and picked up an ivory crochet hook from the marble top of the bureau. She turned down the cover and pressed the blunt end of the ivory against Faye's flabby breast with a steady, increasing pressure until the sleeping woman whined and writhed. Then Kate explored the sensitive places of the body with the hook – under the arm, the groin, the ear, the clitoris, and always she removed the pressure just before Faye awakened fully.

Faye was very near the surface now. She whined and sniffled and tossed. Kate stroked her forehead and ran smooth fingers over her inner arm and spoke softly to her.

'Dear – dear. You're having such a bad dream. Come out of the bad dream, Mother.'

Faye's breathing grew more regular. She heaved a great sigh and turned on her side and settled down with little grunts of comfort.

Kate stood up from the bed and a wave of dizziness rose in her head. She steadied herself, then went to the door and listened, slipped out, and moved cautiously to her own room. She undressed quickly and put on her nightgown and a robe and slippers. She brushed her hair and put it up and covered it with a sleeping-cap, and she sponged her face with Florida water. She went quietly back to Faye's room.

Faye was still sleeping peacefully on her side. Kate opened the door to the hall. She carried the glass of water to the bed and poured cold water in Faye's ear.

Faye screamed, and screamed again. Ethel's frightened face looked out of her room in time to see Kate in robe and slippers at Faye's door. The cook was right behind Kate, and he put out his hand to stop her.

'Now don't go in there, Miss Kate. You don't know what's in there.'

'Nonsense, Faye's in trouble.' Kate burst in and ran to the bed.

Faye's eyes were wild and she was crying and moaning.

'What is it? What is it, dear?'

The cook was in the middle of the room, and three sleep-haggard girls stood in the doorway.

'Tell me, what is it?' Kate cried.

'Oh, darling – the dreams, the dreams! I can't stand them!'

Kate turned to the door. 'She's had a nightmare – she'll be all right. You go back to bed. I'll stay with her a while. Alex, bring a pot of tea.'

Kate was tireless. The other girls remarked on it. She put cold towels on Faye's aching head and held her shoulders and the cup of tea for her. She petted and babied her, but the look of horror would not go out of Faye's eyes. At ten o'clock Alex brought in a can of beer and without a word put it on the bureau top. Kate held a glass of it to Faye's lips.

'It will help, darling. Drink it down.'

227

'I never want another drink.'

'Nonsense! Drink it down like medicine. That's a good girl. Now just lie back and go to sleep.'

'I'm afraid to sleep.'

'Were the dreams so bad?'

'Horrible, horrible!'

'Tell me about them, Mother. Maybe that will help.'

Faye shrank back. 'I wouldn't tell anyone. How I could have dreamed them? They weren't like my dreams.'

'Poor little Mother! I love you,' Kate said. 'You go to sleep. I'll keep your dreams away.'

Gradually Faye slid off to sleep. Kate sat beside the bed, studying her.

CHAPTER 21

I

IN HUMAN affairs of danger and delicacy successful conclusion is sharply limited by hurry. So often men trip by being in a rush. If one were properly to perform a difficult and subtle act, he should first inspect the end to be achieved and then, once he had accepted the end as desirable, he should forget it completely and concentrate solely on the means. By this method he would not be moved to false action by anxiety or hurry or fear. Very few people learn this.

What made Kate so effective was the fact that she had either learned it or had been born with the knowledge. Kate never hurried. If a barrier arose, she waited until it had disappeared before continuing. She was capable of complete relaxation between the times for action. Also, she was mistress of a technique which is the basis of good wrestling – that of letting your opponent do the heavy work towards his own defeat, or of guiding his strength towards his weaknesses.

Kate was in no hurry. She thought to the end very quickly and then put it out of her mind. She set herself to work on method. She built a structure and attacked it, and if it showed the slightest shakiness she tore it down and started afresh. This she did only late at night or otherwise when she was completely alone, so that no change or preoccupation was noticeable in her manner. Her building was constructed of personalities, materials, knowledge, and time. She had access to the first and last, and she set about getting knowledge and materials, but while she did that she set in motion a series of imperceptible springs and pendulums and left them to pick up their own momenta.

First the cook told about the will. It must have been the cook. He thought he did anyway. Kate heard about it from Ethel, and she confronted him in the kitchen where he was kneading bread, his hairy big arms floured to the elbows and his hands yeast-bleached.

'Do you think it was a good thing to tell about being a witness?' she said mildly. 'What do you think Miss Faye is going to think?'

He looked confused. 'But I didn't —'

'You didn't what – tell about it or think it would hurt?'

'I don't think I —'

'You don't think you told? Only three people knew. Do you think I told? Or do you think Miss Faye did?' She saw the puzzled look come into his eyes and knew that by now he was far from sure that he had not told. In a moment he would be sure that he had.

Three of the girls questioned Kate about the will, coming to her together for mutual strength.

Kate said, 'I don't think Faye would like me to discuss it. Alex should have kept his mouth shut.' Their wills wavered, and she said, 'Why don't you ask Faye?'

'Oh, we wouldn't do that!'

'But you dare to talk behind her back! Come on now, let's go in to her and you can ask her the questions.'

'No, Kate, no.'

'Well, I'll have to tell her you asked. Wouldn't you rather be there? Don't you think she would feel better if she knew you weren't talking behind her back?'

'Well —'

'I know I would. I always like a person who comes right out.' Quietly she surrounded and nudged and pushed until they stood in Faye's room.

Kate said, 'They asked me about a certain you-know-what. Alex admits he let it out.'

Faye was slightly puzzled. 'Well, dear, I can't see that it's such a secret.'

Kate said, 'Oh, I'm glad you feel that way. But you can see that I couldn't mention it until you did.'

'You think it's bad to tell, Kate?'

'Oh, not at all. I'm glad, but it seemed to me that it wouldn't be loyal of me to mention it before you did.'

'You're sweet, Kate. I don't see any harm. You see, girls, I'm alone in the world and I have taken Kate as my daughter. She takes such care of me. Get the box, Kate.'

And each girl took the will in her own hands and inspected it. It was so simple they could repeat it word for word to the other girls.

They watched Kate to see how she would change, perhaps become a tyrant, but, if anything, she was nicer to them.

A week later when Kate became ill, she went right on with her supervision of the house, and no one would have known if she hadn't been found standing rigid in the hall with agony printed on her face. She begged the girls not to tell Faye, but they were outraged, and it was Faye who forced her to bed and called Dr Wilde.

He was a nice man and a pretty good doctor. He looked at her tongue, felt her pulse, asked her a few intimate questions, and then tapped his lower lip.

'Right here?' he asked, and exerted a little pressure on the small of her back. 'No? Here? Does this hurt? So. Well, I think you just need a kidney flushing.' He left yellow, green, and red pills to be taken in sequence. The pills did good work.

She did have one little flare-up. She told Faye, 'I'll go to the doctor's office.'

'I'll ask him to come here.'

'To bring me some more pills? Nonsense. I'll go in the morning.'

11

Dr Wilde was a good man and an honest man. He was accustomed to say of his profession that all he was sure of was that sulphur would cure the itch. He was not casual about his practice. Like so many country doctors, he was a combination doctor, priest, psychiatrist, to his town. He knew most of the secrets, weaknesses, and the braveries of Salinas. He never learned to take death easily. Indeed the death of a patient always gave him a sense of failure and hopeless ignorance. He was not a bold man, and he used surgery only as a last and fearful resort. The drugstore was coming in to help the doctors, but Dr Wilde was one of the few to maintain his own dispensary and to compound his own prescriptions. Many years of overwork and interrupted sleep had made him a little vague and preoccupied.

At eight-thirty on a Wednesday morning Kate walked up Main Street, climbed the stairs of the Monterey County Bank Building, and walked along the corridor until she found the door which said, 'Dr Wilde – Office Hours 11–2.'

At nine-thirty Dr Wilde put his buggy in the livery stable and wearily lifted out his black bag. He had been out in the Alisal presiding at the disintegration of old, old lady German. She had not been able to terminate her life neatly. There were codicils. Even now Dr Wilde wondered whether the tough, dry, stringy life was completely gone out of her. She was ninety-seven and a death certificate meant nothing to her. Why, she had corrected the priest who prepared her. The mystery of death was on him. It often was. Yesterday, Allen Day, thirty-seven, six feet one inch, strong as a bull and valuable to four hundred acres and a large family, had meekly surrendered his life to pneumonia after a little exposure and three days of fever. Dr Wilde knew it was a mystery. His eyelids felt grainy. He thought he would take a sponge bath and have a drink before his first office patients arrived with their stomach-aches.

He climbed the stairs and put his worn key in the lock of his office door. The key would not turn. He set his bag on the floor and exerted pressure. The key refused to budge. He grabbed the door-knob and pulled outwards and rattled the key. The door was opened from within. Kate stood in front of him.

'Oh, good morning. Lock was stuck. How did you get in?'

'It wasn't locked. I was early and came in to wait.'

'Wasn't locked?' He turned the key the other way and saw that, sure enough, the little bar slipped out easily.

'I'm getting old, I guess,' he said. 'I'm forgetful.' He sighed. 'I don't know why I lock it, anyway. You could get in with a piece of bailing wire. And who'd want to get in, anyway?' He seemed to see her for the first time. 'I don't have office hours until eleven.'

Kate said, 'I needed some more of those pills and I couldn't come later.'

'Pills? Oh, yes. You're the girl from down at Faye's.'

'That's right.'

'Feeling better?'

'Yes, the pills help.'

'Well, they can't hurt,' he said. 'Did I leave the door to the dispensary open too?'

'What's a dispensary?'

'Over there – that door.'

231

'I guess you must have.'

'Getting old. How is Faye?'

'Well, I'm worried about her. She was real sick a while ago. Had cramps and went a little out of her head.'

'She's had a stomach disorder before,' Dr Wilde said. 'You can't live like that and eat all hours and be very well. I can't, anyway. We just call it stomach trouble. Comes from eating too much and staying up all night. Now – the pills. Do you remember what colour?'

'There were three kinds, yellow, red, and green.'

'Oh yes. Yes, I remember.'

While he poured pills into a round cardboard box she stood in the doorway.

'What a lot of medicines!'

Dr Wilde said, 'Yes – and the older I get, the fewer I use. I got some of those when I started to practise. Never used them. That's a beginner's stock. I was going to experiment – alchemy.'

'What?'

'Nothing. Here you are. Tell Faye to get some sleep and eat some vegetables. I've been up all night. Let yourself out, will you?' He went wavering back into the surgery.

Kate glanced after him and then her eyes flicked over the lines of bottles and containers. She closed the dispensary door and looked round the outer office. One book in the case was out of line. She pushed it back until it was shoulder to shoulder with its brothers.

She picked up her big handbag from the leather sofa and left.

In her own room Kate took five small bottles and a strip of scribbled paper from her handbag. She put the whole works in the toe of a stocking, pushed the wad into a rubber overshoe, and stood it with its fellow in the back of her closet.

III

During the following months a gradual change came over Faye's house. The girls were sloppy and touchy. If they had been told to clean themselves and their rooms a deep resentment would have set in and the house would have reeked of ill temper. But it didn't work that way.

Kate said at table one evening that she had just happened to look in Ethel's room, and it was so neat and pretty she couldn't help buying her a present. When Ethel unwrapped the package right at the table it was a big bottle of Hoyt's German, enough to keep her smelling sweet for a long time. Ethel was pleased and she hoped Kate hadn't seen the dirty clothes under the bed. After supper she not only got the clothes out but brushed the floors and swept the cobwebs out of the corners.

Then Grace looked so pretty one afternoon that Kate couldn't help giving her the rhinestone butterfly pin she was wearing. And Grace had to rush up and put on a clean shirtwaist to set it off.

Alex in the kitchen, who if he had believed what was usually said of him would have considered himself a murderer, found that he had a magic hand with biscuits. He discovered that cooking was something you couldn't learn. You had to feel it.

Cotton Eye learned that nobody hated him. His tub-thumping piano-playing changed imperceptibly.

He told Kate, 'It's funny what you remember when you think back.'

'Like what?' she asked.

'Well, like this,' and he played for her.

'That's lovely,' she said. 'What is it?'

'Well, I don't know. I think it's Chopin. If I could just see the music!'

He told her how he had lost his sight, and he had never told anyone else. It was a bad story. That Saturday night he took the chain off the piano strings and played something he had been remembering and practising in the morning, something called 'Moonlight', a piece by Beethoven, Cotton Eye thought.

Ethel said it sounded like moonlight and did he know the words.

'It don't have words,' said Cotton Eye.

Oscar Trip, up from Gonzales for Saturday night, said, 'Well, it ought to have. It's pretty.'

One night there were presents for everyone because Faye's was the best house, the cleanest, and nicest in the whole county – and who was responsible for that? Why, the girls – who else? And did they ever taste seasoning like in that stew?'

Alex retired into the kitchen and shyly wiped his eyes with the back of his wrist. He bet he could make a plum pudding which would knock their eyes out.

Georgia was getting up at ten every morning and taking piano lessons from Cotton Eye, and her nails were clean.

Coming back from eleven o'clock mass on a Sunday morning, Grace said to Trixie, 'And I was about ready to get married and give up whoring. Can you imagine?'

233

'It's sure nice,' said Trixie. 'Jenny's girls came over for Faye's birthday cake and they couldn't believe their eyes. They don't talk about nothing else but how it is at Faye's. Jenny's sore.'

'Did you see the score on the blackboard this morning?'

'Sure I did – eighty-seven tricks in one week. Let Jenny or the Nigger match that when there ain't no holidays!'

'No holidays, hell. Have you forgot it's Lent? They ain't turning a trick at Jenny's.'

After her illness and her evil dreams Faye was quiet and depressed. Kate knew she was being watched, but there was no help for that. And she had made sure the rolled paper was still in the box and all the girls had seen it or heard about it.

One afternoon Faye looked up from her solitaire game as Kate knocked and entered the room.

'How do you feel, Mother?'

'Fine, just fine.' Her eyes were secretive. Faye wasn't very clever. 'You know, Kate, I'd like to go to Europe.'

'Well, how wonderful! And you deserve it and you can afford it.'

'I don't want to go alone. I want you to go with me.'

Kate looked at her in astonishment. 'Me? You want to take me?'

'Sure, why not?'

'Oh, you sweet dear! When can we go?'

'You want to?'

'I've always dreamed of it. When can we go? Let's go soon.'

Faye's eyes lost their suspicion and her face relaxed. 'Maybe next summer,' she said. 'We can plan it for next summer, Kate!'

'Yes, Mother.'

'You – you don't turn any tricks any more, do you?'

'Why should I? You take such good care of me.'

Faye slowly gathered up the cards and tapped them square, and dropped them in the table drawer.

Kate pulled up a chair. 'I want to ask your advice about something.'

'What is it?'

'Well, you know I'm trying to help you.'

'You're doing everything, darling.'

'You know our biggest expense is food, and it gets bigger in the winter.'

'Yes.'

'Well, right now you can buy fruit and all kinds of vegetables for two bits a lug. And in the winter you know what we pay for canned peaches and canned string beans.'

'You aren't planning to start preserving?'

'Well, why shouldn't we?'

'What will Alex say to that?'

'Mother, you can believe it or not, or you can ask him. Alex suggested it.'

'No!'

'Well, he did. Cross my heart.'

'Well, I'll be damned – Oh, I'm sorry, sweet. It slipped out.'

The kitchen turned into a cannery and all the girls helped. Alex truly believed it was his idea. At the end of the season he had a silver watch with his name engraved on the back to prove it.

Ordinarily both Faye and Kate had their supper at the long table in the dining-room, but on Sunday nights, when Alex was off and the girls dined on thick sandwiches, Kate served supper for two in Faye's room. It was a pleasant and a ladylike time. There was always some little delicacy, very special and good – *foie gras* or a tossed salad, pastry bought at Lang's Bakery just across Main Street. And instead of the white oilcloth and paper napkins of the dining-room, Faye's table was covered with a white damask cloth and the napkins were linen. It had a party feeling, too, candles and – something rare in Salinas – a bowl of flowers. Kate could make pretty floral arrangements using only the blossoms from weeds she picked in the fields.

'What a clever girl she is,' Faye would say. 'She can do anything and she can make do with anything. We're going to Europe. And did you know Kate speaks French? Well, she can. When you get her alone, ask her to say something in French. She's teaching me. Know how you say bread in French?' Faye was having a wonderful time. Kate gave her excitement and perpetual planning.

I V

On Saturday the fourteenth of October the first wild ducks went over Salinas. Faye saw them from her window, a great wedge flying south. When Kate came in before supper, as she always did, Faye told her about it. 'I guess the winter's nearly here,' she said. 'We'll have to get Alex to set up the stoves.'

'Ready for your tonic, Mother dear?'

'Yes, I am. You're making me lazy, waiting on me.'

235

'I like to wait on you,' said Kate. She took the bottle of Lydia Pinkham's Vegetable Compound from the drawer and held it up to the light. 'Not much left,' she said. 'We'll have to get some more.'

'Oh, I think I have three bottles left of the dozen in my closet.'

Kate picked up the glass. 'There's a fly in the glass,' she said. 'I'll just go and wash it out.'

In the kitchen she rinsed the glass. From her pocket she took the eye-dropper. The end was closed with a little piece of potato, the way you plug the spout of a kerosene can. She carefully squeezed a few drops of clear liquid into the glass, a tincture of nux vomica.

Back in Faye's room she poured the three tablespoons of vegetable compound in the glass and stirred it.

Faye drank her tonic and licked her lips. 'It tastes bitter,' she said.

'Does it, dear? Let me taste.' Kate took a spoonful from the bottle and made a face. 'So it does,' she said. 'I guess it's been standing around too long. I'm going to throw it out. Say, that *is* bitter. Let me get you a glass of water.'

At supper Faye's face was flushed. She stopped eating and seemed to be listening.

'What's the matter?' Kate asked. 'Mother, what's the matter?'

Faye seemed to tear her attention away. 'Why, I don't know. I guess a little heart flutter. Just all of a sudden I felt afraid and my heart got to pounding.'

'Don't you want me to help you to your room?'

'No, dear, I feel all right now.'

Grace put down her fork. 'Well, you got a real high flush, Faye.'

Kate said, 'I don't like it. I wish you'd see Dr Wilde.'

'No, it's all right now.'

'You frightened me,' said Kate. 'Have you ever had it before?'

'Well, I'm a little short of breath sometimes. I guess I'm getting too stout.'

Faye didn't feel very good that Saturday night, and about ten o'clock Kate persuaded her to go to bed. Kate looked in several times until she was sure Faye was asleep.

The next day Faye felt all right. 'I guess I'm just short-winded,' she said.

'Well, we're going to have invalid food for my darling,' said Kate. 'I've made some chicken soup for you and we'll have a string-bean salad – the way you like it, just oil and vinegar, and a cup of tea.'

'Honest to God, Kate, I feel pretty good.'

'It wouldn't hurt either of us to eat a little light. You frightened me last night. I had an aunt who died of heart trouble. And that leaves a memory, you know.'

'I never had any trouble with my heart. Just a little short-winded when I climb the stairs.'

In the kitchen Kate set the supper on two trays. She measured out the French dressing in a cup and poured it on the string-bean salad. On Faye's tray she put her favourite cup and set the soup forward on the stove to heat. Finally she took the eye-dropper from her pocket and squeezed two drops of croton oil on the string beans and stirred it in. She went to her room and swallowed the contents of a small bottle of Cascara Sagrada and hurried back to the kitchen. She poured the hot soup in the cups, filled the teapot with boiling water, and carried the trays to Faye's room.

'I didn't think I was hungry,' Faye said. 'But that soup smells good.'

'I made a special salad dressing for you,' said Kate. 'It's an old recipe, rosemary and thyme. See if you like it.'

'Why, it's delicious,' said Faye. 'Is there anything you can't do, darling?'

Kate was stricken first. Her forehead beaded with perspiration and she doubled over, crying with pain. Her eyes were staring and the saliva ran from her mouth. Faye ran to the hallway, screaming for help. The girls and a few Sunday customers crowded into the room. Kate was writhing on the floor. Two of the regulars lifted her on to Faye's bed and tried to straighten her out, but she screamed and doubled up again. The sweat poured from her body and wetted her clothes.

Faye was wiping Kate's forehead with a towel when the pain struck her.

It was an hour before Dr Wilde could be found, playing euchre with a friend. He was dragged down to the Line by two hysterical whores. Faye and Kate were weak from vomiting and diarrhoea and the spasms continued at intervals.

Mr Wilde said, 'What did you eat?' and then he noticed the trays. 'Are these string beans home-canned?' he demanded.

'Sure,' said Grace. 'We did them right here.'

'Did any of you have them?'

'Well, no. You see —'

'Go out and break every jar,' Dr Wilde said. 'Goddam the string beans!' And he unpacked his stomach pump.

On Tuesday he sat with two pale weak women. Kate's bed had been moved into Faye's room. 'I can tell you now,' he said, 'I didn't think you had a chance. You're pretty lucky. And let home-made string beans alone. Buy canned ones.'

'What is it?' Kate asked.

'Botulism. We don't know much about it, but damn few ever get over it. I guess it's because you're young and she's tough.' He asked Faye, 'Are you still bleeding from the bowels?'

'Yes, a little.'

'Well, here are some morphine pills. They'll bind you up. You've probably ruptured something. But they say you can't kill a whore. Now take it easy, both of you.'

That was October 17.

Faye was never really well again. She would make a little gain and then go to pieces. She had a bad time on December 3, and it took even longer for her to gain her strength. February 12 the bleeding became violent and the strain seemed to have weakened Faye's heart. Dr Wilde listened a long time through his stethoscope.

Kate was haggard and her slender body had shrunk to bones. The girls tried to spell her with Faye, but Kate would not leave.

Grace said, 'God knows when's the last sleep she had. If Faye was to die, I think it would kill that girl.'

'She's just as like to blow her brains out,' said Ethel.

Dr Wilde took Kate into the day-darkened parlour and put his black bag on the chair. 'I might as well tell you,' he said. 'Her heart just can't stand the strain, I'm afraid. She's all torn up inside. That goddam botulism. Worse than a rattlesnake.' He looked away from Kate's haggard face. 'I thought it would be better to tell you so you can prepare yourself,' he said lamely, and put his hand on her bony shoulder. 'Not many people have such loyalty. Give her a little warm milk if she can take it.'

Kate carried a basin of warm water to the table beside the bed. When Trixie looked in, Kate was bathing Faye and using the fine linen napkins to do it. Then she brushed the lank blonde hair and braided it.

Faye's skin had shrunk, clinging to jaw and skull, and her eyes were huge and vacant.

She tried to speak, and Kate said, 'Shush! Save your strength. Save your strength.'

She went to the kitchen for a glass of warm milk and put it on

238

the bedside table. She took two little bottles from her pocket and sucked a little from each into the eye-dropper. 'Open up, Mother. This is a new kind of medicine. Now be brave, dear. This will taste bad.' She squeezed the fluid far back on Faye's tongue and held up her head so she could drink a little milk to take away the taste. 'Now you rest and I'll be back in a little while.'

Kate slipped quietly out of the room. The kitchen was dark. She opened the outer door and crept out and moved back among the weeds. The ground was damp from the spring rains. At the back of the lot she dug a small hole with a pointed stick. She dropped in a number of small thin bottles and an eye-dropper. With the stick she crushed the glass to bits and scraped the dirt over them. Rain was beginning to fall as Kate went back to the house.

At first they had to tie Kate down to keep her from hurting herself. From violence she went into a gloomy stupor. It was a long time before she regained her health. And she forgot completely about the will. It was Trixie who finally remembered.

CHAPTER 22

I

ON THE Trask place Adam drew into himself. The unfinished Sanchez house lay open to wind and rain, and the new floor-boards buckled and warped with moisture. The laid-out vegetable gardens rioted with weeds.

Adam seemed clothed in a viscosity that slowed his movements and held his thoughts down. He saw the world through grey water. Now and then his mind fought its way upwards, and when the light broke in it brought him only a sickness of the mind, and he retired into the greyness again. He was aware of the twins because he heard them cry and laugh, but he felt only a thin distaste for them. To Adam they were symbols of his loss. His neighbours drove up into his little valley, and every one of them would have understood anger or sorrow – and so helped him. But they could do nothing with the cloud that hung over him. Adam did not resist them. He simply did not see them, and before long the neighbours stopped driving up the road under the oaks.

For a time Lee tried to stimulate Adam to awareness, but Lee was a busy man. He cooked and washed, he bathed the twins and fed them. Through his hard and constant work he grew fond of the two little boys. He talked to them in Cantonese, and Chinese words were the first they recognized and tried to repeat.

Samuel Hamilton went back twice to try to wedge Adam up and out of his shock. Then Liza stepped in.

'I want you to stay away from there,' she said. 'You come back a changed man. Samuel, you don't change him. He changes you. I can see the look of him in your face.'

'Have you thought of the two little boys, Liza?' he asked.

'I've thought of your own family,' she said snappishly. 'You lay a crêpe on us for days after.'

'All right, Mother,' he said, but it saddened him, because Samuel could not mind his own business when there was pain in any man. It was no easy thing for him to abandon Adam to his desolation.

Adam had paid him for his work, had even paid him for the windmill parts and did not want the windmills. Samuel sold the equipment and sent Adam the money. He had no answer.

He became aware of an anger at Adam Trask. It seemed to Samuel that Adam might be pleasuring himself with sadness But there was little leisure to brood. Joe was off to college – to that school Leland Stanford had built on his farm near Palo Alto. Tom worried his father, for Tom grew deeper and deeper into books. He did his work well enough, but Samuel felt that Tom had not joy enough.

Will and George were doing well in business, and Joe was writing letters home in rhymed verse and making as smart an attack on all the accepted verities as was healthful.

Samuel wrote to Joe, saying, 'I would be disappointed if you had not become an atheist, and I read pleasantly that you have, in your age and wisdom, accepted agnosticism the way you'd take a cookie on a full stomach. But I would ask you with all my understanding heart not to try to convert your mother. Your last letter only made her think you are not well. Your mother does not believe there are many ills incurable by good strong soup. She puts your brave attack on the structure of civilization down to a stomach-ache. It worries her. Her faith is a mountain, and you, my son, haven't even got a shovel yet.'

Liza was getting old. Samuel saw it in her face, and he could not feel old himself, white beard or no. But Liza was living backwards, and that's the proof.

240

There was a time when she looked on his plans and prophecies as the crazy shoutings of a child. Now she felt that they were unseemly in a grown man. They three, Liza and Tom and Samuel, were alone on the ranch. Una was married to a stranger and gone away. Dessie had her dressmaking business in Salinas. Olive had married her young man and Mollie was married and living, believe it or not, in an apartment in San Francisco. There was perfume, and a white bearskin rug in the bedroom in front of the fireplace, and Mollie smoked a gold-tipped cigarette – Violet Milo – with her coffee after dinner.

One day Samuel strained his back lifting a bale of hay, and it hurt his feelings more than his back, for he could not imagine a life in which Sam Hamilton was not privileged to lift a bale of hay. He felt insulted by his back, almost as he would have been if one of his children had been dishonest.

In King City, Dr Tilson felt him over. The doctor grew more testy with his overworked years.

'You sprained your back.'

'That I did,' said Samuel.

'And you drove all the way in to have me tell you that you sprained your back and charge you two dollars?'

'Here's your two dollars.'

'And you want to know what to do about it?'

'Sure I do.'

'Don't sprain it any more. Now take your money back. You're not a fool, Samuel, unless you're getting childish.'

'But it hurts.'

'Of course it hurts. How would you know it was strained if it didn't?'

Samuel laughed. 'You're good for me,' he said. 'You're more than two dollars good for me. Keep the money.'

The doctor looked closely at him. 'I think you're telling the truth, Samuel. I'll keep the money.'

Samuel went in to see Will in his fine new store. He hardly knew his son, for Will was getting fat and prosperous and he wore a coat and waistcoat and a gold ring on his little finger.

'I've got a package made up for Mother,' Will said. 'Some little cans of things from France. Mushrooms and liver paste and sardines so little you can hardly see them.'

'She'll just send them to Joe,' said Samuel.

'Can't you make her eat them?'

'No,' said his father. 'But she'll enjoy sending them to Joe.'

241

Lee came into the store and his eyes lighted up. 'How do, Missy,' he said.

'Hello, Lee. How are the boys?'

'Boys fine.'

Samuel said, 'I'm going to have a glass of beer next door, Lee. Be glad to have you join me.'

Lee and Samuel sat at the little round table in the bar-room and Samuel drew figures on the scrubbed wood with the moisture off his beer glass. 'I've wanted to go and see you and Adam, but I didn't think I could do any good.'

'Well, you can't do any harm. I thought he'd get over it. But he still walks around like a ghost.'

'It's over a year, isn't it?' Samuel asked.

'Three months over.'

'Well, what do you think I can do?'

'I don't know,' said Lee. 'Maybe you could shock him out of it. Nothing else has worked.'

'I'm not good at shocking. I'd probably end up by shocking myself. By the way, what did he name the twins?'

'They don't have any names.'

'You're making a joke, Lee.'

'I am not making jokes.'

'What does he call them?'

'He calls them "they".'

'I mean when he speaks to them.'

'When he speaks to them he calls them "you", one or both.'

'This is nonsense,' Samuel said angrily. 'What kind of a fool is the man?'

'I've meant to come and tell you. He's a dead man unless you can wake him up.'

Samuel said, 'I'll come. I'll bring a horse-whip. No names! You're damn right I'll come, Lee.'

'When?'

'Tomorrow.'

'I'll kill a chicken,' said Lee. 'You'll like the twins, Mr Hamilton. They're fine-looking boys. I won't tell Mr Trask you're coming.'

II

Shyly Samuel told his wife he wanted to visit the Trask place. He thought she would pile up strong walls of objection, and for one of the few times in his life he would disobey her wish no matter how strong her objection. It gave him a sad feeling in the

242

stomach to think of disobeying his wife. He explained his purpose almost as though he were confessing. Liza put her hands on her hips during the telling and his heart sank. When he was finished she continued to look at him, he thought, coldly.

Finally she said, 'Samuel, do you think you can move this rock of a man?'

'Why, I don't know, Mother.' He had not expected this. 'I don't know.'

'Do you think it is such an important matter that those babies have names right now?'

'Well, it seemed so to me,' he said lamely.

'Samuel, do you think why you want to go? Is it your natural incurable nosiness? Is it your black inability to mind your own business?'

'Now, Liza, I know my failings pretty well. I thought it might be more than that.'

'It had better be more than that,' she said. 'This man has not admitted that his sons live. He has cut them off mid-air.'

'That's the way it seems to me, Liza.'

'If he tells you to mind your own business – what then?'

'Well, I don't know.'

Her jaw snapped shut and her teeth clicked. 'If you do not get those boys named, there'll be no warm place in this house for you. Don't you dare come whining back, saying he wouldn't do it or he wouldn't listen. If you do I'll have to go myself.'

'I'll give him the back of my hand,' Samuel said.

'No, that you won't do. You fall short in savagery, Samuel. I know you. You'll give him sweet-sounding words and you'll come dragging back and try to make me forget you ever went.'

'I'll beat his brains out,' Samuel shouted.

He slammed into the bedroom, and Liza smiled at the panels.

He came out soon in his black suit and his hard shiny shirt and collar. He stooped down to her while she tied his black string tie. His white beard was brushed to shining.

'You'd best take a swab at your shoes with a blacking brush,' she said.

In the midst of painting the blacking on his worn shoes he looked sideways up at her. 'Could I take the Bible along?' he asked. 'There's no place for getting a good name like the Bible.'

'I don't much like it out of the house,' she said uneasily. 'And if you're late coming home, what'll I have for my reading? And the children's names are in it.' She saw his face fall. She went into the bedroom and came back with a small Bible, worn and scuffed, its cover held on by brown paper and glue. 'Take this one,' she said.

'But that's your mother's.'

'She wouldn't mind. And all the names but one in here have two dates.'

'I'll wrap it so it won't get hurt,' said Samuel.

Liza spoke sharply, 'What my mother would mind is what I mind, and I'll tell you what I mind. You're never satisfied to let the Testament alone. You're for ever picking at it and questioning it. You turn it over the way a 'coon turns over a wet rock, and it angers me.'

'I'm just trying to understand it, Mother.'

'What is there to understand? Just read it. There it is in black and white. Who wants you to understand it? If the Lord God wanted you to understand it He'd have given you to understand or He'd have set it down different.'

'But, Mother —'

'Samuel,' she said, 'you're the most contentious man this world has ever seen.'

'Yes, Mother.'

'Don't agree with me all the time. It hints of insincerity. Speak up for yourself.'

She looked after his dark figure in the buggy as he drove away. 'He's a sweet husband,' she said aloud, 'but contentious.'

And Samuel was thinking with wonder, 'Just when I think I know her she does a thing like that.'

III

On the last half-mile, turning out of the Salinas Valley and driving up the unscraped road under the great oak trees, Samuel tried to plait a rage to take care of his embarrassment. He said heroic words to himself.

Adam was more gaunt than Samuel remembered. His eyes were dull, as though he did not use them much for seeing. It took a little time for Adam to become aware that Samuel was standing before him. A grimace of displeasure drew down his mouth.

Samuel said, 'I feel small now – coming uninvited as I have.'

Adam said, 'What do you want? Didn't I pay you?'

'Pay?' Samuel asked. 'Yes, you did. Yes, by God, you did. And I'll tell you that pay has been more than I've merited by the nature of it.'

'What? What are you trying to say?'

Samuel's anger grew and put out leaves. 'A man, his whole life, matches himself against pay. And how, if it's my whole life's work to find my worth, can you, sad man, write me down instant in a ledger?'

Adam exclaimed, 'I'll pay. I tell you I'll pay. How much? I'll pay.'

'You have, but not to me.'

'Why did you come, then? Go away!'

'You once invited me.'

'I don't invite you now.'

Samuel put his hands on his hips and leaned forward. 'I'll tell you now, quiet. In a bitter night, a mustard night that was last night, a good thought came and the dark was sweetened when the day sat down. And this thought went from evening star to the late dipper on the edge of the first light – that our betters spoke of. So I invite myself.'

'You are not welcome.'

Samuel said, 'I'm told that out of some singular glory your loins got twins.'

'What business is that of yours?'

A kind of joy lighted Samuel's eyes at the rudeness. He saw Lee lurking inside the house and peeking out at him. 'Don't, for the love of God, put violence on me. I'm a man hopes there'll be a picture of peace on my hatchments.'

'I don't understand you.'

'How could you? Adam Trask, a dog-wolf with a pair of cubs, a scrubby rooster with sweet paternity for a fertilized egg! A dirty clod!'

A darkness covered Adam's cheeks and for the first time his eyes seemed to see. Samuel joyously felt hot rage in his stomach. He cried, 'Oh, my friend, retreat from me! Please, I beg of you!' The saliva dampened the corners of his mouth. 'Please!' he cried. 'For the love of any holy thing you can remember, step back from me. I feel murder nudging my gizzard.'

Adam said, 'Get off my place. Go on – get off. You're acting crazy. Get off. This is my place. I bought it.'

'You bought your eyes and nose,' Samuel jeered. 'You bought your uprightness. You bought your thumb on sideways. Listen to me, because I'm like to kill you after. You bought! You bought out of some sweet inheritance. Think now – do you deserve your children, man?'

'Deserve them? They're here – I guess. I don't understand you.'

Samuel wailed, 'God save me, Liza! It's not the way you think, Adam! Listen to me before my thumb finds the bad place at your throat. The precious twins – untried, unnoticed, undirected – and I say it quiet with my hands down – undiscovered.'

'Get off,' said Adam hoarsely. 'Lee, bring a gun! This man is crazy. Lee!'

Then Samuel's hands were on Adam's throat, pressing the throbbing up to his temples, swelling his eyes with blood. And Samuel was snarling at him. 'Tear away with your jelly fingers. You have not bought these boys, not stolen them, nor passed any bit for them. You have them by some strange and lovely dispensation.' Suddenly he plucked his hard thumbs out of his neighbour's throat.

Adam stood panting. He felt his throat where the blacksmith's hands had been. 'What is it you want of me?'

'You have no love.'

'I had – enough to kill me.'

'No one ever had enough. The stone orchard celebrates too little, not too much.'

'Stay away from me. I can fight back. Don't think I can't defend myself.'

'You have two weapons, and they not named.'

'I'll fight you, old man. You are an old man.'

Samuel said, 'I can't think in my mind of a dull man picking up a rock, who before evening would not put a name to it – like Peter. And you – for a year you've lived with your heart's draining and you've not even laid a number to the boys.'

Adam said, 'What I do is my own business.'

Samuel struck him with a work-heavy fist, and Adam sprawled in the dust. Samuel asked him to rise, and when Adam accepted struck him again, and this time Adam did not get up. He looked stonily at the menacing old man.

The fire went out of Samuel's eyes and he said quietly, 'Your sons have no names.'

Adam replied, 'Their mother left them motherless.'

'And you have left them fatherless. Can't you feel the cold at night of a lone child? What warm is there, what bird song, what possible morning can be good? Don't you remember, Adam, how it was, even a little?'

'I didn't do it,' Adam said.

246

'Have you undone it? Your boys have no names.' He stooped down and put his arms around Adam's shoulders and helped him to his feet. 'We'll give them names,' he said. 'We'll think long and find good names to clothe them.' He whipped the dust from Adam's shirt with his hands.

Adam wore a far-away yet intent look, as though he were listening to some wind-carried music, but his eyes were not dead as they had been. He said, 'It's hard to imagine I'd thank a man for insults and for shaking me out like a rug. But I'm grateful. It's a hurty thanks, but it's thanks.'

Samuel smiled, crinkle-eyed. 'Did it seem natural? Did I do it right?' he asked.

'What do you mean?'

'Well, in a way I promised my wife I'd do it. She didn't believe I would. I'm not a fighting man, you see. The last time I clobbered a human soul it was over a red-nosed girl and a schoolbook in County Derry.'

Adam stared at Samuel, but in his mind he saw and felt his brother Charles, black and murderous, and that sight switched to Cathy and the quality of her eyes over the gun-barrel. 'There wasn't any fear in it,' Adam said, 'it was more like a weariness.'

'I guess I was not angry enough.'

'Samuel, I'll ask you just once and then no more. Have you heard anything? Has there been any news of her – any news at all?'

'I've heard nothing.'

'It's almost a relief,' said Adam.

'Do you have hatred?'

'No. No – only a kind of sinking in the heart. Maybe later I'll sort it out to hatred. There was no interval from loveliness to horror, you see. I'm confused, confused.'

Samuel said, 'One day we'll sit and you'll lay it out on the table, neat like a solitaire deck, but now – why, you can't find all the cards.'

From behind the shed there came the indignant shrieking of an outraged chicken and then a dull thump.

'There's something at the hens,' said Adam.

A second shrieking started. 'It's Lee at the hens,' said Samuel. 'You know, if chickens had government and church and history, they would take a distant and distasteful view of human joy. Let any gay and hopeful thing happen to a man, and some chicken goes howling to the block.'

Now the two men were silent, breaking it only with small

247

false courtesies – meaningless inquiries about health and weather, with answers unlistened to. And this might have continued until they were angry at each other again if Lee had not interfered.

Lee brought out a table and two chairs and set the chairs facing each other. He made another trip for a pint of whisky and two glasses and set a glass on the table in front of each chair. Then he carried out the twins, one under each arm, and put them on the ground beside the table and gave each boy a stick for his hand to shake and make shadows with.

The boys sat solemnly and looked about, stared at Samuel's beard and searched for Lee. The strange thing about them was their clothing, for the boys were dressed in the straight trousers and the frogged and braided jackets of the Chinese. One was in turquoise blue and the other in a faded rose pink, and the frogs and braid were black. On their heads sat round black silken hats, each with a bright red button on its flat top.

Samuel asked, 'Where in the world did you get those clothes, Lee?'

'I didn't get them,' Lee said testily. 'I had them. The only other clothes they have I made myself, out of sail-cloth. A boy should be well dressed on his naming day.'

'You've dropped the pidgin, Lee.'

'I hope for good. Of course, I use it in King City.' He addressed a few short sung syllables to the boys on the ground, and they both smiled up at him and waved their sticks in the air. Lee said, 'I'll pour you a drink. It's some that was here.'

'It's some you bought yesterday in King City,' said Samuel.

Now that Samuel and Adam were seated together and the barriers were down, a curtain of shyness fell on Samuel. What he had beaten in with his fists he could not supplement easily. He thought of the virtues of courage and forbearance, which became flabby when there is nothing to use them on. His mind grinned inward at itself.

The two sat looking at the twin boys in their strange, bright-coloured clothes. Samuel thought, 'Sometimes your opponent can help you more than your friend.' He lifted his eyes to Adam.

'It's hard to start,' he said, 'And it's like a put-off letter that gathers difficulties to itself out of the minutes. Could you give me a hand?'

Adam looked up for a moment and then back at the boys on the ground. 'There's a crashing in my head,' he said. 'Like sounds you hear under water. I'm having to dig myself out of a year.'

248

'Maybe you'll tell me how it was and that will get us started.'

Adam tossed down his drink and poured another and rolled the glass at an angle in his hand. The amber whisky moved high on the side and the pungent fruit odour of its warming filled the air. 'It's hard to remember,' he said, 'It was not agony but a dullness. But no – there were needles in it. You said I had not all the cards in the deck – and I was thinking of that. Maybe I'll never have all the cards.'

'Is it herself trying to come out? When a man says he does not want to speak of something he usually means he can think of nothing else.'

'Maybe it's that. She's all mixed up with the dullness, and I can't remember much except the last picture drawn in fire.'

'She did shoot you, didn't she, Adam?'

His lips grew thin and his eyes black.

Samuel said, 'There's no need to answer.'

'There's no reason not to,' Adam replied. 'Yes, she did.'

'Did she mean to kill you?'

'I've thought of that more than anything else. No, I don't think she meant to kill me. She didn't allow me that dignity. There was no hatred in her, no passion at all. I learned about that in the army. If you want to kill a man, you shoot at head or heart or stomach. No, she hit me where she intended. I can see the gun-barrel moving over. I guess I wouldn't have minded so much if she had wanted my death. That would have been a kind of love. But I was an annoyance, not an enemy.'

'You've given it a lot of thought,' said Samuel.

'I've had lots of time for it. I want to ask you something. I can't remember behind the last ugly thing. Was she very beautiful, Samuel?'

'To you she was because you built her. I don't think you ever saw her – only your own creation.'

Adam mused aloud, 'I wonder who she was – what she was. I was content not to know.'

'And now you want to?'

Adam dropped his eyes. 'It's not curiosity. But I would like to know what kind of blood is in my boys. When they grow up – won't I be looking for something in them?'

'Yes, you will. And I will warn you now that not their blood but your suspicion might build evil in them. They will be what you expect of them.'

'But their blood — '

'I don't very much believe in blood,' said Samuel. 'I think

249

when a man finds good or bad in his children he is seeing only what he planted in them after they cleared the womb.'

'You can't make a racehorse of a pig.'

'No,' said Samuel, 'but you can make a very fast pig.'

'No one hereabouts would agree with you. I think even Mrs Hamilton would not.'

'That's exactly right. She most of all would disagree, and so I would not say it to her and let loose the thunder of her disagreement. She wins all arguments by the use of vehemence and the conviction that a difference of opinion is a personal affront. She's a fine woman, but you have to learn to feel your way with her. Let's speak of the boys.'

'Will you have another drink?'

'That I will, thank you. Names are a great mystery. I've never known whether the name is moulded by the child or the child changed to fit the name. But you can be sure of this – whenever a human has a nickname it is a proof that the name given him was wrong. How do you favour the standard names – John or James or Charles?'

Adam was looking at the twins and suddenly with the mention of the name he saw his brother peering out of the eyes of one of the boys. He leaned forward.

'What is it?' Samuel asked.

'Why,' Adam cried, 'these boys are not alike! They don't look alike.'

'Of course they don't. They're not identical twins.'

'That one – that one looks like my brother. I just saw it. I wonder if the other looks like me.'

'Both of them do. A face has everything in it right back to the beginning.'

'It's not so much now,' said Adam. 'But for a moment I thought I was seeing a ghost.'

'Maybe that's what ghosts are,' Samuel observed.

Lee brought dishes out and put them on the table.

'Do you have Chinese ghosts?' Samuel asked.

'Millions,' said Lee. 'We have more ghosts than anything else. I guess nothing in China ever dies. It's very crowded. Anyway, that's the feeling I got when I was there.'

Samuel said, 'Sit down, Lee. We're trying to think of names.'

'I've got chicken frying. It will be ready pretty soon.'

Adam looked up from the twins and his eyes were warmed and softened. 'Will you have a drink, Lee?'

'I'm nipping at the ng-ka-py in the kitchen,' said Lee and went back to the house.'

Samuel leaned down and gathered up one of the boys and held him on his lap. 'Take that one up,' he said to Adam. 'We ought to see whether there's something that draws names to them.'

Adam held the other child awkwardly on his knee. 'They look some alike,' he said, 'but not when you look close. This one has rounder eyes than that one.'

'Yes, and a rounder head and bigger ears,' Samuel added. 'But this one is more like – like a bullet. This one might go farther but not so high. And this one is going to be darker in the hair and skin. This one will be shrewd, I think, and shrewdness is a limitation on the mind. Shrewdness tells you what you must not do because it would not be shrewd. See how this one supports himself! He's farther along than that one – better developed. Isn't it strange how different they are when you look close?'

Adam's face was changing as though he had opened and come out on his surface. He held up his finger, and the child made a lunge for it and missed and nearly fell off his lap. 'Whoa!' said Adam. 'Take it easy. Do you want to fall?'

'It would be a mistake to name them for qualities we think they have,' Samuel said. 'We might be wrong – so wrong. Maybe it would be good to give them a high mark to shoot at – a name to live up to. The man I'm named after had his name called clear by the Lord God, and I've been listening all my life. And once or twice I've thought I heard my name called – but not clear, not clear.'

Adam, holding the child by his upper arm, leaned over and poured whisky in both glasses. 'I thank you for coming, Samuel,' he said. 'I even thank you for hitting me. That's a strange thing to say.'

'It was a strange thing for me to do. Liza will never believe it, and so I'll never tell her. An unbelieved truth can hurt a man much more than a lie. It takes great courage to back truth unacceptable to our times. There's a punishment for it, and it's usually crucifixion. I haven't the courage for that.'

Adam said, 'I've wondered why a man of your knowledge would work a desert hill place.'

'It's because I haven't courage,' said Samuel. 'I could never quite take the responsibility. When the Lord God did not call my name, I might have called His name – but I did not. There you have the difference between greatness and mediocrity. It's

251

not an uncommon disease. But it's nice for a mediocre man to know that greatness must be the loneliest state in the world.'

'I'd think there are degrees of greatness,' Adam said.

'I don't think so,' said Samuel. 'That would be like saying there is a little bigness. No. I believe when you come to that responsibility the hugeness and you are alone to make your choice. On one side you have warmth and companionship and sweet understanding, and on the other – cold, lonely greatness. There you make your choice. I'm glad I chose mediocrity, but how am I to say what reward might have come with the other? None of my children will be great either, except perhaps Tom. He's suffering over the choosing right now. It's a painful thing to watch. And somewhere in me I want him to say yes. Isn't that strange? A father to want his son condemned to greatness! What selfishness that must be.'

Adam chuckled. 'This naming is no simple business, I see.'

'Did you think it would be?'

'I didn't know it could be so pleasant,' said Adam.

Lee came out with a platter of fried chicken, a bowl of smoking boiled potatoes, and a deep dish of pickled beets, all carried on a pastry board. 'I don't know how good it will be,' he said. 'The hens are a little old. We don't have any pullets. The weasels got the baby chicks this year.'

'Pull up,' said Samuel.

'Wait until I get my ng-ka-py,' said Lee.

While he was gone Adam said, 'It's strange to me – he used to speak differently.'

'He trusts you now,' Samuel said. 'He has a gift of resigned loyalty without hope of reward. He's maybe a much better man than either of us could dream of being.'

Lee came back and took his seat at the end of the table. 'Just put the boys on the ground,' he said.

The twins protested when they were set down. Lee spoke to them sharply in Cantonese and they were silent.

The men ate quietly as nearly all country people do. Suddenly Lee got up and hurried into the house. He came back with a jug of red wine. 'I forgot it,' he said. 'I found it in the house.'

Adam laughed. 'I remember drinking wine here before I bought the place. Maybe I bought the place because of the wine. The chicken's good, Lee. I don't think I've been aware of the taste of food for a long time.'

'You're getting well,' Samuel said. 'Some people think it's an insult to the glory of their sickness to get well. But the time poultice is no respecter of glories. Everyone gets well if he waits around.'

Lee cleared the table and gave each of the boys a clean drumstick. They sat solemnly holding their greasy batons and alternately inspecting and sucking them. The wine and the glasses stayed on the table.

'We'd best get on with the naming,' Samuel said. 'I can feel a little tightening on my halter from Liza.'

'I can't think what to name them,' Adam said.

'You have no family name you want – no inviting trap for a rich relative, no proud name to re-create?'

'No, I'd like them to start fresh, in so far as that is possible.'

Samuel knocked his forehead with his knuckles. 'What a shame,' he said. 'What a shame it is that the proper names for them they cannot have.'

'What do you mean?' Adam asked.

'Freshness, you said. I thought last night — ' He paused. 'Have you thought of your own name?'

'Mine?'

'Of course. Your first-born – Cain and Abel.'

Adam said, 'Oh, no. No, we can't do that.'

'I know we can't. That would be tempting whatever fate there is. But isn't it odd that Cain is maybe the best-known name in the whole world and as far as I know only one man has ever borne it?'

Lee said, 'Maybe that's why the name has never changed its emphasis.'

Adam looked into the ink-red wine in his glass. 'I got a shiver when you mentioned it,' he said.

'Two stories have haunted us and followed us from our beginning,' Samuel said. 'We can carry them along with us like invisible tails – the story of original sin and the story of Cain and Abel. And I don't understand either of them. I don't understand them at all, but I feel them. Liza gets angry with me. She says I should not try to understand them. She says why should we try to explain a verity. Maybe she's right – maybe she's right. Lee, Liza says you're a Presbyterian – do you understand the Garden of Eden and Cain and Abel?'

'She thought I should be something, and I went to Sunday

253

School long ago in San Francisco. People like you to be something, preferably what they are.'

Adam said, 'He asked you if you understood.'

'I think I understand the Fall. I could perhaps feel that in myself. But the brother murder – no. Well, maybe I don't remember the details very well.'

Samuel said, 'Most people don't read the details. It's the details that astonish me. And Abel had no children.' He looked up at the sky. 'Lord, how the day passes! It's like a life – so quickly when we don't watch it and so slowly when we do. No,' he said, 'I'm having enjoyment. And I made a promise to myself that I would not consider enjoyment a sin. I take a pleasure in inquiring into things. I've never been content to pass a stone without looking under it. And it is a black disappointment to me that I can never see the far side of the moon.'

'I don't have a Bible,' Adam said. 'I left the family one in Connecticut.'

'I have,' said Lee. 'I'll get it.'

'No need,' said Samuel. 'Liza let me take her mother's. It's here in my pocket.' He took out the package and unwrapped the battered book. 'This one has been scraped and gnawed at,' he said. 'I wonder what agonies have settled here. Give me a used Bible and I will, I think, be able to tell you about a man by the places that are edged with the dirt of seeking fingers. Liza wears a Bible down evenly. Here we are – this oldest story. If it troubles us it must be that we find the trouble in ourselves.'

'I haven't heard it since I was a child,' said Adam.

'You think it's long then, and it's very short,' said Samuel. 'I'll read it through and then we'll go back. Give me a little wine, my throat's dried out with wine. Here it is – such a little story to have made so deep a wound.' He looked down at the ground. 'See!' he said. 'The boys have gone to their sleep, there in the dust.'

Lee got up. 'I'll cover them,' he said.

'The dust is warm,' said Samuel. 'Now it goes this way. "And Adam knew Eve his wife; and she conceived, and bare Cain, and said, 'I have gotten a man from the Lord.'"'

Adam started to speak and Samuel looked up at him and he was silent and covered his eyes with his hand. Samuel read, '"And she again bare his brother Abel. And Abel was a keeper of sheep, but Cain was a tiller of the ground. And in the process of time it came to pass that Cain brought of the fruit of the ground an offering unto the Lord. And Abel, he also brought of the firstlings of his flock and of the fat thereof. And the Lord had respect unto Abel and to his offering. But unto Cain and to his offering he had not respect." '

Lee said, 'Now where – no, go on, go on. We'll come back.'

Samuel read, ' "And Cain was very wroth, and his countenance fell. And the Lord said unto Cain, 'Why art thou wroth? And why is thy countenance fallen? If thou doest well, shall thou not be accepted? And if thou doest not well, sin lieth at the door. And unto thee shall be his desire, and thou shalt rule over him'.

' "And Cain talked with Abel his brother: and it came to pass, when they were in the field, that Cain rose up against Abel his brother and slew him. And the Lord said unto Cain, 'Where is Abel thy brother?' And he said, 'I know not. Am I my brother's keeper?' And he said, 'What hast thou done? The voice of thy brother's blood crieth unto me from the ground. And now art thou cursed from the earth, which hath opened her mouth to receive thy brother's blood from thy hand. When thou tillest the ground it shall not henceforth yield unto thee her strength; a fugitive and a vagabond shalt thou be in the earth.' And Cain said unto the Lord, 'My punishment is greater than I can bear. Behold, thou hast driven me out this day from the face of the earth, and from thy face shall I be hid. And I shall be a fugitive and a vagabond in the earth; and it shall come to pass that everyone that findeth me shall slay me.' And the Lord said unto him, 'Therefore whosoever slayeth Cain, vengeance shall be taken on him sevenfold.' And the Lord set a mark upon Cain, lest any finding him should kill him. And Cain went out from the presence of the Lord and dwelt in the land of Nod on the east of Eden." '

Samuel closed the loose cover of the book almost with weariness. 'There it is,' he said. 'Sixteen verses, no more. And oh, Lord! I had forgotten how dreadful it is – no single tone of encouragement. Maybe Liza's right. There's nothing to understand.'

Adam sighed deeply. 'It's not a comforting story, is it?'

Lee poured a tumbler full of dark liquor from his round stone bottle and sipped it and opened his mouth to get the double taste on the back of his tongue. 'No story has power, nor will it last, unless we feel in ourselves that it is true and true of us. What a great burden of guilt men have!'

Samuel said to Adam, 'And you have tried to take it all.'

Lee said, 'So do I, so does everyone. We gather our arms full of guilt as though it were precious stuff. It must be that we want it that way.'

Adam broke in, 'It makes me feel better, not worse.'

'How do you mean?' Samuel asked.

'Well, every little boy thinks he invented sin. Virtue we think we learn, because we are told about it. But sin is our own designing.'

'Yes, I can see. But how does this story make it better?'

'Because,' Adam said excitedly, 'we are descended from this. This is our father. Some of our guilt is absorbed in our ancestry. What chance did we have? We are the children of our father. It means we aren't the first. It's an excuse, and there aren't enough excuses in the world.'

'Not convincing ones anyway,' said Lee. 'Else we would long ago have wiped out guilt, and the world would not be filled with sad, punished people.'

Samuel said, 'But do you think of another frame for this picture? Excuse or not, we are snapped back to our ancestry. We have guilt.'

Adam said, 'I remember being a little outraged at God. Both Cain and Abel gave what they had, and God accepted Abel and rejected Cain. I never thought that was a just thing. I never understood it. Do you?'

'Maybe we think out of a different background,' said Lee. 'I remember that this story was written by and for a shepherd people. They were not farmers. Wouldn't the god of shepherds find a fat lamb more valuable than a sheaf of barley? A sacrifice must be the best and most valuable.'

'Yes, I can see that,' said Samuel. 'And Lee, let me caution you about bringing your Oriental reasoning to Liza's attention.'

Adam was excited. 'Yes, but why did God condemn Cain? That's an injustice.'

Samuel said, 'There's an advantage to listening to the words. God did not condemn Cain at all. Even God can have a preference, can't He? Let's suppose God liked lamb better than vegetables. I think I do myself. Cain brought Him a bunch of carrots maybe. And God said, "I don't like this. Try again. Bring me something I like and I'll set you up alongside your brother." But Cain got mad. His feelings were hurt. And when a man's feelings are hurt he wants to strike at something, and Abel was in the way of his anger.'

Lee said, 'St Paul says to the Hebrews that Abel had faith.'

'There's no reference to it in Genesis,' Samuel said. 'No faith or lack of faith. Only a hint of Cain's temper.'

Lee asked, 'How does Mrs Hamilton feel about the paradoxes of the Bible?'

'Why, she does not feel anything because she does not admit they are there.'

'But —'

'Hush, man. Ask her. And you'll come out of it older but not less confused.'

Adam said, 'You two have studied this. I only got it through my skin and not much of it stuck. Then Cain was driven out for murder?'

'That's right – for murder.'

'And God branded him?'

'Did you listen? Cain bore the mark not to destroy him but to save him. And there's a curse called down on any man who shall kill him. It was a preserving mark.'

Adam said, 'I can't get over a feeling that Cain got the dirty end of the stick.'

'Maybe he did,' said Samuel. 'But Cain lived and had children, and Abel lives only in the story. We are Cain's children. And isn't it strange that three grown men, here in a century so many thousands of years away, discuss this crime as though it happened in King City yesterday and hadn't come up for trial?'

One of the twins awakened and yawned and looked at Lee and went to sleep again.

Lee said, 'Remember, Mr Hamilton, I told you I was trying to translate some old Chinese poetry into English? No, don't worry. I won't read it. Doing it, I found some of the old things as fresh and clear as this morning. And I wondered why. And, of course, people are interested only in themselves. If a story is not about the hearer he will not listen. And I here make a rule – a great and lasting story is about everyone or it will not last. The strange and foreign is not interesting – only the deeply personal and familiar.'

Samuel said, 'Apply that to the Cain–Abel story.'

And Adam said, 'I didn't kill my brother —' Suddenly he stopped and his mind went reeling back in time.

'I think I can,' Lee answered Samuel. 'I think this is the best-known story in the world because it is everybody's story. I think it is the symbol story of the human soul. I'm feeling my way now – don't jump on me if I'm not clear. The greatest terror a child can have is that he is not loved, and rejection is the hell he fears. I think everyone in the world to a large or small extent has felt rejection. And with rejection comes anger, and with anger some kind of crime in revenge for the rejection, and with the crime guilt – and there is the story of mankind. I think that if rejection could be amputated, the human would not be what he is. Maybe there would be fewer crazy people. I am sure in myself there would not be many jails. It is all there – the start, the beginning. One child, refused the love he craves, kicks the cat and hides his secret guilt; and another steals so that money will make him loved; and a third conquers the world – and always the guilt and revenge and more guilt. The human is the only guilty animal. Now wait! Therefore I think this old and terrible story is important because it is a chart of the soul – the secret, rejected, guilty soul. Mr Trask, you said you did not kill your brother and then you remembered something. I don't want to know what it was, but was it very far apart from Cain and Abel? And what do you think of my Oriental patter, Mr Hamilton? You know I am no more Oriental than you are.'

Samuel had leaned his elbows on the table and his hands covered his eyes and his forehead. 'I want to think,' he said. 'Damn you, I want to think. I'll want to take this off alone where I can pick it apart and see. Maybe you've tumbled a world for me. And I don't know what I can build in my world's place.'

Lee said softly, 'Couldn't a world be built around accepted truth? Couldn't some pains and insanities be rooted out if the causes were known?'

'I don't know, damn you. You've disturbed my pretty universe. You've taken a contentious game and made an answer of it. Let me alone – let me think! Your damned bitch is having pups in my brain already. Oh, I wonder what my Tom will think of this! He'll cradle it in the palm of his hand. He'll turn it slow in his brain like a roast of pork before the fire. Adam, come out now. You've been long enough in whatever memory it was.'

Adam started. He sighed deeply. 'Isn't it too simple?' he asked. 'I'm always afraid of simple things.'

'It isn't simple at all,' said Lee. 'It's desperately complicated. But at the end there's light.'

'There's not going to be light long,' Samuel said. 'We've sat and let the evening come. I drove over to help name the twins and they're not named. We've swung ourselves on a pole. Lee, you better keep your complications out of the machinery of the set-up churches or there might be a Chinese with nails in his hands and feet. They like complications, but they like their own. I'll have to be driving home.'

Adam said desperately, 'Name me some names.'

'From the Bible?'

'From anyplace.'

'Well, let's see. Of all the people who started out of Egypt only two came to the Promised Land. Would you like them for a symbol?'

'Who?'

'Caleb and Joshua.'

'Joshua was a soldier – a general. I don't like soldiering.'

'Well, Caleb was a captain.'

'But not a general. I kind of like Caleb – Caleb Trask.'

One of the twins woke up and without interval began to wail.

'You called his name,' said Samuel. 'You don't like Joshua, and Caleb's named. He's the smart one – the dark one. See, the other one is awake too. Well, Aaron I've always liked, but he didn't make it to the Promised Land.'

The second boy almost joyfully began to cry.

'That's good enough,' said Adam.

Suddenly Samuel laughed. 'In two minutes,' he said, 'and after a waterfall of words. Caleb and Aaron – now you are people and you have joined the fraternity and you have the right to be damned.'

Lee took the boys up under his arms. 'Have you got them straight?' he asked.

'Of course,' said Adam. 'That one is Caleb and you are Aaron.'

Lee lugged the yelling twins towards the house in the dusk.

'Yesterday I couldn't tell them apart,' said Adam. 'Aaron and Caleb.'

'Thank the good Lord we had produce from our patient thought,' Samuel said. 'Liza would have preferred Joshua. She loves the crashing walls of Jericho. But she likes Aaron too, so I guess it's all right. I'll go and hitch my rig.'

Adam walked to the shed with him. 'I'm glad you came,' he said. 'There's a weight off me.'

Samuel slipped the bit in Doxology's reluctant mouth, set the brow-band, and buckled the throat-latch. 'Maybe you'll now be thinking of the garden in the flat land,' he said. 'I can see it there the way you planned it.'

Adam was long in answering. At last he said, 'I think that kind of energy is gone out of me. I can't feel the pull of it. I have money enough to live. I never wanted it for myself. I have no one to show a garden to.'

Samuel wheeled on him and his eyes were filled with tears. 'Don't think it will ever die,' he cried. 'Don't expect it. Are you better than other men? I tell you it won't ever die until you do.' He stood panting for a moment and then he climbed into the rig and whipped Doxology and he drove away, his shoulders hunched, without saying goodbye.

Part Three

CHAPTER 23

I

THE HAMILTONS were strange, high-strung people, and some of them were tuned too high and they snapped. This happens often in the world.

Of all his daughters Una was Samuel's greatest joy. Even as a little girl she hungered for learning as a child does for cookies in the late afternoon. Una and her father had a conspiracy about learning – secret books were borrowed and read and their secrets communicated privately.

Of all the children Una had the least humour. She met and married an intense dark man – a man whose fingers were stained with chemicals, mostly silver nitrate. He was one of those men who live in poverty so that their lines of questioning may continue. His question was about photography. He believed that the exterior world could be transferred to paper – not in the ghost shadings of black and white but in the colours the human eye perceives.

His name was Anderson and he had little gift for communication. Like most technicians, he had a terror and a contempt for speculation. The inductive leap was not for him. He dug a step and pulled himself up one single step, the way a man climbs the last shoulder of a mountain. He had great contempt, born of fear, for the Hamiltons, for they all half believed they had wings – and they got some bad falls that way.

Anderson never fell, never slipped back, never flew. His steps moved slowly, slowly upwards, and in the end, it is said, he found what he wanted – colour film. He married Una, perhaps, because she had little humour, and this reassured him. And because her family frightened and embarrassed him, he took her away to the north, and it was black and lost where he went – somewhere on the borders of Oregon. He must have lived a very primitive life with his bottles and papers.

Una wrote bleak letters without joy but also without self-pity. She was well and she hoped the family was well. Her husband was near to his discovery.

And then she died and her body was shipped home.

I never knew Una. She was dead before I remember, but George Hamilton told me about it many years later and his eyes filled with tears and his voice croaked in the telling.

'Una was not a beautiful girl like Mollie,' he said. 'But she had the loveliest hands and feet. Her ankles were as slender as grass and she moved like grass. Her fingers were long and the nails narrow and shaped like almonds. And Una had lovely skin too, translucent, even glowing.

'She didn't laugh and play like the rest of us. There was something set apart about her. She seemed always to be listening. When she was reading, her face would be like the face of one listening to music. And when we asked her any question, why, she gave the answer, if she knew it – not pointed up and full of colour and "maybes" and "it-might-bes" the way the rest of us would. We were always full of bull. There was some pure simple thing in Una,' George said.

'And then they brought her home. Her nails were broken to the quick and her fingers cracked and all worn out. And her poor, dear feet —' George could not go on for a while, and then he said with the fierceness of a man trying to control himself, 'Her feet were broken and gravel-cut and briar-cut. Her dear feet had not worn shoes for a long time. And her skin was rough as rawhide.

'We think it was an accident,' he said. 'So many chemicals around. We think it was.'

But Samuel thought and mourned in the thought that the accident was pain and despair.

Una's death struck Samuel like a silent earthquake. He said no brave and reassuring words, he simply sat alone and rocked himself. He felt that it was his neglect that had done it.

And now his tissue, which had fought joyously against time, gave up a little. His young skin turned old, his clear eyes dulled, and a little stoop came to his great shoulders. Liza with her acceptance could take care of tragedy; she had no real hope this side of Heaven. But Samuel had put up a laughing wall against natural laws, and Una's death breached his battlements. He became an old man.

His other children were doing well. George was in the insurance business. Will was getting rich. Joe had gone east and was helping to invent a new profession called advertising. Joe's very faults were virtues in this field. He found that he could communicate his material day-dreaming – and, properly applied, that is all advertising is. Joe was a big man in a new field.

The girls were married, all except Dessie, and she had a successful dressmaking business in Salinas. Only Tom had never got started.

Samuel told Adam Trask that Tom was arguing with greatness. And the father watched his son and could feel the drive and the fear, the advance and the retreat, because he could feel it in himself.

Tom did not have his father's lyric softness or his gay good looks. But you could feel Tom when you came near him – you could feel strength and warmth and an iron integrity. And under all of this was a shrinking – a shy shrinking. He could be as gay as his father, and suddenly in the middle of it would be cut the way you would cut a violin string, and you could watch Tom go whirling into darkness.

He was a dark-faced man; his skin, perhaps from sun, was a black red, as though some Norse or perhaps Vandal blood was perpetuated in him. His hair and beard and moustache were dark red too, and his eyes gleamed startlingly blue against his colouring. He was powerful, heavy of shoulders and arm, but his hips were slim. He could lift and run and hike and ride with anyone, but he had no sense of competition whatever. Will and George were gamblers and often tried to entice their brother into the joys and sorrows of venture.

Tom said, 'I've tried and it just seems tiresome. I've thought why this must be. I get no great triumph when I win and no tragedy when I lose. Without these it is meaningless. It is not a way to make money, that we know, and unless it can simulate birth and death, joy and sorrow, it seems, at least to me – it feels – it doesn't feel at all. I would do it if I felt anything – good or bad.'

Will did not understand this. His whole life was competitive and he lived by one kind of gambling or another. He loved Tom and he tried to give him the things he himself found pleasant. He took him into business and tried to inoculate him with the joys of buying and selling, of outwitting other men, of judging them for a bluff, of living by manoeuvre.

Always Tom came back to the ranch, puzzled, not critical, but feeling that somewhere he had lost track. He felt that he should take joy in the man-pleasures of contest, but he could not pretend to himself that he did.

Samuel had said that Tom always took too much on his plate, whether it was beans or women. And Samuel was wise, but I think he knew only one side of Tom. Maybe Tom opened up a little more for children. What I set down about him will be the result of memory plus what I know to be true plus conjecture built on the combination. Who knows whether it will be correct?

We lived in Salinas and we knew when Tom had arrived – I think he always arrived at night – because under our pillows, Mary's and mine, there would be packages of gum. And gum was valuable in those days just as a nickel was valuable. There were months when he did not come, but every morning as soon as we awakened we put our hands under our pillows to see. And I still do it, and it has been many years since there had been gum there.

My sister Mary did not want to be a girl. It was a misfortune she could not get used to. She was an athlete, a marble player, a pitcher of one-o'-cat, and the trappings of a girl inhibited her. Of course this was long before the compensations for being a girl were apparent to her.

Just as we knew that somewhere on our bodies, probably under the arm, there was a button which if pressed just right would permit us to fly, so Mary had worked out a magic for herself to change her over into the tough little boy she wanted to be. If she went to sleep in a magical position, knees crooked just right, head at a magical angle, fingers all crossed one over the other, in the morning she would be a boy. Every night she tried to find exactly the right combination, but she never could. I used to help her cross her fingers like shiplap.

She was despairing of ever getting it right when one morning there was gum under the pillow. We each peeled a stick and solemnly chewed it; it was Beeman's peppermint, and nothing so delicious has been made since.

Mary was pulling on her long black ribbed stockings when she said with great relief, 'Of course.'

'Of course what?' I asked.

'Uncle Tom,' she said and chewed her gum with great snapping sounds.

'Uncle Tom what?' I demanded.

'He'll know how to get to be a boy.'

There it was – just as simple as that. I wondered why I hadn't thought of it myself.

Mother was in the kitchen overseeing a new little Danish girl who worked for us. We had a series of girls. New-come Danish farm families put their daughters out to service with American families, and they learned not only English but American cooking and table setting and manners and all the little niceties of high life in Salinas. At the end of a couple of years of this, at twelve dollars a month, the girls were highly desirable wives for American boys. Not only did they have American manners but they could still work like horses in the fields. Some of the most elegant families in Salinas today are descended from these girls.

It would be flaxen-haired Mathilde in the kitchen, with Mother clucking over her like a hen.

We charged in. 'Is he up?'

'Sh!' said Mother. 'He got in late. You let him sleep.'

But the water was running in the basin of the back bedroom, so we knew he was up. We crouched like cats at his door, waiting for him to emerge.

There was always a little diffidence between us at first. I think Uncle Tom was as shy as we were. I think he wanted to come running out and toss us in the air, but instead we were all formal.

'Thank you for the gum, Uncle Tom.'

'I'm glad you liked it.'

'Do you think we'll have an oyster loaf late at night while you're here?'

'We'll certainly try, if your mother will let you.'

We drifted into the sitting-room and sat down. Mother's voice called from the kitchen, 'Children, you let him alone.'

'They're all right, Ollie,' he called back.

We sat in a triangle in the living-room. Tom's face was so dark and his eyes so blue. He wore good clothes but he never seemed well dressed. In this he was very different from his father. His red moustache was never neat and his hair would not lie down and his hands were hard from work.

Mary said, 'Uncle Tom, how do you get to be a boy?'

'How? Why, Mary, you're just born a boy.'

'No, that's not what I mean. How do *I* get to be a boy?'

Tom studied her gravely. 'You?' he asked.

Her words poured out. 'I don't want to be a girl, Uncle Tom. I want to be a boy. A girl's all kissing and dolls. I don't want to be a girl. I don't want to be.' Tears of anger welled up in Mary's eyes.

Tom looked down at his hands and picked at a loose piece of callous with a broken nail. He wanted to say something beautiful, I think. He wished for words like his father's words, sweet winged words, cooing and lovely. 'I wouldn't like you to be a boy,' he said.

'Why not?'

'I like you as a girl.'

An idol was crashing in Mary's temple. 'You mean you like girls?'

'Yes, Mary, I like girls very much.'

A look of distaste crossed Mary's face. If it were true, Tom was a fool. She put on her don't-give-me-any-of-that-crap tone. 'All right,' she said, 'but how do I go about being a boy?'

Tom had a good ear. He knew he was reeling down in Mary's estimation and he wanted her to love him and to admire him. At the same time there was a fine steel wire of truthfulness in him that cut off the heads of fast-travelling lies. He looked at Mary's hair, so light that it was almost white, and braided tight to be out of the way, and dirty at the end of the braid, for Mary wiped her hands on her braid before she made a difficult marble shot. Tom studied her cold and hostile eyes.

'I don't think you really want to change.'

'I do.'

Tom was wrong – she really did.

'Well,' he said, 'you can't. And some day you'll be glad.'

'I won't be glad,' said Mary, and she turned to me and said with frigid contempt, 'He doesn't know!'

Tom winced and I shivered at the immensity of her criminal charge. Mary was braver and more ruthless than most. That's why she won every marble in Salinas.

Tom said uneasily, 'If your mother says it's all right, I'll order the oyster loaf this morning and pick it up tonight.'

'I don't like oyster loaves,' said Mary and stalked to our bedroom and slammed the door.

Tom looked ruefully after her. 'She's a girl all right,' he said.

Now we were alone together and I felt that I had to heal the wound Mary had made. 'I love oyster loaves,' I said.

'Sure you do. So does Mary.'

'Uncle Tom, don't you think there's some way for her to be a boy?'

'No, I don't,' he said sadly. 'I would have told her if I had known.'

'She's the best pitcher in the West End.'

Tom sighed and looked down at his hands again, and I could see his failure on him and I was sorry for him, aching sorry. I brought out my hollowed cork with pins stuck down to make bars. 'Would you like to have my fly cage, Uncle Tom?'

Oh, he was a great gentleman. 'Do you want me to have it?'

'Yes. You see, you pull up a pin to get the fly in and then he sits in there and buzzes.'

'I'd like to have it very much. Thank you, John.'

He worked all day with a sharp tiny pocket-knife on a small block of wood, and when we came home from school he had carved a little face. The eyes and ears and lips were movable, and little perches connected them with the inside of the hollow head. At the bottom of the neck there was a hole closed by a cork. And this was very wonderful. You caught a fly and eased him through the hole and set the cork. And suddenly the head became alive. The eyes moved and the lips talked and the ears wiggled as the frantic fly crawled over the little perches. Even Mary forgave him a little, but she never really trusted him until after she was glad she was a girl, and then it was too late. He gave the head not to me but to us. We still have it put away somewhere, and it still works.

Sometimes Tom took me fishing. We started before the sun came up and drove in the rig straight towards Frémont Peak, and as we neared the mountains the stars would pale out and the light would rise to blacken the mountains. I can remember riding and pressing my ear and cheek against Tom's coat. And I can remember that his arm would rest lightly over my shoulders and his hand pat my arm occasionally. Finally we would pull up under an oak tree and take the horse out of the shafts, water him at the stream side, and halter him to the back of the rig.

I don't remember that Tom talked. Now that I think of it, I can't remember the sound of his voice or the kind of words he used. I can remember both about my grandfather, but when I think of Tom it is a memory of a kind of warm silence. Maybe he didn't talk at all. Tom had beautiful tackle and made his own flies. But he didn't seem to care whether we caught trout or not. He needed not to triumph over animals.

I remember the five-fingered ferns growing under little waterfalls, bobbing their green fingers as the droplets struck them. And I remember the smells of the hills, wild azalea and a very distant skunk and the sweet cloy of lupin and horse sweat on harness. I remember the sweeping lovely dance of high buzzards against the sky and Tom looking long up at them, but I can't remember that he ever said anything about them. I remember holding the bite of a line while Tom drove pegs and braided a splice. I remember the smell of crushed ferns in the creel and the delicate sweet odour of fresh damp rainbow trout lying so prettily on the green bed. And finally I can remember coming back to the rig and pouring rolled barley into the leather feed-bag and buckling it over the horse's head behind the ears. And

I have no sound of his voice or words in my ear; he is dark and silent and hugely warm in my memory.

Tom felt his darkness. His father was beautiful and clever, his mother was short and mathematically sure. Each of his brothers and sisters had looks or gifts or fortune. Tom loved all of them passionately, but he felt heavy and earth-bound. He climbed ecstatic mountains and floundered in the rocky darkness between the peaks. He had spurts of bravery but they were bracketed in the battens of cowardice.

Samuel said that Tom was quavering over greatness, trying to decide whether he could take the cold responsibility. Samuel knew his son's quality and felt the potential of violence, and it frightened him, for Samuel had no violence – even when he hit Adam Trask with his fist he had no violence. And the books that came into the house, some of them secretly – well, Samuel rode lightly on top of a book and he balanced happily among ideas the way a man rides white rapids in a canoe. But Tom got into a book, crawled and grovelled between the covers, tunnelled like a mole among the thoughts, and came up with the book all over his face and hands.

Violence and shyness – Tom's loins needed women and at the same time he did not think himself worthy of a woman. For long periods he would welter in a howling celibacy, and then he would take a train to San Francisco and roll and wallow in women, and then he would come silently back to the ranch, feeling weak and unfulfilled and unworthy and he would punish himself with work, would plough and plant unprofitable land, would cut tough oakwood until his back was breaking and his arms were weary rags.

It is probable that his father stood between Tom and the sun, and Samuel's shadow fell on him. Tom wrote secret poetry, and in those days it was only sensible to keep it secret. The poets were pale emasculates, and Western men held them in contempt. Poetry was a symptom of weakness, of degeneracy and decay. To read it was to court catcalls. To write it was to be suspected and ostracized. Poetry was a secret vice, and properly so. No one knows whether Tom's poetry was any good or not, for he showed it to only one person, and before he died he burned every word. From the ashes in the stove there must have been a great deal of it.

Of all his family Tom loved Dessie best. She was gay. Laughter lived on her doorstep.

Her shop was a unique institution in Salinas. It was a

woman's world. Here all the rules, and the fears that created the iron rules, went down. The door was closed to men. It was a sanctuary where women could be themselves – smelly, wanton, mystic, conceited, truthful, and interested. The whalebone corsets came off at Dessie's, the sacred corsets that moulded and warped woman-flesh into goddess-flesh. At Dessie's they were women who went to the toilet and over-ate and scratched and farted. And from this freedom came laughter, roars of laughter.

Men could hear the laughter through the closed door and were properly frightened at what was going on, feeling, perhaps, that they were the butt of the laughter – which to a large extent was true.

I can see Dessie now, her gold pince-nez wobbling on a nose not properly bridged for pince-nez, her eyes streaming with hilarious tears, and her whole front constricted with muscular spasms of laughter. Her hair would come down and drift between her glasses and her eyes, and the glasses would fall off her wet nose and spin and swing at the end of their black ribbon.

You had to order a dress from Dessie months in advance, and you made twenty visits to her shop before you chose material and pattern. Nothing so healthy as Dessie had ever happened to Salinas. The men had their lodges, their clubs, their whorehouses; the women nothing but the Altar Guild and the mincing coquetry of the minister, until Dessie came along.

And then Dessie fell in love. I do not know any details of her love affair – who the man was or what the circumstances, whether it was religion or a living wife, a disease or a selfishness. I guess my mother knew, but it was one of those things put away in the family closet and never brought out. And if other people in Salinas knew, they must have kept it a loyal town secret. All I do know is that it was a hopeless thing, grey and terrible. After a year of it the joy was all drained out of Dessie and the laughter had ceased.

Tom raged crazily through the hills like a lion in horrible pain. In the middle of a night he saddled and rode away, not waiting for the morning train, to Salinas. Samuel followed him and sent a telegram from King City to Salinas.

And when in the morning Tom, his face black, spurred his spent horse up John Street in Salinas, the sheriff was waiting for him. He disarmed Tom and put him in a cell and fed him black coffee and brandy until Samuel came for him.

Samuel did not lecture Tom. He took him home and never

mentioned the incident. And a stillness fell on the Hamilton place.

11

On Thanksgiving of 1911 the family gathered at the ranch – all the children except Joe, who was in New York, and Lizzie, who had left the family and joined another, and Una, who was dead. They arrived with presents and more food than even this clan could eat. They were all married save Dessie and Tom. Their children filled the Hamilton place with riot. The home place flared up – noisier than it had ever been. The children cried and screamed and fought. The men made many trips to the forge and came back self-consciously wiping their moustaches.

Liza's little round face grew redder and redder. She organized and ordered. The kitchen stove never went out. The beds were full, and comforters laid on pillows on the floor were for children.

Samuel dug up his old gaiety. His sardonic mind glowed and his speech took on its old singing rhythm. He hung on with the talk and the singing and the memories, and then suddenly, and it not midnight, he tired. Weariness came down on him, and he went to his bed where Liza had been for two hours. He was puzzled at himself, not that he had to go to bed but that he wanted to.

When the mother and father were gone, Will brought the whisky in from the forge and the clan had a meeting in the kitchen with whisky passed round in round-bottomed jelly glasses. The mothers crept to the bedrooms to see that the children were covered and then came back. They all spoke softly, not to disturb the children and the old people. There were Tom and Dessie, George and his pretty Mamie, who had been a Dempsey, Mollie and William J. Martin, Olive and Ernest Steinbeck, Will and his Deila.

They all wanted to say the same thing – all ten of them. Samuel was an old man. It was as startling a discovery as the sudden seeing of a ghost. Somehow they had not believed it could happen. They drank their whisky and talked softly of the new thought.

His shoulders – did you see how they slump? And there's no spring in his step.

His toes drag a little, but it's not that – it's his eyes. His eyes are old.

270

He would never go to bed until last.

Did you notice he forgot what he was saying right in the middle of a story?

It's his skin told me. It's gone wrinkled, and the backs of his hands have turned transparent.

He favours his right leg.

Yes, but that's the one the horse broke.

I know, but he never favoured it before.

They said these things in outrage. This can't happen, they were saying. Father can't be an old man. Samuel is young as the dawn – the perpetual dawn.

He might get old as midday maybe, but sweet God! the evening cannot come, and the night —? Sweet God, no!

It was natural that their minds leaped on and recoiled, and they would not speak of that, but their minds said, There can't be any world without Samuel.

How could we think about anything without knowing what he thought about it?

What would the spring be like, or Christmas, or rain? There couldn't be a Christmas.

Their minds shrank away from such thinking and they looked for a victim – someone to hurt because they were hurt. They turned on Tom.

You were here. You've been here all along!

How did this happen? When did it happen?

Who did this to him?

Have you by any chance done this with your craziness?

And Tom could stand it because he had been with it. 'It was Una,' he said hoarsely. 'He couldn't get over Una. He told me how a man, a real man, had no right to let sorrow destroy him. He told me again and again how I must believe that time would take care of it. He said it so often I knew he was losing.'

'Why didn't you tell us? Maybe we could have done something.'

Tom leaped up, violent and cringing. 'Goddam it! What was there to tell? That he was dying of sorrow? That the marrow had melted out of his bones? What was there to tell? You weren't here. I had to look at it and see his eyes die down – goddam it.' Tom went out of the room and they heard his clod-hopper feet knocking on the flinty ground outside.

They were ashamed. Will Martin said, 'I'll go out and bring him back.'

'Don't do it,' George said quickly, and the blood kin nodded.

'Don't do it. Let him alone. We know him from the insides of ourselves.'

In a little while Tom came back. 'I want to apologize,' he said. 'I'm very sorry. Maybe I'm a little drunk. Father calls it "jolly" when I do it. One night I rode home' – it was a confession – 'and I came staggering across the yard and I fell into the rosebush and crawled up the stairs on my hands and knees and I was sick on the floor beside my bed. In the morning I tried to tell him I was sorry, and do you know what he said? "Why, Tom, you were just jolly." "Jolly", if *I* did it. A drunken man didn't crawl home. Just jolly.'

George stopped the crazy flow of talk. 'We want to apologize to you, Tom,' he said. 'Why, we sounded as though we were blaming you and we didn't mean to. Or maybe we did mean to. And we're sorry.'

Will Martin said realistically, 'It's too hard a life here. Why don't we get him to sell out and move to town? He could have a long and happy life. Mollie and I would like them to come and live with us.'

'I don't think he'd do it,' said Will. 'He's stubborn as a mule and proud as a horse. He's got a pride like brass.'

Olive's husband, Ernest, said, 'Well, there'd be no harm in asking him. We would like to have him – or both of them – with us.'

Then they were silent again, for the idea of not having the ranch, the dry, stony desert of heart-breaking hillside and un-profitable hollow, was shocking to them.

Will Hamilton from instinct and training in business had become a fine reader of the less profound impulses of men and women. He said, 'If we ask him to close up shop it will be like asking him to close his life, and he won't do it.'

'You're right, Will,' George agreed. 'He would think it was like quitting. He'd feel it was a cowardice. No, he will never sell out, and if he did I don't think he would live a week.'

Will said, 'There's another way. Maybe he could come for a visit. Tom can run the ranch. It's time Father and Mother saw something of the world. All kinds of things are happening. It would freshen him, and then he could come back and go to work again. And after a while maybe he wouldn't have to. He says himself that thing about time doing the job that dynamite can't touch.'

Dessie brushed the hair out of her eyes. 'I wonder if you really think he's that stupid,' she said.

And Will said out of his experience, 'Sometimes a man wants to be stupid if it lets him do a thing his cleverness forbids. We can try it anyway. What do you all think?'

There was a nodding of heads in the kitchen, and only Tom sat rocklike and brooding.

'Tom, wouldn't you be willing to take over the ranch?' George asked.

'Oh, that's nothing,' said Tom. 'It's no trouble to run the ranch because the ranch doesn't run – never has.'

'Then why don't you agree?'

'I'd find a reluctance to insult my father,' Tom said. 'He'd know.'

'But where's the harm in suggesting it?'

Tom rubbed his ears until he forced the blood out of them and for a moment they were white. 'I don't forbid you,' he said. 'But I can't do it.'

George said, 'We could write it in a letter – a kind of invitation full of jokes. And when he got tired of one of us, he could go to another. There's years of visiting among the lot of us.' And that was how they left it.

III

Tom brought Olive's letter from King City, and because he knew what it contained he waited until he caught Samuel alone before he gave it to him. Samuel was working in the forge and his hands were black. He took the envelope by a tiny corner and put it on the anvil, and then he scrubbed his hands in the half-barrel of black water into which he plunged hot iron. He slit the letter open with the point of a horseshoe nail and went into the sunlight to read it. Tom had the wheels off the buckboard and was buttering the axles with yellow axle grease. He watched his father from the corners of his eyes.

Samuel finished the letter and folded it and put back in its envelope. He sat down on the bench in front of the shop and stared into space. Then he opened the letter and read it again and folded it again and put it in his blue shirt pocket. Then Tom saw him stand up and walk slowly up the eastern hill, kicking at the flints on the ground.

There had been a little rain and a fuzz of miserly grass had started up. Half way up the hill Samuel squatted down and took up a handful of the harsh gravelly earth in his palm and spread it with his forefinger, flint and sandstone and bits of shining mica and a frail rootlet and a veined stone. He let it slip from his hand and brushed his palms. He picked up a spear of grass and set it between his teeth and stared up the hill to the sky. A grey nervous cloud was scurrying eastward, searching for trees on which to rain.

Samuel stood up and sauntered down the hill. He looked into the tool-shed and patted the four-by-four supports. He paused near Tom and spun one of the free-running wheels of the buckboard, and he inspected Tom as though he saw him for the first time. 'Why, you're a grown-up man,' he said.

'Didn't you know?'

'I guess I did – I guess I did,' said Samuel and sauntered on. There was the sardonic look on his face his family knew so well – the joke on himself that made him laugh inwardly. He walked by the sad little garden and all round the house – not a new house any more. Even the last added lean-to bedrooms were old and weathered and the putty round the window-panes had shrunk away from the glass. At the porch he turned and surveyed the whole home cup of the ranch before he went inside.

Liza was rolling out pie-crust on the floury board. She was so expert with the rolling-pin that the dough seemed alive. It flattened out and then pulled back a little from tension in itself. Liza lifted the pale sheet of it and laid it over one of the pie tins and trimmed the edges with a knife. The prepared berries lay deep in red juice in a bowl.

Samuel sat down in a kitchen chair and crossed his legs and looked at her. His eyes were smiling.

'Can't you find something to do this time of day?' she asked.

'Oh, I guess I could, Mother, if I wanted to.'

'Well, don't sit there and make me nervous. The paper's in the other room if you're feeling day-lazy.'

'I've read it,' said Samuel.

'All of it?'

'All I want to.'

'Samuel, what's the matter with you? You're up to something. I can see it in your face. Now tell it, and let me get on with my pies.'

He swung his leg and smiled at her. 'Such a little bit of a wife,' he said. 'Three of her is hardly a bite.'

'Samuel, now you stop that. I don't mind a joke in the evening sometimes, but it's not eleven o'clock. Now you go along.'

Samuel said, 'Liza, do you know the meaning of the English word "vacation"?'

'Now don't you make jokes in the morning.'

'Do you, Liza?'

'Of course I do. Don't play me for a fool.'

'What does it mean?'

'Going away for a rest to the sea and the beach. Now, Samuel, get out with your fooling.'

'I wonder how you know the word.'

'Will you tell me what you're after? Why shouldn't I know?'

'Did you ever have one, Liza?'

'Why, I —' She stopped.

'In fifty years, did you ever have a vacation, you little, silly, half-pint, smidgin of a wife?'

'Samuel, please go out of my kitchen,' she said apprehensively.

He took the letter from his pocket and unfolded it. 'It's from Ollie' he said. 'She wants us to come and visit in Salinas. They've fixed over the upstairs rooms. She wants us to get to know the children. She's got us tickets for the Chautauqua season. Billy Sunday's going to wrestle with the Devil and Bryan is going to make his Cross of Gold speech. I'd like to hear that. It's an old fool of a speech but they say he gives it in a way to break your heart.'

Liza rubbed her nose and floured it with her finger. 'Is it very costly?' she asked anxiously.

'Costly? Ollie has bought the tickets. They're a present.'

'We can't go,' said Liza. 'Who'd run the ranch?'

'Tom would – what running there is to do in the winter.'

'He'd be lonely.'

'George would maybe come out and stay a while to go quail hunting. See what's in the letter, Liza.'

'What are those?'

'Two tickets to Salinas on the train. Ollie says she doesn't want to give us a single escape.'

'You can just turn them in and send her back the money.'

'No, I can't. Why, Liza – Mother – now don't. Here – here's a handkerchief.'

'That's a dish-towel,' said Liza.

'Sit here, Mother. There! I guess the shock of taking a rest kind of threw you. Here! I know it's a dish-towel. They say that Billy Sunday drives the Devil all over the stage.'

'That's blasphemy,' said Liza.

'But I'd like to see it, wouldn't you? What did you say? Hold up your head. I didn't hear you. What did you say?'

'I said yes,' said Liza.

Tom was making a drawing when Samuel came in to him. Tom looked at his father with veiled eyes, trying to read the effect of Olive's letter.

Samuel looked at the drawing. 'What is it?'

'I'm trying to work out a gate-opener so a man won't have to get out of his rig. Here's the pull-rod to open the latch.'

'What's going to open it?'

'I figured a strong spring.'

Samuel studied the drawing. 'Then what's going to close it?'

'This bar here. It would slip to this spring with the tension the other way.'

'I see,' said Samuel. 'It might work too, if the gate was truly hung. And it would only take twice as much time to make and keep up as twenty years of getting out of the rig and opening the gate.'

Tom protested, 'Sometimes with a skittish horse —'

'I know,' said his father. 'But the main reason is that it's fun.'

Tom grinned. 'Caught me,' he said.

'Tom, do you think you could look after the ranch if your mother and I took a little trip?'

'Why, sure,' said Tom. 'Where do you plan to go?'

'Ollie wants us to stay with her for a while in Salinas.'

'Why, that would be fine,' said Tom. 'Is Mother agreeable?'

'She is, always forgetting the expense.'

'That's fine,' said Tom. 'How long do you plan to be gone?'

Samuel's jewelled, sardonic eyes dwelt on Tom's face until Tom said, 'What's the matter, Father?'

'It's the little tone, son – so little that I could barely hear it. But it was there. Tom, my son, if you have a secret with your brothers and sisters, I don't mind. I think that's good.'

'I don't know what you mean,' said Tom.

'You may thank God you didn't want to be an actor, Tom, because you would have been a very bad one. You worked it out at Thanksgiving, I guess, when you were all together. And it's working smooth as butter. I see Will's hand in this. Don't tell me if you don't want to.'

'I wasn't in favour of it,' said Tom.

'It doesn't sound like you,' his father said. 'You'd be for scattering the truth out in the sun for me to see. Don't tell the others I know.' He turned away and then came back and put his hand on Tom's shoulders. 'Thank you for wanting to honour

276

me with the truth, my son. It's not clever but it's more permanent.'

'I'm glad you're going.'

Samuel stood in the doorway of the forge and looked at the land. 'They say a mother loves best an ugly child,' he said, and he shook his head sharply. 'Tom, I'll trade your honour for honour. You will please hold this in your dark secret place, nor tell any of your brothers and sisters – I know why I'm going – and, Tom, I know where I'm going, and I am content.'

CHAPTER 24

I

I HAVE wondered why it is that some people are less affected and torn by the verities of life and death than others. Una's death cut the earth from under Samuel's feet and opened his defended keep and let in old age. On the other hand Liza, who surely loved her family as deeply as did her husband, was not destroyed or warped. Her life continued evenly. She felt sorrow but she survived it.

I think perhaps Liza accepted the world as she accepted the Bible, with all of its paradoxes and its reverses. She did not like death but she knew it existed, and when it came it did not surprise her.

Samuel may have thought and played and philosophized about death, but he did not really believe in it. His world did not have death as a member. He, and all around him, was immortal. When real death came it was an outrage, a denial of the immortality he deeply felt, and the one crack in his wall caused the whole structure to crash. I think he had always thought he could argue himself out of death. It was a personal opponent and one he could lick.

To Liza it was simply death – the thing promised and expected. She could go on and in her sorrow put a pot of beans in the oven, bake six pies and plan to exactness how much food would be necessary properly to feed the funeral guests. And she could in her sorrow see that Samuel had a clean white shirt and that his black broadcloth was brushed and free of spots and his shoes blacked. Perhaps it takes these two kinds to make a good marriage, riveted with several kinds of strengths.

Once Samuel accepted, he could probably go farther than Liza, but the process of accepting tore him to pieces. Liza watched him closely after the decision to go to Salinas. She didn't quite know what he was up to, but, like a good and cautious mother, she knew he was up to something. She was a complete realist. Everything else being equal, she was glad to be going to visit her children. She was curious about them and their children. She had no love of places. A place was only a resting stage on the way to Heaven. She did not like work for itself, but she did it because it was there to be done. And she was tired. Increasingly it was more difficult to fight the aches and stiffness which tried to keep her in bed in the morning – not that they ever succeeded.

And she looked forward to Heaven as a place where clothes did not get dirty and where food did not have to be cooked and dishes washed. Privately there were some things in Heaven of which she did not quite approve. There was too much singing, and she didn't see how even the Elect could survive for very long the celestial laziness which was promised. She would find something to do in Heaven. There must be something to take up one's time – some clouds to darn, some weary wings to rub with liniment. Maybe the collars of the robes needed turning now and then, and when you come right down to it, she couldn't believe that even in Heaven there would not be cobwebs in some corner to be knocked down with a cloth-covered broom.

She was gay and frightened about the visit to Salinas. She liked the idea so well that she felt there must be something bordering on sin involved in it. And the Chautauqua? Well, she didn't have to go and probably wouldn't. Samuel would run wild – she would have to watch him. She never lost her feeling that he was young and helpless. It was a good thing that she did not know what went on in his mind, and, through his mind, what happened to his body.

Places were very important to Samuel. The ranch was a relative, and when he left it he plunged a knife into a darling. But having made up his mind, Samuel set about doing it well. He made formal calls on all of his neighbours, the old-timers who remembered how it used to be and how it was. And when he drove away from his old friends they knew they would not see him again, although he did not say it. He took to gazing at the mountains and the trees, even at faces, as though to memorize them for eternity.

He saved his visit to the Trask place for last. He had not been there for months. Adam was not a young man any more. The boys were eleven years old, and Lee – well, Lee did not change much. Lee walked to the shed with Samuel.

'I've wanted to talk to you for a long time,' said Lee. 'But there's so much to do. And I try to get to San Francisco at least once a month.'

'You know how it is,' Samuel said. 'When you know a friend is there you do not go to seek him. Then he's gone and you blast your conscience to shreds that you did not see him.'

'I heard about your daughter. I'm sorry.'

'I got your letter, Lee. I have it. You said good things.'

'Chinese things,' said Lee. 'I seem to get more Chinese as I get older.'

'There's something changed about you, Lee. What is it?'

'It's my queue, Mr Hamilton. I've cut off my queue.'

'That's it.'

'We all did. Haven't you heard? The Dowager Empress is gone. China is free. The Manchus are not overlords and we do not wear queues. It was a proclamation of the new government. There's not a queue left anywhere.'

'Does it make a difference, Lee?'

'Not much. It's easier. But there's a kind of looseness on the scalp that makes me uneasy. It's hard to get used to the convenience of it.'

'How is Adam?'

'He's all right. But he hasn't changed much. I wonder what he was like before.'

'Yes, I've wondered about that. It was a short flowering. The boys must be big.'

'They are big. I'm glad I stayed here. I learned a great deal from seeing the boys grow and helping a little.'

'Did you teach them Chinese?'

'No. Mr Trask didn't want me to. And I guess he was right. It would have been a needless complication. But I'm their friend – yes, I'm their friend. They admire their father, but I think they love me. And they're very different. You can't imagine how different.'

'In what way, Lee?'

'You'll see when they come home from school. They're like two sides of a medal. Cal is sharp and dark and watchful, and his brother – well, he's a boy you like before he speaks and like more afterwards.'

'And you don't like Cal?'

279

'I find myself defending him – to myself. He's fighting for his life and his brother doesn't have to fight.'

'I have the same thing in my brood,' said Samuel. 'I don't understand it. You'd think with the same training and the same blood they'd be alike, but they're not – not at all.'

Later Samuel and Adam walked down the oak-shadowed road to the entrance to the draw where they could look out at the Salinas Valley.

'Will you stay to dinner,' Adam asked.

'I will not be responsible for the murder of more chickens,' said Samuel.

'Lee's got a pot roast.'

'Well, in that case — '

Adam still carried one shoulder lower than the other from the old hurt. His face was hard and curtained, and his eyes looked at generalities and did not inspect details. The two men stopped in the road and looked out at the valley, green-tinged from the early rains.

Samuel said softly, 'I wonder you do not feel a shame at leaving that land fallow.'

'I had no reason to plant it,' Adam said. 'We had that out before. You thought I would change. I have not changed.'

'Do you take pride in your hurt?' Samuel asked. 'Does it make you seem large and tragic?'

'I don't know.'

'Well, think about it. Maybe you're playing a part on a great stage with only yourself as audience.'

A slight anger came into Adam's voice. 'Why do you come to lecture me? I'm glad you've come, but why do you dig into me?'

'To see whether I can raise a little anger in you. I'm a nosy man. But there's all that fallow land, and here beside me is all that fallow man. It seems a waste. And I have a bad feeling about waste because I could never afford it. Is it a good feeling to let your life lie fallow?'

'What else could I do?'

'You could try again.'

Adam faced him. 'I'm afraid to, Samuel,' he said. 'I'd rather just go about it this way. Maybe I haven't the energy or the courage.'

'How about your boys – do you love them?'

'Yes – yes.'

'Do you love one more than the other?'

'Why do you say that?'

'I don't know. Something about your tone.'

'Let's go back to the house,' said Adam. They strolled back under the trees. Suddenly Adam said, 'Did you ever hear that Cathy was in Salinas? Did you ever hear such a rumour?'

'Did you?'

'Yes – but I don't believe it. I can't believe it.'

Samuel walked silently in the sandy wheel-rut of the road. His mind turned sluggishly in the pattern of Adam and almost wearily took up a thought he had hoped was finished. He said at last, 'You have never let her go.'

'I guess not. But I've let the shooting go. I don't think about it any more.'

'I can't tell you how to live your life,' Samuel said, 'although I do be telling you how to live it. I know that it might be better for you to come out from under your might-have-beens, into the winds of the world. And while I tell you, I am myself sifting my memories, the way men pan the dirt under a bar-room floor for the bits of gold dust that fall between the cracks. It's small mining – small mining. You're too young a man to be panning memories, Adam. You should be getting yourself some new ones, so that the mining will be richer when you come to age.'

Adam's face was bent down, and his jawbone jutted below his temples from clenching.

Samuel glanced at him. 'That's right,' he said. 'Set your teeth in it. How we do defend a wrongness! Shall I tell you what to do, so you will not think you invented it? When you go to bed and blow out the lamp – then she stands in the doorway with a little light behind her, and you can see her nightgown stir. And she comes sweetly to your bed, and you, hardly breathing, turn back the covers to receive her and move your head over on the pillow to make room for her head beside yours. You can smell the sweetness of her skin, and it smells like no other skin in the world — '

'Stop it,' Adam shouted at him. 'Goddam you, stop it! Stop nosing over my life! You're like a coyote sniffing around a dead cow.'

'The way I know,' Samuel said softly, 'is that one came to me that selfsame way – night after month after year, right to the very now. And I think I should have double-bolted my mind and sealed off my heart against her, but I did not. All of these years I've cheated Liza. I've given her an untruth, a counterfeit,

281

and I've saved the best for those dark sweet hours. And now I could wish that she may have had some secret caller too. But I'll never know that. I think she would maybe have bolted her heart shut and thrown the key to hell.'

Adam's hands were clenched and the blood was driven out of his white knuckles. 'You make me doubt myself,' he said fiercely. 'You always have. I'm afraid of you. What should I do, Samuel? Tell me! I don't know how you saw the thing so clear. What should I do?'

'I know the "shoulds", although I never do them, Adam. I always know the "shoulds". You should try to find a new Cathy. You should let the new Cathy kill the dream Cathy – let the two of them fight it out. And you, sitting by, should marry your mind to the winner. That's the second-best "should". The best would be to search out and find some fresh new loveliness to cancel out the old.'

'I'm afraid to try,' said Adam.

'That's what you've said. And now I'm going to put a selfishness on you. I'm going away, Adam. I came to say goodbye.'

'What do you mean?'

'My daughter Olive has asked Liza and me to visit with her in Salinas, and we're going – day after tomorrow.'

'Well, you'll be back.'

Samuel went on, 'After we've visited with Olive for maybe a month or two, there will come a letter from George. And his feelings will be hurt if we don't visit him in Paso Robles. And after that Mollie will want us in San Francisco, and then Will, and maybe even Joe in the East, if we should live so long.'

'Well, won't you like that? You've earned it. You've worked hard enough on that dust heap of yours.'

'I love that dust heap,' Samuel said. 'I love it the way a bitch loves her runty pup. I love every flint, the plough-breaking out-croppings, the thin and barren topsoil, the waterless heart of her. Somewhere in my dust heap there's a richness.'

'You deserve a rest.'

'There, you've said it again,' said Samuel. 'That's what I had to accept, and I have accepted. When you say I deserve a rest, you are saying that my life is over.'

'Do you believe that?'

'That's what I have accepted.'

Adam said excitedly, 'You can't do that. Why, if you accept that you won't live!'

'I know,' said Samuel.

'But you can't do that.'

'Why not?'

'I don't want you to.'

'I'm a nosy old man, Adam. And the sad thing to me is that I'm losing my nosiness. That's maybe how I know it's time to visit my children. I'm having to pretend to be nosy a good deal of the time.'

'I'd rather you worked your guts out on your dust heap.'

Samuel smiled at him. 'What a nice thing to hear! And I thank you. It's a good thing to be loved, even late.'

Suddenly Adam turned in front of him so that Samuel had to stop. 'I know what you've done for me,' Adam said. 'I can't return anything. But I can ask you for one more thing. If I asked you, would you do me one more kindness, and maybe save my life?'

'I would if I could.'

Adam swung out his hand and made an arc over the west. 'That land out there – would you help me to make the garden we talked of, the windmills and the wells and the flats of alfalfa? We could raise flower-seeds. There's money in that. Think of what it would be like, acres of sweet peas and gold squares of calendulas. Maybe ten acres of roses for the gardens of the West. Think how they would smell on the west wind!'

'You're going to make me cry,' Samuel said, 'and that would be an unseemly thing in an old man.' And indeed his eyes were wet. 'I thank you, Adam,' he said. 'The sweetness of your offer is a good smell on the west wind.'

'Then you'll do it?'

'No, I will not do it. But I'll see it in my mind when I'm in Salinas, listening to William Jennings Bryan. And maybe I'll get to believe it happened.'

'But I want to do it.'

'Go and see my Tom. He'll help you. He'd plant the world with roses, poor man, if he could.'

'You know what you're doing, Samuel?'

'Yes, I know what I'm doing, know so well that it's half done.'

'What a stubborn man you are!'

'Contentious,' said Samuel. 'Liza says I'm contentious, but now I'm caught in a web of my children – and I think I like it.'

The dinner-table was set in the house. Lee said, 'I'd have liked to serve it under the tree like the other times, but the air is chilly.'

'So it is, Lee,' said Samuel.

The twins came in silently and stood shyly staring at their guest.

'It's a long time since I've seen you, boys. But we named you well. You're Caleb, aren't you?'

'I'm Cal.'

'Well, Cal, then.' And he turned to the other. 'Have you found a way to rip the backbone out of your name?'

'Sir?'

'Are you called Aaron?'

'Yes, sir.'

Lee chuckled. 'He spells it with one *a*. The two *a*'s seem a little fancy to his friends.'

'I've got thirty-five Belgian hares, sir,' Aron said. 'Would you like to see them, sir? The hutch is up by the spring. I've got eight new-borns – just born yesterday.'

'I'd like to see them, Aron.' His mouth twitched. 'Cal, don't tell me you're a gardener?'

Lee's head snapped round and he inspected Samuel. 'Don't do that,' Lee said nervously.

Cal said, 'Next year my father is going to let me have an acre in the flat.'

Aron said, 'I've got a buck rabbit weighs fifteen pounds. I'm going to give it to my father for his birthday.'

They heard Adam's bedroom door opening. 'Don't tell him,' Aron said quickly. 'It's a secret.'

Lee sawed at the pot roast. 'Always you bring trouble for my mind, Mr Hamilton,' he said. 'Sit down, boys.'

Adam came in, turning down his sleeves, and took his seat at the head of the table. 'Good evening, boys,' he said, and they replied in unison, 'Good evening, Father.'

And, 'Don't you tell,' said Aron.

'I won't,' Samuel assured him.

'Don't tell what?' Adam asked.

Samuel said, 'Can't there be a privacy? I have a secret with your son.'

Cal broke in, 'I'll tell you a secret too, right after dinner.'

'I'll like to hear it,' said Samuel. 'And I do hope I don't know already what it is.'

Lee looked up from his carving and glared at Samuel. He began piling meat on the plates.

The boys ate quickly and quietly, wolfed their food. Aron said, 'Will you excuse us, Father?'

Adam nodded, and the two boys went quickly out. Samuel looked after them. 'They seem older than eleven,' he said. 'I seem to remember that at eleven my brood were howlers and screamers and runners in circles. These seem like grown men.'

'Do they?' Adam asked.

Lee said, 'I think I see why that is. There is no woman in the house to put a value on babies. I don't think men care much for babies, and so it was never an advantage to these boys to be babies. There was nothing to gain by it. I don't know whether that is good or bad.'

Samuel wiped up the remains of gravy in his plate with a slice of bread. 'Adam, I wonder whether you know what you have in Lee. A philosopher who can cook, or a cook who can think? He has taught me a great deal. You must have learned from him, Adam.'

Adam said, 'I'm afraid I didn't listen enough – or maybe he didn't talk.'

'Why didn't you want the boys to learn Chinese, Adam?'

Adam thought for a moment. 'It seems a time for honesty,' he said at last. 'I guess it was plain jealousy. I gave it another name, but maybe I didn't want them to be able so easily to go away from me in a direction I couldn't follow.'

'That's reasonable enough and almost too human,' said Samuel. 'But knowing it – that's a great jump. I wonder whether I have ever gone so far.'

Lee brought the grey enamelled coffee-pot to the table and filled the cups and sat down. He warmed the palm of his hand against the rounded side of his cup. And then Lee laughed. 'You've given me great trouble, Mr Hamilton, and you've disturbed the tranquillity of China.'

'How do you mean, Lee?'

'It almost seems that I have told you this,' said Lee. 'Maybe I only composed it in my mind, meaning to tell you. It's an amusing story anyway.'

'I want to hear,' said Samuel, and he looked at Adam. 'Don't you want to hear, Adam? Or are you slipping into your cloud bath?'

'I was thinking of that,' said Adam. 'It's funny – a kind of excitement is coming over me.'

'That's good,' said Samuel. 'Maybe that's the best of all good things that can happen to a human. Let's hear your story, Lee.'

The Chinese reached to the side of his neck and he smiled. 'I wonder whether I'll ever get used to the lack of a queue,' he said. 'I guess I used it more than I knew. Yes, the story. I told you, Mr Hamilton, that I was growing more Chinese. Do you ever grow more Irish?'

'It comes and goes,' said Samuel.

'Do you remember when you read us the sixteen verses of the fourth chapter of Genesis and we argued about them?'

'I do indeed. And that's a long time ago.'

'Ten years nearly,' said Lee. 'Well, the story bit deeply into me and I went into it word for word. The more I thought about the story, the more profound it became to me. Then I compared the translations we have – and they were fairly close. There was only one place that bothered me. The King James version says this – it is when Jehovah has asked Cain why he is angry. Jehovah says, "If thou doest well, shalt thou not be accepted? and if thou doest not well, sin lieth at the door. And unto thee shall be his desire, and *thou shalt* rule over him." It was the "thou shalt" that struck me, because it was a promise that Cain would conquer sin.'

Samuel nodded. 'And his children didn't do it entirely,' he said.

Lee sipped his coffee. 'Then I got a copy of the American Standard Bible. It was very new then. And it was different in this passage. It says, "*Do thou* rule over him." Now this is very different. This is not a promise, it is an order. And I began to stew about it. I wondered what the original word of the original writer had been that these very different translations could be made.'

Samuel put his palms down on the table and leaned forward and the old young light came into his eyes. 'Lee,' he said, 'don't tell me you studied Hebrew!'

Lee said, 'I'm going to tell you. And it's a fairly long story. Will you have a touch of ng-ka-py?'

'You mean the drink that tastes of good rotten apples?'

'Yes. I can talk better with it.'

'Maybe I can listen better,' said Samuel.

While Lee went to the kitchen Samuel asked, 'Adam, did you know about this?'

'No,' said Adam. 'He didn't tell me. Maybe I wasn't listening.'

Lee came back with his stone bottle and three little porcelain cups so thin and delicate that the light shone through them. 'Dlinkee Chinee fashion,' he said and poured the almost black liquor. 'There's a lot of wormwood in this. It's quite a drink,' he said. 'Has about the same effect as absinthe if you drink enough of it.'

Samuel sipped his drink. 'I want to know why you were so interested,' he said.

'Well, it seemed to me that the man who could conceive this great story would know exactly what he wanted to say and there would be no confusion in his statement.'

'You say "the man". Do you then not think this is a divine book written by the inky finger of God?'

'I think the mind that could think this story was a curiously divine mind. We have had a few such minds in China too.'

'I just wanted to know,' said Samuel. 'You're not a Presbyterian after all.'

'I told you I was getting more Chinese. Well, to go on, I went to San Francisco to the headquarters of our family association. Do you know about them? Our great families have centres where any member can get help or give it. The Lee family is very large. It takes care of its own.'

'I have heard of them,' said Samuel.

'You mean Chinee hatchet man fightee Tong war over slave girl?'

'I guess so.'

'It's a little different from that, really,' said Lee. 'I went there because in our family there are a number of ancient reverend gentlemen who are great scholars. They are thinkers in exactness. A man may spend many years pondering a sentence of the scholar you call Confucius. I thought there might be experts in meaning who could advise me.

'They are fine old men. They smoke their two pipes of opium in the afternoon and it rests and sharpens them, and they sit through the night and their minds are wonderful. I guess no other people have been able to use opium well.'

Lee dampened his tongue in the black brew. 'I respectfully submitted my problem to one of these sages, read him the story, and told him what I understood from it. The next night four of them met and called me in. We discussed the story all night long.'

Lee laughed. 'I guess it's funny,' he said. 'I know I wouldn't dare tell it to many people. Can you imagine four old gentlemen, the youngest is over ninety now, taking on the study of Hebrew?

They engaged a learned rabbi. They took to the study as though they were children. Exercise books, grammar, vocabulary, simple sentences. You should see Hebrew written in Chinese ink with a brush! The right to left didn't bother them as much as it would you, since we write up to down. Oh, they were perfectionists! They went to the root of the matter.'

'And you?' said Samuel.

'I went along with them, marvelling at the beauty of their proud clean brains. I began to love my race, and for the first time I wanted to be Chinese. Every two weeks I went to a meeting with them, and in my room here I covered pages with writing. I bought every known Hebrew dictionary. But the old gentlemen were always ahead of me. It wasn't long before they were ahead of our rabbi; he brought a colleague in. Mr Hamilton, you should have sat through some of those nights of argument and discussion. The questions, the inspection, oh, the lovely thinking – the beautiful thinking.

'After two years we felt that we could approach your sixteen verses of the fourth chapter of Genesis. My old gentlemen felt that these words were very important too – "Thou shalt" and "Do thou". And this was the gold from our mining: *"Thou mayest."* "Thou mayest rule over sin." The old gentlemen smiled and nodded and felt the years were well spent. It brought them out of their Chinese shells too, and right now they are studying Greek.'

Samuel said, 'It's a fantastic story. And I've tried to follow and maybe I've missed somewhere. Why is this word so important?'

Lee's hand shook as he filled the delicate cups. He drank his down in one gulp. 'Don't you see?' he cried. 'The American Standard translation *orders* men to triumph over sin, and you can call sin ignorance. The King James translation makes a promise in "Thou shalt", meaning that men will surely triumph over sin. But the Hebrew word, the word *timshel* – "Thou mayest" – that gives a choice. It might be the most important word in the world. That says the way is open. That throws it right back on a man. For if "Thou mayest" – it is also true that "Thou mayest not". Don't you see?'

'Yes, I see. I do see. But you do not believe this is divine law. Why do you feel its importance?'

'Ah!' said Lee. 'I've wanted to tell you this for a long time. I even anticipated your questions and I am well prepared. Any writing which has influenced the thinking and the lives of in-

288

numerable people is important. Now, there are many millions in their sects and Churches who feel the order, "Do thou", and throw their weight into obedience. And there are millions more who feel predestination in "Thou shalt". Nothing they may do can interfere with what will be. But "Thou mayest"! Why, that makes a man great, that gives him stature with the gods, for in his weakness and his filth and his murder of his brother he has still the great choice. He can choose his course and fight it through and win.' Lee's voice was a chant of triumph.

Adam said, 'Do you believe that, Lee?'

'Yes, I do. Yes, I do. It is easy out of laziness, out of weakness, to throw oneself into the lap of deity, saying, "I couldn't help it; the way was set." But think of the glory of the choice! That makes a man a man. A cat has no choice, a bee must make honey. There's no godliness there. And do you know, those old gentlemen who were sliding gently down to death are too interested to die now.'

Adam said, 'Do you mean these Chinese men believe the Old Testament?'

Lee said, 'These old men believe a true story, and they know a true story when they hear it. They are critics of truth. They know that these sixteen verses are a history of humankind in any age or culture or race. They do not believe a man writes fifteen and three-quarter verses of truth and tells a lie with one verb. Confucius tells men how they should live to have good and successful lives. But this – this is a ladder to climb to the stars.' Lee's eyes shone. 'You can never lose that. It cuts the feet from under weakness and cowardliness and laziness.'

Adam said, 'I don't see how you could cook and raise the boys and take care of me and still do all this.'

'Neither do I,' said Lee. 'But I take my two pipes in the afternoon, no more and no less, like the elders. And I feel that I am a man. And I feel that a man is a very important thing – maybe more important than a star. This is not theology. I have no bent towards gods. But I have a new love for that glittering instrument, the human soul. It is a lovely and unique thing in the universe. It is always attacked and never destroyed – because "Thou mayest".'

III

Lee and Adam walked out to the shed with Samuel to see him off. Lee carried a tin lantern to light the way, for it was one of those clear early winter nights when the sky riots with stars and the earth seems doubly dark because of them. A silence lay on the hills. No animal moved about, neither grass-eater nor predator, and the air was so still that the dark limbs and leaves of the live oaks stood unmoving against the Milky Way. The three men were silent. The bail of the tin lantern squeaked a little as the light swung in Lee's hand.

Adam asked, 'When do you think you'll be back from your trip?'

Samuel did not answer.

Doxology stood patiently in the stall, head down, his milky eyes staring at the straw under his feet.

'You've had that horse for ever,' Adam said.

'He's thirty-three,' said Samuel. 'His teeth are worn off. I have to feed him warm mash with my fingers. And he has bad dreams. He shivers and cries sometimes in his sleep.'

'He's about as ugly a crow bait as I ever saw,' Adam said.

'I know it. I think that's why I picked him when he was a colt. Do you know I paid two dollars for him thirty-three years ago? Everything was wrong with him, hoofs like flapjacks, a hock so thick and short and straight there seems no joint at all. He's hammer-headed and sway-backed. He has a pinched chest and a big behind. He has an iron mouth and he still fights the crupper. With a saddle he feels as though you were riding a sled over a gravel pit. He can't trot and he stumbles over his feet when he walks. I have never in thirty-three years found one good thing about him. He even has an ugly disposition. He is selfish and quarrelsome and mean and disobedient. To this day I don't dare walk behind him because he will surely take a kick at me. When I feed him mash he tries to bite my hand. And I love him.'

Lee said, 'And you named him "Doxology".'

'Surely,' said Samuel, 'so ill endowed a creature deserved, I thought, one grand possession. He hasn't very long now.'

Adam said, 'Maybe you should put him out of his misery.'

'What misery?' Samuel demanded. 'He's one of the few happy and consistent beings I've ever met.'

'He must have aches and pains.'

'Well, he doesn't think so. Doxology still thinks he's one hell of a horse. Would you shoot him, Adam?'

'Yes, I think I would. Yes, I would.'

'You'd take the responsibility?'

'Yes, I think I would. He's thirty-three. His life-span is long over.'

Lee had set his lantern on the ground. Samuel squatted beside it and instinctively stretched his hands for warmth to the butterfly of yellow light.

'I've been bothered by something, Adam,' he said.

'What is that?'

'You would really shoot my horse because death might be more comfortable?'

'Well, I meant —'

Samuel said quickly, 'Do you like your life, Adam?'

'Of course not.'

'If I had a medicine that might cure you and also might kill you, should I give it to you? Inspect yourself, man.'

'What medicine?'

'No,' said Samuel. 'If I tell you, believe me when I say it may kill you.'

Lee said, 'Be careful, Mr Hamilton. Be careful.'

'What is this?' Adam demanded. 'Tell me what you're thinking of.'

Samuel said softly, 'I think for once I will not be careful. Lee, if I am wrong – listen – if I am mistaken, I accept the responsibility and I will take what blame there is to take.'

'Are you sure you're right?' Lee asked anxiously.

'Of course I'm not sure. Adam, do you want the medicine?'

'Yes. I don't know what it is, but give it to me.'

'Adam, Cathy is in Salinas. She owns a whorehouse, the most vicious and depraved in this whole end of the country. The evil and ugly, the distorted and slimy, the worst things humans can think up are for sale there. The crippled and crooked come there for satisfaction. But it is worse than that. Cathy, and she is now called Kate, takes the fresh and young and beautiful and so maims them that they can never be whole again. Now, there's your medicine. Let's see what it does to you.'

'You're a liar!' Adam said.

'No, Adam. Many things I am, but a liar I am not.'

Adam whirled on Lee. 'Is this true?'

'I'm no antidote,' said Lee. 'Yes. It's true.'

Adam stood swaying in the lantern light and then he turned and ran. They could hear his heavy steps running and tripping. They heard him falling over the brush and scrambling and clawing his way upwards on the slope. The sound of him stopped only when he had gone over the brow of the hill.

Lee said, 'Your medicine acts like poison.'

'I take responsibility,' said Samuel. 'Long ago I learned this:

when a dog has eaten strychnine and is going to die, you must get an axe and carry him to a chopping block. Then you must wait for his next convulsion, and in that moment – then – chop off his tail. Then, if the poison has not gone too far, your dog may recover. The shock of pain can counteract the poison. Without the shock he will surely die.'

'But how do you know this is the same?' Lee asked.

'I don't. But without it he would surely die.'

'You're a brave man,' Lee said.

'No, I'm an old man. And if I should have anything on my conscience it won't be for long.'

Lee asked, 'What do you suppose he'll do?'

'I don't know,' said Samuel, 'but at least he won't sit around and mope. Here, hold the lantern for me, will you?'

In the yellow light Samuel slipped the bit in Doxology's mouth, a bit worn so thin that it was a flake of steel. The check rein had been abandoned long ago. The old hammerhead was free to drag his nose if he wished, or to pause and crop grass beside the road. Samuel didn't care. Tenderly he buckled the crupper, and the horse edged round to try to kick him.

When Dox was between the shafts of the cart Lee asked, 'Would you mind if I rode along with you a little. I'll walk back.'

'Come along,' said Samuel, and he tried not to notice that Lee helped him up into the cart.

The night was very dark, and Dox showed his disgust for night-travelling by stumbling every few steps.

Samuel said, 'Get on with it, Lee. What is it you want to say?'

Lee did not appear surprised. 'Maybe I'm nosy the way you say you are. I get to thinking. I know probabilities, but tonight you fooled me completely. I would have taken any bet that you of all men would not have told Adam.'

'Did you know about her?'

'Of course,' said Lee.

'Do the boys know?'

'I don't think so, but that's only a matter of time. You know how cruel children are. Some day in the school-yard it will be shouted at them.'

'Maybe he ought to take them away from here,' said Samuel. 'Think about that, Lee.'

'My question isn't answered, Mr Hamilton. How were you able to do what you did?'

'Do you think I was that wrong?'

'No, I don't mean that at all. But I've never thought of you as taking any strong unchanging stand on anything. This has been my judgement. Are you interested?'

'Show me the man who isn't interested in discussing himself,' said Samuel. 'Go on.'

'You're a kind man, Mr Hamilton. And I've always thought it was the kindness that comes from not wanting any trouble. And your mind is as facile as a young lamb leaping in a daisy field. You have never to my knowledge taken a bulldog grip on anything. And then tonight you did a thing that tears down my whole picture of you.'

Samuel wrapped the lines around a stick stuck in the whip socket, and Doxology stumbled on down the rutty road. The old man stroked his beard, and it shone very white in the starlight. He took off his black hat and laid it in his lap. 'I guess it surprised me as much as it did you,' he said. 'But if you want to know why – look into yourself.'

'I don't understand you.'

'If you had only told me about your studies earlier it might have made a great difference, Lee.'

'I still don't understand you.'

'Careful, Lee, you'll get me talking. I told you my Irish came and went. It's coming now.'

Lee said, 'Mr Hamilton, you're going away and you're not coming back. You do not intend to live very much longer.'

'That's true, Lee. How did you know?'

'There's death all around you. It shines from you.'

'I didn't know anyone could see it,' Samuel said. 'You know, Lee, I think of my life as a kind of music, not always good music but still having form and melody. And my life has not been a full orchestra for a long time now. A single note only – and that note unchanging sorrow. I'm not alone in my attitude, Lee. It seems to me that too many of us conceive of a life as ending in defeat.'

Lee said, 'Maybe everyone is too rich. I have noticed that there is no dissatisfaction like that of the rich. Feed a man, clothe him, put him in a good house, and he will die of despair.'

'It was your two-word re-translation, Lee – "Thou mayest". It took me by the throat and shook me. And when the dizziness was over, a path was open, new and bright. And my life which is ending seems to be going on to an ending wonderful. And my music has a new last melody like a bird song in the night.'

Lee was peering at him through the darkness. 'That's what it did to those old men of my family.'

' "Thou mayest rule over sin", Lee. That's it. I do not believe all men are destroyed. I can name you a dozen who were not, and they are the ones the world lives by. It is true of the spirit as it is true of battles – only the winners are remembered. Surely most men are destroyed, but there are others who like pillars of fire guide frightened men through the darkness. "*Thou mayest, Thou mayest!*" What glory! It is true that we are weak and sick and quarrelsome, but if that is all we were, we would, millenniums ago, have disappeared from the face of the earth. A few remnants of fossilized jawbone, some broken teeth in strata of limestone, would be the only mark man would have left of his existence in the world. But the choice, Lee, the choice of winning! I had never understood it or accepted it before. Do you see now why I told Adam tonight? I exercised the choice. Maybe I was wrong, but by telling him I also forced him to live or get off the pot. What is that word, Lee?'

'*Timshel*,' said Lee. 'Will you stop the cart?'

'You'll have a long walk back.'

Lee climbed down. 'Samuel!' he said.

'Here am I.' The old man chuckled. 'Liza hates for me to say that.'

'Samuel, you've gone beyond me.'

'It's time, Lee.'

'Goodbye, Samuel,' Lee said, and he walked hurriedly back along the road. He heard the iron tyres of the cart grinding on the road. He turned and looked after it, and on the slope he saw old Samuel against the sky, his white hair shining with starlight.

CHAPTER 25

I

IT WAS a deluge of a winter in the Salinas Valley, wet and wonderful. The rains fell gently and soaked in and did not freshet. The feed was deep in January, and in February the hills were fat with grass and the coats of the cattle looked tight and sleek. In March the soft rains continued, and each storm waited courteously until its predecessor sank beneath the ground. Then warmth flooded the valley and the earth burst into bloom – yellow and blue and gold.

Tom was alone on the ranch, and even that dust heap was rich and lovely and the flints were hidden in grass and the Hamilton cows were fat and the Hamilton sheep sprouted grass from their damp backs.

At noon on March 15 Tom sat on the bench outside the forge. The sunny morning was over, and grey water-bearing clouds sailed in over the mountains from the ocean, and their shadows slid under them on the bright earth.

Tom heard a horse's clattering hoofs and he saw a small boy, elbows flapping, urging a tired horse towards the house. He stood up and walked towards the road. The boy galloped up to the house, yanked off his hat, flung a yellow envelope on the ground, spun his horse round, and kicked up a gallop again.

Tom started to call after him, and then he leaned wearily down and picked up the telegram. He sat in the sun on the bench outside the forge, holding the telegram in his hand. And he looked at the hills and at the old house, as though to save something, before he tore open the envelope and read the inevitable four words, the person, the event, and the time.

Tom slowly folded the telegram and folded it again and again until it was a square no longer than his thumb. He walked to the house, through the kitchen, through the little living-room, and into his bedroom. He took his dark suit out of the clothes-press and laid it over the back of a chair, and he put a white shirt and a black tie on the seat of the chair. And then he lay down on the bed and turned his face to the wall.

I I

The surreys and the buggies had driven out of the Salinas cemetery. The family and friends went back to Olive's house on Central Avenue to eat and drink coffee, to see how each one was taking it, and to do and say the decent things.

George offered Adam Trask a lift in his rented surrey, but Adam refused. He wandered around the cemetery and sat down on the cement kerb of the Williams family plot. The traditional dark cypresses wept around the edge of the cemetery, and white violets ran wild in the pathways. Someone had brought them in and they had become weeds.

The cold wind blew over the tombstones and cried in the cypresses. There were many cast-iron stars, marking the graves of Grand Army men, and on each star a small wind-bitten flag from a year ago Decoration Day.

Adam sat looking at the mountains to the east of Salinas, with the noble point of Frémont's Peak dominating. The air was crystalline, as it sometimes is when rain is coming. And then the light rain began to blow on the wind although the sky was not properly covered with cloud.

Adam had come up on the morning train. He had not intended to come at all, but something drew him beyond his power to resist. For one thing, he could not believe that Samuel was dead. He could hear the rich, lyric voice in his ears, the tones rising and falling in their foreignness, and the curious music of oddly chosen words tripping out so that you were never sure what the next word would be. In the speech of most men you are absolutely sure what the next word will be.

Adam had looked at Samuel in his casket and knew that he didn't want him to be dead. And since the face in the casket did not look like Samuel's face, Adam walked away to be by himself and to preserve the man alive.

He had to go to the cemetery. Custom would have been outraged else. But he stood well back where he could not hear the words, and when the sons filled in the grave he walked away and strolled in the paths where the white violets grew.

The cemetery was deserted and the dark crooning of the wind bowed the heavy cypress trees. The rain droplets grew larger and drove stinging along.

Adam stood up, shivered, and walked slowly over the white violets and past the new grave. The flowers had been laid evenly to cover the mound of new-turned damp earth, and already the wind had frayed the blossoms and flung the smaller bouquets out into the path. Adam picked them up and laid them back on the mound.

He walked out of the cemetery. The wind and the rain were at his back, and he ignored the wetness that soaked through his black coat. Romie Lane was muddy with pools of water standing in the new wheel-ruts, and the tall wild oats and mustard grew beside the road, with wild turnip forcing its boisterous way up and stickery beads of purple thistles rising above the green riot of the wet spring.

The black 'dobe mud covered Adam's shoes and splashed the bottoms of his dark trousers. It was nearly a mile to the Monterey road. Adam was dirty and soaking when he reached it and turned east into the town of Salinas. The water was standing in the curved brim of his derby hat and his collar was wet and sagging.

At John Street the road angled and became Main Street. Adam stamped the mud off his shoes when he reached the pavement. The buildings cut the wind from him and almost instantly he began to shake with a chill. He increased his speed. Near the other end of Main Street he turned into the Abbot House bar. He ordered brandy and drank it quickly and his shivering increased.

Mr Lapierre behind the bar saw the chill. 'You'd better have another one,' he said. 'You'll get a bad cold. Would you like a hot rum? That will knock it out of you.'

'Yes, I would,' said Adam.

'Well, here. You sip another cognac while I get some hot water.'

Adam took his glass to a table and sat uncomfortably in his wet clothes. Mr Lapierre brought a steaming kettle from the kitchen. He put the squat glass on a tray and brought it to the table. 'Drink it as hot as you can stand it,' he said. 'That will shake the chill out of an aspen.' He drew a chair up, sat down, then stood up. 'You've made me cold,' he said. 'I'm going to have one myself.' He brought his glass back to the table and sat opposite Adam. 'It's working,' he said. 'You were so pale you scared me when you came in. You're a stranger?'

'I'm from near King City,' Adam said.

'Come up for the funeral?'

'Yes – he was an old friend.'

'Big funeral?'

'Oh, yes.'

'I'm not surprised. He had lots of friends. Too bad it couldn't have been a nice day. You ought to have one more and then go to bed.'

'I will,' said Adam. 'It makes me comfortable and peaceful.'

'That's worth something. Might have saved you from pneumonia too.'

After he had served another toddy he brought a damp cloth from behind the bar. 'You can wipe off some of that mud,' he said. 'A funeral isn't very gay, but when it gets rained on – that's really mournful.'

'It didn't rain till after,' said Adam. 'It was walking back I got wet.'

'Why don't you get a nice room right here? You get into bed

297

and I'll send a toddy up to you, and in the morning you'll be fine.'

'I think I'll do that,' said Adam. He could feel the blood stinging his cheeks and running hotly in his arms, as though it were some foreign warm fluid taking over his body. Then the warmth melted through into the cold concealed box where he stored forbidden thoughts, and the thoughts came timidly up to the surface like children who do not know whether they will be received. Adam picked up the damp cloth and leaned down to sponge off the bottoms of his trousers. The blood pounded behind his eyes. 'I might have one more toddy,' he said.

Mr Lapierre said, 'If it's for cold, you've had enough. But if you just want a drink I've got some old Jamaica rum. I'd rather you'd have that straight. It's fifty years old. The water would kill the flavour.'

'I just want a drink,' said Adam.

'I'll have one with you. I haven't opened that jug in months. Not much call for it. This is a whisky-drinking town.'

Adam wiped off his shoes and dropped the cloth on the floor. He took a drink of the dark rum and coughed. The heavy-muscled drink wrapped its sweet aroma around his head and struck at the base of his nose like a blow. The room seemed to tip sideways and then right itself.

'Good, isn't it?' Mr Lapierre asked. 'But it can knock you over. I wouldn't have more than one – unless of course you want to get knocked over. Some do.'

Adam leaned his elbows on the table. He felt a garrulousness coming on him and he was frightened at the impulse. His voice did not sound like his voice, and his words amazed him.

'I don't get up here much,' he said. 'Do you know a place called Kate's?'

'Jesus! That rum is better than I thought,' Mr Lapierre said, and he went on sternly, 'You live on a ranch?'

'Yes. Got a place near King City. My name's Trask.'

'Glad to meet you. Married?'

'No. Not now.'

'Widower?'

'Yes.'

'You go to Jenny's. Let Kate alone. That's not good for you. Jenny's is right next door. You go there and you'll get everything you need.'

'Right next door?'

298

'Sure, you go east a block and a half and turn right. Any-body'll tell you where the Line is.'

Adam's tongue was getting thick. 'What's the matter with Kate's?'

'You go to Jenny's,' said Mr Lapierre.

III

It was a dirty gusty evening. Castroville Street was deep in sticky mud, and Chinatown was so flooded that its inhabitants had laid planks across the narrow street that separated their hutches. The clouds against the evening sky were the grey of rats, and the air was not damp but dank. I guess the difference is that dampness comes down but dankness rises up out of rot and fermentation. The afternoon wind had dropped away and left the air raw and wounded. It was cold enough to shake out the curtains of rum in Adam's head without restoring his timidity. He walked quickly down the unpaved sidewalks, his eyes on the ground to avoid stepping in puddles. The row was dimly lit by the warning lantern where the railroad crossed the street and by one small carbon-filamented globe that burned on the porch of Jenny's.

Adam had his instructions. He counted two houses and nearly missed the third, so high and unbridled were the dark bushes in front of it. He looked in through the gateway at the dark porch, slowly opened the gate, and went up the overgrown path. In the half-darkness he could see the sagging dilapidated porch and the shaky steps.

The paint had long disappeared from the clapboard walls and no work had ever been done on the garden. If it had not been for the vein of light around the edges of the drawn blinds he would have passed on, thinking the house deserted. The stair treads seemed to crumple under his weight and the porch planks squealed as he crossed them.

The front door opened, and he could see a dim figure holding the knob.

A soft voice said, 'Won't you come in?'

The reception-room was dimly lighted by small globes set under rose-coloured shades. Adam could feel a thick carpet under his feet. He could see the shine of polished furniture and the gleam of gold picture frames. He got a quick impression of richness and order.

The soft voice said, 'You should have worn a raincoat. Do we know you?'

'No, you don't,' said Adam.

'Who sent you?'

'A man at the hotel.' Adam peered at the girl before him. She was dressed in black and wore no ornaments. Her face was sharp – pretty and sharp. He tried to think of what animal, what night prowler, she reminded him. It was some secret and predatory animal.

The girl said, 'I'll move nearer to a lamp if you like.'

'No.'

She laughed. 'Sit down – over here. You did come here for something, didn't you? If you'll tell me what you want I'll tell the proper girl.' The low voice had a precise and husky power. And she picked her words as one picks flowers in a mixed garden and took her time choosing.

She made Adam seem clumsy to himself. He blurted out, 'I want to see Kate.'

'Miss Kate is busy now. Does she expect you?'

'No.'

'I can take care of you, you know.'

'I want to see Kate.'

'Can you tell me what you want to see her about?'

'No.'

The girl's voice took on the edge of a blade sharpened on a stone. 'You can't see her. She's busy. If you don't want a girl or something else, you'd better go away.'

'Well, will you tell her I'm here?'

'Does she know you?'

'I don't know.' He felt his courage going. This was a remembered cold. 'I don't know. But will you tell her that Adam Trask would like to see her? She'll know then whether I know her or not.'

'I see. Well, I'll tell her.' She moved silently to a door on the right and opened it. Adam heard a few muffled words and a man looked through the door. The girl left the door open so that Adam would know he was not alone. On one side of the room heavy dark portières hung over a doorway. The girl parted the deep folds and disappeared. Adam sat back in his chair. Out of the side of his eyes he saw the man's head thrust in and then withdrawn.

Kate's private room was comfort and efficiency. It did not look at all like the room where Faye had lived. The walls were clad in saffron silk and the curtains were apple-green. It was a silken room – deep chairs with silk-upholstered cushions, lamps with silken shades, a broad bed at the far end of the room with a gleaming white satin cover on which were piled gigantic pillows. There was no picture on the wall, no photograph or personal thing of any kind. A dressing-table near the bed had no bottle or vial on its ebony top, and its sheen was reflected in triple mirrors. The rug was old and deep and Chinese, an apple-green dragon on saffron. One end of the room was bedroom, the centre social, and the other end was office – filing cabinets of golden oak, a large safe, black with gold lettering, and a roll-top desk with a green-hooded double lamp over it, a swivel chair behind it and a straight chair beside it.

Kate sat in the swivel chair behind the desk. She was still pretty. Her hair was blonde again. Her mouth was little and firm and turned up at the corners as always. But her outlines were not sharp anywhere. Her shoulders had become plump while her hands grew lean and wrinkled. Her cheeks were chubby and the skin under her chin was crêpe. Her breasts were still tiny, but a padding of fat protruded her stomach a little. Her hips were slender, but her legs and feet had thickened a little so that a bulge hung over her low shoes. And through her stockings, faintly, could be seen the wrappings of elastic bandage to support the veins.

Still, she was pretty and neat. Only her hands had really aged, the palms and fingerpads shining and tight, the backs wrinkled and splotched with brown. She was dressed severely in a dark dress with long sleeves, and the only contrast was billowing white lace at her wrists and throat.

The work of the years had been subtle. If one had been nearby it is probable that no change at all would have been noticed. Kate's cheeks were unlined, her eyes sharp and shallow, her nose delicate, and her lips thin and firm. The scar on her forehead was barely visible. It was covered with a powder tinted to match Kate's skin.

Kate inspected a sheaf of photographs on her roll-top desk, all the same size, all taken by the same camera and bright with flash powder. And although the characters were different in each picture, there was a dreary similarity about their postures. The faces of the women were never towards the camera.

Kate arranged the pictures in four piles and slipped each pile into a heavy manila envelope. When the knock came on her door she put the envelopes in a pigeon-hole of her desk. 'Come in. Oh, come in, Eva. Is he here?'

The girl came to the desk before she replied. In the increased light her face showed tight and her eyes were shiny. 'It's a new one, a stranger. He says he wants to see you.'

'Well, he can't, Eva. You know who's coming.'

'I told him you couldn't see him. He said he thought he knew you.'

'Well, who is he, Eva?'

'He's a big gangly man, a little bit drunk. He says his name is Adam Trask.'

Although Kate made no movement or sound Eva knew something had struck home. The fingers of Kate's right hand slowly curled around the palm while the left hand crept like a lean cat towards the edge of the desk. Kate sat still as though she held her breath. Eva was jittery. Her mind went to the box in her dresser drawer where her hypodermic needle lay.

Kate said at last, 'Sit over there in that big chair, Eva. Just sit still a minute.' When the girl did not move Kate whipped one word at her. 'Sit!' Eva cringed and went to the big chair.

'Don't pick your nails,' said Kate.

Eva's hands separated, and each one clung to an arm of the chair.

Kate stared straight ahead at the green glass shade of her desk-lamp. Then she moved so suddenly that Eva jumped and her lips quivered. Kate opened the desk drawer and took out a folded paper. 'Here! Go to your room and fix yourself up. Don't take it all – no, I won't trust you.' Kate tapped the paper and tore it in two; a little white powder spilled before she folded the ends and passed one to Eva. 'Now hurry up! When you come downstairs, tell Ralph I want him in the hall close enough to hear the bell but not the voices. Watch him to see he doesn't creep up. If he hears the bell – no, tell him – no, let him do it his own way. After that bring Mr Adam Trask to me.'

'Will you be all right, Miss Kate?'

Kate looked at her until she turned away. Kate called after her, 'You can have the other half as soon as he goes. Now hurry up.'

After the door had closed Kate opened the right-hand drawer of her desk and took out a revolver with a short barrel. She swung the cylinder sideways and looked at the cartridges, snapped it shut and put it on her desk, and laid a sheet of paper over it. She turned off one of the lights and settled back in her chair. She clasped her hands on the desk in front of her.

When the knock came on the door she called, 'Come in,' hardly moving her lips.

Eva's eyes were wet, and she was relaxed. 'Here he is,' she said, and closed the door behind Adam.

He glanced quickly about before he saw Kate sitting so quietly behind the desk. He stared at her, and then he moved slowly towards her.

Her hands unclasped and her right hand moved towards the paper. Her eyes, cold and expressionless, remained on his eyes.

Adam saw her hair, her scar, her lips, her crêping throat, her arms and shoulders and flat breasts. He sighed deeply.

Kate's hand shook a little. She said, 'What do you want?'

Adam sat down in the straight chair beside the desk. He wanted to shout with relief but he said, 'Nothing now. I just wanted to see you. Sam Hamilton told me you were here.'

The moment he sat down the shake went out of her hand. 'Hadn't you heard before?'

'No,' he said. 'I hadn't heard. It made me a little crazy at first, but now I'm all right.'

Kate relaxed and her mouth smiled and her little teeth showed, the long canines sharp and white. She said, 'You frightened me.'

'Why?'

'Well, I didn't know what you'd do.'

'Neither did I,' said Adam and he continued to stare at her as though she were not alive.

'I expected you for a long time, and when you didn't come I guess I forgot you.'

'I didn't forget you,' he said. 'But now I can.'

'What do you mean?'

He laughed pleasantly. 'Now I see you, I mean. You know, I guess it was Samuel said I'd never seen you, and it's true. I remember your face but I had never seen it. Now I can forget it.'

Her lips closed and straightened and her wide-set eyes narrowed with cruelty. 'You think you can?'

'I know I can.'

She changed her manner. 'Maybe you won't have to,' she said. 'If you feel all right about everything, maybe we could get together.'

'I don't think so,' said Adam.

'You were such a fool,' she said. 'Like a child. You didn't know what things to do with yourself. I can teach you now. You seem to be a man.'

'You have taught me,' he said. 'It was a pretty sharp lesson.'

'Would you like a drink?'

'Yes,' he said.

'I can smell your breath – you've been drinking rum.' She got up and went to a cabinet for a bottle and two glasses, and when she turned back she noticed that he was looking at her fattened ankles. Her quick rage did not change the little smile on her lips.

She carried the bottle to the round table in the middle of the room and filled the two small glasses with rum. 'Come, sit over here,' she said. 'It's more comfortable.' As he moved to a big chair she saw that his eyes were on her protruding stomach. She handed him a glass, sat down, and folded her hands across her middle.

He sat holding his glass, and she said, 'Drink it. It's very good rum.' He smiled at her, a smile she had never seen. She said, 'When Eva told me you were here, I thought at first I would have you thrown out.'

'I would have come back,' he said. 'I had to see you – not that I mistrusted Samuel, but just to prove it to myself.'

'Drink your rum,' she said.

He glanced at her glass.

'You don't think I'd poison you —' She stopped and was angry that she had said it.

Smiling, he still gazed at her glass. Her anger came through to her face. She picked up her glass and touched her lips to it. 'Liquor makes me sick,' she said. 'I never drink it. It poisons me.' She shut her mouth tight and her sharp teeth bit down on her lower lip.

Adam continued to smile at her.

Her rage was rising beyond her control. She tossed the rum down her throat and coughed, and her eyes watered and she wiped her tears away with the back of her hand. 'You don't trust me very much,' she said.

'No, I don't.' He raised his glass and drank his rum, then got up and filled both glasses.

'I will not drink any more,' she said in panic.

'You don't have to,' Adam said. 'I'll just finish this and go along.'

The biting alcohol burned in her throat and she felt the stirring in her that frightened her. 'I'm not afraid of you or anyone else,' she said, and she drank off her second glass.

'You haven't any reason to be afraid of me,' said Adam. 'You can forget me now. But you said you had already.' He felt gloriously warm and safe, better than he had for many years. 'I came up to Sam Hamilton's funeral,' he said. 'That was a fine man. I'll miss him. Do you remember, Cathy, he helped you with the twins?'

In Kate the liquor raged. She fought, and the strain of the fight showed on her face.

'What's the matter?' Adam asked.

'I told you it poisoned me. I told you it made me sick.'

'I couldn't take the chance,' he calmly said. 'You shot me once. I don't know what else you've done.'

'What do you mean?'

'I've heard some scandal,' he said. 'Just dirty scandal.'

For the moment she had forgotten her will-fight against the cruising alcohol, and now she had lost the battle. The redness was up in her brain and her fear was gone and in its place was cruelty without caution. She snatched the bottle and filled her glass.

Adam had to get up to pour his own. A feeling completely foreign to him had arisen. He was enjoying what he saw in her. He liked to see her struggling. He felt good about punishing her, but he was also watchful. 'Now I must be careful,' he told himself. 'Don't talk, don't talk.'

He said aloud, 'Sam Hamilton had been a good friend to me all the years. I'll miss him.'

She had spilled some rum, and it moistened the corners of her mouth. 'I hated him,' she said. 'I would have killed him if I could.'

'Why? He was kind to us.'

'He looked – he looked into me.'

'Why not? He looked into me too, and he helped me.'

'I hate him,' she said. 'I'm glad he's dead.'

'Might have been good if I had looked into you,' Adam said.

Her lips curled. 'You are a fool,' she said. 'I don't hate you. You're just a weak fool.'

As her tension built up, a warm calm settled on Adam.

'Sit there and grin,' she cried. 'You think you're free, don't you? A few drinks and you think you're a man! I could crook my little finger and you'd come back slobbering, crawling on your knees.' Her sense of power was loose and her vixen carefulness abandoned. 'I know you,' she said. 'I know your cowardly heart.'

Adam went on smiling. He tasted his drink, and that reminded her to pour another for herself. The bottle neck chattered against her glass.

'When I was hurt I needed you,' she said. 'But you were slop. And when I didn't need you any more you tried to stop me. Take that ugly smirk off your face.'

'I wonder what it is you hate so much.'

'You wonder, do you?' Her caution was almost entirely gone. 'It isn't hatred, it's contempt. When I was a little girl I knew what stupid lying fools they were – my own mother and father pretending goodness. And they weren't good. I knew them. I could make them do whatever I wanted. I could always make people do what I wanted. When I was half-grown I made a man kill himself. He pretended to be good too, and all he wanted was to go to bed with me – a little girl.'

'But you say he killed himself. He must have been very sorry about something.'

'He was a fool,' said Kate. 'I heard him come to the door and beg. I laughed all night.'

Adam said, 'I wouldn't like to think I'd driven anybody out of the world.'

'You're a fool too. I remember how they talked. "Isn't she a pretty little thing, so sweet, so dainty?" And no one knew me. I made them jump through hoops and they never knew it.'

Adam drained his glass. He felt remote and inspective. He thought he could see her impulses crawling like ants and could read them. The sense of deep understanding that alcohol sometimes gives was on him. He said, 'It doesn't matter whether you liked Sam Hamilton. I found him wise. I remember he said one time that a woman who knows all about men usually knows one part very well and can't conceive the other parts, but that doesn't mean they weren't there.'

'He was a liar and a hypocrite too.' Kate spat out her words. 'That's what I hate, the liars, and they're all liars. That's what it is. I love to show them up. I love to rub their noses in their own nastiness.'

Adam's brows went up. 'Do you mean that in the whole world there's only evil and folly?'

'That's exactly what I mean.'

'I don't believe it,' Adam said quietly.

'You don't believe it! You don't believe it!' She mimicked him. 'Would you like me to prove it?'

'You can't,' he said.

She jumped up and ran to her desk, and brought the brown envelopes to the table. 'Take a look at these,' she said.

'I don't want to.'

'I'll show you anyway.' She took out a photograph. 'Look there. That's a state senator. He thinks he's going to run for Congress. Look at his fat stomach. He's got bubs like a woman. He likes whips. That streak there – that's a whip mark. Look at the expression on his face! He's got a wife and four kids and he's going to run for Congress. You don't believe! Look at this! This piece of white blubber is a council-man; this big red Swede has a ranch out near Blanco. Look here! This is a professor at Berkeley. Comes all the way down here to have the toilet splashed in his face – professor of philosophy. And look at this! This is a minister of the Gospel, a little brother of Jesus. He used to burn a house down to get what he wanted. We give it to him now another way. See that lighted match under his skinny flank?'

'I don't want to see these,' said Adam.

'Well, you have seen them. And you don't believe it! I'll have you begging to get in here. I'll have you screaming at the moon.' She tried to force her will on him, and she saw that he was detached and free. Her rage congealed to poison. 'No one has ever escaped,' she said softly. Her eyes were flat and cold but her fingernails were tearing at the upholstery of the chair, ripping and fraying the silk.

Adam sighed. 'If I had those pictures and those men knew it, I wouldn't think my life was very safe,' he said. 'I guess one of those pictures could destroy a man's whole life. Aren't you in danger?'

'Do you think I'm a child?' she asked.

'Not any more,' said Adam. 'I'm beginning to think you're a twisted human – or no human at all.'

She smiled. 'Maybe you've struck it,' she said. 'Do you think I want to be human? Look at those pictures! I'd rather be a dog than a human. But I'm not a dog. I'm smarter than humans. Nobody can hurt me. Don't worry about danger.' She waved at the filing cabinets. 'I have a hundred beautiful pictures in there, and those men know that if anything should happen to me – anything – one hundred letters, each one with a picture, would be dropped in the mail, and each letter will go where it will do the most harm. No, they won't hurt me.'

Adam asked, 'But suppose you had an accident, or maybe a disease?'

'That wouldn't make any difference,' she said. She leaned closer to him. 'I'm going to tell you a secret none of those men knows. In a few years I'll be going away. And when I do – those envelopes will be dropped in the mail anyway.' She leaned back in her chair, laughing.

Adam shivered. He looked closely at her. Her face and her laughter were childlike and innocent. He got up and poured himself another drink, a short drink. The bottle was nearly empty. 'I know what you hate. You hate something in them you can't understand. You don't hate their evil. You hate the good in them you can't get at. I wonder what you want, what final thing.'

'I'll have all the money I need,' she said. 'I'll go to New York and I won't be old. I'm not old. I'll buy a house, a nice house in a nice neighbourhood, and I'll have nice servants. And first I will find a man, if he's still alive, and very slowly and with the greatest attention to pain I will take his life away. If I do it well and carefully, he will go crazy before he dies.'

Adam stamped on the floor impatiently. 'Nonsense,' he said. 'This isn't true. This is crazy. None of this is true. I don't believe any of it.'

She said, 'Do you remember when you first saw me?'

His face darkened. 'Oh, Lord, yes!'

'You remember my broken jaw and my split lips and my missing teeth?'

'I remember. I don't want to remember.'

'My pleasure will be to find the man who did that,' she said. 'And after that – there will be other pleasures.'

'I have to go,' Adam said.

She said, 'Don't go, dear. Don't go now, my love. My sheets are silk. I want you to feel those sheets against your skin.'

'You don't mean that?'

'Oh, I do, my love. I do. You aren't clever at love, but I can teach you. I will teach you.' She stood up unsteadily and laid her hand on his arm. Her face seemed fresh and young. Adam looked down at her hand and saw it wrinkled as a pale monkey's paw. He moved away in revulsion.

She saw his gesture and understood it and her mouth hardened.

'I don't understand,' he said. 'I know, but I can't believe. I know I won't believe it in the morning. It will be a nightmare dream. But no, it – it can't be a dream – no. Because I remember you are the mother of my boys. You haven't asked about them. You are the mother of my sons.'

Kate put her elbows on her knees and cupped her hands under her chin so that her fingers covered her pointed ears. Her eyes were bright with triumph. Her voice was mockingly soft. 'A fool always leaves an opening,' she said. 'I discovered that when I was a child. I am the mother of your sons. Your sons? I am the mother, yes – but how do you know you are the father?'

Adam's mouth dropped open. 'Cathy, who do you mean?'

'My name is Kate,' she said. 'Listen, my darling, and remember. How many times did I let you come near enough to me to have children?'

'You were hurt,' he said. 'You were terribly hurt.'

'Once,' said Kate, 'just once.'

'The pregnancy made you ill,' he protested. 'It was hard on you.'

She smiled at him sweetly. 'I wasn't too hurt for your brother.'

'My brother?'

'Have you forgotten Charles?'

Adam laughed. 'You are a devil,' he said. 'But do you think I could believe that of my brother?'

'I don't care what you believe,' she said.

Adam said, 'I don't believe it.'

'You will. At first you will wonder, and then you'll be unsure. You'll think back about Charles – all about him. I could have loved Charles. He was like me in a way.'

'He was not.'

'You'll remember,' she said. 'Maybe one day you will remember some tea that tasted bitter. You took my medicine by mistake – remember? Slept as you had never slept before and awakened late – thick-headed?'

'You were too hurt to plan a thing like that.'

'I can do anything,' she said. 'And now, my love, take off your clothes. And I will show you what else I can do.'

Adam closed his eyes and his head reeled with the rum. He opened his eyes and shook his head violently. 'It wouldn't matter – even if it were true,' he said. 'It wouldn't matter at all.' And suddenly he laughed because he knew that this was so. He stood too quickly and had to grab the back of his chair to steady himself against dizziness.

Kate leaped up and put both of her hands on his elbow. 'Let me help you take off your coat.'

Adam twisted her hands from his arm as though they were wire. He moved unsteadily towards the door.

Uncontrolled hatred shone in Kate's eyes. She screamed, a long and shrill animal screech. Adam stopped and turned towards her. The door banged open. The house pimp took three steps, poised, pivoted with his whole weight, and his fist struck Adam under the ear. Adam crashed to the floor.

Kate screamed, 'The boots! Give him the boots!'

Ralph moved closer to the fallen man and measured the distance. He noticed Adam's open eyes staring up at him. He turned nervously to Kate.

Her voice was cold. 'I said give him the boots. Break his face!'

Ralph said, 'He ain't fighting back. The fight's all out of him.'

Kate sat down. She breathed through her mouth. Her hands writhed in her lap. 'Adam,' she said, 'I hate you. I hate you now for the first time. I hate you! Adam, are you listening? I hate you!'

Adam tried to sit up, fell back, and tried again. Sitting on the floor, he looked up at Kate. 'It doesn't matter,' he said. 'It doesn't matter at all.'

He got to his knees and rested with his knuckles against the floor. He said, 'Do you know, I loved you better than anything in the world? I did. It was so strong that it took quite a killing.'

'You'll come crawling back,' she said. 'You'll drag your belly on the floor – begging, begging!'

'You want the boots now, Miss Kate?' Ralph asked.

She did not answer.

Adam moved very slowly towards the door, balancing his steps carefully. His hand fumbled at the door-jamb.

Kate called, 'Adam!'

He turned slowly. He smiled at her as a man might smile at a memory. Then he went out and closed the door gently behind him.

Kate sat staring at the door. Her eyes were desolate.

CHAPTER 26

I

ON THE train back to King City from his trip to Salinas, Adam Trask was in a cloud of vague forms and sounds and colours. He was not conscious of any thought at all.

I believe there are techniques of the human mind whereby, in its dark deep, problems are examined, rejected, or accepted. Such activities sometimes concern facets a man does not know he has.

How often one goes to sleep troubled and full of pain, not knowing what causes the travail, and in the morning a whole new direction and a clearness is there, maybe the result of the black reasoning. And again there are mornings when ecstasy bubbles in the blood, and the stomach and chest are tight and electric with joy, and nothing in the thoughts to justify or cause it.

Samuel's funeral and the talk with Kate should have made Adam sad and bitter, but they did not. Out of the grey throbbing an ecstasy arose. He felt young and free and filled with a hungry gaiety. He got off the train in King City, and, instead of going directly to the livery stable to claim his horse and buggy, he walked to Will Hamilton's new garage.

Will was sitting in his glass-walled office from which he could watch the activity of his mechanics without hearing the clamour of their work. Will's stomach was beginning to fill out richly.

He was studying an advertisement for cigars shipped direct and often from Cuba. He thought he was mourning for his dead father, but he was not. He did have some little worry about Tom, who had gone directly from the funeral to San Francisco. He felt that it was more dignified to lose oneself in business, as he intended to do, than in alcohol, as Tom was probably doing.

He looked up when Adam came into the office and waved his hand to one of the big leather chairs he had installed to lull his customers past the size of the bills they were going to have to pay.

Adam sat down. 'I don't know whether I offered my condolences,' he said.

'It's a sad time,' said Will. 'You were at the funeral?'

'Yes,' said Adam. 'I don't know whether you know how I felt about your father. He gave me things I will never forget.'

'He was respected,' said Will. 'There were over two hundred people at the cemetery – over two hundred.'

'Such a man doesn't really die,' Adam said, and he was discovering it himself. 'I can't think of him as dead. He seems maybe more alive to me than before.'

'That's true,' said Will, and it was not true to him. To Will, Samuel was dead.

'I think of things he said,' Adam went on. 'When he said them I didn't listen very closely, but now they come back, and I can see his face when he said them.'

'That's true,' said Will. 'I was just thinking the same thing. Are you going back to your place?'

'Yes, I am. But I thought I would come in and talk to you about buying an automobile.'

A subtle change came over Will, a kind of silent alertness. 'I would have thought you'd be the last man in the valley to get a car,' he observed, and watched through half-closed eyes for Adam's reaction.

Adam laughed. 'I guess I deserved that,' he said. 'Maybe your father is responsible for a change in me.'

'How do you mean?'

'I don't know as I could explain it. Anyway, let's talk about a car.'

'I'll give you the straight dope on it,' said Will. 'The truth of the matter is I'm having one hell of a time getting enough cars to fill my orders. Why, I've got a list of people who want them.'

'Is that so? Well, maybe I'll just have to put my name on the list.'

'I'd be glad to do that, Mr Trask, and —' He paused. 'You've been so close to the family that – well, if there should be a cancellation I'd be glad to move you up on the list.'

'That's kind of you,' said Adam.

'How would you like to arrange it?'

'How do you mean?'

'Well, I can arrange it so you pay only so much a month.'

'Isn't it more expensive that way?'

'Well, there's interest and carrying charge. Some people find it convenient.'

'I think I'll pay cash,' said Adam. 'There'd be no point in putting it off.'

Will chuckled. 'Not many people feel that way,' he said. 'And there's going to come a time when I won't be able to sell for cash without losing money.'

'I'd never thought of that,' said Adam. 'You will put me on the list, though?'

Will leaned towards him. 'Mr Trask, I'm going to put you on the top of the list. The first car that comes in, you're going to have.'

'Thank you.'

'I'll be glad to do it for you,' said Will.

Adam asked, 'How is your mother holding up?'

Will leaned back in his chair and an affectionate smile came on his face. 'She's a remarkable woman,' he said. 'She's like a rock. I think back on all the hard times we had, and we had plenty of them. My father wasn't very practical. He was always off in the clouds or buried in a book. I think my mother held us together and kept the Hamiltons out of the poorhouse.'

'She's a fine woman,' Adam said.

'Not only fine. She's strong. She stands on her two feet. She's a tower of strength. Did you come back to Olive's house after the funeral?'

'No, I didn't.'

'Well over a hundred people did. And my mother fried all that chicken and saw that everybody had enough.'

'She didn't!'

'Yes, she did. And when you think – it was her own husband.'

'A remarkable woman,' Adam repeated Will's phrase.

'She's practical. She knew they had to be fed and she fed them.'

'I guess she'll be all right, but it must be a great loss to her.'

'She'll be all right,' Will said. 'And she'll outlive us all, little tiny thing that she is.'

On his drive back to the ranch Adam found that he was noticing things he had not seen for years. He saw the wild flowers in the heavy grass, and he saw the red cows against the hillsides, moving up the easy ascending paths and eating as they went. When he came to his own land Adam felt a quick pleasure so sharp that he began to examine it. And suddenly he found himself saying aloud in rhythm with his horse's trotting feet. 'I'm free, I'm free. I don't have to worry any more. I'm free. She's gone. She's gone out of me. Oh, Christ Almighty, I'm free!'

He reached out and stripped the fur from the silver-grey sage beside the road, and when his fingers were sticky with the sap he smelled the sharp pentrating odour on his fingers, breathed it deep into his lungs. He was glad to be going home. He wanted to see how the twins had grown in the two days he had been gone – he wanted to see the twins.

'I'm free, she's gone,' he chanted aloud.

11

Lee came out of the house to meet Adam, and he stood at the horse's head while Adam climbed down from the buggy.

'How are the boys?' Adam asked.

'They're fine. I made them some bows and arrows and they went hunting rabbits in the river bottom. I'm not keeping the pan hot, though.'

'Everything all right here?'

Lee looked at him sharply, was about to exclaim, changed his mind. 'How was the funeral?'

'Lots of people,' Adam said. 'He had lots of friends. I can't get it through my head that he's gone.'

'My people bury them with drums and scatter papers to confuse the devils and put roast pigs instead of flowers on the grave. We're a practical people and always a little hungry. But our devils aren't very bright. We can out-think them. That's some progress.'

'I think Samuel would have liked that kind of funeral,' said Adam. 'It would have interested him.' He noticed that Lee was staring at him. 'Put the horse away, Lee, and then come in and make some tea. I want to talk to you.'

Adam went into the house and took off his black clothes. He could smell the sweet and now sickish odour of rum about himself. He removed all of his clothes and sponged his skin with yellow soap until the odour was gone from his pores. He put on a clean blue shirt and overalls washed until they were soft and pale blue and lighter blue at the knees where the wear came. He shaved slowly and combed his hair while the rattle of Lee at the stove sounded from the kitchen. Then he went to the living-room. Lee had set out one cup and a bowl of sugar on the table beside his big chair. Adam looked around at the flowered curtains washed so long that the blossoms were pale. He saw the worn rugs on the floor and the brown path on the linoleum in the hall. And it was all new to him.

When Lee came in with the teapot Adam said, 'Bring yourself a cup, Lee. And if you've got any of that drink of yours, I could use a little. I got drunk last night.'

Lee said, 'You drunk? I can hardly believe it.'

'Well, I was. And I want to talk about it. I saw you looking at me.'

'Did you?' asked Lee, and he went to the kitchen to bring his cup and glasses and his stone bottle of ng-ka-py.

He said when he came back, 'The only times I've tasted it for years has been with you and Mr Hamilton.'

'Is that the same one we named the twins with?'

'Yes, it is.' Lee poured the scalding green tea. He grimaced when Adam put two spoonfuls of sugar in his cup.

Adam stirred his tea and watched the sugar crystals whirl and disappear into liquid. He said, 'I went down to see her.'

'I thought you might,' said Lee. 'As a matter of fact I don't see how a human man could have waited so long.'

'Maybe I wasn't a human man.'

'I thought of that too. How was she?'

Adam said slowly, 'I can't understand it. I can't believe there is such a creature in the world.'

'The trouble with you Occidentals is that you don't have devils to explain things with. Did you get drunk afterwards?'

'No, before and during. I needed it for courage, I guess.'

'You look all right now.'

'I am all right,' said Adam. 'That's what I want to talk to you about.' He paused and said ruefully, 'This time last year I would have run to Sam Hamilton to talk.'

'Maybe both of us have got a piece of him,' said Lee. 'Maybe that's what immortality is.'

'I seemed to come out of a sleep,' said Adam. 'In some strange way my eyes have cleared. A weight is off me.'

'You even use words that sound like Mr Hamilton,' said Lee. 'I'll build a theory for my immortal relatives.'

Adam drank his cup of black liquor and licked his lips. 'I'm free,' he said. 'I have to tell it to someone. I can live with my boys. I might even see a woman. Do you know what I'm saying?'

'Yes, I know. And I can see it in your eyes and in the way your body stands. A man can't lie about a thing like that. You'll like the boys, I think.'

'Well, at least I'm going to give myself a chance. Will you give me another drink and some more tea?'

Lee poured the tea and picked up his cup.

'I don't know why you don't scald your mouth, drinking it that hot.'

Lee was smiling inwardly. Adam, looking at him, realized that Lee was not a young man any more. The skin on his cheeks was stretched tight, and its surface shone as though it were glazed. And there was a red irritated rim around his eyes.

Lee studied the shell-thin cup in his hand and his was a memory smile. 'Maybe if you're free, you can free me.'

'What do you mean, Lee?'

'Could you let me go?'

'Why, of course you can go. Aren't you happy here?'

'I don't think I've ever known what you people call happiness. We think of contentment as the desirable thing, and maybe that's negative.'

Adam said, 'Call it that, then. Aren't you contented here?'

Lee said, 'I don't think any man is contented when there are things undone he wishes to do.'

'What do you want to do?'

'Well, one thing it's too late for. I wanted to have a wife and sons of my own. Maybe I wanted to hand down the nonsense that passes for wisdom in a parent, to force it on my own helpless children.'

'You're not too old.'

'Oh, I guess I'm physically able to father a child. That's not what I'm thinking. I'm too closely married to a quiet reading-lamp. You know, Mr Trask, once I had a wife. I made her up just as you did, only mine had no life outside my mind. She was good company in my little room. I would talk and she would listen, and then she would talk, would tell me all the happenings of a woman's afternoon. She was very pretty and she made coquettish little jokes. But now I don't know whether I would listen to her. And I wouldn't want to make her sad or lonely. So there's my first plan gone.'

'What was the other?'

'I talked to Mr Hamilton about that. I want to open a bookstore in Chinatown in San Francisco. I would live in the back, and my days would be full of discussions and arguments. I would like to have in stock some of those dragon-carved blocks of ink from the dynasty of Sung. The boxes are worm-bored, and that ink is made from fir smoke and a glue that comes only from wild asses' skin. When you paint with that ink it may physically be black but it suggests to your eye and persuades your seeing that it is all the colours in the world. Maybe a painter would come by and we could argue about method and haggle about price.'

Adam said, 'Are you making this up?'

'No. If you are well and if you are free, I would like to have my little bookshop at last. I would like to die there.'

Adam sat silently for a while, stirring sugar into his lukewarm tea. Then he said, 'Funny. I found myself wishing you were a slave so I could refuse you. Of course you can go if you want to. I'll even lend you money for your bookstore.'

'Oh, I have the money. I've had it a long time.'

'I never thought of your going,' Adam said. 'I took you for granted.' He straightened his shoulders. 'Could you wait a little while?'

'What for?'

'I want you to help me get acquainted with my boys. I want

316

to put this place in shape, or maybe sell it or rent it. I'll want to know how much money I have left and what I can do with it.'

'You wouldn't lay a trap for me?' Lee asked. 'My wish isn't as strong as it once was. I'm afraid I could be talked out of it or, what would be worse, I could be held back just by being needed. Please try not to need me. That's the worst bait of all to a lonely man.'

Adam said, 'A lonely man. I must have been far down in myself not to have thought of that.'

'Mr Hamilton knew,' said Lee. He raised his head and his fat lids let only sparks from his eyes show through. 'We're controlled, we Chinese,' he said. 'We show no emotion. I loved Mr Hamilton. I would like to go to Salinas tomorrow if you will permit it.'

'Do anything you want,' said Adam. 'God knows you've done enough for me.'

'I want to scatter devil papers,' Lee said. 'I want to put a little roast pig on the grave of my father.'

Adam got up quickly and knocked over his cup and went outside and left Lee sitting there.

CHAPTER 27

I

THAT YEAR the rains had come so gently that the Salinas River did not overflow. A slender stream twisted back and forth in its broad bed of grey sand, and the water was not milky with silt but clear and pleasant. The willows that grow in the river-bed were well leafed, and the wild blackberry vines were thrusting their spiky new shoots along the ground.

It was very warm for March, and the kite wind blew steadily from the south and turned up the silver undersides of the leaves.

Against the perfect cover of vine and bramble and tangled drift sticks, a little grey brush rabbit sat quietly in the sun, drying his breast fur, wetted by the grass dew of his early feeding. The rabbit's nose crinkled, and his ears slewed around now and then, investigating small sounds that might possibly be charged with danger to a brush rabbit. There had been a rhythmic vibration in the ground audible through the paws, so that ears swung and nose wrinkled, but that had stopped. Then there had been a movement of willow branches twenty-five yards away and down-wind, so that no odour of fear came to the rabbit.

For the last two minutes there had been sounds of interest but not of danger – a snap and then a whistle like that of the wings of a wild dove. The rabbit stretched out one hind leg lazily in the warm sun. There was a snap and a whistle and a grunting thud on fur. The rabbit sat perfectly still and his eyes grew large. A bamboo arrow was through his chest, and its iron tip deep in the ground on the other side. The rabbit slumped over on his side and his feet ran and scampered in the air for a moment before he was still.

From the willow two crouching boys crept. They carried four-foot bows, and tufts of arrows stuck their feathers up from the quivers behind their left shoulders. They were dressed in overalls and faded blue shirts, but each boy wore one perfect turkey tail-feather tied with tape against his temple.

The boys moved cautiously, bending low, self-consciously toeing-in like Indians. The rabbit's flutter of death was finished when they bent over to examine their victim.

'Right through the heart,' said Cal as though it could not be any other way. Aron looked down and said nothing. 'I'm going to say you did it,' Cal went on. 'I won't take credit. And I'll say it was a hard shot.'

'Well, it was,' said Aron.

'Well, I'm telling you. I'll give you credit to Lee and to Father.'

'I don't know as I want credit – not all of it,' said Aron. 'Tell you what. If we get another one we'll say we each hit one, and if we don't get any more, why don't we say we both shot together and we don't know who hit?'

'Don't you want credit?' Cal asked subtly.

'Well, not full credit. We could divide it up.'

'After all, it was my arrow,' said Cal.

'No, it wasn't.'

'You look at the feathers. See that nick? That's mine.'

'How did it get in my quiver? I don't remember any nick.'

'Maybe you don't remember. But I'm going to give you credit anyway.'

Aron said gratefully, 'No, Cal. I don't want that. We'll say we both shot at once.'

'Well, if that's what you want. But suppose Lee sees it was my arrow?'

'We'll just say it was in my quiver.'

'You think he'll believe that? He'll think you're lying.'

Aron said helplessly, 'If he thinks you shot it, why, we'll just let him think that.'

'I just wanted you to know,' said Cal. 'Just in case he'd think that.' He drew the arrow through the rabbit so that the white feathers were dark red with heart blood. He put the arrow in his quiver. 'You can carry him,' he said magnanimously.

'We ought to start back,' said Aron. 'Maybe Father's back by now.'

Cal said, 'We could cook that old rabbit and have him for our supper and stay out all night.'

'It's too cold at night, Cal. Don't you remember how you shivered this morning?'

'It's not too cold for me,' said Cal. 'I never feel cold.'

'You did this morning.'

'No, I didn't. I was just making fun of you, shivering and chattering like a milk baby. Do you want to call me a liar?'

'No,' said Aron. 'I don't want to fight.'

'Afraid to fight?'

'No. I just don't want to.'

'If I was to say you were scared, would you want to call me a liar?'

'No.'

'Then you're scared, aren't you?'

'I guess so.'

Aron wandered slowly away, leaving the rabbit on the ground. His eyes were very wide and he had a beautiful soft mouth. The width between his blue eyes gave him an expression of angelic innocence. His hair was fine and golden. The sun seemed to light up the top of his head.

He was puzzled – but he was often puzzled. He knew his brother was getting at something, but he didn't know what. Cal was an enigma to him. He could not follow the reasoning of his brother, and he was always surprised at the tangents it took.

Cal looked more like Adam. His hair was dark brown. He was bigger than his brother, bigger of bone, heavier in the shoulder, and his jaw had the square sternness of Adam's jaw. Cal's eyes were brown and watchful, and sometimes they sparkled as though they were black. But Cal's hands were very small for the size of the rest of him. The fingers were short and slender, the nails delicate. Cal protected his hands. There were few things that could make him cry, but a cut finger was one of them. He never ventured with his hands, never touched an insect or carried a snake about. And in a fight he picked up a rock or a stick to fight with.

As Cal watched his brother walking away from him there was a small sure smile on his lips. He called, 'Aron, wait for me!'

When he caught up with his brother he held out the rabbit. 'You can carry it,' he said kindly, putting his arm around his brother's shoulders. 'Don't be mad at me.'

'You always want to fight,' said Aron.

'No, I don't. I was only making a joke.'

'Were you?'

'Sure. Look – you can carry the rabbit. And we'll start back now if you want.'

Aron smiled at last. He was always relieved when his brother let the tension go. The two boys trudged up out of the river bottom and up the crumbling cliff to the level land. Aron's right trouser leg was well bloodied from the rabbit.

Cal said, 'They'll be surprised we got a rabbit. If Father's home, let's give it to him. He likes a rabbit for his supper.'

'All right,' Aron said happily. 'Tell you what. We'll both give it to him and we won't say which one hit it.'

'All right, if you want to,' said Cal.

They walked along in silence for a time and then Cal said, 'All this is our land – way to hell over the river.'

'It's Father's.'

'Yes, but when he dies it's going to be ours.'

This was a new thought to Aron. 'What do you mean, when he dies?'

'Everybody dies,' said Cal. 'Like Mr Hamilton. He died.'

'Oh, yes,' Aron said. 'Yes, he died.' He couldn't connect the two – the dead Mr Hamilton and the live father.

'They put them in a box and then they dig a hole and put the box in,' said Cal.

'I know that.' Aron wanted to change the subject, to think of something else.

Cal said, 'I know a secret.'

'What is it.'

'You'd tell.'

'No, I wouldn't, if you said not.'

'I don't know if I ought.'

'Tell me,' Aron begged.

'You won't tell?'

'No, I won't.'

Cal said, 'Where do you think our mother is?'

320

'She's dead.'

'No, she isn't.'

'She is too.'

'She ran away,' said Cal. 'I heard some men talking.'

'They are liars.'

'She ran away,' said Cal. 'You won't tell I told you?'

'I don't believe it,' said Aron. 'Father said she was in Heaven.

Cal said quietly, 'Pretty soon I'm going to run away and find her. I'll bring her back.'

'Where did the men say she is?'

'I don't know, but I'll find her.'

'She's in Heaven,' said Aron. 'Why would Father tell a lie?' He looked at his brother, begging him silently to agree. Cal didn't answer him. 'Don't you think she's in Heaven with the angels?' Aron insisted. And when Cal still did not answer, 'Who were the men who said it?'

'Just some men. In the post office at King City. They didn't think I could hear. But I got good ears. Lee says I can hear the grass grow.'

Aron said, 'What would she want to run away for?'

'How do I know. Maybe she didn't like us.'

Aron inspected this heresy. 'No,' he said. 'The men were liars. Father said she's in Heaven. And you know how he don't like to talk about her.'

'Maybe that's because she ran away.'

'No. I asked Lee. Know what Lee said? Lee said, "Your mother loved you and she still does." And Lee gave me a star to look at. He said maybe that was our mother and she would love us as long as that light was there. Do you think Lee is a liar?' Through his gathering tears Aron could see his brother's eyes, hard and reasonable. There were no tears in Cal's eyes.

Cal felt pleasantly excited. He had found another implement, another secret tool, to use for any purpose he needed. He studied Aron, saw his quivering lips, but he noticed in time the flaring nostrils. Aron would cry, but sometimes, pushed to tears, Aron would fight too. And when Aron cried and fought at the same time he was dangerous. Nothing could hurt him and nothing could stop him. Once Lee had held him in his lap, clasping his still flailing fists to his sides, until after a long time he relaxed. And his nostrils had flared then.

Cal put his new tool away. He could bring it out any time, and he knew it was the sharpest weapon he had found. He would inspect it at his ease and judge when and how to use it.

He made his decision almost too late. Aron leaped at him and the limp body of the rabbit slashed against his face. Cal jumped back and cried, 'I was just joking. Honest, Aron, it was only a joke.'

Aron stopped. Pain and puzzlement were on his face. 'I don't like that joke,' he said, and he sniffled and wiped his nose on his sleeve.

Cal came close to him and hugged him and kissed him on the cheek. 'I won't do it any more,' he said.

The boys trudged along silently for a while. The light of day began to withdraw. Cal looked over his shoulder at the thunderhead sailing blackly over the mountains on the nervous March wind. 'Going to storm,' he said. 'Going to be a bastard.'

Aron said, 'Did you really hear those men?'

'Maybe I only thought I did,' Cal said quickly. 'Jesus, look at that cloud!'

Aron turned round to look at the black monster. It ballooned in great dark rolls above, and beneath it drew a long trailing skirt of rain, and as they looked the cloud rumbled and flashed fire. Borne on the wind, the cloud-burst drummed hollowly on the fat wet hills across the valley and moved out over the flat lands. The boys turned and ran for home, and the cloud boomed at their backs and the lightning shattered the air into quaking pieces. The cloud caught up with them, and the first stout drops plopped on the ground out of the riven sky. They could smell the sweet odour of ozone. Running, they sniffed the thunder smell.

As they ran across the country road and on to the wheel tracks that led to their own home draw the water struck them. The rain fell in sheets and in columns. Instantly they were soaked through, and their hair plastered down on their foreheads and streamed into their eyes, and the turkey feathers at their temples bent over with the weight of water.

Now that they were as wet as they could get the boys stopped running. There was no reason to run for cover. They looked at each other and laughed for joy. Aron wrung out the rabbit and tossed it in the air and caught it and threw it to Cal. And Cal, feeling silly, put it around his neck with the head and hind feet under his chin. Both boys leaned over and laughed hysterically. The rain roared on the oak trees in the home draw and the wind disturbed their high dignity.

The twins came in sight of the ranch buildings in time to see Lee, his head through the centre hole of a yellow oilskin poncho, leading a strange horse and a flimsy rubber-tyred buggy towards the shed. 'Somebody's here,' said Cal. 'Will you look at that rig?'

They began to run again, for there was a certain deliciousness about visitors. Near the steps they slowed down, moved cautiously round the house, for there was a certain fearsomeness about visitors too. They went in the back way and stood dripping in the kitchen.

They heard voices in the living-room – their father's voice and another, a man's voice. And then a third voice stiffened their stomachs and rippled a little chill up their spines. It was a woman's voice. Those boys had had very little experience with women. They tiptoed into their own room and stood looking at each other.

'Who do you s'pose it is?' Cal said.

An emotion like a light had burst in Aron. He wanted to shout, 'Maybe it's our mother. Maybe she's come back.' And then he remembered that she was in Heaven and people do not come back from there. He said, 'I don't know. I'm going to put on dry clothes.'

The boys put on clean dry clothes, which were exact replicas of the sopping clothes they were taking off. They took off the wet turkey feathers and combed their hair back with their fingers. And all the while they could hear the voices, mostly low-pitched, and then the high woman's voice, and once they froze, listening, for they heard a child's voice – a girl's voice – and this was such an excitement that they did not even speak of hearing it.

Silently they edged into the hall and crept towards the door to the living-room. Cal turned the door-knob very, very slowly and lifted it up so that no creak would betray them.

Only the smallest crack was open when Lee came in by the back door, shuffled along the hall, getting out of his poncho, and caught them there. 'Lilly boy peek?' he said in pidgin, and when Cal closed the door and the latch clicked Lee said quickly, 'Your father's home. You'd better go in.'

Aron whispered hoarsely, 'Who else is there?'

'Just some people going by. The rain drove them in.' Lee put his hand over Cal's on the door-knob and turned it and opened the door.

'Boys come along home,' he said and left them there, exposed in the opening.

Adam cried, 'Come in, boys! Come on in!'

The two carried their heads low and darted glances at the strangers and shuffled their feet. There was a man in city clothes and a woman in the fanciest clothes ever. Her dust-coat and a hat and veil lay on a chair beside her, and she seemed to the boys to be clad entirely in black silk and lace. Black lace even climbed up little sticks and hugged her throat. That was enough for one day, but it wasn't all. Beside the woman sat a girl, a little younger maybe than the twins, but not much. She wore a blue-checked sunbonnet with lace around the front. Her dress was flowery, and a little apron with pockets was tied around her middle. Her skirt was turned back, showing a petticoat of red knitted yarn with tatting around the edge. The boys could not see her face because of the sunbonnet, but her hands were folded in her lap, and it was easy to see the little gold seal ring she wore on her third finger.

Neither boy had drawn a breath and the red rings were beginning to flare at the back of their eyes from holding their breath.

'These are my boys,' their father said. 'They're twins. That's Aron and this is Caleb. Boys, shake hands with our guests.'

The boys moved forward, heads down, hands up, in a gesture very like surrender and despair. Their limp fists were pumped by the gentleman and then by the lacy lady. Aron was first, and he turned away from the little girl, but the lady said, 'Aren't you going to say how do to my daughter?'

Aron shuddered and surrendered his hand in the direction of the girl with the hidden face. Nothing happened. His lifeless sausages were not gripped, or wrung, or squeezed, or racheted. His hand simply hung on the air in front of her. Aron peeked up through his eyelashes to see what was going on.

Her head was down too, and she had the advantage of the sunbonnet. Her small right hand with the signet ring on the middle finger was stuck out too, but it made no move towards Aron's hand.

He stole a glance at the lady. She was smiling, her lips parted. The room seemed crushed with silence. And then Aron heard a ripping snicker from Cal.

Aron reached out and grabbed her hand and pumped it up and down three times. It was as soft as a handful of pearls. He felt a pleasure that burned him. He dropped her hand and concealed his in his overall pocket. As he backed hastily away he saw

324

Cal step up and shake hands formally and say, 'How do.' Aron had forgotten to say it, so he said it now after his brother, and it sounded strange. Adam and his guests laughed.

Adam said, 'Mr and Mrs Bacon nearly got caught in the rain.'

'We were lucky to be lost here,' Mr Bacon said. 'I was looking for the Long ranch.'

'That's farther. You should have taken the next left turn off the country road to the south.' Adam continued to the boys 'Mr Bacon is a county supervisor.'

'I don't know why, but I take the job very seriously,' said Mr Bacon, and he too addressed the boys. 'My daughter's name is Abra, boys. Isn't that a funny name?' He used the tone adults employ with children. He turned to Adam and said in poetic sing-song, ' "Abra was ready ere I called her name; And though I called another, Abra came." Matthew Prior. I won't say I hadn't wanted a son – but Abra's such a comfort. Look up, dear.'

Abra did not move. Her hands were again clasped in her lap. Her father repeated with relish, ' "And though I called another, Abra came." '

Aron saw his brother looking at the little sunbonnet without an ounce of fear. And Aron said hoarsely, 'I don't think Abra's a funny name.'

'He didn't mean funny that way,' Mrs Bacon explained. 'He only meant curious.' And she explained to Adam, 'My husband gets the strangest things out of books. Dear, shouldn't we be going?'

Adam said eagerly, 'Oh, don't go yet, ma'am. Lee is making some tea. It will warm you up.'

'Well, how pleasant!' Mrs Bacon said, and she continued, 'Children, it isn't raining any more. Go outside and play.' Her voice had such authority that they filed out – Aron first and Cal second and Abra following.

III

In the living-room Mr Bacon crossed his legs. 'You have a fine prospect here,' he said. 'Is it a sizeable piece?'

Adam said, 'I have a good strip. I cross the river to the other side. It's a good piece.'

'That's all yours across the county road then?'

'Yes, it is. I'm kind of ashamed to admit it. I've let it go badly. I haven't farmed it at all. Maybe I got too much farming as a child.'

325

Both Mr and Mrs Bacon were looking at Adam now, and he knew he had to make some explanation for letting his good land run free. He said, 'I guess I'm a lazy man. And my father didn't help me when he left me enough to get along on without working.' He dropped his eyes but he could feel the relief on the part of the Bacons. It was not laziness if he was a rich man. Only the poor were lazy. Just as only the poor were ignorant. A rich man who didn't know anything was spoiled or independent.

'Who takes care of the boys?' Mrs Bacon asked.

Adam laughed. 'What taking care of they get, and it isn't much, is Lee's work.'

'Lee?'

Adam became a little irritated with the questioning. 'I only have one man,' he said shortly.

'You mean the Chinese we saw?' Mrs Bacon was shocked.

Adam smiled at her. She had frightened him at first, but now he was more comfortable. 'Lee raised the boys, and he has taken care of me,' he said.

'But didn't they ever have a woman's care?'

'No, they didn't.'

'The poor lambs,' she said.

'They're wild but I guess they're healthy,' Adam said. 'I guess we've all gone wild like the land. But now Lee is going away. I don't know what we'll do.'

Mr Bacon carefully cleared the phlegm from his throat so it wouldn't be run over by his pronouncement. 'Have you thought about the education of your sons?'

'No – I guess I haven't thought about it much.'

Mrs Bacon said, 'My husband is a believer in education.'

'Education is the key to the future,' Mr Bacon said.

'What kind of education?' asked Adam.

Mr Bacon went on, 'All things come to men who know. Yes, I'm a believer in the torch of learning.' He leaned close and his voice became confidential. 'So long as you aren't going to farm your land, why don't you rent it and move to the county seat – near our good public schools?'

For just a second Adam thought of saying, 'Why don't you mind your own goddam business?' but instead he asked, 'You think that would be a good idea?'

'I think I could get you a good reliable tenant,' Mr Bacon said. 'No reason why you shouldn't have something coming in from your land if you don't live on it.'

Lee made a great stir coming in with the tea. He had heard

enough of the tones through the door to be sure Adam was finding them tiresome. Lee was pretty certain they didn't like tea, and if they did, they weren't likely to favour the kind he had brewed. And when they drank it with compliments he knew that the Bacons had their teeth in something. Lee tried to catch Adam's eye but could not. Adam was studying the rug between his feet.

Mrs Bacon was saying, "My husband has served on his school board for many years —' but Adam didn't hear the discussion that followed.

He was thinking of a big globe of the world, suspended and swaying from a limb of one of his oak trees. And for no reason at all that he could make out, his mind leaped to his father, stumping about on his wooden leg, rapping on his leg for attention with a walking-stick. Adam could see the stern and military face of his father as he forced his sons through drill and made them carry heavy packs to develop their shoulders. Through his memory Mrs Bacon's voice droned on. Adam felt the pack loaded with rocks. He saw Charles's face grinning sardonically – Charles – the mean, fierce eyes, the hot temper. Suddenly Adam wanted to see Charles. He would take a trip – take the boys. He slapped his leg with excitement.

Mr Bacon paused in his talk. 'I beg your pardon?'

'Oh, I'm sorry,' Adam said. 'I just remembered something I've neglected to do.' Both Bacons were patiently, politely waiting for his explanation. Adam thought, 'Why not? I'm not running for supervisor. I'm not on the school board. Why not?' He said to his guests, 'I just remembered that I have forgotten to write to my brother for over ten years.' They shuddered under his statement and exchanged glances.

Lee had been refilling the tea-cups. Adam saw his cheeks puff out and heard his happy snort as he passed to the safety of the hallway. The Bacons didn't want to comment on the incident. They wanted to be alone to discuss it.

Lee anticipated that it would be this way. He hurried out to harness up and bring the rubber-tyred buggy to the front door.

IV

When Abra and Cal and Aron went out, they stood side by side on the small covered porch, looking at the rain splashing and dripping down from the wide-spreading oak trees. The cloud-burst had passed into a distant echoing thunder roll, but it had left a rain determined to go on for a long time.

Aron said, 'That lady told us the rain was stopped.'

Abra answered him wisely, 'She didn't look. When she's talking she never looks.'

Cal demanded, 'How old are you?'

'Ten, going on eleven,' said Abra.

'Ho!' said Cal. 'We're eleven, going on twelve.'

Abra pushed her sunbonnet back. It framed her head like a halo. She was pretty, with dark hair in two braids. Her little forehead was round and domed, and her brows were level. One day her nose would be sweet and turned up where now it was still button-form. But two features would be with her always. Her chin was firm and her mouth was as sweet as a flower and very wide and pink. Her hazel eyes were sharp and intelligent and completely fearless. She looked straight into the faces of the boys, straight into their eyes, one after the other, and there was no hint of the shyness she had pretended inside the house.

'I don't believe you're twins,' she said. 'You don't look alike.'

'We are too,' said Cal.

'We are too,' said Aron.

'Some twins don't look alike,' Cal insisted.

'Lots of them don't,' Aron said. 'Lee told us how it is. If the lady has one egg, the twins look alike. If she has two eggs, they don't.'

'We're two eggs,' said Cal.

Abra smiled with amusement at the myths of these country boys. 'Eggs,' she said. 'Ho! Eggs.' She didn't say it loudly or harshly, but Lee's theory tottered and swayed and then she brought it crashing down. 'Which one of you is fried?' she asked. 'And which one is poached?'

The boys exchanged uneasy glances. It was their first experience with the inexorable logic of women, which is overwhelming even, or perhaps especially, when it is wrong. This was new to them, exciting and frightening.

Cal said, 'Lee is a Chinaman.'

'Oh, well,' said Abra kindly, 'why don't you say so? Maybe you're china eggs, then, like they put in a nest.' She paused to let her shaft sink in. She saw opposition, struggle, disappear. Abra had taken control. She was the boss.

Aron suggested, 'Let's go to the old house and play there. It leaks a little but it's nice.'

They ran under the dripping oaks to the old Sanchez house

and plunged in through its open door, which squeaked restlessly on rusty hinges.

The 'dobe house had entered its second decay. The great sala all along the front was half plastered, the line of white half way round and then stopping, just as the workmen had left it over ten years before. And the deep windows with their rebuilt sashes remained glassless. The new floor was streaked with water stain, and a clutter of old papers and darkened nail bags with their nails rusted to prickly balls filled the corner of the room.

As the children stood in the entrance a bat flew from the rear of the house. The grey shape swooped from side to side and disappeared through the doorway.

The boys conducted Abra through the house – opened closets to show wash-basins and toilets and chandeliers, still crated and waiting to be installed. A smell of mildew and of wet paper was in the air. The three children walked on tiptoe, and they did not speak for fear of the echoes from the walls of the empty house.

Back in the big sala the twins faced their guest. 'Do you like it?' Aron asked softly because of the echo.

'Yee-es,' she admitted hesitantly.

'Sometimes we play here,' Cal said boldly. 'You can come here and play with us if you like.'

'I live in Salinas,' Abra said in such a tone that they knew they were dealing with a superior being who hadn't time for bumpkin pleasures.

Abra saw that she had crushed their highest treasure, and while she knew the weaknesses of men she still liked them, and, besides, she was a lady. 'Sometimes, when we are driving by, I'll come and play with you – a little,' she said kindly, and both boys felt grateful to her.

'I'll give you my rabbit,' said Cal suddenly. 'I was going to give it to my father, but you can have it.'

'What rabbit?'

'The one we shot today – right through the heart with an arrow. He hardly even kicked.'

Aron looked at him in outrage. 'It was my —'

Cal interrupted. 'We will let you have it to take home. It's a pretty big one.'

Abra said, 'What would I want with a dirty old rabbit all covered with blood?'

Aron said, 'I'll wash him off and put him in a box and tie him with string, and if you don't want to eat him, you can have a funeral when you get time – in Salinas.'

'I go to real funerals,' said Abra. 'Went to one yesterday. There was flowers high as this roof.'

'Don't you want our rabbit?' Aron asked.

Abra looked at his sunny hair, tight-curled now, and at his eyes that seemed so near to tears, and she felt the longing and the itching burn in her chest that is the beginning of love. Also, she wanted to touch Aron, and she did. She put her hand on his arm and felt him shiver under her fingers. 'If you put it in a box,' she said.

Now that she had got herself in charge, Abra looked around and inspected her conquests. She was well above vanity now that no male principle threatened her. She felt kindly towards these boys. She noticed their thin washed-out clothes patched here and there by Lee. She drew on her fairy tales. 'You poor children,' she said, 'does your father beat you?'

They shook their heads. They were interested but bewildered.

'Are you very poor?'

'How do you mean?' Cal asked.

'Do you sit in the ashes and have to fetch water and faggots?'

'What's faggots?' Aron asked.

She avoided that by continuing, 'Poor darlings,' she began, and she seemed to herself to have a little wand in her hand tipped by a twinkling star. 'Does your wicked step-mother hate you and want to kill you?'

'We don't have a step-mother,' said Cal.

'We don't have any kind,' said Aron. 'Our mother's dead.'

His words destroyed the story she was writing but almost immediately supplied her with another. The wand was gone but she wore a big hat with an ostrich plume and she carried an enormous basket from which a turkey's feet protruded.

'Little motherless orphans,' she said sweetly. 'I'll be your mother. I'll hold you and rock you and tell you stories.'

'We're too big,' said Cal. 'We'd overset you.'

Abra looked away from his brutality. Aron, she saw, was caught up in her story. His eyes were smiling and he seemed almost to be rocking in her arms, and she felt again the tug of love for him. She said pleasantly, 'Tell me, did your mother have a nice funeral?'

'We don't remember,' said Aron. 'We were too little.'

'Well, where is she buried? You could put flowers on her grave. We always do that for Grandma and Uncle Albert.'

'We don't know,' said Aron.

Cal's eyes had a new interest, a gleaming interest that was

close to triumph. He said naïvely, 'I'll ask our father where it is so we can take flowers.'

'I'll go with you,' said Abra. 'I can make a wreath. I'll show you how.' She noticed that Aron had not spoken. 'Don't you want to make a wreath?'

'Yes,' he said.

She had to touch him again. She patted his shoulder and then touched his cheek. 'Your mama will like that,' she said. 'Even in Heaven they look down and notice. My father says they do. He knows a poem about it.'

Aron said, 'I'll go and wrap up the rabbit. I've got the box my pants came in.' He ran out of the old house. Cal watched him go. He was smiling.

'What are you laughing at?' Abra asked.

'Oh, nothing,' he said. Cal's eyes stayed on her.

She tried to stare him down. She was an expert at staring down, but Cal did not look away. At very first he had felt a shyness, but that was gone now, and the sense of triumph at destroying Abra's control made him laugh. He knew she preferred his brother, but that was nothing new to him. Nearly everyone preferred Aron with his golden hair and the openness that allowed his affection to plunge like a puppy. Cal's emotions hid deep in him and peered out, ready to retreat or attack. He was starting to punish Abra for liking his brother, and this was nothing new either. He had done it since he first discovered he could. And secret punishment had grown to be almost a creative thing with him.

Maybe the difference between the two boys can best be described in this way. If Aron should come upon an ant-hill in a little clearing in the brush, he would lie on his stomach and watch the complications of ant life – he would see some of them bringing food in the ant roads and others carrying the white eggs. He would see how two members of the hill on meeting put their antennae together and talked. For hours he would lie absorbed in the economy of the ground.

If, on the other hand, Cal came upon the same ant-hill, he would kick it to pieces and watch while the frantic ants took care of their disaster. Aron was content to be part of his world, but Cal must change it.

Cal did not question the fact that people liked his brother better, but he had developed a means for making it all right with himself. He planned and waited until one time that admiring person exposed himself, and then something happened and the

331

victim never knew how or why. Out of revenge Cal extracted a fluid of power, and out of power, joy. It was the strongest, purest emotion he knew. Far from disliking Aron, he loved him because he was usually the cause for Cal's feeling of triumph. He had forgotten – if he had ever known – that he punished because he wished he could be loved as Aron was loved. It had gone so far that he preferred what he had to what Aron had.

Abra had started a process in Cal by touching Aron and by the softness of her voice towards him. Cal's reaction was automatic. His brain probed for a weakness in Abra, and so clever was he that he found one almost at once in her words. Some children want to be babies and some want to be adults. Few are content with their age. Abra wanted to be an adult. She used adult words and simulated, in so far as she was able, adult attitudes and emotions. She had left babyhood far behind, and she was not capable yet of being one of the grown-ups she admired. Cal sensed this, and it gave him the instrument to knock down her ant-hill.

He knew about how long it would take his brother to find the box. He could see in his mind what would happen. Aron would try to wash the blood off the rabbit, and this would take time. Finding string would take more time, and the careful tying of bow knots still more time. And meanwhile Cal knew he was beginning to win. He felt Abra's certainty wavering and he knew that he could prod it further.

Abra looked away from him at last and said, 'What do you stare at a person for?'

Cal looked at her feet and slowly raised his eyes, going over her as coldly as if she were a chair. This, he knew, could make even an adult nervous.

Abra couldn't stand it. She said, 'See anything green?'

Cal asked, 'Do you go to school?'

'Of course I do.'

'What grade?'

'High fifth.'

'How old are you?'

'Going on eleven.'

Cal laughed.

'What's wrong with that?' she demanded. He didn't answer her. 'Come on, tell me! What's wrong with that?' Still no answer. 'You think you're mighty smart,' she said, and when he continued to laugh at her she said uneasily, 'I wonder what's taking your brother so long. Look, the rain's stopped.'

Cal said, 'I guess he's looking around for it.'

'You mean, for the rabbit?'

'Oh, no. He's got that all right – it's dead. But maybe he can't catch the other. It gets away.'

'Catch what? What gets away?'

'He wouldn't want me to tell,' said Cal. 'He wants it to be a surprise. He caught it last Friday. It bit him too.'

'Whatever are you talking about?'

'You'll see,' said Cal, 'when you open the box. I bet he tells you not to open it right off.' This was not a guess. Cal knew his brother.

Abra knew she was losing not only the battle but the whole war. She began to hate this boy. In her mind she went over the deadly retorts she knew and gave them all up in helplessness, feeling they would have no effect. She retired into silence. She walked out of the door and looked towards the house where her parents were.

'I think I'll go back,' she said.

'Wait,' said Cal.

She turned as he came up with her. 'What do you want?' she asked coldly.

'Don't be mad at me,' he said. 'You don't know what goes on here. You should see my brother's back.'

His change of pace bewildered her. He never let her get set in an attitude, and he had properly read her interest in romantic situations. His voice was low and secret. She lowered her voice to match his.

'What do you mean? What's wrong with his back?'

'All scars,' said Cal. 'It's the Chinaman.'

She shivered and tensed with interest. 'What does he do? Does he beat him?'

'Worse than that,' said Cal.

'Why don't you tell your father?'

'We don't dare. Do you know what would happen if we told?'

'No. What?'

He shook his head. 'No' – he seemed to think carefully – 'I don't even dare tell you.'

At that moment Lee came from the shed leading the Bacons' horse hitched to the high spindly rig with rubber tyres. Mr and Mrs Bacon came out of the house and automatically they all looked up at the sky.

Cal said, 'I can't tell you now. The Chinaman would know if I told.'

Mrs Bacon called, 'Abra! Hurry! We're going.'

Lee held the restive horse while Mrs Bacon was helped up into the rig.

Aron came dashing round the house, carrying a cardboard box intricately tied with string in fancy bow knots. He thrust it at Abra. 'Here,' he said. 'Don't untie it until you get home.'

Cal saw revulsion on Abra's face. Her hands shrank away from the box.

'Take it, dear,' her father said. 'Hurry, we're very late.' He thrust the box into her hands.

Cal stepped close to her. 'I want to whisper,' he said. He put his mouth to her ear. 'You've wet your pants,' he said. She blushed and pulled the sunbonnet up over her head. Mrs Bacon picked her up under the arms and passed her into the buggy.

Lee and Adam and the twins watched the horse pick up a fine trot.

Before the first turn Abra's hand came up and the box went sailing backward into the road. Cal watched his brother's face and saw misery come into Aron's eyes. When Adam had gone back into the house and Lee was moving out with a pan of grain to feed the chickens, Cal put his arm around his brother's shoulders and hugged him reassuringly.

'I wanted to marry her,' Aron said. 'I put a letter in the box, asking her.'

'Don't be sad,' said Cal. 'I'm going to let you use my rifle.'

Aron's head jerked round. 'You haven't got a rifle.'

'Haven't I?' Cal said. 'Haven't I, though?'

CHAPTER 28

I

IT WAS at the supper table that the boys discovered the change in their father. They knew him as a presence – as ears that heard but did not listen, eyes that looked but did not notice. He was a cloud of a father. The boys had never learnt to tell him of their interests and discoveries, or of their needs. Lee had been their contact with the adult world, and Lee had managed not only to raise, feed, clothe, and discipline the boys, but had also given them a respect for their father. He was a mystery to the boys, and his word, his law, was carried down by Lee, who naturally made it up himself and ascribed it to Adam.

This night, the first after Adam's return from Salinas, Cal and Aron were first astonished and then a little embarrassed to find that Adam listened to them and asked questions, looked at them and saw them. The change made them timid.

Adam said, 'I hear you were hunting today.'

The boys became cautious as humans always are, faced with a new situation. After a pause Aron admitted, 'Yes, sir.'

'Did you get anything?'

This time a longer pause, and then, 'Yes, sir.'

'What did you get?'

'A rabbit.'

'With bows and arrows? Who got him?'

Aron said, 'We both shot. We don't know which one hit.'

Adam said, 'Don't you know your own arrows? We used to mark our arrows when I was a boy.'

This time Aron refused to answer and get into trouble. And Cal, after waiting, said, 'Well, it was my arrow, all right, but we think it might have got in Aron's quiver.'

'What makes you think that?'

'I don't know,' Cal said. 'But I think it was Aron hit the rabbit.'

Adam swung his eyes. 'And what do you think?'

'I think maybe I hit it – but I'm not sure.'

'Well, you both seem to handle the situation very well.'

The alarm went out of the faces of the boys. It did not seem to be a trap.

'Where is the rabbit?' Adam asked.

Cal said, 'Aron gave it to Abra as a present.'

'She threw it out,' said Aron.

'Why?'

'I don't know. I wanted to marry her too.'

'You did?'

'Yes, sir.'

'How about you, Cal?'

'I guess I'll let Aron have her,' said Cal.

Adam laughed, and the boys could not recall ever having heard him laugh. 'Is she a nice little girl?' he asked.

'Oh, yes,' said Aron. 'She's nice, all right. She's good and nice.'

'Well, I'm glad of that if she's going to be my daughter-in-law.'

Lee cleared the table and after a quick rattling in the kitchen he came back. 'Ready to go to bed?' he asked the boys.

They glared in protest. Adam said, 'Sit down and let them stay a while.'

'I've got the accounts together. We can go over them later,' said Lee.

'What accounts, Lee?'

'The house and ranch accounts. You said you wanted to know where you stood.'

'Not the accounts for over ten years, Lee!'

'You never wanted to be bothered before.'

'I guess that's right. But sit a while. Aron wants to marry the little girl who was here today.'

'Are they engaged?' Lee asked.

'I don't think she's accepted him yet,' said Adam. 'That may give us some time.'

Cal had quickly lost his awe of the changed feeling in the house and had been examining this ant-hill with calculating eyes, trying to determine just how to kick it over. He made his decision.

'She's a real nice girl,' he said. 'I like her. Know why? Well, she said to ask you where our mother's grave is, so we can take some flowers.'

'Could we, Father?' Aron asked. 'She said she would teach us how to make wreaths.'

Adam's mind raced. He was not good at lying, to begin with, and he hadn't practised. The solution frightened him, it came so quickly to his mind and so glibly to his tongue. Adam said, 'I wish we could do that, boys. But I'll have to tell you. Your mother's grave is clear across the country where she came from.'

'Why?' Aron asked.

'Well, some people want to be buried in the place they came from.'

'How did she get there?' Cal asked.

'We put her on a train and sent her home – didn't we, Lee?'

Lee nodded. 'It's the same with us,' he said. 'Nearly all Chinese get sent home to China after they die.'

'I know that,' said Aron. 'You told us that before.'

'Did I?' Lee asked.

'Sure you did,' said Cal. He was vaguely disappointed.

Adam quickly changed the subject. 'Mr Bacon made a suggestion this afternoon,' he began. 'I'd like you boys to think about it. He said it might be better for you if we moved to

alinas – better schools and lots of other children to play
ith.'

The thought stunned the twins. Cal asked, 'How about here?'

'Well, we'd keep the ranch in case we want to come back.'

Aron said, 'Abra lives in Salinas.' And that was enough for
ron. Already he had forgotten the sailing box. All he could
nink of was a small apron and a sunbonnet and soft little
ngers.

Adam said, 'Well, you think about it. Maybe you should go to
ed now. Why didn't you go to school today?'

'The teacher's sick,' said Aron.

Lee verified it. 'Miss Culp has been sick for three days,' he
aid. 'They don't have to go back until Monday. Come on,
oys.'

They followed him obediently from the room.

II

Adam sat smiling vaguely at the lamp and tapping his knee with
forefinger until Lee came back. Adam said, 'Do they know
nything?'

'I don't know,' said Lee.

'Well, maybe it was just the little girl.'

Lee went to the kitchen and brought back a big cardboard
ox. 'Here are the accounts. Every year has a rubber band round
t. I've been over it. It's complete.'

'You mean all accounts?'

Lee said, 'You'll find a book for each year and receipted bills
or everything. You wanted to know how you stood. Here it is
– all of it. Do you really think you'll move?'

'Well, I'm thinking of it.'

'I wish there were some way you could tell the boys the truth.'

'That would rob them of the good thoughts about their
mother, Lee.'

'Have you thought of the other danger?'

'What do you mean?'

'Well, suppose they find out the truth. Plenty of people know.'

'Well, maybe when they're older it will be easier for them.'

'I don't believe that,' said Lee. 'But that's not the worst
danger.'

'I guess I don't follow you, Lee.'

'It's the lie I'm thinking of. It might infect everything. If they
ever found out you'd lied to them about this, the true thing
would suffer. They wouldn't believe anything then.'

337

'Yes, I see. But what can I tell them? I couldn't tell them the whole truth.'

'Maybe you can tell them a part truth, enough so that you won't suffer if they find out.'

'I'll have to think about that, Lee.'

'If you go to live in Salinas it will be more dangerous.'

'I'll have to think about it.'

Lee went on insistently, 'My father told me about my mother when I was very little, and he didn't spare me. He told me a number of times as I was growing. Of course it wasn't the same, but it was pretty dreadful. I'm glad he told me, though. I wouldn't like not to know.'

'Do you want to tell me?'

'No, I don't want to. But it might persuade you to make some change for your own boys. Maybe if you just said she went away and don't know where.'

'But I do know.'

'Yes, there's the trouble. It's bound to be all truth or part lie. Well, I can't force you.'

'I'll think about it,' said Adam. 'What's the story about your mother?'

'You really want to hear?'

'Only if you want to tell me.'

'I'll make it very short,' said Lee. 'My first memory is of living in a little dark shack alone with my father in the middle of a potato field, and with it the memory of my father telling me the story of my mother. His language was Cantonese, but whenever he told the story he spoke in high and beautiful Mandarin. All right, then. I'll tell you —' And Lee looked back in time.

'I'll have to tell you first that when you built the railroads in the West the terrible work of grading and laying ties and spiking the rails was done by many thousands of Chinese. They were cheap, they worked hard, and if they died no one had to worry. They were recruited largely from Canton, for the Cantonese are short and strong and durable, and also they are not quarrelsome. They were brought in by contract, and perhaps the history of my father was a fairly typical one.

'You must know that a Chinese must pay all of his debts on or before our New Year's Day. He starts every year clean. If he does not, he loses face; but not only that – his family loses face. There are no excuses.'

'That's not a bad idea,' said Adam.

'Well, good or bad, that's the way of it. My father had some

338

bad luck. He could not pay a debt. The family met and discussed the situation. Ours is an honourable family. The bad luck was nobody's fault, but the unpaid debt belonged to the whole family. They paid my father's debt and then he had to repay them, and that was almost impossible.

'One thing the recruiting agents for the railroad companies did – they paid down a lump of money on the signing of the contract. In this way they caught a great many men who had fallen into debt. All of this was reasonable and honourable. There was only one black sorrow.

'My father was a young man recently married, and his tie to his wife was very strong and deep and warm, and hers to him must have been – overwhelming. Nevertheless, with good manners they said goodbye in the presence of the heads of the family. I have often thought that perhaps formal good manners may be a cushion against heartbreak.

'The herds of men went like animals into the black hold of a ship, there to stay until they reached San Francisco six weeks later. And you can imagine what those holds were like. The merchandise had to be delivered in some kind of working condition, so it was not mistreated. And my people have learnt through the ages to live close together, to keep clean and fed under intolerable conditions.

'They were a week at sea before my father discovered my mother. She was dressed like a man and she had braided her hair in a man's queue. By sitting very still and not talking she had not been discovered, and of course there were no examinations or vaccination then. She moved her mat closer to my father. They could not talk except mouth to ear in the dark. My father was angry at her disobedience, but he was glad too.

'Well, there it was. They were condemned to hard labour for five years. It did not occur to them to run away once they were in America, for they were honourable people and they had signed the contract.'

Lee paused. 'I thought I could tell it in a few sentences,' he said. 'But you don't know the background. I'm going to get a cup of water – do you want some?'

'Yes,' said Adam. 'But there's one thing I don't understand. How could a woman do that kind of work?'

'I'll be back in a moment,' said Lee, and he went to the kitchen. He brought back tin cups of water and put them on the table. He asked, 'Now what did you want to know?'

'How could your mother do a man's work?'

Lee smiled. 'My father said she was a strong woman, and I believe a strong woman may be stronger than a man, particularly if she happens to have love in her heart. I guess a loving woman is almost indestructible.'

Adam made a wry grimace.

Lee said, 'You'll see one day, you'll see.'

'I didn't mean to think badly,' said Adam. 'How could I know out of one experience? Go on.'

'One thing my mother did not whisper in my father's ear during that long miserable crossing. And because a great many were deadly seasick, no remark was made of her illness.'

Adam cried, 'She wasn't pregnant!'

'She was pregnant,' said Lee. 'And she didn't want to burden my father with more worries.'

'Did she know about it when she started?'

'No, she did not. I set my presence in the world at the most inconvenient time. It's a longer story than I thought.'

'Well, you can't stop now,' said Adam.

'No, I suppose not. In San Francisco the flood of muscle and bone flowed into cattle cars and the engines puffed up the mountains. They were going to dig hills in the Sierras and burrow tunnels under the peaks. My mother got herded into another car, and my father didn't see her until they got to their camp on a high mountain meadow. It was very beautiful, with green grass and flowers and the snow mountains all around. And only then did she tell my father about me.

'They went to work. A woman's muscles harden just as a man's do and my mother had a muscular spirit too. She did the pick and shovel work expected of her, and it must have been dreadful. But a panic worry settled on them about how she was going to have the baby.'

Adam said, 'Were they ignorant? Why couldn't she have gone to the boss and told him she was a woman and pregnant? Surely they would have taken care of her.'

'You see?' said Lee. 'I haven't told you enough. And that's why this is so long. They were not ignorant. These human cattle were imported for one thing only – to work. When the work was done, those who were not dead were to be shipped back. Only males were brought – no females. The country did not want them breeding. A man and a woman and a baby have a way of digging in, of pulling the earth where they are about them and scratching out a home. And then it takes all hell to root them out. But a crowd of men, nervous, lusting, restless, half sick

340

with loneliness for women – why, they'll go anywhere, and particularly will they go home. And my mother was the only woman in this pack of half-crazy, half-savage men. The longer the men worked and ate, the more restless they became. To the bosses they were not people but animals which could be dangerous if not controlled. You can see why my mother did not ask for help. Why, they'd have rushed her out of the camp and – who knows? – perhaps shot and buried her like a diseased cow. Fifteen men were shot for being a little mutinous.

'No – they kept order the only way our poor species has ever learned to keep order. We think there must be better ways but we never learn them – always the whip, the rope, the rifle. I wish I hadn't started to tell you this — '

'Why should you not tell me?' Adam asked.

'I can see my father's face when he told me. An old misery come back, raw and full of pain. Telling it, my father had to stop and gain possession of himself, and when he continued he spoke sternly and he used hard sharp words almost as though he wanted to cut himself with them.

'These two managed to stay close together by claiming she was my father's nephew. The months went by and fortunately for them there was very little abdominal swelling, and she worked in pain and out of it. My father could only help her a little, apologizing, "My nephew is young and his bones are brittle." They had no plan. They did not know what to do.

'And then my father figured out a plan. They would run into the high mountains to one of the higher meadows, and there beside a lake they would make a burrow for the birthing, and when my mother was safe and the baby born, my father would come back and take his punishment. And he would sign for an extra five years to pay for his delinquent nephew. Pitiful as their escape was, it was all they had and it seemed a brightness. The plan had two requirements – the timing had to be right and a supply of food was necessary.'

Lee said, 'My parents' – and he stopped, smiling over his use of the word, and it felt so good that he warmed it up – 'my dear parents began to make their preparations. They saved a part of their daily rice and hid it under their sleeping mats. My father found a length of string and filed out a hook from a piece of wire, for there were trout to be caught in the mountain lakes. He stopped smoking to save the matches issued. And my mother collected every tattered scrap of cloth she could find and unravelled edges to make thread and sewed this ragbag together

341

with a splinter to make swaddling clothes for me. I wish I had known her.'

'So do I,' said Adam. 'Did you ever tell this to Sam Hamilton?'

'No. I didn't. I wish I had. He loved a celebration of the human soul. Such things were like a personal triumph to him.'

'I hope they got there,' said Adam.

'I know. And when my father would tell me I would say to him, "Get to that lake – get my mother there – don't let it happen again, not this time. Just once let's tell it: how you got to the lake and built a house of fir boughs." And my father became very Chinese then. He said, "There's more beauty in the truth even if it is dreadful beauty. The storytellers at the city gate twist life so that it looks sweet to the lazy and the stupid and the weak, and this only strengthens their infirmities, and teaches nothing, cures nothing, nor does it let the heart soar." '

'Get on with it,' Adam said irritably.

Lee got up and went to the window and he finished the story, looking out at the stars that winked and blew in the March wind.

'A little boulder jumped down a hill and broke my father's leg. They set the leg and gave him cripples' work, straightening used nails with a hammer on a rock. And whether with worry or work – it doesn't matter – my mother went into early labour. And then the half-mad men knew and they went all mad. One hunger sharpened another hunger, and one crime blotted out the one before it, and the little crimes committed against those starving men flared into one gigantic maniac crime.

'My father heard the shout "Woman" and he knew. He tried to run and his leg re-broke under him and he crawled up the ragged slope to the roadbed where it was happening.

'When he got there a kind of sorrow had come over the sky, and the Canton men were creeping away to hide and to forget that men can be like this. My father came to her on the pile of shale. She had not even eyes to see out of, but her mouth still moved and she gave him his instructions. My father clawed me out of the tattered meat of my mother with his fingernails. She died on the shale in the afternoon.'

Adam was breathing hard. Lee continued in a singsong cadence, 'Before you hate those men you must know this. My father always told it at the last: No child ever had such care as I. The whole camp became my mother. It is a beauty – a dreadful kind of beauty. And now good night. I can't talk any more.'

Adam restlessly opened drawers and looked up at the shelves and raised the lids of boxes in his house and at last he was forced to call Lee back and ask, 'Where's the ink and the pen?'

'You don't have any,' said Lee. 'You haven't written a word in years. I'll lend you mine if you want.' He went to his room and brought back a squat bottle of ink and a stub pen and a pad of paper and an envelope and laid them on the table.

Adam asked, 'How do you know I want to write a letter?'

'You're going to try to write to your brother, aren't you?'

'That's right.'

'It will be a hard thing to do after so long,' said Lee.

And it was hard. Adam nibbled and munched on the pen and his mouth became strained grimaces. Sentences were written and the page thrown away and another started. Adam scratched his head with the penholder. 'Lee, if I wanted to take a trip east, would you stay with the twins until I get back?'

'It's easier to go than to write,' said Lee. 'Sure I'll stay.'

'No. I'm going to write.'

'Why don't you ask your brother to come out here?'

'Say, that's a good idea, Lee. I didn't think of it.'

'It also gives you a reason for writing, and that's a good thing.'

The letter came fairly easily then, was corrected and copied fair. Adam read it slowly to himself before he put it in the envelope.

'Dear brother Charles,' it said. 'You will be surprised to hear from me after so long. I have thought of writing many times, but you know how a man puts it off.

'I wonder how this letter finds you. I trust in good health. For all I know you may have five or even ten children by now. Ha! Ha! I have two sons and they are twins. Their mother is not here. Country life did not agree with her. She lives in a town near-by and I see her now and then.

'I have a fine ranch, but I am ashamed to say I do not keep it up very well. Maybe I will do better from now on. I always did make good resolutions. But for a number of years I felt poorly. I am well now.

'How are you and how do you prosper? I would like to see you. Why don't you come to visit here? It is a great country and you might even find a place where you would like to settle. No cold winters here. That makes a difference to "old men" like us. Ha! Ha!

'Well, Charles, I do hope you will think about it and let me know. The trip would do you good. I want to see you. I have much to tell you that I can't write down.

'Well, Charles, write me a letter and tell me all the news of the old home. I suppose many things have happened. As you get older you hear mostly about people you knew that died. I guess that is the way of the world. Write quick and tell me if you will come to visit. Your brother Adam.'

He sat holding the letter in his hand and looking over it at his brother's dark face with its scarred forehead. Adam could see the glinting heat in the brown eyes, and as he looked he saw the lips writhe back from the teeth and the blind destructive animal take charge. He shook his head to rid his memory of the vision, and he tried to rebuild the face smiling. He tried to remember the forehead before the scar, but he could not bring either into focus. He seized the pen and wrote below his signature, 'P.S. Charles, I never hated you no matter what. I always loved you because you were my brother.'

Adam folded the letter and forced the creases sharp with his fingernails. He sealed the envelope flap with his fist. 'Lee!' he called, 'Oh, Lee!'

The Chinese looked in through the door.

'Lee, how long does it take a letter to go east – clear east?'

'I don't know,' said Lee. 'Two weeks maybe.'

CHAPTER 29

AFTER HIS first letter to his brother in over ten years was mailed Adam became impatient for an answer. He forgot how much time had elapsed. Before the letter got as far as San Francisco he was asking aloud in Lee's hearing, 'I wonder why he doesn't answer. Maybe he's mad at me for not writing. But he didn't write either. No – he didn't know where to write. Maybe he's moved away.'

Lee answered. 'It's only been gone a few days. Give it time.'

'I wonder whether he would really come out here?' Adam asked himself, and he wondered whether he wanted Charles. Now that the letter was gone, Adam was afraid Charles might accept. He was like a restless child whose fingers stray to every loose article. He interfered with the twins, asked them innumerable questions about school.

'Well, what did you learn today?'

'Nothing!'

'Oh, come! You must have learned something. Did you read?'

'Yes, sir.'

'What did you read?'

'That old one about the grasshopper and the ant.'

'Well, that's interesting.'

'There's one about an eagle carries a baby away.'

'Yes, I remember that one. I forget what happens.'

'We aren't to it yet. We saw the pictures.'

The boys were disgusted. During one of Adam's moments of fatherly bungling Cal borrowed his pocket-knife, hoping he would forget to ask for it back. But the sap was beginning to run freely in the willows. The bark would slip easily from a twig. Adam got his knife back to teach the boys to make willow whistles, a thing Lee had taught them three years before. To make it worse, Adam had forgotten how to make the cut. He couldn't get a peep out of his whistles.

At noon one day Will Hamilton came roaring and bumping up the road in a new Ford. The engine raced in its low gear, and the high top swayed like a storm-driven ship. The brass radiator and the Prestolite tank on the running-board were blinding with brass polish.

Will pulled up the brake lever, turned the switch straight down, and sat back in the leather seat. The car backfired several times without ignition because it was overheated.

'Here she is!' Will called with false enthusiasm. He hated Fords with a deadly hatred, but they were daily building his fortune.

Adam and Lee hung over the exposed insides of the car while Will Hamilton, puffing under the burden of his new fat, explained the workings of a mechanism he did not understand himself.

It is hard now to imagine the difficulty of learning to start, drive, and maintain an automobile. Not only was the whole process complicated, but one had to start from scratch. Today's children breathe in the theory, habits, and idiosyncrasies of the internal combustion engine in their cradles, but then you started with the blank belief that it would not run at all, and sometimes you were right. Also, to start the engine of a modern car you do just two things, turn a key and touch the starter. Everything

345

else is automatic. The process used to be more complicated. It required not only a good memory, a strong arm, an angelic temper, and a blind hope, but also a certain amount of practice of magic, so that a man about to turn the crank of a Model T might be seen to spit on the ground and whisper a spell.

Will Hamilton explained the car and went back and explained it again. His customers were wide-eyed, interested as terriers, co-operative, and did not interrupt, but as he began for the third time Will saw that he was getting no place.

'Tell you what!' he said brightly. 'You see this isn't my line. I wanted you to see her and listen to her before I made delivery. Now, I'll go back to town and tomorrow I'll send back this car with an expert, and he'll tell you more in a few minutes than I could in a week. But I just wanted you to see her.'

Will had forgotten some of his own instructions. He cranked for a while and then borrowed a buggy and a horse from Adam and drove to town, but he promised to have a mechanic out the next day.

II

There was no question of sending the twins to school the next day. They wouldn't have gone. The Ford stood tall and aloof and dour under the oak tree where Will had stopped it. Its new owners circled it and touched it now and then, the way you touch a dangerous horse to soothe him.

Lee said, 'I wonder whether I'll ever get used to it.'

'Of course you will,' Adam said without conviction. 'Why, you'll be driving all over the county first thing you know.'

'I will try to understand it,' Lee said. 'But drive it I will not.'

The boys made little dives in and out, to touch something and leap away. 'What's this do-hickey, Father?'

'Get your hands off that.'

'But what's it for?'

'I don't know, but don't touch it. You don't know what might happen.'

'Didn't the man tell you?'

'I don't remember what he said. Now you boys get away from it or I'll have to send you to school. Do you hear me, Cal? Don'' open that.'

They had got up and were ready very early in the morning. By eleven o'clock hysterical nervousness had set in. The mechanic drove up in the buggy in time for the midday meal. He wore box-toed shoes and Duchess trousers and his wide square coat came almost to his knees. Beside him in the buggy was a satchel in which were his working clothes and tools. He was nineteen and chewed tobacco, and from his three months in automobile school he had gained a great though weary contempt for human beings. He spat and threw the reins at Lee.

'Put this hay-burner away,' he said. 'How do you tell which end is the front?' And he climbed down the rig as an ambassador comes out of a state train. He sneered at the twins and turned coldly to Adam. 'I hope I'm in time for dinner,' he said.

Lee and Adam stared at each other. They had forgotten about the noonday meal.

In the house the godling grudgingly accepted cheese and bread and cold meat and pie and coffee and a piece of chocolate cake.

'I'm used to a hot dinner,' he said. 'You better keep those kids away if you want any car left.' After a leisurely meal and a short rest on the porch the mechanic took his satchel into Adam's bedroom. In a few minutes he emerged dressed in striped overalls and a white cap which had 'Ford' printed on the front of its crown.

'Well,' he said. 'Done any studying?'

'Studying?' Adam asked.

'Ain't you even read the literature in the book under the seat?'

'I didn't know it was there,' said Adam.

'Oh, Lord,' said the young man disgustedly. With a courageous gathering of his moral forces he moved with decision towards the car. 'Might as well get started,' he said. 'God knows how long it's going to take if you ain't studied.'

Adam said, 'Mr Hamilton couldn't start it last night.'

'He always tries to start it on the magneto,' said the sage. 'All right! All right, come along. Know the principles of a internal combustion engine?'

'No,' said Adam.

'Oh, Jesus Christ!' He lifted the tin flaps. 'This-here is a internal combustion engine,' he said.

Lee said quietly, 'So young to be so erudite.'

The boy swung round towards him, scowling. 'What did you say?' he demanded, and he asked Adam, 'What did the Chink say?'

Lee spread his hands and smiled blandly. 'Say velly smaht fella,' he observed quietly. 'Mebbe go college. Velly wise.'

'Just call me Joe!' the boy said for no reason at all, and he added, 'College! What do them fellas know? Can they set a

347

timer, huh? Can they file a point? College!' And he spat a brown disparaging comment on the ground. The twins regarded him with admiration, and Cal collected spit on the back of his tongue to practise.

Adam said, 'Lee was admiring your grasp of the subject.'

The truculence went out of the boy and magnanimity took its place. 'Just call me Joe,' he said. 'I *ought* to know it. Went to automobile school in Chicago. That's a real school – not like no college.' And he said, 'My old man says you take a good Chink, I mean a good one – why, he's about as good as anybody. They're honest.'

'But not the bad ones,' said Lee.

'Hell no! Not no high binders nor nothing like that. But good Chinks.'

'I hope I may be included in that group?'

'You look like a good Chink to me. Just call me Joe.'

Adam was puzzled at the conversation, but the twins weren't. Cal said experimentally to Aron, 'Jus' call me Joe,' and Aron moved his lips trying out, 'Jus' call me Joe.'

The mechanic became professional again. but his tone was kinder. An amused friendliness took the place of his former contempt. 'This-here,' he said, 'is a internal combustion engine.' They looked down at the ugly lump of iron with a certain awe.

Now the boy went on so rapidly that the words ran together into a great song of the new era. 'Operates through the explosion of gases in a enclosed space. Power of explosion is exerted on piston and through connecting rod and crankshaft through transmission thence to rear wheels. Got that?' They nodded blankly, afraid to stop the flow. 'They's two kinds, two-cycle and four-cycle. This-here is four-cycle. Got that?'

Again they nodded. The twins, looking up into his face with adoration, nodded.

'That's interesting,' said Adam.

Joe went on hurriedly. 'Main difference of a Ford automobile from other kinds is its planetary transmission which operates on a rev-rev-a-lu-shun-ary principle.' He pulled up for a moment, his face showing strain. And when his four listeners nodded again he cautioned them, 'Don't get the idea you know it all. The planetary system is, don't forget, rev-a-lu-shun-ary. You better study up on it in the book. Now, if you got all that we'll go on to Operation of the Automobile.' He said this in bold-face type, capital letters. He was obviously glad to be done with the first part of the lecture, but he was no gladder than his listeners.

The strain of concentration was beginning to tell on them, and it was not made any better by the fact that they had not understood one single word.

'Come around here,' said the boy. 'Now you see that-there? That's the ignition key. When you turn that-there you're ready to go ahead. Now, you push this do-hickey to the left. That puts her on battery – see, where it says Bat. That means battery.' They craned their necks into the car. The twins were standing on the running-board.

'No – wait. I got ahead of myself. First you got to retard the spark and advance the gas, else she'll kick your goddam arm off. This-here – see it? – this-here's the spark. You push it up – get it? – *up*. Clear up. And this here's the gas – you push her down. Now I'm going to explain it and then I'm going to do it. I want you to pay attention. You kids get off the car. You're in my light. Get down, goddam it.' The boys reluctantly climbed down from the running-board; only their eyes looked over the door.

He took a deep breath. 'Now, you ready? Spark retarded, gas advanced. Spark up, gas down. Now switch to battery – left, remember – left.' A buzzing like that of a gigantic bee sounded. 'Hear that? That's the contact in one of the coil boxes. If you don't get that, you got to adjust the points or maybe file them.' He noticed a look of consternation on Adam's face. 'You can study up on that in the book,' he said kindly.

He moved to the front of the car. 'Now this-here is the crank and – see this little wire sticking out of the radiator? – that's the choke. Now watch careful while I show you. You grab the crank like this and push till she catches. See how my thumb is turned down? If I grabbed her the other way with my thumb around her, and she was to kick, why, she'd knock my thumb off. Got it?'

He didn't look up but he knew they were nodding.

'Now,' he said, 'look careful. I push in and bring her up until I got compression, and then, why, I pull out this wire and I bring her around careful to suck gas in. Hear that sucking sound? That's choke. But don't pull her too much or you'll flood her. Now, I let go the wire and give her a hell of a spin, and as soon as she catches I run around and advance the spark and retard the gas and I reach over and throw the switch quick over to magneto – see where it says Mag? – and there you are.'

His listeners were limp. After all this they had just got the engine started.

The boy kept at them. 'I want you to say after me now so you learn it. Spark up – gas down.'

They repeated in chorus, 'Spark up – gas down.'

'Switch to Bat.'

'Switch to Bat.'

'Crank to compression, thumb down.'

'Crank to compression, thumb down.'

'Easy over – choke out.'

'Easy over – choke out.'

'Spin her.'

'Spin her.'

'Spark down – gas up.'

'Spark down – gas up.'

'Switch to Mag.'

'Switch to Mag.'

'Now we'll go over her again. Just call me Joe.'

'Just call you Joe.'

'Not that. Spark up – gas down.'

A kind of weariness settled on Adam as they went over the litany for the fourth time. The process seemed silly to him. He was relieved when a short time later Will Hamilton drove up in his low sporty red car. The boy looked at the approaching vehicle. 'That-there's got sixteen valves,' he said in a reverent tone. 'Special job.'

Will leaned out of his car. 'How's it going?' he asked.

'Just fine,' said the mechanic. 'They catch on quick.'

'Look, Roy, I've got to take you in. The new hearse knocked out a bearing. You'll have to work late to get it ready for Mrs Hawks at eleven tomorrow.'

Roy snapped to efficient attention. 'I'll get my clos',' he said and ran for the house. As he tore back with his satchel Cal stood in his way.

'Hey,' Cal said, 'I thought your name was Joe.'

'How do you mean, Joe?'

'You told us to call you Joe. Mr Hamilton says you're Roy.'

Roy laughed and jumped into the roadster. 'Know why I say call me Joe?'

'No. Why?'

'Because my name is Roy.' In the midst of his laughter he stopped and said sternly to Adam, 'You get that book under the seat and you study up. Hear me?'

'I will,' said Adam.

CHAPTER 30

I

EVEN AS in Biblical times, there were miracles on the earth in those days. One week after the lesson a Ford bumped up the main street of King City and pulled to a shuddering stop in front of the post office. Adam sat at the wheel with Lee beside him and the two boys straight and grand in the back seat.

Adam looked down at the floorboards, and all four chanted in unison, 'Brake on – advance gas – switch off.' The little engine roared and then stopped. Adam sat back for a moment, limp but proud, before he got out.

The postmaster looked out between the bars of his golden grill. 'I see you've got one of those damn things,' he said.

'Have to keep up with the times,' said Adam.

'I predict there'll come a time when you can't find a horse, Mr Trask.'

'Maybe so.'

'They'll change the face of the countryside. They get their clatter into everything,' the postmaster went on. 'We even feel it here. Man used to come for his mail once a week. Now he comes every day, sometimes twice a day. He just can't wait for his damn catalogue. Running around. Always running around.' He was so violent in his dislike that Adam knew he hadn't bought a Ford yet. It was a kind of jealousy coming out. 'I wouldn't have one around,' the postmaster said, and this meant that his wife was at him to buy one. It was the women who put the pressure on. Social status was involved.

The postmaster angrily shuffled through the letters from the T box and tossed out a long envelope. 'Well, I'll see you in the hospital,' he said viciously.

Adam smiled at him and took his letter and walked out.

A man who gets few letters does not open one lightly. He hefts it for weight, reads the name of the sender on the envelope and the address, looks at the handwriting, and studies the postmark and the date. Adam was out of the post office and across the sidewalk to his Ford before he had done all of these things. The left-hand corner of the envelope had printed on it, Bellows and Harvey, Attorneys at Law, and their address was the town in Connecticut from which Adam had come.

He said in a pleasant tone, 'Why I know Bellows and Harvey,

know them well. I wonder what they want?' He looked closely at the envelope. 'I wonder how they got my address?' He turned the envelope over and looked at the back. Lee watched him, smiling. 'Maybe the questions are answered in the letter.'

'I guess so,' Adam said. Once having decided to open the letter, he took out his pocket-knife, opened the big blade and inspected the envelope for a point of ingress, found none, held the letter up to the sun to make sure not to cut the message, tapped the letter to one end of the envelope, and cut off the other end. He blew in the end and extracted the letter with two fingers. He read the letter very slowly.

'Mr Adam Trask, King City, California. Dear Sir,' it began testily, 'For the last six months we have exhausted every means of locating you. We have advertised in newspapers all over the country without success. It was only when your letter to your brother was turned over to us by the local postmaster that we were able to ascertain your whereabouts.' Adam could feel their impatience with him. The next paragraph began a complete change of mood. 'It is our sad duty to inform you that your brother, Charles Trask, is deceased. He died of a lung ailment October 12 after an illness of two weeks, and his body rests in the Odd Fellows cemetery. No stone marks his grave. We presume you will want to undertake this sorrowful duty yourself.'

Adam drew a deep full breath and held it while he read the paragraph again. He breathed out slowly to keep the release from being a sigh. 'My brother Charles is dead,' he said.

'I'm sorry,' said Lee.

Cal said, 'Is he our uncle?'

'He was your Uncle Charles,' said Adam.

'Mine too?' Aron asked.

'Yours too.'

'I didn't know we had him,' Aron said. 'Maybe we can put some flowers on his grave. Abra could help us. She likes to.'

'It's a long way off – clear across the country.'

Aron said excitedly, 'I know! When we take flowers to our mother we'll take some to our Uncle Charles.' And he said a little sadly, 'I wish't I knew I had him before he was dead.' He felt that he was growing rich in dead relatives. 'Was he nice?' Aron asked.

'Very nice,' said Adam. 'He was my only brother, just like Cal is your only brother.'

'Were you twins too?'

'No – not twins.'

Cal asked, 'Was he rich?'

'Of course not,' said Adam. 'Where'd you get that idea?'

'Well, if he was rich we'd get it, wouldn't we?'

Adam said sternly, 'At a time of death it isn't a nice thing to talk about money. We're sad because he died.'

'How can I be sad?' said Cal. 'I never saw him.'

Lee covered his mouth with his hand to conceal a smile. Adam looked back at the letter, and again it changed mood with its paragraph.

'As attorneys for the deceased it is our pleasant duty to inform you that your brother through industry and judgement amassed a considerable fortune, which in land, securities, and cash is well in excess of one hundred thousand dollars. His will, which was drawn and signed in this office, is in our hands and will be sent to you on your request. By its terms it leaves all money, property, and securities to be divided equally between you and your wife. In the event that your wife is deceased, the total goes to you. The will also stipulates that if you are deceased, all property goes to your wife. We judge from your letter that you are still in the land of the living and we wish to offer our congratulations. Your obedient servants, Bellows and Harvey, by George B. Harvey.' And at the bottom of the page was scrawled, 'Dear Adam: Forget not thy servants in the days of thy prosperity. Charles never spent a dime. He pinched a dollar until the eagle screamed. I hope you and your wife will get some pleasure from the money. Is there an opening out there for a good lawyer? I mean myself. Your old friend, Geo. Harvey.'

Adam looked over the edge of the letter at the boys and at Lee. All three were waiting for him to continue. Adam's mouth shut to a line. He folded the letter, put it in its envelope, and placed the envelope carefully in his inside pocket.

'Any complications?' Lee asked.

'No.'

'I just thought you looked concerned.'

'I'm not. I'm sad about my brother.' Adam was trying to arrange the letter's information in his mind, and it was as restless as a setting hen scrounging into the nest. He felt that he would have to be alone to absorb it. He climbed into the car and looked blankly at the mechanism. He couldn't remember a single procedure.

Lee asked, 'Want some help?'

'Funny!' said Adam. 'I can't remember where to start.'

Lee and the boys began softly, 'Spark up – gas down, switch over to Bat.'

'Oh yes. Of course, of course.' And while the loud bee hummed in the coil box Adam cranked the Ford and ran to advance the spark and throw the switch to Mag.

They were driving slowly up the lumpy road of the home draw under the oak trees when Lee said, 'We forgot to get meat.'

'Did we? I guess we did. Well, can't we have something else?'

'How about bacon and eggs?'

'That's fine. That's good.'

'You'll want to mail your answer tomorrow,' said Lee. 'You can buy meat then.'

'I guess so,' said Adam.

While dinner was preparing Adam sat staring into space. He knew he would have to have help from Lee, if only the help of a listener to clear his own thinking.

Cal had led his brother outside and conducted him to the wagon shed where the tall Ford rested. Cal opened the door and sat behind the wheel. 'Come on, get in!' he said.

Aron protested, 'Father told us to stay out of it.'

'He won't ever know. Get in!'

Aron climbed in timidly and eased back in the seat. Cal turned the wheel from side to side. 'Honk, honk,' he said, and then, 'Know what I think? I think Uncle Charles was rich.'

'He was not.'

'I bet you anything he was.'

'You think our father'd tell a lie.'

'I won't say that. I just bet he was rich.' They were silent for a while. Cal steered wildly around imaginary curves. He said, 'I bet you I can find out.'

'How do you mean?'

'What do you bet?'

'Nothing,' said Aron.

'How about your deer's-leg whistle? I bet you this here taw against that deer's-leg whistle that we get sent to bed right after supper. Is it a bet?'

'I guess so,' Aron said vaguely. 'I don't see why.'

Cal said, 'Father will want to talk to Lee. And I'm going to listen.'

'You won't dare.'

'You think I won't.'

'S'pose I was to tell.'

Cal's eyes turned cold and his face darkened. He leaned so

close that his voice dropped to a whisper. 'You won't tell. Because if you do – I'll tell who stole his knife.'

'Nobody stole his knife. He's got his knife. He opened the letter with it.'

Cal smiled bleakly. 'I mean tomorrow,' he said. And Aron saw what he meant and knew he couldn't tell. He couldn't do anything about it. Cal was perfectly safe.

Cal saw the confusion and helplessness on Aron's face and felt his power, and it made him glad. He could out-think and out-plan his brother. He was beginning to think he could do the same thing to his father. With Lee, Cal's tricks did not work, for Lee's bland mind moved effortlessly ahead of him and was always there waiting, understanding, and at the last moment cautioning quietly, 'Don't do it.' Cal had respect for Lee and a little fear of him. But Aron here, looking helplessly at him, was a lump of soft mud in his hands. Cal suddenly felt a deep love for his brother and an impulse to protect him in his weakness. He put his arm around Aron.

Aron did not flinch or respond. He drew back a little to see Cal's face.

Cal said, 'See any green grass growing out of my head?'

Aron said, 'I don't know why you go for to do it.'

'How do you mean? Do what?'

'All the tricky, sneaky things,' said Aron.

'What do you mean, sneaky?'

'Well, about the rabbit, and sneaking here in the car. And you did something to Abra. I don't know what, but it was you made her throw the box away.'

'Ho,' said Cal. 'Wouldn't you like to know!' But he was uneasy.

Aron said slowly, 'I wouldn't want to know that. I'd like to know why you do it. You're always at something. I just wonder why you do it. I wonder what's it good for.'

A pain pierced Cal's heart. His planning suddenly seemed mean and dirty to him. He knew that his brother had found him out. And he felt a longing for Aron to love him. He felt lost and hungry and he didn't know what to do.

Aron opened the door of the Ford and climbed down and walked out of the wagon shed. For a few moments Cal twisted the steering wheel and tried to imagine he was racing down the road. But it wasn't any good, and soon he followed Aron back towards the house.

When supper was finished and Lee had washed the dishes Adam said, 'I think you boys had better go to bed. It's been a big day.'

Aron looked quickly at Cal and slowly took his deer's-leg whistle out of his pocket.

Cal said, 'I don't want it.'

Aron said, 'It's yours now.'

'Well, I don't want it. I won't have it.'

Aron laid the bone whistle on the table. 'It'll be here for you,' he said.

Adam broke in, 'Say, what is this argument? I said you boys should go to bed.'

Cal put on his 'little boy' face. 'Why?' he asked. 'It's too early to go to bed.'

Adam said, 'That wasn't quite the truth I told you. I want to talk privately to Lee. And it's getting dark so you can't go outside, so I want you boys to go to bed – at least to your room. Do you understand?'

Both boys said, 'Yes, sir,' and they followed Lee down the hall to their bedroom at the back of the house. In their night-gowns they returned to say good night to their father.

Lee came back to the living-room and closed the door to the hall. He picked up the deer's-leg whistle and inspected it and laid it down. 'I wonder what went on there,' he said.

'How do you mean, Lee?'

'Well, some bet was made before supper, and just after supper Aron lost the bet and paid off. What were we talking about?'

'All I can remember is telling them to go to bed.'

'Well, maybe it will come out later,' said Lee.

'Seems to me you put too much stock in the affairs of children. It probably didn't mean anything.'

'Yes, it meant something.' Then he said, 'Mr Trask do you think the thoughts of people suddenly become important at a given age? Do you have sharper feelings or clearer thoughts now than when you were ten? Do you see as well, hear as well, taste as vitally?'

'Maybe you're right,' said Adam.

'It's one of the great fallacies, it seems to me,' said Lee, 'that time gives much of anything but years and sadness to a man.'

'And memory.'

'Yes, memory. Without that, time would be unarmed against us. What did you want to talk to me about?'

Adam took the letter from his pocket and put it on the table. 'I want you to read this, to read it carefully, and then – I want to talk about it.' Lee took out his half-glasses and put them on. He opened the letter under the lamp and read it.

Adam asked, 'Well?'

'*Is* there an opening here for a lawyer?'

'How do you mean? Oh, I see. Are you making a joke?'

'No,' said Lee, 'I was not making a joke. In my obscure but courteous Oriental manner I was indicating to you that I would prefer to know your opinion before I offered mine.'

'Are you speaking sharply to me?'

'Yes I am,' said Lee. 'I'll lay aside my Oriental manner. I'm getting old and cantankerous. I am growing impatient. Haven't you heard of all Chinese servants that when they get old they remain loyal but they turn mean?'

'I don't want to hurt your feelings.'

'They aren't hurt. You want to talk about this letter. Then talk, and I will know from your talk whether I can offer an honest opinion or whether it is better to reassure you in your own.'

'I don't understand it,' said Adam helplessly.

'Well, you knew your brother. If you don't understand it, how can I, who never saw him?'

Adam got up and opened the hall door and did not see the shadow that slipped behind it. He went to his room and returned and put a faded brown daguerreotype on the table in front of Lee. 'That is my brother, Charles,' he said, and he went back to the hall door and closed it.

Lee studied the shiny metal under the lamp, shifting the picture this way and that to overcome the highlights. 'It's a long time ago,' Adam said. 'Before I went into the army.'

Lee leaned close to the picture. 'It's hard to make out. But from his expression I wouldn't say your brother had much humour.'

'He hadn't any,' said Adam. 'He never laughed.'

'Well, that wasn't exactly what I meant. When I read the terms of your brother's will it struck me that he might have been a man with a particularly brutal sense of play. Did he like you?'

'I don't know,' said Adam. 'Sometimes I thought he loved me. He tried to kill me once.'

Lee said, 'Yes, that's in his face – both the love and murder. And the two made a miser of him, and a miser is a frightened man hiding in a fortress of money. Did he know your wife?'

357

'Yes.'

'Did he love her?'

'He hated her.'

Lee sighed. 'It doesn't really matter. That's not your problem, is it?'

'No. It isn't.'

'Would you like to bring the problem out and look at it?'

'That's what I want.'

'Go ahead, then.'

'I can't seem to get my mind to work clearly.'

'Would you like me to lay out the cards for you? The un-involved can sometimes do that.'

'That's what I want.'

'Very well, then.' Suddenly Lee grunted and a look of astonishment came over his face. He held his round chin in his thin small hand. 'Holy thorns!' he said. 'I didn't think of that.'

Adam stirred uneasily. 'I wish you'd get off the tack you're sitting on,' he said irritably. 'You make me feel like a column of figures on a blackboard.'

Lee took a pipe from his pocket, a long slender ebony stem with a little cup-like brass bowl. He filled the thimble bowl with tobacco so fine-cut it looked like hair, then lighted the pipe, took four long puffs, and let the pipe go out.

'Is that opium?' Adam demanded.

'No,' said Lee. 'It's a cheap brand of Chinese tobacco, and it has an unpleasant taste.'

'Why do you smoke it, then?'

'I don't know,' said Lee. 'I guess it reminds me of something – something I associate with clarity. Not very complicated.' Lee's eyelids half closed. 'All right, then – I'm going to try and pull out your thoughts like egg noodles and let them dry in the sun. The woman is still your wife and she is still alive. Under the letter of the will she inherits something over fifty thousand dollars. That is a great deal of money. A sizeable chunk of good or evil could be done with it. Would your brother, if he knew where she is and what she is doing, want her to have the money? Courts always try to follow the wishes of the testator.'

'My brother would not want that,' said Adam. And then he remembered the girls upstairs in the tavern and Charles's peri-odic visits.

'Maybe you'll have to think for your brother,' said Lee. 'What your wife is doing is neither good nor bad. Saints can spring from any soil. Maybe with this money she would do some fine thing. There's no springboard to philanthropy like a bad conscience.'

Adam shivered. 'She told me what she would do if she had money. It was closer to murder than to charity.'

'You don't think she should have the money, then?'

'She said she would destroy many reputable men in Salinas. She can do it too.'

'I see,' said Lee. 'I'm glad I can take a detached view of this. The pants of their reputations must have some thin places. Morally, then, you would be against giving her the money?'

'Yes.'

'Well, consider this. She has no name, no background. A whore springs full-blown from the earth. She couldn't very well claim the money, if she knew about it, without your help.'

'I guess that's so. Yes, I can see that she might not be able to claim it without my help.'

Lee took up the pipe and picked out the ash with a little brass pin and filled the bowl again. While he drew in the four slow puffs his heavy lids raised and he watched Adam.

'It's a very delicate moral problem,' he said. 'With your permission I shall offer it for the consideration of my honourable relatives – using no names of course. They will go over it as a boy goes over a dog for ticks. I'm sure they will get some interesting results.' He laid his pipe on the table. 'But you don't have any choice, do you?'

'What do you mean by that?' Adam demanded.

'Well, do you? Do you know yourself so much less than I do?'

'I don't know what to do,' said Adam. 'I'll have to give it a lot of thought.'

Lee said angrily, 'I guess I've been wasting my time. Are you lying to yourself or only to me?'

'Don't speak to me like that!' Adam said.

'Why not? I have always disliked deception. Your course is drawn. What you will do is written – written in every breath you've ever taken. I'll speak any way I want to. I'm crochety. I feel sand under my skin. I'm looking forward to the ugly smell of old books and the sweet smell of good thinking. Faced with two sets of morals, you'll follow your training. What you call thinking won't change it. The fact that your wife is a whore in Salinas won't change a thing.'

Adam got to his feet. His face was angry. 'You are insolent

now that you've decided to go away,' he cried. 'I tell you I haven't made up my mind what to do about the money.'

Lee sighed deeply. He pushed his small body erect with his hands against his knees. He walked wearily to the front door and opened it. He turned back and smiled at Adam. 'Bull shit!' he said amiably, and he went out and closed the door behind him.

III

Cal crept quietly down the dark hall and edged into the room where he and his brother slept. He saw the outline of his brother's head against the pillow in the double bed, but he could not see whether Aron slept. Very gently he eased himself in on his side and turned slowly and laced his fingers behind his head and stared at the myriads of tiny coloured dots that make up darkness. The window-blind bellied slowly in and then the night wind fell and the worn blind flapped quietly against the window.

A grey, quilted melancholy descended on him. He wished with all his heart that Aron had not walked away from him out of the wagon shed. He wished with all his heart that he had not crouched listening at the hall door. He moved his lips in the darkness and made the words silently in his head and yet he could hear them.

'Dear Lord,' he said, 'let me be like Aron. Don't make me mean. I don't want to be. If you will let everybody like me, why, I'll give you anything in the world, and if I haven't got it, why, I'll go for to get it. I don't want to be mean. I don't want to be lonely. For Jesus's sake, Amen.' Slow warm tears were running down his cheeks. His muscles were tight and he fought against making any crying sound or sniffle.

Aron whispered from his pillow in the dark, 'You're cold. You've got a chill.' He stretched out his hand to Cal's arm and felt the goose bumps there. He asked softly, 'Did Uncle Charles have any money?'

'No,' said Cal.

'Well, you were out there long enough. What did Father want to talk about?'

Cal lay still, trying to control his breathing.

'Don't you want to tell me?' Aron asked. 'I don't care if you don't tell me.'

'I'll tell,' Cal whispered. He turned on his side so that his back was towards his brother. 'Father is going to send a wreath to our mother. A great big goddam wreath of carnations.'

Aron half sat up in bed and asked excitedly, 'He is? How's he going to get it clear there?'

'On the train. Don't talk so loud.'

Aron dropped back to a whisper. 'But how's it going to keep fresh?'

'With ice,' said Cal. 'They're going to pack ice all around it.'

Aron asked, 'Won't it take a lot of ice?'

'A whole hell of a lot of ice,' said Cal. 'Go to sleep now.'

Aron was silent, and then he said, 'I hope it gets there fresh and nice.'

'It will,' said Cal. And in his mind he cried, 'Don't let me be mean.'

CHAPTER 31

I

ADAM BROODED around the house all morning, and at noon he went to find Lee, who was spading the dark composted earth of his vegetable garden and planting his spring vegetables, carrots and beets, turnips, peas, and string beans, rutabaga and kale. The rows were straight planted under a tight-stretched string, and the pegs at the row ends carried the seed package to identify the row. On the edge of the garden in a cold frame the tomato and bell pepper and cabbage sets were nearly ready for transplanting, waiting only for the passing of the frost danger.

Adam said, 'I guess I was stupid.'

Lee leaned on his spading fork and regarded him quietly.

'When are you going?' he asked.

'I thought I would catch the two-forty. Then I can get the eight o'clock back.'

'You could put it in a letter, you know,' said Lee.

'I've thought of that. Would you write a letter?'

'No. You're right. I'm the stupid one there. No letters.'

'I have to go,' said Adam. 'I thought in all directions and always a leash snapped me back.'

Lee said, 'You can be unhonest in many ways, but not in that way. Well, good luck. I'll be interested to hear what she says and does.'

'I'll take the rig,' said Adam. 'I'll leave it at the stable at King City. I'm nervous about driving the Ford alone.'

361

It was four-fifteen when Adam climbed the rickety steps and knocked on the weather-beaten door of Kate's place. A new man opened the door, a square-faced Finn, dressed in shirt and trousers; red silk arm-bands held up his full sleeves. He left Adam standing on the porch and in a moment came back and led him to the dining-room.

It was a large undecorated room, the walls and woodwork painted white. A long square table filled the centre of the room, and on the white oilcloth cover the places were set – plates, cups and saucers, and cups upside down in the saucers.

Kate sat at the end of the table with an account book open before her. Her dress was severe. She wore a green eyeshade, and she rolled a yellow pencil restlessly in her fingers. She looked coldly at Adam as he stood in the doorway.

'What do you want now?' she asked.

The Finn stood behind Adam.

Adam did not reply. He walked to the table and laid the letter in front of her on top of the account book.

'What's this?' she asked, and without waiting for a reply she read the letter quickly. 'Go out and close the door,' she told the Finn.

Adam sat at the table beside her. He pushed the dishes aside to make a place for his hat.

When the door was closed Kate said, 'Is this a joke? No, you haven't got a joke in you.' She considered. 'Your brother might be joking. You sure he's dead?'

'All I have is the letter,' said Adam.

'What do you want me to do about it?'

Adam shrugged his shoulders.

Kate said, 'If you want me to sign anything, you're wasting your time. What do you want?'

Adam drew his finger slowly around his black ribbon hatband. 'Why don't you write down the name of the firm and get in touch with them yourself?'

'What have you told them about me?'

'Nothing,' said Adam. 'I wrote to Charles and said you were living in another town, nothing more. He was dead when the letter got there. The letter went to the lawyers. It tells about it.'

'The one who wrote the postscript seems to be a friend of yours. What have you written him?'

'I haven't answered the letter yet.'

'What do you intend to say when you answer it?'

'The same thing – that you live in another town.'

362

'You can't say we've been divorced. We haven't been.'

'I don't intend to.'

'Do you want to know how much it will take to buy me off? I'll take forty-five thousand in cash.'

'No.'

'What do you mean – no? You can't bargain.'

'I'm not bargaining. You have the letter, you know as much as I do. Do what you want.'

'What makes you so cocky?'

'I feel safe.'

She peered at him from under the green transparent eyeshade. Little curls of her hair lay on the bill like vines on a green roof. 'Adam, you're a fool. If you had kept your mouth shut nobody would ever have known I was alive.'

'I know that.'

'You know it. Did you think I might be afraid to claim the money? You're a damn fool if you thought that.'

Adam said patiently, 'I don't care what you do.'

She smiled cynically at him. 'You don't, huh? Suppose I should tell you that there's a permanent order in the sheriff's office, left there by the old sheriff, that if I ever use your name or admit I'm your wife I'll get a floater out of the county and out of the state. Does that tempt you?'

'Tempt me to do what?'

'To get me floated and take all the money.'

'I brought you the letter,' Adam said patiently.

'I want to know why.'

Adam said, 'I'm not interested in what you think or in what you think of me. Charles left you the money in his will. He didn't put any strings on it. I haven't seen the will, but he wanted you to have the money.'

'You're playing a close game with fifty thousand dollars,' she said, 'and you're not going to get away with it. I don't know what the trick is, but I'm going to find out.' And then she said, 'What am I thinking about? You're not smart. Who's advising you?'

'No one.'

'How about that Chinaman? He's smart.'

'He gave me no advice.' Adam was interested in his own complete lack of emotion. He didn't really feel that he was here at all. When he glanced at her he surprised an emotion on her face he had never seen before. Kate was afraid – she was afraid of him. But why?

She controlled her face and whipped the tear from it. 'You're just doing it because you're honest, is that it? You're just too sugar-sweet to live.'

'I hadn't thought of it,' Adam said. 'It's your money and I'm not a thief. It doesn't matter to me what you think about it.'

Kate pushed the eyeshade back on her head. 'You want me to think you're just dropping this money in my lap. Well, I'll find out what you're up to. Don't think I won't take care of myself. Did you think I'd take such a stupid bait?'

'Where do you get your mail?' he asked patiently.

'What's that to you?'

'I'll write the lawyers where to get in touch with you.'

'Don't you do it!' she said. She put the letter in the account book and closed the cover. 'I'll keep this. I'll get legal advice. Don't think I won't. You can drop the innocence now.'

'You do that,' Adam said. 'I want you to have what is yours. Charles willed you the money. It isn't mine.'

'I'll find the trick. I'll find it.'

Adam said, 'I guess you can't understand it. I don't much care. There are so many things I don't understand. I don't understand how you could shoot me and desert your sons. I don't understand how you or anyone could live like this.' He waved his hand to indicate the house.

'Who asked you to understand?'

Adam stood up and took his hat from the table. 'I guess that's all,' he said. 'Goodbye.' He walked towards the door.

She called after him, 'You're changed, Mr Mouse. Have you got a woman at last?'

Adam stopped and slowly turned and his eyes were thoughtful. 'I hadn't considered before,' he said, and he moved towards her until he towered over her and she had to tilt back her head to look into his face. 'I said I didn't understand about you,' he said slowly. 'Just now it came to me what you don't understand.'

'What don't I understand, Mr Mouse?'

'You know about the ugliness in people. You showed me the pictures. You use all the sad, weak parts of a man, and God knows he has them.'

'Everybody —'

Adam went on, astonished at his own thoughts, 'But you — yes, that's right – you don't know about the rest. You don't believe I brought you the letter because I don't want your money. You don't believe I loved you. And the men who come to you

364

here with their ugliness, the men in the pictures – you don't believe those men could have goodness and beauty in them. You see only one side, and you think – more than that, you're sure – that's all there is.'

She cackled at him derisively. 'In sticks and stones. What a sweet dreamer is Mr Mouse! Give me a sermon, Mr Mouse.'

'No. I won't because I seem to know that there's a part of you missing. Some men can't see the colour green, but they may never know they can't. I think you are only a part of a human. I can't do anything about that. But I wonder whether you ever feel that something invisible is all around you. It would be horrible if you knew it was there and couldn't see it or feel it. That would be horrible.'

Kate pushed back her chair and stood up. Her fists were clenched at her sides and hiding in the folds of her skirt. She tried to prevent the shrillness that crept into her voice.

'Our Mouse is a philosopher,' she said. 'But our Mouse is no better at that than he is at other things. Did you ever hear of hallucinations? If there are things I can't see, don't you think it's possible that they are dreams manufactured in your own sick mind?'

'No, I don't,' said Adam. 'No, I don't. And I don't think you do either.' He turned and went out and closed the door behind him.

Kate sat down and stared at the closed door. She was not aware that her fists beat softly on the white oilcloth. But she did know that the square white door was distorted by tears and that her body shook with something that felt like rage and also felt like sorrow.

11

When Adam left Kate's place he had over two hours to wait for the train back to King City. On an impulse he turned off Main Street and walked up Central Avenue to number 130, the high white house of Ernest Steinbeck. It was an immaculate and friendly house, grand enough, but not pretentious, and it sat inside its white fence, surrounded by its clipped lawn, and roses and cotoneasters lapped against its white walls.

Adam walked up the wide veranda steps and rang the bell. Olive came to the door and opened it a little, while Mary and John peeked around the edges of her.

Adam took off his hat. 'You don't know me. I'm Adam Trask.

365

Your father was a friend of mine. I thought I'd like to pay my respects to Mrs Hamilton. She helped me with the twins.'

'Why, of course,' Olive said, and swung the wide doors open. 'We've heard about you. Just a moment. You see, we've made a kind of retreat for Mother.'

She knocked on a door off the wide front hall and called, 'Mother! There's a friend to see you.'

She opened the door and showed Adam into the pleasant room where Liza lived. 'You'll have to excuse me,' she said to Adam. 'Catrina's frying chicken and I have to watch her. John! Mary! Come along. Come along.'

Liza seemed smaller than ever. She sat in a wicker rocking-chair and she was old and old. Her dress was a full wide-skirted black alpaca, and at her throat she wore a pin which spelled 'Mother' in golden script.

The pleasant little bed-sitting-room was crowded with photographs, bottles of toilet water, lace pin-cushions, brushes and combs, and the china and silver bureau-knacks of many birthdays and Christmases.

On the wall hung a huge tinted photograph of Samuel, which had captured a cold and aloof dignity, a scrubbed and dressed remoteness, which did not belong to him living. There was no twinkle in the picture of him, nor any of his inspective joyousness. The picture hung in a heavy gold frame, and to the consternation of all children its eyes followed a child about the room.

On a wicker table beside Liza was the cage of Polly parrot. Tom had bought the parrot from a sailor. He was an old bird, reputed to be fifty years old, and he had lived a ribald life and acquired the vigorous speech of a ship's fo'c'sle. Try as she would, Liza could not make him substitute psalms for the picturesque vocabulary of his youth.

Polly cocked his head sideways, inspecting Adam, and scratched his feathers at the base of his beak with a careful foreclaw. 'Come off it, you bastard,' said Polly unemotionally.

Liza frowned at him. 'Polly,' she said sternly, 'that's not polite.'

'Bloody bastard!' Polly observed.

Liza ignored the vulgarity. She held out her tiny hand. 'Mr Trask,' she said, 'I'm glad to see you. Sit down, won't you?'

'I was passing by, and I wanted to offer my condolences.'

'We got your flowers.' And she remembered, too, every bouquet after all this time. Adam had sent a fine pillow of ever-astings.

'It must be hard to rearrange your life.'

Liza's eyes brimmed over and she snapped her little mouth hut on her weakness.

Adam said, 'Maybe I shouldn't bring up your hurt, but I niss him.'

Liza turned her head away. 'How is everything down your vay?' she asked.

'Good this year. Lots of rainfall. The feed's deep already.'

'Tom wrote me,' she said.

'Button up,' said the parrot, and Liza scowled at him as she aad at her growing children when they were mutinous.

'What brings you to Salinas, Mr Trask?' she asked.

'Why, some business.' He sat down in a wicker chair and it ricked under his weight. 'I'm thinking of moving up here. Thought it might be better for my boys. They get lonely on the anch.'

'We never got lonely on the ranch,' she said harshly.

'I thought maybe the schools would be better here. My twins could have the advantages.'

'My daughter Olive taught at Peach Tree and Pleyto and the Big Sur.' Her tone made it clear that there were no better schools than those. Adam began to feel a warm admiration for her iron gallantry.

'Well, I was just thinking about it,' he said.

'Children raised in the country do better.' It was the law, and she could prove it by her own boys. Then she centred closely on him. 'Are you looking for a house in Salinas?'

'Well, yes, I guess I am.'

'Go see my daughter Dessie,' she said. 'Dessie wants to move back to the ranch with Tom. She's got a nice little house up the street next to Reynaud's Bakery.'

'I'll certainly do that,' said Adam. 'I'll go now. I'm glad to see you doing so well.'

'Thank you,' she said. 'I'm comfortable.' Adam was moving towards the door when she said, 'Mr Trask, do you ever see my son Tom?'

'Well, no, I don't. You see, I haven't been off the ranch.'

'I wish you would go and see him,' she said quickly. 'I think he's lonely.' She stopped as though horrified at this breaking over.

'I will. I surely will. Goodbye, ma'am.'

As he closed the door he heard the parrot say, 'Button up, you bloody bastard!' and Liza, 'Polly, if you don't watch your language, I'll thrash you.'

Adam let himself out of the house and walked up the evening street towards Main. Next to Reynaud's French Bakery he saw Dessie's house, set back in its little garden. The yard was so massed with tall privets that he couldn't see much of the house. A neatly painted sign was screwed to the front gate. It read: Dessie Hamilton, Dressmaker.

The San Francisco Chop House was on the corner of Main and Central and its windows were on both streets. Adam went in to get some dinner. Will Hamilton sat at the corner table, devouring a rib steak. 'Come and sit with me,' he called to Adam. 'Up on business?'

'Yes,' said Adam. 'I went to pay a call on your mother.'

Will laid down his fork. 'I'm just up here for an hour. I didn't go to see her because it gets her excited. And my sister Olive would tear the house down getting a special dinner for me. I just didn't want to disturb them. Besides, I have to go right back. Order a rib steak. They've got good ones. How is Mother?'

'She's got great courage,' said Adam. 'I find I admire her more all the time.'

'That she has. How she kept her good sense with all of us and with my father, I don't know.'

'Rib steak, medium,' said Adam to the waiter.

'Potatoes?'

'No – yes, french fried. Your mother is worried about Tom. Is he all right?'

Will cut off the edging of fat from his steak and pushed it to the side of his plate. 'She's got reason to worry,' he said. 'Something's the matter with Tom. He's moping around like a monument.'

'I guess he depended on Samuel.'

'Too much,' said Will. 'Far too much. He can't seem to come out of it. In some ways Tom is a great big baby.'

'I'll go and see him. Your mother says Dessie is going to move back to the ranch.'

Will laid his knife and fork down on the tablecloth and stared at Adam. 'She can't do it,' he said. 'I won't let her do it.'

'Why not?'

Will covered up. 'Well,' he said, 'she's got a nice business here. Makes a good living. It would be a shame to throw it

368

away.' He picked up his knife and fork, cut off a piece of the fat, and put it in his mouth.

'I'm catching the eight o'clock home,' Adam said.

'So am I,' said Will. He didn't want to talk any more.

CHAPTER 32

I

DESSIE WAS the beloved of the family. Mollie the pretty kitten, Olive the strong-headed, Una with clouds on her head, all were loved, but Dessie was the warm-beloved. Hers was the twinkle and the laughter infectious as chickenpox, and hers the gaiety that coloured a day and spread to people so that they carried it away with them.

I can put it this way. Mrs Clarence Morrison of 122 Church Street, Salinas, had three children and a husband who ran a dry goods store. On certain mornings, at breakfast, Agnes Morrison would say, 'I'm going to Dessie Hamilton's for a fitting after dinner.'

The children would be glad and would kick their copper toes against the table legs until cautioned. And Mr Morrison would rub his palms together and go to his store, hoping some drummer would come by that day. And any drummer who did come by was likely to get a good order. Maybe the children and Mrs Morrison would forget why it was a good day with a promise on its tail.

Mrs Morrison would go to the house next to Reynaud's Bakery at two o'clock and she would stay until four. When she came out her eyes would be wet with tears and her nose red and streaming. Walking home, she would dab her nose and wipe her eyes and laugh all over again. Maybe all Dessie had done was to put several black pins in a cushion to make it look like the Baptist minister, and then had the pin-cushion deliver a short dry sermon. Maybe she had recounted a meeting with Old Man Taylor, who bought old houses and moved them to a big vacant lot he owned until he had so many it looked like a dry-land Sargasso Sea. Maybe she had read a poem from *Chatterbox* with gestures. It didn't matter. It was warm-funny, it was catching-funny.

The Morrison children, coming home from school, would find

no aches, no carping, no headache. Their noise was not a scandal nor their dirty faces a care. And when the giggles overcame them, why, their mother was giggling too.

Mr Morrison, coming home, would tell of the day and get listened to, and he would try to re-tell the drummer's stories – some of them at least. The supper would be delicious – omelettes never fell and cakes rose to balloons of lightness, biscuits fluffed up, and no one could season a stew like Mrs Morrison. After supper, when the children had laughed themselves to sleep, like as not Mr Morrison would touch Agnes on the shoulder in their old, old signal and they would go to bed and make love and be very happy.

The visit to Dessie might carry its charge into two days more before it petered out and the little headaches came back and business was not so good as last year. That's how Dessie was and that's what she could do. She carried excitement in her arms just as Samuel had. She was the darling, she was the beloved of the family.

Dessie was not beautiful. Perhaps she wasn't even pretty, but she had the glow that makes men follow a woman in the hope of reflecting a little of it. You would have thought that in time she would have got over her first love affair and found another love, but she did not. Come to think of it, none of the Hamiltons, with all their versatility, had any versatility in love. None of them seemed capable of light or changeable love.

Dessie did not simply throw up her hands and give up. It was much worse than that. She went right on doing and being what she was – without the glow. The people who loved her ached for her, seeing her try, and they got to trying for her.

Dessie's friends were good and loyal but they were human, and humans love to feel good and they hate to feel bad. In time the Mrs Morrisons found unassailable reasons for not going to the little house by the bakery. They weren't disloyal. They didn't want to be sad as much as they wanted to be happy. It is easy to find a logical and virtuous reason for not doing what you don't want to do.

Dessie's business began to fall off. And the women who had thought they wanted dresses never realized that what they had wanted was happiness. Times were changing and the ready-made dress was becoming popular. It was no longer a disgrace to wear one. If Mr Morrison was stocking ready-mades, it was only reasonable that Agnes Morrison should be seen in them.

The family was worried about Dessie, but what could you do

370

when she would not admit there was anything wrong with her? She did admit to pains in her side, quite fierce, but they lasted only a little while and came only at intervals.

Then Samuel died and the world shattered like a dish. His sons and daughters and friends groped about among the pieces, trying to put some kind of world together again.

Dessie decided to sell her business and go back to the ranch to live with Tom. She hadn't much of any business to sell out. Liza knew about it, and Olive, and Dessie had written to Tom. But Will, sitting scowling at the table in the San Francisco Chop House, had not been told. Will frothed inwardly and finally he balled up his napkin and got up. 'I forgot something,' he said to Adam. 'I'll see you on the train.'

He walked the half-block to Dessie's house and went through the high-grown garden and rang Dessie's bell.

She was having her dinner alone, and she came to the door with her napkin in her hand. 'Why, hello, Will,' she said and put up her pink cheek for him to kiss. 'When did you get in town?'

'Business,' he said. 'Just here between trains. I want to talk to you.'

She led him back to her kitchen and dining-room combined, a warm little room papered with flowers. Automatically she poured a cup of coffee and placed it for him and put the sugar bowl and the cream pitcher in front of it.

'Have you seen Mother?' she asked.

'I'm just here over trains,' he said gruffly. 'Dessie, is it true that you want to go back to the ranch?'

'I was thinking of it.'

'I don't want you to go.'

She smiled uncertainly. 'Why not? What's wrong with that? Tom's lonely down there.'

'You've got a nice business here,' he said.

'I haven't any business here,' she replied. 'I thought you knew that.'

'I don't want you to go,' he repeated sullenly.

Her smile was wistful and she tried her best to put a little mockery in her manner. 'My big brother is masterful. Tell Dessie why not.'

'It's too lonely down there.'

'It won't be lonely with the two of us.'

Will pulled at his lips angrily. He blurted, 'Tom's not himself. You shouldn't be alone with him.'

371

'Isn't he well? Does he need help?'

Will said, 'I didn't want to tell you – I don't think Tom's ever got over – the death. He's strange.'

She smiled affectionately. 'Will, you've always thought he was strange. You thought he was strange when he didn't like business.'

'That's different. But now he's broody. He doesn't talk. He goes walking alone in the hills at night. I went to see him and – he's been writing poetry – pages of it all over the table.'

'Didn't you ever write poetry, Will?'

'I did not.'

'I have,' said Dessie. 'Pages and pages of it all over the table.'

'I don't want you to go.'

'Let me decide,' she said softly. 'I've lost something. I want to try to find it again.'

'You're talking foolish.'

She came round the table and put her arms around his neck. 'Dear brother,' she said, 'please let me decide.'

He went angrily out of the house and barely caught his train.

11

Tom met Dessie at the King City station. She saw him out of the train window, scanning every coach for her. He was burnished, his face shaved so close that its darkness had a shine like polished wood. His red moustache was clipped. He wore a new Stetson hat with a flat crown, a tan Norfolk jacket with a belt buckle of mother-of-pearl. His shoes glinted in the noonday light so that it was sure he had gone over them with his handkerchief just before the train arrived. His hard collar stood up against his strong red neck, and he wore a pale blue knitted tie with a horseshoe tie-pin. He tried to conceal his excitement by clasping his rough brown hands in front of him.

Dessie waved wildly out of the window, crying, 'Here I am, Tom, here I am!' though she knew he couldn't hear her over the grinding wheels of the train as the coach slid past him. She climbed down the steps and saw him look frantically about in the wrong direction. She smiled and walked up behind him.

'I beg your pardon, stranger,' she said quietly. 'Is there a Mr Tom Hamilton here?'

He spun round and he squealed with pleasure and picked her up in a bear hug and danced her around. He held her off the

372

ground with one arm and spanked her bottom with his free hand. He nuzzled her cheek with his harsh moustache. Then he held her back by the shoulders and looked at her. Both of them threw back their heads and howled with laughter.

The station agent leaned out of his window and rested his elbows, protected with black false sleeves, on the sill. He said over his shoulder to the telegrapher, 'Those Hamiltons! Just look at them!'

Tom and Dessie, fingertips touching, were doing a courtly heel-and-toe while he sang Doodle-doodle-doo and Dessie sang Deedle-deedle-dee, and then they embraced again.

Tom looked down at her. 'Aren't you Dessie Hamilton? I seem to remember you. But you've changed. Where are your pigtails?'

It took him quite a fumbling time to get her luggage checks, to lose them in his pockets, to find them and pick up the wrong pieces. At last he had her baskets piled in the back of the buck-board. The two bay horses pawed the hard ground and threw up their heads so that the shined pole jumped and the double-trees squeaked. The harness was polished and the horse brasses glittered like gold. There was a red bow tied half way up the buggy whip and red ribbons were braided into the horses' manes and tails.

Tom helped Dessie into the seat and pretended to peek coyly at her ankle. Then he snapped up the check reins and unfastened the leather tie reins from the bits. He unwrapped the lines from the whip stock, and the horses turned so sharply that the wheel screamed against the guard.

Tom said, 'Would you care to make a tour of King City? It's a lovely town.'

'No,' she said. 'I think I remember it.' He turned left and headed south and lifted the horses to a fine swinging trot.

Dessie said, 'Where's Will?'

'I don't know,' he answered gruffly.

'Did he talk to you?'

'Yes. He said you shouldn't come.'

'He told me the same thing,' said Dessie. 'He got George to write to me too.'

'Why shouldn't you come if you want to?' Tom raged. 'What's Will got to do with it?'

She touched his arm. 'He thinks you're crazy. Says you're writing poetry.'

Tom's face darkened. 'He must have gone into the house

373

when I wasn't there. What's he want anyway? He had no right to look at my papers.'

'Gently, gently,' said Dessie. 'Will's your brother. Don't forget that.'

'How would he like me to go through his papers?' Tom demanded.

'He wouldn't let you,' Dessie said dryly. 'They'd be locked in the safe. Now let's not spoil the day with anger.'

'All right,' he said. 'God knows all right! But he makes me mad. If I don't want to live his kind of life I'm crazy – just crazy.'

Dessie changed the subject, forced the change. 'You know, I had quite a time at the last,' she said. 'Mother wanted to come. Have you ever seen Mother cry, Tom?'

'No, not that I can remember. No, she's not a crier.'

'Well, she cried. Not much, but a lot for her – a choke and two sniffles and a wiped nose and polished her glasses and snapped shut like a watch.'

Tom said, 'Oh, Lord, Dessie, it's good to have you back! It's good. Makes me feel I'm well from a sickness.'

The horses spanked along the county road. Tom said, 'Adam Trask has bought a Ford. Or maybe I should say Will sold him a Ford.'

'I didn't know about the Ford,' said Dessie. 'He's buying my house. Giving me a very good price for it.' She laughed. 'I put a very high price on the house. I was going to come down during negotiations. Mr Trask accepted the first price. It put me in a fix.'

'What did you do, Dessie?'

'Well, I had to tell him about the high price and that I had planned to be argued down. He didn't seem to care either way.'

Tom said, 'Let me beg you never to tell that story to Will. He'd have you locked up.'

'But the house wasn't worth what I asked!'

'I repeat what I said about Will. What's Adam want with your house?'

'He's going to move there. Wants the twins to go to school in Salinas.'

'What'll he do with his ranch?'

'I don't know. He didn't say.'

Tom said, 'I wonder what would have happened if Father'd got hold of a ranch like that instead of Old Dry and Dusty.'

'It isn't such a bad place.'

374

'Fine for everything except making a living.'

Dessie said earnestly, 'Have you ever known any family that had more fun?'

'No, I don't. But that was the family, not the land.'

'Tom, remember when you took Jenny and Belle Williams to the Peach Tree dance on the sofa?'

'Mother never let me forget it. Say, wouldn't it be good to ask Jenny and Belle down for a visit?'

'They'd come too,' Dessie said. 'Let's do it.'

When they turned off the county road she said, 'Somehow I remember it differently.'

'Drier?'

'I guess that's it. Tom, there's so much grass.'

'I'm getting twenty head of stock to eat it.'

'You must be rich.'

'No, and the good year will break the price of beef. I wonder what Will would do. He's a scarcity man. He told me. He said, "Always deal in scarcities." Will's smart.'

The rutty road had not changed except that the ruts were deeper and the round stones stuck up higher.

Dessie said, 'What's the card on that mesquite bush?' She picked it off as they drove by, and it said, 'Welcome Home'.

'Tom, you did it!'

'I did not. Someone's been here.'

Every fifty yards there was another card sticking on a bush, or hanging from the branches of a madrone, or tacked to the trunk of a buckeye, and all of them said, 'Welcome Home'. Dessie squealed with delight over each one.

They topped the rise above the little valley of the old Hamilton place and Tom pulled up to let her enjoy the view. On the hill across the valley, spelled out in whitewashed stones, were the huge words, 'Welcome Home, Dessie'. She put her head against his lapel and laughed and cried at the same time.

Tom looked sternly ahead of him. 'Now who could have done that?' he said. 'A man can't leave the place any more.'

In the dawn Dessie was awakened by the chill of pain that came to her at intervals. It was a rustle and a threat of pain; it scampered up from her side and across her abdomen, a nibbling pinch and then a little grab and then a hard catch and finally a fierce grip as though a huge hand had wrenched her. When that relaxed she felt a soreness like a bruise. It didn't last very long, but while it went on the outside world was blotted out, and she seemed to be listening to the struggle in her body.

When only the soreness remained she saw how the dawn had come silver to the windows. She smelled the good morning wind rippling the curtains, bringing in the odour of grass and roots and damp earth. After that sounds joined the parade of perception – sparrows haggled among themselves, a bawling cow monotonously berating a punching hungry calf, a blue jay's squawk of false excitement, the sharp warning of a cock quail on guard and the answering whisper of the hen quail somewhere near in the tall grass. The chicken yard boiled with excitement over an egg, and a big lady Rhode Island Red, who weighed four pounds, hypocritically protested the horror of being lustfully pinned to the ground by a scrawny wreck of a rooster she could have blasted with one blow of her wing.

The cooing of pigeons brought memory into the procession. Dessie remembered how her father had said, sitting at the head of the table, 'I told Rabbit I was going to raise some pigeons and – do you know? – he said, "No white pigeons." "Why not white?" I asked him, and he said, "They're the rare worst of bad luck. You take a flight of white pigeons and they'll bring sadness and death. Get grey ones." "I like white ones." "Get grey ones," he told me. And as the sky covers me, I'll get white ones.'

And Liza said patiently, 'Why do you be for ever testing, Samuel? Grey ones taste just as good and they're bigger.'

'I'll let no flimsy fairy-tale push me,' Samuel said.

And Liza said with her dreadful simplicity, 'You're already pushed by your own contentiousness. You're a mule of contention, a very mule!'

'Someone's got to do these things,' he said sullenly. 'Else Fate would not ever get nose-thumbed and mankind would still be clinging to the top branches of a tree.'

And of course he got white pigeons and waited truculently for sadness and death until he'd proved his point. And here were the great-great-grand squabs cooing in the morning and rising to fly like a whirling white scarf around the wagon shed.

As Dessie remembered, she heard the words and the house around her grew peopled. Sadness and death, she thought, and death and sadness, and it wrenched in her stomach against the soreness. You just have to wait around long enough and it will come.

She heard the air whooshing into the big bellows in the forge and the practice tap for range of hammer on anvil. She heard Liza open the oven door and the thump of a kneaded loaf on the floury board. Then Joe wandered about, looking in unlikely

376

places for his shoes, and at last found them where he had left them under the bed.

She heard Mollie's sweet high voice in the kitchen, reading a morning text from the Bible, and Una's full cold throaty correction.

And Tom had cut Mollie's tongue with his pocket-knife and died in his heart when he realized his courage.

'Oh, dear Tom,' she said, and her lips moved.

Tom's cowardice was as huge as his courage, as it must be in great men. His violence balanced his tenderness, and himself was a pitted battlefield of his own forces. He was confused now, but Dessie could hold his bit and point him, the way a handler points a thoroughbred at the barrier to show his breeding and his form.

Dessie lay part in pain and a part of her dangled still in sleep while the morning brightened against the window. She remembered that Mollie was going to lead the Grand March at the Fourth of July picnic with no less than Harry Forbes, State Senator. And Dessie had not finished putting the braid on Mollie's dress. She struggled to get up. There was so much braid, and here she lay drowsing.

She cried, 'I'll get it done, Mollie. It will be ready.'

She got up from her bed and threw her robe around her and walked barefoot through the house crowded with Hamiltons. In the hall they were gone to the bedrooms. In the bedrooms, with the beds neat-made, they were all in the kitchen, and in the kitchen – they dispersed and were gone. Sadness and death. The wave receded and left her in dry awakeness.

The house was clean, scrubbed and immaculate, curtains washed, windows polished, but all as a man does it – the ironed curtains did not hang quite straight and there were streaks on the windows and a square showed on the table when a book was moved.

The stove was warming, with orange light showing around the lids and the soft thunder of draughty flame leaping past the open damper. The kitchen clock flashed its pendulum behind its glass skirt, and it ticked like a little wooden hammer striking on an empty wooden box.

From outside came a whistle as wild and raucous as a reed and pitched high and strange. The whistling scattered a savage melody. Then Tom's steps sounded on the porch, and he came in with an armload of oakwood so high he could not see over it. He cascaded the wood into the wood-box.

'You're up,' he said. 'That was to wake you if you were still sleeping.' His face was lighted with joy. 'This is a morning light as down and no time to be slugging.'

'You sound like your father,' Dessie said, and she laughed with him.

His joy hardened to fierceness. 'Yes,' he said loudly. 'And we'll have that time again, right here. I've been dragging myself in misery like a spine-broken snake. No wonder Will thought I was cracked. But now you're back, and I'll show you. I'll breathe life into life again. Do you hear? This house is going to be alive.'

'I'm glad I came,' she said, and she thought in desolation how brittle he was now and how easy to shatter, and how she would have to protect him.

'You must have worked day and night to get the house so clean,' she said.

'Nothing,' said Tom. 'A little twist with the fingers.'

'I know that twist, but it was the bucket and mop and on your knees – unless you've invented some way to do it by chicken power or the harnessed wind.'

'Invented – now that's why I have no time. I've invented a little slot that lets a necktie slip freely in a stiff collar.'

'You don't wear stiff collars.'

'I did yesterday. That's when I invented it. And chickens – I'm going to raise millions of them – little houses all over the ranch and a ring on the roof to dip them in a whitewashed tank. And the eggs will come through on a little conveyor belt – here! I'll draw it.'

'I want to draw some breakfast,' Dessie said. 'What's the shape of a fried egg? How would you colour the fat and lean of a strip of bacon?'

'You'll have it,' he cried, and he opened the stove lid and assaulted the fire with the stove lifter until the hairs on his hand curled and charred. He pitched wood in and started his high whistling.

Dessie said, 'You sound like some goat-foot with a wheat flute on a hill in Greece.'

'What do you think I am?' he shouted.

Dessie thought miserably, If his is real, why can't my heart be light? Why can't I climb out of my grey ragbag? I will, she screeched inside herself. If he can – I will.

She said, 'Tom!'

'Yes.'

'I want a purple egg.'

CHAPTER 33

I

THE GREEN lasted on the hills far into June before the grass turned yellow. The heads of the wild oats were so heavy with seed that they hung over on their stalks. The little springs trickled on late in the summer. The range cattle staggered under their fat and their hides shone with health. It was a year when the people of the Salinas Valley forgot the dry years. Farmers bought more land than they could afford and figured their profits on the covers of their cheque-books.

Tom Hamilton laboured like a giant, not only with his strong arms and rough hands but also with his heart and spirit. The anvil rang in the forge again. He painted the old house white and whitewashed the sheds. He went to King City and studied a flush toilet and then built one of craftily bent tin and carved wood. Because the water came so slowly from the spring, he put a redwood tank beside the house and pumped the water up to it with a hand-made windmill so cleverly made that it turned in the slightest wind. And he made metal and wood models of two ideas to be sent to the patent office in the fall.

That was not all – he laboured with humour and good spirits. Dessie had to rise very early to get in her hand at the housework before Tom had it all done. She watched his great red happiness, and it was not light as Samuel's happiness was light. It did not rise out of his roots and come floating up. He was manufacturing happiness as cleverly as he knew how, moulding it and shaping it.

Dessie, who had more friends than anyone in the whole valley, had no confidants. When her trouble had come upon her she had not talked about it. And the pains were a secret in herself.

When Tom found her rigid and tight from the grabbing pain and cried in alarm, 'Dessie, what's the matter?' she controlled her face and said, 'A little crick, that's all. Just a little crick. I'm all right now.' And in a moment they were laughing.

They laughed a great deal, as though to reassure themselves. Only when Dessie went to her bed did her loss fall on her, bleak and unendurable. And Tom lay in the dark of his room, puzzled as a child. He could hear his heart beating and rasping a little in its beat. His mind fell away from thought and clung for safety to little plans, designs, machines.

Sometimes in the summer evenings they walked up the hill to watch the afterglow clinging to the tops of the western mountains and to feel the breeze drawn into the valley by the rising day-heated air. Usually they stood silently for a while and breathed in peacefulness. Since both were shy they never talked about themselves. Neither knew about the other at all.

It was startling to both of them when Dessie said one evening on the hill, 'Tom, why don't you get married?'

He looked quickly at her and away. He said, 'Who'd have me?'

'Is that a joke or do you really mean it?'

'Who'd have me?' he said again. 'Who'd want a thing like me?'

'It sounds to me as though you really mean it.' Then she violated their unstated code. 'Have you been in love with someone?'

'No,' he said shortly.

'I wish I knew,' she said as though he had not answered.

Tom did not speak again as they walked down the hill. But on the porch he said suddenly, 'You're lonely here. You don't want to stay.' He waited for a moment. 'Answer me. Isn't that true?'

'I want to stay here more than I want to stay anyplace else.' She asked, 'Do you ever go to women?'

'Yes,' he said.

'Is it any good to you?'

'Not much.'

'What are you going to do?'

'I don't know.'

In silence they went back to the house. Tom lighted the lamp in the old living-room. The horsehair sofa he had rebuilt raised its goose-neck against the wall, and the green carpet had tracks worn light between the doors.

Tom sat down by the round centre table. Dessie sat on the sofa, and she could see that he was still embarrassed from his last admission. She thought, How pure he is, how unfit for a world that even she knew more about than he did. A dragon killer, he was, a rescuer of damsels, and his small sins seemed so great to him that he felt unfit and unseemly. She wished her father were here. Her father had felt greatness in Tom. Perhaps he would know now how to release it out of its darkness and let it fly free.

She took another tack to see whether she could raise some

spark in him. 'As long as we're talking about ourselves, have you ever thought that our whole world is the valley and a few trips to San Francisco, and have you ever been farther south than San Luis Obispo? I never have.'

'Neither have I,' said Tom.

'Well, isn't that silly?'

'Lots of people haven't,' he said.

'But it's not law. We could go to Paris and to Rome or to Jerusalem. I would dearly love to see the Colosseum.'

He watched her suspiciously, expecting some kind of joke. 'How could we?' he asked. 'That takes a lot of money.'

'I don't think it does,' she said. 'We wouldn't have to stay in fancy places. We could take the cheapest boats and the lowest class. That's how our father came here from Ireland. And we could go to Ireland.'

Still he watched her, but a burning was beginning in his eyes.

Dessie went on, 'We could take a year for work, save every penny. I can get some sewing to do in King City. Will would help us. And next summer you could sell all the stock and we could go. There's no law forbids it.'

Tom got up and went outside. He looked at the summer stars, at blue Venus and red Mars. His hands flexed at his sides, closed to fists and opened. Then he turned and went back into the house. Dessie had not moved.

'Do you want to go, Dessie?'

'More than anything in the world.'

'Then we will go!'

'Do you want to go?'

'More than anything in the world,' he said, and then, 'Egypt – have you given a thought to Egypt?'

'Athens,' she said.

'Constantinople!'

'Bethlehem!'

'Yes, Bethlehem,' and he said suddenly, 'Go to bed. We've got a year of work – a year. Get some rest. I'm going to borrow money from Will to buy a hundred shoats.'

'What will you feed them?'

'Acorns,' said Tom. 'I'll make a machine to gather acorns.'

After he had gone to his room she could hear him knocking around and talking softly to himself. Dessie looked out of her window at the starlit night and she was glad. But she wondered whether she really wanted to go, or whether Tom did. And as she wondered the whisper of pain grew up from her side.

381

When Dessie got up in the morning Tom was already at his drawing-board, beating his forehead with his fist and growling to himself. Dessie looked over his shoulder. 'Is it the acorn machine?'

'It should be easy,' he said. 'But how to get out the sticks and rocks?'

'I know you're the inventor, but I invented the greatest acorn picker in the world and it's ready to go.'

'What do you mean?'

'Children,' she said. 'Those restless little hands.'

'They wouldn't do it, not even for pay.'

'They would for prizes. A prize for everyone and a big prize for the winner – maybe a hundred-dollar prize. They'd sweep the valley clean. Will you let me try?'

He scratched his head. 'Why not?' he said. 'But how would you collect the acorns?'

'The children will bring them in,' said Dessie. 'Just let me take care of it. I hope you have plenty of storage space.'

'It would be exploiting the young, wouldn't it?'

'Certainly it would,' Dessie agreed. 'When I had my shop I exploited the girls who wanted to learn to sew – and they exploited me. I think I will call this The Great Monterey County Acorn Contest. And I won't let everyone in. Maybe bicycles for prizes – wouldn't you pick up acorns in hope of a bicycle, Tom?'

'Sure I would,' he said. 'But couldn't we pay them too?'

'Not with money,' Dessie said. 'That would reduce it to labour, and they will not labour if they can help it. Nor will I.'

Tom leaned back from his board and laughed. 'Nor will I,' he said. 'All right, you are in charge of acorns and I am in charge of pigs.'

Dessie said, 'Tom, wouldn't it be ridiculous if we made money, we of all people?'

'But you made money in Salinas,' he said.

'Some – not much. But oh, I was rich in promises. If the bills had ever been paid we wouldn't need pigs. We could go to Paris tomorrow.'

'I'm going to drive in and talk to Will,' said Tom. He pushed his chair back from the drawing-board. 'Want to come with me?'

'No, I'll stay and make my plans. Tomorrow I start The Great Acorn Contest.'

On the ride back to the ranch in the late afternoon Tom was depressed and sad. As always, Will had managed to chew up and spit out his enthusiasm. Will had pulled his lip, rubbed his eyebrows, scratched his nose, cleaned his glasses, and made a major operation of cutting and lighting a cigar. The pig proposition was full of holes, and Will was able to put his finger in the holes.

The Acorn Contest wouldn't work, although he was not explicit about why it wouldn't. The whole thing was shaky, particularly in these times. The very best Will was able to do was to think about it.

At one time during the talk Tom had thought to tell Will about Europe, but a quick instinct stopped him. The idea of traipsing around Europe, unless, of course, you were retired and had your capital out in good securities, would be to Will a craziness that would make the pig plan a marvel of business acumen. Tom did not tell him, and he left Will to 'think it over', knowing that the verdict would be against the pigs and the acorns.

Poor Tom did not know and could not learn that dissembling successfully is one of the creative joys of a business man. To indicate enthusiasm was to be idiotic. And Will really did mean to think it over. Parts of the plan fascinated him. Tom had stumbled on a very interesting thing. If you could buy shoats on credit, fatten them on food that cost next to nothing, sell them, pay off your loan, and take your profit, you would really have done something. Will would not rob his brother. He would cut him in on the profits, but Tom was a dreamer and could not be trusted with a good sound plan. Tom, for instance, didn't even know the price of pork and its probable trend. If it worked out, Will could be depended on to give Tom a very substantial present – maybe even a Ford. And how about a Ford as first and only prize for acorns? Everybody in the whole valley would pick acorns.

Driving up the Hamilton road, Tom wondered how to break it to Dessie that their plan was no good. The best way would be to have another plan to substitute for it. How could they make enough money in one year to go to Europe? And suddenly he realized that he didn't know how much they'd need. He didn't know the price of a steamship ticket. They might spend the evening figuring.

He half expected Dessie to run out of the house when he drove up. He would put on his best face and tell a joke. But Dessie didn't run out. Maybe taking a nap, he thought. He watered the horses and stabled them and pitched hay into the manger.

Dessie was lying on the goose-neck sofa when Tom came in. 'Taking a nap?' he asked, and then he saw the colour of her face. 'Dessie,' he cried, 'what's the matter?'

She rallied herself against pain. 'Just a stomach-ache,' she said. 'A pretty severe one.'

'Oh,' said Tom. 'You scared me. I can fix up a stomach-ache.' He went to the kitchen and brought back a glass of pearly liquid. He handed it to her.

'What is it, Tom?'

'Good old-fashioned salts. It may gripe you a little but it'll do the job.'

She drank it obediently and made a face. 'I remember that taste,' she said. 'Mother's remedy in green apple season.'

'Now lie still,' Tom said. 'I'll rustle up some dinner.'

She could hear him knocking about in the kitchen. The pain roared through her body. And on top of the pain there was fear. She could feel the medicine burn down to her stomach. After a while she dragged herself to the new home-made flush toilet and tried to vomit the salts. The perspiration ran from her forehead and blinded her. When she tried to straighten up, the muscles over her stomach were set and she could not break free.

Later Tom brought her some scrambled eggs. She shook her head slowly. 'I can't,' she said, smiling. 'I think I'll just go to bed.'

'The salts should work pretty soon,' Tom assured her. 'Then you'll be all right.' He helped her to bed. 'What do you suppose you ate to cause it?'

Dessie lay in her bedroom and her will battled the pain. About ten o'clock in the evening her will began to lose its fight. She called, 'Tom! Tom!' He opened the door. He had the World Almanac in his hand. 'Tom,' she said, 'I'm sorry. But I'm awfully sick, Tom. I'm terribly sick.'

He sat down on the edge of her bed in the half-darkness. 'Are the gripes bad?'

'Yes, awful?'

'Can you go to the toilet now?'

'No, not now.'

'I'll bring a lamp and sit with you,' he said. 'Maybe you can get some sleep. It'll be gone in the morning. The salts will do the job.'

Her will took hold again and she lay still while Tom read bits out of the *Almanac* to soothe her. He stopped reading when he thought she was sleeping, and he dozed in his chair beside the lamp.

A thin scream awakened him. He stepped beside the struggling bedclothes. Dessie's eyes were milky and crazy, like those of a maddened horse. Her mouth corners erupted thick bubbles and her face was on fire. Tom put his hand under the cover and felt muscles knotted like iron. And then her struggle stopped and her head fell back and the light glinted on her half-closed eyes.

Tom put only a bridle on the horse and flung himself on bareback. He groped and ripped out his belt to beat the frightened horse to an awkward run over the stony, rutted wheel track.

The Duncans, asleep upstairs in the two-storey house on the county road, didn't hear the banging on their door, but they heard the bang and ripping sound as their front door came off, carrying lock and hinges with it. By the time Red Duncan got downstairs with a shotgun Tom was screaming into the wall telephone at the King City central. 'Dr Tilson! Get him! I don't care. Get him! Get him, goddam it.' Red Duncan sleepily had the gun on him.

Dr Tilson said, 'Yes! Yes – yes, I hear. You're Tom Hamilton. What's the matter with her? Is her stomach hard? What did you do? Salts! You goddam fool!'

Then the doctor controlled his anger. 'Tom,' he said, 'Tom, boy. Pull yourself together. Go back and lay cold cloths – cold as you can get them. I don't suppose you have any ice. Well, keep changing the cloths. I'll be out as fast as I can. Do you hear me? Tom, do you hear me?'

He hung the receiver up and dressed. In angry weariness he opened the wall cabinet and collected scalpels and clamps, sponges and tubes of sutures, to put in his bag. He shook his gasoline pressure lantern to make sure it was full and arranged ether can and mask beside it on his bureau. His wife in boudoir cap and nightgown looked in. Dr Tilson said, 'I'm walking over to the garage. Call Will Hamilton. Tell him I want him to drive me to his father's place. If he argues tell him his sister is – dying.'

I I I

Tom came riding back to the ranch a week after Dessie's funeral, riding high and prim, his shoulders straight and chin in, like a guardsman on parade. Tom had done everything slowly, perfectly. His horse was curried and brushed, and his Stetson hat was square on his head. Not even Samuel could have held himself in more dignity than Tom as he rode back to the old house. A hawk driving down on a chicken with doubled fists did not make him turn his head.

At the barn he dismounted, watered his horse, held him a moment at the door, haltered him, and put rolled barley in the box beside the manger. He took off the saddle and turned the blanket inside out to dry. Then the barley was finished and he led the bay horse out and turned him free to graze on every unfenced inch of the world.

In the house the furniture, chairs, and stove seemed to shrink back and away from him in distaste. A stool avoided him as he went to the living-room. His matches were soft and damp, and with a feeling of apology he went to the kitchen for more. The lamp in the living-room was fair and lonely. Tom's first match flame ran quickly round the Rochester wick and then stood up a full inch of yellow flame.

Tom sat down in the evening and looked around. His eyes avoided the horsehair sofa. A slight noise of mice in the kitchen made him turn, and he saw his shadow on the wall and his hat was on. He removed it and laid it on the table beside him.

He thought dawdling, protective thoughts, sitting under the lamp, but he knew that pretty soon his name would be called and he would have to go up before the bench with himself as judge and his own crimes as jurors.

And his name *was* called, shrilly in his ears. His mind walked in to face the accusers: Vanity, which charged him with being ill dressed and dirty and vulgar; and Lust, slipping him the money for his whoring; Dishonesty, to make him pretend to talent and thought he did not have; Laziness and Gluttony arm-in-arm. Tom felt comforted by these because they screened the great Grey One in the back seat, waiting – the grey and dreadful crime. He dredged up lesser things, used small sins almost like virtues to save himself. There were Covetousness of Will's money, Treason towards his mother's God. Theft of time and hope, sick Rejection of love.

Samuel spoke softly but his voice filled the room. 'Be good, be pure, be great, Tom Hamilton.'

Tom ignored his father. He said, 'I'm busy greeting my friends,' and he nodded to Discourtesy and Ugliness and Unfilial Conduct and Unkept Fingernails. Then he started with

Vanity again. The Grey One shouldered up in front. It was too late to stall with baby sins. This Grey One was Murder.

Tom's hand felt the chill of the glass and saw the pearly liquid with the dissolving crystals still turning over and lucent bubbles rising, and he repeated aloud in the empty, empty room, 'This will do the job. Just wait till morning. You'll feel fine then.' That's how it had sounded, exactly how, and the walls and chairs and the lamp had all heard it and they could prove it. There was no place in the whole world for Tom Hamilton to live. But it wasn't for lack of trying. He shuffled possibilities like cards. London? No! Egypt – pyramids in Egypt and the Sphinx? No! Paris? No! Now wait – they do all your sins lots better there. No! Well, stand aside and maybe we'll come back to you. Bethlehem? Dear God, no! It would be lonely there for a stranger.

And here interpolated – it's so hard to remember how you die or when. An eyebrow raised or a whisper – they may be it; or a night mottled with splashed light until powder-driven lead finds your secret and lets out the fluid in you.

Now this is true, Tom Hamilton was dead and he had only to do a few decent things to make it final.

The sofa cricked in criticism, and Tom looked at it and at the smoking lamp to which the sofa referred. 'Thank you,' Tom said to the sofa. 'I hadn't noticed it,' and he turned down the wick until the smoking stopped.

His mind dozed. Murder slapped him aware again. Now Red Tom, Gun Tom, was too tired to kill himself. That takes some doing, with maybe pain and maybe hell.

He remembered that his mother had a strong distaste for suicide, feeling that it combined three things of which she strongly disapproved – bad manners, cowardice, and sin. It was almost as bad as adultery or stealing – maybe just as bad. There must be a way to avoid Liza's disapproval. She could make one suffer if she disapproved.

Samuel wouldn't make it hard, but on the other hand you couldn't avoid Samuel because he was in the air every place. Tom had to tell Samuel. He said, 'My father, I'm sorry. I can't help it. You over-estimated me. You were wrong. I wish I could justify the love and the pride you squandered on me. Maybe you could figure a way out, but I can't. I cannot live. I've killed Dessie and I want to sleep.'

And his mind spoke for his father absent, saying, 'Why, I can understand how that could be. There are so many patterns to choose from in the arc from birth back to birth again. But let's think how we can make it all right with Mother. Why are you so impatient, dear?'

'I can't wait, that's why,' Tom said. 'I can't wait any more.'

'Why, sure you can, my son, my darling. You're grown great as I knew you would. Open the table drawer and then make use of that turnip you call your head.'

Tom opened the drawer and saw a tablet of Crane's Linen Lawn and a package of envelopes to match and two gnawed and crippled pencils and in the dust corner at the back a few stamps. He laid out the tablet and sharpened the pencils with his pocket-knife.

He wrote, 'Dear Mother, I hope you keep yourself well. I am going to plan to spend more time with you. Olive asked me for Thanksgiving and you know I'll be there. Our little Olive can cook a turkey nearly to match yours, but I know you will never believe that. I've had a stroke of good luck. Bought a horse for fifteen dollars – a gelding, and he looks like a blood horse to me. I got him cheap because he has taken a dislike to mankind. His former owner spent more time on his own back than on the gelding's. I must say he's a pretty cute article. He's thrown me twice but I'll get him yet, and if I can break him I'll have one of the best horses in the whole county. And you can be sure I'll break him if it takes all winter. I don't know why I go on about him, only the man I bought him from said a funny thing. He said, "That horse is so mean he'd eat a man right off his back." Well, remember what Father used to say when we went a rabbit hunting? "Come back with your shield or on it." I'll see you Thanksgiving. Your son Tom.'

He wondered whether it was good enough, but he was too tired to do it again. He added, 'P.S. I notice Polly has not re-formed one bit. That parrot makes me blush.'

On another sheet he wrote, 'Dear Will, No matter what you yourself may think – please help me now. For Mother's sake – please. I was killed by a horse – thrown and kicked in the head – please! Your brother Tom.'

He stamped the letters and put them in his pocket and he asked Samuel, 'Is it all right?'

In his bedroom he broke open a new box of shells and put one of them in the cylinder of his well-oiled Smith and Wesson ·38 and he set the loaded chamber one space to the left of the firing-pin.

His horse standing sleepily near the fence came to his whistle and stood drowsing while he saddled up.

It was three o'clock in the morning when he dropped the letters in the post office at King City and mounted and turned his horse south towards the unproductive hills of the old Hamilton place.

He was a gallant gentleman.

Part Four

CHAPTER 34

A CHILD may ask, 'What is the world's story about?' And a grown man or woman may wonder, 'What way will the world go? How does it end and, while we're at it, what's the story about?'

I believe that there is one story in the world, and only one, that has frightened and inspired us, so that we live in a Pearl White serial of continuing thought and wonder. Humans are caught in their lives, in their thoughts, in their hungers and ambitions, in their avarice and cruelty, and in their kindness and generosity too – in a net of good and evil. I think this is the only story we have and that it occurs on all levels of feeling and intelligence. Virtue and vice were warp and woof of our first consciousness, and they will be the fabric of our last, and this despite changes we may impose on field and river and mountain, on economy and manners. There is no other story. A man, after he has brushed off the dust and chips of his life, will have left only the hard, clean questions: Was it good or was it evil? Have I done well – or ill?

Herodotus, in the Persian War, tells a story of how Croesus, the richest and most-favoured king of his time, asked Solon the Athenian a leading question. He would not have asked it if he had not been worried about the answer. 'Who,' he asked, 'is the luckiest person in the world?' He must have been eaten with doubt and hungry for reassurance. Solon told him of three lucky people in old times. And Croesus more than likely did not listen, so anxious was he about himself. And when Solon did not mention him, Croesus was forced to say, 'Do you consider me lucky?'

Solon did not hesitate in his answer. 'How can I tell?' he said. 'You aren't dead yet.'

And this answer must have haunted Croesus dismally as his luck disappeared, and his wealth and his kingdom. And as he was being burned on a tall fire, he may have thought of it and perhaps wished he had not asked or not been answered.

And in our time, when a man dies – if he has had wealth and

391

influence and power and all the vestments that arouse envy, and after the living take stock of the dead man's property and his eminence and works and monuments – the question is still there: Was his life good or was it evil? – which is another way of putting Croesus's question. Envies are gone, and the measuring stick is: 'Was he loved or was he hated? Is his death felt as a loss or does a kind of joy come of it?'

I remember clearly the deaths of three men. One was the richest man of the century, who, having clawed his way to wealth through the souls and bodies of men, spent many years trying to buy back the love he had forfeited and by that process performed great service to the world and, perhaps, had much more than balanced the evils of his rise. I was on a ship when he died. The news was posted on the bulletin board, and nearly everyone received the news with pleasure. Several said, 'Thank God that son of a bitch is dead.'

Then there was a man, smart as Satan, who, lacking some perception of human dignity and knowing all too well every aspect of human weakness and wickedness, used his special knowledge to warp men, to buy men, to bribe and threaten and seduce until he found himself in a position of great power. He clothed his motives in the names of virtue, and I have wondered whether he ever knew that no gift will ever buy back a man's love when you have removed his self-love. A bribed man can only hate his briber. When this man died the nation rang with praise and, just beneath, with gladness that he was dead.

There was a third man, who perhaps made many errors in performance but whose effective life was devoted to making men brave and dignified and good in a time when they were poor and frightened and when ugly forces were loose in the world to utilize their fears. This man was hated by the few. When he died the people burst into tears in the streets and their minds wailed, 'What can we do now? How can we go on without him?'

In uncertainty I am certain that underneath their topmost layers of frailty men want to be good and want to be loved. Indeed, most of their vices are attempted short cuts to love. When a man comes to die, no matter what his talents and influence and genius, if he dies unloved his life must be a failure to him and his dying a cold horror. It seems to me that if you or I must chose between two courses of thought or action, we should remember our dying and try so to live that our death brings no pleasure to the world.

We have only one story. All novels, all poetry, are built on the never-ending contest in ourselves of good and evil. And it occurs to me that evil must constantly re-spawn, while good, while virtue, is immortal. Vice has always a new fresh young face, while virtue is venerable as nothing else in the world is.

CHAPTER 35

I

LEE HELPED Adam and the two boys move to Salinas, which is to say he did it all, packed the things to be taken, saw them on the train, loaded the back seat of the Ford, and, arriving in Salinas, unpacked and saw the family settled in Dessie's little house. When he had done everything he could think of to make them comfortable, and a number of things unnecessary, and more things for the sake of delay, he waited on Adam formally one evening after the twins had gone to bed. Perhaps Adam caught his intention from Lee's coldness and formality.

Adam said, 'All right. I've been expecting it. Tell me.'

That broke up Lee's memorized speech, which he had intended to begin, 'For a number of years I have served you to the best of my ability and now I feel — '

'I've put it off as long as I could,' said Lee. 'I have a speech all ready. Do you want to hear it?'

'Do you want to say it?'

'No,' said Lee. 'I don't. And it's a pretty good speech too.'

'When do you want to go?' Adam asked.

'As soon as possible. I'm afraid I might lose my intention if I don't go soon. Do you want me to wait until you get someone else?'

'Better not,' said Adam. 'You know how slow I am. It might be some time. I might never get around to it.'

'I'll go tomorrow, then.'

'It will tear the boys to pieces,' Adam said. 'I don't know what they'll do. Maybe you'd better sneak off and let me tell them afterwards.'

'It's my observation that children always surprise us,' said Lee.

And so it was. At breakfast the next morning Adam said, 'Boys, Lee is going away.'

'Is he?' said Cal. 'There's a basketball game tonight, costs ten cents. Can we go?'

'Yes. But did you hear what I said?'

'Sure,' said Aron. 'You said Lee's going away.'

'But he's not coming back.'

Cal asked, 'Where's he going?'

'To San Francisco to live.'

'Oh!' said Aron. 'There's a man on Main Street, right on the street, and he's got a little stove and he cooks sausages and puts them in buns. They cost a nickel. And you can take all the mustard you want.'

Lee stood in the kitchen door, smiling at Adam.

When the twins got their books together Lee said, 'Goodbye, boys.'

They shouted, 'Goodbye!' and tumbled out of the house.

Adam stared into his coffee-cup and said in apology, 'What little brutes! I guess that's your reward for over ten years of service.'

'I like it better that way,' Lee said. 'If they pretended sorrow they'd be liars. It doesn't mean anything to them. Maybe they'll think of me sometimes – privately. I don't want them to be sad. I hope I'm not so small-souled as to take satisfaction in being missed.' He laid fifty cents on the table in front of Adam. 'When they start for the basketball game tonight, give them this from me and tell them to buy the sausage buns. My farewell gift may be ptomaine, for all I know.'

Adam looked at the telescope basket Lee brought into the dining-room. 'Is that all your stuff, Lee?'

'Everything but my books. They're in boxes in the cellar. If you don't mind I'll send for them or come for them after I get settled.'

'Why, sure. I'm going to miss you, Lee, whether you want me to or not. Are you really going to get your bookstore?'

'That is my intention.'

'You'll let us hear from you?'

'I don't know. I'll have to think about it. They say a clean cut heals soonest. There's nothing sadder to me than associations held together by nothing but the glue of postage stamps. If you can't see or hear or touch a man, it's best to let him go.'

Adam stood up from the table. 'I'll walk to the depot with you.'

'No!' Lee said sharply. 'No. I don't want that. Goodbye, Mr Trask. Goodbye, Adam.' He went out of the house so fast that

Adam's 'Goodbye' reached him at the bottom of the front steps and Adam's 'Don't forget to write' sounded over the click of the front gate.

That night after the basketball game Cal and Aron each had five sausages on buns, and it was just as well, for Adam had forgotten to provide any supper. Walking home, the twins discussed Lee for the first time.

'I wonder if he went away?' Cal asked.

'He's talked about going before.'

'What do you suppose he'll do without us?'

'I don't know. I bet he comes back,' Aron said.

'How do you mean? Father said he was going to start a bookstore. That's funny. A Chinese bookstore.'

'He'll come back,' said Aron. 'He'll get lonesome for us. You'll see.'

'Bet you ten cents he don't.'

'Before when?'

'Before for ever.'

'That's a bet,' said Aron.

Aron was not able to collect his winnings for nearly a month, but he won six days later.

Lee came on the ten-forty and let himself in with his own key. There was a light in the dining-room, but Lee found Adam in the kitchen, scraping at a thick black crust in the frying-pan with the point of a can opener.

Lee put down his basket. 'If you soak it overnight it will come right out.'

'Will it? I've burned everything I've cooked. There's a saucepan of beets out in the yard. Smelled so bad I couldn't have them in the house. Burned beets are awful – Lee!' he cried, and then, 'Is anything the matter?'

Lee took the black iron pan from him and put it in the sink and ran water in it. 'If we had a new gas stove we could make a cup of coffee in a few minutes,' he said. 'I might as well build up the fire.'

'Stove won't burn,' said Adam.

Lee lifted the lid. 'Have you ever taken the ashes out?'

'Ashes?'

'Oh, go in the other room,' said Lee. 'I'll make some coffee.'

Adam waited impatiently in the dining-room but he obeyed

his orders. At last Lee brought in two cups of coffee and set them on the table. 'Made it in a skillet,' he said. 'Much faster.' He leaned over his telescope basket and untied the rope that held it shut. He brought out the stone bottle. 'Chinese absinthe,' he said. 'Ng-ka-py maybe last ten more years. I forgot to ask whether you had replaced me.'

'You're beating about the bush,' said Adam.

'I know it. And I also know the best way would be just to tell it and get it over with.'

'You lost your money in a fan-tan game.'

'No. I wish that was it. No, I have my money. This damn cork's broken – I'll have to shove it in the bottle.' He poured the black liquor into his coffee. 'I never drank it this way,' he said. 'Say, it's good.'

'Tastes like rotten apples,' said Adam.

'Yes, but remember Sam Hamilton said like good rotten apples.'

Adam said, 'When do you think you'll get around to telling me what happened to you?'

'Nothing happened to me,' said Lee. 'I got lonesome. That's all. Isn't that enough?'

'How about your bookstore?'

'I don't want a bookstore. I think I knew it before I got on the train, but I took all this time to make sure.'

'Then there's your last dream gone.'

'Good riddance.' Lee seemed on the verge of hysteria. 'Missy Tlask, Chinee boy sink gung get dlunk.'

Adam was alarmed. 'What's the matter with you anyway?'

Lee lifted the bottle to his lips and took a deep hot drink and panted the fumes out of his burning throat. 'Adam,' he said, 'I am incomparably, incredibly, overwhelmingly glad to be home. I've never been so goddam lonesome in my life.'

CHAPTER 36

I

SALINAS HAD two grammar schools, big yellow structures with tall windows, and the windows were baleful and the doors did not smile. These schools were called the East End and the West End. Since the East End School was way to hell and gone across town and the children who lived east of Main Street attended there, I will not bother with it.

The West End, a huge building of two storeys, fronted with gnarled poplars, divided the play-yards called girlside and boyside. Behind the school a high board fence separated girlside from boyside, and the back of the play-yard was bounded by a slough of standing water in which tall tules and even cattails grew. The West End had grades from third to eighth. The first- and second-graders went to Baby School some distance away.

In the West End there was a room for each grade – third, fourth, and fifth on the ground floor, sixth, seventh, eighth on the second floor. Each room had the usual desks of battered oak, a platform and square teacher's desk, one Seth Thomas clock and one picture. The pictures identified the rooms, and the pre-Raphaelite influence was overwhelming. Galahad standing in full armour pointed the way for third-graders; Atlanta's race urged on the fourth, the Pot of Basil confused the fifth grade, and so on until the denunciation of Cataline sent the eighth-graders on to high school with a sense of high civic virtue.

Cal and Aron were assigned to the seventh grade because of their age, and they learned every shadow of its picture – Laocoön completely wrapped in snakes.

The boys were stunned by the size and grandeur of the West End after their background in a one-room country school. The opulence of having a teacher for each grade made a deep impression on them. It seemed wasteful. But, as is true of all humans, they were stunned for one day, admiring on the second, and on the third day could not remember very clearly ever having gone to any other school.

The teacher was dark and pretty, and by a judicious raising or withholding of hands the twins had no worries. Cal worked it out quickly and explained it to Aron. 'You take most kids,' he said, 'if they know the answer, why, they hold up their hands, and if they don't know they just crawl under the desk. Know what we're going to do?'

'No. What?'

'Well, you notice the teacher don't always call on somebody with his hand up. She lets drive at the others and, sure enough, they don't know.'

'That's right,' said Aron.

'Now, first week we're going to work like bedamned but we won't stick up our hands. So she'll call on us and we'll know. That'll throw her. So the second week we won't work and we'll stick up our hands and she won't call on us. Third week we'll just sit quiet, and she won't even know whether we got the answer or not. Pretty soon she'll let us alone. She isn't going to waste her time calling on somebody that knows.'

Cal's method worked. In a short time the twins were not only let alone but got themselves a certain reputation for smartness. As a matter of fact, Cal's method was a waste of time. Both boys learned easily enough.

Cal was able to develop his marble game and set about gathering in all the chalkies and immies, glassies and agates, in the school-yard. He traded them for tops just as the marble season ended. At one time he had and used as legal tender at least forty-five tops of various sizes and colours, from the thick clumsy baby tops to the lean and dangerous splitters with their needle points.

Everyone who saw the twins remarked on their difference one from the other and seemed puzzled that this should be so. Cal was growing up dark-skinned, dark-haired. He was quick and sure and secret. Even though he may have tried, he could not conceal his cleverness. Adults were impressed with what seemed to them a precocious maturity, and they were a little frightened at it too. No one liked Cal very much and yet everyone was touched with fear of him and through fear with respect. Although he had no friends he was welcomed by his obsequious class-mates and took up a natural and cold position of leadership in the school-yard.

If he concealed his ingenuity, he concealed his hurts too. He was regarded as thick-skinned and insensitive – even cruel.

Aron drew love from every side. He seemed shy and delicate. His pink-and-white skin, golden hair, and wide-set blue eyes caught attention. In the school-yard his very prettiness caused some difficulty until it was discovered by his testers that Aron was a dogged, steady, and completely fearless fighter, particularly when he was crying. Word got around, and the natural punishers of new boys learned to let him alone. Aron did not attempt to hide his disposition. It was concealed by being the opposite of his appearance. He was unchanging once a course was set. He had few facets and very little versatility. His body was as insensitive to pain as was his mind to subtleties.

Cal knew his brother and could handle him by keeping him off balance, but this only worked up to a certain point. Cal had learned when to sidestep, when to run away. Change of direction confused Aron, but that was the only thing that confused him. He set his path and followed it and he did not see nor was he interested in anything beside his path. His emotions were few and heavy. All of him was hidden by his angelic face, and for this he had no more concern or responsibility than has a fawn for the dappling spots of its young hide.

11

On Aron's first day at school he waited eagerly for the recess. He went over to the girlside to talk to Abra. A mob of squealing girls could not drive him out. It took a full-grown teacher to force him back to the boyside.

At noon he missed her, for her father came by in his high-wheeled buggy and drove her home for her lunch. He waited outside the school-yard gate for her after school.

She came out surrounded by girls. Her face was composed and gave no sign that she expected him. She was far the prettiest girl in the school, but it is doubtful whether Aron had noticed that.

The cloud of girls hung on and hung on. Aron marched along three paces behind them, patient and unembarrassed even when the girls tossed their squealing barbs of insult over their shoulders at him. Gradually some drifted away to their own homes, and only three girls were with Abra when she came to the white gate of her yard and turned in. Her friends stared at him a moment, giggled, and went on their way.

Aron sat down on the edge of the sidewalk. After a moment the latch lifted, the white gate opened, and Abra emerged. She walked across the walk and stood over him. 'What do you want?'

Aron's wide eyes looked up at her. 'You aren't engaged to anybody?'

'Silly,' she said.

He struggled up to his feet. 'I guess it will be a long time before we can get married,' he said.

'Who wants to get married?'

Aron didn't answer. Perhaps he didn't hear. He walked along beside her.

Abra moved with firm and deliberate steps and she faced straight ahead. There was wisdom and sweetness in her expression. She seemed deep in thought. And Aron, walking beside her, never took his eyes from her face. His attention seemed tied to her face by a taut string.

They walked silently past the Baby School, and there the pavement ended. Abra turned right and led the way through the stubble of the summer's hayfield. The black 'dobe clods crushed under their feet.

On the edge of the field stood a little pump-house, and a willow tree flourished beside it, fed by the overspill of water. The long skirts of the willow hung down nearly to the ground.

Abra parted the switches like a curtain and went into the house of leaves made against the willow trunk by the sweeping branches. You could see out through the leaves, but inside it was sweetly protected and warm and safe. The afternoon sunlight came yellow through the ageing leaves.

Abra sat down on the ground, or rather she seemed to drift down, and her full skirts settled in a billow around her. She folded her hands in her lap almost as though she were praying.

Aron sat down beside her. 'I guess it will be a long time before we can get married,' he said again.

'Not so long,' Abra said.

'I wish it was now.'

'It won't be long,' said Abra.

Aron asked, 'Do you think your father will let you?'

It was a new thought to her, and she turned and looked at him. 'Maybe I won't ask him.'

'But your mother?'

'Let's not disturb them,' she said. 'They'd think it was funny or bad. Can't you keep a secret?'

'Oh, yes. I can keep secrets better than anybody. And I've got some too.'

Abra said, 'Well, you just put this one with the others.'

Aron picked up a twig and drew a line on the dark earth. 'Abra, do you know how you get babies?'

'Yes,' she said. 'Who told you?'

400

'Lee told me. He explained the whole thing. I guess we can't have any babies for a long time.'

Abra's mouth turned up at the corners with a condescending wisdom. 'Not so long,' she said.

'We'll have a house together some time,' Aron said, bemused. 'We'll go in and close the door and it will be nice. But that will be a long time.'

Abra put out her hand and touched him on the arm. 'Don't you worry about long times,' she said. 'This is a kind of a house. We can play like we live here while we're waiting. And you will be my husband and you can call me wife.'

He tried it over under his breath and then aloud. 'Wife,' he said.

'It'll be like practising,' said Abra.

Aron's arm shook under her hand, and she put it, palm up, in her lap.

Aron said suddenly, 'While we're practising, maybe we could do something else.'

'What?'

'Maybe you wouldn't like it.'

'What is it?'

'Maybe we could pretend like you're my mother.'

'That's easy,' she said.

'Would you mind?'

'No, I'd like it. Do you want to start now?'

'Sure,' Aron said. 'How do you want to go about it?'

'Oh, I can tell you that,' said Abra. She put a cooing tone in her voice and said, 'Come, my baby, put your head in Mother's lap. Come, my little son. Mother will hold you.' She drew his head down and without warning Aron began to cry and could not stop. He wept quietly, and Abra stroked his cheek and wiped the flowing tears away with the edge of her skirt.

The sun crept down towards its setting place behind the Salinas River, and a bird began to sing wonderfully from the golden stubble of the field. It was as beautiful under the branches of the willow tree as anything in the world can be.

Very slowly Aron's weeping stopped, and he felt good and he felt warm.

'My good little baby,' Abra said. 'Here, let Mother brush your hair back.'

Aron sat up and said almost angrily, 'I don't hardly ever cry unless I'm mad. I don't know why I cried.'

Abra asked, 'Do you remember your mother?'

'No. She died when I was a little bit of a baby.'

'Don't you know what she looked like?'

'No.

'Maybe you saw a picture.'

'No, I tell you. We don't have any pictures. I asked Lee and he said no pictures – no, I guess it was Cal asked Lee.'

'When did she die?'

'Right after Cal and I were born.'

'What was her name?'

'Lee says it was Cathy. Say, what are you asking so much for?'

Abra went on calmly, 'How was she complected?'

'What?'

'Light or dark hair?'

'I don't know.'

'Didn't your father tell you?'

'We never asked him.'

Abra was silent, and after a while Aron asked, 'What's the matter – cat got your tongue?'

Abra inspected the setting sun.

Aron asked uneasily, 'You mad with me' – and he added tentatively – 'wife?'

'No, I'm not mad. I'm just wondering.'

'What about?'

'About something.' Abra's firm face was tight against a seething inner argument. She asked, 'What's it like not to have any mother?'

'I don't know. It's like anything else.'

'I guess you wouldn't even know the difference.'

'I would too. I wish you would talk out. You're like riddles in the *Bulletin*.'

Abra continued in her concentrated imperturbability, 'Do you want to have a mother?'

'That's crazy,' said Aron. ' 'Course I do. Everybody does. You aren't trying to hurt my feelings, are you? Cal tries that sometimes and then he laughs.'

Abra looked away from the setting sun. She had difficulty seeing past the purple spots the light had left on her eyes. 'You said a little while ago you could keep secrets.'

'I can.'

'Well, do you have a double-poison-and-cut-my-throat secret?'

'Sure I have.'

Abra said softly, 'Tell me what it is, Aron.' She put a caress in his name.

'Tell you what?'

'Tell me the deepest down hell-and-goddam secret you know.'

Aron reared back from her in alarm. 'Why, I will not,' he said. 'What right you got to ask me? I wouldn't tell anybody.'

'Come on, my baby – tell Mother,' she crooned.

There were tears crowding up in his eyes again, but this time they were tears of anger. 'I don't know as I want to marry you,' he said. 'I think I'm going home now.'

Abra put her hand on his wrist and hung on. Her voice lost its coquetry. 'I wanted to see. I guess you can keep secrets all right.'

'Why did you go for to do it? I'm mad now. I feel sick.'

'I think I'm going to tell you a secret,' she said.

'Ho!' he jeered at her. 'Who can't keep a secret now?'

'I was going to decide,' she said. 'I think I'm going to tell you this secret because it might be good for you. It might make you glad.'

'Who told you not to tell?'

'Nobody,' she said. 'I only told myself.'

'Well, I guess that's a little different. What's your old secret?'

The red sun leaned its rim on the roof-tree of Tollot's house on the Blanco Road, and Tollot's chimney stuck up like a black thumb against it.

Abra said softly, 'Listen, you remember when we came to your place that time?'

'Sure!'

'Well, in the buggy I went to sleep, and when I woke up my father and mother didn't know I was awake. They said your mother wasn't dead. They said she went away. They said something bad must have happened to her, and she went away.'

Aron said hoarsely. 'She's dead.'

'Wouldn't it be nice if she wasn't?'

'My father says she's dead. He's not a liar.'

'Maybe *he* thinks she's dead.'

He said, 'I think he'd know.' But there was uncertainty in his tone.

Abra said, 'Wouldn't it be nice if we could find her? S'pose she lost her memory or something. I've read about that. And we could find her and that would make her remember.' The glory of the romance caught her like a rip tide and carried her away.

Aron said, 'I'll ask my father.'

'Aron,' she said sternly, 'what I told you is a secret.'

'Who says?'

'I say. Now you just say after me – "I'll take double poison and cut my throat if I tell." '

For a moment he hesitated and then he repeated, 'I'll take double poison and cut my throat if I tell.'

She said, 'Now spit in your palm – like this – that's right. Now you give me your hand – see? – squidge the spit all together. Now rub it dry on your hair.' The two followed the formula, and then Abra said solemnly, 'Now, I'd just like to see you tell that one. I knew one girl that told a secret after that oath and she burned up in a barn fire.'

The sun was gone behind Tollot's house and the gold light with it. The evening star shimmered over Mount Toro.

Abra said, 'They'll skin me alive. Come on. Hurry! I bet my father's got the dog whistle out for me. I'll get whipped.'

Aron looked at her in disbelief. 'Whipped! They don't whip you?'

'That's what you think!'

Aron said passionately, 'You just let them try. If they go for to whip you, you tell them I'll kill them.' His wide-set blue eyes were slitted and glinting. 'Nobody's going to whip my wife,' he said.

Abra put her arms around his neck in the dusk under the willow tree. She kissed him on his open mouth. 'I love you, husband,' she said, and then she turned and bolted, holding up her skirts above her knees, her lace-edged white drawers flashing as she ran towards home.

III

Aron went back to the trunk of the willow tree and sat on the ground and leaned back against the bark. His mind was a greyness and there were churnings of pain in his stomach. He tried to sort out the feeling into thoughts and pictures so the pain would go away. It was hard. His slow deliberate mind could not accept so many thoughts and emotions at once. The door was shut against everything except physical pain. After a while the door opened a little and let in one thing to be scrutinized and then another and another, until all had been absorbed, one at a time. Outside his closed mind a huge thing was clamouring to get in. Aron held it back until last.

First he let Abra in and went over her dress, her face, the feel of her hand on his cheek, the odour that came from her, like milk a little and like cut grass a little. He saw and felt and heard and smelled her all over again. He thought how clean she was, her hands and fingernails, and how straightforward and unlike the gigglers in the school-yard.

Then, in order, he thought of her holding his head and his baby crying, crying with longing, wanting something and in a way feeling that he was getting it. Perhaps the getting it was what had made him cry.

Next he thought of her trick – her testing of him. He wondered what she would have done if he had told her a secret. What secret could he have told her if he had wished? Right now he didn't recall any secret except the one that was beating on the door to get into his mind.

The sharpest question she had asked, 'How does it feel not to have a mother?' slipped into his mind. And how did it feel? It didn't feel like anything. Ah, but in the schoolroom, at Christmas and graduation, when the mothers of other children came to the parties – then was the silent cry and the wordless longing. That's what it was like.

Salinas was surrounded and penetrated with swamps, with tule-filled ponds, and every pond spawned thousands of frogs. With the evening the air was so full of their song that it was a kind of roaring silence. It was a veil, a background, and its sudden disappearance, after a clap of thunder, was a shocking thing. It is possible that if in the night the frog sound should have stopped, everyone in Salinas would have awakened, feeling that there was a great noise. In their millions the frog songs seemed to have a beat and a cadence, and perhaps it is the ears' function to do this just as it is the eyes' business to make stars twinkle.

It was quite dark under the willow tree now. Aron wondered whether he was ready for the big thing, and while he wondered it slipped through and was in.

His mother was alive. Often he had pictured her lying underground, still and cool and unrotted. But this was not so. Somewhere she moved about and spoke, and her hands moved and her eyes were open. And in the midst of this flood of pleasure a sorrow came down on him and a sense of loss, a dreadful loss. Aron was puzzled. He inspected the cloud of sadness. If his mother was alive, his father was a liar. If one was alive, the other was dead. Aron said aloud under the tree, 'My mother is dead. She's buried some place in the East.'

In the darkness he saw Lee's face and heard Lee's soft speech.

405

Lee had built very well. Having a respect that amounted to reverence for the truth he had also its natural opposite, a loathing of a lie. He had made it very clear to the boys exactly what he meant. If something was untrue and you didn't know it, that was error. But if you knew a true thing and changed it to a false thing, both you and it were loathsome.

Lee's voice said, 'I know that sometimes a lie is used in kindness. I don't believe it ever works kindly. The quick pain of truth can pass away, but the slow, eating agony of a lie is never lost. That's a running sore.' And Lee had worked patiently and slowly and he had succeeded in building Adam as the centre, the foundation, the essence of truth.

Aron shook his head in the dark, shook it hard in disbelief. 'If my father is a liar, Lee is a liar too.' He was lost. He had no one to ask. Cal was a liar, but Lee's conviction had made Cal a clever liar. Aron felt that something had to die – his mother or his world.

His solution lay suddenly before him. Abra had not lied. She had told him only what she had heard, and her parents had only heard it too. He got to his feet and pushed his mother back into death and closed his mind against her.

He was late for supper. 'I was with Abra,' he explained. After supper, when Adam sat in his new comfortable chair, reading the *Salinas Index*, he felt a stroking touch on his shoulder and looked up. 'What is it, Aron?' he asked.

'Good night, Father,' Aron said.

CHAPTER 37

I

FEBRUARY IN Salinas is likely to be damp and cold and full of miseries. The heaviest rains fall then and if the river is going to rise, it rises then. February of 1915 was a year heavy with water.

The Trasks were well established in Salinas. Lee, once he had given up his brackish bookish dream, made a new kind of place for himself in the house beside Reynaud's Bakery. On the ranch his possessions had never really been unpacked, for Lee had lived poised to go somewhere else. Here, for the first time in his life, he built a home for himself, feathered with comfort and permanence.

The large bedroom nearest the street door fell to him. Lee dipped into his savings. He had never before spent a needless penny, since all money had been earmarked for his bookstore. But now he bought a little hard bed and a desk. He built bookshelves and unpacked his books, invested in a soft rug and tacked prints on the walls. He placed a deep and comfortable Morris chair under the best reading-lamp he could find. And last he bought a typewriter and set about learning to use it.

Having broken out of his own Spartanism, he remade the Trask household, and Adam gave him no opposition. A gas stove came into the house and electric wires and a telephone. He spent Adam's money remorselessly – new furniture, new carpets, a gas water-heater, and a large ice-box. In a short time there was hardly a house in Salinas so well equipped. Lee defended himself to Adam, saying, 'You have plenty of money. It would be a shame not to enjoy it.'

'I'm not complaining,' Adam protested. 'Only I'd like to buy something too. What shall I buy?'

'Why don't you go to Logan's music store and listen to one of the new phonographs?'

'I think I'll do that,' said Adam. And he bought a Victor victrola, a tall Gothic instrument, and he went regularly to see what new records had come in.

The growing century was shucking Adam out of his shell. He subscribed to the *Atlantic Monthly* and the *National Geographic*. He joined the Masons and seriously considered the Elks. The new ice-box fascinated him. He bought a textbook on refrigeration and began to study it.

The truth was that Adam needed work. He came out of his long sleep needing to do something.

'I think I'll go into business,' he said to Lee.

'You don't need to. You have enough to live on.'

'But I'd like to be doing something.'

'That's different,' said Lee. 'Know what you want to do? I don't think you'd be very good at business.'

'Why not?'

'Just a thought,' said Lee.

'Say, Lee, I want you to read an article. It says they've dug up a mastodon in Siberia. Been in the ice thousands of years. And the meat's still good.'

Lee smiled at him. 'You've got a bug in your bonnet some-

407

where,' he said. 'What have you got in all those little cups in the ice-box?'

'Different things.'

'Is that the business? Some of the cups smell bad.'

'It's an idea,' Adam said, 'I can't seem to stay away from it. I just can't seem to get over the idea that you can keep things if you get them cold enough.'

'Let's not have any mastodon meat in our ice-box,' said Lee.

If Adam had conceived thousands of ideas, the way Sam Hamilton had, they might all have drifted away, but he had only the one. The frozen mastodon stayed in his mind. His little cups of fruit, of pudding, bits of meat, both cooked and raw, continued in the ice-box. He bought every available book on bacteria and began sending for magazines and printed articles of a mildly scientific nature. And, as is usually true of a man of one idea, he became obsessed.

Salinas had a small ice company, not large but enough to supply the few houses with ice-boxes and to service the ice-cream parlours. The horse-drawn ice wagon went its route every day.

Adam began to visit the ice plant, and pretty soon he was taking his little cups to the freezing chambers. He wished with all his heart that Sam Hamilton were alive to discuss cold with him. Sam would have covered the field very quickly, he thought.

Adam was walking back from the ice plant one rainy afternoon, thinking about Sam Hamilton, when he saw Will Hamilton go into the Abbot House Bar. He followed him and leaned against the bar beside him. 'Why don't you come up and have some supper with us?'

'I'd like to,' Will said. 'I tell you what -- I've got a deal I'm trying to put through. If I get finished in time I'll walk by. Is there something important?'

'Well, I don't know. I've been doing some thinking and I'd like to ask your advice.'

Nearly every business proposition in the country came sooner or later to Will Hamilton's attention. He might have excused himself if he had not remembered that Adam was a rich man. An idea was one thing, but backed up with cash was quite another. 'You wouldn't entertain a reasonable offer for your ranch, would you?' he asked.

'Well, the boys, particularly Cal, they like the place. I think I'll hang on to it.'

'I think I can turn it over for you.'

'No, it's rented, paying its own taxes. I'll hold on to it.'

'If I can't get in for supper I might be able to come in afterwards,' said Will.

Will Hamilton was a very substantial business man. No one knew exactly how many pies his thumb had explored, but it was known that he was a clever and comparatively rich man. His business deal had been non-existent. It was a part of his policy always to be busy and occupied.

He had supper alone in the Abbot House. After a considered time he walked round the corner on Central Avenue and rang the bell of Adam Trask's house.

The boys had gone to bed. Lee sat with a darning basket, mending the long black stockings the twins wore at school. Adam had been reading the *Scientific American*. He let Will in and placed a chair for him. Lee brought a pot of coffee and went back to his mending.

Will settled himself into a chair, took out a fat black cigar, and lighted up. He waited for Adam to open the game.

'Nice weather for a change. And how's your mother?' Adam said.

'Just fine. Seems younger every day. The boys must be growing up.'

'Oh, they are. Cal's going to be in his school play. He's quite an actor. Aron's a real good student. Cal wants to go to farming.'

'Nothing wrong with that if you go about it right. Country could use some forward-looking farmers.' Will waited uneasily. He wondered if it could be that Adam's money was exaggerated. Could Adam be getting ready to borrow money? Will quickly worked out how much he would lend on the Trask ranch and how much he could borrow on it. The figures were not the same, nor was the interest rate. And still Adam did not come up with his proposition. Will grew restless. 'I can't stay very long,' he said. 'Told a fellow I'd meet him later tonight.'

'Have another cup of coffee,' Adam suggested.

'No thanks. Keeps me awake. Did you have something you wanted to see me about?'

Adam said, 'I was thinking about your father and I thought I'd like to talk to a Hamilton.'

Will relaxed a little in his chair. 'He was a great old talker.'

'Somehow he made a better man than he was,' said Adam.

Lee looked up from his darning egg. 'Perhaps the best conversationalist in the world is the man who helps others to talk.'

Will said, 'You know, it sounds funny to hear you use all those two-bit words. I'd swear to God you used to talk pidgin.'

'I used to,' said Lee. 'It was vanity, I guess.' He smiled at Adam and said to Will, 'Did you hear that somewhere up in Siberia they dug a mastodon out of the ice? It had been there a hundred thousand years and the meat was still fresh.'

'Mastodon?'

'Yes, a kind of elephant that hasn't lived on the earth for a long time.'

'Meat was still fresh?'

'Sweet as a pork chop,' said Lee. He shoved the wooden egg into the shattered knee of a black stocking.

'That's very interesting,' said Will.

Adam laughed. 'Lee hasn't wiped my nose yet, but that will come,' he said. 'I guess I'm pretty roundabout. The whole thing comes up because I'm tired of just sitting around. I want to get something to take up my time.'

'Why don't you farm your place?'

'No. That doesn't interest me. You see, Will, I'm not like a man looking for a job. I'm looking for work. I don't need a job.'

Will came out of his cautiousness, 'Well, what can I do for you?'

'I thought I'd tell you an idea I had, and you might give me an opinion. You're a business man.'

'Of course,' said Will. 'Anything I can do.'

'I've been looking into refrigeration,' said Adam. 'I got an idea and I can't get rid of it. I go to sleep and it comes right back at me. Never had anything give me so much trouble. It's kind of a big idea. Maybe it's full of holes.'

Will uncrossed his legs and pulled at his trousers where they were binding him. 'Go ahead – shoot,' he said. 'Like a cigar?'

Adam didn't hear the offer, nor did he know the implication. 'The whole country's changing,' Adam said. 'People aren't going to live the way they used to. Do you know where the biggest market for oranges in the winter is?'

'No. Where?'

'New York City. I read that. Now in the cold parts of the country, don't you think people get to wanting perishable things in the winter – like peas and lettuce and cauliflower? In a big part of the country they don't have those things for months and months. And right here in the Salinas Valley we can raise them all the year round.'

'Right here isn't right there,' said Will. 'What's your idea?'

'Well, Lee made me get a big ice-box, and I got kind of interested. I put different kinds of vegetables in there. And I got to arranging them different ways. You know, Will, if you chop ice fine and lay a head of lettuce in it and wrap it in waxed paper, it will keep three weeks and come out fresh and good.'

'Go on,' said Will cautiously.

'Well, you know the railroads built those fruit cars. I went down and had a look at them. They're pretty good. Do you know we could ship lettuce right to the east coast in the middle of winter?'

Will asked, 'Where do you come in?'

'I was thinking of buying the ice plant here in Salinas and trying to ship some things.'

'That would cost a lot of money.'

'I have quite a lot of money,' said Adam.

Will Hamilton pulled his lip angrily. 'I don't know why I got into this,' he said. 'I know better.'

'How do you mean?'

'Look here,' said Will. 'When a man comes to me for advice about an idea, I know he doesn't want advice. He wants me to agree with him. And if I want to keep his friendship I tell him his idea is fine and go ahead. But I like you and you're a friend of my family, so I'm going to stick my neck out.'

Lee put down his darning, moved his sewing basket to the floor, and changed his glasses.

Adam remonstrated, 'What are you getting upset about?'

'I come from a whole goddam family of inventors,' said Will. 'We had ideas for breakfast. We had ideas instead of breakfast. We had so many ideas we forgot to make the money for groceries. When we got a little ahead my father, or Tom, patented something. I'm the only one in the family, except my mother, who didn't have ideas, and I'm the only one who ever made a dime. Tom had ideas about helping people, and some of it was pretty darn near socialism. And if you tell me you don't care about making a profit, I'm going to throw that coffee-pot right at your head.'

'Well, I don't care much.'

'You stop right there, Adam. I've got my neck out. If you want to drop forty or fifty thousand dollars quick, you just go on with your idea. But I'm telling you – let your damned idea lie. Kick dust over it.'

'What's wrong with it?'

411

'Everything's wrong with it. People in the East aren't used to vegetables in the winter. They wouldn't buy them. You get your cars stuck on a siding and you'll lose the shipment. The market is controlled. Oh, Jesus Christ! It makes me mad when babies try to ride into business on an idea.'

Adam sighed. 'You make Sam Hamilton sound like a criminal,' he said.

'Well, he was my father and I loved him, but I wish to God he had let ideas alone.' Will looked at Adam and saw amazement in his eyes, and suddenly Will was ashamed. He shook his head slowly from side to side. 'I didn't mean to run down my people,' he said. 'I think they were good people. But my advice to you stands. Let refrigeration alone.'

Adam turned slowly to Lee. 'Have we got any more of that lemon pie we had for supper?' he asked.

'I don't think so,' said Lee. 'I thought I heard mice in the kitchen. I'm afraid there will be white of egg on the boys' pillows. You've got half a quart of whisky.'

'Have I. Why don't we have that?'

'I got excited,' said Will, and he tried to laugh at himself. 'A drink would do me good.' His face was fiery red and his voice was strained in his throat. 'I'm getting too fat,' he said.

But he had two drinks and relaxed. Sitting comfortably, he instructed Adam. 'Some things don't ever change their value,' he said. 'If you want to put money into something, you look around at the world. This war in Europe is going to go on a long time. And when there's war there's going to be hungry people. I won't say it is so, but it wouldn't surprise me if we got into it. I don't trust this Wilson – he's all theory and big words. And if we do get into it, there's going to be fortunes made in imperishable foods. You take rice and corn and wheat and beans, they don't need ice. They keep, and people can stay alive on them. I'd say if you were to plant your whole damned bottom land to beans and just put them away, why, your boys wouldn't have to worry about the future. Beans are up to three cents now. If we get into the war I wouldn't be surprised if they went to ten cents. And you keep beans dry and they'll be right there, waiting for a market. If you want to turn a profit, you plant beans.'

He went away feeling good. The shame that had come over him was gone and he knew he had given sound advice.

After Will had gone Lee brought out one-third of a lemon pie and cut it in two. 'He's getting too fat,' Lee said.

Adam was thinking. 'I only said I wanted something to do,' he observed.

'How about the ice plant?'

'I think I'll buy it.'

'You might plant some beans too,' said Lee.

Late in the year Adam made his great try, and it was a sensation in a year of sensations, both local and international. As he got ready, business men spoke of him as far-seeing, forward-looking, progress-minded. The departure of six car-loads of lettuce packed in ice was given a civic overtone. The Chamber of Commerce attended the departure. The cars were decorated with big posters which said, 'Salinas Valley Lettuce'. But no one wanted to invest in the project.

Adam untapped energy he did not suspect he had. It was a big job to gather, trim, box, ice, and load the lettuce. There was no equipment for such work. Everything had to be improvised, a great many hands hired and taught to do the work. Everyone gave advice but no one helped. It was estimated that Adam had spent a fortune on his idea, but how big a fortune no one knew. Adam did not know. Only Lee knew.

The idea looked good. The lettuce was consigned to commission merchants in New York at a fine price. Then the train was gone and everyone went home to wait. If it was a success any number of men were willing to dig down to put money in. Even Will Hamilton wondered whether he had not been wrong with his advice.

If the series of events had been planned by an omnipotent and unforgiving enemy it could not have been more effective. As the train came into Sacramento a snow slide closed the Sierras for two days and the six cars stood on a siding, dripping their ice away. On the third day the freight crossed the mountains, and that was the time for unseasonable warm weather throughout the Middle West. In Chicago there developed a confusion of orders – no one's fault, just one of those things that happens – and Adam's six cars of lettuce stood in the yard for five more days. That was enough, and there is no reason to go into it in detail. What arrived in New York was six car-loads of horrible slop with a sizeable charge just to get rid of it.

Adam read the telegram from the commission house and he

settled back in his chair and a strange enduring smile came on his face and did not go away.

Lee kept away from him to let him get a grip of himself. The boys heard the reaction in Salinas. Adam was a fool. These know-it-all dreamers always got into trouble. Business men congratulated themselves on their foresight in keeping out of it. It took experience to be a business man. People who inherited their money always got into trouble. And if you wanted proof – just look at how Adam had run his ranch. A fool and his money were soon parted. Maybe that would teach him a lesson. And he had doubled the output of the ice company.

Will Hamilton recalled that he had not only argued against it but had foretold in detail what would happen. He did not feel pleasure, but what could you do when a man wouldn't take advice from a sound business man? And, God knows, Will had plenty of experience with fly-by-night ideas. In a roundabout way it was recalled that Sam Hamilton had been a fool too. And as for Tom Hamilton – he had been just crazy.

When Lee felt that enough time had passed he did not beat around the bush. He sat directly in front of Adam to get and to keep his attention.

'How do you feel?' he asked.

'All right.'

'You aren't going to crawl back in your hole, are you?'

'What makes you think that?' Adam asked.

'Well, you have the look on your face you used to wear. And you've got that sleep-walker light in your eyes. Does this hurt your feelings?'

'No,' said Adam. 'The only thing I was wondering about was whether I'm wiped out.'

'Not quite,' said Lee. 'You have about nine thousand dollars left and the ranch.'

'Theres' a two-thousand-dollar bill for garbage disposal,' said Adam.

'That's before the nine thousand.'

'I owe quite a bit for the new ice machinery.'

'That's paid.'

'I have nine thousand?'

'And the ranch,' said Lee. 'Maybe you can sell the ice plant.'

Adam's face tightened up and lost the dazed smile. 'I still believe it will work,' he said. 'It was a whole lot of accidents. I'm going to keep the ice plant. Cold does preserve things. Besides, the plant makes some money. Maybe I can figure something out.'

'Try not to figure something that costs money,' said Lee. 'I would hate to leave my gas stove.'

III

The twins felt Adam's failure very deeply. They were fifteen years old and they had known so long that they were sons of a wealthy man that the feeling was hard to lose. If only the affair had not been a kind of carnival it would not have been so bad. They remembered the big placards on the freight cars with horror. If the business men made fun of Adam, the high-school group was much more cruel. Overnight it became the thing to refer to the boys as 'Aron and Cal Lettuce', or simply as 'Lettuce-head'.

Aron discussed his problem with Abra. 'It's going to make a big difference,' he told her.

Abra had grown to be a beautiful girl. Her breasts were rising with the leaven of her years, and her face had the calm and warmth of beauty. She had gone beyond prettiness. She was strong and sure and feminine.

She looked at his worried face and asked, 'Why is it going to make a difference?'

'Well, one thing, I think we're poor.'

'You would have worked anyway.'

'You know I want to go to college.'

'You still can. I'll help you. Did your father lose all his money?'

'I don't know. That's what they say.'

'Who is "they"?' Abra asked.

'Why, everybody. And maybe your father and mother won't want you to marry me.'

'Then I won't tell them about it,' said Abra.

'You're pretty sure of yourself.'

'Yes,' she said, 'I'm pretty sure of myself. Will you kiss me?'

'Right here? Right in the street?'

'Why not?'

'Everybody'd see.'

'I want them to,' said Abra.

Aron said, 'No. I don't like to make things public like that.'

She stepped around in front of him and stopped him. 'You look here, mister. You kiss me now.'

415

'Why?'

She said slowly, 'So everybody will know that I'm Mrs Lettuce-head.'

He gave her a quick embarrassed peck and then forced her beside him again. 'Maybe I ought to call it off myself,' he said.

'What do you mean?'

'Well, I'm not good enough for you now. I'm just another poor kid. You think I haven't seen the difference in your father?'

'You're just crazy,' Abra said. And she frowned a little because she had seen the difference in her father too.

They went into Bell's candy store and sat at a table. The rage was celery tonic that year. The year before it had been root-beer ice-cream sodas.

Abra stirred bubbles delicately with her straw and thought how her father had changed since the lettuce failure. He had said to her, 'Don't you think it would be wise to see someone else for a change?'

'But I'm engaged to Aron.'

'Engaged?' he snorted at her. 'Since when do children get engaged? You'd better look around a little. There are other fish in the sea.'

And she remembered that recently there had been references to suitability of families and once a hint that some people couldn't keep a scandal hidden for ever. This had happened only when Adam was reputed to have lost all of his money.

She leaned across the table. 'You know, what we could really do is so simple it will make you laugh.'

'What?'

'We could run your father's ranch. My father says it's beautiful land.'

'No,' Aron said quickly.

'Why not?'

'I'm not going to be a farmer and you're not going to be a farmer's wife.'

'I'm going to be Aron's wife, no matter what he is.'

'I'm not going to give up college,' he said.

'I'll help you,' Abra said again.

'Where would you get the money?'

'Steal it,' she said.

'I want to get out of this town,' he said. 'Everybody's sneering at me. I can't stand it here.'

'They'll forget it pretty soon.'

'No, they won't either. I don't want to stay two years more to finish high school.'

'Do you want to go away from me, Aron?'

'No. Oh damn it, why did he have to mess with things he doesn't know about?'

Abra reproved him. 'Don't you blame your father. If it had worked everybody'd been bowing to him.'

'Well, it didn't work. He sure fixed me. I can't hold up my head. By God! I hate him!'

Abra said sternly, 'Aron! You stop talking like that!'

'How do I know he didn't lie about my mother?'

Abra's face reddened with anger. 'You ought to be spanked,' she said. 'If it wasn't in front of everybody I'd spank you myself.' She looked at his beautiful face, twisted now with rage and frustration, and suddenly she changed her tactics. 'Why don't you ask about your mother? Just come right out and ask him.'

'I can't, I promised you.'

'You only promised not to say what I told you.'

'Well, if I asked him he'd want to know where I heard.'

'All right,' she cried, 'you're a spoiled baby! I let you out of your promise. Go ahead and ask him.'

'I don't know if I will or not.'

'Sometimes I want to kill you,' she said. 'But, Aron – I do love you so. I do love you so.' There was giggling from the stools in front of the soda fountain. Their voices had risen and they were overheard by their peers. Aron blushed and tears of anger started in his eyes. He ran out of the store and plunged away up the street.

Abra calmly picked up her purse and straightened her skirt and brushed it with her hand. She walked calmly over to Mr Bell and paid for the celery tonics. On her way to the door she stopped by the giggling group. 'You let him alone,' she said coldly. She walked on, and a falsetto followed her – 'Oh, Aron, I do love you so.'

In the street she broke into a run to try to catch up with Aron, but she couldn't find him. She called on the telephone. Lee said that Aron had not come home. But Aron was in his bedroom, lapped in resentments – Lee had seen him creep in and close his door behind him.

Abra walked up and down the streets of Salinas, hoping to catch sight of him. She was angry at him, but she was also bewilderingly lonely. Aron hadn't ever run away from her before. Abra had lost her gift for being alone.

Cal had to learn loneliness. For a very short time he tried to join Abra and Aron, but they didn't want him. He was jealous and tried to attract the girl to himself and failed.

His studies he found easy and not greatly interesting. Aron had to work harder to learn, wherefore Aron had a greater sense of accomplishment when he did learn, and he developed a respect for learning out of all proportion with the quality of the learning. Cal drifted through. He didn't care much for the sports at school or for the activities. His growing restlessness drove him out at night. He grew tall and rangy, and always there was the darkness about him.

CHAPTER 38

I

FROM HIS first memory Cal had craved warmth and affection, just as everyone does. If he had been an only child or if Aron had been a different kind of boy, Cal might have achieved his relationship normally and easily. But from the very first people were won instantly to Aron by his beauty and his simplicity. Cal very naturally competed for attention and affection in the only way he knew – by trying to imitate Aron. And what was charming in the blond ingenuousness of Aron became suspicious and unpleasant in the dark-faced, slit-eyed Cal. And since he was pretending, his performance was not convincing. Where Aron was received, Cal was rebuffed for doing or saying exactly the same thing.

And as a few strokes on the nose will make a puppy head-shy, so a few rebuffs will make a boy shy all over. But whereas a puppy will cringe away or roll on its back, grovelling, a little boy may cover his shyness with nonchalance, with bravado, or with secrecy. And once a boy has suffered rejection, he will find rejection even where it does not exist – or, worse, will draw it forth from people simply by expecting it.

In Cal the process had been so long and so slow that he felt no strangeness. He had built a wall of self-sufficiency around himself, strong enough to defend him against the world. If his wall had any weak places they may have been on the sides nearest Aron and Lee, and particularly nearest Adam. Perhaps in his father's very unawareness Cal had felt safety. Not being noticed at all was better than being noticed adversely.

When he was quite small Cal had discovered a secret. If he moved very quietly to where his father was sitting and if he leaned very lightly against his father's knee, Adam's hand would rise automatically and his fingers would caress Cal's shoulder. It is probable that Adam did not even know he did it, but the caress brought such a raging flood of emotion to the boy that he saved this special joy and used it only when he needed it. It was a magic to be depended upon. It was the ceremonial symbol of a dogged adoration.

Things do not change with a change of scene. In Salinas, Cal had no more friends than he had in King City. Associates he had, and authority and some admiration, but friends he did not have. He lived alone and walked alone.

11

If Lee knew that Cal left the house at night and returned very late, he gave no sign, since he couldn't do anything about it. The night constables sometimes saw him walking alone. Chief Heiserman made it a point to speak to the truant officer, who assured him that Cal not only had no record for playing hooky but actually was a very good student. The chief knew Adam, of course, and since Cal broke no windows and caused no disturbance he told the constables to keep their eyes open but to let the boy alone unless he got into trouble.

Old Tom Watson caught up with Cal one night and asked, 'Why do you walk around so much at night?'

'I'm not bothering anybody,' said Cal defensively.

'I know you're not. But you ought to be home in bed.'

'I'm not sleepy,' said Cal, and this didn't make any sense at all to Old Tom, who couldn't remember any time in his whole life when he wasn't sleepy. The boy looked in on the fan-tan games in Chinatown, but he didn't play. It was a mystery, but then fairly simple things were mysteries to Tom Watson and he preferred to leave them that way.

On his walks Cal often recalled the conversation between Lee and Adam he had heard on the ranch. He wanted to dig out the truth. And his knowledge accumulated slowly, a reference heard in the street, the gibing talk in the pool-hall. If Aron had heard the fragments he would not have noticed, but Cal collected them. He knew that his mother was not dead. He knew also,

419

both from the first conversation and from the talk he heard, that Aron was not likely to be pleased at discovering her.

One night Cal ran into Rabbit Holman, who was up from San Ardo on his semi-annual drunk. Rabbit greeted Cal effusively, as a country man always greets an acquaintance in a strange place. Rabbit, drinking from a pint flask in the alley behind the Abbot House, told Cal all the news he could think of. He had sold a piece of his land at a fine price and he was in Salinas to celebrate, and celebration meant the whole shebang. He was going down the Line and show the whores what a real man could do.

Cal sat quietly beside him, listening. When the whisky got low in Rabbit's pint Cal slipped away and got Louis Schneider to buy him another one. And Rabbit put down his empty pint and reached for it again and came up with the full pint.

'Funny,' he said, 'thought I had only one. Well, it's a good mistake.'

Half way down the second pint Rabbit had not only forgotten who Cal was but how old he was. He remembered, however, that his companion was his very dear old friend.

'Tell you what, George,' he said. 'You let me get a little more of this here lead in my pencil and you and me will go down the Line. Now don't say you can't afford it. The whole shebang's on me. Did I tell you I sold forty acres? Wasn't no good neither.'

And he said, 'Harry, tell you what let's do. Let's keep away from them two-bit whores. We'll go to Kate's place. Costs high, ten bucks, but what the hell! They got a circus down there. Ever seen a circus, Harry? Well, it's a lulu. Kate sure knows her stuff. You remember who Kate is, don't you, George? She's Adam Trask's wife, mother of them damn twins. Jesus! I never forget the time she shot him and ran away. Plugged him in the shoulder and just run off. Well, she wasn't no good as a wife but she's sure as hell a good whore. Funny too – you know how they say a whore makes a good wife? Ain't nothing new for them to experiment with. Help me up a little, will you, Harry? What was I saying?'

'Circus,' said Cal softly.

'Oh, yeah. Well, this circus of Kate's will pop your eyes out. Know what they do?'

Cal walked a little behind so that Rabbit would not notice him. Rabbit told what they did. And what they did wasn't what made Cal sick. That just seemed to him silly. It was the men who watched. Seeing Rabbit's face under the street-lights, Cal knew what the watchers at the circus would look like.

They went through the overgrown yard and up on the unpainted porch. Although Cal was tall for his age he walked high on his toes. The guardian of the door didn't look at him very closely. The dim room with its low secret lamps and the nervous waiting men concealed his presence.

III

Always before, Cal had wanted to build a dark accumulation of things seen and things heard – a kind of a warehouse of materials that, like obscure tools, might come in handy, but after the visit to Kate's he felt a desperate need for help.

One night Lee, tapping away at his typewriter, heard a quiet knock on his door and let Cal in. The boy sat down on the edge of the bed, and Lee let his thin body down in the Morris chair. He was amused that a chair could give him so much pleasure. Lee folded his hands over his stomach as though he wore Chinese sleeves and waited patiently. Cal was looking at a spot in the air right over Lee's head.

Cal spoke softly and rapidly. 'I know where my mother is and what she's doing. I saw her.'

Lee's mind was a convulsive prayer for guidance. 'What do you want to know?' he asked softly.

'I haven't thought yet. I'm trying to think. Would you tell me the truth?'

'Of course.'

The questions whirling in Cal's head were so bewildering he had trouble picking one out. 'Does my father know?'

'Yes.'

'Why did he say she was dead?'

'To save you from pain.'

Cal considered. 'What did my father do to make her leave?'

'He loved her with his whole mind and body. He gave her everything he could imagine.'

'Did she shoot him?'

'Yes.'

'Why?'

'Because he didn't want her to go away.'

'Did he ever hurt her?'

'Not that I know of. It wasn't in him to hurt her.'

'Lee, why did she do it?'

421

'I don't know.'

'Don't know or won't say?'

'Don't know.'

Cal was silent for so long that Lee's fingers began to creep a little, holding to his wrists. He was relieved when Cal spoke again. The boy's tone was different. There was a pleading in it.

'Lee, you knew her. What was she like?'

Lee sighed and his hands relaxed. 'I can only say what I think. I may be wrong.'

'Well, what did you think?'

'Cal,' he said, 'I've thought about it for a great many hours and I still don't know. She is a mystery. It seems to me that she is not like other people. There is something she lacks. Kindness maybe, or conscience. You can only understand people if you feel them in yourself. And I can't feel her. The moment I think about her my feeling goes into darkness. I don't know what she wanted or what she was after. She was full of hatred, but why or towards what I don't know. It's a mystery. And her hatred wasn't healthy. It wasn't angry. It was heartless. I don't know that it is good to talk to you like this.'

'I need to know.'

'Why? Didn't you feel better before you knew?'

'Yes. But I can't stop now.'

'You're right,' said Lee. 'When the first innocence goes, you can't stop – unless you're a hypocrite or a fool. But I can't tell you any more because I don't know any more.'

Cal said, 'Tell me about my father, then.'

'That I can do,' said Lee. He paused. 'I wonder if anyone can hear us talking? Speak softly.'

'Tell me about him,' said Cal.

'I think your father has in him, magnified, the things his wife lacks. I think in him kindness and conscience are so large that they are almost faults. They trip him up and hinder him.'

'What did he do when she left?'

'He died,' said Lee. 'He walked around but he was dead. And only recently has he come half to life again.' Lee saw a strange new expression on Cal's face. The eyes were open wider, and the mouth, ordinarily tight and muscular, was relaxed. In his face, now for the first time, Lee could see Aron's face in spite of the different colouring. Cal's shoulders were shaking a little, like a muscle too long held under strain.

'What is it?' Lee asked.

'I love him,' Cal said.

'I love him too,' said Lee. 'I guess I couldn't have stayed around so long if I hadn't. He is not smart in a worldly sense, but he's a good man. Maybe the best man I have ever known.'

Cal stood up suddenly. 'Good night, Lee,' he said.

'Now you just wait a moment. Have you told anyone?'

'No.'

'Not Aron – no, of course you wouldn't.'

'Suppose he finds out?'

'Then you'd have to stand by to help him. Don't go yet. When you leave this room we may not be able to talk again. You may dislike me for knowing you know the truth. Tell me this – do you hate your mother?'

'Yes,' said Cal.

'I wonder,' said Lee. 'I don't think your father ever hated her. He had only sorrow.'

Cal drifted towards the door, slowly, softly. He shoved his fists deep in his pockets. 'It's like you said about knowing people. I hate her because I know why she went away. I know – because I've got her in me.' His head was down and his voice was heart-broken.

Lee jumped up. 'You stop that!' he said sharply. 'You hear me? Don't let me catch you doing that. Of course you may have that in you. Everybody has. But you've got the other too. Here – look up! Look at me!'

Cal raised his head and said wearily, 'What do you want?'

'You've got the other too. Listen to me! You wouldn't even be wondering if you didn't have it. Don't you dare take the lazy way. It's too easy to excuse yourself because of your ancestry. Don't let me catch you doing it! Now – look close at me so you will remember. Whatever you do, it will be you who do it – not your mother.'

'Do you believe that, Lee?'

'Yes, I believe it, and you'd better believe it or I'll break every bone in your body.'

After Cal had gone Lee went back to his chair. He thought ruefully, 'I wonder what happened to my Oriental repose.'

IV

Cal's discovery of his mother was more a verification than a new thing to him. For a long time he had known without details that the cloud was there. And his reaction was twofold. He had an almost pleasant sense of power in knowing, and he could evaluate actions and expressions, could interpret vague references, could even dip up and reorganize the past. But these did not compensate for the pain in his knowledge.

His body was rearranging itself towards manhood, and he was shaken by the veering winds of adolescence. One moment he was dedicated and pure and devoted; the next he wallowed in filth; and the next he grovelled in shame and emerged re-dedicated.

His discovery sharpened all of his emotions. It seemed to him that he was unique, having such a heritage. He could not quite believe Lee's words or conceive that other boys were going through the same thing.

The circus at Kate's remained with him. At one moment the memory inflamed his mind and body with pubescent fire, and the next moment nauseated him with revulsion and loathing.

He looked at his father more closely and saw perhaps more sadness and frustration in Adam than may have been there. And in Cal there grew up a passionate love for his father and a wish to protect him and to make up to him for the things he had suffered. In Cal's own sensitized mind that suffering was unbearable. He blundered into the bathroom while Adam was bathing and saw the ugly bullet scar and heard himself ask against his will, 'Father, what's that scar?'

Adam's fingers went up as though to conceal the scar. He said, 'It's an old wound, Cal. I was in the Indian campaigns. I'll tell you about it some time.'

Cal, watching Adam's face, had seen his mind leap into the past for a lie. Cal didn't hate the lie but the necessity for telling it. Cal lied for reasons of profit of one kind or another. To be driven to a lie seemed shameful to him. He wanted to shout, 'I know how you got it and it's all right.' But, of course, he did not. 'I'd like to hear about it,' he said.

Aron was caught in the roil of change too, but his impulses were more sluggish than Cal's. His body did not scream at him so shrilly. His passions took a religious direction. He decided on the ministry for his future. He attended all services in the Episcopal church, helped with the flowers and leaves at feast times, and spent many hours with the young and curly-haired clergyman, Mr Rolf. Aron's training in worldliness was gained from a young man of no experience, which gave him the ability for generalization only the inexperienced can have.

Aron was confirmed in the Episcopal church and took his place in the choir on Sundays. Abra followed him. Her feminine mind knew such things were necessary but unimportant.

It was natural that the convert Aron should work on Cal. First Aron prayed silently for Cal, but finally he approached him. He denounced Cal's godlessness, demanded his reformation.

Cal might have tried to go along if his brother had been more clever. But Aron had reached a point of passionate purity that made everyone else foul. After a few lectures Cal found him unbearably smug and told him so. It was a relief to both of them when Aron abandoned his brother to eternal damnation.

Aron's religion inevitably took a sexual turn. He spoke to Abra of the necessity for abstinence and decided that he would live a life of celibacy. Abra in her wisdom agreed with him, feeling and hoping that this phase would pass. Celibacy was the only state she had known. She wanted to marry Aron and bear any number of his children, but for the time being she did not speak of it. She had never been jealous before, but now she began to find in herself an instinctive and perhaps justified hatred for the Reverend Mr Rolf.

Cal watched his brother triumph over sins he had never committed. He thought sardonically of telling him about his mother, to see how he would handle it, but he withdrew the thought quickly. He didn't think Aron could handle it at all.

CHAPTER 39

I

AT INTERVALS Salinas suffered from a mild eructation of morality. The process never varied much. One burst was like another. Sometimes it started in the pulpit and sometimes with a new ambitious president of the Women's Civic Club. Gambling was invariably the sin to be eradicated. There were certain advantages in attacking gambling. One could discuss it, which was not true of prostitution. It was an obvious evil and most of the games were operated by Chinese. There was little chance of treading on the toes of a relative.

From church and club the town's two newspapers caught fire. Editorials demanded a clean-up. The police agreed but pleaded short-handedness and tried for increased budget and sometimes succeeded.

When it got to the editorial stage everyone knew the cards

were down. What followed was as carefully produced as a ballet. The police got ready, the gambling houses got ready, and the papers set up congratulatory editorials in advance. Then came the raid, deliberate and sure. Twenty or more Chinese, imported from Pajaro, a few bums, six or eight drummers, who, being strangers, were not warned, fell into the police net, were booked, jailed, and in the morning fined and released. The town relaxed in its new spotlessness and the houses lost only one night of business plus the fines. It is one of the triumphs of the human that he can know a thing and still not believe it.

In the autumn of 1916 Cal was watching the fan-tan game at Shorty Lim's one night when the raid scooped him up. In the dark no one noticed him, and the Chief was embarrassed to find him in the tank in the morning. The Chief telephoned Adam, got him up from his breakfast. Adam walked the two blocks to the City Hall, picked up Cal, crossed the street to the post office for his mail, and then the two walked home.

Lee had kept Adam's eggs warm and had fried two for Cal.

Aron walked through the dining-room on his way to school. 'Want me to wait for you?' he asked Cal.

'No,' said Cal. He kept his eyes down and ate his eggs.

Adam had not spoken except to say, 'Come along!' at the City Hall after he had thanked the Chief.

Cal gulped down a breakfast he did not want, darting glances up through his eyelashes at his father's face. He could make nothing of Adam's expression. It seemed at once puzzled and angry and thoughtful and sad.

Adam stared down into his coffee-cup. The silence grew until it had the weight of age so hard to lift aside.

Lee looked in. 'Coffee?' he asked.

Adam shook his head slowly. Lee withdrew and this time closed the kitchen door.

In the clock-ticking silence Cal began to be afraid. He felt a strength flowing out of his father he had never known was there. Itching prickles of agony ran up his legs, and he was afraid to move to restore the circulation. He knocked his fork against his plate to make a noise and the clatter was swallowed up. The clock struck nine deliberate strokes and they were swallowed up.

As the fear began to chill, resentment took its place. So might a trapped fox feel anger at the paw which held him to the trap.

Suddenly Cal jumped up. He hadn't known he was going to move. He shouted and he hadn't known he was going to speak.

He cried, 'Do what you're going to do to me! Go ahead! Get it over!'

And his shout was sucked into the silence.

Adam slowly raised his head. It is true Cal had never looked into his father's eyes before, and it is true that many people never look into their father's eyes. Adam's irises were light blue with dark lines leading into the vortices of the pupils. And deep down in each pupil Cal saw his own face reflected, as though two Cals looked out at him.

Adam said slowly, 'I've failed you, haven't I?'

It was worse than an attack. Cal faltered, 'What do you mean?'

'You were picked up in a gambling house. I don't know how you got there, what you were doing there, why you went there.'

Cal sat limply down and looked at his plate.

'Do you gamble, son?'

'No, sir. I was just watching.'

'Had you been there before?'

'Yes, sir. Many times.'

'Why do you go?'

'I don't know. I get restless at night – like an alley cat, I guess.' He thought of Kate and his weak joke seemed horrible to him. 'When I can't sleep I walk around,' he said, 'to try to blot it out.'

Adam considered his words, inspected each one. 'Does your brother walk around too?'

'Oh, no, sir. He wouldn't think of it. He's – he's not restless.'

'You see, I don't know,' said Adam. 'I don't know anything about you.'

Cal wanted to throw his arms about his father, to hug him and to be hugged by him. He wanted some wild demonstration of sympathy and love. He picked up his wooden napkin ring and thrust his forefinger through it. 'I'd tell you if you asked,' he said softly.

'I didn't ask, I didn't ask! I'm as bad a father as my father was.'

Cal had never heard this tone in Adam's voice. It was hoarse and breaking with warmth and he fumbled among his words, feeling for them in the dark.

'My father made a mould and forced me into it,' Adam said. 'I was a bad casting but I couldn't be re-melted. Nobody can be re-melted. And so I remained a bad casting.'

427

Cal said, 'Sir, don't be sorry. You've had too much of that.'

'Have I? Maybe – but maybe the wrong kind. I don't know my sons. I wonder whether I could learn.'

'I'll tell you anything you want to know. Just ask me.'

'Where would I start? Right at the beginning?'

'Are you sad or mad because I was in jail?'

To Cal's surprise Adam laughed. 'You were just there, weren't you? You didn't do nothing wrong.'

'Maybe being there was wrong.' Cal wanted a blame for himself.

'One time I was just there,' said Adam. 'I was a prisoner for nearly a year for just being there.'

Cal tried to absorb this heresy. 'I don't believe it,' he said.

'Sometimes I don't either, but I know that when I escaped I robbed a store and stole some clothes.'

'I don't believe it,' Cal said weakly, but the warmth, the closeness, was so delicious that he clung to it. He breathed shallowly so that the warmth might not be disturbed.

Adam said, 'Do you remember Samuel Hamilton? – sure you do. When you were a baby he told me I was a bad father. He hit me, knocked me down, to impress it on me.'

'That old man?'

'He was a tough old man. And now I know what he meant. I'm the same as my father was. He didn't allow me to be a person, and I haven't seen my sons as people. That's what Samuel meant.' He looked right into Cal's eyes and smiled, and Cal ached with affection for him.

Cal said, 'We don't think you're a bad father.'

'Poor things,' said Adam. 'How could you know? You've never had any other kind.'

'I'm glad I was in jail,' said Cal.

'So am I. So am I.' He laughed. 'We've both been in jail – we can talk together.' A gaiety grew in him. 'Maybe you can tell me what kind of a boy you are – can you?'

'Yes, sir.'

'Will you?'

'Yes, sir.'

'Well, tell me. You see, there's a responsibility in being a person. It's more than just taking up space where air would be. What are you like?'

'No joke?' Cal asked shyly.

'No joke – oh, surely, no joke. Tell me about yourself – that is, if you want to.'

Cal began, 'Well – I'm —' He stopped. 'It's not so easy when you try,' he said.

'I guess it would be – maybe impossible. Tell me about your brother.'

'What do you want to know about him?'

'What you think of him, I guess. That's all you could tell me.'

Cal said, 'He's good. He doesn't do bad things. He doesn't think bad things.'

'Now you're telling me about yourself.'

'Sir?'

'You're saying you do and think bad things.'

Cal's cheeks reddened. 'Well, I do.'

'Very bad things?'

'Yes, sir. Do you want me to tell?'

'No, Cal. You've told. Your voice tells and your eyes tell you're at war with yourself. But you shouldn't be ashamed. It's awful to be ashamed. Is Aron ever ashamed?'

'He doesn't do anything to be ashamed of.'

Adam leaned forward. 'Are you sure?'

'Pretty sure.'

'Tell me, Cal – do you protect him?'

'How do you mean, sir?'

'I mean like this – if you heard something bad or cruel or ugly, would you keep it from him?'

'I – I think so.'

'You think he's too weak to bear things you can bear?'

'It's not that, sir. He's good. He's really good. He never does anyone harm. He never says bad things about anyone. He's not mean and he never complains and he's brave. He doesn't like to fight but he will.'

'You love your brother, don't you?'

'Yes, sir. And I do bad things to him. I cheat him and I fool him. Sometimes I hurt him for no reason at all.'

'And then you're miserable?'

'Yes, sir.'

'Is Aron ever miserable?'

'I don't know. When I didn't want to join the Church he felt bad. And once when Abra got angry and said she hated him he felt awful bad. He was sick. He had fever. Don't you remember? Lee sent for the doctor.'

Adam said with wonder, 'I could live with you and not know any of these things! Why was Abra mad?'

Cal said, 'I don't know if I ought to tell.'

'I don't want you to, then.'

'It's nothing bad. I guess it's all right. You see, sir, Aron wants to be a minister. Mr Rolf – well, he likes High Church, and Aron liked that, and he thought maybe he would never get married and maybe go to a retreat.'

'Like a monk, you mean?'

'Yes, sir.'

'And Abra didn't like that?'

'Like it? She got spitting mad. She can get mad sometimes. She took Aron's fountain pen and threw it on the sidewalk and tramped on it. She said she'd wasted half her life on Aron.'

Adam laughed. 'How old is Abra?'

'Nearly fifteen. But she's – well, more than that some ways.'

'I should say she is. What did Aron do?'

'He just got quiet but he felt awful bad.'

Adam said, 'I guess you could have taken her away from him then.'

'Abra is Aron's girl,' said Cal.

Adam looked deeply into Cal's eyes. Then he called, 'Lee!' There was no answer. 'Lee!' he called again. He said, 'I didn't hear him go out. I want some fresh coffee.'

Cal jumped up. 'I'll make it.'

'Say,' said Adam, 'you should be in school.'

'I don't want to go.'

'You ought to go. Aron went.'

'I'm happy,' Cal said. 'I want to be with you.'

Adam looked down at his hands. 'Make the coffee,' he said softly, and his voice was shy.

When Cal was in the kitchen Adam looked inward at himself with wonder. His nerves and muscles throbbed with an excited hunger. His fingers yearned to grasp, his legs to run. His eyes avidly brought the room into focus. He saw the chairs, the pictures, the red roses on the carpet, and new sharp things – almost people things but friendly things. And in his brain was born sharp appetite for the future – a pleased warm anticipation, as though the coming minutes and weeks must bring delight. He felt a dawn emotion, with a lovely day to slip golden and quiet over him. He laced his fingers behind his head and stretched his legs out stiff.

In the kitchen Cal urged on the water heating in the coffee-pot, and yet he was pleased to be waiting. A miracle once it is familiar is no longer a miracle; Cal had lost his wonder at the golden relationship with his father but the pleasure remained.

The poison of loneliness and the gnawing envy of the unlonely had gone out of him, and his person was clean and sweet, and he knew it was. He dredged up an old hatred to test himself, and he found the hatred gone. He wanted to serve his father, to give him some great gift, to perform some huge task in honour of his father.

The coffee boiled over and Cal spent minutes cleaning up the stove. He said to himself, 'I wouldn't have done this yesterday.'

Adam smiled at him when he carried in the steaming pot. Adam sniffed and said, 'That's a smell could raise me out of a concrete grave.'

'It boiled over,' said Cal.

'It has to boil over to taste good,' Adam said. 'I wonder where Lee went.'

'Maybe to his room. Shall I look?'

'No. He'd have answered.'

'Sir, when I finish school, will you let me run the ranch?'

'You're planning early. How about Aron?'

'He wants to go to college. Don't tell him I told you. Let him tell you, and you be surprised.'

'Why, that's fine,' said Adam. 'But don't you want to go to college too?'

'I bet I could make money on the ranch – enough to pay Aron's way through college.'

Adam sipped his coffee. 'That's a generous thing,' he said. 'I don't know whether I ought to tell you this, but – well, when I asked you earlier what kind of boy Aron was, you defended him so badly I thought you might dislike him or even hate him.'

'I have hated him,' Cal said vehemently. 'And I've hurt him too. But, sir, can I tell you something? I don't hate him now. I won't ever hate him again. I don't think I will hate anyone, not even my mother — ' He stopped, astonished at his slip, and his mind froze up tight and helpless.

Adam looked straight ahead. He rubbed his forehead with the palm of his hand. Finally he said quietly, 'You know about your mother.' It was not a question.

'Yes – yes, sir.

'All about her?'

'Yes, sir.'

Adam leaned back in his chair. 'Does Aron know?'

'Oh, no! No – no, sir. He doesn't know.'

'Why do you say it that way?'

'I wouldn't dare to tell him.'

'Why not?'

Cal said brokenly, 'I don't think he could stand it. He hasn't enough badness in him to stand it.' He wanted to continue, ' – any more than you could, sir,' but he left the last unsaid.

Adam's face looked weary. He moved his head from side to side. 'Cal, listen to me. Do you think there's any chance of keeping Aron from knowing? Think carefully.'

Cal said, 'He doesn't go near places like that. He's not like me.'

'Suppose someone told him?'

'I don't think he would believe it, sir. I think he would lick whoever told him and think it was a lie.'

'You've been there?'

'Yes, sir. I had to know.' And Cal went on excitedly, 'If he went away to college and never lived in this town again —'

Adam nodded. 'Yes. That might be. But he has two more years here.'

'Maybe I could make him hurry it up and finish in one year. He's smart.'

'But you're smarter?'

'A different kind of smart,' said Cal.

Adam seemed to grow until he filled one side of the room. His face was stern and his blue eyes sharp and penetrating. 'Cal!' he said harshly.

'Sir?'

'I trust you, son,' said Adam.

I I

Adam's recognition brought a ferment of happiness to Cal. He walked on the balls of his feet. He smiled more often than he frowned, and the secret darkness was seldom on him.

Lee, noticing the change in him, asked quietly, 'You haven't found a girl, have you?'

'Girl? No. Who wants a girl?'

'Everybody,' said Lee.

And Lee asked Adam, 'Do you know what's got into Cal?'

Adam said, 'He knows about her.'

'Does he?' Lee stayed out of trouble. 'Well, you remember I thought you should have told them.'

'I didn't tell him. He knew.'

'What do you think of that!' said Lee. 'But that's not information to make a boy hum when he studies and play catch with his cap when he walks. How about Aron?'

'I'm afraid of that,' said Adam. 'I don't think I want him to now.'

'It might be too late.'

'I might have a talk with Aron. Kind of feel around.'

Lee considered. 'Something's happened to you too.'

'Has it? I guess it has,' said Adam.

But humming and sailing his cap, driving quickly through his school work, were only the smallest of Cal's activities. In his new joy he appointed himself guardian of his father's content. It was true what he had said about not feeling hatred for his mother. But that did not change the fact that she had been the instrument of Adam's hurt and shame. Cal reasoned that what she could do before, she could do again. He set himself to learn all he could about her. A known enemy is less dangerous, less able to surprise.

At night he was drawn to the house across the tracks. Sometimes in the afternoon he lay hidden in the tall weeds across the street, watching the place. He saw the girls come out, dressed sombrely, even severely. They left the house always in pairs, and Cal followed them with his eyes to the corner of Castroville Street, where they turned left towards Main Street. He discovered that if you didn't know where they had come from you couldn't tell what they were. But he was not waiting for the girls to come out. He wanted to see his mother in the light of day. He found that Kate emerged every Monday at one-thirty.

Cal made arrangements in school, by doing extra and excellent work, to make up for his absences on Monday afternoons. To Aron's questions he replied that he was working on a surprise and was duty bound to tell no one. Aron was not much interested anyway. In his self-immersion Aron soon forgot the whole thing.

Cal, after he had followed Kate several times, knew her route. She always went to the same places – first to the Monterey County Bank, where she was admitted behind the shining bars that defended the safe-deposit vault. She spent fifteen or twenty minutes there. Then she moved slowly along Main Street, looking in the store windows. She stepped into Porter and Irvine's and looked at dresses and sometimes made a purchase – elastic, safety pins, a veil, a pair of gloves. About two-fifteen she entered Minnie Franken's beauty parlour, stayed an hour, and came out with her hair pinned up in tight curls and a silk scarf around her head and tied under her chin.

At three-thirty she climbed the stairs to the offices over the

Farmer's Mercantile and went into the consulting-room of Dr Rosen. When she came down from the doctor's office she stopped for a moment at Bell's candy store and bought a two-pound box of mixed chocolates. She never varied the route. From Bell's she went directly back to Castroville Street and thence to her house.

There was nothing strange about her clothing. She dressed exactly like any well-to-do Salinas woman out shopping on a Monday afternoon – except that she always wore gloves, which was unusual for Salinas.

The gloves made her hands seem puffed and pudgy. She moved as though she were surrounded by a glass shell. She spoke to no one and seemed to see no one. Occasionally a man turned and looked after her and then nervously went about his business. But for the most part she slipped past like an invisible woman.

For a number of weeks Cal followed Kate. He tried not to attract her attention. And since Kate walked always looking straight ahead, he was convinced that she did not notice him.

When Kate entered her own yard Cal strolled casually by and went home by another route. He could not have said exactly why he followed her, except that he wanted to know all about her.

The eighth week he took the route she completed her journey and went into her overgrown yard as usual.

Cal waited a moment, then strolled past the rickety gate.

Kate was standing behind a tall ragged privet. She said to him coldly, 'What do you want?'

Cal froze in his steps. He was suspended in time, barely breathing. Then he began a practice he had learned when he was very young. He observed and catalogued details outside his main object. He noticed how the wind from the south bent over the new little leaves of the tall privet bush. He saw the muddy path beaten to black mush by many feet, and Kate's feet standing far to the side out of the mud. He heard a switch engine in the Southern Pacific yards discharging steam in shrilly dry spurts. He felt the chill air on the growing fuzz on his cheeks. And all the time he was staring at Kate and she was staring back at him. And he saw in the set and colour of her eyes and hair, even in the way she held her shoulders – high in a kind of semi-shrug – that Aron looked very like her. He did not know his own face well enough to recognize her mouth and little teeth and wide cheekbones as his own. They stood thus for a moment, between two gusts of the southern wind.

Kate said, 'This isn't the first time you've followed me. What do you want?'

He dipped his head. 'Nothing,' he said.

'Who told you to do it?' she demanded.

'Nobody – ma'am.'

'You won't tell me, will you?'

Cal heard his own speech with amazement. It was out before he could stop it. 'You're my mother and I wanted to see what you're like.' It was the exact truth and it had leaped out like the stroke of a snake.

'What? What is this? Who are you?'

'I'm Cal Trask,' he said. He felt the delicate change of balance as when a seesaw moves. His was the upper seat now. Although her expression had not changed Cal knew she was on the defensive.

She looked at him closely, observed every feature. A dim remembered picture of Charles leaped into her mind. Suddenly she said, 'Come with me!' She turned and walked up the path, keeping well to the side, out of the mud.

Cal hesitated only for a moment before following her up the steps. He remembered the big dim room, but the rest was strange to him. Kate preceded him down a hall and into her room. As she went past the kitchen entrance she called, 'Tea. Two cups!'

In her room she seemed to have forgotten him. She removed her coat, tugging at the sleeves with reluctant fat gloved fingers. Then she went to a new door cut in the wall in the end of the room where her bed stood. She opened the door and went into a new little lean-to. 'Come in here!' she said. 'Bring that chair with you.'

He followed her into a box of a room. It had no windows, no decorations of any kind. Its walls were painted a dark grey. A solid grey carpet covered the floor. The only furniture in the room was a huge chair puffed with grey silk cushions, a tilted reading-table, and a floor-lamp deeply hooded. Kate pulled the light chain with her gloved hand, holding it deep in the crotch between her thumb and forefinger as though her hand were artificial.

'Close the door!' Kate said.

The light threw a circle on the reading-table and only diffused dimly through the grey room. Indeed the grey walls seemed to suck up the light and destroy it.

Kate settled herself gingerly among the thick down cushions

435

and slowly removed her gloves. The fingers of both hands were bandaged.

Kate said angrily, 'Don't stare. It's arthritis. Oh – so you want to see, do you?' She unwrapped the oily-looking bandage from her right forefinger and stuck the crooked finger under the light. 'There – look at it,' she said. 'It's arthritis.' She whined in pain as she tenderly wrapped the bandage loosely. 'God, those gloves hurt!' she said. 'Sit down.'

Cal crouched on the edge of his chair.

'You'll probably get it,' Kate said. 'My great-aunt had it and my mother was just beginning to get it —' She stopped. The room was very silent.

There was a soft knock on the door. Kate called, 'Is that you, Joe? Set the tray down out there. Joe, are you there?'

A mutter came through the door.

Kate said tonelessly, 'There's a litter in the parlour. Clean it up. Anne hasn't cleaned her room. Give her one more warning. Tell her it's the last. Eva got smart last night. I'll take care of her. And, Joe, tell the cook if he serves carrots again this week he can pack up. Hear me?'

The mutter came through the door.

'That's all,' said Kate. 'The dirty pigs!' she muttered. 'They'd rot if I didn't watch them. Go out and bring in the tea tray.

The bedroom was empty when Cal opened the door. He carried the tray into the lean-to and set it gingerly on the tilted reading-table. It was a large silver tray, and on it were a pewter teapot, two paper-thin white tea-cups, sugar, cream, and an open box of chocolates.

'Pour the tea,' said Kate. 'It hurts my hands.' She put a chocolate in her mouth. 'I saw you looking at this room,' she went on when she had swallowed her candy. 'The light hurts my eyes. I come in her to rest.' She saw Cal's quick glance at her eyes and said with finality, 'The light hurts my eyes.' She said harshly, 'What's the matter? Don't you want tea?'

'No, ma'am,' said Cal. 'I don't like tea.'

She held the thin cup with her bandaged fingers. 'All right. What *do* you want?'

'Nothing, ma'am.'

'Just wanted to look at me?'

'Yes, ma'am.'

'Are you satisfied?'

'Yes, ma'am.'

'How do I look?' She smiled crookedly at him and showed her sharp white little teeth.

'All right.'

'I might have known you'd cover up. Where's your brother?'

'In school, I guess, or home.'

'What's he like?'

'He looks more like you.'

'Oh, he does? Well, *is* he like me?'

'He wants to be a minister,' said Cal.

'I guess that's the way it should be – looks like me and wants to go into the Church. A man can do a lot of damage in the Church. When someone comes here he's got his guard up. But in church a man's wide open.'

'He means it,' said Cal.

She leaned towards him, and her face was alive with interest. 'Fill my cup. Is your brother dull?'

'He's nice,' said Cal.

'I asked you if he's dull.'

'No, ma'am,' said Cal.

She settled back and lifted her cup. 'How's your father?'

'I don't want to talk about him,' Cal said.

'Oh, no! You like him then?'

'I love him,' said Cal.

Kate peered closely at him, and a curious spasm shook her – an aching twist rose in her chest. And then she closed up and her control came back.

'Don't you want some candy?' she asked.

'Yes, ma'am. Why did you do it?'

'Why did I do what?'

'Why did you shoot my father and run away from us?'

'Did he tell you that?'

'No. He didn't tell us.'

She touched one hand with the other and her hands leaped apart as though the contact burned them. She asked, 'Does your father ever have any – girls or young women come to your house?'

'No,' said Cal. 'Why did you shoot him and go away?'

Her cheeks tightened and her mouth straightened, as though a net of muscles took control. She raised her head, and her eyes were cold and shallow.

'You talk older than your age,' she said. 'But you don't talk old enough. Maybe you'd better run along and play – and wipe your nose.'

437

'Sometimes I work my brother over,' he said. 'I make him squirm, I've made him cry. He doesn't know how I do it. I'm smarter than he is. I don't want to do it. It makes me sick.'

Kate picked it up as though it were her own conversation. 'They thought they were so smart,' she said. 'They looked at me and thought they knew about me. And I fooled them. I fooled every one of them. And when they thought they could tell me what to do – oh! that's when I fooled them best. Charles, I really fooled them then.'

'My name is Caleb,' Cal said. 'Caleb got to the Promised Land. That's what Lee says, and it's in the Bible.'

'That's the Chinaman,' Kate said, and she went on eagerly, 'Adam thought he had me. When I was hurt, all broken up, he took me in and he waited on me, cooked for me. He tried to tie me down that way. Most people get tied down that way. They're grateful, they're in debt, and that's the worst kind of handcuffs. But nobody can hold me. I waited and waited until I was strong and then I broke out. Nobody can trap me,' she said. 'I knew what he was doing. I waited.'

The grey room was silent except for her excited wheezing breath.

Cal said, 'Why did you shoot him?'

'Because he tried to stop me. I could have killed him but I didn't. I just wanted him to let me go.'

'Did you ever wish you'd stayed?'

'Christ, no! Even when I was a little girl I could do anything I wanted. They never knew how I did it. Never. They were always so sure they were right. And they never knew – no one ever knew.' A kind of realization came to her. 'Sure, you're my kind. Maybe you're the same. Why wouldn't you be?'

Cal stood up and closed his hands behind his back. He said, 'When you were little, did you' – he paused to get the thought straight – 'did you ever have the feeling like you were missing something? Like as if the others knew something you didn't – like a secret they wouldn't tell you? Did you ever feel that way?'

While he spoke her face began to close against him, and by the time he paused she was cut off and the way open between them was blocked.

She said, 'What am I doing, talking to kids!'

Cal unclasped his hands from behind him and shoved them in his pockets.

'Talking to snot-nosed kids,' she said. 'I must be crazy.'

438

Cal's face was alight with excitement, and his eyes were wide with vision.

Kate said, 'What's the matter with you?'

He stood still, his forehead glistening with sweat, his hands clenched into fists.

Kate, as she had always, drove in the smart but senseless knife of her cruelty. She laughed softly. 'I may have given you some interesting things, like this — ' She held up her crooked hands. 'But if it's epilepsy – fits – you didn't get it from me.' She glanced brightly up at him, anticipating the shock and beginning worry in him.

Cal spoke happily. 'I'm going,' he said. 'I'm going now. It's all right. What Lee said was true.'

'What did Lee say?'

Cal said, 'I was afraid I had you in me.'

'You have,' said Kate.

'No, I haven't. I'm my own. I don't have to be you.'

'How do you know that?' she demanded.

'I just know. It came to me whole. If I'm mean, it's my own mean.'

'This Chinaman has really fed you some pap. What are you looking at me like that for?'

Cal said, 'I don't think the light hurts your eyes. I think you're afraid.'

'Get out!' she cried. 'Go on, get out!'

'I'm going.' He had his hand on the door-knob. 'I don't hate you,' he said. 'But I'm glad you're afraid.'

She tried to shout 'Joe!' but her voice thickened to a croak.

Cal wrenched open the door and slammed it behind him.

Joe was talking to one of the girls in the parlour. They heard the stutter of light quick footsteps. But by the time they looked up a streaking figure had reached the door, opened it, slipped through, and the heavy front door banged. There was only one step on the porch and then a crunch as jumping feet struck earth.

'What in hell was that?' the girl asked.

'God knows,' said Joe. 'Sometimes I think I'm seeing things.'

'Me too,' said the girl. 'Did I tell you Clara's got bugs under her skin?'

'I guess she seen the shadow of the needle,' said Joe. 'Well, the way I figure, the less you know, the better off you are.'

'That's the truth you said there,' the girl agreed.

CHAPTER 40

I

KATE SAT back in her chair against the deep down cushions. Waves of nerves cruised over her body, raising the little hairs and making ridges of icy burn as they went.

She spoke softly to herself. 'Steady now,' she said. 'Quiet down. Don't let it hit you. Don't think for a while. The goddam snot-nose!'

She thought suddenly of the only person who had ever made her feel this panic hatred. It was Samuel Hamilton, with his white beard and his pink cheeks and the laughing eyes that lifted her skin and looked underneath.

With her bandaged forefinger she dug out a slender chain which hung around her neck and pulled the chain's burden up from her bodice. On the chain were strung two safe-deposit keys, a gold watch with a fleur-de-lis pin, and a little steel tube with a ring on its top. Very carefully she unscrewed the top from the tube and, spreading her knees, shook out a gelatine capsule. She held the capsule under the light and saw the white crystals inside – six grains of morphine, a good, sure margin. Very gently she eased the capsule into its tube, screwed on the cap, and dropped the chain inside her dress.

Cal's last words had been repeating themselves over and over in her head. 'I think you're afraid.' She said the words aloud to herself to kill the sound. The rhythm stopped, but a strong picture formed in her mind and she let it form so that she could inspect it again.

II

It was before the lean-to was built. Kate had collected the money Charles had left. The cheque was converted to large notes and the notes in their bales were in the safe-deposit box at the Monterey County Bank.

It was about the time the first pains began to twist her hands. There was enough money now to go away. It was just a matter of getting the most she could out of the house. But also it was better to wait until she felt quite well again.

She never felt quite well again. New York seemed cold and very far away.

A letter came to her signed 'Ethel'. Who the hell was Ethel? Whoever she was, she must be crazy to ask for money. Ethel — there were hundreds of Ethels. Ethels grew on every bush. And this one scrawled illegibly on a lined pad.

Not very long afterwards Ethel came to see Kate, and Kate hardly recognized her.

Kate sat at her desk, watchful, suspicious, and confident. 'It's been a long time,' she said.

Ethel responded like a soldier who comes in his cushion age upon the sergeant who trained him. 'I've been poorly,' she said. Her flesh had thickened and grown heavy all over her. Her clothes had the strained cleanliness that means poverty.

'Where are you — staying now?' Kate asked, and she wondered how soon the old bag would be able to come to the point.

'Southern Pacific Hotel. I got a room.'

'Oh, then you don't work in a house now?'

'I couldn't never get started again,' said Ethel. 'You shouldn't of run me off.' She wiped big tears from the corners of her eyes with the tip of a cotton glove. 'Things are bad,' she said. 'First I had trouble when we got that new judge. Ninety days, and I didn't have no record — not here anyways. I come out of that and I got the old Joe. I didn't know I had it. Give it to a regular — nice fella, worked on the section gang. He got sore an' busted me up, hurt my nose, lost four teeth, an' that new judge he gave me a hundred and eighty. Hell, Kate, you lose all your contacts in a hundred and eighty days. They forget you're alive. I just never could get started.'

Kate nodded her head in cold and shallow sympathy. She knew that Ethel was working up to the bite. Just before it came Kate made a move. She opened her desk drawer and took out some money and held it out to Ethel. 'I never let a friend down,' she said. 'Why don't you go to a new town, start fresh? It might change your luck.'

Ethel tried to keep her fingers from grabbing at the money. She fanned the notes like a poker hand — four tens. Her mouth began to work with emotion.

Ethel said, 'I kind of hoped you'd see your way to let me take more than forty bucks.'

'What do you mean?'

'Didn't you get my letter?'

'What letter?'

'Oh!' said Ethel. 'Well, maybe it got lost in the mail. They don't take no care of things. Anyways, I thought you might look

441

after me. I don't feel good hardly ever. Got a kind of weight dragging my guts down.' She sighed and then she spoke so rapidly that Kate knew it had been rehearsed.

'Well, maybe you remember how I've got like second sight,' Ethel began. 'Always predicting things that come true. Always dreaming stuff and it come out. Fella says I should go in the business. Says I'm a natural medium. You remember that?'

'No,' said Kate, 'I don't.'

'Don't? Well, maybe you never noticed. All the others did. I told 'em lots of things and they come true.'

'What are you trying to say?'

'I had this-here dream. I remember when it was because it was the same night Faye died.' Her eyes flicked up at Kate's cold face. She continued doggedly, 'It rained that night, and it was raining in my dream – anyways, it was wet. Well, in my dream I seen you come out the kitchen door. It wasn't pitch-dark – moon was coming through a little. And the dream thing was you. You went out to the back of the lot and stooped over. I couldn't see what you done. Then you come creeping back.

'Next thing I knew – why, Faye was dead.' She paused and waited for some comment from Kate, but Kate's face was expressionless.

Ethel waited until she was sure Kate would not speak. 'Well, like I said, I always believed in my dreams. It's funny, there wasn't nothing out there except some smashed medicine bottles and a little rubber tit from an eye-dropper.'

Kate said lazily, 'So you took them to a doctor. What did he say had been in the bottles?'

'Oh, I didn't do nothing like that.'

'You should have,' said Kate.

'I don't want to see anybody get in trouble. I've had enough trouble myself. I put that broken glass in an envelope and stuck it away.'

Kate said softly, 'And so you are coming to me for advice?'

'Yes, ma'am.'

'I'll tell you what I think,' said Kate. 'I think you're a worn-out old whore and you've been beaten over the head too many times.'

'Don't you start saying I'm nuts —' Ethel began.

'No, maybe you're not, but you're tired and you're sick. I told you I never let a friend down. You can come back here. You can't work but you can help around, clean and give the cook a

442

hand. You'll have a bed and you'll get your meals. How would that be? And a little spending money.'

Ethel stirred uneasily. 'No, ma'am,' she said. 'I don't think I want to – sleep here. I don't carry that envelope around. I left it with a friend.'

'What *did* you have in mind?'

'Well, I thought if you could see your way to let me have a hundred dollars a month, why, I could make out and maybe get my health back.'

'You said you lived at the Southern Pacific Hotel?'

'Yes, ma'am – and my room is right up the hall from the desk. The night clerk's a friend of mine. He don't never sleep when he's on duty. Nice fella.'

Kate said, 'Don't wet your pants, Ethel. All you've got to worry about is how much does the "nice fella" cost. Now wait a minute.' She counted six more ten-dollar bills from the drawer in front of her and held them out.

'Will it come the first of the month or do I have to come here for it?'

'I'll send it to you,' said Kate. 'And, Ethel,' she continued quietly, 'I still think you ought to have those bottles analysed.'

Ethel clutched the money tightly in her hand. She was bubbling over with triumph and good feeling. It was one of the few things that had ever worked out for her. 'I wouldn't think of doing that,' she said. 'Not unless I had to.'

After she had gone Kate strolled out to the back of the lot behind the house. And even after years she could see from the unevenness of the earth that it must have been pretty thoroughly dug over.

The next morning the judge heard the usual chronicle of small violence and nocturnal greed. He only half listened to the fourth case and at the end of the terse testimony of the complaining witness he asked, 'How much did you lose?'

The dark-haired man said, 'Pretty close to a hundred dollars.'

The judge turned to the arresting officer. 'How much did she have?'

'Ninety-six dollars. She got whisky and cigarettes and some magazines from the night clerk at six o'clock this morning.'

Ethel cried, 'I never seen this guy in my life.'

The judge looked up from his papers. 'Twice for prostitution and now robbery. You're costing too much. I want you out of town by noon.' He turned to the officer. 'Tell the sheriff to run her over the county line.' And he said to Ethel, 'If you come back, I'll give you over to the county for the limit, and that's San Quentin. Do you understand?'

Ethel said, 'Judge, I want to see you alone.'

'Why?'

'I got to see you,' said Ethel. 'This is a frame.'

'Everything's a frame,' said the judge. 'Next.'

While a deputy sheriff drove Ethel to the county line on the bridge over the Pajaro River, the complaining witness strolled down Castroville Street towards Kate's, changed his mind and went back to Kenoe's barber-shop to get a haircut.

III

Ethel's visit did not disturb Kate very much when it happened. She knew about what attention would be paid to a whore with a grievance, and that an analysis of the broken bottles would not show anything recognizable as poison. She had nearly forgotten Faye. The forcible recalling was simply an unpleasant memory.

Gradually, however, she found herself thinking about it. One night when she was checking the items on a grocery bill a thought shot into her mind, shining and winking like a meteor. The thought flashed and went out so quickly that she had to stop what she was doing to try to find it. How was the dark face of Charles involved in the thought? And Sam Hamilton's puzzled and merry eyes? And why did she get a shiver of fear from the flashing thought?

She gave it up and went back to her work, but the face of Charles was behind her, looking over her shoulder. Her fingers began to hurt her. She put the accounts away and made a tour through the house. It was a slow, listless night – a Tuesday night. There weren't even enough customers to put on the circus.

Kate knew how the girls felt about her. They were desperately afraid of her. She kept them that way. It was probable that they hated her, and that didn't matter either. But they trusted her, and that did matter. If they followed the rules she laid down, followed them exactly, Kate would take care of them and protect them. There was no love involved and no respect. She never rewarded them and she punished an offender only twice before she removed her. The girls did have the security of knowing that they would not be punished without cause.

As Kate walked about, the girls became elaborately casual. Kate knew about that too and expected it. But on this side she

444

felt that she was not alone. Charles seemed to walk to the side and behind her.

She went through the dining-room and into the kitchen, opened the ice-box and looked in. She lifted the cover of the garbage can and inspected it for waste. She did this every night, but this night she carried some extra charge.

When she had left the parlour the girls looked at each other and raised their shoulders in bewilderment. Eloise, who was talking to the dark-haired Joe, said, 'Anything the matter?'

'Not that I know of. Why?'

'I don't know. She seems nervous.'

'Well, there was some kind of rat race.'

'What was it?'

'Wait a minute!' said Joe. 'I don't know and you don't know.'

'I get it. Mind my own business.'

'You're goddam right,' said Joe. 'Let's keep it that way, shall we?'

'I don't want to know,' said Eloise.

'Now you're talking,' Joe said.

Kate ranged back from her tour. 'I'm going to bed,' she said to Joe. 'Don't call me unless you have to.'

'Anything I can do?'

'Yes, make me a pot of tea. Did you press that dress, Eloise?'

'Yes, ma'am.'

'You didn't do it very well.'

'Yes, ma'am.'

Kate was restless. She put all of her papers neatly in the pigeonholes of her desk, and when Joe brought the tea tray she had him put it beside her bed.

Lying back among her pillows and sipping the tea, she probed for her thought. What about Charles? And then it came to her.

Charles was clever. In his crazy way Sam Hamilton was clever. That was the fear-driven thought – there were clever people. Both Sam and Charles were dead, but maybe there were others. She worked it out very slowly.

Suppose I had been the one to dig up the bottles? What would I think and what would I do? A rim of panic rose in her breast. Why were the bottles broken and buried? So it wasn't poison! Then why bury them? What had made her do that? She should have dropped them in the gutter on Main Street or tossed them in the garbage can. Dr Wilde was dead. But what kind of records did he keep? She didn't know. Suppose she had found the glass and learned what had been in them? Wouldn't she

445

have asked someone who knew – 'Suppose you gave croton oil to a person. What would happen?'

'Well, suppose you gave little doses and kept it up a long time?' She would know. Maybe somebody else would know.

'Suppose you heard about a rich madam who willed everything to a new girl and then died.' Kate knew perfectly well what her first thought would be. What insanity had made her get Ethel floated? Now she couldn't be found. Ethel should have been paid and tricked into turning over the glass. Where was the glass now? In an envelope – but where? How could Ethel be found?

Ethel would know why and how she had been floated. Ethel wasn't bright, but she might tell somebody who was bright. That chattering voice might tell the story, how Faye was sick, and what she looked like, and about the will.

Kate was breathing quickly and little prickles of fear were beginning to course over her body. She should go to New York or somewhere – not bother to sell the house. She didn't need the money. She had plenty. Nobody could find her. Yes, but if she ran out and the clever person heard Ethel tell the story, wouldn't that cinch it?

Kate got up from her bed and took a heavy dose of bromide.

From that time on the crouching fear had always been at her side. She was almost glad when she learned that the pain in her hands was developing arthritis. An evil voice had whispered that it might be a punishment.

She had never gone out in the town very much, but now she developed a reluctance to go out at all. She knew that men stared secretly after her, knowing who she was. Suppose one of those men should have Charles's face or Samuel's eyes. She had to drive herself to go out once a week.

Then she built the lean-to and had it painted grey. She said it was because the light troubled her eyes and gradually she began to believe the light did trouble her eyes. Her eyes burned after a trip to the town. She spent more and more time in her little room.

It is possible to some people, and it was possible for Kate, to hold two opposing thoughts at the same time. She believed that the light pained her eyes, and also that the grey room was a cave to hide in, a dark burrow in the earth, a place where no eyes could stare at her. Once, sitting in her pillowed chair, she considered having a secret door built so that she would have an avenue of escape. And then a feeling rather than a thought threw out the plan. She would not be protected then. If she could get

446

out, something could get in – that something which had begun to crouch outside the house, to crawl close to the walls at night, and to rise silently, trying to look through the windows. It required more and more will-power for Kate to leave the house on Monday afternoons.

When Cal began to follow her she had a terrible leap of fear. And when she waited for him behind the privet she was very near to panic.

But now her head dug deep in her soft pillows and her eyes felt the gentle weight of the bromide.

CHAPTER 41

I

THE NATION slipped imperceptibly towards war, frightened and at the same time attracted. People had not felt the shaking emotion of war in nearly sixty years. The Spanish affair was more nearly an expedition than a war. Mr Wilson was re-elected President in November on his platform promise to keep us out of war, and at the same time he was instructed to take a firm hand, which inevitably meant war. Business picked up and prices began to rise. British purchasing agents roved about the country, buying food and cloth and metals and chemicals. A charge of excitement ran through the country. People didn't really believe in war even while they planned it. The Salinas Valley lived about as it always had.

II

Cal walked to school with Aron.

'You look tired,' Aron said.

'Do I?'

'I heard you come in last night. Four o'clock. What do you do so late?'

'I was walking around – thinking. How would you like to quit school and go back to the ranch?'

'What for?'

'We could make some money for Father.'

'I'm going to college. I wish I could go now. Everybody is laughing at us. I want to get out of town.'

'You act mad.'

'I'm not mad. But I didn't lose the money. I didn't have a crazy lettuce idea. But people laugh at me just the same. And I don't know if there's enough money for college.'

'He didn't mean to lose the money.'

'But he lost it.'

Cal said, 'You've got this year to finish and next before you can go to college.'

'Do you think I don't know it?'

'If you worked hard, maybe you could take entrance examinations next summer and go in the fall.'

Aron swung round. 'I couldn't do it.'

'I think you could. Why don't you talk to the principal? And I bet the Reverend Rolf would help you.'

Aron said, 'I want to get out of this town. I don't ever want to come back. They still call us Lettuce-heads. They laugh at us.'

'How about Abra?'

'Abra will do what's best.'

Cal asked, 'Would she want you to go away?'

'Abra's going to do what I want her to do.'

Cal thought for a moment. 'I'll tell you what. I'm going to try to make some money. If you knuckle down and pass examinations a year early, why, I'll help you through college.'

'You will?'

'Sure I will.'

'Why, I'll go and see the principal right away.' He quickened his steps.

Cal called, 'Aron, wait! Listen! If he says he thinks you can do it, don't tell Father.'

'Why not?'

'I was just thinking how nice it would be if you went to him and told him you'd done it.'

'I don't see what difference it makes.'

'You don't?'

'No, I don't,' said Aron. 'It sounds silly to me.'

Cal had a violent urge to shout, 'I know who our mother is! I can show her to you.' That would cut through and get inside of Aron.

Cal met Abra in the hall before the school-bell rang.

'What's the matter with Aron?' he demanded.

'I don't know.'

'Yes, you do,' he said.

'He's just in a cloud. I think it's that minister.'

'Does he walk home with you?'

'Sure he does. But I can see right through him. He's wearing wings.'

'He's still ashamed about the lettuce.'

'I know he is,' said Abra. 'I try to talk him out of it. Maybe he's enjoying it.'

'What do you mean?'

'Nothing,' said Abra.

After supper that night Cal said, 'Father, would you mind if I went down to the ranch Friday afternoon?'

Adam turned in his chair. 'What for?'

'Just want to see. Just want to look around.'

'Does Aron want to go?'

'No. I want to go alone.'

'I don't see why you shouldn't. Lee, do you see any reason why he shouldn't go?'

'No,' said Lee. He studied Cal. 'Thinking seriously of going to farming?'

'I might. If you'd let me take it over, I'd farm it, Father.'

'The lease has more than a year to run,' Adam said.

'After that can I farm it?'

'How about school?'

'I'll be through school.'

'Well, we'll see,' said Adam. 'You might want to go to college.'

When Cal started for the front door Lee followed and walked out with him.

'Can you tell me what it's about?' Lee asked.

'I just want to look around.'

'All right, I guess I'm left out.' Lee turned to go back into the house. Then he called, 'Cal!' The boy stopped. 'You worried, Cal?'

'No.'

'I've got five thousand dollars if you ever need it?'

'Why should I need it?'

'I don't know,' said Lee.

III

Will Hamilton liked his glass cage of an office in the garage. His business interests were much wider than the automobile agency, but he did not get another office. He loved the movement that went on outside his square glass cage. And he had put in double glass to kill the noise of the garage.

He sat in his big red leather swivel chair, and most of the

time he enjoyed his life. When people spoke of his brother Joe making so much money in advertising in the East, Will always said he himself was a big frog in a little puddle.

'I'd be afraid to go to a big city,' he said. 'I'm just a country boy.' And he liked the laugh that always followed. It proved to him that his friends knew he was well off.

Cal came in to see him one Saturday morning. Seeing Will's puzzled look, he said, 'I'm Cal Trask.'

'Oh, sure. Lord, you're getting to be a big boy. Is your father down?'

'No. I came alone.'

'Well, sit down. I don't suppose you smoke.'

'Sometimes. Cigarettes.'

Will slid a package of Murads across the desk. Cal opened the box and then closed it. 'I don't think I will right now.'

Will looked at the dark-faced boy and he liked him. He thought, 'This boy is sharp. He's nobody's fool.' 'I guess you'll be going into business pretty soon,' he said.

'Yes, sir. I thought I might run the ranch when I get out of high school.'

'There's no money in that,' said Will. 'Farmers don't make any money. It's the man who buys from him and sells. You'll never make any money farming.' Will knew that Cal was feeling him, testing him, observing him, and he approved of that.

And Cal had made up his mind, but first he asked, 'Mr Hamilton, you haven't any children, have you?'

'Well, no. And I'm sorry about that. I guess I'm sorriest about that.' And then, 'What makes you ask?'

Cal ignored the question. 'Would you give me some advice?'

Will felt a glow of pleasure. 'If I can, I'll be glad to. What is it you want to know?'

And then Cal did something Will Hamilton approved even more. He used candour as a weapon. He said, 'I want to make a lot of money. I want you to tell me how.'

Will overcame his impulse to laugh. Naïve as the statement was, he didn't think Cal was naïve. 'Everybody wants that,' he said. 'What do you mean by a lot of money?'

'Twenty or thirty thousand dollars.'

'Good God!' said Will, and he screeched his chair forward. And now he did laugh, but not in derision. Cal smiled along with Will's laughter.

Will said, 'Can you tell me why you want to make so much?'

'Yes, sir,' said Cal, 'I can.' And Cal opened the box of Murads and took out one of the oval cork-tipped cigarettes and lighted it. 'I'll tell you why,' he said.

Will leaned his chair back in enjoyment.

'My father lost a lot of money.'

'I know,' said Will. 'I warned him not to try to ship lettuce across the country.'

'You did? Why did you?'

'There were no guarantees,' said Will. 'A business man has to protect himself. If anything happened, he was finished. And it happened. Go on.'

'I want to make enough money to give him back what he lost.'

Will gaped at him. 'Why?' he asked.

'I want to.'

Will said, 'Are you fond of him?'

'Yes.'

Will's fleshy face contorted and a memory swept over him like a chilling wind. He did not move slowly over the past, it was all there in one flash, all of the years, a picture, a feeling and a despair, all stopped the way a fast camera stops the world. There was the flashing Samuel, beautiful as dawn with a fancy like a swallow's flight, and the brilliant, brooding Tom who was dark fire, Una who rode the storms, and lovely Mollie, Dessie of laughter, George handsome and with a sweetness that filled a room like the perfume of flowers, and there was Joe, the youngest, the beloved. Each one without effort brought some gift to the family.

Nearly everyone has his box of secret pain, shared with no one. Will had concealed his well, laughed loud, exploited perverse virtues, and never let his jealousy go wandering. He thought of himself as slow, doltish, conservative, uninspired. No great dream lifted him high and no despair forced self-destruction. He was always on the edge, trying to hold on to the rim of the family with what gifts he had – care, and reason, application. He kept the books, hired the attorneys, called the undertaker, and eventually paid the bills. The other didn't even know they needed him. He had the ability to get money and to keep it. He thought the Hamiltons despised him for his one ability. He had loved them doggedly, had always been at hand with his money to pull them out of their errors. He thought they were ashamed of him, and he fought bitterly for their recognition. All of this was in the frozen wind that blew through him.

His slightly bulging eyes were damp as he stared past Cal, and

451

the boy asked, 'What's the matter, Mr Hamilton? Don't you feel well?'

Will had sensed his family but he had not understood them. And they had accepted him without knowing there was anything to understand. And now this boy came along. Will understood him, felt him, sensed him, recognized him. This was the son he should have had, or the brother, or the father. And the cold wind of memory changed to a warmth towards Cal which gripped him in the stomach and pushed up against his lungs.

He forced his attention to the glass office. Cal was sitting back in his chair, waiting.

Will did not know how long his silence had lasted. 'I was thinking,' he said lamely. He made his voice stern. 'You asked me something. I'm a business man. I don't give things away. I sell them.'

'Yes, sir.' Cal was watchful, but he felt that Will Hamilton liked him.

Will said, 'I want to know something and I want the truth. Will you tell me the truth?'

'I don't know,' said Cal.

'I like that. How do you know until you know the question? I like that. That's smart – and honest. Listen – you have a brother. Does your father like him better than you?'

'Everybody does,' said Cal calmly. 'Everybody loves Aron.'

'Do you?'

'Yes, sir. At least – yes, I do.'

'What's the "at least"?'

'Sometimes I think he's stupid, but I like him.'

'Now, how about your father?'

'I love him,' said Cal.

'And he loves your brother better.'

'I don't know.'

'Now, you say you want to give back the money your father lost. Why?'

Ordinarily Cal's eyes were squinted and cautious, but now they were so wide that they seemed to look around and through Will. Cal was as close to his own soul as it is possible to get.

'My father is good,' he said. 'I want to make it up to him because I am not good.'

'If you do that, wouldn't you be good?'

'No,' said Cal. 'I think bad.'

Will had never met anyone who spoke so nakedly. He was near to embarrassment because of the nakedness, and he knew

452

how safe Cal was in his stripped honesty. 'Only one more,' he said, 'and I won't mind if you don't answer it. I don't think I would answer it. Here it is. Suppose you should get this money and give it to your father – would it cross your mind that you were trying to buy his love?'

'Yes, sir. It would. And it would be true.'

'That's all I want to ask. That's all.' Will leaned forward and put his hands against his sweating, pulsing forehead. He could not remember when he had been so shaken. And in Cal there was a cautious leap of triumph. He knew he had won and he closed his face against showing it.

Will raised his head and took off his glasses and wiped the moisture from them. 'Let's go outside,' he said. 'Let's go for a drive.'

Will drove a big Winton now, with a hood as long as a coffin and a powerful panting mutter in its bowels. He drove south from King City over the county road, through the gathering forces of spring, and the meadowlarks flew ahead, bubbling melody from the fence wires. Pico Blanco stood up against the West with a full head of snow, and in the valley the lines of eucalyptus, which stretched across the valley to break the winds, were gleaming silver with new leaves.

When he came to the side road that led into the home draw of the Trask place Will pulled up on the side of the road. He had not spoken since the Winton rolled out of King City. The big motor idled with a deep whisper.

Will, looking straight ahead, said, 'Cal – do you want to be partners with me?'

'Yes, sir.'

'I don't like to take a partner without money. I could lend you the money, but there's only trouble in that.'

'I can get money,' said Cal.

'How much?'

'Five thousand dollars.'

'You – I don't believe it.'

Cal didn't answer.

'I believe it,' said Will. 'Borrowed?'

'Yes, sir.'

'What interest?'

'None.'

'That's a good trick. Where will you get it?'

'I won't tell you, sir.'

Will shook his head and laughed. He was filled with pleasure.

453

'Maybe I'm being a fool, but I believe you – and I'm not a fool.' He gunned his motor and then let it idle again. 'I want you to listen. Do you read the papers?'

'Yes, sir.'

'We're going to be in this war any minute now.'

That's what it looks like.'

'Well, a lot of people think so. Now, do you know the present price of beans? I mean, what you can sell a hundred sacks for in Salinas?'

'I'm not sure. I think about three to three and a half cents a pound.'

'What do you mean you're not sure? How do you know that?'

'Well, I was thinking about asking my father to let me run the ranch.'

'I see. But you don't want to farm. You're too smart. Your father's tenant is named Rantani. He's a Swiss Italian, a good farmer. He's put nearly five hundred acres under cultivation. If we can guarantee him five cents a pound and give him a seed loan, he'll plant beans. So will every other farmer around here. We could contract five thousand acres of beans.'

Cal said, 'What are we going to do with five-cent beans in a three-cent market? Oh, yes! But how can we be sure?'

Will said, 'Are we partners?'

'Yes, sir.'

'Yes, Will!'

'Yes, Will.'

'How soon can you get five thousand dollars?'

'By next Wednesday.'

'Shake!' Solemnly the stout man and the lean dark boy shook hands.

Will, still holding Cal's hand, said, 'Now we're partners. I have a contract with the British Purchasing Agency. And I have a friend in the Quartermaster Corps. I bet we can sell all the dried beans we can find at ten cents a pound or more.'

'When can you sell?'

'I'll sell before we sign anything. Now, would you like to go up to the old place and talk to Rantani?'

'Yes, sir,' said Cal.

Will double-clutched the Winton and the big green car lumbered into the side road.

CHAPTER 42

A W A R comes always to someone else. In Salinas we were aware that the United States was the greatest and most powerful nation in the world. Every American was a rifleman by birth, and one American was worth ten or twenty foreigners in a fight.

Pershing's expedition into Mexico after Villa had exploded one of our myths for a little while. We had truly believed that Mexicans can't shoot straight and besides were lazy and stupid. When our own Troop C came wearily back from the border they said that none of this was true. Mexicans could shoot straight, goddam it! And Villa's horsemen had out-ridden and out-lasted our own boys. The two evenings a month of training had not toughened them very much. And last, the Mexicans seemed to have out-thought and out-ambushed Black Jack Pershing. When the Mexicans were joined by their ally, dysentery, it was godawful. Some of our boys didn't really feel good again for years.

Somehow we didn't connect Germans with Mexicans. We went right back to our myths. One American was as good as twenty Germans. This being true, we had only to act in a stern manner to bring the Kaiser to heel. He wouldn't dare interfere with our trade – but he did. He wouldn't stick out his neck and sink our ships – but he did. It was stupid, but he did, and so there was nothing for it but to fight him.

The war, at first anyway, was for other people. We, I, my family and friends, had kind of ring seats, and it was pretty exciting. And just as war is always for somebody else, so it is also true that someone else always gets killed. And Mother of God! that wasn't true either. The dreadful telegrams began to sneak sorrowfully in, and it was everybody's brother. Here we were, over six thousand miles from the anger and the noise, and that didn't save us.

It wasn't much fun then. The Liberty Belles could parade in white caps and uniforms of white sharkskin. Our uncle could re-write his Fourth of July speech and use it to sell bonds. We in high school could wear olive drab and campaign hats and learn the manual of arms from the physics teacher, but, Jesus Christ! Marty Hopps dead, the Berges boy, from across the street, the handsome one our little sister was in love with from the time she was three, blown to bits!

And the gangling, shuffling, loose-jointed boys carrying suitcases were marching awkwardly down Main Street to the Southern Pacific Depot. They were sheepish, and the Salinas Band marched ahead of them, playing 'Stars and Stripes Forever', and the families walking along beside them were crying, and the music sounded like a dirge. The draftees wouldn't look at their mothers. They didn't dare. We'd never thought the war could happen to us.

There were some in Salinas who began to talk softly in the poolrooms and the bars. These had private information from a soldier – we weren't getting the truth. Our men were being sent in without guns. Troopships were sunk and the government wouldn't tell us. The German army was so far superior to ours that we didn't have a chance. That Kaiser was a smart fellow. He was getting ready to invade America. But would Wilson tell us this? He would not. And usually these carrion talkers were the same ones who had said one American was worth twenty Germans in a scrap – the same ones.

Little groups of British in their outlandish uniforms (but they did look smart) moved about the country, buying everything that wasn't nailed down and paying for it and paying big. A good many of the British purchasing men were crippled, but they wore their uniforms just the same. Among other things they bought beans, because beans are easy to transport and they don't spoil and a man can damn well live on them. Beans are twelve and a half cents a pound and hard to find. And farmers wished they hadn't contracted their beans for a lousy two cents a pound above the going price six months ago.

The nation and the Salinas Valley changed its songs. At first we sang of how we could knock hell out of Heligoland and hang the Kaiser and march over there and clean up the mess them damn foreigners had made. And then suddenly we sang, 'In the war's red curse stand the Red Cross nurse. She's the rose of No Man's Land', and we sang, 'Hello, central, give me Heaven, 'cause my Daddy's there', and we sang, 'Just a baby's prayer at twilight, when lights are low. She climbs upstairs and says her prayers—Oh, God! please tell my daddy thaddy must take care — ' I guess we were like a tough but inexperienced little boy who gets punched in the nose in the first flurry and it hurts and we wished it was over.

CHAPTER 43

I

LATE IN the summer Lee came in off the street, carrying his big market basket. Lee had become American conservative in his clothes since he had lived in Salinas. He regularly wore black broadcloth when he went out of the house. His shirts were white, his collars high and stiff, and he affected narrow black string ties, like those which once were the badge for Southern senators. His hats were black, round of crown and straight of brim, and uncrushed as though he still left room for a coiled queue. He was immaculate.

Once Adam had remarked on the quiet splendour of Lee's clothes, and Lee had grinned at him. 'I have to do it,' he said. 'One must be very rich to dress as badly as you do. The poor are forced to dress well.'

'Poor!' Adam exploded. 'You'll be lending us money before we're through.'

'That might be,' said Lee.

This afternoon he set his heavy basket on the floor. 'I'm going to try to make a winter melon soup,' he said. 'Chinese cooking. I have a cousin in Chinatown, and he told me how. My cousin is in the fire-cracker and fan-tan business.'

'I thought you didn't have any relatives,' said Adam.

'All Chinese are related, and the ones named Lee are closest,' said Lee. 'My cousin is a Suey Dong. Recently he went into hiding for his health and he learned to cook. You stand the melon in a pot, cut off the top carefully, put in a whole chicken, mushrooms, water chestnuts, leeks, and just a touch of ginger. Then you put the top back on the melon and cook it as slowly as possible for two days. Ought to be good.'

Adam was lying back in his chair, his palms clasped behind his head, and he was smiling at the ceiling. 'Good, Lee, good,' he said.

'You didn't even listen,' said Lee.

Adam drew himself upright. He said, 'You think you know your own children and then you find you don't at all.'

Lee smiled. 'Has some detail of their lives escaped you?' he asked.

Adam chuckled. 'I only found out by accident,' he said. 'I

457

knew that Aron wasn't around very much this summer, but I thought he was just out playing.'

'Playing!' said Lee. 'He hasn't played for years.'

'Well, whatever he does.' Adam continued, 'Today I met Mr Kilkenny – you know, from the high school? He thought I knew all about it. Do you know what that boy is doing?'

'No,' said Lee.

'He's covered all next year's work. He's going to take examinations for college and save a year. And Kilkenny is confident that he will pass. Now, what do you think of that?'

'Remarkable,' said Lee. 'Why is he doing it?'

'Why, to save a year!'

'What does he want to save it for?'

'Goddam it, Lee, he's ambitious. Can't you understand that?'

'No,' said Lee. 'I never could.'

Adam said, 'He never spoke of it. I wonder if his brother knows.'

'I guess Aron wants it to be a surprise. We shouldn't mention it until he does.'

'I guess you're right. Do you know, Lee? – I'm proud of him. Terribly proud. This makes me feel good. I wish Cal had some ambition.'

'Maybe he has,' said Lee. 'Maybe he has some kind of a secret too.'

'Maybe. God knows we haven't seen much of him lately either. Do you think it's good for him to be away so much?'

'Cal's trying to find himself,' said Lee. 'I guess this personal hide-and-seek is not unusual. And some people are "it" all their lives – hopelessly "it".'

'Just think,' said Adam. 'A whole year's work ahead. When he tells us we ought to have a present for him.'

'A gold watch,' said Lee.

'That's right,' said Adam. 'I'm going to get one and have it engraved and ready. What should it say?'

'The jeweller will tell you,' said Lee. 'You take the chicken out after two days and cut it off the bone and put the meat back.'

'What chicken?'

'Winter melon soup,' said Lee.

'Have we got enough money to send him to college, Lee?'

'If we're careful and he doesn't develop expensive tastes.'

'He wouldn't,' Adam said.

'I didn't think I would – but I have.' Lee inspected the sleeve of his coat with admiration.

The rectory of St Paul's Episcopal Church was large and rambling. It had been built for ministers with large families. Mr Rolf, unmarried and simple in his tastes, closed up most of the house, but when Aron needed a place to study he gave him a large room and helped him with his studies.

Mr Rolf was fond of Aron. He liked the angelic beauty of his face and his smooth cheeks, his narrow hips, and long straight legs. He liked to sit in the room and watch Aron's face straining with effort to learn. He understood why Aron could not work at home in an atmosphere not conducive to hard clean thought. Mr Rolf felt that Aron was his product, his spiritual son, his contribution to the Church. He saw him through his travail of celibacy and felt that he was guiding him into calm waters.

Their discussions were long and close and personal. 'I know I am criticized,' Mr Rolf said. 'I happen to believe in a Higher Church than some people. No one can tell me that confession is not just as important a sacrament as communion. And you mind my word – I am going to bring it back, but cautiously, gradually.'

'When I have a church I'll do it too.'

'It requires great tact,' said Mr Rolf.

Aron said, 'I wish we had in our Church, well – well, I might as well say it. I wish we had something like the Augustines or the Franciscans. Someplace to withdraw. Sometimes I feel dirty. I want to get away from the dirt and be clean.'

'I know how you feel,' Mr Rolf said earnestly. 'But there I cannot go along with you. I can't think that our Lord Jesus would want His priesthood withdrawn from service to the world. Think how He insisted that we preach the Gospel, help the sick and poor, even lower ourselves into filth to raise sinners from the slime. We must keep the exactness of His example before us.'

His eyes began to glow and his voice took on the throatiness he used in sermons. 'Perhaps I shouldn't tell you this. And I hope you won't find any pride in me telling it. But there is a kind of glory in it. For the last five weeks a woman has been coming to evening service. I don't think you can see her from the choir. She sits always in the last row on the left-hand side – yes, you can see her too. She is off at an angle. Yes, you can see her. She wears a veil and she always leaves before I can get back after recessional.'

'Who is she?' Aron asked.

'Well, you'll have to learn these things. I made very discreet inquiries and you would never guess. She is – well – the owner of a house of ill fame.'

'Here in Salinas?'

'Here in Salinas.' Mr Rolf leaned forward. 'Aron, I can see your revulsion. You must get over that. Don't forget our Lord and Mary Magdalene. Without pride I say I would be glad to raise her up.'

'What does she want here?' Aron demanded.

'Perhaps what we have to offer – salvation. It will require great tact. I can see how it will be. And mark my words – these people are timid. One day there will come a tap on my door and she will beg to come in. Then, Aron, I pray that I may be wise and patient. You must believe me – when that happens, when a lost soul seeks the light, it is the highest and most beautiful experience a priest can have. That's what we are for, Aron. That's what we are for.'

Mr Rolf controlled his breathing with difficulty. 'I pray God I may not fail,' he said.

III

Adam Trask thought of the war in terms of his own dimly remembered campaigns against the Indians. No one knew anything about huge and general war. Lee read European history, trying to discern from the filaments of the past some pattern of the future.

Liza Hamilton died with a pinched little smile on her mouth, and her cheekbones were shockingly high when the red was gone from them.

And Adam waited impatiently for Aron to bring news of his examinations. The massive gold watch lay under his handkerchiefs in the top drawer of his bureau, and he kept it wound and set and checked its accuracy against his own watch.

Lee had his instructions. On the evening of the day of the announcement he was to cook a turkey and bake a cake.

'We'll want to make a party of it,' Adam said. 'What would you think of champagne?'

'Very nice,' said Lee. 'Did you ever read von Clausewitz?'

'Who is he?'

'Not very reassuring reading,' said Lee. 'One bottle of champagne?'

'That's enough. It's just for toasts, you know. Makes a party of it.' It didn't occur to Adam that Aron might fail.

One afternoon Aron came in and asked Lee, 'Where's father?'

'He's shaving.'

'I won't be in for dinner,' said Aron.

In the bathroom he stood behind his father and spoke to the soap-faced image in the mirror. 'Mr Rolf asked me to have dinner at the rectory.'

Adam wiped his razor on a folded piece of toilet paper. 'That's nice,' he said.

'Can I get a bath?'

'I'll be out of here in just a minute,' said Adam.

When Aron walked through the living-room and said good night and went out, Cal and Adam looked after him. 'He got into my cologne,' said Cal. 'I can still smell him.'

'It must be quite a party,' Adam said.

'I don't blame him for wanting to celebrate. That was a hard job.'

'Celebrate?'

'The exams. Didn't he tell you? He passed them.'

'Oh, yes – the exams,' said Adam. 'Yes, he told me. A fine job. I'm proud of him. I think I'll get him a gold watch.'

Cal said sharply, 'He didn't tell you!'

'Oh, yes – yes, he did. He told me this morning.'

'He didn't know this morning,' said Cal, and he got up and went out.

He walked very fast in the gathering darkness, out Central Avenue, past the park and past Stonewall Jackson Smart's house clear to the place beyond the street-lights where the street became a country road and angled to avoid Tollot's farm-house.

At ten o'clock Lee, going out to mail a letter, found Cal sitting on the lowest step of the front porch. 'What happened to you?' he asked.

'I went for a walk.'

'What's the matter with Aron?'

'I don't know.'

'He seems to have some kind of grudge. Want to walk to the post office with me?'

'No.'

'What are you sitting out here for?'

'I'm going to beat the hell out of him.'

'Don't do it,' said Lee.

'Why not?'

'Because I don't think you can. He'd slaughter you.'

'I guess you're right,' said Cal. 'The son of a bitch!'

'Watch your language.'

Cal laughed. 'I guess I'll walk along with you.'

'Did you ever read von Clausewitz?'

'I never even heard of him.'

When Aron came home it was Lee who was waiting for him on the lowest step of the front porch. 'I saved you from a licking,' Lee said. 'Sit down.'

'I'm going to bed.'

'Sit down! I want to talk to you. Why didn't you tell your father you passed the tests?'

'He wouldn't understand.'

'You've got a bug up your arse.'

'I don't like that kind of language.'

'Why do you think I used it? I am not profane by accident. Aron, your father has been living for this.'

'How did he know about it?'

'You should have told him yourself.'

'This is none of your business.'

'I want you to go in and wake him up if he's asleep, but I don't think he'll be asleep. I want you to tell him.'

'I won't do it.'

Lee said softly, 'Aron, did you ever have to fight a little man, a man half your size?'

'What do you mean?'

'It's one of the most embarrassing things in the world. He won't stop and pretty soon you have to hit him and that's worse. Then you're really in trouble all round.'

'What are you talking about?'

'If you don't do as I tell you, Aron, I'm going to fight you. Isn't that ridiculous?'

Aron tried to pass. Lee stood up in front of him, his tiny fists doubled ineffectually, his stance and position so silly that he began to laugh. 'I don't know how to do it, but I'm going to try,' he said.

Aron nervously backed away from him. And when finally he sat down on the steps Lee sighed deeply. 'Thank heaven that's over,' he said. 'It would have been awful. Look, Aron, can't you tell me what's the matter with you? You always used to tell me.'

Suddenly Aron broke down. 'I want to go away. It's a dirty town.'

'No, it isn't. It's just the same as other places.'

'I don't belong here. I wish we hadn't ever come here. I don't now what's the matter with me. I want to go away.' His voice ose to a wail.

Lee put his arm around the broad shoulders to comfort him. You're growing up. Maybe that's it,' he said softly. 'Sometimes think the world tests us most sharply then, and we turn in-ard and watch ourselves with horror. But that's not the worst. Ve think everybody is seeing into us. Then dirt is very dirty nd purity is shining white. Aron, it will be over. Wait only a ttle while and it will be over. That's not much relief to you ecause you don't believe it, but it's the best I can do for you. ry to believe that things are neither so good nor so bad as they eem to you now. Yes, I can help you. Go to bed now, and in he morning get up early and tell your father about the tests. Make it exciting. He's lonelier than you are because he has no ovely future to dream about. Go through the motions. Sam Iamilton said that. Pretend it's true and maybe it will be. Go hrough the motions. Do that. And go to bed. I've got to bake a ake – for breakfast. And, Aron – your father left a present on our pillow.'

CHAPTER 44

I

T W A S only after Aron went away to college that Abra really got to know his family. Aron and Abra had fenced themselves in vith themselves. With Aron gone, she attached herself to the other Trasks. She found that she trusted Adam more, and loved Lee more, than her own father.

About Cal she couldn't decide. He disturbed her sometimes vith anger, sometimes with pain, and sometimes with curiosity. He seemed to be in a perpetual contest with her. She didn't know whether he liked her or not, and so she didn't like him. She was relieved when, calling at the Trask house, Cal was not here, to look secretly at her, judge, appraise, consider, and look away when she caught him at it.

Abra was a straight, strong, fine-breasted woman, developed and ready and waiting to take her sacrament – but waiting. She took to going to the Trask house after school, sitting with Lee, reading him parts of Aron's daily letter.

Aron was lonely at Stanford. His letters were drenched wit' lonesome longing for his girl. Together they were matter-of-fact but from the university, ninety miles away, he made passionat' love to her, shut himself off from the life around him. H' studied, ate, slept, and wrote to Abra, and this was his whol' life.

In the afternoons she sat in the kitchen with Lee and helpe' him to string beans or slip peas from their pods. Sometimes sh' made fudge and very often she stayed to dinner rather than g' home to her parents. There was no subject she could not discus' with Lee. And the few things she could talk about to her fathe' and mother were thin and pale and tired and mostly not eve' true. There Lee was different also. Abra wanted to tell Lee onl' true things even when she wasn't quite sure what was true.

Lee would sit smiling a little, and his quick fragile hand' flew about their work as though they had independent lives' Abra wasn't aware that she spoke exclusively of herself. An' sometimes while she talked Lee's mind wandered out and cam' back and went out again like a ranging dog, and Lee would no' at intervals and make a quiet humming sound.

He liked Abra and he felt strength and goodness in her, an' warmth too. Her features had the bold muscular strength whic' could result finally either in ugliness or in great beauty. Lee' musing through her talk, thought of the round smooth faces o' the Cantonese, his own breed. Even thin they were moon-faced' Lee should have liked that kind best since beauty must be some-what like ourselves, but he didn't. When he thought of Chinese beauty the iron predatory faces of the Manchus came to hi' mind, arrogant and unyielding faces of a people who ha' authority by unquestioned inheritance.

She said, 'Maybe it was there all along. I don't know. He never talked much about his father. It was after Mr Trask had the – you know – the lettuce. Aron was angry then.'

'Why?' Lee asked.

'People were laughing at him.'

Lee's whole mind popped back. 'Laughing at Aron? Why at him? He didn't have anything to do with it.'

'Well, that's the way he felt. Do you want to know what I think?'

'Of course,' said Lee.

'I figured this out and I'm not quite finished figuring. I thought he always felt – well, kind of crippled – maybe un-finished, because he didn't have a mother.'

Lee's eyes opened wide and then drooped again. He nodded. 'I see. Do you figure Cal that way too?'

'No.'

'Then why Aron?'

'Well, I haven't got that yet. Maybe some people need things more than others, or hate things more. My father hates turnips. He always did. Never came from anything. Turnips make him mad, real mad. Well, one time my mother was – well, huffy, and she made a casserole out of mashed turnips with lots of pepper and cheese on top and got it all brown on top. My father ate half a dish of it before he asked what it was. My mother said turnips, and he threw the dish on the floor and got up and went out. I don't think he ever forgave her.'

Lee chuckled. 'He can forgive her because she said turnips. But, Abra, suppose he'd asked and she had said something else and he liked it and had another dish. And then afterwards he found out. Why, he might have murdered her.'

'I guess so. Well, anyway, I figure Aron needed a mother more than Cal did. And I think he always blamed his father.'

'Why?'

'I don't know. That's what I think.'

'You get around, don't you?'

'Shouldn't I?'

'Of course you should.'

'Shall I make some fudge?'

'Not today. We still have some.'

'What can I do?'

'You can pound flour into the top round. Will you eat with us?'

'No. I'm going to a birthday party, thank you. Do you think he'll be a minister?'

'How do I know?' said Lee. 'Maybe it's just an idea.'

'I hope he doesn't,' said Abra, and she clapped her mouth shut in astonishment at having said it.

Lee got up and pulled out the pastry board and laid out the red meat and a flour sifter beside it. 'Use the back of the knife,' he said.

'I know.' She hoped he hadn't heard her.

But Lee asked, 'Why don't you want him to be a minister?'

'I shouldn't say it.'

'You should say anything you want to. You don't have to explain.' He went back to his chair, and Abra sifted flour over

465

the steak and pounded the meat with a big knife. Tap-tap – 'I shouldn't talk like this' – tap-tap.

Lee turned his head away to let her take her own pace.

'He goes all one way,' she said over the pounding. 'If it's Church its got to be High Church. He was talking about how priests shouldn't be married.'

'That's not the way his last letter sounded,' Lee observed.

'I know. That was before.' Her knife stopped its pounding. Her face was young perplexed pain. 'Lee, I'm not good enough for him.'

'Now, what do you mean by that?'

'I'm not being funny. He doesn't think of me. He's made someone up, and it's like he put my skin on her. I'm not like that – not like the made-up one.'

'What's she like?'

'Pure!' said Abra. 'Just absolutely pure. Nothing but pure – never a bad thing. I'm not like that.'

'Nobody is,' said Lee.

'He doesn't know me. He doesn't even want to know me. He wants that – white – ghost.'

Lee rubbled a piece of cracker. 'Don't you like him? You're pretty young, but I don't think that makes any difference.'

' 'Course I like him. I'm going to be his wife. But I want him to like me too. And how can' he, if he doesn't know anything about me? I used to think he knew me. Now I'm not sure he ever did.'

'Maybe he's going through a hard time that isn't permanent. You're a smart girl – very smart. Is it pretty hard trying to live up to the one – in your skin?'

'I'm always afraid he'll see something in me that isn't in the one he made up. I'll get mad or I'll smell bad – or something else. He'll find out.'

'Maybe not,' said Lee. 'But it must be hard living the Lily Maid, the Goddess-Virgin, and the other all at once. Humans just do smell bad sometimes.'

She moved towards the table. 'Lee, I wish —'

'Don't spill flour on my floor,' he said. 'What do you wish?'

'It's from my figuring out. I think Aron, when he didn't have a mother – why, he made her everything good he could think of.'

'That might be. And then you think he dumped it all on you.' She stared at him and her fingers wandered delicately up and down the blade of the knife. 'And you wish you could find some way to dump it all back.'

'Yes.'

'Suppose he wouldn't like you then?'

'I'd rather take a chance on that,' she said. 'I'd rather be myself.'

Lee said, 'I never saw anybody get mixed up in other people's business the way I do. And I'm a man who doesn't have a final answer about anything. Are you going to pound that meat or shall I do it?'

She went back to work. 'Do you think it's funny to be so serious when I'm not even out of high school?' she asked.

'I don't see how it could be any other way,' said Lee. 'Laughter comes later, like wisdom teeth, and laughter at yourself comes last of all in a mad race with death, and sometimes it isn't in time.'

Her tapping speeded up and its beat became erratic and nervous. Lee moved five dried lima beans in patterns on the table – a line, an angle, a circle.

The beating stopped. 'Is Mrs Trask alive?'

Lee's forefinger hung over a bean for a moment and then slowly fell and pushed it to make the *O* into a *Q*. He knew she was looking at him. He could even see in his mind how her expression would be one of panic at her question. His thought raced like a rat new caught in a wire trap. He sighed and gave it up. He turned slowly and looked at her, and his picture had been accurate.

Lee said tonelessly, 'We've talked a lot and I don't remember that we have ever discussed me – ever.' He smiled shyly. 'Abra, let me tell you about myself. I'm a servant. I'm old. I'm Chinese. These three you know. I'm tired and I'm cowardly.'

'You're not —' she began.

'Be silent,' he said. 'I am so cowardly. I will not put my finger in any human pie.'

'What do you mean?'

'Abra, is your father mad at anything except turnips?'

Her face went stubborn. 'I asked you a question.'

'I did not hear a question,' he said softly and his voice became confident. 'You did not ask a question, Abra.'

'I guess you think I'm too young —' Abra began.

Lee broke in, 'Once I worked for a woman of thirty-five who had successfully resisted experience, learning, and beauty. If she had been six she would have been the despair of her parents. And at thirty-five she was permitted to control money and the lives of people around her. No, Abra, age has nothing to do with it. If I had anything at all to say – I would say it to you.'

The girl smiled at him. 'I'm clever,' she said. 'Shall I be clever?'

'God help me – no,' Lee protested.

'Then you don't want me to try to figure it out?'

'I don't care what you do as long as I don't have anything to do with it. I guess no matter how weak and negative a good man is, he has as many sins on him as he can bear. I have enough sins to trouble me. Maybe they aren't very fine sins compared to some, but, the way I feel, they're all I can take care of. Please forgive me.'

Abra reached across the table and touched the back of his hand with floury fingers. The yellow skin on his hand was tight and glazed. He looked down at the white powdery smudges her fingers left.

Abra said, 'My father wanted a boy. I guess he hates turnips and girls. He tells everyone how he gave me my crazy name. "And though I called another, Abra came."'

Lee smiled at her. 'You're such a nice girl,' he said. 'I'll buy some turnips tomorrow if you'll come to dinner.'

Abra asked softly, 'Is she alive?'

'Yes,' said Lee.

The front door slammed, and Cal came into the kitchen. 'Hello, Abra. Lee, is father home?'

'No, not yet. What are you grinning all over for?'

Cal handed him a cheque. 'There. That's for you.'

Lee looked at it. 'I didn't want interest,' he said.

'It's better. I might want to borrow it back.'

'You won't tell me where you got it?'

'No. Not yet. I've got a good idea —' His eyes flicked to Abra.

'I have to go home now,' she said.

Cal said, 'She might as well be in on it. I decided to do it Thanksgiving, and Abra'll probably be around and Aron will be home.'

'Do what?' she asked.

'I've got a present for my father.'

'What is it?' Abra asked.

'I won't tell. You'll find out then.'

'Does Lee know?'

'Yes, but he won't tell.'

'I don't think I ever saw you so – gay,' Abra said. 'I don't

468

think I ever saw you gay at all.' She discovered in herself a warmth for him.

After Abra had gone Cal sat down. 'I don't know whether to give it to him before Thanksgiving dinner or after,' he said.

'After,' said Lee. 'Have you really got the money?'

'Fifteen thousand dollars.'

'Honestly?'

'You mean, did I steal it?'

'Yes.'

'Honestly,' said Cal. 'Remember how we had champagne for Aron? We'll get champagne. And – well, we'll maybe decorate the dining-room. Maybe Abra'll help.'

'Do you really think your father wants money?'

'Why shouldn't he?'

'I hope you're right,' said Lee. 'How have you been doing in school?'

'Not very well. I'll pick up after Thanksgiving,' said Cal.

11

After school the next day Abra hurried and caught up with Cal.

'Hello, Abra,' he said. 'You make good fudge.'

'That last was dry. It should be creamy.'

'Lee is just crazy about you. What have you done to him?'

'I like Lee,' she said, and then, 'I want to ask you something, Cal.'

'Yes?'

'What's the matter with Aron?'

'What do you mean?'

'He just seems to think only about himself.'

'I don't think that's very new. Have you had a fight with him?'

'No. When he had all that about going to Church and not getting married, I tried to fight with him, but he wouldn't.'

'Not get married to you? I can't imagine that.'

'Cal, he writes me love letters now – only they aren't to me.'

'Then who are they to?'

'It's like they were to – himself.'

Cal said, 'I know about the willow tree.'

She didn't seem surprised. 'Do you?' she asked.

'Are you mad at Aron?'

'No, not mad. I just can't find him. I don't know him.'

469

'Wait around,' said Cal. 'Maybe he's going through something.'

'I wonder if I'll be all right. Do you think I could have been wrong all the time?'

'How do I know?'

'Cal,' she said, 'is it true that you go out late at night and even go – to – bad houses?'

'Yes,' he said. 'That's true. Did Aron tell you?'

'No, not Aron. Well, why do you go there?'

He walked beside her and did not answer.

'Tell me,' she said.

'What is it to you?'

'Is it because you're bad?'

'What's it sound like to you?'

'I'm not good either,' she said.

'You're crazy,' said Cal. 'Aron will knock that out of you.'

'Do you think he will?'

'Why, sure,' said Cal. 'He's got to.'

CHAPTER 45

I

JOE VALERY got along by watching and listening and, as he said himself, not sticking his neck out. He had built his hatreds little by little – beginning with a mother who neglected him, a father who alternately whipped and slobbered over him. It had been easy to transfer his developing hatred to the teacher who disciplined him and the policeman who chased him and the priest who lectured him. Even before the first magistrate looked down on him, Joe had developed a fine stable of hates towards the whole world he knew.

Hate cannot live alone. It must have love as a trigger, a goad, or a stimulant. Joe early developed a gentle protective love for Joe. He comforted and flattered and cherished Joe. He set up walls to save Joe from a hostile world. And gradually Joe became proof against wrong. If Joe got into trouble, it was because the world was in angry conspiracy against him. And if Joe attacked the world, it was revenge and they damn well deserved it – the sons of bitches. Joe lavished every care on his love, and he perfected a lonely set of rules which might have gone like this:

1. Don't believe nobody. The bastards are after you.

2. Keep your mouth shut. Don't stick your neck out.

3. Keep your ears open. When they make a slip, grab on to it and wait.

4. Everybody's a son of a bitch and whatever you do they got it coming.

5. Go at everything roundabout.

6. Don't never trust no dame about nothing.

7. Put your faith in dough. Everybody wants it. Everybody will sell out for it.

There were other rules, but they were refinements. His system worked, and since he knew no other, Joe had no basis of comparison with other systems. He knew it was necessary to be smart and he considered himself smart. If he pulled something off, that was smart; if he failed, that was bad luck. Joe was not very successful but he got by with the minimum of effort. Kate kept him because she knew he would do anything in the world if he were paid to do it or was afraid not to do it. She had no illusions about him. In her business Joe was necessary.

When he first got the job with Kate, Joe looked for the weaknesses on which he lived – vanity, voluptuousness, anxiety or conscience, greed, hysteria. He knew they were there because she was a woman. It was a matter of considerable shock to him to learn that, if they were there, he couldn't find them. This dame thought and acted like a man – only tougher, quicker, and more clever. Joe made a few mistakes and Kate rubbed his nose in them. He developed an admiration for her based on fear.

When he found that he couldn't get away with some things, he began to believe he couldn't get away with anything. Kate made a slave of him just as she had always made slaves of women. She fed him, clothed him, gave him orders, punished him.

Once Joe recognized her as more clever than himself, it was a short step to the belief that she was more clever than anybody. He thought that she possessed the two great gifts: she was smart and she got the breaks – and you couldn't want no better than that. He was glad to do her hatchet work – and afraid not to. Kate don't make no mistakes, Joe said. And if you played along with her, Kate took care of you. This went beyond thought and became a habit pattern. When he got Ethel floated over the county line, it was all in the day's work. It was Kate's business and she was smart.

Kate did not sleep well when the arthritic pains were bad. She could almost feel her joints thicken and knot. Sometimes she tried to think of other things, even unpleasant ones, to drive the pain and the distorted fingers from her mind. Sometimes she tried to remember every detail in a room she had not seen for a long time. Sometimes she looked at the ceiling and projected long columns of figures and added them. Sometimes she used memories. She built Mr Edwards's face and his clothes and the word that was stamped on the metal clasp on his braces. She had never noticed it, but she knew the word was 'Excelsior'.

Often in the night she thought of Faye, remembered her eyes and hair and the tone of her voice and how her hands fluttered and the little lump of flesh beside her left thumb-nail, a scar from an ancient cut. Kate went into her feeling about Faye. Did she hate or love her? Did she pity her? Was she sorry she had killed her? Kate inched over her own thought like a measuring worm. She found she had no feeling about Faye. She neither liked nor disliked her or her memory. There had been a time during her dying when the noise and the smell of her had made anger rise in Kate so that she considered killing her quickly to get it over.

Kate remembered how Faye had looked the last time she saw her, lying in her purple casket, dressed in white, with the undertaker's smile on her lips and enough powder and rouge to cover her sallow skin.

A voice behind Kate had said, 'She looks better than she has in years.' And another voice had answered, 'Maybe the same thing would do me some good,' and there was a double snicker. The first voice would be Ethel, and the second Trixie. Kate remembered her own half-humorous reaction. Why, she had thought, a dead whore looks like anybody else.

Yes, the first voice must have been Ethel. Ethel always got into the night thinking, and Ethel always brought a shrinking fear with her, the stupid, clumsy, nosy bitch – the lousy old bag. And it happened very often that Kate's mind would tell her, 'Now wait a moment. Why is she a lousy bag? Isn't it because you made a mistake? Why did you float her? If you'd used your head and kept her here —'

Kate wondered where Ethel was. How about one of those agencies to find Ethel – at least to find where she went? Yes, and then Ethel would tell about that night and show the glass. Then there'd be two noses sniffing instead of one. Yes, but what difference would that make? Every time Ethel got a beer in her she would be telling somebody. Oh, sure, but they would think she was just a buzzed old hustler. Now an agency man – no – no agencies.

Kate spent many hours with Ethel. Did the Judge have any idea it was a frame – too simple? It shouldn't have been an even hundred dollars. That was obvious. And how about the sheriff? Joe said they dropped her over the line into Santa Cruz County. What did Ethel tell the deputy who drove her out? Ethel was a lazy old bat. Maybe she had stayed in Watsonville. There was Pajaro, and that was a railroad section, and then the Pajaro River and the bridge into Watsonville. Lots of section hands went back and forth, Mexicans, some Hindus. That puddle-head Ethel might have thought she could turn enough tricks with the track workers. Wouldn't it be funny if she had never left Watsonville, thirty miles away? She could even slip in over the line and see her friends if she wanted to. Maybe she came to Salinas sometimes. She might be in Salinas right now. The cops weren't likely to keep too much on the look for her. Maybe it would be a good idea to send Joe over to Watsonville to see if Ethel was there. She might have gone on to Santa Cruz. Joe could look there too. It wouldn't take him long. Joe could find any hooker in any town in a few hours. If he found her they would get her back somehow. Ethel was a fool. But maybe when her found her it would be better if Kate went to her. Lock the door. Leave a 'Do not disturb' sign. She could get to Watsonville, do her business and get back. No taxis. Take a bus. Nobody saw anybody on the night buses. People sleeping with their shoes off and coats rolled up behind their heads. Suddenly she knew she would be afraid to go to Watsonville. Well, she could make herself go. It would stop all this wondering. Strange she hadn't thought of sending Joe before. That was perfect. Joe was good at some things, and the dumb bastard thought he was clever. That was the kind easiest to handle. Ethel was stupid, That made her hard to handle.

As her hands and her mind grew more crooked, Kate began to rely more and more on Joe Valery as her assistant-in-chief, as her go-between, and as her executioner. She had a basic fear of the girls in the house – not that they were more untrustworthy than Joe but that the hysteria which lay very close to the surface might at any time crack through their caution and shatter their

sense of self-preservation and tear down not only themselves but
their surroundings. Kate had always been able to handle this
ever-present danger, but now the slow-depositing calcium and
the slow growth of apprehension caused her to need help and to
look for it from Joe. Men, she knew, had a little stronger wall
against self-destruction than the kind of women she knew.

She felt that she could trust Joe, because she had in her files
a notation relating to one Joseph Venuta who had walked away
from a San Quentin road gang in the fourth year of a five-year
sentence for robbery. Kate had never mentioned this to Joe
Valery, but she thought it might have a soothing influence on
him if he got out of hand.

Joe brought the breakfast tray every morning – green China
tea and cream and toast. When he had set it on her bedside
table he made his report and got his orders for the day. He
knew that she was depending on him more and more. And Joe
was very slowly and quietly exploring the possibility of taking
over entirely. If she got sick enough there might be a chance.
But very profoundly Joe was afraid of her.

'Morning,' he said.

'I'm not going to sit up for it, Joe. Just give me the tea.
You'll have to hold it.'

'Hands bad?'

'Yes. They get better after a flare-up.'

'Looks like you had a bad night.'

'No,' said Kate. 'I had a good night. I've got some new medicine.'

Joe held the cup to her lips, and she drank the tea in little
sips, breathed over it to cool it. 'That's enough,' she said when
the cup was only half empty. 'How was the night?'

'I almost came to tell you last night,' said Joe. 'Hick came in
from King City. Just sold his crop. Bought out the house.
Dropped seven hundred not counting what he gave the girls.'

'What was his name?'

'I don't know. But I hope he comes in again.'

'You should get the name, Joe. I've told you that.'

'He was cagey.'

'All the more reason to get his name. Didn't any of the girls
frisk him?'

'I don't know.'

'Well, find out.'

Joe sensed a mild geniality in her and it made him feel good.
'I'll find out,' he assured her. 'I got enough to go on.'

Her eyes went over him, testing and searching, and he knew something was coming. 'You like it here?' she asked softly.

'Sure. I got it good here.'

'You could have it better – or worse,' she said.

'I like it good here,' he said uneasily, and his mind cast about for a fault in himself. 'I got it real nice here.'

She moistened her lips with her arrow-sharp tongue. 'You and I can work together,' she said.

'Any way you want it,' he said ingratiatingly, and a surge of pleasant expectation grew in him. He waited patiently. She took a good long time to begin.

At last she said, 'Joe, I don't like to have anything stolen.'

'I didn't take nothing.'

'I didn't say you did.'

'Who?'

'I'll get to it, Joe. Do you remember that old buzzard we had to move?'

'You mean Ethel what's-her-name?'

'Yes. That's the one. She got away with something. I didn't know it then.'

'What?'

A coldness crept into her voice. 'Not your business, Joe. Listen to me! You're a smart fellow. Where would you go to look for her?'

Joe's mind worked quickly, not with reason but with experience and instinct. 'She was pretty beat up. She wouldn't go far. An old hustler don't go far.'

'You're smart. You think she might be in Watsonville?'

'There or maybe Santa Cruz. Anyways, I'll give odds she ain't farther away than San Jose.'

She caressed her fingers tenderly. 'Would you like to make five hundred, Joe?'

'You want I should find her?'

'Yes. Just find her. When you do, don't let her know. Just bring me the address. Got that? Just tell me where she is.'

'Okay,' said Joe. 'She must of rolled you good.'

'That's not your business, Joe.'

'Yes, ma'am,' he said. 'You want I should start right off?'

'Yes. Make it quick, Joe.'

'Might be a little tough,' he said. 'It's been a long time.'

'That's up to you.'

'I'll go to Watsonville this afternoon.'

'That's good, Joe.'

475

She was thoughtful. He knew she was not finished and that she was wondering whether she should go on. She decided.

'Joe, did – did she do anything – well, peculiar – that day in court?'

'Hell, no. Said she was framed like they always do.'

And then something came back to him that he hadn't noticed at the time. Out of his memory Ethel's voice came, saying, 'Judge, I got to see you alone. I got to tell you something.' He tried to bury his memory deep so that his face would not speak.

Kate said, 'Well, what is it?'

He had been too late. His mind leaped for safety. 'There's something,' he said, to gain time. 'I'm trying to think.'

'Well, think!' Her voice was edged and anxious.

'Well —' He had it. 'Well, I heard her tell the cops – let's see – she said why couldn't they let her go south. She said she had relatives in San Luis Obispo.'

Kate leaned quickly towards him. 'Yes?'

'And the cops said it was too damn far.'

'You're smart, Joe. Where will you go first?'

'Watsonville,' he said. 'I got a friend in San Luis. He'll look around for me. I'll give him a ring.'

'Joe,' she said sharply, 'I want this quiet.'

'For five hundred you'll get it quiet and quick,' said Joe. He felt fine even though her eyes were slitted and inspective again. Her next words jarred his stomach loose from his backbone.

'Joe, not to change the subject – does the name Venuta mean anything to you?'

He tried to answer before his throat tightened. 'Not a thing,' he said.

'Come back as soon as you can,' Kate said. 'Tell Helen to come in. She'll take over for you.'

III

Joe packed his suitcase, went to the depot, and bought a ticket for Watsonville. At Castroville, the first station north, he got off and waited four hours for the Del Monte express from San Francisco to Monterey, which is the end of a spur line. In Monterey he climbed the stairs of the Central Hotel, registered as John Vicker. He went downstairs and ate a steak at Pop Ernst's, bought a bottle of whisky, and retired to his room.

He took off his shoes and his coat and waistcoat, removed his collar and tie, and lay down on the bed. The whisky and a glass

476

ere on the table beside the brass bed. The overhead light shin-
ng in his face didn't bother him. He didn't notice it. Methodic-
lly he primed his brain with half a tumbler of whisky and then
e crossed his hands behind his head and crossed his ankles and
e brought out thoughts and impressions and perceptions and
nstincts and began matching them.

It had been a good job and he had thought he had her fooled.
Vell, he'd under-rated her. But how in hell had she got on to
he was wanted? He thought he might go to Reno or maybe to
eattle. Seaport towns – always good. And then – now wait a
minute. Think about it.

Ethel didn't steal nothing. She had something. Kate was
cared of Ethel. Five hundred was a lot of dough to dig out a
eat-up whore. What Ethel wanted to tell the judge was, num-
er one, true; and, number two, Kate was scared of it. Might be
ble to use that. Hell! – not with her holding that jail-break over
im. Joe wasn't going to serve out the limit with penalties.

But no harm in thinking about it. Suppose he was to gamble
our years against – well, let's say ten grand. Was that a bad bet?
No need to decide. She knew it before and she didn't turn him
n. Suppose she thought he was a good dog.

Maybe Ethel might be a hole-card.

Now – wait – just think about it. Maybe it was the breaks.
Maybe he ought to draw his hand and see. But she was so god-
lam smart. Joe wondered if he could play against her. But how,
f he just played along?

Joe sat up and filled his glass full. He turned off his light and
aised his blind. And as he drank his whisky he watched a skinny
ittle woman in a bathrobe washing her stockings in a basin in a
oom on the other side of the air-shaft. And the whisky mut-
ered in his ears.

It might be the breaks. God knows, Joe had waited long
nough. God knows, he hated the bitch with her sharp little
eeth. No need to decide right now.

He raised his window quietly and threw the writing pen from
he table against the window across the air-shaft. He enjoyed the
cene of fear and apprehension before the skinny dame yanked
er blind down.

With the third glass of whisky the pint was empty. Joe felt a
vish to go out in the street and look the town over. But then his
liscipline took over. He had made a rule, and kept to it, never
o leave his room when he was drinking. That way a man never
got in trouble. Trouble meant cops, and cops meant a check-up,

and that would surely mean a trip across the bay to San Quenti and no road gang for good behaviour this time. He put the stree out of his mind.

Joe had another pleasure he saved for times when he wa alone, and he was not aware it was a pleasure. He indulged now. He lay on the brass bed and went back in time over hi sullen and miserable childhood and his fretful and vicious grow ing up. No luck – he never got the breaks. The big shots got th breaks. A few snatch jobs he got away with, but the tray c pocket-knives? Cops came right in his house and got him. Ther he was on the books and they never let him alone. Guy in Dal City couldn't shag a crate of strawberries off a truck withou they'd pick up Joe. In school he didn't have no luck neither Teachers against him, principal against him. Guy couldn't tak that crap. Had to get out.

Out of his memory of bad luck warm sadness grew, and h pushed it with more memories until the tears came to his eye and his lips quivered with pity for the lonely lost boy he hac been. And here he was now – look at him – a rap against him working in a whorehouse when other men had homes and cars They were safe and happy and at night their blinds were pullec down against Joe. He wept quietly until he fell asleep.

Joe got up at ten in the morning and ate a monster breakfas at Pop Ernst's. In the early afternoon he took a bus to Watson ville and played three games of snooker with a friend who cam to meet him in answer to a phone call. Joe won the last game anc racked his cue. He handed his friend two ten-dollar notes.

'Hell,' said his friend, 'I don't want your money.'

'Take it,' said Joe.

'It ain't like I give you anything.'

'You give me plenty. You say she ain't here and you're the baby that would know.'

'Can't tell me what you want her for?'

'Wilson, I tol' you right first an' I tell you now, I don't know I'm jus' doing a job of work.'

'Well, that's all I can do. Seems like there was this conven tion – what was it? – dentists, or maybe Owls. I don't know whether she said she was going or I just figured it myself I got it stuck in my mind. Give Santa Cruz a whirl. Know anybody?'

'I got a few acquaintances,' said Joe.

'Look up H. V. Mahler. Hal Mahler. He runs Hal's pool room. Got a game in back.'

'Thanks,' said Joe.

'No – look, Joe. I don't want your money.'

'It ain't my money – buy a cigar,' said Joe.

The bus dropped him two doors from Hal's place. It was uppertime but the stud game was still going. It was an hour before Hal got up to go to the can and Joe could follow and make a connection. Hal peered at Joe with large pale eyes made huge by thick glasses. He buttoned his fly slowly and adjusted his black alpaca sleeve guards and squared his green eyeshade. 'Stick around till the game breaks,' he said. 'Care to sit in?'

'How many playing for you, Hal?'

'Only one.'

'I'll play for you.'

'Five bucks an hour,' said Hal.

'An' ten per cent if I win?'

'Well, okay. Sandy-haired fella Williams is the house.'

At one o'clock in the morning Hal and Joe went to Barlow's Grill. 'Two rib steaks and french fries. You want soup?' Hal asked Joe.

'No. And no french fries. They bind me up.'

'Me too,' said Hal. 'But I eat them just the same. I don't get enough exercise.'

Hal was a silent man until he was eating. He rarely spoke unless his mouth was full. 'What's your pitch?' he asked around steak.

'Just a job. I make a hundred bucks and you get twenty-five – 'kay?'

'Got to have like proof – like papers?'

'No. Be good but I'll get by without them.'

'Well, she comes in and wants me to steer for her. She wasn't no good. I don't take twenty a week off her. I probably wouldn't of knew what become of her only Bill Primus seen her in my place and when they found her he come in an' ast me about her. Nice fella, Bill. We got a nice force here.'

Ethel was not a bad woman – lazy, sloppy, but good-hearted. She wanted dignity and importance. She was just not very bright and not very pretty and, because of these two lacks, not very lucky. It would have bothered Ethel if she had known that when they pulled her out of the sand where waves had left her half buried her skirts were pulled around her arse. She would have liked more dignity.

Hal said, 'We got some crazy bohunk bastards in the sardine fleet. Get loaded with ink an' they go nuts. Way I figure, one of

479

them sardine crews took her out an' then just pushed her over
board. I don't see how else she'd get in the water.'

'Maybe she jumped off the pier?'

'Her?' said Hal through potatoes. 'Hell, no! She was too laz[y]
to kill herself. You want to check?'

'If you say it's her, it's her,' said Joe, and he pushed a twent[y]
and five across the table.

Hal rolled the notes like a cigarette and put them in his waist[-]
coat pocket. He cut out the triangle of meat from the rib stea[k]
and put it in his mouth. 'It was her,' he said. 'Want a piece o[f]
pie?'

Joe meant to sleep until noon, but he awakened at seven an[d]
lay in bed for quite a long time. He planned not to get back t[o]
Salinas until after midnight. He needed more time to think.

When he got up he looked in the mirror and inspected th[e]
expression he planned to wear. He wanted to look disappointe[d]
but not too disappointed. Kate was so goddam clever. Let he[r]
lead. Just follow suit. She was about as wide open as a fist. Jo[e]
had to admit that he was scared to death of her.

His caution said to him, 'Just go in and tell her and get you[r]
five hundred.'

And he answered his caution savagely. 'Breaks. How man[y]
breaks did I ever get? Part of the breaks is knowing a brea[k]
when you get it. Do I want to be a lousy pimp all my life? Jus[t]
play it close. Let her do the talking. No harm in that. I ca[n]
always tell her later like I just found out if it don't go good.'

'She could have you in a cell block in six hours flat.'

'Not if I play 'em close. What I got to lose? What breaks di[d]
I ever get?'

I V

Kate was feeling better. The new medicine seemed to be doin[g]
her some good. The pain in her hands was abated, and it seeme[d]
to her that her fingers were straighter, the knuckles not so swollen. She had had a good night's sleep, the first in a long time[,]
and she felt good, even a little excited. She planned to have [a]
boiled egg for breakfast. She got up and put on a dressing-gow[n]
and brought a hand mirror back to the bed. Lying high agains[t]
the pillows, she studied her face.

The rest had done wonders. Pain makes you set your jaw, and
your eyes grow falsely bright with anxiety, and the muscles over
the temples and along the cheeks, even the weak muscles near t[o]

480

he nose stand out a little, and that is the look of sickness and of
esistance to suffering.

The difference in her rested face was amazing. She looked ten
ears younger. She opened her lips and looked at her teeth.
Time to go for a cleaning. She took care of her teeth. The gold
ridge where the molars were gone was the only repair in her
nouth. It was remarkable how young she looked, Kate thought.
ust one night's sleep and she snapped back. That was another
hing that fooled them. They thought she would be weak and
elicate. She smiled to herself – delicate like a steel trap. But
hen she always took care of herself – no liquor, no drugs, and
ecently she had stopped drinking coffee. And it paid off. She
ad an angelic face. She put the mirror a little higher so that
he crêpe at her throat did not reflect.

Her thought jumped to that other angelic face so like hers –
what was his name? – what the hell was his name – Alec? She
ould see him, moving slowly past, his white surplice edged with
ace, his sweet chin down and his hair glowing under the candle-
ight. He held the oaken staff and its brass cross angled ahead of
im. There was something frigidly beautiful about him, some-
hing untouched and untouchable. Well, had anything or any-
ody ever really touched Kate – really got through and soiled
er? Certainly not. Only the hard outside had been brushed by
ontacts. Inside she was intact – as clean and bright as this boy
Alec – was that his name?

She chuckled – mother of two sons – and she looked like a
child. And if anyone had seen her with the blond one – could
hey have any doubt? She thought how it would be to stand
eside him in a crowd and let people find out for themselves.
What would – Aron, that was his name – what would he do if he
knew? His brother knew. That smart little son of a bitch –
wrong word – must not call him that. Might be too true. Some
people believed it. And not smart bastard either – born in holy
wedlock. Kate laughed aloud. She felt good. She was having a
good time.

The smart one – the dark one – bothered her. He was like
Charles. She had respected Charles – and Charles would probably have killed her if he could.

Wonderful medicine – it not only stopped the arthritic pain,
it gave her back her courage. Pretty soon she could sell out and
go to New York as she had always planned. Kate thought of her
fear of Ethel. How sick she must have been – the poor dumb old
bag! How would it be to murder her with kindness? When Joe

found her, how about – well, how about taking her to New York? Keep her close.

A funny notion came to Kate. That would be a comical murder, and a murder no one under any circumstances could solve or even suspect. Chocolates – boxes of chocolates, bowls of fondant, bacon, crisp bacon – fat; port wine, and then butter, everything soaked in butter and whipped cream; no vegetables, no fruit – and no amusement either. Stay in the house, dear. I trust you. Look after things. You're tired. Go to bed. Let me fill your glass. I got these new sweets for you. Would you like to take the box to bed? Well, if you don't feel good why don't you take a physic? These cachous are nice, don't you think? The old bitch would blow up and burst in six months. Or how about a tapeworm? Did anyone ever use tapeworms? Who was the man who couldn't get water to his mouth in a sieve – Tantalus?

Kate's lips were smiling sweetly and gaiety was coming over her. Before she went it might be good to give a party for her sons. Just a simple little party with a circus afterwards for her darlings – her jewels. And then she thought of Aron's beautiful face so like her own and a strange pain – a little collapsing pain – arose in her chest. He wasn't smart. He couldn't protect himself. The dark brother might be dangerous. She had felt his quality. Cal had beaten her. Before she went away she would teach him a lesson. Maybe – why, sure – maybe a dose of the clap might set that young man back on his heels.

Suddenly she knew that she did not want Aron to know about her. Maybe he could come to her in New York. He would think she had always lived in an elegant little house on the East Side. She would take him to the theatre, to the opera, and people would see them together and wonder at their loveliness, and recognize that they were either brother and sister or mother and son. No one could fail to know. They could go together to Ethel's funeral. She would need an oversize coffin and six wrestlers to carry it. Kate was so filled with amusement at her thoughts that she did not hear Joe's knocking on the door. He opened it a crack and looked in and saw her gay and smiling face.

'Breakfast,' he said and nudged the door open with the edge of the linen-covered tray. He pushed the door closed with his knee. 'Want it there?' he asked and gestured towards the grey room with his chin.

'No. I'll have it right here. And I want a boiled egg and a piece of cinnamon toast. Four and a half minutes on the egg. Make sure. I don't want it gooey.'

'You must feel better, ma'am.'

'I do,' she said. 'That new medicine is wonderful. You look ragged by dogs, Joe. Don't you feel well?'

'I'm all right,' he said and set the tray on the table in front of he big deep chair. 'Four and a half minutes?'

'That's right. And if there's a good apple – a crisp apple – ring that too.'

'You ain't et like this since I knew you,' he said.

In the kitchen, waiting for the cook to boil the egg, he was apprehensive. Maybe she knew. He'd have to be careful. But ell! she couldn't hate him for something he didn't know. No crime in that.

Back in her room he said, 'Didn't have no apples. He said his was a good pear.'

'I'd like that even better,' said Kate.

He watched her chip off the egg and dip a spoon into the shell. 'How is it?'

'Perfect!' said Kate. 'Just perfect.'

'You look good,' he said.

'I feel good. You look like hell. What's the matter?'

Joe went into it warily. 'Ma'am, there ain't nobody needs five hundred like I do.'

She said playfully, 'There isn't *anyone* who needs — '

'What?'

'Forget it. What are you trying to say? You couldn't find her – is that it? Well, if you did a good job looking, you'll get your five hundred. Tell me about it.' She picked up the salt shaker and scattered a few grains into the open eggshell.

Joe put an artificial joy on his face. 'Thanks,' he said. 'I'm in a spot. I need it. Well, I looked in Pajaro and Watsonville. Got a line on her in Watsonville but she'd went to Santa Cruz. Got a smell of her there but she was gone.'

Kate tasted the egg and added more salt. 'That all?'

'No,' said Joe. 'I went it blind there. Dropped down to San Luis an' she had been there too but gone.'

'No trace? No idea where she went?'

Joe fiddled with his fingers. His whole pitch, maybe his whole life, depended on his next words, and he was reluctant to say them.

'Come on,' she said at last. 'You got something – what is it?'

'Well, it ain't much. I don't know what to think of it.'

'Don't think. Just tell. I'll think,' she said sharply.

'Might not even be true.'

'For Christ's sake!' she said angrily.

'Well, I talked to the last guy that seen her. Guy named Joe, like me —'

'Did you get his grandmother's name?' she asked sarcastically.

'This guy Joe says she loaded up on beer one night an' she said how she's going to come back to Salinas an' lay low. Then she dropped out of sight. This guy Joe didn't know nothing more.'

Kate was startled out of control. Joe read her quick start, the apprehension, and then the almost hopeless fear and weariness. Whatever it was, Joe had something. He had got the breaks at last.

She looked up from her lap and her twisted fingers. 'We'll forget the old fart,' she said. 'You'll get your five hundred, Joe.'

Joe breathed shallowly, afraid that any sound might drag her out of her self-absorption. She had believed him. More than that, she was believing things he had not told her. He wanted to get out of the room as quickly as possible. He said, 'Thank you, ma'am,' but very softly, and he moved silently towards the door.

His hand was on the knob when she spoke with elaborate casualness. 'Joe, by the way —'

'Ma'am?'

'If you should hear anything about – her, let me know, will you?'

'I sure will. Want me to dig into it?'

'No. Don't bother. It isn't that important.'

In his room, with the door latched, Joe sat down and folded his arms. He smiled to himself. And instantly he began to work out the future course. He decided to let her brood on it till, say, next week. Let her relax, and then bring up Ethel again. He did not know what his weapon was or how he was going to use it. But he did know that it was very sharp and he itched to use it. He would have laughed out loud if he had known that Kate had gone to the grey room and locked its door, and that she sat still in the big chair and her eyes were closed.

CHAPTER 46

SOMETIMES, BUT not often, a rain comes to the Salinas Valley in November. It is so rare that the *Journal* or the *Index* or both carry editorials about it. The hills turn to a soft green over-night and the air smells good. Rain at this time is not particularly good in an agricultural sense unless it is going to continue, and this is extremely unusual. More commonly, the dryness comes back and the fuzz of grass withers or a little frost curls it and there's that amount of seed wasted.

The war years were wet years, and there were many people who blamed the strange intransigent weather on the firing of the great guns in France. This was seriously considered in articles and in arguments.

We didn't have many troops in France that first winter, but we had millions in training, getting ready to go.

Painful as the war was, it was exciting too. The Germans were not stopped. In fact, they had taken the initiative again, driving methodically towards Paris, and God knew when they could be stopped – if they could be stopped at all. General Pershing would save us if we could be saved. His trim, beautifully uniformed soldierly figure made its appearance in every paper every day. His chin was granite and there was no wrinkle on his tunic. He was the epitome of a perfect soldier. No one knew what he really thought.

We knew we couldn't lose and yet we seemed to be going about losing. You couldn't buy flour, white flour, any more without taking four times the quantity of brown flour. Those who could afford it ate bread and biscuits made with white flour and made mash for the chickens with the brown.

In the old Troop C armoury the Home Guard drilled, men over fifty and not the best soldier material, but they took setting-up exercises twice a week, wore Home Guard buttons and overseas caps, snapped orders at one another, and wrangled eternally about who should be officers. William C. Burt died right on the armoury floor in the middle of a push-up. His heart couldn't take it.

There were Minute Men too, so called because they made one-minute speeches in favour of America in moving-picture theatres and in churches. They had buttons too.

The women rolled bandages and wore Red Cross uniforms

and thought of themselves as Angels of Mercy. And everybod knitted something for someone. There were wristlets, short tube of wool to keep the wind from whistling up soldiers' sleeves, an there were knitted helmets with only a hole in front to look ou of. These were designed to keep the new tin helmets from freez ing to the head.

Every bit of really first-grade leather was taken for officers boots and for Sam Browne belts. These belts were handsome an only officers could wear them. They consisted of a wide bel and a strap that crossed the chest and passed under the lef epaulette. We copied them from the British, and even the Britis had forgotten their original purpose, which was possibly to sup port a heavy sword. Swords were not carried except on parade but an officer would not be caught dead without a Sam Browne belt. A good one cost as much as twenty-five dollars.

We learned a lot from the British – and if they had not been good fighting men we wouldn't have taken it. Men began to wear their handkerchiefs in their sleeves and some foppish lieu tenants carried swagger sticks. One thing we resisted for a long time, though. Wrist-watches were just too silly. It didn't seem likely that we would ever copy the Limeys in that.

We had our internal enemies too, and we exercised vigilance San Jose had a spy scare, and Salinas was not likely to be lef behind – not the way Salinas was growing.

For about twenty years Mr Fenchel had done hand tailoring in Salinas. He was short and round and he had an accent that made you laugh. All day he sat cross-legged on his table in the little shop on Alisal Street, and in the evening he walked home to his small white house far out on Central Avenue. He was for ever painting his house and the white picket fence in front of it. Nobody had given his accent a thought until the war came along, but suddenly we knew. It was German. We had our own personal German. It didn't do him any good to bankrupt him self buying war bonds. That was too easy a way to cover up.

The Home Guards wouldn't take him in. They didn't want a spy knowing their secret plans for defending Salinas. And who wanted to wear a suit made by an enemy? Mr Fenchel sat all day on his table and he didn't have anything to do, so he basted and ripped and sewed and ripped on the same piece of cloth over and over.

We used every cruelty we could think of on Mr Fenchel. He was our German. He passed our house every day, and there had been a time when he spoke to every man and woman and child and dog, and everyone had answered. Now no one spoke to him, and I can see now in my mind his tubby loneliness and his face full of hurt pride.

My little sister and I did our part with Mr Fenchel, and it is one of those memories of shame that still makes me break into a sweat and tighten up around the throat. We were standing in our front yard on the lawn one evening and we saw him coming with little fat steps. His black homburg was brushed and squarely set on his head. I don't remember that we discussed our plan but we must have, to have carried it out so well.

As he came near, my sister and I moved slowly across the street side by side. Mr Fenchel looked up and saw us moving towards him. We stopped in the gutter as he came by.

He broke into a smile and said, 'Gut efning, Chon. Gut efning, Mary.'

We stood stiffly side by side and we said in unison, 'Hoch der Kaiser!'

I can see his face now, his startled innocent blue eyes. He tried to say something and then he began to cry. Didn't even try to pretend he wasn't. He just stood there sobbing. And do you know? – Mary and I turned round and walked stiffly across the street and into our front yard. We felt horrible. I still do when I think of it.

We were too young to do a good job on Mr Fenchel. That took strong men – about thirty of them. One Saturday night they collected in a bar and marched in a column of fours out Central Avenue, saying, 'Hup! Hup!' in unison. They tore down Mr Fenchel's white picket fence and burned the front out of his house. No Kaiser-loving son of a bitch was going to get away with it with us. And then Salinas could hold up its head with San Jose.

Of course that made Watsonville get busy. They tarred and feathered a Pole they thought was a German. He had an accent.

We of Salinas did all of the things that are inevitably done in a war, and we thought the inevitable thoughts. We screamed over good rumours and died of panic at bad news. Everybody had a secret that he had to spread obliquely to keep its identity as a secret. Our pattern of life changed in the usual manner. Wages and prices went up. A whisper of shortage caused us to buy and store food. Nice quiet ladies clawed one another over a can of tomatoes.

It wasn't all bad or cheap or hysterical. There was heroism too. Some men who could have avoided the army enlisted, and others objected to the war on moral or religious grounds and took the walk up Golgotha which normally comes of that. There were people who gave everything they had to the war because it was the last war and by winning it we would remove war like a thorn from the flesh of the world and there wouldn't be any more such horrible nonsense.

There is no dignity in death in battle. Mostly that is a splashing about of human meat and fluid, and the result is filthy, but there is a great and almost sweet dignity in the sorrow, the helpless, the hopeless sorrow, that comes down over a family with the telegram. Nothing to say, nothing to do, and only one hope – I hope he didn't suffer – and what a forlorn and last-choice hope that is. And it is true that there were some people who, when their sorrow was beginning to lose its savour, gently edged it towards pride and felt increasingly important because of their loss. Some of these even made a good thing of it after the war was over. That is only natural, just as it is natural for a man whose function is the making of money to make money out of a war. No one blamed a man for that, but it was expected that he should invest a part of his loot in war bonds. We thought we invented all of it in Salinas, even the sorrow.

CHAPTER 47

I

IN THE Trask house next to Reynaud's bakery, Lee and Adam put up a map of the western front with lines of coloured pins snaking down, and this gave them a feeling of participation. Then Mr Kelly died and Adam Trask was appointed to take his place on the draft board. He was the logical man for the job. The ice plant did not take up much of his time, and he had a clear service record and an honourable discharge himself.

Adam Trask had seen a war – a little war of manoeuvre and butchery, but at least he had experienced the reversal of the rules where a man is permitted to kill all the humans he can. Adam didn't remember his war very well. Certain sharp pictures stood out in his memory, a man's face, the piled and burning bodies, the clang of sabre scabbards at fast trot, the uneven, tearing sound of firing carbines, the thin cold voice of a bugle in the night. But Adam's pictures were frozen. There was no motion

r emotion in them – illustrations in the pages of a book, and
ot very well drawn.

Adam worked hard and honestly and sadly. He could not get
ver the feeling that the young men he passed to the army were
nder sentence of death. And because he knew he was weak, he
rew more and more stern and painstaking and much less likely
o accept an excuse or a borderline disability. He took the lists
ome with him, called on parents, in fact, did much more work
han was expected of him. He felt like a hanging judge who
ates the gallows.

Henry Stanton watched Adam grow more gaunt and more
ilent, and Henry was a man who liked fun – needed it. A sour-
ussed associate could make him sick.

'Relax,' he told Adam. 'You're trying to carry the weight of
he war. Now, look – it's not your responsibility. You got put in
ere with a set of rules. Just follow the rules and relax. You
ren't running the war.'

Adam moved the slats of the blind so that the late afternoon
un would not shine in his eyes, and he gazed down at the
arsh parallel lines the sun threw on his desk. 'I know,' he said
early. 'Oh, I know that! But, Henry, it's when there's a
hoice, and it's my own judgement of the merits, that's when it
ets me. I passed Judge Kendal's boy, and he was killed in
raining.'

'It's not your business, Adam. Why don't you take a few
drinks at night? Go to a movie – sleep on it.' Henry put his
humbs in the armholes of his waistcoat and leaned back in his
hair. 'While we're talking about it, Adam, it seems to me it
lon't do a candidate a damn bit of good for you to worry. You
pass boys I could be talked into letting off.'

'I know,' said Adam. 'I wonder how long it will last?'

Henry inspected him shrewdly and took a pencil from his
stuffed waistcoat pocket and rubbed the eraser against his big
white front teeth. 'I see what you mean,' he said softly.

Adam looked at him, startled. 'What do I mean?' he demanded.

'Now don't get huffy. I never thought I was lucky before,
just having girls.'

Adam traced one of the slat shadows on his desk with his
forefinger. 'Yes,' he said in a voice as soft as a sigh.

'It's a long time before your boys will be called up.'

'Yes.' Adam's finger entered a line of light and slid slowly
back.

Henry said, 'I'd hate to — '

'Hate to what?'

'I was just wondering how I'd feel if I had to pass my own sons.'

'I'd resign,' said Adam.

'Yes, I can see that. A man would be tempted to reject them – I mean, his own.'

'No,' said Adam. 'I'd resign because I couldn't reject them. A man couldn't let his own go free.'

Henry laced his fingers and made one big fist of his two hands and laid the fist on the desk in front of him. His face was querulous. 'No,' he said, 'you're right. A man couldn't.' Henry liked fun and avoided when he could any solemn or serious matter, for he confused these with sorrow. 'How's Aron doing at Stanford?'

'Fine. He writes that it's hard but he thinks he'll make out all right. He'll be home for Thanksgiving.'

'I'd like to see him. I saw Cal on the street last night. There's a smart boy.'

'Cal didn't take college tests a year ahead,' said Adam.

'Well, maybe that's not what he's cut out for. I didn't go to college. Did you?'

'No,' said Adam. 'I went into the army.'

'Well, it's good experience. I'll bet you wouldn't take a good bit for the experience.'

Adam stood up slowly and picked his hat from the deer-horns on the wall. 'Good night, Henry,' he said.

II

Walking home, Adam pondered his responsibility. As he passed Reynaud's Bakery Lee came out, carying a golden loaf of French bread.

'I have a hunger for some garlic bread,' Lee said.

'I like it with steak,' said Adam.

'We're having steak. Was there any mail?'

'I forgot to look in the box.'

They entered the house and Lee went to the kitchen. In a moment Adam followed him and sat at the kitchen table. 'Lee,' he said, 'suppose we send a boy to the army and he is killed, are we responsible?'

'Go on,' said Lee. 'I would rather have the whole thing at once.'

'Well, suppose there's a slight doubt that the boy should be in the army and we send him and he gets killed.'

'I see. Is it responsibility or blame that bothers you?'

'I don't want blame.'

'Sometimes responsibility is worse. It doesn't carry any pleasant egotism.'

'I was thinking about that time when Sam Hamilton and you and I had a long discussion about a word,' said Adam. 'What was that word?'

'Now I see. The word was *timshel*.'

'*Timshel* – and you said —'

'I said that word carried a man's greatness if he wanted to take advantage of it.'

'I remember Sam Hamilton felt good about it.'

'It set him free,' said Lee. 'It gave him the right to be a man, separate from every other man.'

'That's lonely.'

'All great and precious things are lonely.'

'What is the word again?'

'*Timshel* – thou mayest.'

III

Adam looked forward to Thanksgiving when Aron would come home from college. Even though Aron had been away such a short time Adam had forgotten him and changed him the way any man changes someone he loves. With Aron gone, the silences were the result of his going, and every little painful event was somehow tied to his absence. Adam found himself talking and boasting about his son, telling people who weren't very interested how smart Aron was and how he had jumped a year in school. He thought it would be a good thing to have a real celebration at Thanksgiving to let the boy know his effort was appreciated.

Aron lived in a furnished room in Palo Alto, and he walked the mile to and from the campus every day. He was miserable. What he had expected to find at the university had been vague and beautiful. His picture – never really inspected – had been of clean-eyed young men and immaculate girls, all in academic robes and converging on a white temple on the crown of a wooded hill in the evening. Their faces were shining and dedicated and their voices rose in chorus and it was never any time but evening. He had no idea where he had got his picture of academic life – perhaps from the Doré illustrations of Dante's

Inferno with its massed and radiant angels. Leland Stanford University was not like that. A formal square of brown sandstone blocks set down in a hayfield; a church with an Italian mosaic front; classrooms of varnished pine; and the great world of struggle and anger re-enacted in the rise and fall of fraternities. And those bright angels were youths in dirty corduroy trousers, some study-raddled and some learning the small vices of their fathers.

Aron, who had not known he had a home, was nauseatingly homesick. He did not try to learn the life around him or to enter it. He found the natural noise and fuss and horseplay of undergraduates horrifying, after his dream. He left the college dormitory for a dreary furnished room where he could decorate another dream which had only now come into being. In the new and neutral hiding place he cut the university out, went to his classes and left as soon as he could, to live in his new-found memories. The house next to Reynaud's Bakery became warm and dear, Lee the epitome of friend and counsellor, his father the cool, dependable figure of godhead, his brother clever and delightful, and Abra – well, of Abra he made his immaculate dream and, having created her, fell in love with her. At night when his studying was over he went to his nightly letter to her as one goes to a scented bath. And as Abra became more radiant, more pure and beautiful, Aron took an increasing joy in a concept of his own wickedness. In a frenzy he poured joyous abjectness on paper to send to her, and he went to bed purified, as a man is after sexual love. He set down every evil thought he had and renounced it. The results were love letters that dripped with longing and by their high tone made Abra very uneasy. She could not know that Aron's sexuality had taken a not unusual channel.

He had made a mistake. He could admit the mistake but as yet he could not reverse himself. He made a compact with himself. At Thanksgiving he would go home, and then he would be sure. He might never come back. He remembered that Abra had once suggested that they go to live on the ranch, and that became his dream. He remembered the great oaks and the clear living air, the clean sage-laced wind from the hills and the brown oak leaves scudding. He could see Abra there, standing under a tree, waiting for him to come in from his work. And it was evening. There, after work of course, he could live in purity and peace with the world, cut off by the little draw. He could hide from ugliness – in the evening.

CHAPTER 48

I

LATE IN November the Nigger died and was buried in black austerity, as her will demanded. She lay for a day in Muller's Funeral Chapel in an ebony and silver casket, her lean and severe profile made even more ascetic by the four large candles set at the four corners of the casket.

Her little black husband crouched like a cat by her right shoulder, and for many hours he seemed as still as she. There were no flowers, as ordered, no ceremony, no sermon, and no grief. But a strange, and catholic selection of citizens tiptoed to the chapel door and peered in and went away – lawyers and labourers and clerks and bank tellers, most of them past middle age. Her girls came in one at a time and looked at her for decency and for luck and went away.

An institution was gone from Salinas, dark and fatal sex, as hopeless and deeply hurtful as human sacrifice. Jenny's place would still jangle with honky-tonk and rock with belching laughter. Kate's would rip the nerves to a sinful ecstasy and leave a man shaken and weak and frightened at himself. But the sombre mystery of connexion that was like a voodoo offering was gone for ever.

The funeral was also by order of the will, the hearse and one automobile with the small black man crouched back in a corner. It was a grey day, and when Muller's service had lowered the casket with oiled and silent winches the hearse drove away and the husband filled the grave himself with a new shovel. The caretaker cutting dry weeds a hundred yards away, heard a whining carried on the wind.

Joe Valery had been drinking a beer with Butch Beavers at the Owl, and he went with Butch to have a look at Nigger. Butch was in a hurry because he had to go out to Natividad to auction a small herd of white-face Herefords for the Tavernettis.

Coming out of the mortuary, Joe found himself in step with Alf Nichelson – crazy Alf Nichelson, who was a survival from an era that was past. Alf was a jack-of-all-trades, carpenter, tinsmith, blacksmith, electrician, plasterer, scissor grinder, and cobbler. Alf could do anything, and as a result was a financial

493

failure although he worked all the time. He knew everything about everybody back to the beginning of time.

In the past, in the period of his success, two kinds of people had access to all homes and all gossip – the seamstress and the handy man. Alf could tell you about everybody on both sides of Main Street. He was a vicious male gossip, insatiably curious and vindictive without malice.

He looked at Joe and tried to place him. 'I know you,' he said. 'Don't tell me.'

Joe edged away. He was wary of people who knew him.

'Wait a minute. I got it. Kate's. You work at Kate's.'

Joe sighed with relief. He had thought Alf might have known him earlier. 'That's right,' he said shortly.

'Never forget a face,' said Alf. 'Seen you when I built that crazy lean-to for Kate. Now why in hell did she want that for? No window.'

'Wanted it dark,' said Joe. 'Eyes bother her.'

Alf sniffed. He hardly ever believed anything simple or good about anybody. You could say good morning to Alf and he'd work it around to a password. He was convinced that everyone lived secretly and that only he could see through them.

He jerked his head back at Muller's. 'Well, it's a milestone,' he said. 'Nearly all the old-timers gone. When Fartin' Jenny goes that'll be the end. And Jenny's getting along.'

Joe was restless. He wanted to get away – and Alf knew he did. Alf was an expert in people who wanted to get away from him. Come to think of it, maybe that's why he carried his bag of stories. No one really went away when he could hear some juicy stuff about someone. Everybody is a gossip at heart. Alf was not liked for his gift but he was listened to. And he knew that Joe was on the point of making an excuse and getting out. It occurred to him that he didn't know much about Kate's place lately. Joe might trade him some new stuff for some old stuff. 'The old days was pretty good,' he said. ' 'Course you're just a kid.'

'I got to meet a fella,' said Joe.

Alf pretended not to hear him. 'You take Faye,' he said. 'She was a case,' and, parenthetically, 'You know Faye run Kate's place. Nobody really knows how Kate come to own it. It was pretty mysterious, and there were some that had their suspicions.' He saw with satisfaction that the fella Joe was going to meet would wait a long time.

'What was they suspicious about?' Joe asked.

494

'Hell, you know how people talk. Probably nothing in it. But got to admit it looked kind of funny.'

'Like to have a beer?' Joe asked.

'Now you got something there,' said Alf. 'They say a fella mps from a funeral to the bedroom. I ain't as young as I was. uneral makes me thirsty. The Nigger was quite a citizen. I uld tell you stuff about her. I've knew her for thirty-five – no, irty-seven years.'

'Who was Faye?' Joe asked.

They went into Mr Griffin's saloon. Mr Griffin didn't like ɩything about liquor, and he hated drunks with a deadly scorn. ʃe owned and operated Griffin's Saloon on Main Street, and on Saturday night he might refuse to serve twenty men he thought ɑd had enough. The result was that he got the best trade in his ɔol, orderly, quiet place. It was a saloon in which to make deals ɩd to talk quietly without interruption.

Joe and Alf sat at the round table at the back and had three ɛers apiece. Joe learned everything true and untrue, founded ɩd unfounded, every ugly conjecture. Out of it he got com-ɭete confusion but a few ideas. Something might have been not xactly on the level about the death of Faye. Kate might be the ife of Adam Trask. He hid that quickly – Trask might want to ɑy off. The Faye thing might be too hot to touch. Joe had to ɩink about that – alone.

At the end of a couple of hours Alf was restive. Joe had not ɭayed ball. He had traded nothing, not one single piece of in-ɔrmation or guess. Alf found himself thinking, Fella that close-ɩouthed must have something to hide. Wonder who would have line on him?

Alf said finally, 'Understand, I like Kate. She gives me a job ow and then and she's generous and quick to pay. Probably ɩothing to all the palaver about her. Still, when you think of it, ɩe's a pretty cold piece of woman. She's got a real bad eye. You ɩink?'

'I get along fine,' said Joe.

Alf was angry at Joe's perfidy, so he put in a needle. 'I had a ɩnny idea,' he said. 'It was when I built that lean-to without no vindow. She laid that cold eye on me one day and the idea ɔome to me. If she knew all the things I heard, and she was to ɔffer me a drink or even a cup-cake – why, I'd say, "No, thank ɔu, ma'am."'

'Me and her get along just fine,' said Joe. 'I got to meet a ɡuy.'

Joe went to his room to think. He was uneasy. He jumped up and looked in his suitcase and opened all the bureau drawers. He thought somebody had been going through his things. Just came to him. There was nothing to find. It made him nervous. He tried to arrange the things he had heard.

There was a tap on the door and Thelma came in, her eyes swollen and her nose red. 'What's got into Kate?'

'She's been sick.'

'I don't mean that. I was in the kitchen shaking up a milk-shake in a fruit jar and she came in and worked me over.'

'Was you maybe shaking up a little bourbon in it?'

'Hell, no. Just vanilla extract. She can't talk like that to me.'

'She did, didn't she?'

'Well, I won't take it.'

'Oh, yes, you will,' said Joe. 'Get out, Thelma!'

Thelma looked at him out of her dark, handsome, brooding eyes, and she regained the island of safety a woman depends on. 'Joe,' she asked, 'are you really just pure son of a bitch or do you just pretend to be?'

'What do you care?' Joe asked.

'I don't,' said Thelma. 'You son of a bitch.'

11

Joe planned to move slowly, cautiously, and only after long con-sideration. 'I got the breaks, I got to use 'em right,' he told him-self.

He went in to get his evening orders and took them from the back of Kate's head. She was at her desk, green eyeshade low, and she did not look round at him. She finished her terse orders and then went on, 'Joe, I wonder if you've been attending to business. I've been sick. But I'm well again or very nearly well.'

'Something wrong?'

'Just a symptom. I'd rather Thelma drank whisky than vanilla extract, and I don't want her to drink whisky. I think you've been slipping.'

His mind scurried for a hiding place. 'Well, I been busy,' he said.

'Busy?'

'Sure. Doing that stuff for you.'

'What stuff?'

'You know – about Ethel.'

496

'Forget Ethel!'

'Okay,' said Joe. And then it came without his expecting it. 'I met a fella yesterday said he seen her.'

If Joe had not known her he would not have given the little pause, the rigid ten seconds of silence, its due.

At the end of it Kate asked softly, 'Where?'

'Here.'

She turned her swivel chair slowly round to face him. 'I shouldn't have let you work in the dark, Joe. It's hard to confess a fault but I owe it to you. I don't have to remind you I got Ethel floated out of the county. I thought she'd done something to me.' A melancholy came into her voice. 'I was wrong. I found out later. It's been working on me ever since. She didn't do anything to me. I want to find her and make it up to her. I guess you think it's strange for me to feel that way.'

'No, ma'am.'

'Find her for me, Joe. I'll feel better when I've made it up to her – the poor old girl.'

'I'll try, ma'am.'

'And, Joe – if you need any money, let me know. And if you find her, just tell her what I said. If she doesn't want to come here, find out where I can telephone her. Need any money?'

'Not right now, ma'am. But I'll have to go out of the house more than I ought.'

'You go ahead. That's all, Joe.'

He wanted to hug himself. In the hall he gripped his elbows and let his joy run through him. And he began to believe he had planned the whole thing. He went through the darkened parlour with its low early evening spatter of conversation. He stepped outside and looked up at the stars swimming in schools through the wind-driven clouds.

Joe thought of his bumbling father – because he remembered something the old man had told him. 'Look out for a soup carrier,' Joe's father had said. 'Take one of them dames that's always carrying soup for somebody – she wants something, and don't you forget it.'

Joe said under his breath, 'A soup carrier. I thought she was smarter than that.' He went over her tone and words to make sure he hadn't missed anything. No – a soup carrier. And he thought of Alf saying, 'If she was to offer a drink or even a cup-cake —'

Kate sat at her desk. She could hear the wind in the tall privet in the yard, and the wind and the darkness was full of Ethel – fat, sloppy Ethel oozing near like a jellyfish. A dull weariness came over her.

She went into the lean-to, the grey room, and closed the door and sat in the darkness, listening to the pain creep back into her fingers. Her temples beat with pounding blood. She felt for the capsule hanging in its tube on the chain round her neck, she rubbed the metal tube, warm from her breast, against her cheek, and her courage came back. She washed her face and put on make-up, combed and puffed her hair in a loose pompadour. She moved into the hall and at the door of the parlour she paused, as always, listening.

To the right of the door two girls and a man were talking. As soon as Kate stepped inside the talk stopped instantly. Kate said, 'Helen, I want to see you if you aren't busy right now.'

The girl followed her down the hall and into her room. She was a pale blonde with a skin like a clean and polished bone. 'Is something the matter, Miss Kate?' she asked fearfully.

'Sit down. No. Nothing's the matter. You went to the Nigger's funeral.'

'Didn't you want me to?'

'I don't care about that. You went.'

'Yes, ma'am.'

'Tell me about it.'

'What about it?'

'Tell me what you remember – how it was.'

Helen said nervously, 'Well, it was kind of awful and – kind of beautiful.'

'How do you mean?'

'I don't know. No flowers, no nothing, but there was – there was a – well, a kind of – dignity. The Nigger was just laying there in a black wood coffin with the biggest goddam silver handles. Made you feel – I can't say it. I don't know how to say it.'

'Maybe you said it. What did she wear.'

'Wear, ma'am?'

'Yes – wear. They didn't bury her naked, did they?'

A struggle of effort crossed Helen's face. 'I don't know,' she said at last. 'I don't remember.'

'Did you go to the cemetery?'

'No, ma'am. Nobody did – except him.'

'Who?'

'Her man.'

Kate said quickly – almost too quickly, 'Have you got any regulars tonight?'

'No, ma'am. Day before Thanksgiving. Bound to be slow.'

'I'd forgotten,' said Kate. 'Get back out.' She watched the girl out of the room and moved restlessly back to her desk. And as she looked at an itemized bill for plumbing her left hand strayed to her neck and touched the chain. It was comfort and reassurance.

CHAPTER 49

I

BOTH LEE and Cal tried to argue Adam out of going to meet the train, the Lark night train from San Francisco to Los Angeles.

Cal said, 'Why don't we let Abra go alone? He'll want to see her first.'

'I think he won't know anybody else is there,' said Lee. 'So it doesn't matter whether we go or not.'

'I want to see him get off the train,' said Adam. 'He'll be changed. I want to see what change there is.'

Lee said, 'He's only been gone a couple of months. He can't be very changed, nor much older.'

'He'll be changed. Experience will do that.'

'If you go we'll all have to go,' said Cal.

'Don't you want to see your brother?' Adam asked sternly.

'Sure, but he won't want to see me – not right at first.'

'He will too,' said Adam. 'Don't you under-rate Aron.'

Lee threw up his hands. 'I guess we'll all go,' he said.

'Can you imagine?' said Adam. 'He'll know so many new things. I wonder if he'll talk different. You know, Lee, in the East a boy takes on the speech of his school. You can tell a Harvard man from a Princeton man. At least that's what they say.'

'I'll listen,' said Lee. 'I wonder what dialect they speak at Stanford.' He smiled at Cal.

Adam didn't think it was funny. 'Did you put some fruit in his room?' he asked. 'He loves fruit.'

'Pears and apples and muscat grapes,' said Lee.

'Yes, he loves muscats. I remember he loves muscats.'

Under Adam's urging they got to the Southern Pacific Depot half an hour before the train was due. Abra was already there.

'I can't come to dinner tomorrow, Lee,' she said. 'My father wants me home. I'll come as soon after as I can.'

'You're a little breathless,' said Lee.

'Aren't you?'

'I guess I am,' said Lee. 'Look up the track and see if the block's turned green.'

Train schedules are a matter of pride and of apprehension to nearly everyone. When, far up the track, the block signal snapped from red to green and the long, stabbing probe of the headlight sheered round the bend and blared on the station, men looked at their watches and said, 'On time.'

There was pride in it, and relief too. The split second has been growing more and more important to us. And as human activities become more and more intermeshed and integrated, the split tenth of a second will emerge, and then a new name must be made for the split hundredth, until one day, although I don't believe it, we'll say, 'Oh, the hell with it. What's wrong with an hour?' But it isn't silly, this preoccupation with small time units. One thing late or early can disrupt everything around it, and the disturbance runs outwards in bands like the waves from a dropped stone in a quiet pool.

The Lark came rushing in as though it had no intention of stopping. And only when the engine and baggage cars were well past did the air brakes give their screaming hiss and the straining iron protest to a halt.

The train delivered quite a crowd for Salinas, returning relatives home for Thanksgiving, their hands entangled in cartons and gift-wrapped paper boxes. It was a moment or two before his family could locate Aron. And then they saw him, and he seemed bigger than he had been.

He was wearing a flat-topped, narrow-brimmed hat, very stylish, and when he saw them he broke into a run and yanked off his hat, and they could see that his bright hair was clipped to a short brush of a pompadour that stood straight up. And his eyes shone so that they laughed with pleasure to see him.

Aron dropped his suitcase and lifted Abra from the ground in a great hug. He set her down and gave Adam and Cal his two hands. He put his arms around Lee's shoulders and nearly crushed him.

On the way home they all talked at once. 'Well, how are you?' 'You look fine.' 'Abra, you're so pretty.'

'I am not. Why did you cut your hair?'

'Oh, everybody wears it that way.'

'But you have such nice hair.'

They hurried up to Main Street and one short block and round the corner on Central past Reynaud's with stacked French bread in the window and black-haired Mrs Reynaud waved her flour-pale hand at them, and they were home.

Adam said, 'Coffee, Lee?'

'I made it before we left. It's on the simmer.' He had the cups laid out too. Suddenly they were together – Aron and Abra on the couch, Adam in his chair under the light, Lee passing coffee, and Cal braced in the doorway to the hall. And they were silent, for it was too late to say hello and too early to begin other things.

Adam did say, 'I'll want to hear all about it. Will you get good marks?'

'Finals aren't until next month, Father.'

'Oh, I see. Well, you'll get good marks, all right. I'm sure you will.'

In spite of himself a grimace of impatience crossed Aron's face.

'I'll bet you're tired,' said Adam. 'Well, we can talk tomorrow.'

Lee said, 'I'll bet he's not. I'll bet he'd like to be alone.'

Adam looked at Lee and said, 'Why, of course – of course. Do you think we should all go to bed?'

Abra solved it for them. 'I can't stay out long,' she said. 'Aron, why don't you walk me home? We'll be together tomorrow.'

On the way Aron clung to her arm. He shivered. 'There's going to be a frost,' he said.

'You're glad to be back.'

'Yes, I am. I have a lot to talk about.'

'Good things?'

'Maybe. I hope you think so.'

'You sound serious.'

'It is serious.'

'When do you have to go back?'

'Not until Sunday night.'

'We'll have lots of time. I want to tell you some things too.

We have tomorrow and Friday and Saturday and all day Sunday. Would you mind not coming in tonight?'

'Why not?'

'I'll tell you later.'

'I want to know now.'

'Well, my father's got one of his streaks.'

'Against me?'

'Yes. I can't go to dinner with you tomorrow, but I won't eat much at home, so you can tell Lee to save a plate for me.'

He was turning shy. She could feel it in the relaxing grip on her arm and in his silence, and she could see it in his raised face. 'I shouldn't have told you that tonight.'

'Yes, you should,' he said slowly. 'Tell me the truth. Do you still want to be with me?'

'Yes, I do.'

'Then all right. I'll go away now. We'll talk tomorrow.'

He left her on the porch with the feeling of a light-brushed kiss on her lips. She felt hurt that he had agreed so easily, and she laughed sourly at herself that she could ask a thing and be hurt when she got it. She watched the tall quick step through the radiance of the corner street-light. She thought, I must be crazy. I've been imagining things.

11

In his bedroom after he had said good night, Aron sat on the edge of his bed and peered down at his hands cupped between his knees. He felt let down and helpless, packed like a bird's egg in the cotton of his father's ambition for him. He had not known its strength until tonight, and he wondered whether he would have the strength to break free of its soft, persistent force. His thoughts would not coagulate. The house seemed cold with a dampness that made him shiver. He got up and softly opened the door. There was a light under Cal's door. He tapped and went in without waiting for a reply.

Cal sat at a new desk. He was working with tissue paper and a bolt of red ribbon, and as Aron came in he hastily covered something on his desk with a large blotter.

Aron smiled. 'Presents?'

'Yes,' said Cal, and left it at that.

'Can I talk to you?'

'Sure! Come on in. Talk low or Father will come in. He hates to miss a moment.'

Aron sat down on the bed. He was silent so long that Cal asked, 'What's the matter – you got trouble?'

'No, not trouble. I just wanted to talk to you. Cal, I don't want to go on at college.'

Cal's head jerked round. 'You don't? Why not?'

'I just don't like it.'

'You haven't told Father, have you? He'll be disappointed. It's bad enough that I don't want to go. What do you want to do?'

'I thought I'd like to take over the ranch.'

'How about Abra?'

'She told me a long time ago that's what she'd like.'

Cal studied him. 'The ranch has got a lease to run.'

'Well, I was just thinking about it.'

Cal said, 'There's no money in farming.'

'I don't want much money. Just to get along.'

'That's not good enough for me,' said Cal. 'I want a lot of money and I'm going to get it too.'

'How?'

Cal felt older and surer than his brother. He felt protective towards him. 'If you'll go on at college, why, I'll get started and lay in a foundation. Then when you finish we can be partners. I'll have one kind of thing and you'll have another. That might be pretty good.'

'I don't want to go back. Why do I have to go back?'

'Because Father wants you to.'

'That won't make me go.'

Cal stared fiercely at his brother, at the pale hair and the wide-set eyes, and suddenly he knew why his father loved Aron, knew it beyond doubt. 'Sleep on it,' he said quickly. 'It would be better if you finished out the term at least. Don't do anything now.'

Aron got up and moved towards the door. 'Who's the present for?' he asked.

'It's for Father. You'll see it tomorrow – after dinner.'

'It's not Christmas.'

'No,' said Cal, 'it's better than Christmas.'

When Aron had gone back to his room Cal uncovered his present. He counted the fifteen new banknotes once more, and they were so crisp they made a sharp, cracking sound. The Monterey County Bank had to send to San Francisco to get them, and only did so when the reason for them was told. It was a matter of shock and disbelief to the bank that a seventeen-year-old boy should, first, own them, and, second, carry them

about. Bankers do not like money to be lightly handled even i
the handling is sentimental. It had taken Will Hamilton's wor
to make the bank believe that the money belonged to Cal, that i
was honestly come by, and that he could do what he wante
with it.

Cal wrapped the notes in tissue and tied it with red ribbor
finished in a blob that was faintly recognizable as a bow. Th
package might have been a handkerchief. He concealed it unde
the shirts in his bureau and went to bed. But he could not sleep
He was excited and at the same time shy. He wished the day wa
over and the gift given. He went over what he planned to say.

'This is for you.'

'What is it?'

'A present.'

From then on he didn't know what would happen. He tossed
and rolled in bed, and at dawn he got up and dressed and crep
out of the house.

On Main Street he saw Old Martin sweeping the streets with
a stable broom. The city council was discussing the purchase of
a mechanical sweeper. Old Martin hoped he would get to drive
it, but he was cynical about it. Young men got the cream of
everything. Bacigalupi's garbage wagon went by, and Martin
looked after it spitefully. *There* was a good business. Those
wops were getting rich.

Main Street was empty except for a few dogs sniffing at closed
entrances and the sleepy activity around the San Francisco Chop
House. Pet Bulene's new taxi was parked in front, for Pet had
been alerted the night before to take the Williams girls to the
morning train for San Francisco.

Old Martin called to Cal, 'Got a cigarette, young fella?'

Cal stopped and took out his cardboard box of Murads.

'Oh, fancy ones!' Martin said. 'I ain't got a match either.'

Cal lighted the cigarette for him, careful not to set fire to the
grizzle around Martin's mouth.

Martin leaned on the handle of his brush and puffed discon-
solately. 'Young fellas gets the cream,' he said. 'They won't let
me drive it.'

'What?' Cal asked.

'Why, the new sweeper. Ain't you heard? Where you been,
boy?' It was incredible to him that any reasonably informed
human did not know about the sweeper. He forgot Cal. Maybe
the Bacigalupis would give him a job. They were coining money.
Three wagons and a new truck.

Cal turned down Alisal Street, went into the post office, and looked in the glass window of box 632. It was empty. He wandered back home and found Lee up and stuffing a very large turkey.

'Up all night?' Lee asked.

'No. I just went for a walk.'

'Nervous?'

'Yes.'

'I don't blame you. I would be too. It's hard to give people things – I guess it's harder to be given things, though. Seems silly, doesn't it? Want some coffee?'

'I don't mind.'

Lee wiped his hands and poured coffee for himself and for Cal. 'How do you think Aron looks?'

'All right, I guess.'

'Did you get to talk to him?'

'No,' said Cal. It was easier that way. Lee would want to know what he said. It wasn't Aron's day. It was Cal's day. He had carved this day out for himself and he wanted it. He meant to have it.

Aron came in, his eyes still misty with sleep. 'What time do you plan to have dinner, Lee?'

'Oh, I don't know – three-thirty or four.'

'Could you make it about five?'

'I guess so, if Adam says it's all right. Why?'

'Well, Abra can't get here before then. I've got a plan I want to put to my father and I want her to be here.'

'I guess that will be all right,' said Lee.

Cal got up quickly and went to his room. He sat at his desk with the student light turned on and he churned with uneasiness and resentment. Without effort, Aron was taking his day away from him. It would turn out to be Aron's day. Then, suddenly, he was bitterly ashamed. He covered his eyes with his hands and he said, 'It's just jealousy. I'm jealous. That's what I am. I'm jealous. I don't want to be jealous.' And he repeated over and over, 'Jealous – jealous – jealous,' as though bringing it into the open might destroy it. And having gone this far, he proceeded with his self-punishment. 'Why am I giving the money to my father? Is it for his good? No. It's for my good. Will Hamilton said it – I'm trying to buy him. There's not one decent thing about it. There's not one decent thing about me. I sit here wallowing in jealousy of my brother. Why not call things by their names?'

505

He whispered hoarsely to himself. 'Why not be honest? I know why my father loves Aron. It's because he looks like her. My father never got over her. He may not know it, but it's true. I wonder if he does know it. That makes me jealous of her too. Why don't I take my money and go away? They wouldn't miss me. In a little while they'd forget I ever existed – all except Lee. And I wonder whether Lee likes me. Maybe not.' He doubled his fists against his forehead. 'Does Aron have to fight himself like this? I don't think so, but how do I know? I could ask him. He wouldn't say.'

Cal's mind careened in anger at himself and in pity for himself. And then a new voice came into it, saying coolly and with contempt, 'If you're being honest – why not say you are enjoying this beating you're giving yourself? That would be the truth. Why not be just what you are and do just what you do?' Cal sat in shock from this thought. Enjoying? – of course. By whipping himself he protected himself against whipping by someone else. His mind tightened up. Give the money, but give it lightly. Don't depend on anything. Don't foresee anything. Just give it and forget it. And forget it now. Give – give. Give the day to Aron. Why not? He jumped up and hurried out to the kitchen.

Aron was holding open the skin of the turkey while Lee forced stuffing into the cavity. The oven cricked and snapped with growing heat.

Lee said, 'Let's see, eighteen pounds, twenty minutes to the pound – that's eighteen times twenty – that's three hundred and sixty minutes, six hours even – eleven to twelve, twelve to one—' He counted on his fingers.

Cal said, 'When you get through, Aron, let's take a walk.'

'Where to?' Aron asked.

'Just around town. I want to ask you something.'

Cal led his brother across the street to Berges and Garrisiere, who imported fine wines and liquors. Cal said, 'I've got a little money, Aron. I thought you might like to buy some wine for dinner. I'll give you the money.'

'What kind of wine?'

'Let's make a real celebration. Let's get champagne – it can be your present.'

Joe Garrisiere said, 'You boys aren't old enough.'

'For dinner? Sure we are.'

'Can't sell it to you. I'm sorry.'

Cal said, 'I know what you can do. We can pay for it and you can send it to our father.'

506

'That I can do,' Joe Garrisiere said. 'We've got some Œil de Perdrix — ' His lips pursed as though he were tasting it.

'What's that?' Cal asked.

'Champagne – but very pretty, same colour as a partridge eye – pink but a little darker than pink, and dry too. Four-fifty a bottle.'

'Isn't that high?' Aron asked.

'Sure it's high!' Cal laughed. 'Send three bottles over, Joe.' To Aron he said, 'It's your present.'

III

To Cal the day was endless. He wanted to leave the house and couldn't. At eleven o'clock Adam went to the closed draft-board office to brood over the records of a new batch of boys coming up.

Aron seemed perfectly calm. He sat in the living-room, looking at cartoons in old numbers of the *Review of Reviews*. From the kitchen the odour of the bursting juices of roasting turkey began to fill the house.

Cal went into his room and took out his present and laid it on his desk. He tried to write a card to put on it. 'To my father from Caleb' – 'To Adam Trask from Caleb Trask.' He tore the cards in tiny pieces and flushed them down the toilet.

He thought, Why give it to him today? Maybe tomorrow I could go to him quietly and say, 'This is for you,' and then walk away. That would be easier. 'No,' he said aloud. 'I want the others to see.' It had to be that way. But his lungs were compressed and the palms of his hands were wet with stage fright. And then he thought of the morning when his father got him out of jail. The warmth and closeness – they were things to remember – and his father's trust. Why, he had even said it. 'I trust you.' He felt much better then.

At about three o'clock he heard Adam come in and there was a low sound of voices conversing in the living-room. Cal joined his father and Aron.

Adam was saying, 'The times are changed. A boy must be a specialist or he will get nowhere. I guess that's why I'm so glad you're going to college.'

Aron said, 'I've been thinking about that, and I wonder.'

'Well, don't think any more. Your first choice is right. Look at me. I know a little bit about a great many things and not enough about any one of them to make a living in these times.'

Cal sat down quietly. Adam did not notice him. His face was concentrated on his thought.

'It's natural for a man to want his son to succeed,' Adam went on. 'And maybe I can see better than you can.'

Lee looked in. 'The kitchen scales must be way off,' he said. 'The turkey's going to be done earlier than the chart says. I'll bet that bird doesn't weigh eighteen pounds.'

Adam said, 'Well, you can keep it warm,' and he continued, 'Old Sam Hamilton saw this coming. He said there couldn't be any more universal philosophers. The weight of knowledge is too great for one mind to absorb. He saw a time when one man would know only one little fragment, but he would know it well.'

'Yes,' Lee said from the doorway, 'and he deplored it. He hated it.'

'Did he now?' Adam asked.

Lee came into the room. He held his big basting spoon in his right hand, and he cupped his left under the bowl for fear it would drip on the carpet. He came into the room and forgot and waved his spoon and drops of turkey fat fell to the floor. 'Now you question it, I don't know,' he said. 'I don't know whether he hated it or I hate it for him.'

'Don't get so excited,' said Adam. 'Seems to me we can't discuss anything any more but you take it as a personal insult.'

'Maybe the knowledge is too great and maybe men are growing too small,' said Lee. 'Maybe, kneeling down to atoms, they're becoming atom-sized in their souls. Maybe a specialist is only a coward, afraid to look out of his little cage. And think what any specialist misses – the whole world over his fence.'

'We're only talking about making a living.'

'A living – or money,' Lee said excitedly. 'Money's easy to make if it's money you want. But with a few exceptions people don't want money. They want luxury and they want love and they want admiration.'

'All right. But do you have any objection to college? That's what we're talking about.'

'I'm sorry,' said Lee. 'You're right, I do seem to get too excited. No, if college is where a man can go to find his relation to his whole world, I don't object. Is it that? Is it that, Aron?'

'I don't know,' said Aron.

A hissing sound came from the kitchen. Lee said, 'The goddam giblets are boiling over,' and he bolted through the door.

508

Adam gazed after him affectionately. 'What a good man! What a good friend!'

Aron said, 'I hope he lives to be a hundred.'

His father chuckled. 'How do you know he's not a hundred now?'

Cal asked, 'How is the ice plant doing, Father?'

'Why, all right. Pays for itself and makes a little profit. Why?'

'I thought of a couple of things to make it really pay.'

'Not today,' said Adam quickly. 'Monday, if you remember, but not today. You know,' Adam said, 'I don't remember when I've felt so good. I feel – well, you might call it fulfilled. Maybe it's only a good night's sleep and a good trip to the bathroom. And maybe it's because we're all together and at peace.' He smiled at Aron. 'We didn't know what we felt about you until you went away.'

'I was homesick,' Aron confessed. 'The first few days I thought I'd die of it.'

Abra came in with a little rush. Her cheeks were pink and she was happy. 'Did you notice there's snow on Mount Toro?' she asked.

'Yes, I saw it,' Adam said. 'They say that means a good year to come. And we could use it.'

'I just nibbled,' said Abra. 'I wanted to be hungry for here.'

Lee apologized for the dinner like an old fool. He blamed the gas oven which didn't heat like a good wood stove. He blamed the new breed of turkeys which lacked a something turkeys used to have. But he laughed with them when they told him he was acting like an old woman fishing for compliments.

With the plum pudding Adam opened the champagne, and they treated it with ceremony. A courtliness settled over the table. They proposed toasts. Each one had his health drunk, and Adam made a little speech to Abra when he drank her health.

Her eyes were shining and under the table Aron held her hand. The wine dulled Cal's nervousness and he was not afraid about his present.

When Adam had finished his plum pudding he said, 'I guess we never had such a good Thanksgiving.'

Cal reached in his jacket pocket, took out the red-ribboned package, and pushed it over in front of his father.

'What's this?' Adam asked.

'It's a present.'

Adam was pleased. 'Not even Christmas and we have presents. I wonder what it can be!'

'A handkerchief,' said Abra.

Adam slipped off the grubby bow and unfolded the tissue paper. He stared down at the money.

Abra said, 'What is it?' and stood up to look. Aron leaned forward. Lee, in the doorway, tried to keep the look of worry from his face. He darted a glance at Cal and saw the light of joy and triumph in his eyes.

Very slowly Adam moved his fingers and fanned the gold certificates. His voice seemed to come from far away. 'What is it? What —' He stopped.

Cal swallowed. 'It's – I made it – to give to you – to make up for losing the lettuce.'

Adam raised his head slowly. 'You made it? How?'

'Mr Hamilton – we made it – on beans.' He hurried on, 'We bought futures at five cents and when the price jumped — It's for you, fifteen thousand dollars. It's for you.'

Adam touched the new notes so that their edges came together, folded the tissue over them and turned the ends up. He looked helplessly at Lee. Cal caught a feeling – a feeling of calamity, of destruction in the air, and a weight of sickness overwhelmed him. He heard his father say, 'You'll have to give it back.'

Almost as remotely his own voice said, 'Give it back? Give it back to who?'

'To the people you got it from.'

'The British Purchasing Agency? They can't take it back. They're paying twelve and a half cents for beans all over the country.'

'Then give it to the farmers you robbed.'

'Robbed?' Cal cried. 'Why, we paid them two cents a pound over the market. We didn't rob them.' Cal felt suspended in space, and time seemed very slow.

His father took a long time to answer. There seemed to be long spaces between his words. 'I send boys out,' he said. 'I sign my name and they go out. And some will die and some will lie helpless without arms or legs. Not one will come back untorn. Son, do you think I could make a profit on that?'

'I did it for you,' Cal said. 'I wanted you to have the money to make up your loss.'

'I don't want the money, Cal. And the lettuce – I don't think

510

did that for a profit. It was a kind of game to see if I could get he lettuce there, and I lost. I don't want the money.'

Cal looked straight ahead. He could feel the eyes of Lee and Aron and Abra crawling on his cheeks. He kept his eyes on his father's lips.

'I like the idea of a present,' Adam went on. 'I thank you for the thought — '

'I'll put it away. I'll keep it for you,' Cal broke in.

'No. I won't want it ever. I would have been happy if you could have given me – well, what your brother has – pride in the thing he's doing, gladness in his progress. Money, even clean money, doesn't stack up with that.' His eyes widened a little and he said, 'Have I made you angry, son? Don't be angry. If you want to give me a present – give me a good life. That would be something I could value.'

Cal felt that he was choking. His forehead streamed with perspiration and he tasted salt on his tongue. He stood up suddenly and his chair fell over. He ran from the room, holding his breath.

Adam called after him, 'Don't be angry, son.'

They let him alone. He sat in his room, his elbows on his desk. He thought he would cry but he did not. He tried to let weeping start but tears could not pass the hot iron in his head.

After a time his breathing steadied and he watched his brain go to work slyly, quietly. He fought the quiet hateful pain down and it slipped aside and went about its work. He fought it more weakly, for hate was seeping all through his body, poisoning every nerve. He could feel himself losing control.

Then there came a point where the control and the fear were gone and his brain cried out in an aching triumph. His hand went to a pencil and he drew tight little spirals one after another on his blotting pad. When Lee came in an hour later there were hundreds of spirals, and they had become smaller and smaller. He did not look up.

Lee closed the door gently. 'I brought you some coffee,' he said.

'I don't want it – yes, I do. Why, thank you, Lee. It's kind of you to think of it.'

Lee said, 'Stop it! Stop it, I tell you!'

'Stop what? What do you want me to stop?'

Lee said uneasily, 'I told you once when you asked me that it was all in yourself. I told you you could control it – if you wanted.'

511

'Control what? I don't know what you're talking about?'

Lee said, 'Can't you hear me? Can't I get through to you? Cal, don't you know what I'm saying?'

'I hear you, Lee. What are you saying?'

'He couldn't help it, Cal. That's his nature. It was the only way he knew. He didn't have any choice. But you have. Don't you hear me? You have a choice.'

The spirals had become so small that the pencil lines ran together and the result was a shiny black dot.

Cal said quietly, 'Aren't you making a fuss about nothing? You must be slipping. You'd think from your tone that I'd killed somebody. Come off it, Lee. Come off it.'

It was silent in the room. After a moment Cal turned from his desk and the room was empty. A cup of coffee on the bureau top sent up a plume of vapour. Cal drank the coffee scalding as it was and went into the living-room.

His father looked up apologetically at him.

Cal said, 'I'm sorry, Father. I didn't know how you felt about it.' He took the package of money from where it lay on the mantel and put it in the inside pocket of his coat where it had been before. 'I'll see what I can do about this.' He said casually, 'Where are the others?'

'Oh, Abra had to go. Aron walked with her. Lee went out.'

'I guess I'll go for a walk,' said Cal.

IV

The November night was well fallen. Cal opened the front door a crack and saw Lee's shoulders and head outlined against the white walls of the French Laundry across the street. Lee was sitting on the steps, and he looked lumpy in his heavy coat.

Cal closed the door quietly and went back through the living-room. 'Champagne makes you thirsty,' he said. His father didn't look up.

Cal slipped out by the kitchen door and moved through Lee's waning kitchen garden. He climbed the high fence, found the two-by-twelve plank that served as a bridge across the slough of dark water, and came out between Lang's Bakery and the tin-smith shop on Castroville Street.

He walked to Stone Street where the Catholic church is and turned left, went past the Carriaga house, the Wilson house, the Zabala house, and turned left on Central Avenue at the Stein-

512

beck house. Two blocks out Central he turned left past the West End School.

The poplar trees in front of the school-yard were nearly bare, but in the evening wind a few yellowed leaves still twisted down.

Cal's mind was numb. He did not even know that the air was cold with frost slipping down from the mountains. Three blocks ahead he saw his brother cross under a street-light, coming towards him. He knew it was his brother by stride and posture and because he knew it.

Cal slowed his steps, and when Aron was close he said, 'Hi. I came looking for you.'

Aron said, 'I'm sorry about this afternoon.'

'You couldn't help it – forget it.' He turned and two walked side by side. 'I want you to come with me,' Cal said. 'I want to show you something.'

'What is it?'

'Oh, it's a surprise. But it's very interesting. You'll be interested.'

'Well, will it take long?'

'No, not very long. Not very long at all.'

They walked past Central Avenue towards Castroville Street.

v

Sergeant Axel Dane ordinarily opened the San Jose recruiting office at eight o'clock, but if he was a little late Corporal Kemp opened it, and Kemp was not likely to complain. Axel was not an unusual case. A hitch in the US Army in the time of peace between the Spanish war and the German war had unfitted him for the cold, ordered life of a civilian. One month between hitches convinced him of that. Two hitches in the peacetime army completely unfitted him for war, and he had learned enough method to get out of it. The San Jose recruiting station proved he knew his way about. He was dallying with the youngest Ricci girl and she lived in San Jose.

Kemp hadn't the time in, but he was learning the basic rule. Get along with the topkick and avoid all officers when possible. He didn't mind the gentle riding Sergeant Dane handed out.

At eight-thirty Dane entered the office to find Corporal Kemp asleep at his desk and a tired-looking kid sat waiting. Dane glanced at the boy and then went behind the rail and put his hand on Kemp's shoulder.

'Darling,' he said, 'the skylarks are singing and a new dawn is here.'

Kemp raised his head from his arms, wiped his nose on the back of his hand, and sneezed. 'That's my sweet,' the sergeant said. 'Arise, we have a customer.'

Kemp squinted his crusted eyes. 'The war will wait,' he said.

Dane looked more closely at the boy. 'God! he's beautiful. I hope they take good care of him. Corporal, you may think that he wants to bear arms against the foe, but I think he's running away from love.'

Kemp was relieved that the sergeant wasn't quite sober. 'You think some dame hurt him?' He played any game his sergeant wished. 'You think it's the Foreign Legion?'

'Maybe he's running away from himself.'

Kemp said, 'I saw that picture. There's one mean son of a bitch of a sergeant in it.'

'I don't believe it,' said Dane. 'Step up, young man. Eighteen, aren't you?'

'Yes, sir.'

Dane turned to his man. 'What do you think?'

'Hell!' said Kemp. 'I say if they're big enough, they're old enough.'

The sergeant said, 'Let's say you're eighteen. And we'll stick to it, shall we?'

'Yes, sir.'

'You just take this form and fill it out. Now you figure out what year you were born, and you put it down right here, and you remember it.'

CHAPTER 50

I

JOE DIDN'T like for Kate to sit still and stare straight ahead – hour after hour. That meant she was thinking, and since her face had no expression Joe had no access to her thoughts. It made him uneasy. He didn't want his first real good break to get away from him.

He had only one plan himself – and that was to keep her stirred up until she gave herself away. Then he could jump in any direction. But how about it if she sat looking at the wall? Was she stirred up or wasn't she?

Joe knew she hadn't been to bed, and when he asked whether or not she wanted breakfast she shook her head so slowly that it was hard to know whether she had heard him or not.

He advised himself cautiously, 'Don't do nothing! Just stick around and keep your eyes and ears open.' The girls in the house knew something had happened but no two of them had the same story, the goddam chicken-heads.

Kate was not thinking. Her mind drifted among impressions the way a bat drifts and swoops in the evening. She saw the face of the blond and beautiful boy, his eyes mad with shock. She heard his ugly words aimed not so much at her as at himself. And she saw his dark brother leaning against the door and laughing.

Kate had laughed too – the quickest and best self-protection. What would her son do? What had he done after he went quietly away?

She thought of Cal's eyes with their look of sluggish and ful-filled cruelty, peering at her as he slowly closed the door.

Why had he brought his brother? What did he want? What was he after? If she knew she could take care of herself. But she didn't know.

The pain was creeping in her hands again and there was a new place. Her right hip ached angrily when she moved. She thought, 'So the pain will move in towards the centre, and sooner or later all the pains will meet in the centre and join like rats in a clot.'

In spite of his advice to himself, Joe couldn't let it alone. He carried a pot of tea to her door, knocked softly, opened the door, and went in. As far as he could see she hadn't moved.

He said, 'I brought you some tea, ma'am.'

'Put it on the table,' she said, and then as a second thought, 'Thank you, Joe.'

'You don't feel good, ma'am?'

'The pain's back. The medicine fooled me.'

'Anything I can do?'

She raised her hands. 'Cut these off – at the wrists.' She grimaced with the extra pain lifting her hands had caused. 'Makes you feel hopeless,' she said plaintively.

Joe had never heard a tone of weakness in her before and his instinct told him it was time to move in. He said, 'Maybe you don't want me to bother you but I got some word about that

515

other.' He knew by the little interval before she answered that she had tensed.

'What other?' she asked softly.

'That dame, ma'am.'

'Oh! You mean Ethel?'

'Yes, ma'am.'

'I'm getting tired of Ethel. What is it now?'

'Well, I'll tell you like it happened. I can't make nothing out of it. I'm in Kellogg's cigar store and a fella came up to me. "You're Joe," he says, an' I tell him, "Who says?" "You was lookin' for somebody," he says. "Tell me about it," I says. Never seen the guy before. So he says, "That party tol' me she wants to talk to you." An' I told him, "Well, why don't she?" He gives me the long look an' he says, "Maybe you forgot what the judge said." I guess he means about her coming back.' He looked at Kate's face, still and pale, the eyes looking straight ahead.

Kate said, 'And then he asked you for some money?'

'No, ma'am. He didn't. He says something don't make no sense. He says, "Does Faye mean anything to you?" "Not a thing," I tol' him. He says, "Maybe you better talk to her." "Maybe," I says, an' I come away. Don't make no sense to me. I figured I'd ask you.'

Kate asked, 'Does the name Faye mean anything to you?'

'Not a thing.'

Her voice became very soft. 'You mean you never heard that Faye used to own this house?'

Joe felt a sickening jolt in the pit of his stomach. What a god-dam fool! Couldn't keep his mouth shut. His mind floundered. 'Why – why come to think of it, I believe I did hear that – seemed like the name was like Faith.'

The sudden alarm was good for Kate. It took the blond head and the pain from her. It gave her something to do. She responded to the challenge with something like pleasure.

She laughed softly. 'Faith,' she said under her breath. 'Pour me some tea, Joe.'

She did not appear to notice that his hand shook and that the teapot spout rattled against the cup. She did not look at him even when he set the cup before her and then stepped back out of range of her eyes. Joe was quaking with apprehension.

Kate said in a pleading voice, 'Joe, do you think you could help me? If I gave you ten thousand dollars, do you think you could fix everything up?' She waited just a second, then swung round and looked full in his face.

His eyes were moist. She caught him licking his lips. And at her sudden move he stepped back as though she had struck at him. Her eyes would not let him go.

'Did I catch you out, Joe?'

'I don't know what you're getting at, ma'am.'

'You go and figure it out – and then you come and tell me. You're good at figuring things out. And send Therese in, will you?'

He wanted to get out of this room where he was out-pointed and out-fought. He'd made a mess of things. He wondered if he'd bollixed up the breaks. And then the bitch had the nerve to say, 'Thank you for bringing tea. You're a nice boy.'

He wanted to slam the door, but he didn't dare.

Kate got up stiffly, trying to avoid the pain of moving her hip. She went to her desk and slipped out a sheet of paper. Holding the pen was difficult.

She wrote, moving her whole arm. 'Dear Ralph: Tell the sheriff it wouldn't do any harm to check on Joe Valery's finger-prints. You remember Joe. He works for me. Y'rs, Kate.' She was folding the paper when Therese came in, looking frightened.

'You want me? Did I do something? I tried my best. Ma'am, I ain't been well.'

'Come here,' Kate said, and while the girl waited beside the desk Kate slowly addressed the envelope and stamped it. 'I want you to run a little errand for me,' she said. 'Go to Bell's candy store and get a five-pound box of mixed chocolates and a one-pound box. The big one is for you girls. Stop at Krough's drugstore and get me two medium toothbrushes and a can of tooth-powder – you know, that can with a spout?'

'Yes, ma'am.' Therese was greatly relieved.

'You're a good girl,' Kate went on. 'I've had my eye on you. I'm not well, Therese. If I see that you do this well, I'll seriously consider putting you in charge when I go to the hospital.'

'You will – are – are you going to the hospital?'

'I don't know yet, dear. But I'll need your help. Now here's some money for the candy. Medium toothbrushes – remember.'

'Yes, ma'am. Thank you. Shall I go now?'

'Yes, and kind of creep out, will you? Don't let the other girls know what I told you.'

'I'll go out the back way.' She hurried towards the door.

Kate said, 'I nearly forgot. Will you drop this in a mail-box?'

'Sure I will, ma'am. Sure I will. Anything else?'

'That's all, dear.'

When the girl was gone Kate rested her arms and hands on the desk so that each crooked finger was supported. Here it was. Maybe she had always known. She must have – but there was no need to think of that now. She would come back to that. They would put Joe away, but there'd be someone else, and there was always Ethel. Sooner or later, sooner or later – but no need to think about that now. She tiptoed her mind around the whole subject and back to an exclusive thing that peeped out and then withdrew. It was when she had been thinking of her yellow-haired son that the fragment had first come to her mind. His face – hurt, bewildered, despairing – had brought it. Then she remembered.

She was a very small girl with a face as lovely and fresh as her son's face – a very small girl. Most of the time she knew she was smarter and prettier than anyone else. But now and then a lonely fear would fall upon her so that she seemed surrounded by a tree-tall forest of enemies. Then every thought and word and look was aimed to hurt her, and she had no place to run and no place to hide. And she would cry in panic because there was no escape and no sanctuary. Then one day she was reading a book. She could read when she was five years old. She remembered the book – brown, with a silver title, and the cloth was broken and the boards thick. It was *Alice in Wonderland*.

Kate moved her hands slowly and lifted her weight a little from her arms. And she could see the drawings – Alice with long straight hair. But it was the bottle which said 'Drink me' that had changed her life. Alice had taught her that.

When the forest of her enemies surrounded her she was prepared. In her pocket she had a bottle of sugar water and on its red-framed label she had written, 'Drink me'. She would take a sip from the bottle and she would grow smaller and smaller. Let her enemies look for her then! Cathy would be under a leaf or looking out of an ant-hole, laughing. They couldn't find her then. No door could close her out and no door could close her in. She could walk upright under a door.

And always there was Alice to play with, Alice to love her and trust her. Alice was her friend, always waiting to welcome her to tinyness.

All this so good – so good that it was almost worth while to be miserable. But good as it was, there was one more thing always held in reserve. It was her threat and her safety. She had only to drink the whole bottle and she would dwindle and disappear and cease to exist. And better than all, when she stopped eing, she never would have been. This was her darling safety. Sometimes in her bed she would drink enough of 'Drink me' so that she was a dot as small as the tiniest gnat. But she had never gone clear out – never had to. That was her reserve – guarded from everyone.

Kate shook her head sadly, remembering the cut-off little girl. She wondered why she had forgotten that wonderful trick. It had saved her from so many disasters. The light filtering down at one through a clover-leaf was glorious. Cathy and Alice walked among towering grass, arms around each other – best friends. And Cathy never had to drink all of 'Drink me' because she had Alice.

Kate put her head down on the blotter between her crooked hands. She was cold and desolate, alone and desolate. Whatever she had done, she had been driven to do. She was different – she had something more than other people. She raised her head and made no move to wipe her streaming eyes. That was true. She was smarter and stronger than other people. She had something they lacked.

And right in the middle of her thought, Cal's dark face hung in the air in front of her and his lips were smiling with cruelty. The weight pressed down on her, forcing her breath out.

They had something she lacked, and she didn't know what it was. Once she knew this, she was ready; and once ready, she knew she had been ready for a long time – perhaps all her life. Her mind functioned like a wooden mind, her body moved crookedly like a badly operated marionette, but she went steadily about her business.

It was noon – she knew from the chatter of the girls in the dining-room. The slugs had only just got up.

Kate had trouble with the door-knob and turned it finally by rolling it between her palms.

The girls choked in the middle of laughter and looked up at her. The cook came in from the kitchen.

Kate was a sick ghost, crooked and in some way horrible. She leaned across the dining-room wall and smiled at her girls, and her smile frightened them even more, for it was like the frame for a scream.

'Where's Joe?' Kate asked.

'He went out, ma'am.'

'Listen,' she said. 'I've had no sleep for a long time. I'm going to take some medicine and sleep. I don't want to be disturbed, I don't want any supper. I'll sleep the clock round. Tell Joe I don't want anybody to come near me for anything until to-morrow morning. Do you understand?'

'Yes, ma'am,' they said.

'Good night then. It's afternoon but I mean good night.'

'Good night, ma'am,' they chorused obediently.

Kate turned and walked crabwise back to her room.

She closed her door and stood looking around, trying to form her simple procedure. She went back to her desk. This time she forced her hand, in spite of the pain, to write plainly. 'I leave everything I have to my son Aron Trask.' She dated the sheet and signed it 'Catherine Trask'. Her fingers dwelt on the page, and then she got up and left her will face upward on the desk.

At the centre table she poured cold tea into her cup and carried the cup to the grey room in the lean-to and set it on the reading-table. Then she went to her dressing-table and combed her hair, rubbed a little rouge all over her face, covered it lightly with powder, and put on the pale lipstick she always used. Last she filed her nails and cleaned them.

When she closed the door to the grey room the outside light was cut off and only the reading-lamp threw its cone on the table. She arranged the pillows, patted them up, and sat down. She leaned her head experimentally against the down pillow. She felt rather gay, as though she was going to a party. Gingerly she fished the chain out from her bodice, unscrewed the little tube, and shook the capsule into her hand. She smiled at it.

'Eat me,' she said and put the capsule in her mouth.

She picked up the tea-cup. 'Drink me,' she said and swallowed the bitter cold tea.

She forced her mind to stay on Alice – so tiny and waiting. Other faces peered in from the sides of her eyes – her father and mother, and Charles, and Adam, and Samuel Hamilton, and then Aron, and she could see Cal smiling at her.

He didn't have to speak. The glint of his eyes said, 'You missed something. They had something and you missed it.'

She thrust her mind back to Alice. In the grey wall opposite there was a nail-hole. Alice would be in there. And she would put her arm around Cathy's waist, and Cathy would put her arm around Alice's waist, and they would walk away – best friends – and tiny as the head of a pin.

A warm numbness began to creep into her arms and legs. The pain was going from her hands. Her eyelids felt heavy – very heavy. She yawned.

She thought or said or thought, 'Alice doesn't know. I'm going right on past.'

Her eyes closed and a dizzy nausea shook her. She opened her eyes and stared about in terror. The grey room darkened and the cone of light flowed and rippled like water. And then her eyes closed again and her fingers curled as though they held small breasts. And her heart beat solemnly and her breathing slowed as she grew smaller and smaller and then disappeared – and she had never been.

I I

When Kate dismissed him Joe went to the barber-shop, as he always did when he was upset. He had his hair cut and an egg shampoo and tonic. He had a facial massage and a mud pack, and around the edges he had his nails manicured, and he had his shoes shined. Ordinarily this and a new necktie set Joe up, but he was still depressed when he left the barber with a fifty-cent tip.

Kate had trapped him like a rat – caught him with his pants down. Her fast thinking left him confused and helpless. The trick she had of leaving it to you whether she meant anything or not was no less confusing.

The night started dully, but then sixteen members and two pledges from Sigma Alpha Epsilon, Stanford chapter, came in hilarious from a pledge hazing in San Juan. They were full of horse-play.

Florence, who smoked the cigarette in the circus, had a hard cough. Every time she tried, she coughed and lost it. And the pony stallion had diarrhoea.

The college boys shrieked and pounded each other in their amusement. And then they stole everything that wasn't nailed down.

After they had left, two of the girls got into a tired and monotonous quarrel, and Therese turned up with the first symptom of the old Joe. Oh, Christ, what a night!

And down the hall that brooding dangerous thing was silent behind its closed door. Joe stood by the door before he went to bed and he could hear nothing. He closed the house at two-thirty and was in bed by three – but he couldn't sleep. He sat up in bed and read seven chapters of *The Winning of Barbara Worth*, and when it was daylight went down to the silent kitchen and made a pot of coffee.

He rested his elbows on the table and held the coffee mug with both hands. Something had gone wrong and Joe couldn't figure what it was. Maybe she'd found out that Ethel was dead. He'd have to watch his step. And then he made up his mind, and made it up firmly. He would go in to see her at nine and he'd keep his ears open. Maybe he hadn't heard right. Best thing would be to lay it on the line and not be a hog. Just say he'd take a thousand bucks and get the hell out, and if she said no he'd get the hell out anyway. He was sick of working with dames. He could get a job dealing faro in Reno – regular hours and no dames. Maybe get himself an apartment and fix it up – big chairs and a davenport. No point in beating his brains out in this lousy town. Better if he got out of the state anyway. He considered going right now – just get up from this table, climb the stairs, two minutes to pack a suitcase, and gone. Three or four minutes at the most. Don't tell nobody nothing. The idea appealed to him. The breaks about Ethel might not be as good as he had thought at first, but a thousand bucks was at stake. Better wait.

When the cook came in he was in a bad mood. He had a developing carbuncle on the back of his neck and the skin from the inside of an eggshell stretched over it to draw it to a head. He didn't want anybody in his kitchen, feeling the way he did.

Joe went back to his room and read some more and then he packed his suitcase. He was going to get out any way it went.

At nine o'clock he knocked gently on Kate's door and pushed it open. Her bed had not been slept in. He set down the tray and went to the door of the lean-to and knocked and knocked again and then called. Finally he opened the door.

The cone of light fell on the reading-stand. Kate's head was deeply cushioned on a pillow.

'You must have slept all night here,' Joe said. He walked around in front of her, saw bloodless lips and eyes shining dully between half-closed lids, and he knew she was dead.

He moved his head from side to side and went quickly into the other room to make sure that the door to the hall was closed. With great speed he went through the dresser, drawer by drawer, opened her purses, the little box by her bed – and he stood still. She didn't have a goddam thing – not even a silver-backed hair-brush.

He crept to the lean-to and stood in front of her – not a ring, not a pin. Then he saw the little chain around her neck and fted it clear and unsnapped the clasp – a small gold watch, a ttle tube, and two safe-deposit keys, numbers 27 and 29.

'So that's where you got it, you bitch,' he said.

He slipped the watch off the thin chain and put it in his ocket. He wanted to punch her on the nose. Then he thought f her desk.

The two-line holograph will attracted him. Somebody might ay for that. He put it in his pocket. He took a handful of apers from a pigeon-hole – bills and receipts; next hole, in-urance; next, a small book with records of every girl. He put hat in his pocket too. He took the rubber band from a packet of rown envelopes, opened one, and pulled out a photograph. On he back of the picture, in Kate's neat, sharp handwriting, a ame and address and a title.

Joe laughed aloud. This was the real breaks. He tried another nvelope and another. A gold mine – guy could live for years on hese. Look at that fat-arsed councilman! He put the band back. n the top drawer eight ten-dollar notes and a bunch of keys. Ie pocketed the money too. As he opened the second drawer nough to see that it held writing paper and sealing wax and ink here was a knock on the door. He walked to it and opened it a rack.

The cook said, 'Fella out here wants to see ya.'

'Who is he?'

'How the hell do I know?'

Joe looked back at the room and then stepped out, took the key from the inside, locked the door, and put the key in his pocket. He might have overlooked something.

Oscar Noble was standing in the big front room, his grey hat on his head and his red mackinaw buttoned up tight around his throat. His eyes were pale grey – the same colour as his stubble whiskers. The room was in semi-darkness. No one had raised the blinds yet.

Joe came lightly along the hall, and Oscar asked, 'You Joe?'

'Who's asking?'

'The sheriff wants to have a talk with you.'

Joe felt ice creeping into his stomach. 'Pinch?' he asked. 'Got a warrant?'

'Hell, no,' said Oscar. 'We got nothing on you. Just checking up. Will you come along?'

'Sure,' said Joe. 'Why not?'

They went out together. Joe shivered. 'I should of got a coat.'

'Want to go back for one?'

'I guess not,' said Joe.

They walked towards Castroville Street. Oscar asked, 'Ever been mugged or printed?'

Joe was quiet for a time. 'Yes,' he said at last.

'What for?'

'Drunk,' said Joe. 'Hit a cop.'

'Well, we'll soon find out,' said Oscar and turned the corner.

Joe ran like a rabbit, across the street and over the track towards the stores and alleys of Chinatown.

Oscar had to take a glove off and unbutton his mackinaw to get his gun out. He tried a snap shot and missed.

Joe began to zigzag. He was fifty yards away by now and nearing an opening between two buildings.

Oscar stepped to a telephone pole at the kerb, braced his left elbow against it, gripped his right wrist with his left hand, and drew a bead on the entrance to the little alley. He fired just as Joe touched the front sight.

Joe splashed forward on his face and skidded a foot.

Oscar went into a Filipino pool-room to phone, and when he came out there was quite a crowd around the body.

CHAPTER 51

I

IN 1903 Horace Quinn beat Mr R. Keef for the office of sheriff. He had been well trained as the chief deputy sheriff. Most of the voters figured that since Quinn was doing most of the work he might as well have the title. Sheriff Quinn held the office until 1919. He was sheriff so long that we growing up in Monterey County thought the words 'Sheriff' and 'Quinn' went together naturally. We could not imagine anyone else being sheriff. Quinn grew old in his office. He limped from an early injury. We knew he was intrepid, for he had held his own in various gun-fights; besides, he looked like a sheriff – the only kind we knew about. His face was broad and pink, his white moustache shaped like the horns of a longhorn steer. He was broad of shoulder, and in his age he developed a portliness which only gave him more authority. He wore a fine Stetson hat, a Norfolk jacket, and in his later years carried his gun in a

oulder holster. His old belt holster tugged at his stomach too
uch. He had known his county in 1903 and he knew it and
ntrolled it even better in 1917. He was an institution, as much
part of the Salinas Valley as its mountains.

In all the years since Adam's shooting Sheriff Quinn had kept
ack of Kate. When Faye died, he knew instinctively that Kate
as probably responsible, but he also knew he hadn't much of
ny chance of convicting her, and a wise sheriff doesn't butt his
ead against the impossible. They were only a couple of whores,
ter all.

In the years that followed, Kate played fair with him and he
radually achieved a certain respect for her. Since there were
oing to be houses anyway, they had better be run by responsible
eople. Every so often Kate spotted a wanted man and turned
im in. She ran a house which did not get into trouble. Sheriff
uinn and Kate got along together.

The Saturday after Thanksgiving, about noon, Sheriff Quinn
oked through the papers from Joe Valery's pockets. The ·38
ug had splashed off one side of Joe's heart and had flattened
gainst the ribs and torn out a section as big as a fist. The
anila envelopes were glued together with blackened blood. The
heriff dampened the papers with a wet handkerchief to get
hem apart. He read the will, which had been folded, so that the
lood was on the outside. He laid it aside and inspected the
hotographs in the envelopes. He sighed deeply.

Every envelope contained a man's honour and peace of mind.
ffectively used, these pictures could cause half a dozen suicides.
lready Kate was on the table at Muller's with the formalin
unning into her veins, and her stomach was in a jar in the
oroner's office.

When he had seen all of the pictures he called a number. He
aid into the phone, 'Can you drop over to my office? Well, put
our lunch off, will you? Yes, I think you'll see it's important.
'll wait for you.'

A few minutes later when the nameless man stood beside his
esk in the front office of the old red county jail behind the
court-house, Sheriff Quinn stuck the will out in front of him.
As a lawyer, would you say this is any good?'

His visitor read the two lines and breathed deep through his
ose. 'Is this who I think it is?'

'Yes.'

'Well, if her name was Catherine Trask and this is her handwriting, and if Aron Trask is her son, this is as good as gold.'

525

Quinn lifted the ends of his fine wide moustache with the back of his forefinger. 'You knew her, didn't you?'

'Well, not to say know. I knew who she was.'

Quinn put his elbows on his desk and leaned forward. 'Sit down, I want to talk to you.'

His visitor drew up a chair. His fingers picked at a cotton button.

The sheriff asked, 'Was Kate blackmailing you?'

'Certainly not. Why should she?'

'I'm asking you as a friend. You know she's dead. You can tell me.'

'I don't know what you're getting at – nobody's blackmailing me.'

Quinn slipped a photograph from its envelope, turned it like a playing card, and skidded it across the desk.

His visitor adjusted his glasses and the breath whistled in his nose. 'Jesus Christ,' he said softly.

'You didn't know she had it?'

'Oh, I knew it all right. She let me know. For Christ's sake, Horace – what are you going to do with this?'

Quinn took the picture from his hand.

'Horace, what are you going to do with it?'

'Burn it.' The sheriff ruffled the edges of the envelopes with his thumb. 'Here's a deck of hell,' he said. 'These could tear the county to pieces.'

Quinn wrote a list of names on a sheet of paper. Then he hoisted himself up on his game leg and went to the iron stove against the north wall of his office. He crunched up the *Salinas Morning Journal* and lighted it and dropped it in the stove, and when it flared up he dropped the manila envelopes on the flame, set the damper, and closed the stove. The fire roared and the flames winked yellow behind the little isinglass windows in the front of the stove. Quinn brushed his hands together as though they were dirty. 'The negatives were in there,' he said. 'I've been through her desk. There weren't any other prints.'

His visitor tried to speak but his voice was a husky whisper. 'Thank you, Horace.'

The sheriff limped to his desk and picked up his list. 'I want you to do something for me. Here's a list. Tell everyone on this list I've burned the pictures. You know them all, God knows. And they could take it from you. Nobody's holy. Get each man alone and tell him exactly what happened. Look here!' He pened the stove door and poked the black sheets until they ere reduced to powder. 'Tell them that,' he said.

His visitor looked at the sheriff, and Quinn knew that there as no power on earth that could keep this man from hating im. For the rest of their lives there would be a barrier between tem, and neither one could ever admit it.

'Horace, I don't know how to thank you.'

And the sheriff said in sorrow, 'That's all right. It's what I'd ant my friends to do for me.'

'The goddam bitch,' his visitor said softly, and Horace Quinn new that part of the curse was for him.

And he knew he wouldn't be sheriff much longer. These uilt-feeling men could get him out, and they would have to. He ighed and sat down. 'Go to your lunch now,' he said. 'I've got ork to do.'

At quarter to one Sheriff Quinn turned off Main Street on Central Avenue. At Reynaud's Bakery he bought a loaf of French read, still warm and giving off its wonderful smell of fernented dough.

He used the hand-rail to help himself up the steps of the Trask porch.

Lee answered the door, a dish-towel tied around his middle. He's not home,' he said.

'Well, he's on his way. I called the draft board. I'll wait for im.'

Lee moved aside and let him in and seated him in the livingoom. 'You like a nice cup of hot coffee?' he asked.

'I don't mind if I do.'

'Fresh made,' said Lee, and went into the kitchen.

Quinn looked around the comfortable sitting-room. He felt hat he didn't want his office much longer. He remembered hearng a doctor say, 'I love to deliver a baby, because if I do my vork well, there's joy at the end of it.' The sheriff had thought ften of that remark. It seemed to him that if he did his work vell there was sorrow at the end of it for somebody. The fact hat it was necessary was losing its weight with him. He would be retiring soon whether he wanted to or not.

Every man has a retirement picture in which he does those hings he never had time to do – makes the journeys, reads the neglected books he always pretended to have read. For many years the sheriff dreamed of spending the shining time hunting and fishing – wandering in the Santa Lucia range, camping by half-remembered streams. And now that it was almost time he

knew he didn't want to do it. Sleeping on the ground wou
make his leg ache. He remembered how heavy a deer is and ho
hard it is to carry the dangling limp body from the place of t
kill. And, frankly, he didn't care for venison anyway. Madan
Reynaud could soak it in wine and lace it with spice but, hell,
old shoe would taste good with that treatment.

Lee had brought a percolator. Quinn could hear the wat
spluttering against the glass dome, and his long-trained mir
made the suggestion that Lee hadn't told the truth about havir
fresh-made coffee.

It was a good mind the old man had – sharpened in its wor
He could bring up old faces in his mind and inspect them, ar
also scenes and conversations. He could play them over like
record or a film. Thinking of venison, his mind had gone abov
cataloguing the sitting-room and his mind nudged him sayin
'Hey, there's something wrong here – something strange.'

The sheriff heeded the voice and looked at the room – flowere
chintz, lace curtains, white drawn-work table cover, cushions c
the couch covered with a bright and impudent print. It was
feminine room in a house where only men lived.

He thought of his own sitting-room. Mrs Quinn had chose
bought, cleaned, every single thing in it except a pipe-stan
Come to think of it, she had bought the pipe-stand for hin
There was a woman's room too. But it was a fake. It was tc
feminine – a woman's room designed by a man – and overdon
too feminine. That would be Lee. Adam wouldn't even see it, l
alone put it together – no – Lee trying to make a home, an
Adam not even seeing it.

Horace Quinn remembered questioning Adam so very lon
ago, remembered him as a man in agony. He could still se
Adam's haunted and horrified eyes. He had thought then o
Adam as a man of such honesty that he couldn't conceive any
thing else. And in the years he had seen much of Adam. The
both belonged to the Masonic Order. They went through th
chairs together. Horace followed Adam as Master of the Lodg
and both of them wore their Past Master's pins. And Adam ha
been set apart – an invisble wall cut him off from the world. Yo
couldn't get into him – he couldn't get out to you. But in tha
old agony there had been no wall.

In his wife Adam had touched the living world. Horac
thought of her now, grey and washed, the needles in her throa
and the rubber formalin tubes hanging down from the ceiling.

Adam could do no dishonesty. He didn't want anything. Yo

d to crave something to be dishonest. The sheriff wondered
at went on behind the wall, what pressures, what pleasures
d achings.

He shifted his behind to ease the pressure on his leg. The
use was still except for the bouncing coffee. Adam was long
ming from the draft board. The amused thought came to the
eriff, 'I'm getting old, and I kind of like it.'

Then he heard Adam at the front door. Lee heard him too
d darted into the hall. 'The sheriff's here,' said Lee, to warn
m perhaps.

Adam came in smiling and held out his hand. 'Hello, Horace
ave you got a warrant?' It was a damn good try at a joke.

'Howdy,' Quinn said. 'Your man is going to give me a cup of
ffee.'

Lee went to the kitchen and rattled dishes.

Adam said, 'Anything wrong, Horace?'

'Everything's always wrong in my business. I'll wait till the
ffee comes.'

'Don't mind Lee. He listens anyway. He can hear through a
osed door. I don't keep anything from him because I can't.'

Lee came in with a tray. He was smiling remotely to himself,
d when he had poured the coffee and gone out Adam asked
gain, 'Is there anything wrong, Horace?'

'No, I don't think so. Adam, was that woman still married to
u?'

Adam became rigid. 'Yes,' he said. 'What's the matter?'

'She killed herself last night.'

Adam's face contorted and his eyes swelled and glistened with
ars. He fought his mouth, and then he gave up and put his
ce down in his hands and wept. 'Oh, my poor darling!' he
id.

Quinn sat quietly and let him have it out, and after a time
dam's control came back and he raised his head. 'Excuse me,
orace,' he said.

Lee came in from the kitchen and put a damp towel in his
ands, and Adam sponged his eyes and handed it back.

'I didn't expect that,' Adam said, and his face was ashamed.
What shall I do? I'll claim her. I'll bury her.'

'I wouldn't,' said Horace. 'That is, unless you feel you have
. That's not what I came about.' He took the folded will from
is pocket and held it out.

Adam shrank from it. 'Is – is that her blood?'

'No, it's not. It's not her blood at all. Read it.'

529

Adam read the two lines and went right on staring at the paper and beyond it. 'He doesn't know – she is his mother.'

'You never told him?'

'No.'

'Jesus Christ!' said the sheriff.

Adam said earnestly, 'I'm sure he wouldn't want anything of hers. Let's just tear it up and forget it. If he knew, I don't think Aron would want anything of hers.'

''Fraid you can't,' Quinn said. 'We do quite a few illegal things. She had a safe-deposit box. I don't have to tell you where I got the will or the key. I went to the bank. Didn't wait for court order. Thought it might have a bearing.' He didn't tell Adam he thought there might be more pictures. 'Well, Old Bob let me open the box. We can always deny it. There's over a hundred thousand dollars in gold certificates. There's money in there in bales – and there isn't one goddam thing in there but money.'

'Nothing?'

'One other thing – a marriage certificate.'

Adam leaned back in his chair. The remoteness was coming down again, the soft protective folds between himself and the world. He saw his coffee and took a sip of it. 'What do you think I ought to do?' he asked steadily and quietly.

'I can only tell you what I'd do,' Sheriff Quinn said. 'You don't have to take my advice. I'd have the boy in right now. I'd tell him everything – every single thing. I'd even tell him why you didn't tell him before. He's – how old?'

'Seventeen.'

'He's a man. He's got to take it some time. Better if he gets the whole thing at once.'

'Cal knows,' said Adam. 'I wonder why she made the will to Aron.'

'God knows. Well, what do you think?'

'I don't know, and so I'm going to do what you say. Will you stay with me?'

'Sure I will.'

'Lee,' Adam called, 'tell Aron I want him. He has come home hasn't he?'

Lee came to the doorway. His heavy lids closed for a moment and then opened. 'Not yet. Maybe he went back to school.'

'He would have told me. You know, Horace, we drank a lot of champagne on Thanksgiving. Where's Cal?'

'In his room,' said Lee.

'Well, call him in. Get him in. Cal will know.'

Cal's face was tired and his shoulders sagged with exhaustion, but his face was pinched and closed and crafty and mean.

Adam asked, 'Do you know where your brother is?'

'No, I don't,' said Cal.

'Weren't you with him at all?'

'No.'

'He hasn't been home for two nights. Where is he?'

'How do I know?' said Cal. 'Am I supposed to look after him?'

Adam's head sank down, his body jarred, just a little quiver. At the back of his eyes a tiny sharp incredibly bright blue light flashed. He said thickly, 'Maybe he did go back to college.' His lips seemed heavy and he murmured like a man talking in his sleep. 'Don't you think he went back to college?'

Sheriff Quinn stood up. 'Anything I got to do I can do later. You get a rest, Adam. You've had a shock.'

Adam looked up at him. 'Shock – oh, yes. Thank you, George. Thank you very much.'

'George?'

'Thank you very much,' said Adam.

When the sheriff had gone, Cal went to his room. Adam leaned back in his chair, and very soon he went to sleep and his mouth dropped open and he snored across his palate.

Lee watched him for a while before he went back to his kitchen. He lifted the bread-box and took out a tiny volume bound in leather, and the gold tooling was almost completely worn away – *The Meditations of Marcus Aurelius* in English translation.

Lee wiped his steel-rimmed spectacles on a dish-towel. He opened the book and leafed through. And he smiled to himself, consciously searching for reassurance.

He read slowly, moving his lips over the words. 'Everything is only for a day, both that which remembers and that which is remembered.

'Observe constantly that all things take place by change, and accustom thyself to consider that the nature of the universe loves nothing so much as to change things which are and to make new things like them. For everything that exists is in a manner the seed of that which will be.'

Lee glanced down the page. 'Thou wilt die soon and thou art not yet simple nor free from perturbations, nor without suspicion of being hurt by external things, nor kindly disposed to-

wards all; nor dost thou yet place wisdom only in acting
justly.'

Lee looked up from the page, and he answered the book as he
would answer one of his ancient relatives. 'That is true,' he said
'It's very hard. I'm sorry. But don't forget that you also say
"Always run the short way and the short way is the natural"—
don't forget that.' He let the pages slip past his fingers to the
flyleaf where was written with a broad carpenter's pencil, 'Sam'
Hamilton'.

Suddenly Lee felt good. He wondered whether Sam'l Hamil
ton had ever missed his book or known who stole it. It had
seemed to Lee the only clean pure way was to steal it. And h
still felt good about it. His fingers caressed the smooth leather
of the binding as he took it back and slipped it under the bread
box. He said to himself, 'But of course he knew who took it
Who else would have stolen *Marcus Aurelius*?' He went into the
sitting-room and pulled a chair near to the sleeping Adam.

11

In his room Cal sat at his desk, elbows down, palms holding his
aching head together, hands pushing against the sides of his
head. His stomach churned and the sour-sweet smell of whisky
was on him and in him, living in his pores, in his clothing, beat
ing sluggishly in his head.

Cal had never drunk before, had never needed to. But going
to Kate's had been no relief from pain and his revenge had been
no triumph. His memory was all swirling clouds and broken
pieces of sound and sight and feeling. What now was true and
what was imagined he could not separate. Coming out of Kate's
he had touched his sobbing brother and Aron had cut him down
with a fist like a whip. Aron had stood over him in the dark, and
then suddenly turned and ran, screaming like a broken-hearted
child. Cal could still hear the hoarse cries over running foot
steps. Cal had lain still where he had fallen under the tall privet
in Kate's front yard. He heard the engines puffing and snorting
by the round-house and the crash of freight cars being as
sembled. Then he had closed his eyes and, hearing light steps
and feeling a presence, he looked up. Someone was bending over
him and he thought it was Kate. The figure moved quietly
away.

After a while Cal had stood up and brushed himself and
walked towards Main Street. He was surprised at how casual his

532

eling was. He sang softly under his breath, 'There's a rose that
ows in no man's land and 'tis wonderful to see —'

On Friday Cal brooded the whole day long. And in the even-
g Joe Laguna bought the quart of whisky for him. Cal was too
ung to purchase. Joe wanted to accompany Cal, but Joe was
tisfied with the dollar Cal gave him and went back for a pint
grappa.

Cal went to the alley behind the Abbot House and found the
adow behind a post where he had sat the night he first saw
s mother. He sat cross-legged on the ground, and then, in
ite of revulsion and nausea, he forced the whisky into him-
lf. Twice he vomited and then went on drinking until the
rth tipped and swayed and the street-light spun majestically
a circle.

The bottle slipped from his hand finally and Cal passed out,
it even unconscious he still vomited weakly. A serious, short-
aired dog-about-town with a curling tail sauntered into the
ley, making his stations, but he smelled Cal and took a wide
rcle around him. Joe Laguna found him and smelled him too.
e shook the bottle leaning against Cal's leg and Joe held it up
the street-light and saw that it was one-third full. He looked
r the cork and couldn't find it. He walked away, his thumb
ver the neck to keep the whisky from sloshing out.

When in the cold dawn a frost awakened Cal to a sick world
e struggled home like a broken bug. He hadn't far to go, just
the alley mouth and then across the street.

Lee heard him at the door and smelled his nastiness as he
umped along the hall to his room and fell over on his bed.
al's head shattered with pain and he was wide awake. He had
o resistance against sorrow and no device to protect himself
gainst shame. After a while he did the best he could. He bathed
icy water and scrubbed and scratched his body with a block
f pumice stone, and the pain of his scraping seemed good to
im.

He knew that he had to tell his guilt to his father and beg his
orgiveness. And he had to humble himself to Aron, not only
ow but always. He could not live without that. And yet, when
e was called out and stood in the room with Sheriff Quinn and
is father, he was as raw and angry as a surly dog and his hatred
f himself turned outward towards everyone – a vicious cur he
vas, unloved, unloving.

Then he was back in his room and his guilt assaulted him and
e had no weapon to fight it off.

A panic for Aron arose in him. He might be injured, might be in trouble. It was Aron who couldn't take care of himself. Cal knew he had to bring Aron back, had to find him and rebuild him back the way he had been. And this had to be done even though Cal sacrificed himself. And then the idea of sacrifice took hold of him the way it does with the guilty-feeling man. A sacrifice might reach Aron and bring him back.

Cal went to his bureau and got the flat package from under his handkerchiefs in his drawer. He looked around the room and brought a porcelain tray to his desk. He breathed deeply and found the cool air good-tasting. He lifted one of the crisp notes, creased it in the middle so that it made an angle, and then he scratched a match under his desk and lighted the note. The heavy paper curled and blackened, the flame ran upwards, and only when the fire was about his fingertips did Cal drop the charred chip in the pin-tray. He stripped off another note and lighted it.

When six were burned Lee came in without knocking. ' I smelled smoke,' and then he saw what Cal was doing. 'Oh!' he said.

Cal braced himself for intervention but none came. Lee folded his hands across his middle and he stood silently – waiting. Cal doggedly lighted note after note until all were burned, and then he crushed the black chips down to powder and waited for Lee to comment, but Lee did not speak or move.

At last Cal said, 'Go ahead – you want to talk to me. Go ahead!'

'No,' said Lee, 'I don't. And if you have no need to talk to me – I'll stay a while and then I'll go away. I'll sit down here.' He squatted in a chair, folded his hands, and waited. He smiled to himself, the expression that is called inscrutable.

Cal turned from him. 'I can out-sit you,' he said.

'In a contest maybe,' said Lee. 'But in day to day, year to year – who knows? – century to century sitting – no, Cal. You'd lose.'

After a few moments Cal said peevishly, 'I wish you'd get on with your lecture.'

'I don't have a lecture.'

'What the hell are you doing here, then? You know what I did, and I got drunk last night.'

'I suspect the first and I can smell the second.'

'Smell?'

'You still smell,' said Lee.

'First time,' said Cal. 'I don't like it.'

'I don't either,' said Lee. 'I've got a bad stomach for liquor. Besides it makes me playful, intellectual but playful.'

'How do you mean, Lee?'

'I can only give you an example. In my younger days I played tennis. I liked it, and it was also a good thing for a servant to do. He could pick up his master's flubs at doubles and get no thanks but a few dollars for it. Once, I think it was sherry that time, I developed the theory that the fastest and most elusive animals in the world are bats. I was apprehended in the middle of the night in the bell tower of the Methodist Church in San Leandro. I had a racquet, and I seemed to have explained to the arresting officer that I was improving my back-hand on bats.'

Cal laughed with such amusement that Lee almost wished he had done it.

Cal said, 'I just sat behind a post and drank like a pig.'

'Always animals —'

'I was afraid if I didn't get drunk I'd shoot myself,' Cal interrupted.

'You'd never do that. You're too mean,' said Lee. 'By the way, where *is* Aron?'

'He ran away. I don't know where he went.'

'He's not too mean,' said Lee nervously.

'I know it. That's what I thought about. You don't think he would, do you, Lee?'

Lee said testily, 'Goddam it, whenever a person wants reassurance he tells a friend to think what he wants to be true. It's like asking a waiter what's good tonight. How the hell do I know?'

Cal cried, 'Why did I do it – why did I do it?'

'Don't make it complicated,' Lee said. 'You know why you did it. You were mad at him, and you were mad at him because your father hurt your feelings. That's not difficult. You were just mean.'

'I guess that's what I wonder – why I'm mean. Lee, I don't want to be mean. Help me, Lee!'

'Just a second,' Lee said. 'I thought I heard your father.' He started out of the door.

Cal heard voices for a moment and then Lee came back to the room. 'He's going to the post office. We never get any mail in mid-afternoon. Nobody does. But every man in Salinas goes to the post office in the afternoon.'

'Some get a drink on the way,' said Cal.

'I guess it is a kind of habit and a kind of rest. They see their friends.' And Lee said, 'Cal – I don't like your father's looks. He's got a dazed look. Oh, I forgot. You don't know. Your mother committed suicide last night.'

Cal said, 'Did she?' and then he snarled, 'I hope it hurt. No, I don't want to say that. I don't want to think that. There it is again. There it is! I don't – want it – like that.'

Lee scratched a spot on his head, and that started his whole head to itching, and he scratched it all over, taking his time. It gave him the appearance of deep thought. He said, 'Did burning the money give you much pleasure?'

'I – I guess so.'

'And are you taking pleasure from this whipping you're giving yourself? Are you enjoying your despair?'

'Lee!'

'You're pretty full of yourself. You're marvelling at the tragic spectacle of Caleb Trask – Caleb the magnificent, the unique Caleb whose suffering should have its Homer. Did you ever think of yourself as a snot-nose kid – mean sometimes, incredibly generous sometimes? Dirty in your habits, and curiously pure in your mind. Maybe you have a little more energy than most, just energy, but outside of that you're very like all the other snot-nose kids. Are you trying to attract dignity and tragedy to yourself because your mother was a whore? And if anything should have happened to your brother, will you be able to sneak for yourself the eminence of being a murderer, snot-nose?'

Cal turned slowly back to his desk. Lee watched him, holding his breath the way a doctor watches for the reaction to a hypodermic. Lee could see the reactions flaring through Cal – the rage at insult, the belligerence, and the hurt feelings following behind, and out of that – just the beginning of relief.

Lee sighed. He had worked so hard, so tenderly, and his work seemed to have succeeded. He said softly, 'We're a violent people, Cal. Does it seem strange to you that I include myself? Maybe it's true that we are all descended from the restless, the nervous, the criminals, the arguers and brawlers, but also the brave and independent and generous. If our ancestors had not been that, they would have stayed in their home plots in the other world and starved over the squeezed-out soil.'

Cal turned his head towards Lee, and his face had lost its tightness. He smiled, and Lee knew he had not fooled the boy entirely. Cal knew now it was a job – a well-done job – and he was grateful.

Lee went on, 'That's why I include myself. We all have that heritage, no matter what old land our fathers left. All colours and blends of Americans have somewhat the same tendencies. It's a breed – selected out by accident. And so we're over-brave and over-fearful – we're kind and cruel as children. We're over-friendly and at the same time frightened of strangers. We boast and are impressed. We're over-sentimental and realistic. We are mundane and materialistic – and do you know of any other nation that acts for ideals? We eat too much. We have no taste, no sense of proportion. We throw our energy about like waste. In the old lands they say of us that we go from barbarism to decadence without an intervening culture. Can it be that our critics have not the key or the language of our culture? That's what we are, Cal – all of us. You aren't any different.'

'Talk away,' said Cal, and he smiled and repeated, 'Talk away.'

'I don't need to any more,' said Lee. 'I'm finished now. I wish your father would come back. He worries me.' And Lee went nervously out.

In the hall just outside the front door he found Adam leaning against the wall, his hat low over his eyes and his shoulders slumped.

'Adam, what's the matter with you?'

'I don't know. Seem tired. Seem tired.'

Lee took him by the arm, and it seemed that he had to guide him towards the living-room. Adam fell heavily into his chair, and Lee took the hat from his head. Adam rubbed the back of his left hand with his right. His eyes were strange, very clear but unmoving. And his lips were dry and thickened and his speech had the sound of a dream talker, slow and coming from a distance. He rubbed his hand harshly. 'Strange thing,' he said, 'I must have fainted – in the post office. I never faint. Mr Pioda helped me up. Just for a second it was, I guess. I never faint.'

Lee asked, 'Was there any mail?'

'Yes – yes – I think there was mail.' He put his left hand in his pocket and in a moment took it out. 'My hand is kind of numb,' he said apologetically and reached across with his right hand and brought out a yellow government postcard.

'Thought I read it,' he said. 'I must have read it.' He held it up before his eyes and then dropped the card in his lap. 'Lee, I guess I've got to get glasses. Never needed them in my life. Can't read it. Letters jump around.'

'Shall I read it?'

'Funny – well, I'll go first thing for glasses. Yes, what does it say?'

And Lee read, ' "Dear Father, I'm in the army. I told them I was eighteen. I'll be all right. Don't worry about me. Aron." '

'Funny,' said Adam. 'Seems like I read it. But I guess I didn't.' He rubbed his hand.

CHAPTER 52

I

THAT WINTER of 1917–18 was a dark and frightened time. The Germans smashed everything in front of them. In three months the British suffered three hundred thousand casualties. Many units of the French army were mutinous. Russia was out of the war. The German east divisions, rested and re-equipped, were thrown at the western front. The war seemed hopeless.

It was May before we had as many as twelve divisions in the field, and summer had come before our troops began to move across the sea in numbers. The Allied generals were fighting each other. Submarines slaughtered the crossing ships.

We learned then that the war was not a quick heroic change, but a slow, incredibly complicated matter. Our spirits sank in those winter months. We lost the flare of excitement and we had not yet put on the doggedness of a long war.

Ludendorff was unconquerable. Nothing stopped him. He mounted attack after attack on the broken armies of France and England. And it occurred to us that we might be too late, that soon we might be standing alone against the invincible Germans.

It was not uncommon for people to turn away from the war, some to fantasy and some to vice and some to crazy gaiety. Fortune-tellers were in great demand, and saloons did a roaring business. But people also turned inward to their private joys and tragedies to escape the pervasive fear and despondency. Isn't it strange that today we have forgotten this? We remember World War I as quick victory, with flags and bands, marching and horseplay and returning soldiers, fights in the bar-rooms with the goddam Limeys who thought they won the war. How quickly we forget that in that winter Ludendorff could not be beaten and that many people were preparing in their minds and spirits for a lost war.

dam Trask was more puzzled than sad. He didn't have to
esign from the draft board. He was given leave of absence for
l health. He sat by the hour rubbing the back of his left
and. He brushed it with a harsh brush and soaked it in hot
ater.

'It's circulation,' he said. 'As soon as I get the circulation back
'll be all right. It's my eyes that bother me. I never had trouble
ith my eyes. Guess I'll have to get my eyes tested for glasses.
Me with glasses! Be hard to get used to. I'd go today but I feel
little dizzy.'

He felt more dizzy than he would admit. He could not move
bout the house without a hand braced against a wall. Lee often
ad to give him a hand-up out of his chair or help him out of
ed in the morning and tie his shoes because he could not tie
nots with his numb left hand.

Almost daily he came back to Aron. 'I can understand why a
oung man might want to enlist,' he said. 'If Aron had talked to
e I might have tried to persuade him against it, but I wouldn't
ave forbidden it. You know that, Lee.'

'I know it.'

'That's what I can't understand. Why did he sneak away?
Why doesn't he write? I thought I knew him better than that.
Has he written to Abra? He'd be sure to write to her.'

'I'll ask her.'

'You do that. Do that right away.'

'The training is hard. That's what I've heard. Maybe they
don't give him time.'

'It doesn't take any time to write a card.'

'When you went in the army, did you write to your father?'

'Think you've got me there, don't you? No, I didn't, but I
had a reason. I didn't want to enlist. My father forced me. I was
esentful. You see, I had a good reason. But Aron – he was doing
ine in college. Why, they've written, asking about him. You read
he letter. He didn't take any clothes. He didn't take the gold
watch.'

'He wouldn't need any clothes in the army, and they don't
want gold watches there either. Everything's brown.'

'I guess you're right. But I don't understand it. I've got to
do something about my eyes. Can't ask you to read everything to me.' His eyes really troubled him. 'I can see a letter,'
he said. 'But the words jumble all around.' A dozen times a

day he seized a paper or a book and stared at it and put down.

Lee read the papers to him to keep him from getting restless and often in the middle of the reading Adam went to sleep.

He would awaken and say, 'Lee? Is that you, Cal? You know I never had any trouble with my eyes. I'll just go tomorrow an get my eyes tested.'

About the middle of February Cal went into the kitchen an said, 'Lee, he talks about it all the time. Let's get his eye tested.'

Lee was stewing apricots. He left the stove and closed th kitchen door and went back to the stove. 'I don't want him t go,' he said.

'Why not?'

'I don't think it's his eyes. Finding out might trouble him Let him be for a while. He's had a bad shock. Let him ge better. I'll read to him all he wants.'

'What do you think it is?'

'I don't want to say. I've thought maybe Dr Edwards migh just come by for a friendly call – just to say hello.'

'Have it your own way,' said Cal.

Lee said, 'Cal, have you seen Abra?'

'Sure, I see her. She walks away.'

'Can't you catch her?'

'Sure – and I could throw her down and punch her in th face and make her talk to me. But I won't.'

'Maybe if you'd just break the ice. Sometimes the barrier is s weak it just falls over when you touch it. Catch up with her Tell her I want to see her.'

'I won't do it.'

'You feel awful guilty, don't you?'

Cal did not answer.

'Don't you like her?'

Cal did not answer.

'If you keep this up, you're going to feel worse, not better You'd better open up. I'm warning you. You'd better open up.'

Cal cried, 'Do you want me to tell Father what I did? I'll do it if you tell me to.'

'No, Cal. Not now. But when he gets well you'll have to. You'll have to for yourself. You can't carry this alone. It will kill you.'

'Maybe I deserve to be killed.'

'Stop that!' Lee said coldly. 'That can be the cheapest kind of self-indulgence. You stop that!'

'How do you go about stopping it?' Cal asked.

Lee changed the subject. 'I don't understand why Abra hasn't been here – not even once.'

'No reason to come now.'

'It's not like her. Something's wrong there. Have you seen her?'

Cal scowled. 'I told you I have. You're getting crazy too. Tried to talk to her three times. She walked away.'

'Something's wrong. She's a good woman – a real woman.'

'She's a girl,' said Cal. 'It sounds funny you calling her a woman.'

'No,' Lee said softly. 'A few are women from the moment they're born. Abra has the loveliness of woman, and the courage – and the strength – and the wisdom. She knows things and she accepts things. I would have bet she couldn't be small or mean or even vain except when it's pretty to be vain.'

'You sure do think well of her.'

'Well enough to think she wouldn't desert us.' And he said, 'I miss her. Ask her to come to see me.'

'I told you she walked away from me.'

'Well, chase her, then. Tell her I want to see her. I miss her.'

Cal asked, 'Shall we go back to my father's eyes now?'

'No,' said Lee.

'Shall we talk about Aron?'

'No.'

III

Cal tried all the next day to find Abra alone, and it was only after school that he saw her ahead of him, walking home. He turned a corner and ran along the parallel street and then back, and he judged time and distance so that he turned in front of her as she strolled along.

'Hello,' he said.

'Hello. I thought I saw you behind me.'

'You did. I ran around the block to get in front of you. I want to talk to you.'

She regarded him gravely. 'You could have done that without running around the block.'

'Well, I tried to talk to you in school. You walked away.'

'You were mad. I don't want to talk to you mad.'

'How do you know I was?'

'I could see it in your face and the way you walked. You're not mad now.'

'No, I'm not.'

'Do you want to take my books?' She smiled.

A warmth fell on him. 'Yes – yes, I do.' He put her schoolbooks under his arm and walked beside her. 'Lee wants to see you. He asked me to tell you.'

She was pleased. 'Does he? Tell him I'll come. How's your father?'

'Not very well. His eyes bother him.'

They walked along in silence until Cal couldn't stand it any more. 'You know about Aron?'

'Yes.' She paused. 'Open my binder and look next to the first page.'

He shifted the books. A penny postcard was in the binder. 'Dear Abra,' it said. 'I don't feel clean. I'm not fit for you. Don't be sorry. I'm in the army. Don't go near my father. Goodbye, Aron.'

Cal snapped the book shut. 'The son of a bitch,' he said under his breath.

'What?'

'Nothing.'

'I heard what you said.'

'Do you know why he went away?'

'No. I guess I could figure out – put two and two together. I don't want to. I'm not ready to – that is, unless you want to tell me.'

Suddenly Cal said, 'Abra – do you hate me?'

'No, Cal, but you hate me a little. Why is that?'

'I – I'm afraid of you.'

'No need to be.'

'I've hurt you more than you know. And you're my brother's girl.'

'How have you hurt me? And I'm *not* your brother's girl.'

'All right,' he said bitterly, 'I'll tell you – and I don't want you to forget you asked me to. Our mother was a whore. She ran a house here in town. I found out about it a long time ago. Thanksgiving night I took Aron down and showed her to him. I —'

Abra broke in excitedly, 'What did he do?'

'He went mad – just crazy. He yelled at her. Outside he

542

nocked me down and ran away. Our dear mother killed herself; my father – he's – there's something wrong with him. Now you know about me. Now you have some reason to walk away from me.'

'Now I know about him,' she said calmly.

'My brother?'

'Yes, your brother.'

'He was good. Why did I say *was*? He *is* good. He's not mean or dirty like me.'

They had been walking very slowly. Abra stopped and Cal stopped and she faced him.

'Cal,' she said, 'I've known about your mother for a long, long time.'

'You have?'

'I heard my parents talking when they thought I was asleep. I want to tell you something, and it's hard to tell and it's good to tell.'

'You want to?'

'I have to. It's not so terribly long ago that I grew up and I wasn't a little girl any more. Do you know what I mean?'

'Yes,' said Cal.

'You sure you know?'

'Yes.'

'All right, then. It's hard to say now. I wish I'd said it then. I didn't love Aron any more.'

'Why not?'

'I've tried to figure it out. When we were children we lived in a story that we made up. But when I grew up the story wasn't enough. I had to have something else, because the story wasn't true any more.'

'Well — '

'Wait – let me get it all out. Aron didn't grow up. Maybe he never will. He wanted the story and he wanted it to come out his way. He couldn't stand to have it come out any other way.'

'How about you?'

'I don't want to know how it comes out. I only want to be here while it's going on. And, Cal – we were kind of strangers. We kept it going because we were used to it. But I didn't believe the story any more.'

'How about Aron?'

'He was going to have it come out his way if he had to tear the world up by the roots.'

Cal stood looking at the ground.

543

Abra said, 'Do you believe me?'

'I'm trying to study it out.'

'When you're a child you're the centre of everything. Ever[y]thing happens to you. Other people? They're only ghosts fu[r]nished for you to talk to. But when you grow up you take yo[ur] place and you're your own size and shape. Things go out of y[ou] to others and come in from other people. It's worse, but i[t's] much better too. I'm glad you told me about Aron.'

'Why?'

'Because now I know I didn't make it all up. He couldn[t] stand to know about his mother because that's not how [he] wanted the story to go – and he wouldn't have any other stor[y.] So he tore up the world. It's the same way he tore me up – Ab[ra] – when he wanted to be a priest.'

Cal said, 'I'll have to think.'

'Give me my books,' she said. 'Tell Lee I'll come. I feel fr[ee] now. I want to think too. I think I love you, Cal.'

'I'm not good.'

'Because you're not good.'

Cal walked quickly home. 'She'll come tomorrow,' he tol[d] Lee.

'Why, you're excited,' said Lee.

IV

Once in the house Abra walked on her toes. In the hall sh[e] moved close to the wall where the floor did not creak. She pu[t] her foot on the lowest step on the carpeted stairs, changed he[r] mind, and went to the kitchen.

'Here you are,' her mother said. 'You didn't come straigh[t] home.'

'I had to stay after class. Is Father better?'

'I guess so.'

'What does the doctor say?'

'Same thing as he said at first – overwork. Just needs [a] rest.'

'He hasn't seemed tired,' said Abra.

Her mother opened a bin and took out three baking potatoe[s] and carried them to the sink. 'Your Father's very brave, dear. [I] should have known. He's been doing so much war work on top of his own work. The doctor says sometimes a man collapses al[l] at once.'

'Shall I go in and see him?'

'You know, Abra, I've got a feeling that he doesn't want to see anybody. Judge Knudsen phoned and your father said to tell him he was asleep.'

'Can I help you?'

'Go change your dress, dear. You don't want to get your pretty dress soiled.'

Abra tiptoed past her father's door and went to her own room. It was harsh-bright with varnish, papered brightly. Framed photographs of her parents on the bureau, poems framed on the walls, and her cupboard – everything in its place, the floor varnished, and her shoes standing diligently side by side. Her mother did everything for her, insisted on it – planned for her, dressed her.

Abra had long ago given up having any private thing in her room, even any personal thing. This was of such long standing that Abra did not think of her room as a private place. Her privacies were of the mind. The few letters she kept were in the sitting-room itself, filed among the pages of the two-volume *Memoirs of Ulysses S. Grant*, which to the best of her knowledge had never been opened by anyone but herself since it came off the press.

Abra felt pleased, and she did not inspect the reason. She knew certain things without question, and such things she did not speak about. For example, she knew that her father was not ill. He was hiding from something. Just as surely she knew that Adam Trask was ill, for she had seen him walking along the street. She wondered whether her mother knew her father was not ill.

Abra slipped off her dress and put on a cotton pinafore, which was understood to be for working around the house. She brushed her hair, tiptoed past her father's room, and went downstairs. At the foot of the stairs she opened her binder and took out Aron's postcard. In the sitting-room she shook Aron's letters out of Volume II of the *Memoirs*, folded them tightly, and, raising her skirt tucked them under the elastic which held up her panties. The package made her a little bumpy. In the kitchen she put on a full apron to conceal the bulge.

'You can scrape the carrots,' her mother said. 'Is that water hot?'

'Just coming to a boil.'

'Drop a bouillon cube in that cup, will you, dear? The doctor says it'll build your father up.'

When her mother carried the steaming cup upstairs, Abra

545

opened the incinerator end of the gas stove, put in the lette
and lighted them.

Her mother came back, saying, 'I smell fire.'

'I lit the trash. It was full.'

'I wish you'd ask me when you want to do a thing like tha
her mother said. 'I was saving the trash to warm the kitchen
the morning.'

'I'm sorry, Mother,' Abra said. 'I didn't think.'

'You should try to think of these things. It seems to r
you're getting very thoughtless lately.'

'I'm sorry, Mother.'

'Saved is earned,' said her mother.

The telephone rang in the dining-room. Her mother went
answer it. Abra heard her mother say, 'No, you can't see hi
It's doctor's orders. He can't see anyone – no, not anyone.'

She came back to the kitchen. 'Judge Knudsen again,' s
said.

CHAPTER 53

I

ALL DURING school next day Abra felt good about going
see Lee. She met Cal in the hall between classes. 'Did you te
him I was coming?'

'He's started some kind of tarts,' said Cal. He was dressed i
his uniform – choking high collar, ill-fitting tunic, and wrappe
leggings.

'You've got drill,' Abra said. 'I'll get there first. What kind (
tarts?'

'I don't know. But leave me a couple, will you? Smelled li
strawberry. Just leave me two.'

'Want to see a present I got for Lee? Look!' She opened
little cardboard box. 'It's a new kind of potato peeler. Takes o
just the skin. It's easy. I got it for Lee.'

'There go my tarts,' said Cal, and then, 'If I'm a little lat
don't go before I get there, will you?'

'Would you like to carry my books home?'

'Yes,' said Cal.

She looked at him long, full in the eyes, until he wanted t
drop his gaze, and then she walked away towards her class.

dam had taken to sleeping late, or, rather, he had taken to
eeping very often – short sleeps during the night and during
he day. Lee looked in on him several times before he found him
wake.

'I feel fine this morning,' Adam said.

'If you can call it morning. It's nearly eleven o'clock.'

'Good Lord! I have to get up.'

'What for?' Lee asked.

'What for? Yes, what for! But I feel good, Lee. I might walk
own to the draft board. How is it outside?'

'Raw,' said Lee.

He helped Adam get up. Buttons and shoe-laces and getting
nings on frontways gave Adam trouble.

While Lee helped him Adam said, 'I had a dream – very real.
dreamed about my father.'

'A great old gentleman, from all I hear,' said Lee. 'I read that
ortfolio of clippings your brother's lawyer sent. Must have been
great old gentleman.'

Adam looked calmly at Lee. 'Did you know he was a thief?'

'You must have had a dream,' said Lee. 'He's buried at Arl-
ngton. One clipping said the Vice-President was at his funeral,
nd the Secretary of War. You know the *Salinas Index* might
ke to do a piece about him – in wartime, you know. How would
ou like to go over the material?'

'He was a thief,' said Adam. 'I didn't think so once, but I do
ow. He stole from the GAR.'

'I don't believe it,' said Lee.

There were tears in Adam's eyes. Very often these days tears
ame suddenly to Adam. Lee said, 'Now you sit right here and
'll bring you some breakfast. Do you know who's coming to see
is this afternoon? Abra.'

Adam said, 'Abra?' and then, 'Oh, sure, Abra. She's a nice
irl.'

'I love her,' said Lee simply. He got Adam seated in front of
he card table in his bedroom. 'Would you like to work on the
ut-out puzzle while I get your breakfast?'

'No, thank you. Not this morning. I want to think about the
ream before I forget it.'

When Lee brought the breakfast tray Adam was asleep in his
hair. Lee awakened him and read the *Salinas Journal* to him
while he ate and then helped him to the toilet.

The kitchen was sweet with tarts, and some of the berries h
boiled over in the oven and burned, making the sharp, bitt
sweet smell pleasant and astringent.

There was a quiet rising joy in Lee. It was the joy of chan
Time's drawing down for Adam, he thought. Time must
drawing down for me, but I don't feel it. I feel immortal. On
when I was very young I felt mortal – but not any more. Dea
has receded. He wondered if this was a normal way to feel.

And he wondered what Adam meant, saying his father was
thief. Part of the dream, maybe. And then Lee's mind played
the way it often did. Suppose it was true – Adam, the mo
rigidly honest man it was possible to find, living all his life
stolen money. Lee laughed to himself – now this second wi
and Aron, whose purity was a little on the self-indulgent sid
living all his life on the profits from a whorehouse. Was th
some kind of joke or did things balance so that if one went to
far in one direction an automatic slide moved on the scale ar
the balance was re-established?

He thought of Sam Hamilton. He had knocked on so ma
doors. He had the most schemes and plans, and no one woul
give him any money. But of course – he had so much, he was
rich. You couldn't give him any more. Riches seem to come
the poor in spirit, the poor in interest and joy. To put
straight – the very rich are a poor bunch of bastards. He wor
dered if that were true. They acted that way sometimes.

He thought of Cal burning the money to punish himself. An
the punishment hadn't hurt him as badly as the crime. Le
said to himself, 'If there should happen to be a place wher
one day I'll come up with Sam Hamilton, I'll have a lot o
good stories to tell him,' and his mind went on, 'But so wi
he!'

Lee went in to find Adam and found him trying to open th
box that held the clippings about his father.

III

The wind blew cold that afternoon. Adam insisted on going t
look in on the draft board. Lee wrapped him up and starte
him off. 'If you feel faint at all, just sit down wherever you are,
Lee said.

'I will,' Adam agreed. 'I haven't felt dizzy all day. Migh
stop in and have Victor look at my eyes.'

'You wait till tomorrow. I'll go with you.'

'We'll see,' said Adam, and he started out, swinging his arms with bravado.

Abra came in with shining eyes and a red nose from the frosty wind, and she brought such pleasure that Lee giggled softly when he saw her.

'Where are the tarts?' she demanded. 'Let's hide them from Cal.' She sat down in the kitchen. 'Oh, I'm so glad to be back.'

Lee started to speak and choked and then what he wanted to say seemed good to say – to say carefully. He hovered over her. 'You know, I haven't wished for many things in my life,' he began. 'I learned very early not to wish for things. Wishing just brought earned disappointment.'

Abra said gaily, 'But you wish for something now. What is it?'

He blurted out, 'I wish you were my daughter —' He was shocked at himself. He went to the stove and turned out the gas under the tea-kettle, then lighted it again.

She said softly, 'I wish you were my father.'

He glanced quickly at her and away. 'You do?'

'Yes, I do.'

'Why?'

'Because I love you.'

Lee went quickly out of the kitchen. He sat in his room, gripping his hands tightly together until he stopped choking. He got up and took a small carved ebony box from the top of his bureau. A dragon climbed towards heaven on the box. He carried the box to the kitchen and laid it on the table between Abra's hands. 'This is for you,' he said, and his tone had no inflexion.

She opened the box and looked down on a small, dark green jade button, and carved on its surface was a human right hand, a lovely hand, the fingers curved and in repose. Abra lifted the button out and looked at it, and then she moistened it with the tip of her tongue and moved it gently over her full lips, and pressed the cool stone against her cheek.

Lee said, 'That was my mother's only ornament.'

Abra got up and put her arms around him and kissed him on the cheek, and it was the only time such a thing had ever happened in his whole life.

Lee laughed. 'My Oriental calm seems to have deserted me,' he said. 'Let me make the tea, darling. I'll get hold of myself that way.' From the stove he said, 'I've never used that word - never once to anybody in the world.'

Abra said, 'I woke up with joy this morning.'

'So did I,' said Lee. 'I know what made me feel happy. You were coming.'

'I was glad about that too, but —'

'You are changed,' said Lee. 'You aren't any part a little girl any more. Can you tell me?'

'I burned all of Aron's letters.'

'Did he do bad things to you?'

'No. I guess not. Lately I never felt good enough. I always wanted to explain to him that I was not good.'

'And now that you don't have to be perfect, you can be good. Is that it?'

'I guess so. Maybe that's it.'

'Do you know about the mother of the boys?'

'Yes. Do you know I haven't tasted a single one of the tarts?' Abra said. 'My mouth is dry.'

'Drink some tea, Abra. Do you like Cal?'

'Yes.'

Lee said, 'He's crammed full to the top with every good thing and every bad thing. I've thought that one single person could almost with the weight of a finger —'

Abra bowed her head over her tea. 'He asked me to go to the Alisal when the wild azaleas bloom.'

Lee put his hands on the table and leaned over. 'I don't want to ask you whether you are going,' he said.

'You don't have to,' said Abra. 'I'm going.'

Lee sat opposite her at the table. 'Don't stay away from this house for long,' he said.

'My father and mother don't want me here.'

'I only saw them once,' Lee said cynically. 'They seemed to be good people. Sometimes, Abra, the strangest medicines are effective. I wonder if it would help if they knew Aron had just inherited over a hundred thousand dollars.'

Abra nodded gravely and fought to keep the corners of her mouth from turning up. 'I think it would help,' she said. 'I wonder how I could get the news to them.'

'My dear,' said Lee, 'if I heard such a piece of news I think my first impulse would be to telephone someone. Maybe you'd have a bad connexion.'

Abra nodded. 'Would you tell her where the money came from?'

'That I would not,' said Lee.

She looked at the alarm clock hung on a nail on the wall.

'Nearly five,' she said. 'I'll have to go. My father isn't well. I thought Cal might get back from drill.'

'Come back very soon,' Lee said.

Cal was on the porch when she came out.

'Wait for me,' he said, and he went into the house and dropped his books.

'Take good care of Abra's books,' Lee called from the kitchen.

The winter night blew in with frosty wind, and the street-lamps with their spluttering carbons swung restlessly and made the shadows dart back and forth like a runner trying to steal second base. Men coming home from work buried their chins in their overcoats and hurried towards warmth. In the still night the monotonous scattering of music of the skating rink could be heard from many blocks away.

Cal said, 'Will you take your books for a minute, Abra? I want to unhook this collar. It's cutting my head off.' He worked the hooks out of the eyes and sighed with relief. 'I'm all chafed,' he said and took her books back. The branches of the big palm tree in Berges' front yard were lashing with a dry clatter, and a cat meowed over and over and over in front of some kitchen door closed against it.

Abra said, 'I don't think you make much of a soldier. You're too independent.'

'I could be,' said Cal. 'This drilling with old Krag-Jorgensens seems silly to me. When the time comes, and I take an interest, I'll be good.'

'The tarts were wonderful,' said Abra. 'I left one for you.'

'Thanks. I'll bet Aron makes a good soldier.'

'Yes, he will – and the best-looking soldier in the army. When are we going for the azaleas?'

'Not until spring.'

'Let's go early and take a lunch.'

'It might be raining.'

'Let's go anyway, rain or shine.'

She took her books and went into her yard. 'See you tomorrow,' she said.

He did not turn towards home. He walked in the nervous night past the high school and past the skating rink – a floor with a big tent over it, and a mechanical orchestra clanging away. Not a soul was skating. The old man who owned it sat miserably in his booth, flipping the end of a roll of tickets against his forefinger.

Main Street was deserted. The wind skidded papers on the sidewalk. Tom Meek, the constable, came out of Bell's candy store and fell into step with Cal. 'Better hook that tunic collar, soldier,' he said softly.

'Hello, Tom. The damn thing's too tight.'

'I don't see you around the town at night lately.'

'No.'

'Don't tell me you reformed.'

'Maybe.'

Tom prided himself on his ability to kid people and make it sound serious. He said, 'Sounds like you got a girl.'

Cal didn't answer.

'I hear your brother faked his age and joined the army. Are you picking off his girl?'

'Oh, sure – sure,' said Cal.

Tom's interest sharpened. 'I nearly forgot,' he said. 'I hear Will Hamilton is telling around you made fifteen thousand dollars in beans. That true?'

'Oh, sure,' said Cal.

'You're just a kid. What are you going to do with all that money?'

Cal grinned at him. 'I burned it up.'

'How do you mean?'

'Just set a match to it and burned it.'

Tom looked into his face. 'Oh, yeah! Sure. Good thing to do. Got to go in here. Good night.' Tom Meek didn't like people to kid him. 'The young punk son of a bitch,' he said to himself. 'He's getting too smart for himself.'

Cal moved slowly along Main Street, looking in store windows. He wondered where Kate was buried. If he could find out, he thought he might take a bunch of flowers, and he laughed at himself for the impulse. Was it good or was he fooling himself? The Salinas wind would blow over a tombstone, let alone a bunch of carnations. For some reason he remembered the Mexican name for carnations. Somebody must have told him when he was a kid. They were called Nails of Love – and marigolds, the Nails of Death. It was a word like nails – *claveles*. Maybe he'd better put marigolds on his mother's grave. 'I'm beginning to think like Aron,' he said to himself.

CHAPTER 54

I

THE WINTER seemed reluctant to let go its bite. It hung on cold and wet and windy long after its time. And people repeated, 'It's those damned big guns they're shooting off in France – spoiling the weather in the whole world.'

The grain was slow coming up in the Salinas Valley, and the wild flowers came so late that some people thought they wouldn't come at all.

We knew – or at least we were confident – that on May Day, when all the Sunday School picnics took place in the Alisal, the wild azaleas that grew in the skirts of the stream would be in bloom. They were a part of May Day.

May Day was cold. The picnic was drenched out of existence by a freezing rain, and there wasn't an open blossom on the azalea trees. Two weeks later they still weren't out.

Cal hadn't known it would be like this when he had made azaleas the signal for his picnic, but once the symbol was set it could not be violated.

The Ford sat in Windham's shed, its tyres pumped up, and with two new dry cells to make it start easily on Bat. Lee was alerted to make sandwiches when the day came, and he got tired of waiting and stopped buying sandwich bread every two days.

'Why don't you just go anyway?' he said.

'I can't,' said Cal. 'I said azaleas.'

'How will you know?'

'The Silacci boys live out there, and they come into school every day. They say it will be a week or ten days.'

'Oh, Lord!' said Lee. 'Don't overtrain your picnic.'

Adam's health was slowly improving. The numbness was going from his hand. And he could read a little – a little more each day.

'It's only when I get tired that the letters jump,' he said. 'I'm glad I didn't get glasses to ruin my eyes. I knew my eyes were all right.'

Lee nodded and was glad. He had gone to San Francisco for the books he needed and had written for a number of articles. He knew about as much as was known about the anatomy of the brain and the symptoms and severities of lesion and thrombus. He had studied and asked questions with the same unwavering intensity as when he had trapped and pelted and cured a Hebrew verb. Dr H. C. Murphy had got to know Lee very well and had gone from a professional impatience with a Chinese servant to a genuine admiration for a scholar. Dr Murphy had even borrowed some of Lee's news articles and reports on diagnosis and practice. He told Dr Edwards, 'That Chink knows more about the pathology of cerebral haemorrhage than I do, and I bet as much as you do.' He spoke with a kind of affectionate anger that this should be so. The medical profession is unconsciously irritated by lay knowledge.

When Lee reported Adam's improvement he said, 'It does seem to me that the absorption is continuing —'

'I had a patient,' Dr Murphy said, and he told a hopeful story.

'I'm always afraid of recurrence,' said Lee.

'That you have to leave with the Almighty,' said Dr Murphy. 'We can't patch an artery like an inner tube. By the way, how do you get him to let you take his blood pressure?'

'I bet on his and he bets on mine. It's better than horse racing.'

'Who wins?'

'Well, I could,' said Lee. 'But I don't. That would spoil the game – and the chart.'

'How do you keep him from getting excited?'

'It's my own invention,' said Lee. 'I call it conversational therapy.'

'Must take all your time.'

'It does,' said Lee.

11

On May 28, 1918, American troops carried out their first important assignment of World War I. The First Division, General Bullard commanding, was ordered to capture the village of Cantigny. The village, on high ground, dominating the Avre River valley. It was defended by trenches, heavy machine-guns, and artillery. The front was a little over a mile wide.

At 6.45 am, May 28, 1918, the attack was begun after one hour of artillery preparation. Troops involved were the 28th Infantry (Col. Ely), one battalion of the 18th Infantry (Parker), a company of the First Engineers, the divisional artillery (Summerall), and a support of French tanks and flame throwers.

The attack was a complete success. American troops entrenched on the new line and repulsed two powerful German counter-attacks.

The First Division received the congratulations of Clemenceau, Foch, and Pétain.

III

It was the end of May before the Silacci boys brought the news that the salmon-pink blossoms of the azaleas were breaking free. It was on a Wednesday, as the nine o'clock bell was ringing, that they told him.

Cal rushed to the English classroom, and just as Miss Norris took her seat on the little stage he waved his handkerchief and blew his nose loudly. Then he went down to the boys' toilet and waited until he heard through the wall the flush of water on the girlside. He went out through the basement door, walked close to the red brick wall, slipped round the pepper tree, and, once out of sight of school, walked slowly along until Abra caught up with him.

'When'd they come out?' she asked.

'This morning.'

'Shall we wait until tomorrow?'

He looked up at the gay yellow sun, the first earth-warming sun of the year. 'Do you want to wait?'

'No,' she said.

'Neither do I.'

They broke into a run – bought bread at Reynaud's and oggled Lee into action.

Adam heard loud voices and looked into the kitchen. 'What's the hullaballoo?' he asked.

'We're going on a picnic,' said Cal.

'Isn't it a school day?'

Abra said, 'Sure it is. But it's a holiday too.'

Adam smiled at her. 'You're pink as a rose,' he said.

Abra cried, 'Why don't you come with us? We're going to the Alisal to get azaleas.'

'Why, I'd like to,' Adam said, and then, 'No, I can't. I promised to go down to the ice plant. We're putting in some new tubing. It's a beautiful day.'

'We'll bring you some azaleas,' Abra said.

'I like them. Well, have a good time.'

When he was gone Cal said, 'Lee, why don't you come with us?'

Lee looked sharply at him. 'I hadn't thought you were a fool,' he said.

'Come on!' Abra cried.

'Don't be ridiculous,' said Lee.

I V

It's a pleasant little stream that gurgles through the Alisal against the Gabilan Mountains on the east side of the Salinas Valley. The water bumbles over round stones and washes the polished roots of the trees that hold it in.

The smell of azaleas and the sleepy smell of sun working with chlorophyll filled the air. On the bank the Ford car sat, still breathing softly from its overheating. The back seat was piled with azalea branches.

Cal and Abra sat on the bank among the luncheon papers. They dangled their feet in the water.

'They always wilt before you get them home,' said Cal.

'But they're such a good excuse, Cal,' she said. 'If you won't I guess I'll have to —'

'What?'

She reached over and took his hand. 'That,' she said.

'I was afraid to.'

'Why?'

'I don't know.'

'I wasn't.'

'I guess girls aren't afraid of near as many things.'

'I guess not.'

'Are you ever afraid?'

'Sure,' she said. 'I was afraid of you after you said I wet my pants.'

'That was mean,' he said. 'I wonder why I did it,' and suddenly he was silent.

Her fingers tightened round his hand. 'I know what you're thinking. I don't want you to think about that.'

Cal looked at the curling water and turned a round brown stone with his toe.

Abra said, 'You think you've got it all, don't you? You think you attract bad things —'

'Well —'

'Well, I'm going to tell you something. My father's in trouble.'

'How in trouble?'

556

'I haven't been listening at doors but I've heard enough. He's not sick. He's scared. He's done something.'

He turned his head. 'What?'

'I think he's taken some money from his company. He doesn't know whether his partners are going to put him in jail or let him try to pay it back.'

'How do you know?'

'I heard them shouting in his bedroom where he's sick. And my mother started the phonograph to drown them out.'

He said, 'You aren't making it up?'

'No. I'm not making it up.'

He shuffled near and put his head against her shoulder and his arm crept timidly around her waist.

'You see, you're not the only one —' She looked sideways at his face. 'Now I'm afraid,' she said weakly.

v

At three o'clock in the afternoon Lee was sitting at his desk, turning over the pages of a seed catalogue. The pictures of sweet peas were in colour.

'Now these would look nice on the back fence. They'd screen off the slough. I wonder if there's enough sun.' He looked up at the sound of his own voice and smiled at himself. More and more he caught himself speaking aloud when the house was empty.

'It's age,' he said aloud. 'The slowing thoughts and —' He stopped and grew rigid for a moment. 'That's funny – listening for something. I wonder whether I left the tea-kettle on the gas. No – I remember.' He listened again. 'Thank heaven I'm not superstitious. I could hear ghosts walk if I'd let myself. I could —'

The front-door bell rang.

'There it is. That's what I was listening for. Let it ring. I'm not going to be led around by feelings. Let it ring.'

But it did not ring again.

A black weariness fell on Lee, a hopelessness that pressed his shoulders down. He laughed at himself. 'I can go and find it's an advertisement under the door or I can sit here and let my silly old mind tell me death is on the doorstep. Well, I want the advertisement.'

Lee sat in the living-room and looked at the envelope in his lap. And suddenly he spat at it. 'All right,' he said, 'I'm coming

– goddam you,' and he ripped it open and in a moment laid it on the table and turned it over with the message down.

He stared between his knees at the floor. 'No,' he said, 'that's not my right. Nobody has the right to remove any single experience from another. Life and death are promised. We have a right to pain.'

His stomach contracted. 'I haven't got the courage. I'm a cowardly yellow-belly. I couldn't stand it.'

He went into the bathroom and measured three teaspoons of elixir of bromide into a glass and added water until the red medicine was pink. He carried the glass to the living-room and put it on the table. He folded the telegram and shoved it in his pocket. He said aloud, 'I hate a coward! God, how I hate a coward!' His hands were shaking and a cold perspiration dampened his forehead.

At four o'clock he heard Adam fumbling at the door-knob. Lee licked his lips. He stood up and walked slowly to the hall. He carried the glass of pink fluid and his hand was steady.

CHAPTER 55

A L L O F the lights were on in the Trask house. The door stood partly open, and the house was cold. In the sitting-room Lee was shrivelled up like a leaf in the chair beside the lamp. Adam's door was open and the sound of voices came from his room.

When Cal came in he asked, 'What's going on?'

Lee looked at him and swung his head towards the table where the open telegram lay. 'Your brother is dead,' he said. 'Your father has had a stroke.'

Cal started down the hall.

Lee said, 'Come back. Dr Edwards and Dr Murphy are in there. Let them alone.'

Cal stood in front of him. 'How bad? How bad, Lee, how bad?'

'I don't know.' He spoke as though recalling an ancient thing. 'He came home tired. But I had to read him the telegram. That was his right. For about five minutes he said it over and over to himself out loud. And then it seemed to get through into his brain and to explode there.'

'Is he conscious?'

Lee said wearily, 'Sit down and wait, Cal. Sit down and wait.
t used to it. I'm trying to.'

Cal picked up the telegram and read its bleak and dignified
nouncement.

Dr Edwards came out, carrying his bag. He nodded curtly,
nt out, and closed the door smartly behind him.

Dr Murphy set his bag on the table and sat down. He sighed.
r Edwards asked me to tell you.'

'How is he?' Cal demanded.

'I'll tell you all we know. You're the head of the family now,
l. Do you know what a stroke is?' He didn't wait for Cal to
swer. 'This one is a leakage of blood in the brain. Certain areas
the brain are affected. There have been earlier small leakages.
e knows that.'

'Yes,' said Lee.

Dr Murphy glanced at him and then back at Cal. 'The left
de is paralysed. The right side partly. Probably there is no
ght in the left eye, but we can't determine that. In other
ords, your father is nearly helpless.'

'Can he talk?'

'A little – with difficulty. Don't tire him.'

Cal struggled for words. 'Can he get well?'

'I've heard of reabsorption cases this bad but I've never seen
ne.'

'You mean he's going to die?'

'We don't know. He might live for a week, a month, a year,
en two years. He might die tonight.'

'Will he know me?'

'You'll have to find that out for yourself. I'll send a nurse
night and then you'll have to get permanent nurses.' He stood
p. 'I'm sorry, Cal. Bear up! You'll have to bear up.' And he
id, 'It always surprises me how people bear up. They always
o. Edwards will be in tomorrow. Good night.' He put his
and out to touch Cal's shoulder, but Cal had moved away and
alked towards his father's room.

Adam's head was propped up on pillows. His face was calm,
e skin pale; his mouth was straight, neither smiling nor dis-
pproving. His eyes were open, and they had great depth and
larity, as though one could see deep into them and as though
ey could see deep into their surroundings. And the eyes were
alm, aware but not interested. They turned slowly towards Cal
s he entered the room, found his chest, and then rose to his
ce and stayed there.

Cal sat down in the straight chair beside the bed. He sa
'I'm sorry, Father.'

The eyes blinked slowly the way a frog blinks.

'Can you hear me, Father? Can you understand me?' T
eyes did not change or move. 'I did it,' Cal cried. 'I'm respo
sible for Aron's death and for your sickness. I took him
Kate's. I showed him his mother. That's why he went away.
don't want to do bad things – but I do them.'

He put his head down on the side of the bed to escape the te
rible eyes, and he could still see them. He knew they would
with him, a part of him, all of his life.

The door-bell rang. In a moment Lee came to the bedroo
followed by the nurse – a strong, broad woman with heavy bla
eyebrows. She opened breeziness as she opened her suitcase.

'Where's my patient! There he is! Why, you look fine! Wh
am I doing here? Maybe you better get up and take care of m
you look good. Would you like to take care of me, big handson
man?' She thrust a muscular arm under Adam's shoulder ar
effortlessly hoisted him towards the head of the bed and he
him up with her right arm while with her left she patted o
the pillows and laid him back.

'Cool pillows,' she said. 'Don't you love cool pillows? Nov
where's the bathroom? Have you got a duck and bedpan? Ca
you put a cot in here for me?'

'Make a list,' said Lee. 'And if you need any help – wit
him —'

'Why would I need help? We'll get along just fine, won't we
sugar-sweetie?'

Lee and Cal returned to the kitchen. Lee said, 'Before sh
came I was going to urge you to have some supper – you know
like the kind of person who uses food for any purpose good o
bad? I bet she's that way. You can eat or not eat, just as yo
wish.'

Cal grinned at him. 'If you'd tried to make me, I'd have bee
sick. But since you put it that way, I think I'll make a sand
wich.'

'You can't have a sandwich.'

'I want one.'

'It all works out,' said Lee, 'true to outrageous form. It's kind
of insulting that everyone reacts about the same way.'

'I don't want a sandwich,' Cal said. 'Are there any tart
left?'

'Plenty – in the bread-box. They may be a little soaky.'

'I like them soaky,' Cal said. He brought the whole plate to he table and set it in front of him.

The nurse looked into the kitchen. 'These look good,' she said nd took one, bit into it, and talked among her chewings. 'Can phone Krough's drugstore for the things I need? Where's the hone? Where do you keep the linen? Where's the cot you're oing to bring in? Are you through with this paper? Where did ou say the phone is?' She took another tart and retired.

Lee asked softly, 'Did he speak to you?'

Cal shook his head back and forth as though he couldn't top.

'It's going to be dreadful. But the doctor is right. You can tand anything. We're wonderful animals that way.'

'I am not.' Cal's voice was flat and dull. 'I can't stand it. No, I can't stand it. I won't be able to. I'll have to – I'll have to –'

Lee gripped his fist fiercely. 'Why, you mouse – you nasty cur. With goodness all around you – don't you dare suggest a thing ike that! Why is your sorrow more refined than my sorrow?'

'It's not sorrow. I told him what I did. I killed my brother. I'm a murderer. He knows it.'

'Did he say it? Tell the truth – did he say it?'

'He didn't have to. It was in his eyes. He said it with his eyes. There's nowhere I can go to get away – there's no place.'

Lee sighed and released his wrist. 'Cal' – he spoke patiently – 'listen to me. Adam's brain centres are affected. Anything you see in his eyes may be pressure on that part of his brain which governs his seeing. Don't you remember? – he couldn't read. That wasn't his eyes – that was pressure. You don't know he accused you. You don't know that.'

'He accused me. I know it. He said I'm a murderer.'

'Then he will forgive you. I promise.'

The nurse stood in the doorway. 'What are you promising, Charley? You promised me a cup of coffee.'

'I'll make it now. How is he?'

'Sleeping like a baby. Have you got anything to read in this house?'

'What would you like?'

'Something to take my mind off my feet.'

'I'll bring the coffee to you. I've got some dirty stories written by a French queen. They might be too –'

'You bring 'em with the coffee,' she said. 'Why don't you get some shut-eye, sonny? Me and Charley'll hold the fort. Don't forget the book, Charley.'

561

Lee set the percolator on the gas jet. He came to the table and said, 'Cal!'

'What do you want?'

'Go to Abra.'

11

Cal stood on the neat porch and kept his finger on the bell until the harsh overlight flashed on and the night bolt rasped and Mrs Bacon looked out. 'I want to see Abra,' Cal said.

Her mouth dropped open in amazement. 'You want what?'

'I want to see Abra.'

'You can't. Abra's gone to her room. Go away.'

Cal shouted, 'I tell you I want to see Abra.'

'You go away or I'll call the police.'

Mr Bacon called, 'What is it? Who is it?'

'Never you mind – go back to bed. You aren't well. I'll handle this.'

She turned back to Cal. 'Now you get off the porch. And if you ring the bell again I'll phone the police. Now, get!' The door slammed, the bolt scraped, and the hard overlight went off.

Cal stood smiling in the dark, for he thought of Tom Meek lumbering up, saying, 'Hello, Cal. What you up to?'

Mrs Bacon shouted from inside, 'I see you. Now go on! Get off the porch!'

He walked slowly down the walk and turned towards home, and he hadn't gone a block before Abra caught up with him. She was panting from her run. 'Got out the back way,' she said.

'They'll find you gone.'

'I don't care.'

'You don't?'

'No.'

Cal said, 'Abra, I've killed my brother and my father is paralysed because of me.'

She took his arm and clung to it with both hands.

Cal said, 'Didn't you hear me?'

'I heard you.'

'Abra, my mother was a whore.'

'I know. You told me. My father was a thief.'

'I've got her blood, Abra. Don't you understand?'

'I've got his,' she said.

562

They walked along in silence while he tried to rebalance himself. The wind was cold, and they quickened their steps to keep warm. They passed the last street-light on the very edge of Salinas, and blackness lay ahead of them and the road was unpaved and sticky with black 'dobe mud.

They had come to the end of the pavement, to the end of the street-lights. The road under their feet was slippery with spring mud, and the grass that brushed against their legs was wet with dew.

Abra asked, 'Where are we going?'

'I wanted to run away from my father's eyes. They're right in front of me all the time. When I close my eyes I still see them. I'll always see them. My father is going to die, but his eyes will still be looking at me, telling me I killed my brother.'

'You didn't.'

'Yes, I did. And his eyes say I did.'

'Don't talk like that. Where are we going?'

'A little farther. There's a ditch and a pump house – and a willow tree. Do you remember the willow tree?'

'I remember it.'

He said, 'The branches come down like a tent and their tips touch the ground.'

'I know.'

'In the afternoons – the sunny afternoons – you and Aron would part the branches and go inside – and no one could see you.'

'You watched?'

'Oh, sure. I watched.' And he said, 'I want you to go inside the willow tree with me. That's what I want to do.'

She stopped and her hand pulled him to a stop. 'No,' she said. 'That's not right.'

'Don't you want to go in with me?'

'Not if you're running away – no, I don't.'

Cal said, 'Then I don't know what to do. What shall I do? Tell me what to do.'

'Will you listen?'

'I don't know.'

'We're going back,' she said.

'Back? Where?'

'To your father's house,' said Abra.

The light of the kitchen poured down on them. Lee had lighted
the oven to warm the chilly air.

'She made me come,' said Cal.

'Of course she did. I knew she would.'

Abra said, 'He would have come by himself.'

'We'll never know that,' said Lee.

He left the kitchen and in a moment returned. 'He's still
sleeping.' Lee set a stone bottle and three little translucent porcelain cups on the table.

'I remember that,' said Cal.

'You ought to.' Lee poured the dark liquor. 'Just sip it and let
it run around your tongue.'

Abra put her elbows on the kitchen table. 'Help him,' she said.
'You can accept things, Lee. Help him.'

'I don't know whether I can accept things or not,' Lee said.
'I've never had a chance to try. I've always found myself with
some – not less uncertain but less able to take care of uncertainty. I've had to do my weeping – alone.'

'Weeping — ? You?'

He said, 'When Samuel Hamilton died the world went out
like a candle. I relighted it to see his lovely creations, and I saw
his children tossed and torn and destroyed as though some
vengefulness was at work. Let the ng-ka-py run back on your
tongue.'

He went on, 'I had to find out my stupidities for myself.
These were my stupidities: I thought the good are destroyed
while the evil survive and prosper.

'I thought that once an angry and disgusted God poured molten fire from a crucible to destroy or to purify his little handiwork of mud.

'I thought I had inherited both the scars of the fire and the
impurities which made the fire necessary – all inherited, I
thought. All inherited. Do you feel that way?'

'I think so,' said Cal.

'I don't know,' Abra said.

Lee shook his head. 'That isn't good enough. That isn't good
enough thinking. Maybe —' And he was silent.

Cal felt the heat of the liquor in his stomach. 'Maybe what,
Lee?'

'Maybe you'll come to know that every man in every generation is re-fired. Does a craftsman, even in his old age, lose his hunger to make a perfect cup – thin, strong, translucent?' He held his cup to the light. 'All impurities burned out and ready for a glorious flux, and for that – more fire. And then either the slag heap or, perhaps what no one in the world ever quite gives up, perfection.' He drained his cup and he said loudly, 'Cal, listen to me. Can you think that whatever made us – would stop trying?'

'I can't take it in,' Cal said. 'Not now I can't.'

The heavy steps of the nurse sounded in the living-room. She billowed through the door and she looked at Abra, elbows on the table, holding her cheeks between her palms.

The nurse said, 'Have you got a pitcher? They get thirsty. I like to keep a pitcher of water handy. You see,' she explained, 'they breathe through their mouths.'

'Is he awake?' Lee asked. 'There's a pitcher.'

'Oh, yes, he's awake and rested. And I've washed his face and combed his hair. He's a good patient. He tried to smile at me.'

Lee stood up. 'Come along, Cal. I want you to come too, Abra. You'll have to come.'

The nurse filled her pitcher at the sink and scurried ahead of them.

When they trooped into the bedroom Adam was propped high on his pillows. His white hands lay palms down on either side of him, and the sinews from knuckle to wrist were tight drawn. His face was waxen, and his sharp features were sharpened. He breathed slowly between pale lips. His blue eyes reflected back the night-light focused on his head.

Lee and Cal and Abra stood at the foot of the bed, and Adam's eyes moved slowly from one face to the other, and his lips moved just a little in greeting.

The nurse said, 'There he is. Doesn't he look nice? He's my darling. He's my sugar pie.'

'Hush!' said Lee.

'I won't have you tiring my patient.'

'Go out of the room,' said Lee.

'I'll have to report this to the doctor.'

Lee whirled towards her. 'Go out of the room and close the door. Go and write your report.'

'I'm not in the habit of taking orders from Chinks.'

Cal said, 'Go out now, and close the door.'

She slammed the door just loud enough to register her anger. Adam blinked at the sound.

Lee said, 'Adam!'

The blue wide eyes looked for the voice and finally foun Lee's brown and shining eyes.

Lee said, 'Adam, I don't know what you can hear or under stand. When you had the numbness in your hand and you eyes refused to read, I found out everything I could. But som things no one but you can know. You may, behind your eye be alert and keen, or you may be living in a confused gre dream. You may, like a newborn child, perceive only light an movement.

'There's damage in your brain, and it may be that you are new thing in the world. Your kindness may be meanness nov and your bleak honesty fretful and conniving. No one know these things except you, Adam! Can you hear me?'

The blue eyes wavered, closed slowly, then opened.

Lee said, 'Thank you, Adam. I know how hard it is. I'n going to ask you to do a much harder thing. Here is your son Caleb – your only son. Look at him, Adam!'

The pale eyes looked until they found Cal. Cal's mouth move dryly and made no sound.

Lee's voice cut in, 'I don't know how long you will live Adam. Maybe a long time. Maybe an hour. But your son wil live. He will marry and his children will be the only remnan left of you.' Lee wiped his eyes with his fingers.

'He did a thing in anger, Adam, because he thought you ha rejected him. The result of his anger is that his brother an your son is dead.'

Cal said, 'Lee – you can't.'

'I have to,' said Lee. 'If it kills him I have to. I have th choice,' and he smiled sadly and quoted, ' "If there's blame, it' my blame." ' Lee's shoulders straightened. He said sharply 'Your son is marked with guilt out of himself – out of himself - almost more than he can bear. Don't crush him with rejection Don't crush him, Adam.'

Lee's breath whistled in his throat. 'Adam, give him you blessing. Don't leave him alone with his guilt. Adam, can you hear me? Give him your blessing!'

A terrible brightness shone in Adam's eyes and he closed them and kept them closed. A wrinkle formed between hi brows.

Lee said, 'Help him, Adam – help him. Give him his chance. Let him be free. That's all a man has over the beasts. Free him! Bless him!'

The whole bed seemed to shake under the concentration.

Adam's breath came quick with his effort and then, slowly, his right hand lifted – lifted an inch and then fell back.

Lee's face was haggard. He moved to the head of the bed and wiped the sick man's damp face with the edge of the sheet. He looked down at the closed eyes. Lee whispered, 'Thank you, Adam – thank you, my friend. Can you move your lips? Make your lips form his name.'

Adam looked up with sick weariness. His lips parted and failed and tried again. Then his lungs filled. He expelled the air and his lips combed the rushing sigh. His whispered word seemed to hang in the air.

'*Timshel!*'

His eyes closed and he slept.

John Steinbeck
Of Mice and Men 50p

The story of Lennie, one of Steinbeck's most poignant characters.
A simple-minded giant who relies on George, his mentor and
protector; but who cannot in the end save Lennie from his
worst enemy — his own strength.

The Grapes of Wrath 95p

'This is a terrible and indignant book; yet it is not without
passages of lyrical beauty, and the ultimate impression is that of
the dignity of the human spirit under the stress of the most
desperate conditions' GUARDIAN

Tortilla Flat 70p

These tales of the ludicrous adventures of *paisano* Danny and
his friends are often described as Steinbeck's funniest.

The Moon is Down 60p

A great novel of courage, defiance and human dignity under
stress tells how invasion came to a small Norwegian town — and
how the inhabitants met their conquerors.

Journal of a Novel 80p
The *East of Eden* Letters

A unique and concentrated portrait of Steinbeck the author and
the man. Steinbeck wrote *East of Eden* in 1951. It was his longest
and most ambitious novel. The *East of Eden* letters were never
intended for publication. They provide an insight into the mind
and art of a great writer — his everyday hopes and fears, the
small worries and the deep convictions.

Joe Esterhas
F. I. S. T. 80p

Soon to be a sensational new film starring Sylvester 'Rocky' Stallone ... F. I. S. T. is the Federation of Inter-State Truckers ... *F. I. S. T.* is the story of Johnny Kovak, whose combination of punch and persuasion took him to the top of the truckers' union ... of the wife he betrayed and the ambitions he tarnished ... and of the dangerous allies who brought him down. A story peopled with characters as big and powerful as the trucks they drive.

Piers Paul Read
Monk Dawson 80p

'A Voltairean journey through contemporary panaceas ... we follow Dawson from his Roman Catholic public school through every stage ... His success, sexual, social, religious and professional, is due to his conviction that he has found the meaning of life, in a world always uncertain of it ...' SUNDAY TELEGRAPH

'A remarkable novel ... profoundly moving' GRAHAM GREENE

Rebecca West
The Birds Fall Down £1.25

An engrossing recreation of the momentous events that led up to the Russian Revolution ... seen through the eyes of Laura, eighteen-year-old-daughter of an English MP and grandchild of an exiled Russian royalist – a vivid canvas, shot through with intrigue, conspiracy and murder, bringing to life the days of tumult that changed the world.

'One of the most fascinating true stories ever to have been used as a basis for fiction' BERNARD LEVIN

'An outstanding achievement' SUNDAY TELEGRAPH

Tom Sharpe
Wilt 75p

'Henry Wilt works humbly at his Polytechnic dinning Eng. Lit.
into the unreceptive skulls of rude mechanicals, his nights in
fantasies of murdering his gargantuan, feather-brained wife,
half-consummated when he dumps a life-sized inflatable doll
in a building site hole, and is grilled by the police, his wife being
missing, stranded on a mud bank with a gruesome American dyke'
GUARDIAN

'Superb farce' TRIBUNE

A. G. Macdonell
England, their England 80p

One of the great classics of English humour . . . The story of
Donald Cameron, returning home from the First World War and
setting out to write his book about the curious habits and
traditional customs of the English. En route there are superb
scenes of village life, a weekend country-house party at the
redoutable Lady Ormerode's, international conferences, and a
description of village cricket immortal in the annals of English
humour.

Nancy Arrowsmith with George Moorse
A Field Guide to the Little People 95p

'A delightfully eccentric and succinct guide to some eighty
elves, goblins, dwarves and other unorthodox adjuncts of the
landscape' OBSERVER

'The elves of this collection all come from centuries of popular
tradition. You can check here on their pedigrees, origins,
appearance, and habitat' GUARDIAN

. Somerset Maugham

f Human Bondage £1.25

this, perhaps the most famous of Somerset Maugham's novels,
follow the story of Philip Carey, an orphaned cripple, in his quest
life and love. Turning from the bohemian life of a Parisian art
dent and the demands of the tragic Fanny, he studies medicine in
ndon, where Mildred, superficial but irresistible, nearly brings
out his ruin.

he Moon and Sixpence 75p

sed on the life of Paul Gauguin, *The Moon and Sixpence* is the
ory of Charles Strickland, a London stockbroker who suddenly
andons his wife and family, to become a painter in Tahiti. Here is
 portrayal of the mentality of genius — and a brilliant affirmation of
augham's power as a novelist.

he Narrow Corner 75p

his tale of the sea came from a passage in *The Moon and Sixpence*
which Maugham had written twelve years earlier. The villainous
aptain Nichols brings his passenger, Fred Blake, a fugitive from the
w, to the remote island of Kanda after a violent storm — and what
tarts as a thrilling tale of sea adventure becomes a tragic tale of love
s Fred and the beautiful young Louise bring sorrow on her island
ome . . .

The Razor's Edge 80p

he story of three of Maugham's most brilliant characters — Isabel,
whose choice between passion and wealth has lifelong   .
epercussions . . . her uncle, Elliott Templeton, a classic American
nob . . . and Larry Darrell, Isabel's ex-fiancé who leaves his
stockbroking life in Chicago to seek spiritual peace in a Guru's
ashram in Southern India.

Farley Mowat
The Serpent's Coil 70p

The great sea saga of ships and men and the savage fury of a
North Atlantic hurricane . . . the crushing embrace of the
'serpent's coil'.

'The true story of the Liberty ship *Leicester* which sailed for
New York from England in the summer of 1948, ran into a
hurricane and was abandoned with the loss of six lives in mid-
Atlantic . . . and of the tug *Foundation Josephine* which tracked
the derelict over many thousands of miles . . .' NEW YORKER

Thomas Hardy
The Return of the Native 70p

Against the background of the lonely villages of Wessex, Hardy tel▶
the story of Eustacia Vye, proud, passionate and condemned to
live in her grandfather's isolated cottage of Egdon Heath. Young
Clym Yeobright returns from Paris, falls in love with Eustacia,
and the pair are wed. But Clym's devotion to the countryside
and Eustacia's overpowering urge to flee bring a conflict that
dooms their marriage.